The Mammot

SWORD & HONOR

The Mammoth Book of
SWORD & HONOR

Edited by

Mike Ashley

CARROLL & GRAF PUBLISHERS, INC.
New York

Carroll & Graf Publishers, Inc.
19 West 21st Street
New York
NY 10010–6805

First published in the UK by Robinson Publishing,
an imprint of Constable & Robinson Ltd 2000

First Carroll & Graf edition 2000

ISBN 0–7867–0727–5

Printed and bound in the EU

CONTENTS

CONTENTS VII

INTRODUCTION

Mike Ashley

I am thankful that I have never had to take part in any military action, but I have the utmost admiration for those who, whether by choice or not, put their lives at risk for others.

In this anthology I wanted to bring together stories that not only demonstrated the bravery and courage of men and women in times of conflict, but also the horror and madness and often the futility of war. These two aspects are reflected in the book's title – *Sword and Honour*. Trying to do what's right in the most extreme of circumstances.

I also wanted stories set during the Age of the British Empire in the nineteenth century. There is something about the Victorian period of Empire that continues to appeal, at the same time as we might abhor many of its actions and the treatment of our fellow humans. There are those moments of crass stupidity that nevertheless lead to remarkable heroism, as in the Charge of the Light Brigade, or those moments when a few men defend a garrison against overwhelming odds, as at Rorke's Drift. In stories like this I want to know how people felt, how they coped, how they reacted, and what became of them.

That's what these stories are about – real people in horrendous situations out of which come remarkable actions. Not all of the stories are about the British Empire. Indeed we start with several stories recapturing the Napoleonic Empire, and there are also five stories set during the American Civil War, plus another in the earlier war between the United States and Mexico. The boundaries are in time rather than geography. I have confined the episodes strictly to conflicts of the nineteenth century. The stories begin in 1805 just before the Battle of Austerlitz and end in 1898 at the Battle of Omdurman. There is also a brief appendix where ten British soldiers who lived through some of these campaigns and were awarded the Victoria Cross, reflect upon their actions.

Several of the stories have been specially written for this anthology, whilst the reprints are, on the whole, not well known or are not readily available today. Authors range from George MacDonald Fraser and John Jakes to Joseph Conrad and Mark Twain. But it is not an all male preserve. I am delighted to include stories by Daphne Wright, Pamela Brooks and Amy Myers as well as rare reprints by Bella Spencer, L.T. Meade and Clotilde Graves.

Several of the stories are written by people who directly experienced the conflicts featured here, and are contemporary with Victorian and Edwardian attitudes and values. Some of the words and expressions used may no longer be politically correct, but I have kept the stories as originally written in order to reflect the period.

I am most grateful to Bernard Cornwell for providing his insightful foreword, which I believe admirably sets the mood for the whole anthology. So, with no more ado I shall step aside and let battle commence.

Mike Ashley

FOREWORD

Bernard Cornwell

Why write about war?

War is, after all, a tragedy. It is reprehensible, frequently unforgivable.

War is about orphans and widows, cruelty and misery. A suspicion attaches to those of us who describe war that, secretly or not, we are in love with war. That we glorify it.

It is a heavy accusation. Glibly, I suppose, we can justify our subject by saying that detective novelists do not approve of murder and it is a rare detective novel that does not contain a murder, but I do not think that defence suffices. The resolution of a detective novel almost always ends with the solution of the murder and the apprehension of the murderer, which implies due punishment. The murder itself is not celebrated, yet in war stories many killings are the result of heroism and bring the hero glory. Mark Adkin, when he wrote *The Sharpe Companion*, reckoned that Richard Sharpe, by age 42, had killed 65 men in close combat, and that was before I wrote Sharpe's Indian adventures or *Sharpe's Trafalgar*, a book in which, amidst other slaughter, he commits a cold-blooded murder. A hero?

It might be well to remember the words of Robert E. Lee. Watching the Confederate lines at the Battle of Fredericksburg, in 1862, he saw a Pennsylvanian division pierce his defences, threatening Lee with disaster, but a spirited Confederate counterattack drove the Pennsylvanians back in disarray. "It is well," Lee remarked to General Longstreet, "that war is so terrible, or else we should grow too fond of it." To me, that phrase sums up the dilemma of those of us who write about war. It is terrible, more awful than our worst nightmares, but it fascinates. Why?

War, at its sharp end, is a place where the rules that govern human behaviour cease to exist. We lead our ordinary lives surrounded by rules. Thou shalt not kill, steal, covet or kidnap, and our society has constructed a framework of police, courts and laws to enforce those rules which serve to make our lives tolerably safe. Yet in war we are encouraged to kill, to plunder the enemy and to capture his territory, families and wealth. I suspect that many of us are fascinated by this reversal of normality and wonder how we would behave in a world where the rules that govern our safety have been abandoned. Most of us are fortunate and never find out, so we seek the vicarious thrills of the fictional soldier's world. Fiction, I do not talk here of literary fiction, depends on adventure, and it is the essence of adventure that the hero or heroine is put at risk, and war provides the writer and the reader with a ready background filled with appalling risks, for war is the one competition where the loser can lose everything. That makes winning a more exquisite pleasure because the pleasures of contest are sharpened by its risks.

War, then, is life taken to its extremes. Life with the gloves off, life without a seat belt, life without rules. To win in war is to have risked everything and that makes for a fascinating, if terrible, environment for fiction. The drama is heightened by the penalties of failure.

I doubt many people would argue that the ghastly environment of war makes for a dramatic background for a tale, but that does not justify using the background if it encourages people to believe that war is a good thing. War is frequently necessary, but that does not make it good. It may be morally justified, as was the campaign against Hitler's Reich, but that does not cleanse war of its barbarity. War is hell. I have seen very little of it, but I did once see an infantry engagement and, at the end of it, there were seven dead. I was working for the BBC and I remember standing over the dead and directing my cameraman to film the corpses, which he did, and when I got home and was in the cutting room I wanted twelve seconds of those pictures which I planned to show in utter silence. The film editor told me there were not even five usable seconds. "Of course there are," I told her, "I was there. I told the cameraman to give me yards of footage, and he did."

"Yes," she said, "but in every shot you can see the decapitated woman."

I smiled. "I was there," I said again, "and there was no headless woman."

Wordlessly, she put the film on the machine, ran it, and there she was. Her head had been shot clean away, and her hands too, I suspect because she had them raised in surrender. I had been there. I had stood directly by her body, I had deliberately stared at each corpse, and I simply had not seen what was in front of my eyes. War is such hell that sometimes we blank out its reality. It is as bad as that.

Yet men frequently go to war with enthusiasm. It appeals. Robert E. Lee saw that appeal as his troops sealed his front line and went on to give him victory. There is the joy of commanding what Lawrence of Arabia called "tides of men". There is the delight of imposing your will on the enemy. There is the supreme satisfaction of risking everything to gain victory. There is the fascination of machines and weapons. There is the age-old human impetus to compete and win. But if men sometimes go to war enthusiastically, they rarely stay in that frame of mind. The reality of war wins. The horror, the dirt, the pain, the weeping, the squalor will soon exhaust enthusiasm.

We think of Wellington's contests with the Emperor and
Marshals of France as a time when war was glorious, of cavalry
in plumes and breastplates sweeping across wide fields, of flags
flying, and of thin red lines resisting the oncoming Eagles, and,
from a distance, if the cannon smoke would have let us see
anything at all, such a contest must have been spectacular. Yet
its reality was that the plumed men died in mud and blood,
calling for their mothers, while the infantry choked up their
lives or died at the hands of surgeons who were little better than
educated butchers.

Yet out of that hell of mud and blood and terrible sadness
there does spring something admirable. Call it heroism, though
here I do not have in mind people like Richard Sharpe. I am
thinking of ordinary men, some officers, many not, who do their
duty, fight their war, and do not allow the rules of ordinary life
to be entirely abandoned. There were Americans at My Lai who
tried to stop the massacre, and risked their own lives to save the
civilians being cut down by other Americans. Those men were
heroes. We are often told that we fight wars to save civilization,
and we do not save civilization by abandoning it. A retired
Warrant Officer of the Scots Guards, whom I met when he was
running a programme to rescue drug addicts, told me that a
soldier "fought for the people who cannot fight for themselves." I like that definition. He was a tough man, few
stronger, and he was using his strength to fight for the derelicts
of our society. The men and women of the Task Force which
retook the Falkland Islands in 1982 were fighting for the
islanders who were unable to resist an invasion by a military
dictatorship. They fought for people who were unable to fight
for themselves. That is a soldier's job, and that, I think, is the
saving grace of military fiction. It plunges its protagonists into
the most horrific, dramatic situations that we can imagine, and
in the centre of the horror, they keep their humanity.

Sharpe is a terrific soldier, none better, but he is not a killing
machine. To his own surprise he has a conscience. The weak
must be protected, the bully punished. Wars are vile, yet even in
the worst of combats, some small spark of human goodness

shines, and shines brighter because of the contrast with its surroundings. That can be inspiring, and I believe that most folk who read war stories, like these that Mike Ashley has collected, want to see that contrast. These are not tales of Armageddon, of the end of all things, of destruction and savagery without hope of salvation, but rather tales of ordinary folk who can inspire us because, in the cauldron of battle, they kept faith with humanity.

THE FIRST CONFLICT

Richard Howard

The first five of our stories deal with the struggle in Europe as Napoleon Bonaparte sought to deliver his grand plan of conquest. Four of these stories look at the situation through the eyes of the French themselves. We so often consider Britain's war against Napoleon, but forget the effect he had right across Europe, and in particular at the bloody battle of Austerlitz on 2 December 1805. This decisive victory for Bonaparte sealed the fate of the Austrians and sent the Russians back behind their borders. Richard Howard is the author of a series of novels featuring Alain Lausard, rescued from the dungeons of the Bastille in 1795 when the Revolutionary Army was in desperate need of troops. The series has included Bonaparte's Sons *(1997)*, Bonaparte's Invaders *(1998)*, Bonaparte's Conquerors *(1999) and* Bonaparte's Warriors *(2000), in which the following episode appears.*

It is November, 1805 and the armies of France, led by Napoleon Bonaparte, have marched across Europe to face the combined threat of Russia and Austria. It is a campaign that will culminate in the triumphant battle of Austerlitz, but first, men like Alain Lausard and his dragoons, must fight skirmishes with their enemies. They must suffer the rigours of cold, hunger and exhaustion. As Napoleon plots his greatest strategic manoeuvre to date, Lausard and his men find themselves confronted by the first of many enemy troops . . .

Lausard heard a high-pitched whinney then a loud crash as the horse fell forward. It was the leading offside animal in the team of four. As it slumped to the ground it pulled the traces with it, causing the other animals dragging the bridging wagon to stumble too. Lausard looked and saw the team driver, for one insane moment, reaching for his whip but then, realizing that no amount of beating would have roused the animal, the grey clad corporal leapt down and wandered across to the stricken horse. He cut the traces with a knife and stood back as the animal slumped to the ground. Lausard and the other dragoons walked their horses past the stranded wagon, keeping to the furthest edges of the road. The sergeant looked back and saw that other vehicles in the column were already coming to a halt, their passage blocked by the bridging wagon. Men were already trying to guide the vehicle off the road but the ground on either side of the road sloped away sharply. Particularly on one side where it led down to a shallow stream.

"It would be a kindness to shoot that horse," Lausard observed.

"Little wonder the poor beast is exhausted," Tigana mused, looking back at the fallen horse. It was lying on its side, head occasionally lifting as if soliciting help from those around it.

"More than twenty days on the march," Delacor muttered. "With barely a decent rest for man or horse. It seems that Bonaparte is trying to kill us before the Austrians do."

"Or the Russians," Tabor added. "There are Russians ahead of us too aren't there?"

"Does it matter from which country the bullet comes that kills you?" Sonnier grunted.

"There are Russians aren't there?" Tabor persisted.

"Yes, my friend, there are," Bonet told him, gently.

"If they shot it we could eat it," Joubert interjected. "When was the last time we had any food? I'm dying of hunger."

"We should eat *you*, fat man," Delacor said. "There's enough meat on you to feed the entire squadron."

Some of the others laughed.

Lausard patted the neck of his own horse and the animal tossed its head. Like the others of the squadron and, indeed, every animal in the army, it was tired and badly in need of food. But, the sergeant reasoned, so too were the *men* of *La Grande Armée*. The march from Boulogne had been accomplished in remarkably good order. Something he would have expected from such highly trained troops. But the distance they had been forced to cover had taken its toll on even the hardiest campaigner. Many of the men in the army, like himself, had been used to long marches before. In the blistering heat of Egypt and the numbing snowstorms of the Alps but, never before had any of them marched seven hundred miles in such a short space of time. Had Lausard not been so exhausted, he may well have taken the time to marvel at the sheer magnitude of the achievement. From the Channel to the Rhine in less than a month. It was an incredible feat. The one saving grace of the incredible manoeuvre had been that the late Autumn weather had remained fine. Most of the journey had been completed in moderate temperatures and with very little rain. Just as well, Lausard had thought. With over 3,500 wagons carrying everything from supplies to bridging equipment, as well as the additional bulk provided by artillery caissons and the guns themselves, the last thing the French needed was bad weather. Had the rain fallen and turned the roads into quagmires, the sergeant had no doubt that the march would have taken three times as long.

"There's only one good thing about being part of the advance guard," Joubert muttered. "At least we reach any supplies before the rest of the army."

"We also reach the *enemy* before the rest of the army," Roussard reminded him.

"And why the hell is it always us?" Delacor demanded. "Three squadrons in our regiment and which one is picked to be part of the advance guard? Us. As usual."

"You know why that is," Lausard told him. "At least you should by now. It is because we are expendable."

"After all these years they still will not let us forget who we were," Rocheteau grunted. "They still punish us for what we were over ten years ago. Haven't we done enough to prove ourselves by now?"

"Personally, I'd rather be ahead of the rest," Lausard commented. "The sooner we reach the enemy the better."

"I agree," Delacor added. "And it keeps us away from those complaining dog-faces too."

"And the stinking Imperial Guard," Giresse grunted. "They are given privileges far above their worth. The best supplies. The best billets. The best pay."

"They are Bonaparte's personal bodyguard," Lausard reminded him. "What do you expect?"

"Are they any better than us, Alain?" Rocheteau wanted to know.

The sergeant shook his head.

"I would back our squadron against any troops in the army," he said, smiling. "Guard or otherwise."

A number of the men nearby cheered. The sound was met with a furious scowl from Captain Milliere who was riding slightly ahead of them.

"Word is that the Emperor has been forced to call up 80,000 conscripts one year early to boost the strength of the army," Bonet offered.

"Then it's a pity he didn't put some of *them* in the advance guard instead of us," Roussard grunted.

"It hasn't been popular with the public," the former schoolmaster continued.

"Does it matter?" Lausard said. "What difference does one year make? Some will die at nineteen instead of twenty. That is all."

"I can remember *my* nineteenth birthday," Giresse said. "I stole some money and spent the entire day and night in a brothel just off the Rue Saint Denis." He smiled wistfully.

"How close do you think we are to the Austrians, Alain?" Rocheteau wanted to know.

"We'll be closer once we've crossed the Rhine," Lausard said, flatly. "If we can *get* across. They may already have the bridges defended, fortified or mined. It will not be easy. The Austrians are good troops."

"What about the Russians?" Charvet wanted to know.

"If they are all like Rostov here, then they will pose a far greater threat," Lausard smiled, looking at his companion and nodding in his direction. "Are all your people like you, my friend?"

"They are not my people anymore," the Russian told him. "The Tsars let my family and I starve. I owe them nothing but hatred."

"Just remember whose side you're on when the fighting starts," Lausard said and some of the other men laughed.

Karim patted the Russian gently on the shoulder and smiled.

The trees on either side of them began to thicken and the ground began to slope upwards more sharply until it levelled out on a wide plateau of land that gave a good view in all directions for at least ten miles. The column rode on at a trot until Captain Milliere raised an arm and slowed it to a walk. The road dipped before them, widening as it led up to a wide bridge. The areas around the bridge were unguarded and afforded the French a clear view of the countryside on both sides. Lausard looked at the murky water that flowed swiftly beneath the structure.

"The Rhine," he murmured.

"And what awaits us on the other side?" Roussard wanted to know.

Lausard didn't answer. He merely coaxed his horse on towards the crossing point. The column continued to move forward.

★　　★　　★

Napoleon Bonaparte stood gazing into the flames of the camp-fire, his hands clasped behind his back. Despite the chill of the night he wore no overcoat over his blue grenadier's uniform. Unlike the chasseurs who walked their horses back and forth around his tent and who were dressed, to a man, in long green capes. The grenadiers of the Old Guard, huge men with bristling moustaches and immaculately clean uniforms who guarded the entrance to the Imperial tent, also wore long blue coats to protect them from the cold. Napoleon seemed oblivious to the elements. He continued watching the dancing flames, as if hypnotized by them, then finally turned to face the gaggle of officers gathered near the entrance to the tent.

"The fox has taken the bait," he smiled. "General Mack has advanced west, beyond Munich towards Ulm as I anticipated. He is walking into the trap I set. All that remains for us is to spring that trap when the time is right."

"Have our leading units reached their first objective yet, Sire?" Duroc wanted to know.

Napoleon nodded.

"Freudenstadt was taken without a fight," the Corsican revealed. "Mack moved more men in that direction as I intended. The Austrians are in the Black Forest defiles. God will it that they stay there. My only fear is that we shall scare them too much. The next fortnight will see many things happen."

"Is Mack still unaware of the size of the army facing him?" Duroc enquired.

"Of its size *and* of its intention," Napoleon told the Grand Marshal. "A combination of the Black Forest itself, the Jura mountains and Murat's cavalry screen has served to mask both our strength and our intent from him. It is going well for us, my friends."

"What news of the Russians?" Duroc enquired.

It was Berthier who spoke.

"Still more than ten days march from their ally," said the Chief of Staff. "General Mack can expect no support from Kutusov or Bennigsen. He is already close to being isolated."

"The advance guard will continue to proceed between Stuttgart and Ansbach. Lannes and d'Hilliers will press on through Pforzheim to join Ney's VIth Corps. They will create the flank around which the more northerly formations will pivot as they move towards the Danube. We have opened a door and invited General Mack and his Austrians through. All that remains for us to do is to slam it shut behind him.''

The outbuildings of the farm were visible through the trees. Lausard could make out a barn, stables and a small hut that he guessed was the home of pigs. The undergrowth inside the woods was sparse, and he found it easy to walk his mount over the mossy carpet beneath the canopy of leaves, as did the dragoons behind him. To his right, Captain Milliere held up a hand to slow the progress of the horsemen. One or two of the mounts snorted impatiently but were silenced by reassuring pats from their riders. As Lausard watched, Milliere dismounted, pulling his carbine from the boot on his saddle. The firing mechanism was bound with oilskin which the officer quickly stripped off. He also fitted the fifteen inch bayonet then advanced through the trees in an effort to get closer to the farm. Lausard waited a moment then imitated his actions, signalling to Karim, Delacor, Sonnier and Charvet to follow him. Other troopers took the bridles of their dismounted colleagues, watching as the men moved swiftly and silently through the trees. The five dragoons spread out in a line, each man no more than five feet from his companion, using what little cover the woods offered as they drew nearer the collection of buildings. The ground sloped down sharply and Lausard almost lost his footing. Charvet put out a large hand to aid the sergeant and he remained upright as the men continued their advance.

Twenty feet from the nearest of the outbuildings, the woods ceased abruptly and there was nothing but open ground between the dragoons and their objective. A narrow stream coursed through a nearby gulley and Lausard could hear it rushing over the stones, swelled by recent rainfall. He was not the only one to notice something steaming close to the opposite bank of the stream. He was also not alone in realizing that the pile was horse droppings.

"They're fresh," whispered Karim.

"Someone got here before us," Milliere murmured.

The Circassian suddenly broke free of the cover of the woods and scuttled down to the bank of the stream. Bent low to the ground he moved with incredible speed, occasionally ducking low to the earth to inspect the many indentations there. Then, he hurried back to the cover of the trees.

"There are dozens of hoofprints," he said. "All of them on the far side of the stream."

"They could be *our* light cavalry?" Milliere offered.

Karim shook his head.

"If they belonged to French horses they would be on *this* side of the stream," he said, jabbing a finger at the ground beneath him. "The only tracks are on the far side. The stream was approached from the opposite direction to that which we now face."

"It must be an Austrian patrol," Milliere offered.

Before the officer could say another word, Lausard broke cover and, followed by Sonnier, Delacor and Charvet, ran headlong across the open ground towards the rear of the barn. As the men reached the stream, they gathered themselves and leapt over it, landing with unexpected grace on the other bank, barely breaking stride as they hurried up the incline towards the cover of the building. Once there, all four pressed themselves against the wooden wall. Lausard raised a hand in Milliere's direction and the officer nodded.

Sonnier and Delacor moved one way. Lausard and Charvet the other. The dragoons on the other bank watched intently.

It was as Lausard crept slowly to the end of the barn wall that he heard the sound of horses.

It was difficult to tell how many but now he also heard voices and the occasional laugh. The language was German. He stood up and peered cautiously around the edge of the barn into the farmyard itself.

He counted fifteen Austrian hussars.

Some were mounted, others wandered about in the muddy yard searching for provisions. He could see that two of the men were carrying sacks they'd taken from the barn. One of the sacks had a large hole in it and potatoes were dropping from it. One of the hussars called to his companion who was leaving a trail of the vegetables across the yard and the other men laughed. They were clad in light blue uniforms, and their pelisses, trimmed with black and yellow lace, were fastened to keep them warm. Their green shakos were covered by oilskins to protect them from the inclement weather. They all wore the familiar black and yellow barrel sashes and red sabertaches, edged red and black. Even on campaign, these spectacular troops retained an air of visual brilliance. It also made them easy targets. Lausard could see that, in addition to the sacks of vegetables they had already collected, the Austrians had slaughtered several pigs and bundled their carcasses into a wagon. Three or four others now nuzzled around in the yard, some chewing on the dropped potatoes.

Lausard stood up, his back pressed against the wall of the barn and lifted his carbine across his chest exaggeratedly then he slowly, and again, with great deliberation, loaded it. Watching from the other side of the stream, hidden by the trees, Milliere understood. When Lausard lifted the carbine above his head and waved it first towards the dragoons then back towards the farm, the officer hurried back to his waiting men and scrambled into the saddle.

Charvet and Delacor had also loaded their carbines by now, and they crouched behind the barn waiting for Lausard's order. He looked again at the hussars, then back towards the dragoons who were advancing at a walk in a broken line, swords still sheathed but carbines at the ready.

The jingling of harnesses began to fill the air and Lausard saw one of the Austrian troopers turn his head in the direction of the stream. He barked a couple of words in his own language and the other men stopped dead, listening intently. Lausard felt his heart beating more swiftly. The blood seemed to be coursing through his veins with increased speed. It was a feeling he had not known for a long time. And it was one he had missed. He swung the carbine up to his shoulder and fired.

The recoil slammed the Charleville back against his shoulder and a cloud of sulphurous smoke filled the air. The ball struck the Austrian in the chest and he fell backwards from his saddle. Immediately, Sonnier also fired. Another hussar hit the ground, blood pouring from the wound in his stomach. The advancing dragoons suddenly quickened their pace and the first half a dozen drove their horses up the incline and into the farmyard. They fired from the saddle at the surprised Austrians who were momentarily thrown into confusion, not knowing whether to fight back or run, unsure of how large a force of Frenchmen confronted them. As more spilled into the farmyard, they could see their situation was serious.

Delacor fired his carbine then ran at the nearest hussar and swung the weapon like a club, grinning maniacally as the butt shattered his nose. He slammed it down repeatedly on the back of the man's head before running the bayonet into the motion-less hussar.

Rocheteau shot an Austrian sergeant in the arm then pulled one pistol from its holster, pressing the barrel against the man's cheek as he fired. The lead ball punched in most of the left side of the man's face.

The Austrians on foot had no chance.

Giresse rode one down and shot another in the back, sliding his carbine back into its boot in order to draw his sword. He pulled the three-foot-long steel free in time to parry a sabre blow from one of the mounted hussars. Sparks flew from the point of contact and Giresse ducked over the pommel of his saddle to avoid the second slash. He turned in the saddle and drove his straight blade into the Austrian's side, driving it between ribs until it burst from the other side of the man's body. He tore it free and stabbed again. This time into the chest. The hussar slumped forward over the neck of his horse, blood streaming down the front of the animal. It reared, hurling his body into the mud.

Lausard stuck his bayonet into the thigh of another Austrian, driving so deep that the wickedly sharp point momentarily pinned the man to his own saddle. He shrieked and struck out at the sergeant with his sabre, but Lausard ducked beneath the swing, wrenched the bayonet out and drove it upwards into his opponent's stomach, pushing on the weapon until he unseated the hussar who fell to the ground and rolled over once before the sergeant stabbed him again to finish the job.

Any remaining hussars now bolted, hurtling away into the enveloping safety of the trees.

Rocheteau rode up, holding the reins of Lausard's horse, keeping the animal steady while the sergeant swung himself into the saddle.

Lieutenant Royere led a dozen dragoons in pursuit of the fleeing Austrians, many firing after their foes. Royere himself shot another from the saddle, the man toppling sideways, slamming into a tree with a savage impact that broke his neck. His foot caught in the stirrup and he was dragged through the woods as his terrified horse careered on.

Lausard looked around at the bodies of the dead Austrians. Several of the dragoons, Delacor and Rocheteau among them, were rifling the pockets of the corpses, comparing finds. Rocheteau grinned as he came upon a gold crucifix around the neck of one man. He tore it free and dropped it into the pocket of his tunic. Delacor seemed happy with an engraved snuff box he took from the same trooper. Elsewhere, men were gathering potatoes and carrots and stuffing them into their portmanteaus. Food was a treasure of a different kind for the dragoons. Tabor, Rostov and Gaston were already carving the dead pigs into more manageable portions with their swords. Tigana was inspecting the horses the Austrians had left behind.

"Are they of any use to us?" Milliere wanted to know.

"Two need re-shoeing, Captain," he called. "But they're in good enough condition. They'll do for remounts."

The officer nodded and rode across to join Lausard who was wiping blood from his face. He looked around at the eight or nine dead Austrians lying in the yard. The corpses were still being scavenged by Rocheteau and several other dragoons.

Each fresh find, be it a watch or a plug of tobacco, was greeted by a cheer.

"Is this the war you promised me, Captain?" Lausard said, flatly.

SPIKING THE GUNS

C. J. Cutcliffe Hyne

Charles John Cutcliffe Hyne (1865–1944) was a prolific writer, an all-round sportsman and an inveterate traveller, reputed to have notched up over 10,000 new miles a year. Down the mines at the age of twelve and off to sea in his early twenties, Hyne eventually turned to writing in his mid-twenties and was soon churning out stories for any available market. He struck paydirt when he introduced the character Captain Kettle into his magazine serial The Great Sea Swindle *and he was soon writing a long series of stories about his roguish merchant seaman for* Pearson's Magazine. *The first book* The Adventures of Captain Kettle *followed in 1898. The following story is one of Hyne's earliest efforts from* The Strand Magazine *for September 1893.*

"The regiment will be annihilated," observed the Adjutant, coolly. And then, in the same immovable tones, he asked someone to pass him a biscuit.

"Curse you," shouted the Colonel, "do you think I don't know that? Do you imagine I fear getting killed tomorrow? Do you suppose I want to live on after what has happened? It's the eternal disgrace of the thing that's cutting me."

"Once comfortably shot," remarked the senior Major with easy philosophy, "it doesn't much matter to me personally where, or for why, I go down. Not a soul will be left behind to care."

This last remark added tinder to the blaze. The Major was a peasant's son who had hacked and thrust his way up from the ranks by sheer hard fighting. His commanding officer was a noble of the old *régime*. He had hoped, and reasonably expected, that the previous day's engagement would give him a brigade; and so the fiasco had fallen all the more bitterly.

It seemed as though the very stars in their courses had been battling against us. Everything had gone wrong. The blame was not ours; but this, in an army where want of luck was the greatest crime, told nothing in our favour. Many men had fallen, and panic had seized the heels of the rest. Which of us initiated the run cannot be said; but in the rush of some, all had been carried along, few (except, perhaps, one or two of the older officers) resisting very strenuously. The Colonel, burning with shame, had gone in to report. What precisely had been said to him we did not know; but we guessed with some accuracy, although he did not repeat the detail. The gist of his interview was that the regiment was to attack again on the morrow; and if unsuccessful then, once more on the day after; and so on till the bridge was taken.

Yesterday the thing had been barely possible. Yet today it was far different. During the night the defences had been more than trebled. The Austrians swarmed. Enough artillery was mounted there now to have demolished an entire army corps advancing against it from the open.

The deduction was clear. The bravest men will turn tail

sometimes; and in our army, which was the bravest in the world, there had, during the latter part of the campaign, been more than one case of wavering. An example accordingly was to be made. Our corps had been singled out for the condign punishment. We were doomed to march on the morrow to our annihilation.

Of course, the matter had not been put so at headquarters. There the words ran: "Most important strategic point. Must be taken at whatever cost. Your regiment will again have the honour, Colonel," and so on. But, summed up bluntly, it was neither more nor less than I have said. We all understood the order to the letter, and there was not a man in the regiment who would hesitate a moment in carrying out his share. Each private soldier, each officer, would march with firm determination, to march then his last. That gives the case in a nutshell.

But the secure knowledge that there would be no skulkers along this road to execution did not pacify the Colonel. If anything, it increased his bitterness. It would make his ungrateful memory last the longer. He sat at the table-end of that inn room where we had messed, with folded arms and nervous fingers kneading at his muscles. By a singular irony we were lodged in comfort there – we, who had got to go out and die on the morrow – and he must needs taunt us with it, as though it were shame for such as we to have so tolerable a billet.

Myself, I was stretched out on a sofa away by the far wall, and lay there mutely, having but little taste for the wordy savageries which were being so freely dealt about. And the night grew older without my being disturbed. But the angry man at the end of the table singled me out at last, perhaps because my outward calm and listlessness jarred upon him.

"Tired, Eugène?" he asked.

"A little, sir."

"Ah, I can understand it. I noted your activity today. You have mistaken your vocation, *mon cher*. You should not have come into the army. You should have been a professional runner."

An answer burned on my tongue. But I kept it there, gave a

shrug, and said nothing. What use could further wrangling be? But the silence was an ill move. It only angered him further, and he threw at me an insult which was more than human man could endure.

"Do you think you will again feel inclined to use those powers of yours tomorrow, Eugène? Or had I better have you hand-cuffed to some steady old soldier?"

A dozen of the other officers sprang to their feet at this ghastly taunt, for when such a thing as this was said to one of their number, it touched all. The old Major was their spokes-man.

"Colonel, we make all allowances, but you are going too far with the youngster."

The Colonel scowled round tight-lipped for a minute, and then:

"I am quite capable of commanding this regiment of lost sheep, without unasked-for advice from subordinates, Major. Lieutenant Ramard, you heard my question, I presume? Please have the civility to answer."

During the minute's respite I had been thinking and acting – that is, writing. I got up and handed the Colonel a slip of paper. On it were the words:

"*I acknowledge that I, E. Ramard, Lieutenant of the 22nd———, am a coward.*

(*Signed*) "EUGÈNE RAMARD."

He read it.

"There, sir," I said, "kindly add the date, as I have forgotten what it is, and please leave that behind with the baggage when we march tomorrow. If I do not do better work for France than any man in the regiment, it is my wish that this paper be published." The Colonel nodded grimly, and then frowned.

"Have I your permission now, sir, to withdraw from this room?"

A refusal was framing itself – I could see it; but the lowering faces around made him curb his passion, and he nodded again, but reluctantly.

II

In the dark, wet air outside, and not before, did I realize fully what I had done. The screed on the slip of paper had been the spasm of the instant. It seemed to me now the outcome of a moment's insanity. I had had no plan, no trace of scheme in my head whilst I was scribbling. The words and the pledge were an empty boast, made in the wild hope that I could hold them good. But how could such a thing be done? The most furious, desperate courage, by itself, would avail nothing. There would be a thousand men around, each to the full as brave as I – for no one can march farther than death – and to do "better work for France" than any of them! Ah, no, the thing was impossible. With them I should fall, and amongst all of them I alone would be branded infamous. The paper would be brought to light; the curt, bald confession would be read with no explanation of how or why it was written; and men would form their own opinions – all hostile, all against me.

To leave behind nothing but the name of a self-avowed coward! Oh, agony! bitter agony!

I wandered wherever my blind feet led me, wrenched by torments that God alone knew the strength of, and from which there seemed no human means of escape. The heavy rain-squalls moaned down the village streets. The place, with its armed tenantry, slept. Only the dripping sentries were open-eyed. These, taking me for an officer on ordinary rounds, saluted with silent respect. No soul interfered with me. Not even a dog barked.

The thought came: You die only to gain a wreath of craven plumes. Why not pass away from here – escape – desert – vanish – be known no more – and yet live? No one withholds from you new life and new country. France alone, of all the world, is utterly hopeless for you.

The thought gained. I say it freely now, for the dead, dull blackness of my prospect then showed no spot of relief. In my walkings to and fro I gradually verged nearer and nearer to the outer cordon. As an officer I knew the words for the night; sign and countersign both. I could pass the pickets.

Farther and farther towards the scattered outskirts of the hamlet did my doubting feet lead me. In one more patrol up and down I think my mind would have been made up, and, after that, whatever deluge the Fates desired. But a sound fell on my ear, faint and not unmusical. I was dully conscious of some new scheme beginning to frame itself. I changed my path, and walked faster.

Presently the cause of the sound disclosed itself. A field forge, an anvil, a couple of grimy farriers, and half-a-dozen troopers with horses. The cavalrymen were resting on the ground, watering-bridle in hand, awaiting their turns. The smiths were slaving, sweating, swearing, doing the work of thrice their number. It was a queer enough group, and I gazed at it for many minutes, still unable to frame the gauzy idea that had reanimated me. Then one of the farriers who had been fitting a hissing shoe on to a hind hoof, chilled the hot iron in a rain puddle, and humped up the horse's fetlock on to his apron again.

I started.

The fellow picked up a hammer, took a nail from his mouth, and drove the nail first gently, and then smartly home. "There, vicious one," swore he. "I put that spike through the vent in a matter of seconds, but with these four others beside it, thou'lt not rid thyself of it in as many weeks."

I strode forward.

"Five louis for that hammer and a score of nails!"

The military smith dropped the hoof from his lap, came to attention, and saluted. But he looked at me queerly, and answered nothing. I could see he thought me mad. Very likely excitement had made me look so.

"Ten louis. There is the money, in gold."

"My officer, the things are yours."

Steel spikes, brittle rods that would snap off short, would have been better. But time was growing narrow, and I must take what offered. These soft bent nails would serve my purpose. And now for the river. The current was swift, and I could not swim a stroke. I must go up-stream, and trust to find some tree-trunk or wooden balk that would aid me in floating down.

III

Of the matters that happened after this I cannot speak with any minuteness. To think back at, the whole time seems like a blurred dream, broken by snatches of dead sleep. I know I gained my point on the river-bank, some mile above the village, and entered the water there, finding it chill as ice. I think it was a small fence-gate that aided my choking passage. I can only recollect clearly that the thing I clung to was terribly unstable; and that on being landed by a chance eddy on a strip of shoal, I lay there for fully half an hour, listening to a sentry plodding past and past through the mud ten yards away, unable to move a limb. Then I gathered strength; and crawling, not only from caution but through sheer helplessness, made my stealthy way still further along the shore.

Four batteries commanded the approaches to the bridge. Two were on either flank, to deliver a converging fire; two, one above the other, were in a direct line with it, so that the causeway could be swept from end to end.

It was in the lower of these last that I found myself – by what route come, I cannot say. Only then my senses seemed to return to me. I was lying in an embrasure. Overhead was the round, black chase of a sixty-pounder. I crawled farther and looked down the line. Six more guns loomed through the night, making seven in all.

The rain was coming down in torrents, sending up spurts of mud. There were men within a dozen yards, wakeful men; and then, and not before, did it flash upon me that my farrier's hammer was a useless weapon. Fool that I was to bring it. Idiot I must have been to forget that the first clink would awaken the redoubt. My life? No, pah! I didn't count that. But it would mean only one gun spiked effectually, if so much. I drew back into the embrasure, and knitted my forehead afresh. The right thought was tardy, but it came. I drew off my boot. It was new, and it was heavy – badinage had been poured out by my comrades over its heaviness. The strong-sewn heel would drive like a calker's mallet.

Then I got to work. The guns were loaded and primed. The locks were covered with leather aprons. I used infinite caution; crawling like a cat, crouching in deepest shadows, stopping, making detours; not for mere life's sake, be it understood, but because life was wanted for work yet undone.

The seven guns were put out of action, and still the night was dark and the Austrians were ignorant behind the curtain of pelting rain . . . And then on to the upper battery . . . Two, four, eight guns!

Three I spiked, and the night began to grey. Three more, and men were stirring. I got reckless, and sprang openly at another. The air was filling with shouts, and stinking powder smoke, and crashes, and the red flash of cannon.

The French were advancing to the storm in the wet, grey dawn. Both flanking batteries, fully manned, had opened upon them; but of the guns which had direct command of the bridge, only one spoke.

Into the roar of artillery, the wind brought up yells, and oaths, and bubbling shrieks. And then the eagles came through the smoke. There was no stopping that rush.

Somehow I found myself amongst comrades, fighting with a claw-backed farrier's hammer; knowing nothing of order, or reason, or how these things came to pass; but heated only by an insane desire to kill, and kill, and kill! And then I grappled with a man who was struggling off with a flag, and wrestled with him in a crimson slough, and choked him down into it, whilst heavily-shod feet trampled madly on both of us. And afterwards there was more shouting and cheering; and mighty hand-claps between my shoulder-blades; and the old Major, who gave me cognac out of a silver flask – cognac which seemed to have been sadly over-watered.

And that is all I remembered till I woke up in the afternoon from the sofa in that village inn. *Reveille* had sounded. We mustered under arms, and the roll was called. Many did not answer.

And then: "Stand out, Lieutenant Ramard!" said the Colonel.

I advanced, and saluted.

"You will consider yourself under arrest, sir, for desertion before the enemy. Presently, you will surrender your sword, and report yourself at head-quarters."

The Colonel turned and exchanged some words with a little, pale man near him, who sat awkwardly on a white stallion.

He resumed: "The Emperor has considered your case, sir, confirms the arrest, and orders you to be reduced to the ranks." The Colonel paused, and continued:

"But as a reward for your gallantry, your commission of captain will be made out with promotion to the first vacant majority, and you will also receive a decoration."

And then I was ordered to advance again, and the Emperor transferred a Cross of the Legion from his own breast to mine.

"Captain of the Twenty-second," he said, "thou art my brother."

I never asked for the Colonel's apology.

HOW THE REDOUBT WAS TAKEN

Prosper Mérimée

Prosper Mérimée (1803–70) is not as well remembered today as he should be, not least because his story "Carmen" (1847) was the basis for Georges Bizet's opera Carmen *(1875). He was a prolific writer of short stories and novels as well as being a serious archeologist, historian and government inspector of historic monuments. His first work appeared in 1825 and he continued to write up until his death, though he produced little of much consequence after 1854. The following story, first published in his collection* Mosaïque *(1833), is believed to be based on the capture of the fort at Schwardino during Napoleon's Russian campaign of 1812.*

A friend of mine, a soldier, who died in Greece of fever some years since, described to me one day his first engagement. His story so impressed me that I wrote it down from memory. It was as follows:

I joined my regiment on September 4. It was evening. I found the Colonel in the camp. He received me rather brusquely but having read the General's introductory letter he changed his manner, and addressed me courteously.

By him I was presented to my Captain, who had just come in from reconnoitring. This Captain, whose acquaintance I had scarcely time to make, was a tall, dark man, of harsh, repelling aspect. He had been a private soldier, and had won his cross and epaulettes upon the field of battle. His voice, which was hoarse and feeble, contrasted strangely with his gigantic stature. This voice of his he owed, as I was told, to a bullet which had passed completely through his body at the Battle of Jena.

On learning that I had just come from college at Fontaine-bleau, he remarked, with a wry face, "My Lieutenant died last night."

I understood what he implied – "It is for you to take his place, and you are good for nothing."

A sharp retort was on my tongue, but I restrained it.

The moon was rising behind the redoubt of Cheverino, which stood two cannon-shots from our encampment. The moon was large and red, as is common at her rising; but that night she seemed to me of extraordinary size. For an instant the redoubt stood out coal-black against the glittering disk. It resembled the cone of a volcano at the moment of eruption.

An old soldier, at whose side I found myself, observed the colour of the moon.

"She is very red," he said. "It is a sign that it will cost us dear to win this wonderful redoubt."

I was always superstitious, and this piece of augury, coming at that moment, troubled me. I sought my couch, but could not sleep. I rose, and walked about awhile, watching the long line of fires upon the heights beyond the village of Cheverino.

When the sharp night air had thoroughly refreshed my blood I went back to the fire. I rolled my mantle round me, and I shut my eyes, trusting not to open them till day-break. But sleep refused to visit me. Insensibly my thoughts grew doleful. I told myself that I had not a friend among the hundred thousand men who filled that plain. If I were wounded, I should be placed in hospital, in the hands of ignorant and careless surgeons. I called to mind what I had heard of operations. My heart beat violently, and I mechanically arranged, as a kind of crude cuirass, my handkerchief and pocket-book upon my breast. Then, over-powered with weariness, my eyes closed drowsily, only to open the next instant with a start at some new thought of horror.

Fatigue, however, at last gained the day. When the drums beat at daybreak I was fast asleep. We were drawn up in rank. The roll was called, then we stacked our arms, and everything announced that we should pass another uneventful day.

But about three o'clock an aide-de-camp arrived with orders. We were commanded to take arms.

Our sharpshooters marched into the plain. We followed slowly, and in twenty minutes we saw the outposts of the Russians falling back and entering the redoubt. We had a battery of artillery on our right, another on our left, but both some distance in advance of us. They opened a sharp fire upon the enemy, who returned it briskly, and the redoubt of Cheverino was soon concealed by volumes of thick smoke. Our regiment was almost covered from the Russians' fire by a piece of rising ground. Their bullets (which besides were rarely aimed at us, for they preferred to fire upon our cannoneers) whistled over us, or at worst knocked up a shower of earth and stones.

Just as the order to advance was given, the Captain looked at me intently. I stroked my sprouting moustache with an air of unconcern; in truth, I was not frightened, and only dreaded lest I might be thought so. These passing bullets aided my heroic coolness, while my self-respect assured me that the danger was a real one, since I was veritably under fire. I was delighted at my self-possession, and already looked forward to the pleasure of describing in Parisian drawing-rooms the capture of the redoubt of Cheverino.

The Colonel passed before our company. "Well," he said to me, "you are going to see warm work in your first action."

I gave a martial smile, and brushed my cuff, on which a bullet, which had struck the earth at thirty paces distant, had cast a little dust.

It appeared that the Russians had discovered that their bullets did no harm, for they replaced them by a fire of shells, which began to reach us in the hollows where we lay. One of these, in its explosion, knocked off my shako and killed a man beside me.

"I congratulate you," said the Captain, as I picked up my shako. "You are safe now for the day."

I knew the military superstition which believes that the axiom *non bis in idem* is as applicable to the battlefield as to the courts of justice. I replaced my shako with a swagger.

"That's a crude way to make one raise one's hat," I said, as lightly as I could. And this wretched piece of wit was, in the circumstances, received as excellent.

"I compliment you," said the Captain. "You will command a company to-night; for I shall not survive the day. Every time I have been wounded the officer below me has been touched by some spent ball; and," he added, in a lower tone, "all their names began with P."

I laughed sceptically; most people would have done the same; but most would also have been struck, as I was, by these prophetic words. But, conscript though I was, I felt that I could trust my thoughts to no one, and that it was my duty to seem always calm and bold.

At the end of half an hour the Russian fire had sensibly diminished. We left our cover to advance on the redoubt.

Our regiment was composed of three battalions. The second had to take the enemy in flank; the two others formed the storming party. I was in the third.

On issuing from behind the cover, we were received by several volleys, which did but little harm. The whistling of the balls amazed me. "But after all," I thought, "a battle is less terrible than I expected."

We advanced at a smart run, our musketeers in front. All at once the Russians uttered three hurras – three distinct hurras – and then stood silent, without firing.

"I don't like that silence," said the Captain. "It bodes no good."

I began to think our people were too eager. I could not help comparing, mentally, their shouts and clamour with the striking silence of the enemy.

We quickly reached the foot of the redoubt. The palisades were broken and the earthworks shattered by our balls. With a roar of "Vive l'Empereur!" our soldiers rushed across the ruins.

I raised my eyes. Never shall I forget the sight which met my view. The smoke had mostly lifted, and remained suspended, like a canopy, at twenty feet above the redoubt. Through a bluish mist could be perceived, behind their shattered parapet, the Russian Grenadiers, with rifles lifted, as motionless as statues. I can see them still – the left eye of every soldier glaring at us, the right hidden by his lifted gun. In an embrasure as a few feet distant, a man with a fusee stood by a cannon.

I shuddered. I believed that my last hour had come.

"Now for the dance to open!" cried the Captain. These were the last words I heard him speak.

There came from the redoubt a roll of drums. I saw the muzzles lowered. I shut my eyes; I heard a most appalling crash of sound, to which succeeded groans and cries. Then I looked up, amazed to find myself still living. The redoubt was once more wrapped in smoke. I was surrounded by the dead and wounded. The Captain was extended at my feet; a ball had carried off his head, and I was covered with his blood. Of all the company, only six men, except myself, remained erect.

This carnage was succeeded by a kind of stupor. The next instant the Colonel, with his hat on his sword's point, had scaled the parapet with a cry of "Vive l'Empereur!" The survivors followed him. All that followed is to me a kind of dream. We rushed into the redoubt, I know not how; we fought hand to hand in the midst of smoke so thick that no man could perceive his enemy. I found my sabre dripping blood; I heard a shout of "Victory"; and, in the clearing smoke, I saw the earthworks piled with dead and dying. The cannons were covered with a heap of corpses. About two hundred men in the French uniform were standing, without order, loading their muskets or wiping their bayonets. Eleven Russian prisoners were with them.

The Colonel was lying, bathed in blood, upon a broken cannon. A group of soldiers crowded round him. I approached them.

"Who is the oldest Captain?" he was asking of a Sergeant.

The Sergeant shrugged his shoulders most expressively.

"Who is the oldest Lieutenant?"

"This gentleman, who came last night," replied the Sergeant, calmly.

The Colonel smiled bitterly.

"Come, sir," he said to me, "you are now in chief command. Fortify the gorge of the redoubt at once with waggons, for the enemy is out in force. But General C—— is coming to support you."

"Colonel," I asked him, "are you badly wounded?"

"Pish, my dear fellow! The redoubt is taken!"

THE DUEL

Joseph Conrad

*Born Jósef Kornzeniowski, in what was then Russian
Poland, Joseph Conrad (1857–1924) – the name he
adopted when he became a British subject in 1886 – spent
all his youth at sea and could not speak English until he
was twenty. Yet he went on to become one of Britain's
greatest writers. "The Duel", first serialised in* Pall Mall
Magazine *in 1908 is considered amongst his best works and
was adapted into a beautifully photographed and superbly
realized film,* The Duellists *(1977), by Ridley Scott.
Conrad was fascinated with the Napoleonic period, perhaps because he had been so imbued with the legend of
Napoleon in his boyhood. He long planned to write a novel
set in the period, and had started researching it in 1904,
but died before he completed it. What was written appeared as* Suspense *(1925). Early in his research he
encountered a story about two hussars in Napoleon's army
whose determination to resolve a point of honour spread
over sixteen years. That was the basis for "The Duel"*

which takes us from the earliest days of Napoleon's Empire through to beyond his death.

Napoleon I, whose career had the quality of a duel against the whole of Europe, disliked duelling between the officers of his army. The great military emperor was not a swashbuckler, and had little respect for tradition.

Nevertheless, a story of duelling, which became a legend in the army, runs through the epic of imperial wars. To the surprise and admiration of their fellows, two officers, like insane artists trying to gild refined gold or paint the lily, pursued a private contest through the years of universal carnage. They were officers of cavalry, and their connection with the high-spirited but fanciful animal which carries men into battle seems particularly appropriate. It would be difficult to imagine for heroes of this legend two officers of infantry of the line, for example, whose fantasy is tamed by much walking exercise and whose valour necessarily must be of a more plodding kind. As to gunners or engineers, whose heads are kept cool on a diet of mathematics, it is simply unthinkable.

The names of the two officers were Feraud and D'Hubert, and they were both lieutenants in a regiment of hussars, but not in the same regiment.

Feraud was doing regimental work, but Lieut. D'Hubert had the good fortune to be attached to the person of the general commanding the division, as *officier d'ordonnance*. It was in Strasbourg, and in this agreeable and important garrison they were enjoying greatly a short interval of peace. They were enjoying it, though both intensely war-like, because it was a sword-sharpening, fire-lock-cleaning peace, dear to a military heart and undamaging to military prestige, inasmuch that no one believed in its sincerity or duration.

Under those historical circumstances, so favourable to the proper appreciation of military leisure, Lieut. D'Hubert, one fine afternoon, made his way along a quiet street of a cheerful

suburb towards Lieut. Feraud's quarters, which were in a
private house with a garden at the back, belonging to an old
maiden lady.

His knock at the door was answered instantly by a young
maid in Alsatian costume. Her fresh complexion and her long
eyelashes, lowered demurely at the sight of the tall officer,
caused Lieut. D'Hubert, who was accessible to esthetic impressions, to relax the cold, severe gravity of his face. At the
same time he observed that the girl had over her arm a pair of
hussar's breeches, blue with a red stripe.

"Lieut. Feraud in?" he inquired benevolently.

"Oh, no, sir! He went out at six this morning."

The pretty maid tried to close the door. Lieut. D'Hubert
stepped into the anteroom, jingling his spurs.

"Come, my dear! You don't mean to say he has not been
home since six o'clock this morning?"

Saying these words, Lieut. D'Hubert opened without ceremony the door of a room so comfortable and neatly ordered that
only from internal evidence in the shape of boots, uniforms, and
military accoutrements did he acquire the conviction that it was
Lieut. Feraud's room. And he saw also that Lieut. Feraud was
not at home. The truthful maid had followed him, and raised
her candid eyes to his face.

"H'm!" said Lieut. D'Hubert, greatly disappointed, for he
had already visited all the haunts where a lieutenant of hussars
could be found of a fine afternoon. "So he's out? And do you
happen to know, my dear, why he went out at six this morning?"

"No," she answered readily. "He came home late last night,
and snored. I heard him when I got up at five. Then he dressed
himself in his oldest uniform and went out. Service, I suppose."

"Service? Not a bit of it!" cried Lieut. D'Hubert. "Learn, my
angel, that he went out thus early to fight a duel with a civilian."

She heard this news without a quiver of her dark eyelashes. It
was very obvious that the actions of Lieut. Feraud were generally above criticism. She only looked up for a moment in mute
surprise, and Lieut. D'Hubert concluded from this absence of

emotion that she must have seen Lieut. Feraud since that morning. He looked around the room.

"Come!" he insisted, with confidential familiarity. "He's perhaps somewhere in the house now?"

She shook her head.

"So much the worse for him!" continued Lieut. D'Hubert, in a tone of anxious conviction. "But he has been home this morning."

This time the pretty maid nodded slightly.

"He has!" cried Lieut. D'Hubert. "And went out again? What for? Couldn't he keep quietly indoors! What a lunatic! My dear girl—"

Lieut. D'Hubert's natural kindness of disposition and strong sense of comradeship helped his powers of observation. He changed his tone to a most insinuating softness, and, gazing at the hussar's breeches hanging over the arm of the girl, he appealed to the interest she took in Lieut. Feraud's comfort and happiness. He was pressing and persuasive. He used his eyes, which were kind and fine, with excellent effect. His anxiety to get hold at once of Lieut. Feraud, for Lieut. Feraud's own good, seemed so genuine that at last it overcame the girl's unwillingness to speak. Unluckily she had not much to tell. Lieut. Feraud had returned home shortly before ten, had walked straight into his room, and had thrown himself on his bed to resume his slumbers. She had heard him snore rather louder than before far into the afternoon. Then he got up, put on his best uniform, and went out. That was all she knew.

She raised her eyes, and Lieut. D'Hubert stared into them incredulously.

"It's incredible. Gone parading the town in his best uniform! My dear child, don't you know he ran that civilian through this morning? Clean through, as you spit a hare."

The pretty maid heard the gruesome intelligence without any signs of distress. But she pressed her lips together thoughtfully.

"He isn't parading the town," she remarked in a low tone. "Far from it."

"The civilian's family is making an awful row," continued

Lieut. D'Hubert, pursuing his train of thought. "And the general is very angry. It's one of the best families in the town. Feraud ought to have kept close at least—"

"What will the general do to him?" inquired the girl anxiously.

"He won't have his head cut off, to be sure," grumbled Lieut. D'Hubert. "His conduct is positively indecent. He's making no end of trouble for himself by this sort of bravado."

"But he isn't parading the town," the maid insisted in a shy murmur.

"Why, yes! Now I think of it, I haven't seen him anywhere about. What on earth has he done with himself?"

"He's gone to pay a call," suggested the maid, after a moment of silence.

Lieut. D'Hubert started.

"A call! Do you mean a call on a lady? The cheek of the man! And how do you know this, my dear?"

Without concealing her woman's scorn for the denseness of the masculine mind, the pretty maid reminded him that Lieut. Feraud had arrayed himself in his best uniform before going out. He had also put on his newest dolman, she added, in a tone as if this conversation were getting on her nerves, and turned away brusquely.

Lieut. D'Hubert, without questioning the accuracy of the deduction, did not see that it advanced him much on his official quest. For his quest after Lieut. Feraud had an official character. He did not know any of the women this fellow, who had run a man through in the morning, was likely to visit in the afternoon. The two young men knew each other but slightly. He bit his gloved finger in perplexity.

"Call!" he exclaimed. "Call on the devil!"

The girl, with her back to him, and folding the hussar's breeches on a chair, protested with a vexed little laugh:

"Oh dear, no! On Madame de Lionne."

Lieut. D'Hubert whistled softly. Madame de Lionne was the wife of a high official who had a well-known *salon* and some pretensions to sensibility and elegance. The husband was a civilian, and old; but the society of the *salon* was young and military. Lieut. D'Hubert had whistled, not because the idea of pursuing Lieut. Feraud into that very *salon* was disagreeable to him, but because, having arrived in Strasbourg only lately, he had not had the time as yet to get an introduction to Madame de Lionne. And what was that swashbuckler Feraud doing there, he wondered. He did not seem the sort of man who—

"Are you certain of what you say?" asked Lieut. D'Hubert.

The girl was perfectly certain. Without turning round to look at him, she explained that the coachman of their next door neighbours knew the *maître-d'hotel* of Madame de Lionne. In this way she had her information. And she was perfectly certain. In giving this assurance she sighed. Lieut. Feraud called there nearly every afternoon, she added.

"Ah, bah!" exclaimed D'Hubert ironically. His opinion of Madame de Lionne went down several degrees. Lieut. Feraud did not seem to him specially worthy of attention on the part of a woman with a reputation for sensibility and elegance. But there was no saying. At bottom they were all alike – very practical rather than idealistic. Lieut. D'Hubert, however, did not allow his mind to dwell on these considerations.

"By thunder!" he reflected aloud. "The general goes there sometimes. If he happens to find the fellow making eyes at the lady there will be the devil to pay! Our general is not a very accommodating person, I can tell you."

"Go quickly, then! Don't stand here now I've told you where he is!" cried the girl, colouring to the eyes.

"Thanks, my dear! I don't know what I would have done without you."

After manifesting his gratitude in an aggressive way, which at first was repulsed violently, and then submitted to with a sudden and still more repellent indifference, Lieut. D'Hubert took his departure.

He clanked and jingled along the streets with a martial swagger. To run a comrade to earth in a drawing-room where he was not known did not trouble him in the least. A uniform is a passport. His position as *officier d'ordonnance* of the general added to his assurance. Moreover, now that he knew where to find Lieut. Feraud, he had no option. It was a service matter.

Madame de Lionne's house had an excellent appearance. A man in livery, opening the door of a large drawing-room with a waxed floor, shouted his name and stood aside to let him pass. It was a reception day. The ladies wore big hats surcharged with a profusion of feathers; their bodies sheathed in clinging white gowns from the armpits to the tips of the low satin shoes, looked sylph-like and cool in a great display of bare necks and arms. The men who talked with them, on the contrary, were arrayed heavily in multi-coloured garments with collars up to their ears and thick sashes round their waists. Lieut. D'Hubert made his unabashed way across the room, and, bowing low before a sylph-like form reclining on a couch, offered his apologies for this intrusion, which nothing could excuse but the extreme urgency of the service order he had to communicate to his comrade Feraud. He proposed to himself to return presently in a more regular manner and beg forgiveness for interrupting the interesting conversation . . .

A bare arm was extended towards him with gracious nonchalance even before he had finished speaking. He pressed the hand respectfully to his lips, and made the mental remark that it was bony. Madame de Lionne was a blonde, with too fine a skin and a long face.

"*C'est ça!*" she said, with an ethereal smile, disclosing a set of large teeth. "Come this evening to plead for your forgiveness."

"I will not fail, madame."

Meantime Lieut. Feraud, splendid in his new dolman and the extremely polished boots of his calling, sat on a chair within the foot of a couch, one hand resting on his thigh, the other twirling his moustache to a point. At a significant glance from D'Hubert he rose without alacrity and followed him into the recess of a window.

"What is it you want with me?" he asked, with astonishing indifference. Lieut. D'Hubert could not imagine that in the innocence of his heart and simplicity of his conscience Lieut. Feraud took a view of his duel in which neither remorse nor yet a rational apprehension of consequences had any place. Though he had no clear recollection how the quarrel had originated (it was begun in an establishment where beer and wine are drunk late at night), he had not the slightest doubt of being himself the outraged party. He had had two experienced friends for his seconds. Everything had been done according to the rules governing that sort of adventures. And a duel is obviously fought for the purpose of some one being at least hurt, if not killed outright. The civilian got hurt. That also was in order. Lieut. Feraud was perfectly tranquil; but Lieut. D'Hubert took it for affectation, and spoke with a certain vivacity.

"I am directed by the general to give you the order to go at once to your quarters, and remain there under close arrest."

It was now the turn of Lieut. Feraud to be astonished. "What the devil are you telling me there?" he murmured faintly, and fell into such profound wonder that he could only follow mechanically the motions of Lieut. D'Hubert. The two officers, one tall, with an interesting face and a moustache the colour of ripe corn, the other, short and sturdy, with a hooked nose and a thick crop of black curly hair, approached the mistress of the house to take their leave. Madame de Lionne, a woman of eclectic taste, smiled upon these armed young men with impartial sensibility and an equal share of interest. Madame de Lionne took her delight in the infinite variety of human species. All the other eyes in the drawing-room followed the departing officers; and when they had gone out one or two men who had already heard of the duel, imparted the information to the sylph-like ladies, who received it with faint shrieks of humane concern.

Meantime the two hussars walked side by side, Lieut. Feraud trying to master the hidden reason of things which in this instance eluded the grasp of his intellect; Lieut. D'Hubert feeling annoyed at the part he had to play, because the general's instructions were that he should see personally that Lieut. Feraud carried out his orders to the letter, and at once.

"The chief seems to know this animal," he thought, eyeing his companion, whose round face, the round eyes and even the twisted up jet black little moustache seemed animated by a mental exasperation against the incomprehensible. And louder he observed rather reproachfully, "The general is in a devilish fury with you!"

Lieut. Feraud stopped short on the edge of the pavement, and cried in the accents of unmistakable sincerity, "What on earth for?" The innocence of the fiery Gascon soul was depicted in the manner in which he seized his head in both hands as if to prevent it bursting with perplexity.

"For the duel," said Lieut. D'Hubert curtly. He was annoyed greatly by this sort of perverse fooling.

"The duel! The . . ."

Lieut. Feraud passed from one paroxysm of astonishment into another. He dropped his hands and walked on slowly, trying to reconcile this information with the state of his own feelings. It was impossible. He burst out indignantly, "Was I to let that sauerkraut-eating civilian wipe his boots on the uniform of the 7th Hussars?"

Lieut. D'Hubert could not remain altogether unmoved by that simple sentiment. This little fellow was a lunatic, he thought to himself, but there was something in what he said.

"Of course, I don't know how far you were justified," he began soothingly. "And the general himself may not be exactly informed. Those people have been deafening him with their lamentations."

"Ah! the general is not exactly informed," mumbled Lieut. Feraud, walking faster and faster as his choler at the injustice of his fate began to rise. "He is not exactly . . . And he orders me under close arrest, with God knows what afterwards!"

"Don't excite yourself like this," remonstrated the other. "Your adversary's people are very influential, you know, and it looks bad enough on the face of it. The general had to take notice of their complaint at once. I don't think he means to be over-severe with you. It's the best thing for you to be kept out of sight for a while."

"I am very much obliged to the general," muttered Lieut. Feraud through his teeth. "And perhaps you would say I ought to be grateful to you too for the trouble you have taken to hunt me up in the drawing-room of a lady who—"

"Frankly," interrupted Lieut. D'Hubert, with an innocent laugh, "I think you ought to be. I had no end of trouble to find out where you were. It wasn't exactly the place for you to disport yourself in under the circumstances. If the general had caught you there making eyes at the goddess of the temple . . . oh, my word! . . . He hates to be bothered with complaints against his officers, you know. And it looked uncommonly like sheer bravado."

The two officers had arrived now at the street door of Lieut. Feraud's lodgings. The latter turned towards his companion. "Lieutenant D'Hubert," he said, "I have something to say to you, which can't be said very well in the street. You can't refuse to come up."

The pretty maid had opened the door. Lieut. Feraud brushed past her brusquely, and she raised her scared and questioning eyes to Lieut. D'Hubert, who could do nothing but shrug his shoulders slightly as he followed with marked reluctance.

In his room Lieut. Feraud unhooked the clasp, flung his new dolman on the bed, and, folding his arms across his chest, turned to the other hussar.

"Do you imagine I am a man to submit tamely to injustice?" he inquired, in a boisterous voice.

"Oh, do be reasonable!" remonstrated Lieut. D'Hubert.

"I am reasonable! I am perfectly reasonable!" retorted the other with ominous restraint. "I can't call the general to account for his behaviour, but you are going to answer me for yours."

"I can't listen to this nonsense," murmured Lieut. D'Hubert, making a slightly contemptuous grimace.

"You call this nonsense? It seems to me a perfectly plain statement. Unless you don't understand French."

"What on earth do you mean?"

"I mean," screamed suddenly Lieut. Feraud, "to cut off your ears to teach you to disturb me with the general's orders when I am talking to a lady!"

A profound silence followed this mad declaration; and

through the open window Lieut. D'Hubert heard the little birds singing sanely in the garden. He said, preserving his calm, "Why! if you take that tone, of course I shall hold myself at your disposition whenever you are at liberty to attend to this affair; but I don't think you will cut my ears off."

"I am going to attend to it at once," declared Lieut. Feraud, with extreme truculence. "If you are thinking of displaying your airs and graces tonight in Madame de Lionne's salon you are very much mistaken."

"Really!" said Lieut. D'Hubert, who was beginning to feel irritated, "you are an impracticable sort of fellow. The general's orders to me were to put you under arrest, not to carve you into small pieces. Good-morning!" And turning his back on the little Gascon, who, always sober in his potations, was as though born intoxicated with the sunshine of his vine-ripening country, the Northman, who could drink hard on occasion, but was born sober under the watery skies of Picardy, made for the door. Hearing, however, the unmistakable sound behind his back of a sword drawn from the scabbard, he had no option but to stop.

"Devil take this mad southerner!" he thought, spinning round and surveying with composure the warlike posture of Lieut. Feraud, with a bare sword in his hand.

"At once! – at once!" stuttered Feraud, beside himself.

"You had my answer," said the other, keeping his temper very well.

At first he had been only vexed, and somewhat amused; but now his face got clouded. He was asking himself seriously how he could manage to get away. It was impossible to run from a man with a sword, and as to fighting him, it seemed completely out of the question. He waited awhile, then said exactly what was in his heart.

"Drop this! I won't fight with you. I won't be made ridiculous."

"Ah, you won't?" hissed the Gascon. "I suppose you prefer to be made infamous. Do you hear what I say? . . . Infamous! Infamous! Infamous!" he shrieked, rising and falling on his toes and getting very red in the face.

Lieut. D'Hubert on the contrary became very pale at the sound of the unsavoury word for a moment, then flushed pink to the roots of his fair hair. "But you can't go out to fight; you are under arrest, you lunatic!" he objected, with angry scorn.

"There's the garden: it's big enough to lay out your long carcass in," spluttered the other, with such ardour that somehow the anger of the cooler man subsided.

"This is perfectly absurd," he said, glad enough to think he had found a way out of it for the moment. "We shall never get any of our comrades to serve as seconds. It's preposterous."

"Seconds! Damn the seconds! We don't want any seconds. Don't you worry about any seconds. I shall send word to your friends to come and bury you when I am done. And if you want any witnesses, I'll send word to the old girl to put her head out of a window at the back. Stay! There's the gardener. He'll do. He's as deaf as a post, but he has two eyes in his head. Come along! I will teach you, my staff officer, that the carrying about of a general's orders is not always child's play."

While thus discoursing he had unbuckled his empty scabbard. He sent it flying under the bed, and, lowering the point of the sword, brushed past the perplexed Lieut. D'Hubert, exclaiming, "Follow me!" Directly he had flung open the door a faint shriek was heard, and the pretty maid, who had been listening at the keyhole, staggered away, putting the backs of her hand over her eyes. Feraud did not seem to see her, but she ran after him and seized his left arm. He shook her off, and then she rushed towards Lieut. D'Hubert and clawed at the sleeve of his uniform.

"Wretched man!" she sobbed, "Is this what you wanted to find him for?"

"Let me go," entreated Lieut. D'Hubert, trying to disengage himself gently. "It's like being in a madhouse," he protested, with exasperation. "Do let me go. I won't do him any harm."

A fiendish laugh from Lieut. Feraud commented that assurance. "Come along!" he shouted, with a stamp of his foot.

And Lieut. D'Hubert did follow. He could do nothing else. Yet in vindication of his sanity it must be recorded that as he passed through the ante-room the notion of opening the street door and bolting out presented itself to this brave youth, only of course to be instantly dismissed, for he felt sure that the other would pursue him without shame or compunction. And the prospect of an officer of hussars being chased along the street by another officer of hussars with a naked sword could not be for a moment entertained. Therefore he followed into the garden. Behind them the girl tottered out too. With ashy lips and wild scared eyes, she surrendered herself to a dreadful curiosity. She had also the notion of rushing if need be between Lieut. Feraud and death.

The deaf gardener, utterly unconscious of approaching footsteps, went on watering his flowers till Lieut. Feraud thumped him on the back. Beholding suddenly an enraged man flourishing a big sabre, the old chap trembling in all his limbs dropped the watering-pot. At once Lieut. Feraud kicked it away with great animosity, and, seizing the gardener by the throat, backed him against a tree. He held him there, shouting in his ear, "Stay here, and look on! You understand? You've got to look on! Don't dare budge from the spot!"

Lieut. D'Hubert came slowly down the walk, unclasping his dolman with unconcealed disgust. Even then, with his hand already on the hilt of his sword, he hesitated to draw till a roar "En garde, fichtre. What do you think you came here for?" and the rush of his adversary forced him to put himself as quickly as possible in a posture of defence.

The clash of arms filled that prim garden, which hitherto had known no more warlike sound than the click of clipping shears; and presently the upper part of an old lady's body was projected out of a window upstairs. She tossed her arms above her white cap, scolding in a cracked voice. The gardener remained glued to the tree, his toothless mouth open in idiotic astonishment, and a little farther up the path the pretty girl, as if spellbound to a small grass plot, ran a few steps this way and that wringing her hands and muttering crazily. She did not rush between the combatants: the onslaughts of Lieut. Feraud were so fierce that her heart failed her. Lieut. D'Hubert, his faculties concentrated upon defence, needed all his skill and science of the sword to stop the rushes of his adversary. Twice already he had to break ground. It bothered him to feel his foothold made insecure by the round, dry gravel of the path rolling under the hard soles of his boots. This was most unsuitable ground, he thought, keeping a watchful, narrowed gaze, shaded by long eyelashes, upon the fiery stare of his thick-set adversary. This absurd affair would ruin his reputation of a sensible, well-behaved, promising officer. It would damage at any rate his immediate prospects, and lose him the good-will of his general. These worldly preoccupations were no doubt mis-placed in view of the solemnity of the moment. A duel, whether regarded as a ceremony in the cult of honour, or even when reduced in its moral essence to a form of manly sport, demands a perfect singleness of intention, a homicidal austerity of mood. On the other hand this vivid concern for his future had not a bad effect inasmuch as it began to rouse the anger of Lieut. D'Hubert. Some seventy seconds had elapsed since they had crossed blades, and Lieut. D'Hubert had to break ground again in order to avoid impaling his reckless adversary like a beetle for a cabinet of specimens. The result was that misapprehending the motive, Lieut. Feraud with a triumphant sort of snarl pressed his attack.

"This enraged animal will have me against the wall directly," thought Lieut. D'Hubert. He imagined himself much closer to the house than he was, and he dared not turn his head; it seemed to him he was keeping his adversary off with his eyes rather more than with his point. Lieut. Feraud crouched and bounded with a fierce tigerish agility fit to trouble the stoutest heart. But what was more appalling than the fury of a wild beast, accom-plishing in all innocence of heart a natural function, was the fixity of savage purpose man alone is capable of displaying. Lieut. D'Hubert in the midst of his worldly preoccupations perceived it at last. It was an absurd and damaging affair to be drawn into, but whatever silly intention the fellow had started with it was clear enough that by this time he meant to kill – nothing less. He meant it with an intensity of will utterly beyond the inferior faculties of a tiger.

As is the case with constitutionally brave men, the full view of the danger interested Lieut. D'Hubert. And directly he got properly interested, the length of his arm and the coolness of his head told in his favour. It was the turn of Lieut. Feraud to recoil, with a bloodcurdling grunt of baffled rage. He made a swift feint, and then rushed straight forward.

"Ah! you would, would you?" Lieut. D'Hubert exclaimed mentally. The combat had lasted nearly two minutes, time enough for any man to get embittered, apart from the merits of the quarrel. And all at once it was over. Trying to close breast to breast under his adversary's guard Lieut. Feraud received a slash on his shortened arm. He did not feel it in the least, but it checked his rush, and his feet slipping on the gravel he fell backwards with great violence. The shock jarred his boiling brain into the perfect quietude of insensibility. Simultaneously with his fall the pretty servant-girl shrieked; but the old maiden lady at the window ceased her scolding, and began to cross herself piously.

Beholding his adversary stretched out perfectly still, his face to the sky, Lieut. D'Hubert thought he had killed him outright. The impression of having slashed hard enough to cut his man clean in two abode with him for a while in an exaggerated memory of the right good will he had put into the blow. He dropped on his knees hastily by the side of the prostrate body. Discovering that not even the arm was severed, a slight sense of disappointment mingled with the feeling of relief. The fellow deserved the worst. But truly he did not want the death of that sinner. The affair was ugly enough as it stood, and Lieut. D'Hubert addressed himself at once to the task of stopping the bleeding. In this task it was his fate to be ridiculously impeded by the pretty maid. Rending the air with screams of horror, she attacked him from behind and, twinning her fingers in his hair, tugged back at his head. Why she should choose to hinder him at this precise moment he could not in the least understand. He did not try. It was all like a very wicked and harassing dream. Twice to save himself from being pulled over he had to rise and fling her off. He did this stoically, without a word, kneeling down again at once to go on with his work. But the third time, his work being done, he seized her and held her arms pinned to her body. Her cap was half off, her face was red, her eyes blazed with crazy boldness. He looked mildly into them while she called him a wretch, a traitor and a murderer many times in succession. This did not annoy him so much as the conviction that she had managed to scratch his face abundantly. Ridicule would be added to the scandal of the story. He imagined the adorned tale making its way through the garrison of the town, through the whole army on the frontier, with every possible distortion of motive and sentiment and circumstance, spreading a doubt upon the sanity of his conduct and the distinction of his taste even to the very ears of his honourable family. It was all very well for that fellow Feraud, who had no connections, no family to speak of, and no quality but courage, which, anyhow, was a matter of course, and possessed by every single trooper in the whole mass of French cavalry. Still holding down the arms of the girl in a strong grip, Lieut. D'Hubert glanced over his shoulder. Lieut. Feraud had opened his eyes. He did not move. Like a man just waking from a deep sleep he stared without any expression at the evening sky.

Lieut. D'Hubert's urgent shouts to the old gardener produced no effect – not so much as to make him shut his toothless mouth. Then he remembered that the man was stone deaf. All that time the girl struggled, not with maidenly coyness, but like a pretty dumb fury, kicking his shins now and then. He continued to hold her as if in a vice, his instinct telling him that were he to let her go she would fly at his eyes. But he was greatly humiliated by his position. At last she gave up; she was more exhausted than appeased, he feared. Nevertheless, he attempted to get out of this wicked dream by way of negotiation.

"Listen to me," he said, as calmly as he could. "Will you promise to run for a surgeon if I let you go?"

With real affliction he heard her declare that she would do nothing of the kind. On the contrary, her sobbed out intention was to remain in the garden, and fight tooth and nail for the protection of the vanquished man. This was shocking.

"My dear child!" he cried in despair, "is it possible that you

think me capable of murdering a wounded adversary? Is it . . .
Be quiet, you little wild cat, you!"

They struggled. A thick, drowsy voice said behind him,
"What are you after with that girl?"

Lieut. Feraud had raised himself on his good arm. He was
looking sleepily at his other arm, at the mess of blood on his
uniform, at a small red pool on the ground, at his sabre lying a
foot away on the path. Then he laid himself down gently again
to think it all out, as far as a thundering headache would permit
of mental operations.

Lieut. D'Hubert released the girl, who crouched at once by
the side of the other lieutenant. The shades of night were falling
on the little trim garden with this touching group, whence
proceeded low murmurs of sorrow and compassion, with other
feeble sounds of a different character, as if an imperfectly awake
invalid were trying to swear. Lieut. D'Hubert went away.

He passed through the silent house, and congratulated himself upon the dusk concealing his gory hands and scratched face
from the passers-by. But this story could by no means be
concealed. He dreaded the discredit and ridicule above everything, and was painfully aware of sneaking through the back
streets in the manner of a murderer. Presently the sounds of a
flute coming out of the open window of a lighted upstairs room
in a modest house interrupted his dismal reflections. It was
being played with a persevering virtuosity, and through the
fioritures of the tune one could hear the regular thumping of the
foot beating time on the floor.

Lieut. D'Hubert shouted a name, which was that of an army
surgeon whom he knew fairly well. The sounds of the flute
ceased, and the musician appeared at the window, his instrument still in his hand, peering into the street.

"Who calls? You, D'Hubert? What brings you this way?"

He did not like to be disturbed at the hour when he was
playing the flute. He was a man whose hair had turned grey
already in the thankless task of tying up wounds on battlefields
where others reaped advancement and glory.

"I want you to go at once and see Feraud. You know Lieut.

Feraud? He lives down the second street. It's but a step from here."

"What's the matter with him?"

"Wounded."

"Are you sure?"

"Sure!" cried D'Hubert. "I come from there."

"That's amusing," said the elderly surgeon. Amusing was his favourite word; but the expression of his face when he pronounced it never corresponded. He was a stolid man. "Come in," he added. "I'll get ready in a moment."

"Thanks! I will. I want to wash my hands in your room."

Lieut. D'Hubert found the surgeon occupied in unscrewing his flute, and packing the pieces methodically in a case. He turned his head.

"Water there – in the corner. Your hands do want washing."

"I've stopped the bleeding," said Lieut. D'Hubert. "But you had better make haste. It's rather more than ten minutes ago, you know."

The surgeon did not hurry his movements.

"What's the matter? Dressing came off? That's amusing. I've been at work in the hospital all day, but I've been told this morning by somebody that he had come off without a scratch."

"Not the same duel, probably," growled moodily Lieut. D'Hubert, wiping his hands on a coarse towel.

"Not the same . . . What? Another. It would take the very devil to make me go out twice in one day." The surgeon looked narrowly at Lieut. D'Hubert. "How did you come by that scratched face? Both sides too – and symmetrical. It's amusing."

"Very!" snarled Lieut. D'Hubert. "And you will find his slashed arm amusing too. It will keep both of you amused for quite a long time."

The doctor was mystified and impressed by the brusque bitterness of Lieut. D'Hubert's tone. They left the house together, and in the street he was still more mystified by his conduct.

"Aren't you coming with me?" he asked.

"No," said Lieut. D'Hubert. "You can find the house by yourself. The front door will be standing open very likely."

"All right. Where's his room?"

"Ground floor. But you had better go right through and look in the garden first."

This astonishing piece of information made the surgeon go off without further parley. Lieut. D'Hubert regained his quarters nursing a hot and uneasy indignation. He dreaded the chaff of his comrades almost as much as the anger of his superiors. The truth was confoundedly grotesque and embarrassing, even putting aside the irregularity of the combat itself, which made it come abominably near a criminal offence. Like all men without much imagination, a faculty which helps the processes of reflective thought, Lieut. D'Hubert became frightfully harassed by the obvious aspects of his predicament. He was certainly glad that he had not killed Lieut. Feraud outside all rules, and without the regular witnesses proper to such a transaction. Uncommonly glad. At the same time he felt as though he would have liked to wring his neck for him without ceremony.

He was still under the sway of these contradictory sentiments when the surgeon amateur of the flute came to see him. More than three days had elapsed. Lieut. D'Hubert was no longer *officier d'ordonnance* to the general commanding the division. He had been sent back to his regiment. And he was resuming his connection with the soldiers' military family by being shut up in close confinement, not at his own quarters in town but in a room in the barracks. Owing to the gravity of the incident, he was forbidden to see anyone. He did not know what had happened, and what was being said, or what was being thought. The arrival of the surgeon was a most unexpected thing to the worried captive. The amateur of the flute began by explaining that he was there only by special favour of the colonel.

"I represented to him that it would be only fair to let you have some authentic news of your adversary," he continued. "You'll be glad to hear he's getting better fast."

Lieut. D'Hubert's face exhibited no conventional signs of gladness. He continued to walk the floor of the dusty bare room.

"Take this chair, doctor," he mumbled.

The doctor sat down.

"This affair is variously appreciated – in town and in the army. In fact, the diversity of opinions is amusing."

"Is it," mumbled Lieut. D'Hubert, tramping steadily from wall to wall. But within himself he marvelled that there could be two opinions on the matter. The surgeon continued.

"Of course, as the real facts are not known—"

"I should have thought," interrupted D'Hubert, "that the fellow would have put you in possession of facts."

"He said something," admitted the other, "the first time I saw him. And, by the bye, I did find him in the garden. The thump on the back of his head had made him a little incoherent then. Afterwards he was rather reticent than otherwise."

"Didn't think he would have the grace to be ashamed," mumbled D'Hubert, resuming his pacing, while the doctor murmured, "It's very amusing. Ashamed! Shame was not exactly his frame of mind. However, you may look at the matter otherwise."

"What are you talking about? What matter?" asked D'Hubert, with a sidelong look at the heavy-faced, grey-haired figure seated on a wooden chair.

"Whatever it is," said the surgeon a little impatiently. "I don't want to pronounce any opinion on your conduct—"

"By heavens, you had better not!" burst out D'Hubert.

"There! – there! Don't be so quick in flourishing the sword. It doesn't pay in the long run. Understand once for all that I would not carve any of you youngsters except with the tools of my trade. But my advice is good. If you go on like this you will make for yourself an ugly reputation."

"Go on like what?" demanded Lieut. D'Hubert, stopping short, quite startled. "I! – I! – make for myself a reputation . . . What do you imagine?"

"I told you I don't wish to judge of the rights and wrongs of this incident. It's not my business. Nevertheless—"

"What on earth has he been telling you?" interrupted Lieut. D'Hubert, in a sort of awed scare.

"I told you already, that at first, when I picked him up in the garden, he was incoherent. Afterwards he was naturally reticent. But I gather at least that he could not help himself."

"He couldn't?" shouted Lieut. D'Hubert in a great voice. Then, lowering his tone impressively, "And what about me? Could I help myself?"

The surgeon stood up. His thoughts were running upon the flute, his constant companion with a consoling voice. In the vicinity of field ambulances, after twenty-four hours' hard work, he had been known to trouble with its sweet sounds the horrible stillness of battlefields, given over to silence and the dead. The solacing hour of his daily life was approaching, and in peace time he held on to the minutes as a miser to his hoard.

"Of course! – of course!" he said perfunctorily. "You would think so. It's amusing. However, being perfectly neutral and friendly to you both, I have consented to deliver his message to you. Say that I am humouring an invalid if you like. He wants you to know that this affair is by no means at an end. He intends to send you his seconds directly he has regained his strength – providing, of course, the army is not in the field at that time."

"He intends, does he? Why, certainly," sputtered Lieut. D'Hubert in a passion.

The secret of his exasperation was not apparent to the visitor; but this passion confirmed the surgeon in the belief which was gaining ground outside that some very serious difference had risen between these two young men, something serious enough to wear an air of mystery, some fact of the utmost gravity. To settle their urgent difference about that fact, those two young men had risked being broken and disgraced at the outset almost of their career. The surgeon feared that the forthcoming inquiry would fail to satisfy the public curiosity. They would not take the public into their confidence as to that something which had passed between them of a nature so outrageous as to make them face a charge of murder – neither more nor less. But what could it be?

The surgeon was not very curious by temperament; but that question haunting his mind caused him twice that evening to hold the instrument off his lips and sit silent for a whole minute – right in the middle of a tune – trying to form a plausible conjecture.

II

He succeeded in this object no better than the rest of the garrison and the whole of society. The two young officers, of no especial consequence till then, became distinguished by the universal curiosity as to the origin of their quarrel. Madame de Lionne's *salon* was the centre of ingenious surmises; that lady herself was for a time assailed by inquiries as being the last person known to have spoken to these unhappy and reckless young men before they went out together from her house to a savage encounter with swords, at dusk, in a private garden. She protested she had not observed anything unusual in their demeanour. Lieut. Feraud had been visibly annoyed at being called away. That was natural enough; no man likes to be disturbed in a conversation with a lady famed for her elegance and sensibility. But in truth the subject bored Madame de Lionne, since her personality could by no stretch of reckless gossip be connected with this affair. And it irritated her to hear it advanced that there might have been some woman in the case. This irritation arose, not from her elegance or sensibility, but from a more instinctive side of her nature. It became so great at last that she peremptorily forbade the subject to be mentioned under her roof. Near her couch the prohibition was obeyed, but farther off in the *salon* the pall of the imposed silence continued to be lifted more or less. A personage with a long, pale face, resembling the countenance of a sheep, opined, shaking his head, that it was a quarrel of long standing envenomed by time. It was objected to him that the men themselves were too young for such a theory. They belonged also to different and distant parts of France. There were other physical impossibilities, too. A sub-commissary of the Intendance, an agreeable and cultivated bachelor in kerseymere breeches, Hessian boots, and a blue coat embroidered with silver lace, who affected to believe in the transmigration of souls, suggested that the two men met perhaps in some previous existence. The feud was in the forgotten past. It might have been something quite inconceivable in the present state of their being; but their souls remembered the animosity, and manifested an instinctive antagonism. He developed this theme jocularly. Yet the affair was so absurd from the worldly, the military, the honourable, or the prudential point of view, that this weird explanation seemed rather more reasonable than any other.

The two officers had confided nothing definite to any one. Humiliation at having been worsted arms in hand, and an uneasy feeling of having been involved in a scrape by the injustice of fate, kept Lieut. Feraud savagely dumb. He mistrusted the sympathy of mankind. That would, of course, go to that dandified staff officer. Lying in bed, he raved aloud to the pretty maid who administered to his needs with devotion, and listened to his horrible imprecations with alarm. That Lieut. D'Hubert should be made to "pay for it," seemed to her just and natural. Her principal care was that Lieut. Feraud should not excite himself. He appeared so wholly admirable and fascinating to the humility of her heart that her only concern was to see him get well quickly, even if it were only to resume his visits to Madame de Lionne's *salon*.

Lieut. D'Hubert kept silent for the immediate reason that there was no one, except a stupid young soldier servant, to speak to. Further, he was aware that the episode, so grave professionally, had its comic side. When reflecting upon it, he still felt that he would like to wring Lieut. Feraud's neck for him. But this formula was figurative rather than precise, and expressed more a state of mind than an actual physical impulse. At the same time, there was in that young man a feeling of comradeship and kindness which made him unwilling to make the position of Lieut. Feraud worse than it was. He did not want to talk at large about this wretched affair. At the inquiry he would have, of course, to speak the truth in self-defence. This prospect vexed him.

But no inquiry took place. The army took the field instead. Lieut. D'Hubert, liberated without remark, took up his regimental duties; and Lieut. Feraud, his arm just out of the sling, rode unquestioned with his squadron to complete his convalescence in the smoke of battlefields and the fresh air of night bivouacs. This bracing treatment turned out so well, that at the first rumour of an armistice being signed he could turn without misgivings to the thoughts of his private warfare.

This time it was to be regular warfare. He sent two friends to Lieut. D'Hubert, whose regiment was stationed only a few miles away. Those friends had asked no questions of their principal. "I owe him one, that pretty staff officer," he had said grimly, and they went away quite contentedly on their mission. Lieut. D'Hubert had no difficulty in finding two friends equally discreet and devoted to their principal. "There's a crazy fellow to whom I must give a lesson," he had declared curtly; and they asked for no better reasons.

On these grounds an encounter with duelling-swords was arranged one early morning in a convenient field. At the third set-to Lieut. D'Hubert found himself lying on his back on the dewy grass with a hole in his side. A serene sun rising over a landscape of meadows and woods hung on his left. A surgeon – not the flute player, but another – was bending over him, feeling around the wound.

"Narrow squeak. But it will be nothing," he pronounced.

Lieut. D'Hubert heard these words with pleasure. One of his seconds, sitting on the wet grass, and sustaining his head on his lap, said, "The fortune of war, *mon pauvre vieux*. What will you have? You had better make it up like two good fellows. Do!"

"You don't know what you ask," murmured Lieut. D'Hubert, in a feeble voice. "However, if he . . ."

In another part of the meadow the seconds of Lieut. Feraud were urging him to go over and shake hands with his adversary.

"You have paid him off now – *que diable*. It's the proper thing to do. This D'Hubert is a decent fellow."

"I know the decency of these generals' pets," muttered Lieut. Feraud through his teeth, and the sombre expression of his face discouraged further efforts at reconciliation. The seconds, bowing from a distance, took their men off the field. In the afternoon Lieut. D'Hubert, very popular as a good comrade uniting great bravery with a frank and equable temper, had many visitors. It was remarked that Lieut. Feraud did not, as is customary, show himself much abroad to receive the felicitations of his friends. They would not have failed him, because he too was liked for the exuberance of his southern nature and the simplicity of his character. In all the places where officers were in the habit of assembling at the end of the day the duel of the morning was talked over from every point of view. Though Lieut. D'Hubert had got worsted this time, his sword play was commended. No one could deny that it was very close, very scientific. It was even whispered that if he got touched it was because he wished to spare his adversary. But by many the vigour and dash of Lieut. Feraud's attack were pronounced irresistible.

The merits of the two officers as combatants were frankly discussed; but their attitude to each other after the duel was criticized lightly and with caution. It was irreconcilable, and that was to be regretted. But after all they knew best what the care of their honour dictated. It was not a matter for their comrades to pry into over-much. As to the origin of the quarrel, the general impression was that it dated from the time they were holding garrison in Strasbourg. The musical surgeon shook his head at that. It went much farther back, he thought.

"Why, of course! You must know the whole story," cried several voices, eager with curiosity. "What was it?"

He raised his eyes from his glass deliberately. "Even if I knew ever so well, you can't expect me to tell you since both the principals choose to say nothing."

He got up and went out, leaving the sense of mystery behind him. He could not stay any longer, because the witching hour of flute playing was drawing near.

After he had gone a very young officer observed solemnly, "Obviously! His lips are sealed."

Nobody questioned the high correctness of that remark.

Somehow it added to the impressiveness of the affair. Several older officers of both regiments, prompted by nothing but sheer kindness and love of harmony, proposed to form a Court of Honour, to which the two young men would leave the task of their reconciliation. Unfortunately they began by approaching Lieut. Feraud, on the assumption that, having just scored heavily, he would be found placable and disposed to moderation.

The reasoning was sound enough. Nevertheless, the move turned out unfortunate. In that relaxation of moral fibre, which is brought about by the ease of soothed vanity, Lieut. Feraud had condescended in the secret of his heart to review the case, and even had come to doubt not the justice of his cause, but the absolute sagacity of his conduct. This being so, he was disinclined to talk about it. The suggestion of the regimental wise men put him in a difficult position. He was disgusted at it, and this disgust, by a paradoxical logic, reawakened his animosity against Lieut. D'Hubert. Was he to be pestered with this fellow for ever – the fellow who had an infernal knack of getting round people somehow? And yet it was difficult to refuse point blank that mediation sanctioned by the code of honour.

He met the difficulty by an attitude of grim reserve. He twisted his moustache and used vague words. His case was perfectly clear. He was not ashamed to state it before a proper Court of Honour, neither was he afraid to defend it on the ground. He did not see any reason to jump at the suggestion before ascertaining how his adversary was likely to take it.

Later in the day, his exasperation growing upon him, he was heard in a public place saying sardonically, "that it would be the very luckiest thing for Lieut. D'Hubert, because the next time of meeting he need not hope to get off with the mere trifle of three weeks in bed."

This boastful phrase might have been prompted by the most profound Machiavellism. Southern natures often hide, under the outward impulsiveness of action and speech, a certain amount of astuteness.

Lieut. Feraud, mistrusting the justice of men, by no means

desired a Court of Honour; and the above words, according so well with his temperament, had also the merit of serving his turn. Whether meant so or not, they found their way in less than four-and-twenty hours into Lieut. D'Hubert's bedroom. In consequence Lieut. D'Hubert, sitting propped up with pillows, received the overtures made to him next day by the statement that the affair was of a nature which could not bear discussion.

The pale face of the wounded officer, his weak voice, which he had yet to use cautiously, and the courteous dignity of his tone had a great effect on his hearers. Reported outside, all this did more for deepening the mystery than the vapourings of Lieut. Feraud. This last was greatly relieved at the issue. He began to enjoy the state of general wonder, and was pleased to add to it by assuming an attitude of fierce discretion.

The colonel of Lieut. D'Hubert's regiment was a grey-haired, weather-beaten warrior, who took a simple view of his responsibilities. "I can't," he said to himself, "let the best of my subalterns get damaged like this for nothing. I must get to the bottom of this affair privately. He must speak out if the devil were in it. The colonel should be more than a father to these youngsters." And indeed he loved all his men with as much affection as a father of a large family can feel for every individual member of it. If human beings by an oversight of providence came into the world as mere civilians, they were born again into a regiment as infants are born into a family, and it was that military birth alone which counted.

At the sight of Lieut. D'Hubert standing before him very bleached and hollow-eyed the heart of the old warrior felt a pang of genuine compassion. All his affection for the regiment – that body of men which he held in his hand to launch forward and draw back, who ministered to his pride and commanded all his thoughts – seemed centred for a moment on the person of the most promising subaltern. He cleared his throat in a threatening manner, and frowned terribly. "You must understand," he began, "that I don't care a rap for the life of a single man in the regiment. I would send the eight hundred and forty-three of you men and horses galloping into the pit of perdition with no more compunction than I would kill a fly!"

"Yes, Colonel. You would be riding at our head," said Lieut. D'Hubert with a wan smile.

The colonel, who felt the need of being very diplomatic, fairly roared at this. "I want you to know, Lieut. D'Hubert, that I could stand aside and see you all riding to Hades if need be. I am a man to do even that if the good of the service and my duty to my country required it from me. But that's unthinkable, so don't you even hint at such a thing." He glared awfully, but his tone softened. "There's some milk yet about that moustache of yours, my boy. You don't know what a man like me is capable of. I would hide behind a haystack if . . . Don't grin at me, sir! How dare you? If this were not a private conversation I would . . . Look here! I am responsible for the proper expenditure of lives under my command for the glory of our country and honour of the regiment. Do you understand that? Well, then, what the devil do you mean by letting yourself be spitted like this by that fellow of the 7th Hussars? It's simply disgraceful!"

Lieut. D'Hubert felt vexed beyond measure. His shoulders moved slightly. He made no other answer. He could not ignore his responsibility.

The colonel veiled his glance and lowered his voice still more. "It's deplorable!" he murmured. And again he changed his tone. "Come!" he went on persuasively, but with that note of authority which dwells in the throat of a good leader of men, "this affair must be settled. I desire to be told plainly what it is all about. I demand, as your best friend, to know."

The compelling power of authority, the persuasive influence of kindness, affected powerfully a man just risen from a bed of sickness. Lieut. D'Hubert's hand, which grasped the knob of a stick, trembled slightly. But his northern temperament, sentimental yet cautious, and clear-sighted, too, in its idealistic way, checked his impulse to make a clean breast of the whole deadly absurdity. According to the precept of transcendental wisdom, he turned his tongue seven times in his mouth before he spoke. He made then only a speech of thanks.

The colonel listened, interested at first, then looked mystified. At last he frowned. "You hesitate? – *mille tonnerres*! Haven't I told you that I will condescend to argue with you – as a friend?"

"Yes, Colonel!" answered Lieut. D'Hubert gently. "But I am afraid that after you have heard me out as a friend you will take action as my superior officer."

The attentive colonel snapped his jaws. "Well, what of that?" he said frankly. "Is it so damnably disgraceful?"

"It is not," negatived Lieut. D'Hubert, in a faint but firm voice.

"Of course, I shall act for the good of the service. Nothing can prevent me doing that. What do you think I want to be told for?"

"I know it is not from idle curiosity," protested Lieut. D'Hubert. "I know you will act wisely. But what about the good fame of the regiment?"

"It cannot be affected by any youthful folly of a lieutenant," said the colonel severely.

"No. It cannot be. But it can be by evil tongues. It will be said that a lieutenant of the 4th Hussars, afraid of meeting his adversary, is hiding behind his colonel. And that would be worse than hiding behind a haystack – for the good of the service. I cannot afford to do that, Colonel."

"Nobody would dare to say anything of the kind," began the colonel very fiercely, but ended the phrase on an uncertain note. The bravery of Lieut. D'Hubert was well known. But the colonel was well aware that the duelling courage, the single combat courage, is rightly or wrongly supposed to be courage of a special sort. And it was eminently necessary that an officer of his regiment should possess every kind of courage – and prove it, too. The colonel stuck out his lower lip, and looked far away with a peculiar glazed stare. This was the expression of his perplexity – an expression practically unknown to his regiment; for perplexity is a sentiment which is incompatible with the rank of colonel of cavalry. The colonel himself was overcome by the unpleasant novelty of the sensation. As he was not accustomed to think except on professional matters connected with the welfare of men and horses, and the proper use thereof on the field of glory, his intellectual efforts degenerated into mere mental repetitions of profane language. "*Mille tonnerres!* . . . *Sacré nom de nom* . . ." he thought.

Lieut. D'Hubert coughed painfully, and added in a weary voice. "There will be plenty of evil tongues to say that I've been cowed. And I am sure you will not expect me to pass that over. I may find myself suddenly with a dozen duels on my hands instead of this one affair."

The direct simplicity of this argument came home to the colonel's understanding. He looked at his subordinate fixedly. "Sit down, Lieutenant!" he said gruffly. "This is the very devil of a . . . Sit down!"

"*Mon Colonel*," D'Hubert began again, "I am not afraid of evil tongues. There's a way of silencing them. But there's my peace of mind, too. I wouldn't be able to shake off the notion that I've ruined a brother officer. Whatever action you take, it is bound to go farther. The inquiry has been dropped – let it rest now. It would have been absolutely fatal to Feraud."

"Hey! What! Did he behave so badly?"

"Yes. It was pretty bad," muttered Lieut. D'Hubert. Being still very weak, he felt a disposition to cry.

As the other man did not belong to his own regiment, the colonel had no difficulty in believing this. He began to pace up and down the room. He was a good chief, a man capable of discreet sympathy. But he was human in other ways too, and this became apparent because he was not capable of artifice.

"The very devil, Lieutenant," he blurted out, in the innocence of his heart, "is that I have declared my intention to get to the bottom of this affair. And when a colonel says something . . . you see . . ."

Lieut. D'Hubert broke in earnestly. "Let me entreat you, Colonel, to be satisfied with taking my word of honour that I was put into a damnable position where I had no option; I had no choice whatever, consistent with my dignity as a man and an officer . . . After all, Colonel, this fact is the very bottom of this affair. Here you've got it. The rest is mere detail . . ."

The colonel stopped short. The reputation of Lieut. D'Hubert for good sense and good temper weighed in the balance. A cool head, a warm heart, open as the day. Always correct in his behaviour. One had to trust him. The colonel repressed manfully an immense curiosity. "H'm! You affirm that as a man and an officer . . . No option? Eh?"

"As an officer – an officer of the 4th Hussars, too," insisted Lieut. D'Hubert, "I had not. And that is the bottom of the affair, Colonel."

"Yes. But still I don't see why, to one's colonel. . . . A colonel is a father – *que diable!*"

Lieut. D'Hubert ought not to have been allowed out as yet. He was becoming aware of his physical insufficiency with humiliation and despair. But the morbid obstinacy of an invalid possessed him, and at the same time he felt with dismay his eyes filling with water. This trouble seemed too big to handle. A tear fell down the thin, pale cheek of Lieut. D'Hubert.

The colonel turned his back on him hastily. You could have heard a pin drop. "This is some silly woman story – is it not?"

Saying these words the chief spun round to seize the truth which is not a beautiful shape living in a well, but a shy bird best caught by stratagem. This was the last move of the colonel's diplomacy. He saw the truth shining unmistakably in the gesture of Lieut. D'Hubert raising his weak arms and his eyes to heaven in supreme protest.

"Not a woman affair – eh?" growled the colonel, staring hard. "I don't ask you who or where. All I want to know is whether there is a woman in it?"

Lieut. D'Hubert's arms dropped, and his weak voice was pathetically broken.

"Nothing of the kind, *mon Colonel*."

"On your honour?" insisted the old warrior.

"On my honour."

"Very well," said the Colonel thoughtfully, and bit his lip. The arguments of Lieut. D'Hubert, helped by his liking for the man, had convinced him. On the other hand, it was highly improper that his intervention, of which he had made no secret, should produce no visible effect. He kept Lieut. D'Hubert a few minutes longer, and dismissed him kindly.

"Take a few days more in bed, Lieutenant. What the devil does the surgeon mean by reporting you fit for duty?"

On coming out of the colonel's quarters, Lieut. D'Hubert said nothing to the friend who was waiting outside to take him home. He said nothing to anybody. Lieut. D'Hubert made no confidences. But on the evening of that day the colonel, strolling under the elms growing near his quarters, in the company of his second in command, opened his lips.

"I've got to the bottom of this affair," he remarked.

The lieut.-colonel, a dry, brown chip of a man with a short side-whiskers, pricked up his ears at that without letting a sign of curiosity escape him.

"It's no trifle," added the colonel oracularly. The other waited for a long while before he murmured—

"Indeed, sir!"

"No trifle," repeated the colonel, looking straight before him. "I've however forbidden D'Hubert either to send to or receive a challenge from Feraud for the next twelve months."

He had imagined this prohibition to save the prestige a colonel should have. The result of it was to give an official seal to the mystery surrounding this deadly quarrel. Lieut. D'Hubert repelled by an impassive silence all attempts to worm the truth out of him. Lieut. Feraud, secretly uneasy at first, regained his assurance as time went on. He disguised his ignorance of the meaning of the imposed truce by slight sardonic laughs, as though he were amused by what he intended to keep to himself. "But what will you do?" his chums used to ask him. He contented himself by replying "*Qui vivra verra*" with a little truculent air. And everybody admired his discretion.

Before the end of the truce Lieut. D'Hubert got his troop. The promotion was well earned, but somehow no one seemed to expect the event. When Lieut. Feraud heard of it at a gathering of officers, he muttered through his teeth, "Is that so?" At once he unhooked his sabre from a peg near the door, buckled it on carefully, and left the company without another word. He walked home with measured steps, struck a light with his flint and steel, and lit his tallow candle. Then snatching an unlucky glass tumbler off the mantelpiece he dashed it violently on the floor.

Now that D'Hubert was an officer of superior rank there could be no question of a duel. Neither of them could send or receive a challenge without rendering himself amenable to a court-martial. It was not to be thought of. Lieut. Feraud, who for many days now had experienced no real desire to meet Lieut. D'Hubert arms in hand, chafed again at the systematic injustice of fate. "Does he think he will escape me in that way?" he thought indignantly. He saw in this promotion an intrigue, a conspiracy, a cowardly manœuvre. That colonel knew what he was doing. He had hastened to recommend his favourite for a step. It was outrageous that a man should be able to avoid the consequences of his acts in such a dark and tortuous manner.

Of a happy-go-lucky disposition, of a temperament more pugnacious than military, Lieut. Feraud had been content to give and receive blows for sheer love of armed strife, and without much thought of advancement; but now an urgent desire to get on sprang up in his breast. This fighter by vocation resolved in his mind to seize showy occasions and to court the favourable opinion of his chiefs like a mere worldling. He knew he was as brave as any one, and never doubted his personal charm. Nevertheless, neither the bravery nor the charm seemed to work very swiftly. Lieut. Feraud's engaging, careless truculence of a *beau sabreur* underwent a change. He began to make bitter allusions to "clever fellows who stick at nothing to get on." The army was full of them, he would say; you had only to look round. But all the time he had in view one person only, his adversary, D'Hubert. Once he confided to an appreciative friend. "You see, I don't know how to fawn on the right sort of people. It isn't in my character."

He did not get his step till a week after Austerlitz. The Light Cavalry of the Grand Army had its hands very full of interesting work for a little while. Directly the pressure of professional occupation had been eased Captain Feraud took measures to arrange a meeting without loss of time. "I know my bird," he observed grimly. "If I don't look sharp he will take care to get himself promoted over the heads of a dozen better men than himself. He's got the knack for that sort of thing."

This duel was fought in Silesia. If not fought to a finish, it was, at any rate, fought to a standstill. The weapon was the cavalry sabre, and the skill, the science, the vigour, and the determination displayed by the adversaries compelled the admiration of the beholders. It became the subject of talk on both shores of the Danube, and as far as the garrisons of Gratz and Laybach. They crossed blades seven times. Both had many cuts which bled profusely. Both refused to have the combat stopped, time after time, with what appeared the most deadly animosity. This appearance was caused on the part of Captain D'Hubert by a rational desire to be done once for all with this worry; on the part of Captain Feraud by a tremendous exaltation of his pugnacious instincts and the incitement of wounded vanity. At last, dishevelled, their shirts in rags, covered with gore and hardly able to stand, they were led away forcibly by their marvelling and horrified seconds. Later on, besieged by comrades avid of details, these gentlemen declared that they could not have allowed that sort of hacking to go on indefinitely. Asked whether the quarrel was settled this time, they gave it out as their conviction that it was a difference which could only be settled by one of the parties remaining lifeless on the ground. The sensation spread from army corps to army corps, and penetrated at last to the smallest detachments of the troops cantoned between the Rhine and the Save. In the cafés in Vienna it was generally estimated, from details to hand, that the adversaries would be able to meet again in three weeks' time on the outside. Something really transcendent in the way of duelling was expected.

These expectations were brought to naught by the necessities of the service which separated the two officers. No official notice had been taken of their quarrel. It was now the property of the army, and not to be meddled with lightly. But the story of the duel, or rather their duelling propensities, must have stood somewhat in the way of their advancement, because they were still captains when they came together again during the war with Prussia. Detached north after Jena, with the army commanded by Marshal Bernadotte, Prince of Ponte Corvo, they entered Lübeck together.

It was only after the occupation of that town that Captain Feraud found leisure to consider his future conduct in view of the fact that Captain D'Hubert had been given the position of third aide-de-camp to the marshal. He considered it a great part of a night, and in the morning summoned two sympathetic friends.

"I've been thinking it over calmly," he said, gazing at them with blood-shot, tired eyes. "I see that I must get rid of that intriguing personage. Here he's managed to sneak on to the personal staff of the marshal. It's a direct provocation to me. I can't tolerate a situation in which I am exposed any day to receive an order through him. And God knows what order too! That sort of thing has happened once before – and that's once too often. He understands this perfectly, never fear. I can't tell you any more. Now you know what it is you have to do."

This encounter took place outside the town of Lübeck, on very open ground, selected with special care in deference to the general sentiment of the cavalry division belonging to the army corps, that this time the two officers should meet on horseback. After all, this duel was a cavalry affair, and to persist in fighting on foot would look like a slight on one's own arm of the service. The seconds, startled by the unusual nature of the suggestion, hastened to refer to their principals. Captain Feraud jumped at it with alacrity. For some obscure reason, depending, no doubt, on his psychology, he imagined himself invincible on horseback. All alone within the four walls of his room he rubbed his hands and muttered triumphantly, "Aha! my pretty staff officer, I've got you now."

Captain D'Hubert on his side, after staring hard for a considerable time at his friends shrugged his shoulders slightly.

This affair had hopelessly and unreasonably complicated his existence for him. One absurdity or less in the development did not matter – all absurdity was distasteful to him; but, urbane as ever, he produced a faintly ironic smile, and said in his calm voice, "It certainly will do away to some extent with the monotony of the thing."

When left alone, he sat down at a table and took his head into his hands. He had not spared himself of late and the marshal had been working all his aides-de-camp particularly hard. The last three weeks of campaigning in horrible weather had affected his health. When over-tired he suffered from a stitch in his wounded side, and that uncomfortable sensation always depressed him. "It's that brute's doing, too," he thought bitterly.

The day before he had received a letter from home, announcing that his only sister was going to be married. He reflected that from the time she was nineteen and he twenty-six, when he went away to garrison life in Strasbourg, he had had but two short glimpses of her. They had been great friends and confidants; and now she was going to be given away to a man whom he did not know – a very worthy fellow no doubt, but not half good enough for her. He would never see his old Léonie again. She had a capable little head, and plenty of tact; she would know how to manage the fellow, to be sure. He was easy in his mind about her happiness, but he felt ousted from the first place in her thoughts, which had been his ever since the girl could speak. A melancholy regret of the days of his childhood settled upon Captain D'Hubert, third aide-de-camp to the Prince of Ponte Corvo.

He threw aside the letter of congratulation he had begun to write as in duty bound, but without enthusiasm. He took a fresh piece of paper, and traced on it the words: "This is my last will and testament." Looking at these words he gave himself up to unpleasant reflection; a presentiment that he would never see the scenes of his childhood weighed down the equable spirits of Captain D'Hubert. He jumped up, pushing his chair back, yawned elaborately in sign that he didn't care anything for presentiments, and throwing himself on the bed went to sleep.

During the night he shivered from time to time without waking up. In the morning he rode out of town between his two seconds, talking of indifferent things, and looking right and left with apparent detachment into the heavy morning mists shrouding the flat green fields bordered by hedges. He leaped a ditch, and saw the forms of many mounted men moving in the fog. "We are to fight before a gallery, it seems," he muttered to himself bitterly.

His seconds were rather concerned at the state of the atmosphere, but presently a pale, sickly sun struggled out of the low vapours, and Captain D'Hubert made out, in the distance, three horsemen riding a little apart from the others. It was Captain Feraud and his seconds. He drew his sabre, and assured himself that it was properly fastened to his wrist. And now the seconds, who had been standing in close group with the heads of their horses together, separated at an easy canter, leaving a large, clear field between him and his adversary. Captain D'Hubert looked at the pale sun, at the dismal fields, and the imbecility of the impending fight filled him with desolation. From a distant part of the field a stentorian voice shouted commands at proper intervals: *Au pas–Au trot–Charrrgez!* . . . Presentiments of death don't come to a man for nothing, he thought at the very moment he put spurs to his horse.

And therefore he was more than surprised when, at the very first set-to, Captain Feraud laid himself open to a cut over the forehead, which blinding him with blood, ended the combat almost before it had fairly begun. It was impossible to go on. Captain D'Hubert, leaving his enemy swearing horribly and reeling in the saddle between his two appalled friends, leaped the ditch again into the road and trotted home with his two seconds, who seemed rather awestruck at the speedy issue of that encounter. In the evening Captain D'Hubert finished the congratulatory letter on his sister's marriage.

He finished it late. It was a long letter. Captain D'Hubert gave reins to his fancy. He told his sister that he would feel rather lonely after this great change in her life; but then the day would come for him too to get married. In fact, he was thinking already of the time when there would be no one left to fight with in Europe and the epoch of wars would be over. "I expect then," he wrote, "to be within measurable distance of a marshal's baton, and you will be an experienced married woman. You shall look out a wife for me. I will be, probably, bald by then, and a little *blasé*. I shall require a young girl, pretty of course, and with a large fortune, which should help me to close my glorious career in the splendour befitting my exalted rank." He ended with the information that he had just given a lesson to a worrying, quarrelsome fellow who imagined he had a grievance against him. "But if you, in the depth of your province," he continued, "ever hear it said that your brother is of a quarrelsome disposition, don't you believe it on any account. There is no saying what gossip from the army may reach your innocent ears. Whatever you hear you may rest assured that your ever-loving brother is not a duellist." Then Captain D'Hubert crumpled up the blank sheet of paper headed with the words "This is my last will and testament," and threw it in the fire with a great laugh at himself. He didn't care a snap for what that lunatic could do. He had suddenly acquired the conviction that his adversary was utterly powerless to affect his life in any sort of way; except, perhaps, in the way of putting special excitement into delightful, gay intervals between the campaigns.

From this on, there were, however, to be no peaceful intervals in the career of Captain D'Hubert. He saw the fields of Eylau and Friedland, marched and counter-marched in the snow, in the mud, in the dust of Polish plains, picking up distinction and advancement on all the roads of North-eastern Europe. Meantime Captain Feraud, despatched southwards with his regiment, made unsatisfactory war in Spain. It was only when the preparations for the Russian campaign began that he was ordered north again. He left the country of mantillas and oranges without regret.

The first signs of a not unbecoming baldness added to the lofty aspect of Colonel D'Hubert's forehead. This feature was no longer white and smooth as in the days of his youth; the kindly open glance of his blue eyes had grown a little hard as if from much peering through the smoke of battles. The ebony crop on Colonel Feraud's head, coarse and crinkly like a cap of horse-hair, showed many silver threads about the temples. A detestable warfare of ambushes and inglorious surprises had not improved his temper. The beak-like curve of his nose was unpleasantly set off by a deep fold on each side of his mouth. The round orbits of his eyes radiated wrinkles. More than ever he recalled an irritable and staring bird – something like a cross between a sparrow and an owl. He was still extremely outspoken in his dislike of "intriguing fellows." He seized every opportunity to state that he did not pick up his rank in the ante-rooms of marshals. The unlucky persons, civil or military, who, with an intention of being pleasant begged Colonel Feraud to tell them how he came by that very apparent scar on the forehead, were astonished to find themselves snubbed in various ways, some of which were simply rude and others mysteriously sardonic. Young officers were warned kindly by their more experienced comrades not to stare openly at the colonel's scar. But indeed an officer need have been very young in his profession not to have heard the legendary tale of that duel originating in a mysterious, unforgivable offence.

III

The retreat from Moscow submerged all private feelings in a sea of disaster and misery. Colonels without regiments, D'Hubert and Feraud carried the musket in the ranks of the so-called sacred battalion – a battalion recruited from officers of all arms who had no longer any troops to lead.

In that battalion promoted colonels did duty as sergeants; the generals captained the companies; a marshal of France, Prince of the Empire, commanded the whole. All had provided themselves with muskets picked up on the road, and with cartridges taken from the dead. In the general destruction of the bonds of discipline and duty holding together the companies, the battalions, the regiments, the brigades, and divisions of an armed host, this body of men put its pride in preserving some semblance of order and formation. The only stragglers were those who fell out to give up to the frost their exhausted souls. They plodded on, and their passage did not disturb the mortal silence of the plains, shining with the livid light of snows under a sky the colour of ashes. Whirlwinds ran along the fields, broke against the dark column, enveloped it in a turmoil of flying icicles, and subsided, disclosing it creeping on its tragic way without the swing and rhythm of the military pace. It struggled onwards, the men exchanging neither words nor looks; whole ranks marched touching elbows day after day, and never raising their eyes from the ground, as if lost in despairing reflections. In the dumb, black forests of pines the crackling of overloaded branches was the only sound they heard. Often from daybreak to dusk no one spoke in the whole column. It was like a *macabre* march of struggling corpses towards a distant grave. Only an alarm of Cossacks could restore to their eyes a semblance of martial resolution. The battalion faced about and deployed, or formed square under the endless fluttering of snowflakes. A cloud of horsemen with fur caps on their heads, levelled long lances, and yelled "Hurrah! Hurrah!" around their menacing immobility whence, with muffled detonations, hundreds of dark red flames darted through the air thick with falling snow. In a very few moments the horsemen would disappear, as if carried off yelling in the gale, and the sacred battalion standing still, alone in the blizzard, heard only the howling of the wind, whose blasts searched their very hearts. Then, with a cry or two of *Vive l'Empereur!* it would resume its march, leaving behind a few lifeless bodies lying huddled up, tiny black specks on the white immensity of the snows.

Though often marching in the ranks, or skirmishing in the woods side by side, the two officers ignored each other; this not so much from inimical intention as from a very real indifference. All their store of moral energy was expended in resisting the terrific enmity of nature and the crushing sense of irretrievable disaster. To the last they counted among the most active, the least demoralized of the battalion; their vigorous vitality invested them both with the appearance of an heroic pair in the eyes of their comrades. And they never exchanged more than a casual word or two, except one day, when skirmishing in front of the battalion against a worrying attack of cavalry, they found themselves cut off in the woods by a small party of Cossacks. A score of fur-capped, hairy horsemen rode to and fro, brandishing their lances in ominous silence; but the two officers had no mind to lay down their arms, and Colonel Feraud suddenly spoke up in a hoarse, growling voice, bringing his firelock to the shoulder. "You take the nearest brute, Colonel D'Hubert; I'll settle the next one. I am a better shot than you are."

Colonel D'Hubert nodded over his levelled musket. Their shoulders were pressed against the trunk of a large tree; on their front enormous snowdrifts protected them from a direct charge. Two carefully aimed shots rang out in the frosty air, two Cossacks reeled in their saddles. The rest, not thinking the game good enough, closed round their wounded comrades and galloped away out of range. The two officers managed to rejoin their battalion halted for the night. During that afternoon they had leaned upon each other more than once, and towards the end, Colonel D'Hubert, whose long legs gave him an advantage in walking through soft snow, peremptorily took the musket of Colonel Feraud from him and carried it on his shoulder, using his own as a staff.

On the outskirts of a village half buried in the snow an old wooden barn burned with a clear and an immense flame. The sacred battalion of skeletons, muffled in rags, crowded greedily the windward side, stretching hundreds of numbed, bony hands to the blaze. Nobody had noted their approach. Before entering the circle of light playing on the sunken, glassy-eyed, starved faces Colonel D'Hubert spoke in his turn.

"Here's your musket, Colonel Feraud. I can walk better than you."

Colonel Feraud nodded, and pushed on towards the warmth of the fierce flames. Colonel D'Hubert was more deliberate, but not the less bent on getting a place in the front rank. Those they

shouldered aside tried to greet with a faint cheer the reappearance of the two indomitable companions in activity and endurance. Those manly qualities had never perhaps received a
higher tribute than this feeble acclamation.

This is the faithful record of speeches exchanged during the
retreat from Moscow by Colonels Feraud and D'Hubert. Colonel Feraud's taciturnity was the outcome of concentrated
rage. Short, hairy, black faced with layers of grime and the
thick sprouting of a wiry beard, a frost-bitten hand wrapped up
in filthy rags carried in a sling, he accused fate of unparalleled
perfidy towards the sublime Man of Destiny. Colonel D'Hubert, his long moustaches pendent in icicles on each side of his
cracked blue lips, his eyelids inflamed with the glare of snows,
the principal part of his costume consisting of a sheepskin coat
looted with difficulty from the frozen corpse of a camp follower
found in an abandoned cart, took a more thoughtful view of
events. His regularly handsome features, now reduced to mere
bony lines and fleshless hollows, looked out of a woman's black
velvet hood, over which was rammed forcibly a cocked hat
picked up under the wheels of an empty army fourgon, which
must have contained at one time some general officer's luggage.
The sheepskin coat being short for a man of his inches ended
very high up, and the skin of his legs, blue with the cold, showed
through the tatters of his nether garments. This under the
circumstances provoked neither jeers nor pity. No one cared
how the next man felt or looked. Colonel D'Hubert himself,
hardened to exposure, suffered mainly in his self-respect from
the lamentable indecency of his costume. A thoughtless person
may think that with a whole host of inanimate bodies bestrew-
ing the path of retreat there could not have been much difficulty
in supplying the deficiency. But to loot a pair of breeches from a
frozen corpse is not so easy as it may appear to a mere theorist.
It requires time and labour. You must remain behind while
your companions march on. Colonel D'Hubert had his scruples
as to falling out. Once he had stepped aside he could not be sure
of ever rejoining his battalion; and the ghastly intimacy of a
wrestling match with the frozen dead opposing the unyielding

rigidity of iron to your violence was repugnant to the delicacy of his feelings. Luckily, one day, grubbing in a mound of snow between the huts of a village in the hope of finding there a frozen potato or some vegetable garbage he could put between his long and shaky teeth, Colonel D'Hubert uncovered a couple of mats of the sort Russian peasants use to line the sides of their carts with. These, beaten free of frozen snow, bent about his elegant person and fastened solidly round his waist, made a bellshaped nether garment, a sort of stiff petticoat which rendered Colonel D'Hubert a perfectly decent, but a much more noticeable figure than before.

Thus accoutred, he continued to retreat, never doubting of his personal escape, but full of other misgivings. The early buoyancy of his belief in the future was destroyed. If the road of glory led through such unforeseen passages, he asked himself – for he was reflective – whether the guide was altogether trustworthy. It was a patriotic sadness, not unmingled with some personal concern, and quite unlike the unreasoning indignation against men and things nursed by Colonel Feraud. Recruiting his strength in a little German town for three weeks, Colonel D'Hubert was surprised to discover within himself a love of repose. His returning vigour was strangely pacific in its aspirations. He meditated silently upon this bizarre change of mood. No doubt many of his brother officers of field rank went through the same moral experience. But these were not the times to talk of it. In one of his letters home Colonel D'Hubert wrote, "All your plans, my dear Léonie, for marrying me to the charming girl you have discovered in your neighbourhood, seem farther off than ever. Peace is not yet. Europe wants another lesson. It will be a hard task for us, but it shall be done, because the Emperor is invincible."

Thus wrote Colonel D'Hubert from Pomerania to his married sister Léonie, settled in the south of France. And so far the sentiments expressed would not have been disowned by Colonel Feraud, who wrote no letters to anybody, whose father had been in life an illiterate blacksmith, who had no sister or brother, and whom no one desired ardently to pair off for a life of peace with a charming young girl. But Colonel D'Hubert's letter contained also some philosophical generalities upon the uncertainty of all personal hopes, when bound up entirely with the prestigious fortune of one incomparably great it is true, yet still remaining but a man in his greatness. This view would have appeared rank heresy to Colonel Feraud. Some melancholy forebodings of a military kind, expressed cautiously, would have been pronounced as nothing short of high treason by Colonel Feraud. But Léonie, the sister of Colonel D'Hubert, read them with profound satisfaction, and, folding the letter thoughtfully, remarked to herself that "Armand was likely to prove eventually a sensible fellow." Since her marriage into a Southern family she had become a convinced believer in the return of the legitimate king. Hopeful and anxious she offered prayers night and morning, and burnt candles in churches for the safety and prosperity of her brother.

She had every reason to suppose that her prayers were heard. Colonel D'Hubert passed through Lutzen, Bautzen and Leipsic, losing no limb, and acquiring additional reputation. Adapting his conduct to the need of that desperate time, he had never voiced his misgivings. He concealed them under a cheerful courtesy of such pleasant character that people were inclined to ask themselves with wonder whether Colonel D'Hubert was aware of any disasters. Not only his manners, but even his glances remained untroubled. The steady amenity of his blue eyes disconcerted all grumblers, and made despair itself pause.

This bearing was remarked favourably by the Emperor himself; for Colonel D'Hubert, attached now to the Major-General's staff, came on several occasions under the imperial eye. But it exasperated the higher strung nature of Colonel Feraud. Passing through Magdeburg on service, this last allowed himself, while seated gloomily at dinner with the *Commandant de Place*, to say of his life-long adversary: "This man does not love the Emperor," and his words were received by the other guests in profound silence. Colonel Feraud, troubled in his conscience at the atrocity of the aspersion, felt the need to back it up by a good argument. "I ought to know him," he cried, adding some oaths. "One studies one's adversary. I have met him on the ground half a dozen times, as all the army knows. What more do you want? If that isn't opportunity enough for any fool to size up his man, may the devil take me if I can tell what is." And he looked around the table obstinate and sombre.

Later on in Paris, while extremely busy reorganising his regiment, Colonel Feraud learned that Colonel D'Hubert had been made a general. He glared at his informant incredulously, then folded his arms and turned away muttering, "Nothing surprises me on the part of that man."

And aloud he added, speaking over his shoulder, "You would oblige me greatly by telling General D'Hubert at the first opportunity that his advancement saves him for a time from a pretty hot encounter. I was only waiting for him to turn up here."

The other officer remonstrated.

"Could you think of it, Colonel Feraud, at this time, when every life should be consecrated to the glory and safety of France?"

But the strain of unhappiness caused by military reverses had spoiled Colonel Feraud's character. Like many other men, he was rendered wicked by misfortune.

"I cannot consider General D'Hubert's existence of any account either for the glory or safety of France," he snapped viciously. "You don't pretend, perhaps, to know him better than I do – I who have met him half a dozen times on the ground – do you?"

His interlocutor, a young man, was silenced. Colonel Feraud walked up and down the room.

"This is not the time to mince matters," he said. "I can't believe that that man ever loved the Emperor. He picked up his general's stars under the boots of Marshal Berthier. Very well. I'll get mine in another fashion, and then we shall settle this business which has been dragging on too long."

General D'Hubert, informed indirectly of Colonel Feraud's attitude, made a gesture as if to put aside an importunate person. His thoughts were solicited by graver cares. He had had no time to go and see his family. His sister, whose royalist hopes were rising higher every day, though proud of her brother, regretted his recent advancement in a measure, because it put on him a prominent mark of the usurper's favour, which later on could have an adverse influence upon his career. He wrote to her that no one but an inveterate enemy could say he had got his promotion by favour. As to his career, he assured her that he looked no farther forward into the future than the next battle-field.

Beginning the campaign of France in this dogged spirit, General D'Hubert was wounded on the second day of the battle under Laon. While being carried off the field he heard that Colonel Feraud, promoted this moment to general, had been sent to replace him at the head of his brigade. He cursed his luck impulsively, not being able at the first glance to discern all the advantages of a nasty wound. And yet it was by this heroic method that Providence was shaping his future. Travelling slowly south to his sister's country home, under the care of a trusty old servant, General D'Hubert was spared the humiliating contacts and the perplexities of conduct which assailed the men of Napoleonic empire at the moment of its downfall. Lying in his bed, with the windows of his room open wide to the sunshine of Provence, he perceived the undisguised aspect of the blessing conveyed by that jagged fragment of a Prussian shell, which, killing his horse and ripping open his thigh, saved him from an active conflict with his conscience. After the last fourteen years spent sword in hand in the saddle, and with the sense of his duty done to the very end, General D'Hubert found resignation an easy virtue. His sister was delighted with his reasonableness. "I leave myself altogether in your hands, my dear Léonie," he had said to her.

He was still laid up when, the credit of his brother-in-law's family being exerted on his behalf, he received from the royal government not only the confirmation of his rank, but the assurance of being retained on the active list. To this was added an unlimited convalescent leave. The unfavourable opinion entertained of him in Bonapartist circles, though it rested on nothing more solid than the unsupported pronouncement of General Feraud, was directly responsible for General D'Hubert's retention on the active list. As to General Feraud, his rank was confirmed too. It was more than he dared to expect; but Marshal Soult, then Minister of War to the restored king, was partial to officers who had served in Spain. Only not even the marshal's protection could secure for him active employment. He remained irreconcilable, idle, and sinister. He sought in obscure restaurants the company of other half-pay officers who cherished dingy, but glorious old tricolour cockades in their breast-pockets, and buttoned with the forbidden eagle buttons their shabby uniforms, declaring themselves too poor to afford the expense of the prescribed change.

The triumphant return from Elba, a historical fact as marvellous and incredible as the exploits of some mythological demi-god, found General D'Hubert still quite unable to sit a horse. Neither could he walk very well. These disabilities, which Madame Léonie accounted most lucky, helped to keep her brother out of all possible mischief. His frame of mind at that time, she noted with dismay, became very far from reasonable. This general officer, still menaced by the loss of a limb, was discovered one night in the stables at the château by a groom, who, seeing a light, raised an alarm of thieves. His crutch was lying half-buried in the straw of the litter, and the general was hopping on one leg in a loose box around a snorting horse he was trying to saddle. Such were the effects of imperial magic upon a calm temperament and a pondered mind. Beset in the light of stable lanterns, by the tears, entreaties, indignation, remonstrances and reproaches of his family, he got out of the difficult situation by fainting away there and then in the arms of his nearest relatives, and was carried off to bed. Before he got out of it again, the second reign of Napoleon, the Hundred Days of feverish agitation and supreme effort, passed away like a terrifying dream. The tragic year 1815, begun in the trouble and unrest of consciences, was ending in vengeful proscriptions.

How General Feraud escaped the clutches of the Special

Commission and the last offices of a firing squad he never knew himself. It was partly due to the subordinate position he was assigned during the Hundred Days. The Emperor had never given him active command, but had kept him busy at the cavalry depôt in Paris, mounting and despatching hastily drilled troopers into the field. Considering this task as unworthy of his abilities, he had discharged it with no offensively noticeable zeal; but for the greater part he was saved from the excesses of royalist reaction by the interference of General D'Hubert.

This last, still on convalescent leave, but able now to travel, had been despatched by his sister to Paris to present himself to his legitimate sovereign. As no one in the capital could possibly know anything of the episode in the stable he was received there with distinction. Military to the very bottom of his soul, the prospect of rising in his profession consoled him from finding himself the butt of Bonapartist malevolence, which pursued him with a persistence he could not account for. All the rancour of that embittered and persecuted party pointed to him as the man who had *never* loved the Emperor – a sort of monster essentially worse than a mere betrayer.

General D'Hubert shrugged his shoulders without anger at this ferocious prejudice. Rejected by his old friends, and mistrusting profoundly the advances of Royalist society, the young and handsome general (he was barely forty) adopted a manner of cold, punctilious courtesy, which at the merest shadow of an intended slight passed easily into harsh haughtiness. Thus prepared, General D'Hubert went about his affairs in Paris feeling inwardly very happy with the peculiar uplifting happiness of a man very much in love. The charming girl looked out by his sister had come upon the scene, and had conquered him in the thorough manner in which a young girl by merely existing in his sight can make a man of forty her own. They were going to be married as soon as General D'Hubert had obtained his official nomination to a promised command.

One afternoon, sitting on the *terrasse* of the *Café Tortoni*, General D'Hubert learned from the conversation of two strangers occupying a table near his own, that General Feraud, included in the batch of superior officers arrested after the second return of the king, was in danger of passing before the Special Commission. Living all his spare moments, as is frequently the case with expectant lovers, a day in advance of reality, and in a state of bestarred hallucination, it required nothing less than the name of his perpetual antagonist pronounced in a loud voice to call the youngest of Napoleon's generals away from the mental contemplation of his betrothed. He looked round. The strangers wore civilian clothes. Lean and weather-beaten, lolling back in their chairs, they scowled at people with moody and defiant abstraction from under their hats pulled low over their eyes. It was not difficult to recognize them for two of the compulsorily retired officers of the Old Guard. As from bravado or carelessness they chose to speak in loud tones, General D'Hubert, who saw no reason why he should change his seat, heard every word. They did not seem to be the personal friends of General Feraud. His name came up amongst others. Hearing it repeated, General D'Hubert's tender anticipations of a domestic future adorned with a woman's grace were traversed by the harsh regret of his warlike past, of that one long, intoxicating clash of arms, unique in the magnitude of its glory and disaster – the marvellous work and the special possession of his own generation. He felt an irrational tenderness towards his old adversary and appreciated emotionally the murderous absurdity their encounter had introduced into his life. It was like an additional pinch of spice in a hot dish. He remembered the flavour with sudden melancholy. He would never taste it again. It was all over. "I fancy it was being left lying in the garden that had exasperated him so against me from the first," he thought indulgently.

The two strangers at the next table had fallen silent after the third mention of General Feraud's name. Presently the elder of the two, speaking again in a bitter tone, affirmed that General Feraud's account was settled. And why? Simply because he was not like some big-wigs who loved only themselves. The Royalists knew they could never make anything of him. He loved *The Other* too well.

The Other was the Man of St. Helena. The two officers nodded and touched glasses before they drank to an impossible return. Then the same who had spoken before, remarked with a sardonic laugh, "His adversary showed more cleverness."

"What adversary?" asked the younger, as if puzzled.

"Don't you know? They were two hussars. At each promotion they fought a duel. Haven't you heard of the duel going on ever since 1801?"

The other had heard of the duel, of course. Now he understood the allusion. General Baron D'Hubert would be able now to enjoy his fat king's favour in peace.

"Much good may it do to him," mumbled the elder. "They were both brave men. I never saw this D'Hubert – a sort of intriguing dandy, I am told. But I can well believe what I've heard Feraud say of him – that he *never* loved the Emperor."

They rose and went away

General D'Hubert experienced the horror of a somnambulist who wakes up from a complacent dream of activity to find himself walking on a quagmire. A profound disgust of the ground on which he was making his way overcame him. Even the image of the charming girl was swept from his view in the flood of moral distress. Everything he had ever been or hoped to be would taste of bitter ignominy unless he could manage to save General Feraud from the fate which threatened so many braves. Under the impulse of this almost morbid need to attend to the safety of his adversary, General D'Hubert worked so well with hands and feet (as the French saying is), that in less than twenty-four hours he found means of obtaining an extraordinary private audience from the Minister of Police.

General Baron D'Hubert was shown in suddenly without preliminaries. In the dusk of the Minister's cabinet, behind the forms of writing-desk, chairs and tables, between two bunches of wax candles blazing in sconces, he beheld a figure in a gorgeous coat posturing before a tall mirror. The old *conventionnel* Fouché, Senator of the Empire, traitor to every man, to every principle and motive of human conduct, Duke of Otranto, and the wily artisan of the second Restoration, was trying the fit of a court suit in which his young and accomplished *fiancée* had declared her intention to have his portrait painted on porcelain. It was a caprice, a charming fancy which the first Minister of Police of the second Restoration was anxious to gratify. For that man, often compared in wiliness of conduct to a fox, but whose ethical side could be worthily symbolized by nothing less emphatic than a skunk, was as much possessed by his love as General D'Hubert himself.

Startled to be discovered thus by the blunder of a servant, he met this little vexation with the characteristic impudence which had served his turn so well in the endless intrigues of his self-seeking career. Without altering his attitude a hair's-breadth, one leg in a silk stocking advanced, his head twisted over his left shoulder, he called out calmly, "This way, General. Pray approach. Well? I am all attention."

While General D'Hubert, ill at ease as if one of his own little weaknesses had been exposed, presented his request as shortly as possible, the Duke of Otranto went on feeling the fit of his collar, settling the lapels before the glass, and buckling his back in an effort to behold the set of the gold embroidered coat-skirts behind. His still face, his attentive eyes, could not have expressed a more complete interest in those matters if he had been alone.

"Exclude from the operations of the Special Court a certain Feraud, Gabriel Florian, General of brigade of the promotion of 1814?" he repeated, in a slightly wondering tone, and then turned away from the glass. "Why exclude *him* precisely?"

"I am surprised that your Excellency, so competent in the evaluation of men of his time, should have thought worth while to have that name put down on the list."

"A rabid Bonapartist!"

"So is every grenadier and every trooper of the army, as your Excellency well knows. And the individuality of General Feraud can have no more weight than that of any casual grenadier. He is a man of no mental grasp, of no capacity whatever. It is inconceivable that he should ever have any influence."

"He has a well-hung tongue, though," interjected Fouché.

"Noisy, I admit, but not dangerous."

"I will not dispute with you. I know next to nothing of him. Hardly his name, in fact."

"And yet your Excellency has the presidency of the Commission charged by the king to point out those who were to be tried," said General D'Hubert, with an emphasis which did not miss the minister's ear.

"Yes, General," he said, walking away into the dark part of the vast room, and throwing himself into a deep armchair that swallowed him up, all but the soft gleam of gold embroideries and the pallid patch of the face – "yes, General. Take this chair there."

General D'Hubert sat down.

"Yes, General," continued the arch-master in the arts of intrigue and betrayals, whose duplicity, as if at times intolerable to his self-knowledge, found relief in bursts of comical openness. "I did hurry on the formation of the proscribing Commission, and I took its presidency. And do you know why? Simply from fear that if I did not take it quickly into my hands my own name would head the list of the proscribed. Such are the times in which we live. But I am minister of the king yet, and I ask you plainly why I should take the name of this obscure Feraud off the list? You wonder how his name got there! Is it possible that you should know men so little? My dear General, at the very first sitting of the Commission names poured on us like rain off the roof of the Tuileries. Names! We had our choice of thousands. How do you know that the name of this Feraud, whose life or death don't matter to France, does not keep out some other name?"

The voice out of the armchair stopped. Opposite General D'Hubert sat still, shadowy and silent. Only his sabre clinked slightly. The voice in the armchair began again. "And we must try to satisfy the exigencies of the Allied Sovereigns, too. The Prince de Talleyrand told me only yesterday that Nesselrode had informed him officially of His Majesty the Emperor Alexander's dissatisfaction at the small number of examples the Government of the king intends to make – especially amongst military men. I tell you this confidentially."

"Upon my word!" broke out General D'Hubert, speaking through his teeth, "if your Excellency deigns to favour me with any more confidential information I don't know what I will do. It's enough to break one's sword over one's knee, and fling the pieces . . ."

"What government you imagined yourself to be serving?" interrupted the minister sharply.

After a short pause the crestfallen voice of General D'Hubert answered, "The Government of France."

"That's paying your conscience off with mere words, General. The truth is that you are serving a government of returned exiles, of men who have been without country for twenty years. Of men also who have just got over a very bad and humiliating fright . . . Have no illusions on that score."

The Duke of Otranto ceased. He had relieved himself, and had attained his object of stripping some self-respect off that man who had inconveniently discovered him posturing in a gold-embroidered court costume before a mirror. But they were a hot-headed lot in the army; it occurred to him that it would be inconvenient if a well-disposed general officer, received in audience on the recommendation of one of the Princes, were to do something rashly scandalous directly after a private interview with the minister. In a changed tone he put a question to the point. "Your relation – this Feraud?"

"No. No relation at all."

"Intimate friend?"

"Intimate . . . yes. There is between us an intimate connexion of a nature which makes it a point of honour with me to try . . ."

The minister rang a bell without waiting for the end of the phrase. When the servant had gone out, after bringing in a pair of heavy silver candelabra for the writing-desk, the Duke of Otranto rose, his breast glistening all over with gold in the strong light, and taking a piece of paper out of a drawer, held it in his hand ostentatiously while he said with persuasive gentleness, "You must not speak of breaking your sword across your knee, General. Perhaps you would never get another. The

Emperor will not return this time . . . *Diable d'homme!* There was just a moment, here in Paris, soon after Waterloo, when he frightened me. It looked as though he were ready to begin all over again. Luckily one never does begin all over again, really. You must not think of breaking your sword, General."

General D'Hubert, looking on the ground, moved slightly his hand in a hopeless gesture of renunciation. The Minister of Police turned his eyes away from him, and scanned deliberately the paper he had been holding up all the time.

"There are only twenty general officers selected to be made an example of. Twenty. A round number. And let's see, Feraud . . . Ah, he's there. Gabriel Florian. *Parfaitement*. That's your man. Well, there will be only nineteen examples made now."

General D'Hubert stood up feeling as though he had gone through an infectious illness. "I must beg your Excellency to keep my interference a profound secret. I attach the greatest importance to his never learning . . ."

"Who is going to inform him, I should like to know?" said Fouché, raising his eyes curiously to General D'Hubert's tense, set face. "Take one of these pens, and run it through the name yourself. This is the only list in existence. If you are careful to take up enough ink no one will be able to tell what was the name struck out. But, *par exemple*, I am not responsible for what Clarke will do with him afterwards. If he persists in being rabid he will be ordered by the Minister of War to reside in some provincial town under the supervision of the police."

A few days later General D'Hubert was saying to his sister, after the first greetings had been got over, "Ah, my dear Léonie! it seemed to me I couldn't get away from Paris quick enough."

"Effect of love," she suggested, with a malicious smile.

"And horror," added General D'Hubert, with profound seriousness. "I have nearly died there of . . . of nausea."

His face was contracted with disgust. And as his sister looked at him attentively, he continued, "I have had to see Fouché. I have had an audience. I have been in his cabinet. There remains with one, who had the misfortune to breathe the air of the same room with that man, a sense of diminished dignity, an uneasy feeling of being not so clean, after all, as one hoped one was. . . . But you can't understand."

She nodded quickly several times. She understood very well on the contrary. She knew her brother thoroughly, and liked him as he was. Moreover, the scorn and loathing of mankind were the lot of the *Jacobin* Fouché, who, exploiting for his own advantage every weakness, every virtue, every generous illusion of mankind, made dupes of his whole generation, and died obscurely as Duke of Otranto.

"My dear Armand," she said compassionately, "what could you want from that man?"

"Nothing less than a life," answered General D'Hubert. "And I've got it. It had to be done. But I feel yet as if I could never forgive the necessity to the man I had to save."

General Feraud, totally unable (as in the case with most of us) to comprehend what was happening to him, received the Minister of War's order to proceed at once to a small town of Central France with feelings whose natural expression consisted in a fierce rolling of the eye and savage grinding of the teeth. The passing away of the state of war, the only condition of society he had ever known, the horrible view of a world at peace, frightened him. He went away to his little town firmly convinced that this could not last. There he was informed of his retirement from the army, and that his pension (calculated on the scale of a colonel's rank) was made dependent on the correctness of his conduct, and on the good reports of the police. No longer in the army! He felt suddenly strange to the earth, like a disembodied spirit. It was impossible to exist. But at first he reacted from sheer incredulity. This could not be. He waited for thunder, earthquakes, natural cataclysms; but nothing happened. The leaden weight of an irremediable idleness descended upon General Feraud, who having no resources within himself sank into a state of awe-inspiring hebetude. He haunted the streets of the little town, gazing before him with lacklustre eyes, disregarding the hats raised on his passage; and people, nudging each other as he went by, whispered, "That's poor General Feraud. His heart is broken. Behold how he loved the Emperor."

The other living wreckage of Napoleonic tempest clustered round General Feraud with infinite respect. He, himself, imagined his soul to be crushed by grief. He suffered from quickly succeeding impulses to weep, to howl, to bite his fists till blood came, to spend days on his bed with his head thrust under the pillow; but these arose from sheer ennui, from the anguish of an immense, indescribable, inconceivable boredom. His mental inability to grasp the hopeless nature of his case as a whole saved him from suicide. He never even thought of it once. He thought of nothing. But his appetite abandoned him, and the difficulty he experienced to express the overwhelming nature of his feelings (the most furious swearing could do no justice to it) induced gradually a habit of silence – a sort of death to a southern temperament.

Great, therefore, was the sensation amongst the *anciens militaires* frequenting a certain little café full of flies, when one stuffy afternoon "that poor General Feraud" let out suddenly a volley of formidable curses.

He had been sitting quietly in his own privileged corner looking through the Paris gazettes with just as much interest as a condemned man on the eve of execution could be expected to show in the news of the day. A cluster of martial, bronzed faces, amongst which there was one lacking an eye, and another the tip of a nose frost-bitten in Russia, surrounded him anxiously.

"What's the matter, General?"

General Feraud sat erect, holding the folded newspaper at arm's length in order to make out the small print better. He read to himself, over again, fragments of the intelligence which had caused, what may be called, his resurrection.

"*We are informed that General D'Hubert, till now on sick leave in the south, is to be called to the command of the 5th Cavalry brigade in . . .*"

He dropped the paper stonily . . . "Called to the command" . . . and suddenly gave his forehead a mighty slap. "I had almost forgotten him," he muttered, in a conscience-stricken tone.

A deep-chested veteran shouted across the café. "Some new villainy of the Government, General?"

"The villainies of these scoundrels," thundered General Feraud, "are innumerable. One more one less!" . . . He lowered his tone. "But I will set good order to one of them at least."

He looked all round the faces. "There's a pomaded, curled staff-officer, the darling of some of the marshals who sold their father for a handful of English gold. He will find out presently that I am alive yet," he declared, in a dogmatic tone. "However, this is a private affair. An old affair of honour. Bah! Our honour does not matter. Here we are driven off with a split ear like a lot of cast troop horses – good only for a knacker's yard. But it would be like striking a blow for the Emperor . . . Messieurs, I shall require the assistance of two of you."

Every man moved forward. General Feraud, deeply touched by this demonstration, called with visible emotion upon the one-eyed veteran cuirassier and the officer of the Chasseurs à Cheval who had left the tip of his nose in Russia. He excused his choice to the others.

"A cavalry affair this – you know."

He was answered with a varied chorus of "*Parfaitement, mon Général . . . C'est juste . . . Parbleu, c'est connu . . .*" Everybody was satisfied. The three left the café together, followed by cries of "*Bonne chance.*"

Outside they linked arms, the general in the middle. The three rusty cocked hats worn *en bataille* with a sinister forward slant barred the narrow street nearly right across. The overheated little town of grey stones and red tiles was drowsing away its provincial afternoon under a blue sky. The loud blows of a cooper hooping a cask reverberated regularly between the houses. The general dragged his left foot a little in the shade of the walls.

"This damned winter of 1813 has got into my bones for good. Never mind. We must take pistols, that's all. A little lumbago. We must have pistols. He's game for my bag. My eyes are as keen as ever. You should have seen me in Russia picking off the dodging Cossacks with a beastly old infantry musket. I have a natural gift for firearms."

In this strain General Feraud ran on, holding up his head, with owlish eyes and rapacious beak. A mere fighter all his life, a cavalry man, a *sabreur*, he conceived war with the utmost simplicity, as, in the main, a massed lot of personal contests, a sort of gregarious duelling. And here he had in hand a war of his own. He revived. The shadow of peace passed away from him like the shadow of death. It was the marvellous resurrection of the named Feraud, Gabriel Florian, *engagé volontaire* of 1793, General of 1814, buried without ceremony by means of a service order signed by the War Minister of the Second Restoration.

IV

No man succeeds in everything he undertakes. In that sense we are all failures. The great point is not to fail in ordering and sustaining the effort of our life. In this matter vanity is what leads us astray. It hurries us into situations from which we must come out damaged; whereas pride is our safeguard, by the reserve it imposes on the choice of our endeavour as much as by the virtue of its sustaining power.

General D'Hubert was proud and reserved. He had not been damaged by his casual love affairs, successful or otherwise. In his war-scarred body his heart at forty remained unscratched. Entering with reserve into his sister's matrimonial plans, he had felt himself falling irremediably in love as one falls off a roof. He was too proud to be frightened. Indeed, the sensation was too delightful to be alarming.

The inexperience of a man of forty is a much more serious thing than the inexperience of a youth of twenty, for it is not helped out by the rashness of hot blood. The girl was mysterious, as young girls are by the mere effect of their guarded ingenuity; and to him the mysteriousness of that young girl appeared exceptional and fascinating. But there was nothing mysterious about the arrangements of the match which Madame Léonie had promoted. There was nothing peculiar either. It was a very appropriate match, commending itself extremely to the young lady's mother (the father was dead) and tolerable to the young lady's uncle – an old *émigré* lately returned from Germany, and pervading, cane in hand, a lean ghost of the *ancien régime*, the garden walks of the young lady's ancestral home.

General D'Hubert was not the man to be satisfied merely with the woman and the fortune – when it came to the point. His pride (and pride aims always at true success) would be satisfied with nothing short of love. But as true pride excludes vanity, he could not imagine any reason why this mysterious creature with deep and brilliant eyes of a violet colour should have any feeling for him warmer than indifference. The young lady (her name was Adèle) baffled every attempt at a clear understanding on that point. It is true that the attempts were clumsy and made timidly, because by then General D'Hubert had become acutely aware of the number of his years, of his wounds, of his many moral imperfections, of his secret unworthiness – and had incidentally learned by experience the meaning of the word funk. As far as he could make out she seemed to imply that, with an unbounded confidence in her mother's affection and sagacity, she felt no unsurmountable dislike for the person of General D'Hubert; and that this was quite sufficient for a well-brought-up young lady to begin married life upon. This view hurt and tormented the pride of General D'Hubert. And yet he asked himself with a sort of sweet despair, what more could he expect? She had a quiet and luminous forehead. Her violet eyes laughed while the lines of her lips and chin remained composed in admirable gravity. All this was set off by such a glorious mass of fair hair, by a complexion so marvellous, by such a grace of expression, that General D'Hubert really never found the opportunity to examine with sufficient detachment the lofty exigencies of his pride. In fact he became shy of that line of inquiry since it had led once or twice to a crisis of solitary passion in which it was borne upon him that he loved her enough to kill her rather than lose her. From such passages, not unknown to men of forty, he would come out broken, exhausted, remorseful, a little dismayed. He derived, however, considerable comfort from the quietist practice of sitting now and then half the night by an open window and meditating upon the wonder of her existence, like a believer lost in the mystic contemplation of his faith.

It must not be supposed that all these variations of his inward state were made manifest to the world. General D'Hubert found no difficulty in appearing wreathed in smiles. Because, in fact, he was very happy. He followed the established rules of his condition, sending over flowers (from his sister's garden and hot-houses) early every morning, and a little later following himself to lunch with his intended, her mother, and her *émigré* uncle. The middle of the day was spent in strolling or sitting in the shade. A watchful deference, trembling on the verge of tenderness was the note of their intercourse on his side – with a playful turn of the phrase concealing the profound trouble of his whole being caused by her inaccessible nearness. Late in the afternoon General D'Hubert walked home between the fields of vines, sometimes intensely miserable, sometimes supremely happy, sometimes pensively sad; but always feeling a special intensity of existence, that elation common to artists, poets, and lovers – to men haunted by a great passion, a noble thought, or a new vision of plastic beauty.

The outward world at that time did not exist with any special distinctness for General D'Hubert. One evening, however, crossing a ridge from which he could see both houses, General D'Hubert became aware of two figures far down the road. The day had been divine. The festal decoration of the inflamed sky lent a gentle glow to the sober tints of the southern land. The grey rocks, the brown fields, the purple, undulating distances harmonised in luminous accord, exhaled already the scents of the evening. The two figures down the road presented themselves like two rigid and wooden silhouettes all black on the ribbon of white dust. General D'Hubert made out the long, straight military *capotes* buttoned closely right up to the black stocks, the cocked hats, the lean, carven brown countenances – old soldiers – *vieilles moustaches*! The taller of the two had a black patch over one eye; the other's hard, dry countenance presented some bizarre, disquieting peculiarity, which on nearer approach proved to be the absence of the tip of the nose. Lifting their hands with one movement, to salute the slightly lame civilian walking with a thick stick, they inquired for the house where the General Baron D'Hubert lived, and what was the best way to get speech with him quietly.

"If you think this quiet enough," said General D'Hubert, looking round at the vine-fields, framed in purple lines, and dominated by the nest of grey and drab walls of a village clustering around the top of a conical hill, so that the blunt church tower seemed but the shape of a crowning rock – "if you think this spot quiet enough, you can speak to him at once. And I beg you, comrades, to speak openly, with perfect confidence."

They stepped back at this, and raised again their hands to their hats with marked ceremoniousness. Then the one with the chipped nose, speaking for both, remarked that the matter was confidential enough, and to be arranged discreetly. Their general quarters were established in that village over there, where the infernal clod-hoppers – damn their false, Royalist hearts! – looked remarkably cross-eyed at three unassuming military men. For the present he should only ask for the name of General D'Hubert's friends.

"What friends?" said the astonished General D'Hubert, completely off the track. "I am staying with my brother-in-law over there."

"Well, he will do for one," said the chipped veteran.

"We're the friends of General Feraud," interjected the other, who had kept silent till then, only glowering with his one eye at the man who had *never* loved the Emperor. That was something to look at. For even the gold-laced Judases who had sold him to the English, the marshals and princes, had loved him at some time or other. But this man had *never* loved the Emperor. General Feraud had said so distinctly.

General D'Hubert felt an inward blow in his chest. For an infinitesimal fraction of a second it was as if the spinning of the earth had become perceptible with an awful, slight rustle in the eternal stillness of space. But this noise of blood in his ears passed off at once. Involuntarily he murmured, "Feraud! I had forgotten his existence."

"He's existing at present, very uncomfortably, it is true, in the infamous inn of that nest of savages up there," said the one-eyed cuirassier drily. "We arrived in your parts an hour ago on post horses. He's awaiting our return with impatience. There is hurry, you know. The General has broken the ministerial order to obtain from you the satisfaction he's entitled to by the laws of honour, and naturally he's anxious to have it all over before the *gendarmerie* gets on his scent."

The other elucidated the idea a little further. "Get back on the quiet – you understand? Phitt. No one the wiser. We have broken out, too. Your friend the king would be glad to cut off our scurvy pittances at the first chance. It's a risk. But honour before everything."

General D'Hubert had recovered his powers of speech. "So you come here like this along this road to invite me to a throat-cutting match with that – that . . ." A laughing sort of rage took possession of him. "Ha! ha! ha! ha!"

His fists on his hips, he roared without restraint, while they stood before him lank and straight, as though they had been shot up with a snap through a trapdoor in the ground. Only four-and-twenty months ago the masters of Europe, they had already the air of antique ghosts, they seemed less substantial in their faded coats than their own narrow shadows falling so black across the white road: the military and grotesque shadows of twenty years of war and conquests. They had an outlandish appearance of two imperturbable bronzes of the religion of the sword. And General D'Hubert, also one of the ex-masters of Europe, laughed at these serious phantoms standing in his way.

Said one, indicating the laughing General with a jerk of the head. "A merry companion, that."

"There are some of us that haven't smiled from the day *The Other* went away," remarked his comrade.

A violent impulse to set upon and beat those unsubstantial wraiths to the ground frightened General D'Hubert. He ceased laughing suddenly. His desire now was to get rid of them, to get them away from his sight quickly before he lost control of himself. He wondered at the fury he felt rising in his breast. But he had no time to look into that peculiarity just then.

"I understand your wish to be done with me as quickly as possible. Don't let us waste time in empty ceremonies. Do you see that wood there at the foot of that slope. Yes, the wood of pines. Let us meet there tomorrow at sunrise. I will bring with me my sword or my pistols, or both if you like."

The seconds of General Feraud looked at each other.

"Pistols, General," said the cuirassier.

"So be it. Au revoir – tomorrow morning. Till then let me advise you to keep close if you don't want the *gendarmerie* making inquiries about you before it gets dark. Strangers are rare in this part of the country."

They saluted in silence. General D'Hubert, turning his back on their retreating forms, stood still in the middle of the road for a long time, biting his lower lip and looking on the ground. Then he began to walk straight before him, thus retracing his steps till he found himself before the park gate of his intended's house. Dusk had fallen. Motionless he stared through the bars at the front of the house, gleaming clear beyond the thickets and trees. Footsteps scrunched on the gravel, and presently a tall stooping shape emerged from the lateral alley following the inner side of the park wall.

Le Chevalier de Valmassigue, uncle of the adorable Adèle, ex-brigadier in the army of the Princes, book-binder in Altona, afterwards shoemaker (with a great reputation for elegance in the fit of ladies' shoes) in another small German town, wore silk stockings on his lean shanks, low shoes with silver buckles, a brocaded waistcoat. A long-skirted coat *à la française* covered loosely his thin, bowed back. A small three-cornered hat rested on a lot of powdered hair, tied in a queue.

"*Monsieur le Chevalier*," called General D'Hubert softly.

"What? You here again, *mon ami*? Have you forgotten something?"

"By heavens! that's just it. I have forgotten something. I am come to tell you of it. No – outside. Behind this wall. It's too ghastly a thing to be let in at all where she lives."

The Chevalier came out at once with that benevolent resignation some old people display towards the fugue of youth. Older by a quarter of a century than General D'Hubert, he looked upon him in the secret of his heart as a rather troublesome youngster in love. He had heard his enigmatical words very well, but attached no undue importance to what a mere man of forty so hard hit was likely to do or say. The turn of mind of the generation of Frenchmen grown up during the years of his exile was almost unintelligible to him. Their sentiments appeared to him unduly violent, lacking fineness and measure, their language needlessly exaggerated. He joined calmly the General on the road, and they made a few steps in silence, the General trying to master his agitation, and get proper control of his voice.

"It is perfectly true; I forgot something. I forgot till half an hour ago that I had an urgent affair of honour on my hands. It's incredible, but it is so!"

All was still for a moment. Then in the profound evening silence of the countryside the clear, aged voice of the Chevalier was heard trembling slightly. "Monsieur! That's an indignity."

It was his first thought. The girl born during his exile, the posthumous daughter of his poor brother murdered by a band of Jacobins, had grown since his return very dear to his old heart, which had been starving on mere memories of affection for so many years. "It is an inconceivable thing, I say! A man settles such affairs before he thinks of asking for a young girl's hand. Why! If you had forgotten for ten days longer, you would have been married before your memory returned to you. In my time men did not forget such things – nor yet what is due to the feelings of an innocent young woman. If I did not respect them myself, I would qualify your conduct in a way which you would not like."

General D'Hubert relieved himself frankly by a groan. "Don't let that consideration prevent you. You run no risk of offending her mortally."

But the old man paid no attention to this lover's nonsense. It's doubtful whether he even heard. "What is it?" he asked. "What's the nature of . . .?"

"Call it a youthful folly, *Monsieur le Chevalier*. An inconceivable incredible result of . . ." He stopped short. "He will never believe the story," he thought. "He will only think I am taking him for a fool, and get offended," General D'Hubert spoke up again. "Yes, originating in youthful folly, it has become . . ."

The Chevalier interrupted. "Well, then it must be arranged."

"Arranged?"

"Yes, no matter at what cost to your *amour propre*. You should have remembered you were engaged. You forgot that too, I suppose. And then you go and forget your quarrel. It's the most hopeless exhibition of levity I ever heard of."

"Good heavens, Monsieur! You don't imagine I have been picking up this quarrel last time I was in Paris, or anything of the sort, do you?"

"Eh! What matters the precise date of your insane conduct," exclaimed the Chevalier testily. "The principal thing is to arrange it."

Noticing General D'Hubert getting restive and trying to place a word, the old *émigré* raised his hand, and added with dignity, "I've been a soldier too. I would never dare suggest a doubtful step to the man whose name my niece is to bear. I tell you that *entre galants hommes* an affair can always be arranged."

"But, *saperlotte, Monsieur le Chevalier*, it's fifteen or sixteen years ago. I was a lieutenant of hussars then."

The old Chevalier seemed confounded by the vehemently despairing tone of this information. "You were a lieutenant of hussars sixteen years ago," he mumbled in a dazed manner.

"Why, yes! You did not suppose I was made a general in my cradle like a royal prince."

In the deepening purple twilight of the fields spread with vine leaves, backed by a low band of sombre crimson in the west, the voice of the old ex-officer in the army of the Princes sounded collected, punctiliously civil.

"Do I dream? Is this a pleasantry? Or am I to understand that you have been hatching an affair of honour for sixteen years?"

"It has clung to me for that length of time. That is my precise meaning. The quarrel itself is not to be explained easily. We met on the ground several times during that time, of course."

"What manners! What horrible perversion of manliness! Nothing can account for such inhumanity but the sanguinary madness of the Revolution which has tainted a whole generation," mused the returned *émigré* in a low tone. "Who's your adversary?" he asked a little louder.

"My adversary? His name is Feraud."

Shadowy in his *triorne* and old-fashioned clothes, like a bowed, thin ghost of the *ancien régime*, the Chevalier voiced a ghostly memory. "I can remember the feud about little Sophie Derval, between Monsieur de Brissac, Captain in the Bodyguards, and d'Anjorrant, (not the pock-marked one, the other – the Beau d'Anjorrant, as they called him). They met three times in eighteen months in a most gallant manner. It was the fault of that little Sophie too, who *would* keep on playing . . ."

"This is nothing of the kind," interrupted General D'Hubert. He laughed a little sardonically. "Not at all so simple," he added. "Nor yet half so reasonable," he finished inaudibly between his teeth, and ground them with rage.

After this sound nothing troubled the silence for a long time till the Chevalier asked, without animation, "What is he – this Feraud?"

"Lieutenant of hussars, too – I mean, he's a general. A Gascon. Son of a blacksmith, I believe."

"There! I thought so. That Bonaparte had a special predilection for the *canaille*. I don't mean this for you, D'Hubert. You are one of us, though you have served this usurper, who . . ."

"Let's leave him out of this," broke in General D'Hubert.

The Chevalier shrugged his peaked shoulders. "Feraud of sorts. Offspring of a blacksmith and some village troll. See what comes of mixing yourself up with that sort of people."

"You have made shoes yourself, Chevalier."

"Yes. But I am not the son of a shoemaker. Neither are you,

Monsieur D'Hubert. You and I have something that your Bonaparte's princes, dukes, and marshals have not, because there's no power on earth that could give it to them," retorted the *émigré*, with the rising animation of a man who has got hold of a hopeful argument. "Those people don't exist – all these Ferauds. Feraud! What is Feraud? A *va-nu-pieds* disguised into a general by a Corsican adventurer masquerading as an emperor. There is no earthly reason for a D'Hubert to *s'encanailler* by a duel with a person of that sort. You can make your excuses to him perfectly well. And if the *manant* takes into his head to decline them, you may simply refuse to meet him."

"You say I may do that?"

"I do. With the clearest conscience."

"*Monsieur le Chevalier*! To what do you think you have returned from your emigration?"

This was said in such a startling tone that the old man raised sharply his bowed head, glimmering silvery white under the points of the little *tricorne*. For a time he made no sound.

"God knows!" he said at last, pointing with a slow and grave gesture at a tall, roadside cross mounted on a block of stone, and stretching its arms of forged iron all black against the darkening red band in the sky – "God knows! If it were not for this emblem, which I remember seeing on this spot as a child, I would wonder to what we who had remained faithful to God and our king have returned. The very voices of the people have changed."

"Yes, it is a changed France," said General D'Hubert. He seemed to have regained his calm. His tone was slightly ironic. "Therefore I cannot take your advice. Besides, how is one to refuse to be bitten by a dog that means to bite? It's impracticable. Take my word for it – Feraud isn't a man to be stayed by apologies or refusals. But there are other ways. I could, for instance, send a messenger with a word to the brigadier of the *gendarmerie* in Senlac. He and his two friends are liable to arrest on my simple order. It would make some talk in the army, both the organised and the disbanded – especially the disbanded. All *canaille*! All once upon a time the companions in arms of

Armand D'Hubert. But what need a D'Hubert care what people that don't exist may think. Or, better still, I might get my brother-in-law to send for the mayor of the village and give him a hint. No more would be needed to get the three 'brigands' set upon with flails and pitchforks and hunted into some nice, deep, wet ditch – and nobody the wiser! It has been done only ten miles from here to three poor devils of the disbanded Red Lancers of the Guard going to their homes. What says your conscience, *Chevalier*? Can a D'Hubert do that thing to three men who do not exist?"

A few stars had come out on the blue obscurity, clear as crystal, of the sky. The dry, thin voice of the Chevalier spoke harshly. "Why are you telling me all this?"

The General seized the withered old hand with a strong grip. "Because I owe you my fullest confidence. Who could tell Adèle but you? You understand why I dare not trust my brother-in-law nor yet my own sister. *Chevalier*! I have been so near doing these things that I tremble yet. You don't know how terrible this duel appears to me. And there's no escape from it."

He murmured after a pause, "It's a fatality," dropped the Chevalier's passive hand, and said in his ordinary conversational voice, "I shall have to go without seconds. If it is my lot to remain on the ground, you at least will know all that can be made known of this affair."

The shadowy ghost of the *ancien régime* seemed to have become more bowed during the conversation. "How am I to keep an indifferent face this evening before these two women," he groaned. "General! I find it very difficult to forgive you."

General D'Hubert made no answer.

"Is your cause good, at least?"

"I am innocent."

This time he seized the Chevalier's ghostly arm above the elbow, and gave it a mighty squeeze. "I must kill him!" he hissed, and opening his hand strode away down the road.

The delicate attentions of his adoring sister had secured for the General perfect liberty of movement in the house where he was a guest. He had even his own entrance through a small door

in one corner of the orangery. Thus he was not exposed that
evening to the necessity of dissembling his agitation before the
calm ignorance of the other inmates. He was glad of it. It
seemed to him that if he had to open his lips he would break
out into horrible and aimless imprecations, start breaking
furniture, smashing china and glass. From the moment he
opened the private door, and while ascending the twenty-eight
steps of a winding staircase, giving access to the corridor on
which his room opened, he went through a horrible and
humiliating scene in which an infuriated madman with blood-
shot eyes and a foaming mouth played inconceivable havoc with
everything inanimate that may be found in a well-appointed
dining-room. When he opened the door of his apartment the fit
was over, and his bodily fatigue was so great that he had to catch
at the backs of the chairs while crossing the room to reach a low
and broad divan on which he let himself fall heavily. His moral
prostration was still greater. That brutality of feeling which he
had known only when charging the enemy, sabre in hand,
amazed this man of forty, who did not recognize in it the
instinctive fury of his menaced passion. But in his mental
and bodily exhaustion this passion got cleared, distilled, refined
into a sentiment of melancholy despair at having, perhaps, to
die before he had taught this beautiful girl to love him.

That night, General D'Hubert stretched out on his back with
his hands over his eyes, or lying on his breast with his face
buried in a cushion, made the full pilgrimage of emotions.
Nauseating disgust at the absurdity of the situation, doubt of
his own fitness to conduct his existence, and mistrust of his best
sentiments (for what the devil did he want to go to Fouché for?)
– he knew them all in turn. "I am an idiot, neither more nor
less," he thought – "A sensitive idiot. Because I overheard two
men talking in a café . . . I am an idiot afraid of lies – whereas in
life it is only the truth that matters."

Several times he got up and, walking in his socks in order not
to be heard by anybody downstairs, drank all the water he could
find in the dark. And he tasted the torments of jealousy, too.
She would marry somebody else. His very soul writhed. The

tenacity of that Feraud, the awful persistence of that imbecile brute, came to him with the tremendous force of a relentless destiny. General D'Hubert trembled as he put down the empty water ewer. "He will have me," he thought. General D'Hubert was tasting every emotion that life has to give. He had in his dry mouth the faint sickly flavour of fear, not the excusable fear before a young girl's candid and amused glance, but the fear of death and the honourable man's fear of cowardice.

But if true courage consists in going out to meet an odious danger from which our body, soul and heart recoil together, General D'Hubert had the opportunity to practise it for the first time in his life. He had charged exultingly at batteries and at infantry squares, and ridden with messages through a hail of bullets without thinking anything about it. His business now was to sneak out unheard, at break of day, to an obscure and revolting death. General D'Hubert never hesitated. He carried two pistols in a leather bag which he slung over his shoulder. Before he had crossed the garden his mouth was dry again. He picked two oranges. It was only after shutting the gate after him that he felt a slight faintness.

He staggered on, disregarding it, and after going a few yards regained the command of his legs. In the colourless and pellucid dawn the wood of pines detached its columns of trunks and its dark green canopy very clearly against the rocks of the grey hillside. He kept his eyes fixed on it steadily, and sucked at an orange as he walked. That temperamental good-humoured coolness in the face of danger which had made him an officer liked by his men and appreciated by his superiors was gradually asserting itself. It was like going into battle. Arriving at the edge of the wood he sat down on a boulder, holding the other orange in his hand, and reproached himself for coming so ridiculously early on the ground. Before very long, however, he heard the swishing of bushes, footsteps on the hard ground, and the sounds of a disjointed, loud conversation. A voice somewhere behind him said boastfully, "He's game for my bag."

He thought to himself, "Here they are. What's this about game? Are they talking of me?" And becoming aware of the other orange in his hand, he thought further, "These are very good oranges. Léonie's own tree. I may just as well eat this orange now instead of flinging it away."

Emerging from a wilderness of rocks and bushes, General Feraud and his seconds discovered General D'Hubert engaged in peeling the orange. They stood still, waiting till he looked up. Then the seconds raised their hats, while General Feraud, putting his hands behind his back, walked aside a little way.

"I am compelled to ask one of you, messieurs, to act for me. I have brought no friends. Will you?"

The one-eyed cuirassier said judicially, "That cannot be refused."

The other veteran remarked, "It's awkward all the same."

"Owing to the state of the people's minds in this part of the country there was no one I could trust safely with the object of your presence here," explained General D'Hubert, urbanely.

They saluted, looked round, and remarked both together:

"Poor ground."

"It's unfit."

"Why bother about ground, measurements, and so on. Let us simplify matters. Load the two pairs of pistols. I will take those of General Feraud, and let him take mine. Or, better still, let us take a mixed pair. One of each pair. Then let us go into the wood and shoot at sight, while you remain outside. We did not come here for ceremonies, but for war – war to the death. Any ground is good enough for that. If I fall, you must leave me where I lie and clear out. It wouldn't be healthy for you to be found hanging about here after that."

It appeared after a short parley that General Feraud was willing to accept these conditions. While the seconds were loading the pistols, he could be heard whistling, and was seen to rub his hands with perfect contentment. He flung off his coat briskly, and General D'Hubert took off his own and folded it carefully on a stone.

"Suppose you take your principal to the other side of the wood and let him enter exactly in ten minutes from now," suggested General D'Hubert calmly, but feeling as if he were giving directions for his own execution. This, however, was his last moment of weakness. "Wait. Let us compare watches first."

He pulled out his own. The officer with the chipped nose went over to borrow the watch of General Feraud. They bent their heads over them for a time.

"That's it. At four minutes to six by yours. Seven to by mine."

It was the cuirassier who remained by the side of General D'Hubert, keeping his one eye fixed immovably on the white face of the watch he held in the palm of his band. He opened his mouth, waiting for the beat of the last second long before he snapped out the word, "*Avancez*."

General D'Hubert moved on, passing from the glaring sunshine of the Provençal morning into the cool and aromatic shade of the pines. The ground was clear between the reddish trunks, whose multitude, leaning at slightly different angles, confused his eye at first. It was like going into battle. The commanding quality of confidence in himself woke up in his breast. He was all to his affair. The problem was how to kill the adversary. Nothing short of that would free him from this imbecile nightmare. "It's no use wounding that brute," thought General D'Hubert. He was known as a resourceful officer. His comrades years ago used also to call him The Strategist. And it was a fact that he could think in the presence of the enemy. Whereas Feraud had always been a mere fighter – but a dead shot, unluckily.

"I must draw his fire at the greatest possible range," said General D'Hubert to himself.

At that moment he saw something white moving far off between the trees – the shirt of his adversary. He stepped out at once between the trunks, exposing himself freely; then, quick as lightning, leaped back. It had been a risky move but it succeeded in its object. Almost simultaneously with the pop of a shot a small piece of bark chipped off by the bullet stung his ear painfully.

General Feraud, with one shot expended, was getting cau-

tious. Peeping round the tree, General D'Hubert could not see
him at all. This ignorance of the foe's whereabouts carried with
it a sense of insecurity. General H'Hubert felt himself abominably exposed on his flank and rear. Again something white
fluttered in his sight. Ha! The enemy was still on his front, then.
He had feared a turning movement. But apparently General
Feraud was not thinking of it. General D'Hubert saw him pass
without special haste from one tree to another in the straight
line of approach. With great firmness of mind General D'Hubert stayed his hand. Too far yet. He knew he was no marksman. His must be a waiting game – to kill.

Wishing to take advantage of the greater thickness of the
trunk, he sank down to the ground. Extended at full length,
head on to his enemy, he had his person completely protected.
Exposing himself would not do now, because the other was too
near by this time. A conviction that Feraud would presently do
something rash was like balm to General D'Hubert's soul. But
to keep his chin raised off the ground was irksome, and not
much use either. He peeped round, exposing a fraction of his
head with dread, but really with little risk. His enemy, as a
matter of fact, did not expect to see anything of him so far down
as that. General D'Hubert caught a fleeting view of General
Feraud shifting trees again with deliberate caution. "He de-
spises my shooting," he thought, displaying that insight into the
mind of his antagonist which is of such great help in winning
battles. He was confirmed in his tactics of immobility. "If I
could only watch my rear as well as my front!" he thought
anxiously, longing for the impossible.

It required some force of character to lay his pistols down;
but, on a sudden impulse, General D'Hubert did this very
gently – one on each side of him. In the army he had been looked
upon as a bit of a dandy because he used to shave and put on a
clean shirt on the days of battle. As a matter of fact he had
always been very careful of his personal appearance. In a man of
nearly forty, in love with a young and charming girl, this praise-
worthy self-respect may run to such little weaknesses as, for
instance, being provided with an elegant little leather folding-

case containing a small ivory comb, and fitted with a piece of looking-glass on the outside. General D'Hubert, his hands being free, felt in his breeches' pockets for that implement of innocent vanity excusable in the possessor of long silky moustaches. He drew it out, and then with the utmost coolness and promptitude turned himself over on his back. In this new attitude, his head a little raised, holding the little looking-glass just clear of his tree, he squinted into it with his left eye, while the right kept a direct watch on the rear of his position. Thus was proved Napoleon's saying, that "for a French soldier, the word impossible does not exist." He had the right tree nearly filling the field of his little mirror.

"If he moves from behind it," he reflected with satisfaction, "I am bound to see his legs. But in any case he can't come upon me unawares."

And sure enough he saw the boots of General Feraud flash in and out, eclipsing for an instant everything else reflected in the little mirror. He shifted its position accordingly. But having to form his judgment of the change from that indirect view he did not realise that now his feet and a portion of his legs were in plain sight of General Feraud.

General Feraud had been getting gradually impressed by the amazing cleverness with which his enemy was keeping cover. He had spotted the right tree with bloodthirsty precision. He was absolutely certain of it. And yet he had not been able to glimpse as much as the tip of an ear. As he had been looking for it at the height of about five feet ten inches from the ground it was no great wonder – but it seemed very wonderful to General Feraud.

The first view of these feet and legs determined a rush of blood to his head. He literally staggered behind his tree, and had to steady himself against it with his hand. The other was lying on the ground then! On the ground! Perfectly still, too! Exposed! What could it mean? . . . The notion that he had knocked over his adversary at the first shot entered then General Feraud's head. Once there it grew with every second of attentive gazing, overshadowing every other supposition – irresistible, triumphant, ferocious.

"What an as I was to think I could have missed him," he muttered to himself. "He was exposed *en plein* – the fool! – for quite a couple of seconds."

General Feraud gazed at the motionless limbs, the last vestiges of surprise fading before an unbounded admiration of his own deadly skill with the pistol.

"Turned up his toes! By the god of war, that was a shot!" he exulted mentally. "Got it through the head, no doubt, just where I aimed, staggered behind that tree, rolled over on his back and died."

And he stared! He stared, forgetting to move, almost awed, almost sorry. But for nothing in the world would he have had it undone. Such a shot! – such a shot! Rolled over on his back and died!

For it was this helpless position, lying on the back, that shouted its direct evidence at General Feraud! It never occured to him that it might have been deliberately assumed by a living man. It was inconceivable. It was beyond the range of sane supposition. There was no possibility to guess the reason for it. And it must be said, too, that General D'Hubert's turned-up feet looked thoroughly dead. General Feraud expanded his lungs for a stentorian shout to his seconds, but, from what he felt to be an excessive scrupulousness, refrained for a while.

"I will just go and see first whether he breathes yet," he mumbled to himself, leaving carelessly the shelter of his tree. This move was immediately perceived by the resourceful General D'Hubert. He concluded it to be another shift, but when he lost the boots out of the field of the mirror he became uneasy. General Feraud had only stepped a little out of the line, but his adversary could not possibly have supposed him walking up with perfect unconcern. General D'Hubert, beginning to wonder what had become of the other, was taken unawares so completely that the first warning of danger consisted in the long, early-morning shadow of his enemy falling aslant on his outstretched legs. He had not even heard a footfall on the soft ground between the trees!

It was too much even for his coolness. He jumped up

thoughtlessly, leaving the pistols on the ground. The irresistible instinct of an average man (unless totally paralysed by discomfiture) would have been to stoop for his weapons, exposing himself to the risk of being shot down in that position. Instinct, of course, is irreflective. It is its very definition. But it may be an inquiry worth pursuing whether in reflective mankind the mechanical promptings of instinct are not affected by the customary mode of thought. In his young days, Armand D'Hubert, the reflective, promising officer, had emitted the opinion that in warfare one should "never cast back on the lines of a mistake." This idea, defended and developed in many discussions, had settled into one of the stock notions of his brain, had become a part of his mental individuality. Whether it had gone so inconceivably deep as to affect the dictates of his instinct, or simply because, as he himself declared afterwards, he was "too scared to remember the confounded pistols," the fact is that General D'Hubert never attempted to stoop for them. Instead of going back on his mistake, he seized the rough trunk with both hands, and swung himself behind it with such impetuosity that, going right round in the very flash and report of the pistol-shot, he reappeared on the other side of the tree face to face with General Feraud. This last, completely unstrung by such a show of agility on the part of a dead man, was trembling yet. A very faint mist of smoke hung before his face which had an extraordinary aspect, as if the lower jaw had become unhinged.

"Not missed!" he cracked hoarsely from the depths of a dry throat.

This sinister sound loosened the spell that had fallen on General D'Hubert's senses." Yes, missed – *à bout portant*," he heard himself saying, almost before he had recovered the full command of his faculties. The revulsion of feeling was accompanied by a gust of homicidal fury, resuming in its violence the accumulated resentment of a lifetime. For years General D'Hubert had been exasperated and humiliated by an atrocious absurdity imposed upon him by this man's savage caprice. Besides, General D'Hubert had been in this last instance too unwilling to confront death for the reaction of his anguish not to take the shape of a desire to kill. "And I have my two shots to fire yet," he added pitilessly.

General Feraud snapped-to his teeth, and his face assumed an irate, undaunted expression. "Go on!" he said grimly.

These would have been his last words if General D'Hubert had been holding the pistols in his hands. But the pistols were lying on the ground at the foot of a pine. General D'Hubert had the second of leisure necessary to remember that he had dreaded death not as a man, but as a lover; not as a danger, but as a rival; not as a foe to life, but as an obstacle to marriage. And behold! there was the rival defeated! – utterly defeated, crushed, done for!

He picked up the weapons mechanically, and, instead of firing them into General Feraud's breast, he gave expression to the thought uppermost in his mind, "You will fight no more duels now."

His tone of leisurely, ineffable satisfaction was too much for General Feraud's stoicism. "Don't dawdle, then, damn you for a cold-blooded staff-coxcomb!" he roared out suddenly, out of an impassive face held erect on a rigidly still body.

General D'Hubert uncocked the pistols carefully. This proceeding was observed with mixed feelings by the other general. "You missed me twice," the victor said coolly, shifting both pistols to one hand; "the last time within a foot or so. By every rule of single combat your life belongs to me. That does not mean that I want to take it now."

"I have no use for your forbearance," muttered General Feraud gloomily.

"Allow me to point out that this is no concern of mine," said General D'Hubert, whose every word was dictated by a consummate delicacy of feeling. In anger he could have killed that man, but in cold blood he recoiled from humiliating by a show of generosity this unreasonable being – a fellow-soldier of the *Grande Armée*, a companion in the wonders and terrors of the great military epic. "You don't set up the pretension of dictating to me what I am to do with what's my own."

General Feraud looked startled, and the other continued, "You've forced me on a point of honour to keep my life at your disposal, as it were, for fifteen years. Very well. Now that the matter is decided to my advantage, I am going to do what I like with your life on the same principle. You shall keep it at my disposal as long as I choose. Neither more or less. You are on your honour till I say the word."

"I am! But, *sacrebleu*! This is an absurd position for a General of the Empire to be placed in!" cried General Feraud, in accents of profound and dismayed conviction. "It amounts to sitting all the rest of my life with a loaded pistol in a drawer waiting for your word. It's – it's idiotic; I shall be an object of – of – derision."

"Absurd? – idiotic? Do you think so?" queried General D'Hubert with sly gravity. "Perhaps. But I don't see how that can be helped. However, I am not likely to talk at large of this adventure. Nobody need ever know anything about it. Just as no one to this day, I believe, knows the origin of our quarrel . . . Not a word more," he added hastily. "I can't really discuss this question with a man who, as far as I am concerned, does not exist."

When the two duellists came out into the open, General Feraud walking a little behind, and rather with the air of walking in a trance, the two seconds hurried towards them, each from his station at the edge of the wood. General D'Hubert addressed them, speaking loud and distinctly, "Messieurs, I make it a point of declaring to you solemnly, in the presence of General Feraud, that our difference is at last settled for good. You may inform all the world of that fact."

"A reconciliation, after all!" they exclaimed together.

"Reconciliation? Not that exactly. It is something much more binding. Is it not so, General?"

General Feraud only lowered his head in sign of assent. The two veterans looked at each other. Later in the day, when they found themselves alone out of their moody friend's earshot, the cuirassier remarked suddenly, "Generally speaking, I can see with my one eye as far as most people; but this beats me. He won't say anything."

"In this affair of honour I understand there has been from first to last always something that no one in the army could quite make out," declared the chasseur with the imperfect nose. "In mystery it began, in mystery it went on, in mystery it is to end, apparently."

General D'Hubert walked home with long, hasty strides, by no means uplifted by a sense of triumph. He had conquered, yet it did not seem to him that he had gained very much by his conquest. The night before he had grudged the risk of his life which appeared to him magnificent, worthy of preservation as an opportunity to win a girl's love. He had known moments when, by a marvellous illusion, this love seemed to be already his, and his threatened life a still more magnificent opportunity of devotion. Now that his life was safe it had suddenly lost its special magnificence. It had acquired instead a specially alarming aspect as a snare for the exposure of unworthiness. As to the marvellous illusion of conquered love that had visited him for a moment in the agitated watches of the night, which might have been his last on earth, he comprehended now its true nature. It had been merely a paroxysm of delirious conceit. Thus to this man, sobered by the victorious issue of a duel, life appeared robbed of its charm, simply because it was no longer menaced.

Approaching the house from the back, through the orchard and the kitchen garden, he could not notice the agitation which reigned in front. He never met a single soul. Only while walking softly along the corridor, he became aware that the house was awake and more noisy than usual. Names of servants were being called out down below in a confused noise of coming and going. With some concern he noticed that the door of his own room stood ajar, though the shutters had not been opened yet. He had hoped that his early excursion would have passed unperceived. He expected to find some servant just gone in; but the sunshine filtering through the usual cracks enabled him to see lying on the low divan something bulky, which had the appearance of two women clasped in each other's arms. Tearful and desolate murmurs issued mysteriously from that appearance. General D'Hubert pulled open the nearest pair of shutters violently.

One of the women then jumped up. It was his sister. She stood for a moment with her hair hanging down and her arms raised straight up above her head, and then flung herself with a stifled cry into his arms. He returned her embrace, trying at the same time to disengage himself from it. The other woman had not risen. She seemed, on the contrary, to cling closer to the divan, hiding her face in the cushions. Her hair was also loose; it was admirably fair. General D'Hubert recognized it with staggering emotion. Mademoiselle de Valmassigue! Adèle! In distress!

He became greatly alarmed, and got rid of his sister's hug definitely. Madame Léonie then extended her shapely bare arm out of her *peignoir*, pointing dramatically at the divan. "This poor, terrified child has rushed here from home, on foot, two miles – running all the way."

"What on earth has happened?" asked General D'Hubert in a low, agitated voice.

But Madame Léonie was speaking loudly. "She rang the great bell at the gate and roused all the household – we were all asleep yet. You may imagine what a terrible shock . . . Adèle, my dear child, sit up."

General D'Hubert's expression was not that of a man who "imagines" with facility. He did, however, fish out of the chaos of surmises the notion that his prospective mother-in-law had died suddenly, but only to dismiss it at once. He could not conceive the nature of the event or the catastrophe which could induce Mademoiselle de Valmassigue, living in a house full of servants, to bring the news over the fields herself, two miles, running all the way.

"But why are you in this room?" he whispered, full of awe.

"Of course, I ran up to see, and this child . . . I did not notice it . . . she followed me. It's that absurd Chevalier," went on Madame Léonie, looking towards the divan . . . "Her hair is all come down. You may imagine she did not stop to call her maid to dress it before she started . . . Adèle, my dear, sit up . . . He blurted it all out to her at half-past five in the morning. She woke up early and opened her shutters to breathe the fresh air, and saw him sitting collapsed on a garden bench at the end of

the great alley. At that hour – you may imagine! And the
evening before he had declared himself indisposed. She hurried
on some clothes and flew down to him. One would be anxious
for less. He loves her, but not very intelligently. He had been up
all night, fully dressed, the poor old man, perfectly exhausted.
He wasn't in a state to invent a plausible story . . . What a
confidant you chose there! My husband was furious. He said,
'We can't interfere now.' So we sat down to wait. It was awful.
And this poor child running with her hair loose over here
publicly! She has been seen by some people in the fields.
She has roused the whole household too. It's awkward for
her. Luckily you are to be married next week . . . Adèle, sit
up. He has come home on his own legs . . . We expected to see
you coming on a stretcher, perhaps – what do I know? Go and
see if the carriage is ready. I must take this child home at once.
It isn't proper for her to stay here a minute longer."

General D'Hubert did not move. It was as though he had
heard nothing. Madame Léonie changed her mind. "I will go
and see myself," she cried. "I want also my cloak. – Adèle –"
she began, but did not add "sit up." She went out saying, in a
very loud and cheerful tone: "I leave the door open."

General D'Hubert made a movement towards the divan, but
then Adèle sat up, and that checked him dead. He thought, "I
haven't washed this morning. I must look like an old tramp.
There's earth on the back of my coat and pine-needles in my
hair." It occurred to him that the situation required a good deal
of circumspection on his part.

"I am greatly concerned, mademoiselle," he began vaguely,
and abandoned that line. She was sitting up on the divan with
her cheeks unusually pink and her hair, brilliantly fair, falling
all over her shoulders – which was a very novel sight to the
general. He walked away up the room, and looking out of the
window for safety said, "I fear you must think I behaved like a
madman," in accents of sincere despair. Then he spun round,
and noticed that she had followed him with her eyes. They were
not cast down on meeting his glance. And the expression of her
face was novel to him also. It was, one might have said,

reversed. Those eyes looked at him with grave thoughtfulness, while the exquisite lines of her mouth seemed to suggest a restrained smile. This change made her transcendental beauty much less mysterious, much more accessible to a man's comprehension. An amazing ease of mind came to the general – and even some ease of manner. He walked down the room with as much pleasurable excitement as he would have found in walking up to a battery vomiting death, fire, and smoke; then stood looking down with smiling eyes at the girl whose marriage with him (next week) had been so carefully arranged by the wise, the good, the admirable Léonie.

"Ah! mademoiselle," he said, in a tone of courtly regret, "if only I could be certain that you did not come here this morning, two miles, running all the way, merely from affection for your mother!"

He waited for an answer imperturbable but inwardly elated. It came in a demure murmur, eyelashes lowered with fascinating effect. "You must not be *méchant* as well as mad."

And then General D'Hubert made an aggressive movement towards the divan which nothing could check. That piece of furniture was not exactly in the line of the open door. But Madame Léonie, coming back wrapped up in a light cloak and carrying a lace shawl on her arm for Adèle to hide her incriminating hair under, had a swift impression of her brother getting up from his knees.

"Come along, my dear child," she cried from the doorway.

The general now himself again in the fullest sense, showed the readiness of a resourceful cavalry officer and the peremptoriness of a leader of men. "You don't expect her to walk to the carriage," he said indignantly. "She isn't fit. I shall carry her downstairs."

This he did slowly, followed by his awed and respectful sister; but he rushed back like a whirlwind to wash off all the signs of the night of anguish and the morning of war, and to put on the festive garments of a conqueror before hurrying over to the other house. Had it not been for that, General D'Hubert felt capable of mounting a horse and pursuing his late adversary in order simply to embrace him from excess of happiness. "I owe it all to this stupid brute," he thought. "He has made plain in a morning what might have taken me years to find out – for I am a timid fool. No self-confidence whatever. Perfect coward. And the Chevalier! Delightful old man!" General D'Hubert longed to embrace him also.

The Chevalier was in bed. For several days he was very unwell. The men of the Empire and the post-revolution young ladies were too much for him. He got up the day before the wedding, and, being curious by nature, took his niece aside for a quiet talk. He advised her to find out from her husband the true story of the affair of honour, whose claim, so imperative and so persistent, had led her to within an ace of tragedy. "It is right that his wife should be told. And next month or so will be your time to learn from him anything you want to know, my dear child."

Later on, when the married couple came on a visit to the mother of the bride, Madame la Générale D'Hubert communicated to her beloved old uncle the true story she had obtained without any difficulty from her husband.

The Chevalier listened with deep attention to the end, took a pinch of snuff, flicked the grains of tobacco from the frilled front of his shirt, and asked calmly, "And that's all it was!"

"Yes, uncle," replied Madame la Générale, opening her pretty eyes very wide. "Isn't it funny? *C'est insensé* – to think what men are capable of!"

"H'm!" commented the old *émigré*. "It depends what sort of men. That Bonaparte's soldiers were savages. It is *insensé*. As a wife, my dear, you must believe implicitly what your husband says."

But to Léonie's husband the Chevalier confided his true opinion. "If that's the tale the fellow made up for his wife, and during the honeymoon too, you may depend on it that no one will ever know now the secret of this affair."

Considerably later still, General D'Hubert judged the time come, and the opportunity propitious to write a letter to General Feraud. This letter began by disclaiming all animosity. "I've never," wrote the General Baron D'Hubert, "wished for your death during all the time of our deplorable quarrel. Allow me," he continued, "to give you back in all form your forfeited life. It is proper that we two, who have been partners in so much military glory, should be friendly to each other publicly."

The same letter contained also an item of domestic information. It was in reference to this last that General Feraud answered from a little village on the banks of the Garonne, in the following words:

"If one of your boy's names had been Napoleon – or Joseph – or even Joachim, I could congratulate you on the event with a better heart. As you have thought proper to give him the names of Charles Henri Armand, I am confirmed in my conviction that you *never* loved the Emperor. The thought of that sublime hero chained to a rock in the middle of a savage ocean makes life of so little value that I would receive with positive joy your instructions to blow my brains out. From suicide I consider myself in honour debarred. But I keep a loaded pistol in my drawer."

Madame la Générale D'Hubert lifted up her hands in despair after perusing that answer.

"You see? He *won't* be reconciled," said her husband. "He must never, by any chance, be allowed to guess where the money comes from. It wouldn't do. He couldn't bear it."

"You are a *brave homme*, Armand," said Madame la Générale appreciatively.

"My dear, I had the right to blow his brains out; but as I didn't, we can't let him starve. He has lost his pension and he is utterly incapable of doing anything in the world for himself. We must take care of him, secretly, to the end of his days. Don't I owe him the most ecstatic moment of my life? . . . Ha! ha! ha! Over the fields, two miles, running all the way! I couldn't believe my ears! . . . But for his stupid ferocity, it would have taken me years to find you out. It's extraordinary how in one way or another this man has managed to fasten himself on my deeper feelings."

GALLANT'S GAMBLE

Charles Partington

Our last Napoleonic story introduces the English. The story is set in the period up to Waterloo and introduces a new character, Jack Gallant, of whom I hope we'll see a lot more. Charles Partington (b. 1940) is a printer by profession, but has been selling stories, mostly of horror and science fiction, for thirty years. He was also the publisher of the avant garde magazine Something Else *in 1980.*

The *Guinevere* was sinking. The twelve hundred ton merchant vessel was listing badly and settling ever lower in the raging waters, driven onto the treacherous shoals off the Dunkirk Sands by the unrelenting squall.

After her captain had been washed overboard, the crew, aware that nothing could be done to save the *Guinevere*, abandoned ship. By the time the platoon of furious Riflemen had smashed their way though the locked hatchway and gained the upper deck, the crew, a rag-bag collection of hands pressed into service just before the merchant ship left Devon, had made good their escape in the only serviceable jolly boat.

Now, Jack Gallant, clinging to the rat-lines at mid-station, watched helplessly as the boat, disappearing into the storm-lashed night, pulled steadily away. Gallant, recently promoted to the rank of Corporal, largely because of his ability to read and write, was one of the youngest Riflemen in the platoon. Though only nineteen years old, he was already taller than most men. Beneath his gold-buttoned red coat, muslin shirt and breeches, his lithely-muscled body was iron hard. Luxuriant dark locks, now wet with spray, framed his strong-boned face and the glance of his quizzical grey eyes projected a sense of glowering inner calm and assurance. But there was anxiety in those eyes now.

Releasing his grip on the shroud lines, he dropped back onto the deck and glanced up at the stern-castle. There, Major Hallam had set Captain Jennings, and a six-man detail of Riflemen, the task of trying to cut free the other jolly boat from under the fallen yard-arm and the entangling web of rigging and sailcloth that imprisoned it. There was much shouting and cursing and progress was desperately slow in the frightful conditions. Gallant could see that despite all their efforts, Hallam's plan wasn't going to work. If something wasn't done quickly, most of the men in the platoon, strangers to the sea and poor swimmers at best, would drown when the ship foundered.

A loud thudding and stamping of iron-shod hoofs came from the lower orlop deck. There, the mule-teams the *Guinevere* had been transporting to Flushing as part of her cargo, were rearing and kicking frantically, trying to break free from their tethers. Gallant stared at these wild-eyed, frothing beasts, and the glimmerings of a plan formed in his racing mind.

Skidding and slipping along the spray-drenched deck, dragging himself hand over hand along the guide-rails, Gallant began to make his way towards the mules.

"Corporal Gallant!" Major Hallam's voice rang out from the quarterdeck. "Where the hell do you think you're going?"

"To free the mules, Sir!" Gallant cried. "The men can . . ." But another monstrous wave broke over the ship's side, submerging him in an icy spray of water and carrying away his words.

"Get back and lend a hand here!" Hallam roared. "Let the Lord worry about the fate of those dumb beasts!"

Gallant shook his head, ignoring him. But he was taking a risk, and he knew it. Hallam was a drink-sodden disciplinarian, quite capable of shooting dead any soldier who dared disobey his orders.

Trying to avoid being kicked or stamped on by the nervous animals, the young Rifleman drew his knife and cut through a tether, freeing one of the braying mules. "Send two of the men down here, Major Hallam!" he shouted. "They can hold onto the mule while she swims ashore. It's the best chance we've got."

There was a roar of approval from the Riflemen who had been watching from the foot of the fore-castle. Major Hallam grew red in the face with rage trying to order them back, but they ignored him, clattering down the steps and running across the tilted orlop deck. From deep in the bowels of the ship, timbers groaned ominously and the air was filled with the noise of crackings and splinterings. The *Guinevere* was settling deeper with every passing second.

Clinging tightly to the bit, Gallant led the blindfolded and skittish mule towards the deck rails. "Right, who's going first?" he asked.

Two of the Riflemen stepped forward, hesitantly. But the sea, surging across the lower deck, stiffened their resolve.

"Grab tight hold of the harness, lads!" Jack Gallant ordered, whipping off the blindfold and cracking the mule as hard as he could on its rump. "You're in for a rough ride!"

The beast snorted in surprise and leaped forward, dragging the men with her, down into the surging waters. They hit with a tremendous splash, submerging for an instant in the white-crested sea, before resurfacing. The wild-eyed mule came up first, snorting and whinnying, followed by the men still clinging to her harness. Then with powerful kicks from its legs, the beast began swimming towards the distant shore, towing the men behind her.

"Right!" Jack Gallant roared. "Cut the rest of those mules free! With any luck we can all get off this bloody ship!"

Three of the Riflemen, still labouring to free the jolly boat, remained with Major Hallam and Captain Jenner on the quarter-deck. Even so, Jack Gallant and six of the best swimmers in the platoon had to take their chances in the sea. Two of the mules had broken legs and had to be left on board, and another dashed over the side in blind panic the moment its tether was cut. But all around the foundering *Guinevere*, the sea was littered with floating debris. Jack Gallant waited until the last of his companions had leapt overboard, then he took a deep breath and plunged after them. The water was icy. He could feel the heat being sucked from his body. Buffeted by the waves, he was tossed around helplessly until he managed to grasp hold of a section of spar large enough to support his weight. Fortunately the easterly squall was blowing him towards the distant French shore.

The almost full moon shone its light fitfully from behind breaks in the racing clouds. illuminating a nightmare scene. One moment Gallant was in utter darkness, lost in a black trough of hissing water, the next, dragged up to the peak of each gathering wave, he could clearly see the mules struggling towards the distant shoreline. All around him, the water shimmered with the cold fires of luminescence; death seemed very close.

Still clinging desperately to the section of splintered, rope-entangled spar, Jack Gallant heard the weakened cries of two of his drowning comrades above the howling of the wind and the booming of the waves. He recognised the voices, they belonged to Collins and Pell. Gallant struggled to get closer to them. Collins was already beyond help, but a vagary of the swirling currents momentarily swept Pell within reach of the Rifleman's outstretched fingers. Just in time, he grabbed hold of the Welshman by one of his flapping shoulder straps, dragging him onto the spar. The old man barely had enough strength left to speak, he just clung there, nodding thankfully. Gallant shook the salt water from his eyes and glanced back at the rapidly disintegrating ship, but a powerful vortex of water spun the spar round and around, threatening to suck both men under. In those frenzied moments, he lost sight of the doomed merchant ship in the scudding sea-fret.

When finally they reached the beach, numbed to near-exhaustion by the freezing water, a grim sight met Jack Gallant's eyes. The shore-line was littered with the corpses of men and animals. Pell had passed out. Crouching beside him on the sand, Gallant shivered and endured the agony of cramped muscles. After a minute or two, he lifted his head and looked around.

There was no sign of Major Hallam, but Captain Jenner had survived the sinking of the *Guinevere*. He was already on his feet, yelling and striking at the dazed survivors with his stick, trying to instil a sense of order and purpose into the minds of the confused and demoralised Riflemen. Most of the mules had bolted, but two were braying mournfully in the tidal-way, shaking excess sea-water from their dripping coats. Jenner had already dispatched men to retrieve them. Other soldiers were breaking open the boxes and packets washed up on the shoreline, looking for food and munitions. Weapons were being stripped from the bodies of dead comrades.

Jack Gallant looked up as Captain Jenner came tramping towards him across the seaweed-strewn sand. He glanced down at the Welshman, concern on his face. "How is he?"

"Pell's alright, Sir," Gallant told him.

Jenner tapped the tip of his stick against his boot. Stiffly, he said, "You did well back there on the *Guinevere*, Jack. The men won't forget." He wiped a trickle of blood from his forehead, "Now there's work to do, Jack, Corporal. I need to know who made it ashore. Can you do a head-count for me?"

Ignoring his aching joints, Gallant saluted then dragged himself to his feet. Jenner returned to his other duties.

Out of an original complement of forty riflemen and three officers, only twenty-two had struggled ashore. There was no sign of Major Hallam or the men who had remained on board with him.

As near as Captain Jenner had been able to estimate, they were some eighty miles south of Brussels. Their orders required that they join Wellingtn's troops, cantoned around the city, as quickly as possible. Though the roads, villages and farms of Picardy and Argonne undoubtedly swarmed with units of the French, Captain Jenner was convinced they could make it to the Dutch port on foot. But every man-jack of them knew it wasn't going to be easy. They were facing a hard and dangerous slog. Forming his men up in a loose line, he led them off the beach, across an area of scrub-covered dunes into open farmland.

Stumbling and trudging along muddy tracks and pot-holed roads, they managed to cover thirteen miles before the dawn broke. The high winds had lessened and the rain fell only sporadically. The three-quarters moon, whenever it shone through breaks in the scudding clouds, revealed waterlogged fields and impenetrable forests of alder and wild cherry. Startled herds of mangy Charolais cattle fled as they approached. Dogs barked in the distance, and somewhere in the darkness a church bell rang ominously, but never once were they challenged.

The Riflemen were clumping along a barely existent track that seemed to be leading them nowhere, when Captain Jenner suddenly called a halt.

His sharp eyes had spotted the remains of an isolated cattle shed. Its sagging roof and part-timbered walls would provide some shelter from the elements and the untended grove of crab apple trees at its rear would offer reasonable cover should a hurried withdrawal prove necessary.

"Pearce!" Jenner yelled. "Reconnaissance duty. And be careful. The rest of you lend cover. But don't fire unless it's necessary."

Pearce nodded. He put down the axe and tent poles he was carrying then unstrapped his knapsack and water bottle. Un-encumbered, he checked the flint and priming pan of his rifle. Then, vaulting over the low stone wall, he started moving across the field towards the distant barn. Behind him, the patrol raised the muzzles of their own weapons, a mix of ancient Brown Besses and gleaming Baker rifles, squinting down the sights to cover his advance.

Pearce reached the barn unchallenged. After peering through a crack in the planking, he dragged the door wide open. A flock of pigeons fluttered out from holes in the roof and went winging towards the grove as he stepped inside. A good sign. Nevertheless, tension mounted and fingers tightened expectantly on triggers. Moments later, Pearce reappeared, grinning and waving his cap, gesturing for the rest of the troop to join him.

"Right boys," Captain Jenner urged. "What say we get in out of this damned rain?"

Everyone tramped tiredly into the barn, except Rifleman Tait, who had been detailed to look after the mules, and Harris who was to take the first watch. The place stank of rotting straw and animal droppings, but it offered shelter from the elements and a reasonably dry floor on which to sleep. There was even a blacksmith's ash-filled iron brazier. A hot meal and mugs of strong black tea laced with brandy or metheglin would lift everyone's spirits.

The men hung around patiently, scratching at fleas and yawning, waiting for Captain Jenner to select his billet, before they sought a place to bed down. After stacking their rifles in a pyramid in the middle of the floor, the men stripped off their heavy knapsacks, water bottles, cartridge pouches and bayonets. Their greatcoats were either draped across beams or spread out on the wooden floor to dry. The cursing had stopped and the familiar droll witticisms and licentious humour had begun flying round as their tempers improved. Jack Gallant dropped his gear at the base of one of the roof supports. Leaning his rifle against the stanchion, he glanced across at Jenner and began unfastening the brass buttons of his red tunic. The Captain had decided to bunk down in a rickety cattle pen at the rear of the barn. Though it provided some privacy, a large heap of stinking bedding and lice-infested rags had been dumped in one corner. "Duffy!" the Captain yelled. "Get rid of these for me, will you?"

Duffy, a little black-eyed private from Ulster, was busy unlacing his gaiters. "Comin', Captain!" He answered.

Unbuckling his belt from which hung his pearl-handled matched pistols and his heavy sabre, Jenner hooked it over one of the planks, then stretched and yawned. "Get a move on, man!" he exhorted again. Extending a foot, he started kicking the rags out of the pen.

There was a sudden groan of surprise and the heap of rags reared up. A filthy face, confused by sleep and creased in terror, appeared from within the folds. Jack Gallant grabbed for his rifle, but even as he aimed and pulled the trigger, the rusted prongs of a pitchfork, held in the man's hands, were thrust deep into Captain Jenner's unprotected chest. The roar as Gallant's rifle fired was deafening. At such close range, the heavy musket ball shattered the man's head, killing him instantly. The force of the impact threw him backwards, sending him crashing through the rotten planks onto the floor, where he lay twitching in a pool of spreading blood.

Captain Jenner, his eyes wide in disbelief, had sunk to his knees. His face was grey with pain. The pitchfork, rammed deep into his chest, had punctured his right lung and penetrated vital stomach organs. Blood was already seeping through his ruffled blouse and staining his braid-edged jacket. Gallant and the men who gathered around him knew immediately that the Captain's wounds were fatal.

Carefully, they lowered him to the floor, placing a greatcoat under the officer's head for a pillow. Weakly, he lifted a finger, gesturing for Gallant to come close. The young Rifleman leaned over him. "Sir . . .?" he asked.

Captain Jenner pointed to where his belt lay on the floor. "Corporal, take charge of my sabre and pistols," he whispered hoarsely. "In my coat pocket are the orders of command, maps and a compass. You'll need them. There's also some personal documents; letters and such-like. I'd like them returned to my wife, if possible." His words were interrupted by a long shuddering sigh. "Try and get the men to Wellington, Jack. It's the only chance they've got."

Gallant nodded. He reached inside the Captain's coat. All the papers were folded inside a tooled-leather wallet. The topmost prong of the fork had stabbed right through it before entering his chest.

"Can't do it, Sir," he said.

"Why not?" Jenner demanded.

"The fork . . ." Gallant explained.

The Captain closed his eyes and grimaced. "Then pull the damned thing out."

Gallant glanced up at Pearce. The Yorkshireman knew more than most about tending wounds. He shook his head.

"For God's sake . . ." Jenner complained, his voice barely audible as he started coughing up bubbles of blood. "We all know I'm dying. What difference does it make . . .? Pull the bloody thing out! That's an order!"

Gallant wiped his lips and steeled himself. Grasping the metal shaft with both hands, he took a deep breath and pulled. The rusted metal came out reluctantly, snagging and tearing. Blood began flowing even more freely. Captain Jenner let out a low moan and slumped into unconsciousness.

"Best if he don't wake up ag'in . . ." someone observed.

Gallant nodded. Removing the wallet, he slipped it into his own pocket. Then he picked up Captain Jenner's belt from which hung the holstered pistols and his heavy sabre. Conscious that he was being watched, Gallant buckled the belt around his waist. The men wandered off and set about preparing their hot food and alcohol-laced tea. They were inured to the concept of death and suffering. But Gallant knew the death of the Captain had placed a heavy responsibility on his young shoulders. For everyone's sake, he had to succeed.

Outside, it began to rain heavily.

Captain Dalton Jenner never regained consciousness, he died at four o'clock the following afternoon. Duffy helped Gallant carry the Captain's blanket-wrapped body outside. They buried him in an unmarked grave in the soggy earth of the apple grove. Jethro Creevey recited a simple prayer. The

Riflemen stood round in small groups, silently paying their respects.

From the moment they had been washed ashore, a constant trickle of desertions had reduced the troop to a small core of fourteen men. It was mostly the younger, less-experienced men who had left, those who had panicked, mistakenly reckoning that they had a better chance of surviving the rigours and dangers of the French countryside alone. One of these "bastard cowards!" as Sam Tait termed them, had even run off with the mules while the guard slept, taking a good part of the supplies along with him. The guard had received a severe thrashing for his stupidity.

The men who remained, the battle-hardened campaigners, stayed not just out of a strong sense of loyalty and duty – but because they knew with absolute certainty that they had a better chance of surviving any skirmish if they stood shoulder to shoulder with their comrades. Fourteen rifles were much better protection in a fire-fight than any single weapon.

For the present the men seemed content to abide by Captain Jenner's instruction that the young Corporal should lead the troop. Yes, he was lacking experience, but Gallant was the only soldier among them who could read and write. Someone had to be able to plot their route across France, and the Riflemen were long practised at avoiding unnecessary responsibilities, especially those associated with command.

For what was left of the afternoon they ate then rested. When darkness fell, Jack Gallant led them out of the rear of the barn, through the apple grove into the hushed French countryside.

After plodding determinedly for nearly two hours across drenched grasslands and meadows, they climbed a hillside dotted with scrub and thorn-tipped gorse and emerged onto a narrow road surfaced with hard flint and limestone. The men rested, sipping from their brandy flasks and chewing on bits of cold meat and bread, while Jack Gallant took a compass reading by moonlight and studied his map. As best as he could estimate, the village of Bellefond was somewhere nearby; though whether it lay behind or in front of them, he was uncertain. Deep wheel ruts suggested that during the hours of daylight the road was in frequent use. If this was anything like the English roads he was accustomed to, traffic would practically cease during the hours of darkness. But on any of these French roads, there was always an increased risk of running into a patrol of infantry, or even grenadiers. Still, out here in the largely uninhabited lowlands, Jack Gallant considered it a risk worth taking, bearing in mind how much distance they could cover before daylight again drove them to seek cover. He ordered the men back to their feet, cautioned them to remain vigilant and not to enter into raucous conversation with the next man in line, and led them off down the moonlit road.

About two miles further on, an ammunition wagon drawn by a team of furiously galloping horses came thundering towards them from the rear. Cursing and yelling out warnings to each other, the entire platoon leapt into the muddy ditches on either side of the road to avoid being crushed under its clattering wheels.

Clinging to the reins with one hand, a thin-faced, cloaked and hatted driver drove the team on, cracking his whip furiously over the horse's sweat-streaked flanks. Crouching behind him in the wagon were seven white-jacketed grenadiers, who cursed the scattering Englishmen as they drove past. Gallant caught a glimpse of an eighth soldier, sporting a long moustache, sitting in the rear of the jolting wagon. He wore a richly decorated jacket and a peaked bear-skinned cap on his head, which immediately identified him as an officer of the French hussars.

Struggling to regain their feet in the ditch, the English Riflemen fired off a ragged fusillade of shots in the direction of the disappearing wagon, but the balls either flew wide or thudded harmlessly into the backboard.

As the wagon sped away, a girl lifted her head, staring at the English soldiers with an expression of helpless pleading on her face. "Help us!" she screamed. "Help us!" But the hussar reached over, roughly thrusting her down below the backboard again. Jack Gallant stood like a man transfixed, watching until the sound of the wagon's rumbling wheels faded into the distance.

All round him, plastered with mud and soaked through with stinking ditch water, the men were gradually reassembling on the road. The troopers who had fired off a round, set about reloading their weapons, but Jethro Creevey was standing, cap in hand, scratching the back of his head and looking puzzled.

"Lost somefin', Jethro?" Tait asked, emptying muddy water from one of his boots.

"No," Creevey said. "I thought I saw something drop from beneath that wagon." He searched the road carefully. "Just about here. All sort of bright and shiny in the moonlight, it was."

"Leave it alone, old man," Padfield grumbled, wiping the blade of his bayonet clean. "Probably wus' nothing more than a woodscrew or some-such."

Jethro let out a sudden whoop. "'Here it is," he yelled. "Knew I was right!"

"What you found then?" Duffy asked, curious now.

"A silver florin, boys! Look see!" Creevey bit into the coin, then held it up for their inspection. "Some bloody woodscrew, eh, Padfield?"

The Riflemen gathered around the old man, trying to convince him that his find, a considerable sum for a poorly paid foot soldier, should be divided equally between them. While they were arguing, Pearce, who had wandered further along the road, found two more coins. Though only copper halfpennies, each one would buy a tankard of ale back in England.

"What do you make of it, Jack?" Sam Tait asked. "English coins lying all over a French road. Seems a bit odd, don't it?"

Gallant nodded thoughtfully. "Reckon someone in that ammunition wagon was trying to attract our attention."

"The girl, you mean?" Tait questioned.

Gallant rubbed his aching neck. "Maybe, Sam, though I fancy there was another prisoner in the wagon. Perhaps we should push on a way and see what happens."

"Be light in a couple of hours," Tait warned, studying the

sky. "And we haven't got a chance of overtaking that wagon on foot."

"I know."

To put an end to their heated bickering, Gallant got the troop to agree that any money found would be split equally between them. Then, formed up in a single line again, they resumed their march. More coins of various denominations were picked up at intervals along the road, including a fine Oxford silver crown. The men were delighted. But Gallant couldn't get the girl's face out of his thoughts . . .

After a steady slog, they reached a point where the dirt road suddenly sloped steeply into a valley. It was just growing light. Warning everyone to remain hidden behind the low wall bordering the road, Gallant crawled on his belly towards a dense thicket of goat willow, where he took out his spyglass. Clearly revealed below was a small ramshackle farm lying on the edge of a series of ploughed fields. Smoke curled up from the building's ancient chimneys. Standing in the courtyard was the ammunition wagon. One of its rear wheels lay shattered on the muddy cobbles. The team had been unhitched and was grazing in a nearby pasture. Curiously, Gallant could see only three horses, there should have been four. He refocused on the yard. Two of the white-coated grenadiers were clearly visible, at ease, but with their muskets within reach. Next, he turned his glass on the outbuildings. The hussar was seated on an upturned barrel beside an open barn door. He was smoking a long-handled pipe and drinking from a wine bottle. Then another of the French soldiers emerged from the farmhouse. He wasn't alone. Jack Gallant stiffened angrily. The grenadier was dragging the girl he'd seen in the back of the wagon towards a red barn. She was manacled and obviously very tired. The grenadier shoved her into the barn, stepped in behind her, then reappeared a moment later on his own. After slamming the barn door shut, he saluted the hussar, then sauntered across the courtyard to join the other guards.

Pearce came crawling up beside him. "Seen anything interesting, Jack?" he asked.

Gallant nodded and handed him the spyglass. "Remember the girl we saw in the back of that wagon?"

Pearce nodded. "What about her?"

"The Frenchies are holding her prisoner in that red barn behind the farmhouse."

The Yorkshireman studied the scene for a moment. "'Ope you're not thinkin' 'bout trying to rescue her, Jack?" he said cautiously.

"Why not?" Gallant questioned. "We outnumber them more than two to one, don't we?"

"Maybe we do," Pearce conceded. "But our boys are about done in, while those Frenchies 'ave just been sittin' on their arses while their 'orses did the work. *And* don't forget, they've got the advantage of cover." He handed the glass back. "You might want to let the troop rest up a while and get something to eat before they see action."

Despite his anxiety for the girl's well-being, Gallant could see that Pearce's suggestion made sense. "Can you organise it, Michael?" he asked. "Get them off the road, into cover?"

Pearce nodded slowly. "Guess so. But what are you going to be doing?"

Gallant snapped the spyglass shut. "I'm going to work my way down there, see if I can learn a bit more about what's going on. One of the horses is missing and I can't see the driver anywhere. Doesn't take a genius to work out that he may have gone for help."

"Well don't go getting yourself killed," Pearce warned him, bluntly. "No girl's worth it. And besides, Jack, the army don't pay us enough to be heroes."

Gallant waited until the daylight strengthened and drifts of mist began to form in the valley below. Then he started to make his way down through the trees towards the farmhouse. Every sound he made seemed magnified in the echoing silence. His boots splashed loudly in the muddy pools lying between the furrows, he was breathing hard and his heart was hammering like a drum. At every moment he expected to see a French soldier rear up in front of him out of the fog and challenge him with a raised musket. But his luck held. Somehow he reached the farm unseen. He was sweating profusely as he made his way around to the rear of the fog-enshrouded buildings. Then, drawing one of his pistols, he tip-toed across the cobbles and let himself into the rear of the barn though a loudly creaking door.

It was much darker inside. A tethered cow moved uneasily as he crept past it. Several small birds ascended to the rafters on thrumming wings. Gripping the pistol firmly, he half-cocked the hammer and crept quietly forward. At the front of the barn, the light from a hanging cresset cast an uneven glow on the straw-covered floor. As the pitchy wood in its iron basket spluttered and flared, Gallant saw the girl. His heart immediately went out to her. She'd been manacled to an iron ring set in the wall. Her head drooped dispiritedly and she looked desperately tired. Gallant remained crouched in the gloom, barely breathing, listening and watching intently. But there was no sign of the French grenadiers or the hussar. Finally, convinced that she was alone, Gallant stepped forward and approached the girl.

At that moment, her head snapped up and she opened her mouth to scream. Gallant hurriedly clapped a hand over her mouth. "It's alright," he whispered. "I'm English! My name's Jack Gallant. I've got a platoon of Riflemen waiting up on the hill. We followed the trail of English coins you dropped from the wagon." He took his hand away slowly. "We're going to get you out of here! Understand?"

She gasped and breathed deeply. "Yes . . . But don't worry about me . . ." She glanced at his Chevrons. ". . . Corporal Gallant," she said urgently. "It's imperative that you free my uncle first."

"Your uncle?"

She nodded. "Dr Randal Rainsley. They've got him imprisoned somewhere in the house. The French are desperate to get him to their ship yards in Bordeaux . . ."

"Bordeaux?" This was becoming complicated. All he'd tried to do was rescue this girl, if possible. All this about . . .

"Listen!" she urged, staring worriedly at the door. "My

uncle is a brilliant naval cartographer. He's developing a new type of oceanographic map of revolutionary precision and complexity. Because the charts are written in a cipher understood only by my uncle, the French kidnapped him with all his research notes and equipment after a surprise raid on Seleham Hall. But the cutter we were imprisoned in was blown off course. It grounded two nights ago, south of Nieupoort during a frightful squall. Now the French soldiers are taking us to a place called Valmy Bay where we are to rendezvous with another French ship."

"But Miss . . ." Gallant insisted, realising he didn't know her name.

"Cross," she snapped testily. "Isabel Cross, if it matters."

"Yes . . . Well, Miss Cross, first let me get these manacles off you. Then . . ."

"Damn you, Sir! Will you not listen?" the girl demanded. "My situation is of no importance. You cannot release me, for that would instantly warn the French soldiers that something is wrong. Only my uncle's safety is of immediate concern. Waiting in Bordeaux, is Professor Andre d'Hericourt. Of all Frenchmen, he alone is clever enough to stand a chance of breaking the cipher. But d'Hericourt is very old and too weak to travel any distance. That's why the French are determined to get Dr Rainsley to Bordeaux. You must free my uncle before the French reinforcements arrive to take us on to Valmy Bay. England's future may well depend upon it."

At that moment the door was thrust open and one of the grenadiers came lurching drunkenly into the barn. Jack Gallant immediately withdrew from sight behind some bales of hay, watching carefully. The grenadier was clutching an almost empty wine bottle. He stood for a moment, blinking and swaying uncertainly. Deeply folded layers of fat in his bulllike neck, heavy jowls and narrow piggy eyes, were revealed in the flickering light cast by the cresset. Finally the grenadier's alcohol-dimmed mind located Isabel Cross. With a grunt of satisfaction he lurched towards her, hands outstretched. His intentions were obvious.

This was no time for misplaced heroics, Jack Gallant knew. The noise of a struggle, indeed, any cry for help, would immediately bring the rest of the French soldiers running to the barn. No, this had to be handled quietly and quickly. Unsheathing his sabre, Gallant stepped from behind the bales of hay and placed himself in front of the girl. The grenadier tried to stop and opened his mouth to yell out a warning, but Gallant's gleaming blade arced swiftly through the air and opened his throat. As the grenadier sank to his knees, Jack Gallant stepped to one side then drove the blade into the man's ribs, plunging it deep into his heart. The bottle dropped from the Frenchman's unfeeling fingers and a bubbling death rattle escaped from his collapsing lungs. In an instant, the grenadier was lying dead on the floor.

Stepping over the motionless body, Jack Gallant walked to the door and started to close it. "Hell!" he muttered, looking out.

"What's wrong, Mr Gallant?" the girl asked, her face white with shock.

"The fog's lifting. How the hell am I going to get back to my men now . . .?"

"So how do I look, Miss? Think I'll get away with it?"

"Perhaps . . ." Isabel Cross admitted. "*If* they're all as drunk as he was."

After hiding the body, Gallant had stripped off the grenadier's topcoat and breeches and pulled them on over his own uniform. Now he picked up the man's musket and dusted off his cap, pulling the peak well down to conceal his face. As a disguise, it just might work. Hell, it had to work!

Reluctant to leave the girl, he hesitated in the doorway before stepping outside. "You'll be alright, Miss Cross?" he asked, worriedly.

"I'll be fine now that swine's dead. Hurry, Mr Gallant, there's not much time. When you reach your men, be sure to tell them that a large reward will be paid to each of them if you succeed in freeing my uncle. Now, *please*, do get a move on!"

With what he hoped looked like an alcoholic swagger, Jack Gallant stepped out into the sunlight. Crossing the yard, he began to amble as slowly as his racing nerves would allow towards the fields and the distant trees. He'd covered maybe fifty yards when a cry rang out behind him from the farmyard. "*Arret, mon ami!*"

An icy shiver speared down Gallant's spine. Surely they couldn't have found the soldier's body already, could they? He turned and looked lazily back. One of the other grenadiers, musket in hand, was waving to him. Gallant was only too aware that at this distance he still presented an easy target. Trying to stay in character, he cupped one hand to his right ear, acting as if he couldn't hear properly. Burping noisily, he shrugged, then pointed to the trees before carrying on walking. At any instant he expected to hear a shot being fired, followed by the whiz of a musket ball. The man could hardly miss at that distance.

The grenadier bellowed at him again. "*Depeche' toi!*"

Gallant threw his arms out in a wild gesture and plodded on across the muddy field. Behind him, the grenadier laughed loudly.

By the time Gallant reached the first of the trees and disappeared into their concealing foliage, his nerves were jangling uncontrollably and he was drenched in sweat. But he was still alive. He'd made it. Gallant struggled up the hill knowing that if they were going to save Dr Rainsley and Isabel, the platoon would have to act quickly and decisively. But the prospect of a large reward for the doctor's safe return to England would no doubt be a sufficient inducement to spur his men into action.

Half way up the slope, Gallant sensed something moving in the bushes ahead of him. Fearing that he was about to be ambushed, he drew both pistols from their holsters, cocked their hammers and took aim. But before he could fire, a young boy, obviously petrified with fear and babbling incoherently in

French, stuck his head out of the leafy branches. The tracks of recent tears ran down his filthy, starved face.

Gallant considered his options. If he let the boy go, there was a strong possibility that he'd go running down the hill as fast as his spindly little legs could carry him to inform the French troops that he'd seen an English soldier. Then *any* chance of launching of a surprise attack on the farmhouse would be lost. Gallant glanced up the hill. Padfield or Pearce, hard, obdurate men, would know exactly what to do in such a situation. And they wouldn't hesitate. They'd slit the boy's throat without a moment's thought. But Gallant didn't want to hurt the boy if he didn't have to. Instead, he tied the boy's hands behind his back with a strap from his satchel, gagged him with his own frayed woollen scarf, then pushed him on up the hill, making sure he never got more than a couple of paces ahead.

As they neared the summit, an expertly placed rifle-shot came whining perilously close to his ears, shattering a branch behind his head. Gallant shoved the boy to the ground, dropping beside him.

"What the hell are you doing!" he cried out in disbelief, lifting his head from the leaf-mould and trying to see which of his men was doing the shooting. "It's me, boys! Jack Gallant! Have you all gone blind up there?"

Another shot came ripping through the sun-dappled leaves. The ball thudded heavily into the soft earth beside his out-stretched leg. "Don't matter who you say you are," a voice echoed down at him. "You look more like a French grenadier than an English Rifleman to us, sport."

Gallant gasped and understood. He was still wearing the dead grenadier's cap, topcoat and britches! Dragging off the cap and coat to reveal his scarlet jacket, Gallant stood up and began yelling out the names of his troopers at the top of his voice. He had to bellow out half their names before he convinced the nervous marksmen that he was who he said he was.

"Right, Jack," someone shouted down. "Come on up here. Just don't do anything sudden-like till we get a clear view of your face."

"Okay," Gallant agreed. "But listen, Harris. It is Harris, isn't it?"

"Yeah it's Harris, Jack. Go on I'm listening."

"I've got a prisoner with me. A young boy. His hands are tied and he isn't armed. He can't do you no harm, so don't go shooting at him, either . . ."

Dragging the boy to his feet, Jack Gallant pushed him on ahead and together they scrambled up to the summit.

Watching from behind a moss-encrusted rock as Gallant stepped out of the trees with his prisoner, Tait cried, "Put down your rifles, boys. It's Jack alright!"

The boy was handed to Joe Zally, the only one of the Riflemen who claimed to understand a few words of French. "Find out what you can from him, Joe," Gallant asked, slumping down beside the fire and gratefully accepting a mug of hot black tea. "And see he gets something to eat, the boy looks half-starved."

Then with the rest of the troop gathered around him, Gallant told them all he had learned from Isabel Cross about the plight of her uncle. When he revealed that he intended to launch an attack on the farmhouse to free the naval cartographer and his niece, serious mutterings of dissent surfaced. Tait complained that neither Major Hallam nor Captain Jenner would ever have considered attempting anything so foolhardy.

"He's right, Jack," Padfield complained. "It's too damned reckless an enterprise, if you ask me."

But Gallant knew he could win them over. "So you're not interested in the reward then, boys?" he suggested.

"Reward?" Padfield sniffed. The men looked at each other uncertainly.

"What kind o' reward would that be, then, Jack?" Duffy questioned, thrusting himself forward, his black eyes narrowing thoughtfully.

Jack Gallant shrugged. No actual figure had been mentioned, but Miss Cross had said that a *large* reward would be paid to each man who helped free Dr Rainsley. "A hundred guineas," Gallant told him.

"Split equally between us?" Creevey butted in, licking his lips. He was obviously tempted.

Gallant shook his head. "No, Jethro, not *shared*. That's a hundred guineas for each of you."

A roar of disbelief went up. This represented a fortune to the Riflemen. "A hundred guineas, Jack? You guarantee it?"

"You have Dr Randal Rainsley's word on it as a gentleman."

"What if some of us get killed in the fighting, Jack?" Creevey asked.

It was a fair question. At least four of them had common-law wives and a string of kids to consider.

"The money will be paid to your next of kin," Gallant assured him.

"Then that's good enough for me, Jack. I'm with you."

"You can count me in too, Jack!"

"An' me!"

It seemed that to a man they were all with him now. Gallant leaned back and sipped his tea, silently praying that Dr Randal Rainsley valued his own neck just as highly.

Joe Zally came up to the fire.

"Learned anything from the boy?" Gallant asked.

"Some . . ." Zally admitted. "From what I can gather, the boy's family were thrown out of the farmhouse when the grenadiers arrived. His kin went off to a neighbour's farm in the next valley, but the boy, Pierre, refused to leave. He hung around, watching the house from a distance. Seems he hates the French soldiers, even more than he hates us."

"Why's that?" Gallant asked.

"After driving his family out, Pierre said the grenadiers ransacked the place. Then they killed and ate his best friend, Bernard."

"His best friend?" Gallant repeated, horrified but intrigued.

Joe Zally grinned, exposing the rotted stumps of his teeth. "Not as bad as it sounds, Jack. Bernard was his pet goose. Now Pierre's determined to get even with the grenadiers before they leave."

"Maybe we can help him . . ." Jack Gallant suggested.

From the edge of the tree line at the bottom of the hill, it was a little more than five hundred yards across the open fields to the nearest of the farmyard buildings. This was just within range of the troops' heavy Baker rifles. Unfortunately, they had only three of these recently issued weapons. The rest of the Riflemen were armed with the dependable, but inferior, Brown Besses. And even the best marksman couldn't guarantee a hit with them at that distance.

Gallant ordered the troop to remain concealed while he discussed the situation with Pearce, Tait and Padfield. Typically, Padfield was for a direct frontal charge with bayonets fixed. "Take the Frenchies by surprise, we should," he insisted. "It'll scare the bloody daylights out of 'em when we come a'charging at 'em over the fields."

"We ain't the bloody cavalry, Harry!" Tait protested. "Half of us'll be lying dead or wounded long before we reach the yard. "'Ow many musket balls you willing to take to earn your 'undred guineas?"

"Tait's right, Jack," Pearce agreed. "Somehow, a number of us got to get round to their rear if we're to have any chance at all of beating 'em."

Jack Gallant nodded sombrely, studying the bleakly open landscape for anything that might provide them with some form of advantage. "See that shallow brook to the left?" he said. "Perhaps we could . . ."

But before he could finish, Tait had jabbed him urgently in the ribs. "Back under cover, Jack. Quickly!" he warned, pointing along the road below. "Look there!"

Sweeping round the bend at a steady canter and heading for the farmhouse, came a group of twenty mounted hussars, members of a French Light Horse cavalry brigade. Sunlight glistened on their sabres and their brass-embellished rifles and each man wore a plumed helmet and gold-embroidered jacket. Clearly, these were members of an elite unit. Following close behind them came a closed landau drawn by four trace-horses.

Gallant studied the driver of the landau through his telescope. He recognised the thin-faced, black-cloaked man immediately. This was the same man who'd driven the ammunition wagon! So, Gallant's suspicions had been right all along; he *had* ridden off to bring help! Rattling along behind the landau came a loaded dray pulled by four sweating heavy horses.

"Shit!" Pearce stared angrily as the hussars reached the farm. Reining their steaming mounts to a halt in the muddy court-yard, they began to dismount. "That's put paid to our 'undred guineas, an' no mistake, Jack!"

Gallant nodded, watching gloomily as the landau and the cart pulled to a halt beside the farmhouse door. However willing they still might be to follow his lead, Gallant knew that his ragged troop of Riflemen, now heavily outnumbered, were no match for these highly trained hussars. It looked almost certain now that there would be no last minute rescue of Isabel Cross and her uncle.

"Look!" Pearce whispered. "Is that Dr Rainsley?"

An old man was being led out of the farmhouse by two of the white-coated grenadiers. Through the telescope, Gallant could see that the doctor's hands were bound behind him. The French soldiers dragged the white-haired cartographer across the yard and roughly bundled him into the landau. Then while a bulging portmanteau and several wooden boxes tied with rope were loaded and secured onto the baggage rack, Dr Rainsley's niece was brought out from the barn. The hussars clustered around her whistling, yelling and roughly manhandling her. But the slim-built young Englishwoman did her best to ignore them. Head held high, blinking in the bright sunlight, she pushed through them and climbed into the waiting carriage. The door was slammed shut and locked behind her. Up on the dickey box, the thin-faced driver released the brake and cracked his whip, urging the team forward. Bringing the landau round in a tight turn, he headed it through the open gates and out onto the road. The driver of the cart performed the same manoeuvre, though with some difficulty. Swinging up into their saddles, the hus-sars spurred their mounts after the carriage, forming up on each side in a protective escort and together, they clattered off down the road.

Now plumes of dense black smoke and flickering tongues of fire began pouring from the farmhouse. Laughing loudly and heavily encumbered by sacks and boxes filled with items of value looted from the farmhouse, the grenadiers began to leave. Their muskets were slung over their shoulders and they appeared to be in no hurry, sauntering out onto the road and frequently stopping to drink from the bottles of wine they carried. Behind them, the blaze was strengthening quickly, becoming an all-consuming inferno. The house would be a burned-out, soot-blackened shell within minutes.

"The bastards!" Gallant cursed. "Why in God's name did they set fire to the house?"

Pearce spat contemptuously. "I reckon it's to hide any trace of their looting, Jack. And it ain't only the Frenchies 'oo go in for it."

As Gallant glowered down at the six grenadiers, the boy pushed past Pearce and stood just beyond the trees, his thin body trembling, his face a drawn white mask as he stared mutely at this final outrage, the destruction of his home. Then, turning quickly, he grabbed the knife hanging at the Rifleman's belt. Letting out a strangled scream, he began racing towards the grenadiers brandishing the weapon.

Down on the road, the French soldiers looked up and saw the boy running towards them. There were bursts of drunken laughter, but two of the grenadiers tossed away their almost empty wine bottles, put down their sacks and started unslinging their muskets.

Jack Gallant had seen enough, as had the rest of his Riflemen. "Right lads, aim and fire at will!" he yelled. "Kill those French bastards, but don't hit the boy!"

A staccato volley of loud explosions erupted from the trees, as eleven of the English weapons sent their heavy lead balls whining through the still morning air. Down on the road, the grenadiers barely had time to cower or turn away before the shots struck them. Taken in the chest, two went down immediately, dead before they hit the road. A third Frenchman took a ball to his head, which disintegrated, splattering his blood and brains onto the man standing behind him. He lost an arm, ripped off above the elbow as a ball shattered bone, sinew and muscle like it was jelly. Screaming like a stuck pig, he started running. But another shot finished him and he lay, his sound limbs thrashing helplessly in a spreading pool of blood. The last two grenadiers, still crouching in abject terror on the road, extended their hands in an attitude of prayer, seeking mercy. They didn't get it. Another volley of shots rang out from the English rifles and both men were driven backwards by multiple impacts, their brutally ruined bodies slumping across the blood-smeared road.

"Stop firing!" Gallant roared out. The smell of burning sulphur filled his nostrils as a ragged cloud of powder smoke drifted out of the trees on each side of him. "Zally!" he yelled.

The Rifleman stuck his head out from behind a nearby bush, patted his rifle and flashed him a toothless grin. "Yes, Jack?" he asked.

"Go down and get that boy, will you?"

"Gonna kill him too?"

Gallant shook his head. "I just want to talk to him . . ." he explained.

The boy had been sent into shock at the sight of sudden violent death, but a nip of brandy wiped the dazed expression from his young face. Gallant was sympathetic but time was running out.

"Joe, ask Pierre if he knows where Valmy Bay is."

Recognising the name, the boy jerked his head round, stabbing a thin finger at the road the landau and its escort had taken.

"Find out how long it will take them to get there," Gallant ordered.

Zally shrugged. "I'll do my best, Jack," he offered. A stumbling dialogue took place between the boy and the old Rifleman. Finally, Joe Zally said, "Well, if I've understood him correctly, it's normally no more than a two hour journey by wagon to Valmy Bay."

"Normally?" Gallant queried. "What does that mean?"

Zally scratched his whiskey chin. "The road's been impassable this past two days. It's either been blocked by a landslide or by a bridge that came down during the recent bad weather. The boy's not sure which. Whatever, the landau and the cart are certain to be delayed some."

Gallant's eyes burned with faint hope. "Joe, ask him if there's any way we can reach the bay ahead of them."

Another exchange incomprehensible to all but the two of them began. It ended with the boy pointing at a hill to their right.

Zally swatted away an insect that was buzzing persistently at the back of his neck. "He says there's a short cut that way, Jack. An old footpath that leads over the hill."

Gallant glanced from the hill, back to the boy and nodded. "Will he guide us?" he asked.

But the moment Zally started to put the question to him, Pierre started to back away. Spinning on his heels, he slipped beneath the Rifleman's flailing hands and began running through the trees. In just a few seconds, he'd disappeared from sight.

"Seems like he don't want to 'elp us no more, Jack," Padfield observed, grinning ruefully.

Gallant flashed his brooding blue eyes at the Rifleman. "Then we'll just have to find our own way there, won't we?" he snapped. "Now if you're still interested in earning your hundred guineas, take Duffy down there and bring back the uniforms of those dead Frenchmen."

"Okay Jack . . ." Padfield hesitated, scratching at a bushy eyebrow. "But even we if do reach the bay in time, what can our lads do against twenty hussars?"

Gallant frowned. "I'll let you know when we get there," he told him. "Now get a move on . . ."

"Ain't right, Jack. Don't seem nat'ral!"

"It's unlucky!"

"Treason to the English crown, that's what you're asking us to do!"

Duffy uttered a stream of profanities as he struggled to pull on a grenadier's coat. "Major Hallam would *never* 'ave allowed it, Jack!"

Gallant had expected complaints from those required to wear the bullet-holed, bloodstained and ill-fitting French uniforms. Riflemen grumbled about everything. But the advantage it gave the troop was obvious to even the most obtuse of them. As Gallant painstakingly explained, with three grenadiers apparently marching at the front of the column and three at the rear, it would look from a distance as if the English Redcoats had been taken prisoner. "And that," he told them, "should stop any French patrol we might encounter from shooting at us."

Still grumbling, the men set off towards the hill.

Away from the damper lowland pastures, the walking was easy. Apart from a few sheep, the entire country seemed deserted. The men cheered up a bit. Soon they were questioning each other about how they'd spend their hundred guineas. Whores and boozing figured predominantly. No one seemed worried now about the fighting they might have to do.

At the top of the gentle slope, a series of low summits stretched away to the near distance. Black-headed gulls wheeled high above them and the air tasted of ozone. The sea was near. After another short march, the path became lost in a swampy hollow, where the clinging mud came up to their knees and the air was alive with biting midges, On the far side of this morass, the footpath re-emerged, splitting into two and running away in different directions.

While Gallant consulted the maps and his compass, the platoon rested. Laying down their weapons, they chewed on dry biscuits and drank from their water bottles, some watching him curiously, while others lay back in the grassy hummocks with their eyes closed.

The maps carried too little detail to be of any real use, but clearly both of these westward leading footpaths would take them to the coast. However, only one would take them to Valmy Bay. A wrong decision here could take them miles off course. But all Gallant could do was trust to luck and providence.

"Jethro," he said, "You still got that silver florin you picked up from the ammunition wagon?"

Creevey nodded and patted a pocket. "Sure 'ave, Jack."

"Spin it for me. If it lands heads we'll take the right fork, tails the left."

Creevey dug the coin out of his jacket and tossed it up. The florin was a glittering blur as it spun in the bright sunlight. Catching it easily, he slapped the double-shilling piece down on the back of his left hand.

"Well?" Gallant asked. "Which is it?"

"Tails it is, Jack. We're for the left-hand path." Creevey answered.

"The devil's route . . ." someone muttered.

The platoon picked up their weapons and set off again.

Less than half an hour later, they found themselves approaching the edge of cliff. Before them lay the curving horizon, where the sea and sky met indeterminately. Below, was a small bay protected by a semi-circle of granite cliffs. No one spoke for a moment, but the same question hung unasked on every Rifleman's lips. Had they come to the right place. *Was* this Valmy Bay?

Out in the English Channel, the air was clear, but a light fog hung over the calm waters of the sheltered inlet.

"There, Jack!" Duffy cried. "Look!"

Anchored several hundred yards off the beach was a square-sterned French barquentine. The vessel's upper deck and masts were just visible through the drifting fog banks. Dragged partly out of the water on the sands below was the barquentine's dory. The three-man crew were loading it with wooden boxes and sacks, presumably provisions for the coming voyage.

Their escort duties completed, the hussars were already cantering back across the sands towards the road. Trundling along behind them came the landau and the now empty wagon.

But where were Miss Cross and her uncle? Gallant took out his telescope. Sliding the brass sections fully open, he trained the instrument on the three-masted merchantman. It swam up into view and his heart leapt. There they were, standing by the wheelhouse. The thin-faced man was arguing violently with them. Gallant watched, enraged, as the Frenchman struck Isabel Cross hard across the face, knocking her to her knees on the deck. Though his hands were bound behind him, her uncle tried to protest, but he was threatened into silence by a dagger pressed close against his throat. Two of the crew dragged Isabel Cross to her feet again, then both of the English prisoners were bundled roughly from sight into one of the quarter-deck cabins.

His face a mask of anger, Gallant turned as Jethro tugged at his elbow. "Hey, lookee there, Jack!" the Rifleman cried. He was pointing to an English frigate approaching from the north, but still some distance away. Under reduced canvas, the forty-gunner was making leisurely progress in the light breeze. If the captain of the barquentine decided to head his ship around the headland within the next thirty or forty minutes, they might well escape unseen.

"What the hell do we do now?" Pearce asked.

Old Jethro spat disgustedly and shook his head. "Damned if I know, young fella," he admitted. "But maybe Jack can think of somethin'."

Gallant licked his cold-cracked lips. "Guess there's only one thing we *can* do," he told them. "It's one hell of a gamble, lads. Different work to the kind you're used to and maybe it's not work risking your necks for a hundred guineas. So if any of you don't fancy the odds involved in boarding that French ship, then the army won't hold it against you, lads, I promise . . ."

"And how we going' to take the Frenchie, Jack?" Pearce asked.

"We're going to use their dory," he answered.

Gallant couldn't risk alerting the barquentine's crew by firing at the dory from the cliff-top. Surprise was the only advantage he had, and now every second counted.

After disguising himself in one of the grenadier's uniforms, Gallant started clambering down to the beach, along a twisting defile of rocks that partially screened him from view for most of the descent. He was armed with a French musket and Captain Jenner's sabre and pistols. The Riflemen were under strict instructions not to do anything till they got his signal.

Once down on level with the beach, the fog appeared to be thicker, enabling him to approach to within twenty yards of the dory before one of the sailors looked up and noticed him. At first all three of them seemed completely taken in by Gallant's ruse. The Englishman's heart was hammering wildly and his muslin shirt was damp with icy sweat at the thought of what he was about to do, as he sauntered ever closer across the tide-rippled sand. Only when one of the sailors barked a question at him – brusquely repeated when he received no answer – did they become suspicious.

Fear flared suddenly in their eyes. But before they could even think of reacting, Gallant raised the musket to his shoulder and aimed, shooting directly at the heart of one of the men. The force of the lead ball smashed through his rib cage, throwing him backwards across the dory into the sea. Dropping the musket, Gallant's fingers closed around the handles of the pistols stuck in his belt, drawing and pointing them in one fluid motion. But he took time to fire, even though the muzzle of an ancient flintlock was now aimed straight at his own head. The French crewman hurried his shot. The blast of the black powder was like a wind from hell on Gallant's neck as the ball thundered past, grazing his skin. But the Englishman didn't flinch. His first shot, from Captain Jenner's pearl-handled weapon blew a ragged hole in the sailor's skull. The shot from the pistol in his left hand, took the last sailor low in the stomach, inflicting a dreadful but not immediately fatal wound. He slumped to the damp sand, writhing and howling frenziedly, blood spreading in a ominous pool from beneath him. Gallant finished him with one quick slash of his heavy blade.

Trembling with emotion, Gallant turned and waved to his men. But having watched what had happened, they were already hurrying down the defile towards him.

The dory was quickly unloaded of its supplies, but even then, with thirteen men cramped together in the small craft, the gunwales were low down in the water when they pushed off. Jethro Creevey had been left on the beach to perform a vital service. Two distress rockets had been found in the dory's aft locker. Gallant had given Creevey the task of running as far round the beach as he could in ten minutes. He was then instructed to set the rockets off. With luck, that would help distract the crew of the barquentine, already confused by the sound of firing on the beach, allowing Gallant and the rest of the Riflemen to scramble aboard. The rockets might also attract the attention of the frigate's lookouts. Her captain would be sure to alter course to investigate. Jethro wasn't too pleased at being out of the fighting, his cursing made that plain to all, but he understood the importance of his role.

Now, undercover of the slowly drifting fog, they rowed as silently as possible out towards the barquentine. Gallant glanced at his men. Their expressions were grim. Hard-edged eyes in unshaven faces stared back at him. Every one of them knew how desperate the coming hand-to-hand fighting was going to be. There was a series of clicks as bayonets were slotted onto rifle muzzles. The long gleaming blades stood out wickedly against the drifting white mist. Loads were checked with meticulous care. Fresh powder was applied, the flint inspected and the heavy lead balls and wads rammed firmly home. Any miss-fire would almost certainly result in the Rifleman's death. Nothing could be left to chance.

The hull of the barquentine loomed up out of the mist. Gallant hissed for his men to ship oars, allowing the dory to drift silently alongside her. A rope ladder came bobbing into view. Rifleman Harris stretched out from the prow of the little boat and grabbed it, pulling them in close and Sam Tait made ready to step onto the swaying rungs. But Gallant held him back. "Wait for Jethro!" he hissed.

Long seconds passed. Rushing wavelets slapped and gurgled against the creaking timbers of the barquentine. Voices and sounds of activity could be heard from the deck above. Then suddenly, two brilliant trails of fire rose high above the fog bank, exploding in twin spheres of glowing red sparks, burning with the brilliance of miniature suns. There were urgent cries from above and the sound of footsteps running to the other side of the ship.

"Now!" Gallant urged, his voice a dry whisper. "Up the ladder men!"

Gallant and four of his Riflemen reached the deck before the crew realised they were being boarded. For a second they stood, mouths agape, astonished at this curious mixture of French and English uniformed soldiers standing rifles in hand on their deck.

Gallant wasn't going to allow any advantage to slip from between his fingers. "Fire!" he roared, bringing up the musket he carried and pulling the trigger. Heavy percussions smote the air. Sulphurous clouds belched from the muzzles of the English rifles and the heavy shot – spewing out at velocity of over five hundred and ten paces per second – ripped flesh and smashed bones, killing instantly or wounding grievously. More of the Riflemen were joining Gallant on the barquentine's deck now, but the rest of the ship's complement came charging out of the companionways, armed with blunderbusses, handspikes, belaying pins and axes. The fighting became a series of confused, hand-to-hand struggles, while shot zipped and whined through the air, shattering anything it met, and men fell dying in tangled bleeding heaps. A pot-bellied cook in carcass-stained whites took a hit to the shoulder from Gallant's pistol, but still he came on, roaring, burying an iron meat hook in Harris's face, all but ripping the Rifleman's jaw off, before Tait spilled his guts with a savage thrust from his bayonet.

Gallant was struggling towards the quarter deck cabins where Dr Rainsley and his niece had been imprisoned, but two of the French crew were barring his way. Gallant forced his opponents backwards, his sabre whistling through the air in great arcs, cutting and slashing as the blood rang in his ears and the thought of personal danger was submerged in the heat of his rising blood-lust.

Then came the sound of distant, heavy guns, followed seconds later, it seemed, by a flock of demons that came whining and shrieking high in the ship's masts, shattering the spars and booms, tearing the sails and reducing the rigging to severed, flapping wreckage. The roar of cannon came again and the deck became a tangled mass of ripped canvas and splintered stays and yard-arms.

The French crew stared in horror at the race-built English frigate bearing down on them, firing repeated broadsides of cross-bar shot from her thirty-pound cannons, intended to disable the barquentine rather than sink her. The English captain obviously saw this unescorted French merchantman as a valuable prize well worth the taking. Aware that further struggle was utterly pointless, and having no desire to end up incarcerated in an English gaol, or be lined up and shot, the French crew began to rapidly abandon their ship, leaping over the side or clambering down the remains of shattered masts into the now swiftly flowing tidal waters.

Four of Gallant's Riflemen were lying dead on the deck. Three more were wounded, one of them seriously. But the rest sent up a rousing, hallooing cheer, waving and shouting greetings at the crew of the English frigate as she steered ever closer.

It was then that Isabel Cross and Dr Rainsley were thrust out of a door in the bullet-scarred quarter-deck and emerged into daylight. Their hands were still bound. Close behind them, holding a pistol to Dr Rainsley's head, came the thin-faced man. Seen close up, his face was almost fleshless. His thin lips were little more than a gash and his pale eyes gleamed with hatred. He waved the pistol menacingly at Dr Rainsley. Isabel Cross stayed by her uncle's side. Using his terrified captives as shields, the thin-faced man manoeuvred himself over to the starboard deck rail. Gallant and Joe Zally made as if to rush forward, but Isabel Cross shook her head. "He'll kill my uncle," she warned. "Keep your men back, Gallant. There's nothing any of you can do."

The thin-faced man glanced anxiously over the deck-rail, staring at the wreckage of shrouds, ropes and masts trailing in the water. What the hell was he planning to do now? Gallant wondered. Escape seemed impossible.

Then a shot rang out.

Pearce, who had been standing quietly by with blood dripping down the stock of his Baker rifle from a wound in his lower left arm, had taken the opportunity to fire off a round. His marksmanship was legendary. He never missed a standing target.

The ball slammed squarely into the Frenchman's chest. The violent impact drove him against the deckrail, shattering several of the already weakened wooden struts. He reached out and grasped the balustrade, steadying himself. Pain and disbelief contorted his skeletal face. Then in a last vengeful and cowardly act, the dying Frenchman pushed Isabel Cross overboard. It was done quickly, before anyone could act or even think of acting. The girl's hands were still tightly bound behind her. She screamed in terror as she hit the water, then immediately sank like a stone below the swirling surface. Dr Rainsley gave out a despairing groan and slumped to his knees.

Everyone stood in stunned silence, not believing what they had just seen. But Gallant acted. Racing to the deckrail, he was already stripping off his jacket and unbuckling the heavy belt holding his pistol holsters and sabre.

Joe Zally tried to hold him back, crying, "No, Jack, it's too late! You can't save her now!" but Gallant knocked the old man's hands loose. Taking a deep breath, he dived off the deck, plummeting into the swelling waters of the bay.

The water was intensely cold and murky, and in the bubbling, swirling current of the running tide it was difficult to see anything more than an arm's length away. Striking down below the surface in a despairing bid to save her, he swam to the silted bottom, a place of dense waving mats of seaweed and darting shoals of silvery fish. His lungs were bursting and the powerful sweep of the tide dragged him away from the shadowy hull of the barquentine floating far overhead. He turned his head, desperately looking this way then that, but there was no sign of her in that glimmering, aqueous murk. Though he struggled, a swirling eddy gripped him, sending him plunging helplessly over the barnacled, rock-strewn bottom tearing patches of skin from his arms and legs. Then, just as he was ready to give up, as the agony of his oxygen-starved lungs and the poundings of his tortured heart drove him to the edge of consciousness, he found her. Her face, fringed by masses of dark waving hair, suddenly swam up before him in the watery gloom. She drifted towards him, like some ghostly Siren, her eyes staring blankly. Then the pull of the waters threatened to drag her away from him again. Barely knowing what he was doing, Gallant reached out and grabbed her. Pulling the girl close, he struck up for the glittering wave-tossed surface so far above his head, his mind growing dim as a pounding red haze confused his thoughts and choking salt water entered his lungs. Above his head the light was growing stronger . . .

Then he was on the surface, coughing and retching, gasping in lungfuls of sweet air. A heavy rope was drifting by him. He reached out grasping it weakly with his right hand. His numbed left arm was still clasped firmly around the unconscious girl's waist.

There were shouts of encouragement from above. Gallant looked up. Shaking the stinging salt-water from his red-rimmed eyes, he saw a row of unfamiliar faces staring down at him. The tidal race had carried them below and beyond the hull of the English frigate. More lines came splashing down around him. Then two of the frigate's crew were in the water beside him, supporting Gallant and the girl with strong hands until a boat could be launched. Isabel Cross gave a faint moan, turned her head then began panting and gasping, dragging air into her lungs. She was alive! Relief swept over him. "Thank God," he muttered. "Thank God . . .!"

An hour later they were standing on the frigate's deck, watching as the prize crew hauled up jury-rigged sails and headed the barquentine out of the bay into the English Channel.

Dr Rainsley clapped a hand on Jack Gallant's shoulder, breaking his thoughts. "You saved our lives, Mr Gallant," he said, his voice filled with emotion. "And for that, we'll both be eternally grateful. If there's ever anything I can do to repay the debt we owe you, you have only to ask."

Jack Gallant shook his head. "You don't owe me anything, Sir," he said. "But Miss Cross did mention that my Riflemen would receive a reward for ensuring that the secrets of your charts didn't fall into Professor d'Hericourt's hands."

"Quite so," Dr Rainsley agreed. "The debt owed to your men will be honoured to the last penny. You have my word on it. Without their help, we would not be standing here now."

Gallant nodded his thanks.

Isabel Cross came running up to the deck rail. "Have you told him yet, Uncle?" she asked excitedly. There was colour in her cheeks again and her eyes shone. She was obviously little the worse for her recent ordeal.

"Told me what?" Gallant asked.

Dr Rainsley blew out his cheeks. "High Commissioner Lord Cavanah has arranged for me to survey the inshore waters around the Gulf of Cambay up to Porbandar, in the Indian sub-continent. Treacherous waters, many of our ships have been lost there recently. But a vital naval shipping route. As some of my work involves charting river-mouths considered unnavigable to ships of the line, Lord Cavanah insists that we take a detachment of Riflemen for protection. What do you say Jack? Are you and your men willing to accompany us?"

Gallant shook his head. "Our orders are to join the Duke of Wellington's forces at Flushing, Sir!" he reminded him.

"Of course," Dr Rainsley agreed. "And that's where we're heading now, up channel. But you misunderstand me. We're not planning to sail for the sub-continent until spring of next year, I still have much work to do. By then, your tour of duty in Europe will be coming to an end. In the light of your sterling work here, it would be most comforting to Isabel and I, if you were in command of our rifle escort."

"It's impossible, Sir," Jack Gallant explained. "I'm just a plain Corporal. And our orders are to join the Duke of Wellington's forces at Brussels."

But Dr Rainsley smiled. "And so you shall! And when you return from destroying Napoleon, I shall see to it that you are promoted to the rank of Captain. My word goes a long way in London, young man. So, now, Captain Jack Gallant. How does that sound?"

Isabel gave the young Rifleman's arm a squeeze and stood on tip-toe to kiss his cheek. "It'll sound just fine," she breathed. "Won't it, Jack!"

Gallant nodded slowly, a strange look in his eyes.

"What's wrong, Jack?" Dr Rainsley asked. "You *will* come with us, won't you?"

"Yes, but . . ."

"But what?" Isabel persisted.

"Well . . .," Gallant shrugged uncertainly. "India! I was just wondering how I was going to break the news to the rest of the lads . . ."

"EVERY MAN A KING"

Clayton Emery

Clayton Emery (b. 1953) has a fascination with Robin Hood. He has written the fantasy novel Tales of Robin Hood *(1988), contributed to the anthology* The Fantastic Adventures of Robin Hood *(1991) and started a series featuring Robin Hood and Maid Marian as medieval sleuths in* Ellery Queen's Mystery Magazine. *But he has written much more besides. Several fantasy novels based on role-playing games such as* Arcane Age: Sword Play *(1996),* Cardmaster *(1997) and* Star of Cursrah *(1999), as well as the light-hearted young adult novel about the teenager Alex Mack and her father,* Father-Daughter Disaster! *(1997). He has also written stories set in Colonial America of 1700, but for this anthology he turned to the War of 1812 between Britain and the United States.*

At a whistle, dark-clad men with stovepipe shakos and browned rifles filtered among the looming trees and impassable thickets, silent and grim as tigers on the hunt.

As always, Walker and Johnson worked in tandem, as always they were on the left of the line. One was fair and lanky, the other short and craggy, but their cautious squints were identical. Spread out to eyeshot, these men of the 95th Rifles leapfrogged their partners to penetrate the swamp. They splashed through tea-dark water, skidded on slimy roots, ducked curtains of Spanish moss, and circled giant trees felled across the meandering paths.

This winter wilderness was Louisiana in the new year 1815. Charges that the British were buying scalps, impressing sailors, and bombarding ships had escalated into battles along the Canadian border, the Atlantic shore, and in Washington, DC itself. After two years of little gain, this expedition hoped to seize New Orleans and halt shipping on the Mississippi. Thus soldiers of the British Army found themselves stumbling through swamps and canebrakes after invisible and resolute Americans.

Rifle upright alongside a tree trunk, Johnson watched ahead and right while Walker angled past, watching left and rearward. A black creek split a tussock of brown thatch. Walker peered ahead, splashed in the creek, and swung left. Yet some oddity turned him back. A veteran's instinct saved his life.

A dun shadow like a panther leapt from the cane. Walker glimpsed a checkerboard face and a glittering arc sweeping for his skull. Ankle-deep and hedged by cane, Walker ducked low and rammed high as if bayoneting.

The rifle barrel slammed the Indian square in the gut. Jerking back his weapon, Walker slammed the oak butt aside the Choctaw's head. A tomahawk bounced off Walker's shoulder.

But underfoot, the creek bed writhed like an earthquake. Stumbling, toppling, Walker's rifle smacked mud as another warpainted savage stepped from the cane and levelled a musket gaudy with brass tacks. Walker fumbled his fouled rifle as the Indian squeezed the trigger.

Twin guns crashed in the close forest. The Choctaw lurched sideways as a lead ball punched his ribs. From the canebrake a white heron fluttered and sputtered into the air. Under Walker's numb feet, the creek bed broke water and crawled away. A black-gray alligator big as a draft horse slithered a few feet, clawed a new bed, and sank to show only bulging eyes and wrinkled nostrils.

Johnson jogged up, spitting a cartridge tip and ramming a charge on the run. Still sitting in mud, Walker pricked his lock clear, wiped the steel dry, reprimed the pan, and plucked black hair from the brass buttplate. Only then did he rise and resettle his tackle and straighten his shako. "Thanks."

"Alligators and Indians," hissed Johnson. The riflemen whispered though now the forest was loud. Johnson's shot had drawn fire from deeper in the swamp. "What kind of cross-patch country is this?"

"How many times have you saved my life? A hundred?" Shaky, Walker drew his sword-bayonet and slipped the blade under the man's chin. The Choctaw's face was red with a blue chin and mask like a raccoon's, and now red blood gouted into black water. Thus the soldiers paid back in part near fifty British sentries throat-slit by night.

"At a shilling a save, I'd be rich as Croesus. You ready?"

Leapfrogging, they steered for the skirmish hotting up the swamp. The thud of reports slammed the air, for a mile distant a larger battle raged on the banks of the Mississippi. There, cannons belched and rockets corkscrewed and red ranks fired on command. Yet Britain's crack troops fought in the swamp, for here the killing would be man to man.

Sparks flickered in the gloom as evening crept up. Guns banged and smoke wafted. Johnson ducked behind a cypress tree nine feet thick, a mountain of wood whose branches tangled with neighbours. Johnson grinned like a wolf, eyes glittering at adventure.

Or maybe his friend was just wrung out, thought Walker, like all of them. Plagued by poor planning, the British Army was stranded ninety miles from the fleet, sick from miasmas and short rations, frozen by night and broiled by day, and sniped and bombarded the clock round. The toll was grinding down older men like Walker and Johnson and their friend Scott, survivors of a score of European campaigns. Those Indians almost got him, Walker worried. He was growing slow and clumsy. Yet he wanted to fight too, for this battle was personal.

Chuffs and whipcracks sputtered in a ragged line ahead. American bullets cut strips in the air like single-minded hornets. Sergeant Durell's whistle piped twice, then once: the signal to fall back where necessary, then scatter and advance.

Ranging ahead of Johnson, Walker pressed his face to a bush and blurred his eyes to better catch movement, the same way a deer saw. A dun hump twitched behind a tree trunk. Raising his Baker rifle to the line of sight – the weapon balanced cool and sweet to snuggle his shoulder like a lover – Walker sipped air and slowly squeezed the trigger. A sear tripped, the hammer snapped, flint struck steel and flashed, then the thick gun slammed his shoulder as a ball invisibly winged away. Powder smoke lingered in the still air, but Walker saw the dun hump was the shattered spine of a Yankee too far from his line.

"Killing Americans is almost too easy." Walker rammed a tight-patched ball that squeaked in the barrel. "Ready."

"We'll be on the buggers before they know't." Johnson sidled to another tree as, rightward, dozens of pairs of dark-jacketed men jog-trotted, firing off and on. The American fusillade grew more furious, hurried and desperate.

Passing Johnson, Walker ducked lacy Spanish moss, for cottonmouth snakes slept amidst it. More to fear were the mankilling coral snakes like red-and-yellow bracelets, and spiders and bears and panthers. Walker almost missed Spain's barren hills.

Bullets zipped and smacked trees. Walker and Johnson closed warily. In weeks of fighting, the 95th had seen Americans punch out a man's eye at two hundred yards, same as the best British riflemen.

Keeping low behind a buttonbush, Walker finally made out the Americans in stained hunting smocks and old faded jackets.

The militiamen hunkered in the vee of two fallen trees. Busy loading and firing, the citizen-soldiers hadn't posted pickets, so didn't know the British riflemen had flanked them. An American officer in civilian clothes howled orders no one heeded.

Walker squinted. "How many you reckon?"

"Sixty." Johnson checked his priming. "Take 'em easy."

"Don't jinx us." As greenjackets flitted forward, Walker spotted Sergeant Durell in a sash and stripes, but carrying a rifle. Walker waggled five fingers and one. The sergeant blew a long blast to make ready, then a single peep: advance but hold your fire. Walker and Johnson drew bayonets amid a chorus of tiny clicks like crickets. The blades were long as swords because the Baker rifles were short.

"Here we go!" hissed Johnson.

At a peep, half the British riflemen unleashed a thundering volley of cover fire while the other half dashed ahead.

The surprise was complete. Americans gaped in shock as the British leapt like wolves over and around the fallen logs. Undisciplined, the militiamen fired wild or ducked or spun and tangled. They were torn to pieces like sheep in a pen.

Vaulting a log, Walker raced after two fleet Americans. He swiped his overlong bayonet left and hooked back to rake the face or neck. The victim shrilled and dropped. Reversing the stroke, Walker swung right, batted aside a long rifle, and smashed the American's jaw. The man flopped to the rooty ground yet still fumbled for a tomahawk at his belt. Walker stamped his groin and, as the man curled, pricked his windpipe. Whirling, Walker found the first victim floundering with hands to his face. His nose and cheek were laid open so teeth showed. Walker shoved his bayonet through the man's liver and twisted. Blood spurted, and Walker left him to die.

Reloading, the rifleman stepped a circle, but only the 95th stood upright. Forty-odd militiamen sprawled on the wet ground with hands jammed in the air. A dozen more bled to death. Another dozen still ran, having chucked their rifles or muskets. Walker snapped his rifle to his shoulder, swung the barrel until it marked a man's spine, and squeezed. The heavy weapon bucked as the victim pitched forward. More rifles cracked. Dead men cannoned into trees.

The forest grew still except for the moaning of wounded.

Walker wiped his bayonet on a dead man's jacket. Riflemen pitched the militia's muskets and even some matchlocks into a pond. Johnson weighed a Kentucky rifle, tall as a man but slim as a snake. "You might kill a squirrel with this toy, but try beating an Imperial Guardsman to death. It's rubbish." Checking the gun was empty, Johnson whacked it across a tree trunk. The lock popped off and the stock splintered.

Looting dead and living, the soldiers slit pouches and pockets and filthy blanketrolls. Scott joined them, burly and dark, with a black eyepatch piped with white, gift of an eye-gouging Irish fusilier in a stew in Southwark. With Scott came his partner, Miller, handsome and quiet, born in Surrey and enlisted to escape poverty, an honest man and good, but not one of the trio that had marched together forever. The British riflemen found ham, jerky, and firecakes that they shared and bolted.

Miller held up scraps of printed money, "These worth anything?"

"Starting fires, maybe," snorted someone.

"'Ere." Michaud offered a gentlemen's flask of engraved silver. Walker swigged a fiery liquor that made him gasp.

Trotting the line, Sergeant Durell pointed two ways. "Corporal Dollar, take this detail and chivvy the prisoners back to camp. Let's get along, 95th." Forty-odd pairs of riflemen vanished into the gloom like ghosts, or shadows of ghosts.

"No hurry, lads." Dollar lit a pipe, as did they all, sucking the smoke greedily. Many took turns to prop their rifles and move off to squat, for dysentery added to their miseries. The veterans welcomed the rest. Johnson coughed steadily as he smoked. Scott blew smoke to speed away mosquitoes that drilled in their sweaty faces. Walker shivered while his stomach churned at the unaccustomed rich rations.

In the distance a triple *pom pom-pom* was answered by a *boom*. Along the river, British batteries swapped shot and shell with American emplacements and US Navy gunboats. Here, deep in the forest, the artillery duel sounded boxed in, but it stirred the men to march. With rifles cradled, the 95th prodded the prisoners along the torturous paths through the swamp, all stumbling on roots and skidding on grass as darkness settled.

From the rear, Walker noted the prisoners were as mixed as Wellington's Spanish army. A fat man wore a natty brushed hat and dove-gray coat, a scarecrow wore a foxskin cap and filthy hunting shirt, and a third, dark as a gypsy, wore a knit hat and crimson shirt and blue-gold sash. The skinny frontiersman suddenly growled at Johnson, "You didn't have to bust my rifle all to hell and gone there, cap'n."

"It'll keep you cowards from sniping our sentries," retorted Johnson. "It's not cricket to shoot a man on post, you know. We never did in Europe, not even in Portugal."

"We ain't a-playin' at war, commander. We aim to push you out 'n keep you out!"

Walker snorted. With their antique accents, all Americans sounded like country bumpkins. And he had no wish to talk to them.

Scott prodded the swarthy man's flashy shirt. "Sir, you remind me of a pirate."

"*Au secours*. I am a privateer, *s'il vous plait*." Despite his predicament, dark eyes twinkled. "M' cap'n has a commission signed by the governor of Cartagena."

"Where the hell's that?" asked Scott.

A brown finger trolled south. "Venezuela."

"That's not part of the United States!" said Johnson.

A Gallic shrug. "No more'n Lou'siana."

"Gentlemen, if I might." The fat man in fine clothes huffed as he trudged. The American commander, General Andrew Jackson, called "Old Hickory," had declared martial law in New Orleans, drafted every man who could stand, then announced he'd burn the city rather than surrender it. This was some hapless merchant with soft hands. "You needn't escort us to your lines. We're all sophisticates here. I'm sure we can strike some bargain." The fat man stuck a hand inside his coat. "Now I propose—"

Walker's rifle exploded. A cat claw tore the fat man's arm and knocked him sprawling. Everyone stopped in shock. Walker reloaded, motions swift and easy as a windmill.

A silver case had flipped from the merchant's hand. Gingerly the pirate retrieved it: a cigar holder. He passed the stogies to the nearest men, including Walker and Johnson and Scott. They cupped their hands as a mizzling rain dripped from naked branches and moss. The riflemen hitched their rifle locks under their armpits, dry but ready.

The pirate watched the fat man writhe. "I'm glad, me, you shot him and not m'self. This shirt she's new, and 'bout the only t'ing I 'xpect for pay out of this American army." Oddly, he chuckled.

Puzzled, Johnson asked, "What's so funny?"

"Thi' shirt. We wear heem because Lafitte he asks it. He wants us to wear uniform like Monsieur Jackson's soldiers. Me, I do not mind. When I go to my house, my wife she will scream, 'What have you bring?' and I will say, 'My han'some self in a new red shirt!'"

The scarecrow asked Walker, "What kind'a rifle is that? That shot were slicker'n a greased eel in a bucket o' snot."

"It's a Baker rifle," said Scott. "Someone wrap his arm, will you? Finest rifle in the world."

"Th' finest rifle in the world you busted acrost a tree, but never mind." The frontiersman spit a fleck of tobacco. "You need good Kentucky whiskey to sip with a seegar."

"Taffia," countered the Frenchman. "Rum."

Scott asked, "Why isn't a pirate in the navy? And pick up that bag of guts."

"We are *privateers*, but *les citoyens* sent their navy to blow up our ships."

Scott squinted. "Then why are you fighting alongside them?"

The pirate wet his lips to blow a smoke ring. "Tha's the way we do business here in N'Orl'ns."

"I'm fr'm Tennessee," announced the scarecrow. "Over the mountain and through the woods. God's country!" Men scoffed.

"By gadfrey, this stings!" The wounded businessman was propped on his feet, a kerchief around his arm. "I feel mighty poorly. Queasy-like."

"Women love scars," said Johnson. "Trust me."

"This country'll never amount to beans," declared Scott. "You blokes are a gammon pie."

"We beat you bully boys last time, n' we can do it agin." snapped the Tennessean.

"Not likely," snarled Walker. "We burnt your Washington to the ground."

"Washin'ton?" The frontiersman piffed. "That's no skin off'n my nose."

"You got no king!" added Scott. "A man's got to have a king, same as a god!"

"God is far away and ver' busy," said the Frenchman. "And in America, we say, every man is a king."

"That makes us kings, then," snapped Walker. At the Americans' puzzlement, he explained, "We were born here, us three. Johnson's from Boston and Scott's from the Carolinas."

"I'm from Halifax," said Johnson.

"And I was born of a virgin!" laughed Scott.

The pirate asked Walker, "N' where are you from, m' friend?"

"Pennsylvania! And I'm not your friend! Our parents were loyal, but they were pushed out by *patriots* during the rebellion! Our own *neighbours* kicked down our doors and drove us at bayonet point to the docks! We lost everything! We were beached in Canada with nothing, not a scrap of food nor a page of the Bible!"

"Like criminals." Johnson flicked away his cigar. "We were just youngsters, but I remember my mother crying every night. It broke her heart."

"We're Canadians now." Scott's one dark eye blinked. "Or something."

Corporal Dollar called back, "Silence in the ranks!"

Men marched. The Tennessean sniffed. "My folks were druv out 'a Scotland for sidin' with Bonnie Prince Charlie. My grandpap had a 'T' burnt into his cheek for 'Traitor'. That's why we fought King George."

"*Eh bien*," added the pirate, "m' family were driv out of Acadia in '49 by *les Anglais*. We became the Cajuns. Many of us still curse the English, but my wife, she say that was long time ago."

"Not long enough," said Walker.

They plodded on in grey gloom. Johnson said, "That reminds me. What did you think of Bermuda? It looked so green from shipside it hurt your eyes."

Walker stifled a groan, tired of the eternal argument. With Napoleon defeated, and as this campaign concluded, the British army would be whittled back to the bone. Well past forty, too old to re-enlist, the three friends would soon be discharged and dumped on the docks. Where to go then?

"Any of the Sugar Islands would suit me," Johnson rambled. "With a little hard work a man could own his own plantation."

"And die in six months of the fever," argued Scott. "And it's hot."

"What about South America?" asked Johnson. "The Dagos are revolting against the Spanish. There's bound to be fighting."

"It's even hotter," said Scott. "What about Poland? Remember all those lancers? They must fight a lot. Or the Germanies. Got good food. Even in Russia."

"Can't pull a trigger with your fingers frozen off," said Johnson.

Years ago, stranded in Canada, barely boys, uprooted and alone, the three friends had joined the 60th Royal Americans. Not just three friends, but many others, most now dead. Trained at Cowes, fitted with elite green jackets and black tackle, they'd fought in Ireland and Dutch Guiana, then marched five thousand miles across Portugal and Spain to fight at Corunna, Rolica, Vimiero, Talavera, Bussaco, and Badajoz. Transferred to the 95th Rifles, they'd fought at Vittoria, in the Pyrenees, and finally in France herself. Now they fought Americans, which Walker considered God's roundabout justice and a fitting end to a long career.

Johnson prodded Walker. "You're quiet. Where do you favour?"

Walker just shook his head. "Anyplace I can get plum puddin' for Christmas."

"Hey," Scott asked the prisoners, "are the women good to look at in New Orleans? So far we've only seen Indian women."

"Women?" grinned the pirate. "We got them in all colours. Creoles, quadroons, octoroons, Cajun women with white throats like the swans. When Lafitte goes at town, we screw so many women we go bowlegged like spavined mules!"

"We'll never see New Orleans," muttered Johnson. "Hey, why don't we go to India?"

"What's wrong with France?" asked Scott. "Now that Boney's off the throne, the country'll be wide open. Lots of fat widows with farms't need tending."

"We ruined France," said Walker.

"Let's go back to Canada, then," said Scott. "We can build ships or fish."

"You can. You've got family there still." Walker hunched against the drizzle and hoped it meant no frost. Lately, between arthritis and ancient wounds, he could barely crawl off his bedroll come morning.

"Twenty-four years since we left Canada," said Johson. "Who knows what's there?"

Talk died. Walker tramped with wet feet. He didn't like to ponder a bleak future or dwell on an unhappy past. But still, these American voices recalled glimpses from his childhood. Green grass dotted with daisies that caught between his toes. An apple tree dripping white blossoms. A stone-lined cellar cool and damp. A swimming hole. Snow on windowsills and on the hills, dazzling in the sun. Pumpkin pie and mulled cider. Not much else, and that torn away in an instant. Walker shook his head. "It's bad luck to talk about home. It'll take you down the low road."

"You know, *mes amis* . . . " The pirate had dawdled, and now stopped in the trail, as did some others. His dark face was hard to see. "Those ones up there can talk to your *chef*. They do not need all of us."

"That's true," piped the Tennessean. "I don't know nothin' worth the tellin'. Whyn't we just part ways and no hard feelin's?"

Casually, the prisoners stepped back a pace.

Walker cocked his rifle.

In unison, the men resumed marching.

The pirate shook his head. "I am hoping you tell my wife why I am so late, me. You will t'ink you got yourself up a tree with an alligator wait to bite off your toes . . ."

Quitting the dark woods, the troop detoured into an abandoned grove to pick oranges winter-withered but still sweet. Scott stumbled over a Royal Engineer dead beneath a tree, a spyglass near his hand, obviously been spied himself by a marksman. They emptied his pockets, matched fingers for the spyglass, then wedged his bicorn in a tree for a burial detail to find.

Just before camp, Johnson said, "Look, you two. We don't know where we'll go when this's over. One place is good as the next. What matter's is we go together, right?" To that, all three nodded.

The British had camped on a squelchy field of cane stubble and slash not far from the wide placid river. The air was nippy and smudged by charcoal smoke. Normally, after supper call, soldiers would talk and smoke and polish gear, but tonight men rustled on the parade ground. A messenger cantered by. Drum rolls summoned officers. Lanterns were lit before the Adjutant General's tent. A distant *poom!* warned of a cannonball that slammed into the ground and was swallowed up. A passing sergeant-major snapped, "Look lively, lads. The big push is on."

The three veterans looked at one another. Walker said only, "Oh, my . . ."

"Gotta be near dawn."

Cold fog swirled and clung. A canteen clonked on a bayonet

hilt. A cannon wheel squeaked. Ducks gabbled on the invisible river.

Walker whispered, "If we break their line, we take the city."

Johnson bit down a yawn. Chivvied into formation, they'd stood for hours. "I wish Old Nosey was leading us. Packy's done a balls-up job."

Stalled and starved for weeks, the British Army had received a new commander, General Packenham, who'd so far aborted two battles by sending troops forward to be killed by artillery, then pulling them back. The 95th Rifles knew the swamps were passable, and the Royal Navy had cited six approaches by water, but the British Army's Council of War dithered on how to attack. Meanwhile, day by day, the American Army fortified the only clear path to the city. "Line Jackson" was a half-mile entrenchment stretching from the Mississippi to a cypress swamp, a deep canal and wall of earth studded with cannons and rifle walks. To assault it was to die, but their general lacked imagination and the soldiers feared the worst.

"The Dirtyshirts could have fifty thousand," hissed a voice in the ranks.

"Their regulars are in Florida fighting the Spanish."

"Buggers. We only got six thousand."

"It's cold as the bleeding Pyrenees."

"Six of our niggers froze to death."

"It'll be the tabletop."

"Not an inch of cover. A killing ground."

"Look where we are. How are we supposed to skirmish except by swimming?"

"Steady on!" snarled a sergeant.

Shivering to keep warm, Walker's back and legs and wits felt thick and slow. He thought: *I'm too old for campaigning.*

Dawn illumined the mist. A Congreve rocket sizzled and exploded overhead. Immediately drums rumbled all around, the heads muffled by damp, but thrilling. Bagpipes skirled. Walker felt his blood quicken, and knew Johnson and Scott's did too.

In the fog a voice barked, and British cannons exploded. American artillery replied, a clash of giants. Cannonballs whistled and droned. Somewhere they struck earth, ricocheted, and slammed into British lines to grunts and screams. Nothing hit near the riflemen, who stood hard at the British left along the river.

Unable to hear, Walker saw the sergeant-major bellow, "Company! To the front – march!" Soldiers clamped their jaws against cold and fear, for the ground underfoot was even as a tennis lawn.

Cannons crashed all around, hard to pinpoint. Line Jackson bristled with cannons, and the United States Navy manned batteries across the river. British Light Infantry and Royal Marines were to cross and seize those batteries, otherwise, marching along the chest-high levee at the muddy Mississippi, the 95th would catch hell from the front and the side.

The riflemen stamped past a shrouded line of British artillery. Unseen but heard, two more British columns marched like spears across the empty field. A horseman vaulted a canal, for the plain was cut by ditches running arrow-straight from the river.

"95th! Prime and load!" Hands moved in perfect accord to tear cartridges, prime pans, swing the butts to charge the cartridges, then ram with quick whisks. As one, rifles snapped to shoulders.

Greenjackets began to die as, from the fog, cannonballs smashed into ranks. Walker and Johnson held their breath as men were blown to flinders a dozen yards ahead, but they kept marching. They hopped a canal bottomed by mud and prayed for a miracle: the cannons would run out of powder, the general would call a parley, the line would retreat, something, please God be kind to forlorn soldiers.

More men were knocked to jelly, until the green column balked, then stopped. Walker said, "We've got to –"

"Skirmishers!" shrilled a young voice. "Detach and take cover!"

Greenjackets jumped from the ranks and scampered left to hug the levee, heads and bellies flat but rifles upright. Cannon fire slammed all around them. Mounted officers dashed hither and yon shrieking, but it was young Colonel Rennie the riflemen attended, for he'd given the order that spared their lives. So far.

"John!" gasped Walker. "Let's kill someone!"

"Fire as ye bear!"

Coming to one knee, his foot touching the levee, Walker searched for a target and was surprised to glimpse the American breastwork at a hundred misty yards. Figures in homespun shirts topped the rampart to snipe the enemy. Had to be militia, thought Walker: no soldier would quit the embrace of solid earth. Walker swung his front sight onto a frontiersman likewise taking aim and squeezed the trigger. As if by magic, the American was bowled off the rampart.

Walker shouted "Ready!" even as he bit salty gunpowder. Johnson's rifle barked. Leaving his ramrod stuck in the ground, Walker hoisted his rifle, found a climbing target, led him, and killed him. And reloaded, shouting "Ready!" Johnson's rifle barked, every gun with its own voice.

Colonel Rennie had stampeded about for orders, but many officers were already killed. Abandoning his terrified horse, gilt sword in hand, Rennie scampered to the levee and cowered with the riflemen, getting mud on his immaculate white breeches. He scanned what battlefield was visible in fog and gunsmoke. Close by, Walker could almost read his thoughts: *If the army still advances, they must too, else be traitors.*

"95th!" Rennie gasped. "We'll advance! All right, men? Follow me, quick time!"

There was no other response. Feeling giddy, battle-mad, Walker jumped up and dashed after Rennie with his rifle at the trail. Sizzling cannonballs smashed into the company as they crowded the levee and leapt canals. Even the American river was an enemy, Walker gauged, for the US Navy could fire across it while the British couldn't advance or flee that way. Thus the riflemen charged the corner of a trap. Johnson panted and coughed beside Walker while Scott and Miller thrummed ahead. The men ran forever with their feet sticking in mud, getting nowhere, as if caught in a nightmare.

The fog had lifted to a man's eyes, though curtains of mist

persisted. Walker saw the American rampart was so fresh-dug it
was still damp. It encroached on a canal that entered the river,
and that corner was anchored by an arrow-headed redoubt built
of broken bricks. The only things taller were a mansion
screened by trees and the triangular sails of gunboats. Beyond
stretched more plantations, fields, and canals, and finally the
city of New Orleans. But that towering line of dirt might have
been a castle wall fronting a moat. Muskets and rifles bristled
atop and cannons belched fire. Two six-pounders bellowed
from the redoubt, and somewhere behind a howitzer farted
and lobbed bombs. Parts of the mucky line were floored by
cotton bales that falling rockets had ignited.

Running in the shifting mist, Walker glimpsed lines of redcoats advancing: the big clot of the 44th and the black round
faces of 5th West Indians, some lugging scaling ladders, others
fascines of cane to chuck in the last canal. The lines marched
forward, solid as a red dragon, but the American cannons had
switched to firing grapeshot: Walker heard cannons blat rather
than bang. Handfuls of redcoats were pulped or swept away.
The ranks magically refilled, like blood flowing into a wound,
but red jackets littered the dragon's wake.

Racing after Colonel Rennie, Walker realized that, insane as
this head-on attack was, some part had gone madder. The 93rd
Highlanders in tartan trews, who should have followed Rennie,
suddenly detached and obliqued toward the field's centre,
though Walker couldn't imagine why. The 44th under Mullins
actually retreated, tangling other regiments and blocking the
British artillery's aim. Horses skittered hither and thither, reins
dangling and saddles empty, the officers dead, so no cool head
would straighten out the mess. The US Navy still fired from
across the river, so the Lights and Marines had failed to scotch
them. Long-eighteen naval guns blew tons of mud from the levee.

Still, it was onto the levee that Colonel Rennie led the
riflemen as the ground got soggy. The Monmouths and Ist
West Indians pounded hard behind, following a leader rather
than stand still. Their courageous charge drew down death.
Musket fire rattled from blue-jacketed soldiers with black

shakos who, oddly, had flowers pinned to their bosoms. Young and green, they flinched every time the six-pounders barked. Atop the earthwork, irregulars in blue hunting shirts and floppy hats levelled slim rifles. Walker saw Ryan spin and fall as a bullet smacked his chest. Yet the brickwork loomed closer, a miraculous haven almost within their grasp. Riflemen growled like chained dogs eager to bite the enemy.

Fog lifted but smoke thickened, and not a cup of breeze stirred it. A band behind the American lines thumped "Yankee Doodle" while, bad luck for the Scots, bagpipes sagged to a stop. The crash of guns was mind-jarring. Americans elbowed each other aside to shoot, hurling a sheet of flame and smoke at the redcoats.

"After me, Lights!" shouted Colonel Rennie, lacking his hat and looking very young with his hair streaming. A cannonball smashed the levee, and the colonel stumbled. Walker saw blood pulse down his silk stockings, but Rennie recovered and shrieked, "*Light Battalion, take that redoubt!*"

Howling, snatching bayonets from scabbards, the 95th took the redoubt. Some greenjackets leapt like tigers from the levee, some scrambled up the erratic walls of broken brick, and some seemed to fly. West Indians and Scotsmen slapped scaling ladders against the higher walls and scrambled upward. Bullets flew from the blueshirts on the breastwork, and Britons were murdered as they pressed in ranks mad to mount the ladders. The first black man to top the brick wall was smacked off the ladder by a scruffy frontiersman swinging a hand-made rifle like a club.

Walker and Johnson trampled a dozen dead companions to scramble up brick walls that crumbled under the onslaught. Walker recognized Ensley, Knobby, and Langlois, his wife back in camp now a widow. A blue-jacketed soldier raised his rifle as Walker fixed his sword bayonet. Johnson's rifle barked and the man's chest tore open. Walker hopped atop the wall, bayonet lunging and lusting to kill.

Amazingly, in the heat, Walker took note of the terrain as he'd been trained, and saw immediately that seizing this redoubt would buy nothing. The back of the arrowhead gaped open above the big canal, which was a death trap ten feet wide, bottomed by mire, and infested with sharp stakes. The canal abutted the tall earthwork, and behind that gunned a thousand Americans.

Even invading the redoubt was grabbing a hornet's nest, for the brickwork teemed with troops. The bluejackets were the US 7th Infantry, Walker saw as he shoved a bayonet between a man's buttons. The six-pounders were naval guns hauled across the mud and manned by US sailors and marines. Jammed between were frontiersmen, citizens, slaves, and pirates, half fighting and half fleeing over a single thick plank that spanned the canal to the rampart. Against them, West Indians in red, Scotsmen in trews, and riflemen in green fought like demons just to stay alive.

Walker saw one-eyed Scott crouch and lunge like a French dancing master. He punched a bluecoat's belly with his bayonet, then bulled into the victim to pink another soldier crowding behind. Johnson was caught reloading, so shot his ramrod through a black man's brisket. Walker jumped into a gap as an American sergeant's spontoon lunged for his face. The veteran skipped his bayonet down the long haft and sliced the sergeant's fingers, then rammed his blade under the man's chin. He hacked down a young lad in blue and bashed his head when the boy grabbed his ankle.

Mind whirling in the fury of action, Walker was nonetheless amazed by a thought: *Americans make pitiful soldiers, but they fight like bulldogs when riled.*

Then the way stood clear. Red and green loomed upright while blue writhed in blood or dashed for the rampart. The British had taken the redoubt!

"Spike the guns!" barked Colonel Rennie. "The rest of you, follow me!"

Out the open back of the brickwork charged the young officer, shouting encouragement and blasphemy, then skipped across the single plank to assault the rampart. Howling men in green and red charged after, but grit and luck only carried them so far. Rennie was a prime target. Blue-shirted men fired from the rampart, six guns banging as one. The colonel's broken body was flung off the plank, and half a dozen men toppled with him into the canal.

Clear of the brick walls, a glance showed Walker the larger assault had failed. The 93rd would never see the Highlands again. The misled 44th were spilled across the field like a crop of flax. Only a trickling column of red had reached the earthworks' farthest end. With no sign of any reserves, every Briton in the centre had died or run. Rennie's brave capture of the redoubt would get no support. The 95th Rifles would die for nothing. Walker gasped, "It's bad as Badajoz!"

Encouraged by the vast numbers of British dead, the blue-shirted riflemen surged down the rampart, crazy-mad to retake the redoubt. Greybeards, Walker saw, cold-hearted veterans, and young bucks of the 7th Infantry out to prove they could fight too. Bullets knocked British soldiers off the single plank like pigeons. With the way clear, screaming Americans dashed across with tomahawks and swords and clubbed rifles.

Johnson and Walker were almost pushed into the canal by the milling mass behind. Johnson hollered, "What a cock-up! Damn Packenham! *Huzzah!*" Lunging, Johnson pinked a young soldier in the liver and steered him into another man rushing. Walker clashed muskets with a man big as a black-smith, gave ground as a feint, then twisted and toppled the man into the canal.

Even as he dodged and stabbed, soldier's instinct made Walker look up. From high atop the rampart a longrifle sighted on him. Walker flinched aside, but hard-pressed Johnson came too. Walker shouted a warning as the gun flamed. The bullet smacked Johnson's eyebrow and snapped his neck. He slipped under Walker's feet, trampled by the crowd.

Walker backstepped as a pack of West Indians tumbled like ninepins against his legs. Smoke boiled until Walker retched. Sweat ran into his eyes, or perhaps blood, and he clawed them clear. He looked for Scott and saw him fighting without Miller. Scott swung his head to watch everywhere, but backed his blind side into an American officer who wheeled and skewered Scott's ribs. One eye flew wide as Scott sank out of sight as if drowning.

Alone, drained of life and spirit, Walker backed into bricks with a handful of greenjackets, as blue and homespun swarmed. Walker wished he might load and shoot just once more, but his hands were slick with blood to the elbows. A spontoon lunged for his guts. Walker blundered aside but bumped another rifleman. The spontoon chipped bricks. Half-turned, wedged by bodies, Walker couldn't swing his bayonet. He braced to shove—

A bullet slammed his leg like a sledgehammer. Walker crumpled and skidded to one hand. An American musket cracked Walker's shoulder. Blood bubbled beneath him, his own. A bayonet sheared past his nose and jammed in his shoulder. Searing pain made Walker yelp and struggle, but the blade twisted deeper.

We'll all go together, Walker thought of his friends, *straight to Hell*. Then a musket crushed his skull.

Walker awoke to see Jesus of the Sacred Heart peering from a whitewashed wall. Outside a window, a tree wore white blossoms that glowed in the sun. Birds sang.

"You be awake." A fat black woman in the doorway wore a turban and apron. She fetched a ewer and a mug. Walker burned with thirst, parched as a desert, but she only allowed him a few delicious sips. Her voice was sweet as molasses. "You a lucky mon. You near died 'a the black vomit." Yellow fever.

Lightheaded, sinking, Walker raised a hand and found it rail-thin, shrunken, yellow. He didn't recall any disease, just a vague nightmare of agony. He tried to sit up, but found only one foot to lever against the bedstead. His right leg had been sawed off at the knee. Slowly he remembered. He was alive while Johnson and Scott and others were dead. Walker didn't think it fair, somehow. Lonely and exhausted, he cried, then slept.

When he awoke, an American dragoon officer stood by his bed. Tall and tanned, he boasted a leather helmet with a white horsetail and a blue jacket rich with silver frogs. The Negro woman brought beef broth and white bread with butter, and helped Walker eat.

"Good morning, private. Welcome back to the land of the living." The officer wore a sabre long as his leg, and rested his left hand on the pommel. "You caught the little end of the horn, I'd say, but you've crossed the River Jordan." The officer tapped a small sack by Walker's bedstead. "As liaison for the British wounded, I signed your discharge papers and insisted on a bonus for your lost limb. You got a month's pay, but you'd fare no better in the American Army, I dare say. This woman has kindly tended you on her own hook. Families are doing that all over New Orleans. She won't accept payment, but you might give her a few coins when you leave."

"Sir – " His voice unused for months, Walker croaked. "Sir, am I a prisoner?"

"Ah. No. You don't know, do you?" The lieutenant rubbed his nose. "England and the US signed a peace treaty at Christmas, but it took two months for word to reach us. That little fandango we threw by the levee was – unnecessary. The British force pulled out a month ago."

"Oh." Walker's thoughts churned like milk a-clabber. Johnson and Scott dead for naught. The British Army, his only home, abandoning him. "I feel like a dog whose master has died."

"It's hard, son. But you're not a dog, you're a man." Saluting, the officer marched out.

Day by day Walker slept and rested. When the negro woman washed him, he discovered a scar on his shoulder, lumps on his skull, and a dimple in his left hand. He rested and stared at walls and missed his friends.

An old Frenchman with crooked hands delivered two crutches carved from tulip wood. Walker practiced walking, planting the foot and swinging the wood, swinging the foot and planting the wood. He stumped back and forth and eventually into the street. The British Army had finally entered New Orleans, he thought, except he wasn't a soldier. Houses were like English houses, stuccoed and galleried. Sidewalks were tile, gutters wood, and an open sewer ran down the middle. People of every color and clothing bustled by. They smiled at Walker, kind to a cripple, he thought at first. Yet they were happy in their busyness.

Once when the dragoon visited, Walker asked, "Sir, is it true that in America every man's a king?"

Bemused, the young officer hesitated. "Well, in a way. Mostly we've learned to do without kings. In America, we believe all men are created equal."

"Equal." Walker didn't know what to think. "Thank you, sir."

Finally the day came when, as Walker was being washed, his wedding tackle grew stiff as a cannon rammer. The Negro woman flushed darker and chuckled. Walker smiled sadly. "I guess it's time to go."

Creaking, off-balance, taking half the day, Walker dressed. His green jacket and trousers and old shirt had been washed and mended, his shoes and gaiters blacked, though he only needed the one. His equipment was gone: rifle, knapsack, blanket, even his jackknife. His shako had gotten wet and, off his head, had shrunk, so he left it. He hid ten silver shillings in the bedclothes. Planting his single foot, swinging the crutches, Walker met the black woman in the doorway.

"Thank you for saving my life."

Shy, she shrugged round shoulders. Yellow eyes glistened, but she didn't speak.

Slowly Walker stumped into the sunshine and squinted about.

The dragoon lieutenant must have been alerted, for he jangled up the street. "I say, son, you're fit. But where are you going?"

Walker hadn't been sure, but now he knew.

"Sir, I've thought about what people have said, and I'm going to Pennsylvania."

Leaving the puzzled American behind, limping slow but sure, the other American stumped away north.

ZODOMIRSKY'S DUEL

Alexandre Dumas

Dumas (1802–70) was one of the great writers of the nineteenth century, indeed of any century. Who can forget his immortal novels The Three Musketeers *(1844) and* The Count of Monte Cristo *(1845), just two of around one hundred books that Dumas produced, some of incredible length, and all at a breathtaking pace. His father had been a general serving under Napoleon, and Dumas remained fascinated with the Revolutionary and Napoleonic period in France. Novels covering this time include* The Chevalier of the Red House *(1846),* Memoirs of a Physician *(1848), and* The Queen's Necklace *(1850). He also wrote a study of Napoleon. He was so prolific that it was years before all of his work was translated into English and there was a flurry of interest in his lesser known works during the 1890s. That was when the following story appeared in* The Strand Magazine.

I

At the time of this story our regiment was stationed in the dirty little village of Valins, on the frontier of Austria.

It was the fourth of May in the year 182–, and I, with several other officers, had been breakfasting with the Aide-de-Camp in honour of his birthday, and discussing the various topics of the garrison.

"Can you tell us without being indiscreet," asked Sub-Lieutenant Stamm of Andrew Michaelovitch, the aide-de-camp, "what the Colonel was so eager to say to you this morning?"

"A new officer," he replied, "is to fill the vacancy of captain."

"His name?" demanded two or three voices.

"Lieutenant Zodomirsky, who is betrothed to the beautiful Mariana Ravensky."

"And when does he arrive?" asked Major Belayef.

"He *has* arrived. I have been presented to him at the Colonel's house. He is very anxious to make your acquaintance, gentlemen, and I have therefore invited him to dine with us. But that reminds me, Captain, you must know him," he continued, turning to me, "you were both in the same regiment at St Petersburg."

"It is true," I replied. "We studied there together. He was then a brave, handsome youth, adored by his comrades, in everyone's good graces, but of a fiery and irritable temper."

"Mademoiselle Ravensky informed me that he was a skilful duellist," said Stamm. "Well, he will do very well here; a duel is a family affair with us. You are welcome, Monsieur Zodomirsky. However quick your temper, you must be careful of it before me, or I shall take upon myself to cool it."

And Stamm pronounced these words with a visible sneer.

"How is it that he leaves the Guards? Is he ruined?" asked Cornet Naletoff.

"I have been informed," replied Stamm, "that he has just inherited from an old aunt about twenty thousand roubles. No, poor devil! He is consumptive."

"Come, gentlemen," said the Aide-de-Camp, rising, "let us pass to the saloon and have a game of cards. Koloff will serve dinner whilst we play."

We had been seated some time, and Stamm, who was far from rich, was in the act of losing sixty roubles, when Koloff announced—

"Captain Zodomirsky."

"Here you are, at last!" cried Michaelovitch, jumping from his chair. "You are welcome."

Then, turning to us, he continued – "These are your new comrades, Captain Zodomirsky; all good fellows and brave soldiers."

"Gentlemen," said Zodomirsky, "I am proud and happy to have joined your regiment. To do so has been my greatest desire for some time, and if I am welcome, as you courteously say, I shall be the happiest man in the world.

"Ah! good day, Captain," he continued, turning to me and holding out his hand. "We meet again. You have not forgotten an old friend, I hope?"

As he smilingly uttered these words, Stamm, to whom his back was turned, darted at him a glance full of bitter hatred. Stamm was not liked in the regiment; his cold and taciturn nature had formed no friendship with any of us. I could not understand his apparent hostility towards Zodomirsky, whom I believed he had never seen before.

Someone offered Zodomirsky a cigar. He accepted it, lit it at the cigar of an officer near him, and began to talk gaily to his new comrades.

"Do you stay here long?" asked Major Belayef.

"Yes, monsieur," replied Zodomirsky." I wish to stay with you as long as possible," and as he pronounced these words he saluted us all round with a smile. He continued, "I have taken a house near that of my old friend Ravensky whom I knew at St Petersburg. I have my horses there, an excellent cook, a passable library, a little garden, and a target; and there I shall be quiet as a hermit, and happy as a king. It is the life that suits me."

"Ha! you practise shooting!" said Stamm, in such a strange voice, accompanied by a smile so sardonic, that Zodomirsky regarded him in astonishment.

"It is my custom every morning to fire twelve balls," he replied.

"You are very fond of that amusement, then?" demanded Stamm, in a voice without any trace of emotion; adding, "I do not understand the use of shooting, unless it is to hunt with."

Zodomirsky's pale face was flushed with a sudden flame. He turned to Stamm, and replied in a quiet but firm voice, "I think, monsieur, that you are wrong in calling it lost time to learn to shoot with a pistol; in our garrison life an imprudent word often leads to a meeting between comrades, in which case he who is known for a good shot inspires respect among those indiscreet persons who amuse themselves in asking useless questions."

"Oh! that is not a reason, Captain. In duels, as in everything else, something should be left to chance. I maintain my first opinion, and say that an honourable man ought not to take too many precautions."

"And why?" asked Zodomirsky.

"I will explain to you," replied Stamm. "Do you play at cards, Captain?"

"Why do you ask that question?"

"I will try to render my explanation clear, so that all will understand it. Everyone knows that there are certain players who have an enviable knack, whilst shuffling the pack, of adroitly making themselves master of the winning card. Now, I see no difference, myself, between the man who robs his neighbour of his money and the one who robs him of his life." Then he added, in a way to take nothing from the insolence of his observation, "I do not say this to you, in particular, Captain, I speak in general terms."

"It is too much as it is, monsieur!" cried Zodomirsky, "I beg Captain Alexis Stephanovitch to terminate this affair with you." Then, turning to me, he said, "You will not refuse me this request?"

"So be it, Captain," replied Stamm quickly. "You have told

me yourself you practise shooting every day, whilst I practise only on the day I fight. We will equalise the chances. I will settle details with Monsieur Stephanovitch."

Then he rose and turned to our host.

"*Au revoir*, Michaelovitch," he said. "I will dine at the Colonel's." And with these words he left the room.

The most profound silence had been kept during this altercation; but, as soon as Stamm disappeared, Captain Pravdine, an old officer, addressed himself to us all.

"We cannot let them fight, gentlemen," he said.

Zodomirsky touched him gently on his arm.

"Captain," he said, "I am a newcomer amongst you; none of you know me. I have yet, as it were, to win my spurs; it is impossible for me to let this quarrel pass without fighting. I do not know what I have done to annoy this gentleman, but it is evident that he has some spite against me."

"The truth of the matter is that Stamm is jealous of you, Zodomirsky," said Cornet Naletoff. "It is well known that he is in love with Mademoiselle Ravensky."

"That, indeed, explains all," he replied. "However, gentlemen, I thank you for your kind sympathy in this affair from the bottom of my heart."

"And now to dinner, gentlemen!" cried Michaelovitch. "Place yourselves as you choose. The soup, Koloff; the soup!"

Everybody was very animated. Stamm seemed forgotten; only Zodomirsky appeared a little sad. Zodomirsky's health was drunk; he seemed touched with this significant attention, and thanked the officers with a broken voice.

"Stephanovitch," said Zodomirsky to me, when dinner was over, and all had risen, "since M. Stamm knows you are my second and has accepted you as such, see him, and arrange everything with him; accept all his conditions; then meet Captain Pravdine and me at my rooms. The first who arrives will wait for the other. We are now going to Monsieur Ravensky's house."

"You will let us know the hour of combat?" said several voices.

"Certainly, gentlemen. Come and bid a last farewell to one of us."

We all parted at the Ravenskys' door, each officer shaking hands with Zodomirsky as with an old friend.

II

Stamm was waiting for me when I arrived at his house. His conditions were these – two sabres were to be planted at a distance of one pace apart; each opponent to extend his arm at full length and fire at the word "*three*." One pistol alone was to be loaded.

I endeavoured in vain to obtain another mode of combat.

"It is not a victim I offer to M. Zodomirsky," said Stamm, "but an adversary. He will fight as I propose, or I will not fight at all; but in that case I shall prove that M. Zodomirsky is brave only when sure of his own safety."

Zodomirsky's orders were imperative. I accepted.

When I entered Zodomirsky's rooms, they were vacant; he had not arrived. I looked round with curiosity. They were furnished in a rich but simple manner, and with evident taste. I drew a chair near the balcony and looked out over the plain. A storm was brewing; some drops of rain fell already, and thunder moaned.

At this instant the door opened, and Zodomirsky and Pravdine entered. I advanced to meet them.

"We are late, Captain," said Zodomirsky, "but it was unavoidable.

"And what says Stamm," he continued.

I gave him his adversary's conditions. When I had ended, a sad smile passed over his face; he drew his hand across his forehead and his eyes glittered with feverish lustre.

"I had foreseen this," he murmured. "You have accepted, I presume?"

"Did you not give me the order yourself?"

"Absolutely," he replied.

Zodomirsky threw himself in a chair by the table, in which

position he faced the door. Pravdine placed himself near the window, and I near the fire. A presentiment weighed down our spirits. A mournful silence reigned.

Suddenly the door opened and a woman muffled in a mantle which streamed with water, and with the hood drawn over her face, pushed past the servant, and stood before us. She threw back the hood, and we recognized Mariana Ravensky!

Pravdine and I stood motionless with astonishment. Zodomirsky sprang towards her.

"Great heavens! what has happened, and why are you here?"

"Why am I here, George?" she cried. "Is it *you* who ask me, when this night is perhaps the last of your life? Why am I here? To say farewell to you. It is only two hours since I saw you, and not one word passed between us of tomorrow. Was that well, George?"

"But I am not alone here," said Zodomirsky in a low voice. "Think, Mariana. Your reputation – your fair fame—"

"Are you not all in all to me, George? And in such a time as this, what matters anything else?"

She threw her arm about his neck and pressed her head against his breast.

Pravdine and I made some steps to quit the room.

"Stay, gentlemen," she said, lifting her head. "Since you have seen me here, I have nothing more to hide from you, and perhaps you may be able to help me in what I am about to say. Then, suddenly flinging herself at his feet—

"I implore you, I command you, George," she cried, "not to fight this duel with Monsieur Stamm. You will not end two lives by such a useless act! Your life belongs to me; it is no longer yours. George, do you hear? You will not do this."

"Mariana! Mariana! in the name of heaven do not torture me thus! Can I refuse to fight? I should be dishonoured – lost! If I could do so cowardly an act, shame would kill me more surely than Stamm's pistol."

"Captain," she said to Pravdine, "you are esteemed in the regiment as a man of honour; you can, then, judge about affairs of honour. Have pity on me, Captain, and tell him he *can* refuse such a duel as this. Make him understand that it is not a duel, but an assassination; speak, speak, Captain, and if he will not listen to me, he will to you."

Pravdine was moved. His lips trembled and his eyes were dimmed with tears. He rose, and, approaching Mariana, respectfully kissed her hand, and said with a trembling voice—

"To spare you any sorrow, Mademoiselle, I would lay down my life; but to counsel M. Zodomirsky to be unworthy of his uniform by refusing this duel is impossible. Each adversary, your betrothed as well as Stamm, has a right to propose his conditions. But whatever be the conditions, the Captain is in circumstances which render this duel absolutely necessary. He is known as a skilful duellist; to refuse Stamm's conditions were to indicate that he counts upon his skill."

"Enough, Mariana, enough," cried George. "Unhappy girl! you do not know what you demand. Do you wish me, then, to fall so low that you yourself would be ashamed of me? I ask you, are you capable of loving a dishonoured man?"

Mariana had let herself fall upon a chair. She rose, pale as a corpse, and began to put her mantle on.

"You are right, George, it is not I who would love you no more, but you who would hate me. We must resign ourselves to our fate. Give me your hand, George; perhaps we shall never see each other again. Tomorrow! tomorrow! my love."

She threw herself upon his breast, without tears, without sobs, but with a profound despair.

She wished to depart alone, but Zodomirsky insisted on leading her home.

Midnight was striking when he returned.

"You had better both retire," said Zodomirsky as he entered. "I have several letters to write before sleeping. At five we must be at the rendezvous."

I felt so wearied that I did not want telling twice. Pravdine passed into the saloon, I into Zodomirsky's bedroom, and the master of the house into his study.

The cool air of the morning woke me. I cast my eyes upon the window, where the dawn commenced to appear. I heard Pravdine also stirring. I passed into the saloon, where Zodomirsky immediately joined us. His face was pale but serene.

"Are the horses ready?" he inquired.

I made a sign in the affirmative.

"Then, let us start," he said.

We mounted into the carriage, and drove off.

III

"Ah," said Pravdine all at once, "there is Michaelovitch's carriage. Yes, yes, it is he with one of ours, and there is Naletoff, on his Circassian horse. Good! the others are coming behind. It is well we started so soon."

The carriage had to pass the house of the Ravenskys. I could not refrain from looking up; the poor girl was at her window, motionless as a statue. She did not even nod to us.

"Quicker! quicker!" cried Zodomirsky to the coachman. It was the only sign by which I knew that he had seen Mariana.

Soon we distanced the other carriages, and arrived upon the place of combat – a plain where two great pyramids rose, passing in this district by the name of the "Tomb of the Two Brothers." The first rays of the sun darting through the trees began to dissipate the mists of night.

Michaelovitch arrived immediately after us, and in a few minutes we formed a group of nearly twenty persons. Then we heard the crunch of other steps upon the gravel. They were those of our opponents. Stamm walked first, holding in his hand a box of pistols. He bowed to Zodomirsky and the officers.

"Who gives the word to fire, gentlemen?" he asked.

The two adversaries and the seconds turned towards the officers, who regarded them with perplexity.

No one offered. No one wished to pronounce that terrible "three," which would sign the fate of a comrade.

"Major," said Zodomirsky to Belayef, "will you render me this service?"

Thus asked, the Major could not refuse and he made a sign that he accepted.

"Be good enough to indicate our places, gentlemen," continued Zodomirsky, giving me his sabre and taking off his coat, "then load, if you please."

"That is useless," said Stamm, "I have brought the pistols; one of the two is loaded, the other has only a gun-cap."

"Do you know which is which?" said Pravdine.

"What does it matter?" replied Stamm, "Monsieur Zodomirsky will choose."

"It is well," said Zodomirsky.

Belayef drew his sabre and thrust it in the ground midway between the two pyramids. Then he took another sabre and planted it before the first. One pace alone separated the two blades. Each adversary was to stand behind a sabre, extending his arm at full length. In this way each had the muzzle of his opponent's pistol at six inches from his heart. Whilst Belayef made these preparations Stamm unbuckled his sabre, and divested himself of his coat. His seconds opened his box of pistols, and Zodomirsky, approaching, took without hesitation the nearest to him. Then he placed himself behind one of the sabres.

Stamm regarded him closely; not a muscle of Zodomirsky's face moved, and there was not about him the least appearance of bravado, but of the calmness of courage.

"He is brave," murmured Stamm.

And taking the pistol left by Zodomirsky he took up his position behind the other sabre, in front of his adversary.

They were both pale, but whilst the eyes of Zodomirsky burned with implacable resolution, those of Stamm were uneasy and shifting. I felt my heart beat loudly.

Belayef advanced. All eyes were fixed on him.

"Are you ready, gentlemen?" he asked.

"We are waiting, Major," replied Zodomirsky and Stamm together, and each lifted his pistol before the breast of the other.

A death-like silence reigned. Only the birds sang in the bushes near the place of combat. In the midst of this silence the Major's voice resounding made everyone tremble.

"One."

"Two."

"*Three*."

Then we heard the sound of the hammer falling on the cap of Zodomirsky's pistol. There was a flash, but no sound followed it.

Stamm had not fired, and continued to hold the mouth of his pistol against the breast of his adversary.

"Fire!" said Zodomirsky, in a voice perfectly calm.

"It is not for you to command, Monsieur," said Stamm, "it is I who must decide whether to fire or not, and that depends on how you answer what I am about to say."

"Speak, then; but in the name of heaven speak quickly."

"Never fear, I will not abuse your patience."

We were all ears.

"I have not come to kill you, Monsieur," continued Stamm, "I have come with the carelessness of a man to whom life holds nothing, whilst it has kept none of the promises it has made to him. You, Monsieur, are rich, you are beloved, you have a promising future before you: life must be dear to you. But fate has decided against you: it is you who must die and not I. Well, Monsieur Zodomirsky, give me your word not to be so prompt in the future to fight duels, and I will not fire."

"I have not been prompt to call you out, Monsieur," replied Zodomirsky in the same calm voice; "you have wounded me by an outrageous comparison, and I have been compelled to challenge you. Fire, then; I have nothing to say to you."

"My conditions cannot wound your honour," insisted Stamm. "Be our judge, Major," he added turning to Belayef. "I will abide by your opinion; perhaps M. Zodomirsky will follow my example."

"M. Zodomirsky has conducted himself as bravely as possible; if he is not killed, it is not his fault." Then, turning to the officers round, he said—

"Can M. Zodomirsky accept the imposed condition?"

"He can! he can!" they cried, "and without staining his honour in the slightest."

Zodomirsky stood motionless.

"The Captain consents," said old Pravdine, advancing. "Yes, in the future he will be less prompt."

"It is you who speak, Captain, and not M. Zodomirsky," said Stamm.

"Will you affirm my words, Monsieur Zodomirsky?" asked Pravdine, almost supplicating in his eagerness.

"I consent," said Zodomirsky, in a voice scarcely intelligible.

"Hurrah! hurrah!" cried all the officers enchanted with this termination. Two or three threw up their caps.

"I am more charmed than anyone," said Stamm, "that all has ended as I desired. Now, Captain, I have shown you that before a resolute man the art of shooting is nothing in a duel, and that if the chances are equal a good shot is on the same level as a bad one. I did not wish in any case to kill you. Only I had a great desire to see how you would look death in the face. You are a man of courage; accept my compliments. The pistols were not loaded." Stamm, as he said these words, fired off his pistol. There was no report!

Zodomirsky uttered a cry which resembled the roar of a wounded lion.

"By my father's soul!" he cried, "this is a new offence, and more insulting than the first. Ah! it is ended, you say? No, Monsieur, it must recommence, and this time the pistols shall be loaded, if I have to load them myself."

"No, Captain," replied Stamm, tranquilly, "I have given you your life, I will not take it back. Insult me if you wish, I will not fight with you."

"Then it is with me whom you will fight, Monsieur Stamm," cried Pravdine, pulling off his coat. "You have acted like a scoundrel; you have deceived Zodomirsky and his seconds, and, in five minutes if your dead body is not lying at my feet, there is no such thing as justice."

Stamm was visibly confused. He had not bargained for this.

"And if the Captain does not kill you, I will!" said Naletoff.

"Or I!" "Or I!" cried with one voice all the officers.

"The devil! I cannot fight with you all," replied Stamm.

"Choose one amongst you, and I will fight with him, though it will not be a duel, but an assassination."

"Reassure yourself, Monsieur," replied Major Belayef, "we will do nothing that the most scrupulous honour can complain of. All our officers are insulted, for under their uniform you have conducted yourself like a rascal. You cannot fight with all; it is even probable you will fight with none. Hold yourself in readiness, then. You are to be judged. Gentlemen, will you approach?"

We surrounded the Major, and the fiat went forth without discussion. Everyone was of the same opinion.

Then the Major, who had played the *role* of president, approached Stamm, and said to him—

"Monsieur, you are lost to all the laws of honour. Your crime was premeditated in cold blood. You have made M. Zodomirsky pass through all the sensations of a man condemned to death, whilst you were perfectly at ease, you who knew that the pistols were not loaded. Finally, you have refused to fight with the man whom you have doubly insulted."

"Load the pistols! load them!" cried Stamm, exasperated. "I will fight with anyone!"

But the Major shook his head with a smile of contempt.

"No, Monsieur Lieutenant," he said, "you will fight no more with your comrades. You have stained your uniform. We can no longer serve with you. The officers have charged me to say that, not wishing to make your deficiencies known to the Government, they ask you to give in your resignation on the cause of bad health. The surgeon will sign all necessary certificates. Today is the 3rd of May: you have from now to the 3rd of June to quit the regiment."

"I will quit it, certainly; not because it is your desire, but mine," said Stamm, picking up his sabre and putting on his coat.

Then he leapt upon his horse, and galloped off towards the village, casting a last malediction to us all.

We all pressed round Zodomirsky. He was sad; more than sad, gloomy.

"Why did you force me to consent to this scoundrel's conditions, gentlemen?" he said. "Without you, I should never have accepted them."

"My comrades and I," said the Major, "will take all the responsibility. You have acted nobly, and I must tell you in the name of us all, M. Zodomirsky, that you are a man of honour." Then, turning to the officers: "Let us go, gentlemen, we must inform the Colonel of what has passed."

We mounted into the carriages. As we did so we saw Stamm in the distance galloping up the mountain side from the village upon his horse. Zodomirsky's eyes followed him.

"I know not what presentiment torments me," he said, "but I wish his pistol had been loaded, and that he had fired."

He uttered a deep sigh, then shook his head, as if with that he could disperse his gloomy thoughts.

"Home," he called to the driver.

We took the same route that we had come by, and consequently again passed Mariana Ravensky's window. Each of us looked up, but Mariana was no longer there.

"Captain," said Zodomirsky, "will you render me a service?"

"Whatever you wish," I replied.

"I count upon you to tell my poor Mariana the result of this miserable affair."

"I will do so. And when?"

"Now. The sooner the better. Stop!" cried Zodomirsky to the coachman. He stopped, and I descended, and the carriage drove on.

Zodomirsky had hardly entered when he saw me appear in the doorway of the saloon. Without doubt my face was pale, and wore a look of consternation, for Zodomirsky sprang towards me, crying—

"Great heavens, Captain! What has happened?"

I drew him from the saloon.

"My poor friend, haste, if you wish to see Mariana alive. She was at her window; she saw Stamm gallop past. Stamm being alive, it followed that you were dead. She uttered a cry, and fell. From that moment she has never opened her eyes."

"Oh, my presentiments!" cried Zodomirsky, "my presentiments!" and he rushed, hatless and without his sabre, into the street.

On the staircase of Mlle Ravensky's house he met the doctor, who was coming down.

"Doctor," he cried, stopping him, "she is better, is she not?"

"Yes," he answered, "better, because she suffers no more."

"Dead!" murmured Zodomirsky, growing white, and supporting himself against the wall. "Dead!"

"I always told her, poor girl! that, having a weak heart, she must avoid all emotion—"

But Zodomirsky had ceased to listen. He sprang up the steps, crossed the hall and the saloon, calling like a madman—

"Mariana! Mariana!"

At the door of the sleeping chamber stood Mariana's old nurse, who tried to bar his progress. He pushed by her, and entered the room.

Mariana was lying motionless and pale upon her bed. Her face was calm as if she slept. Zodomirsky threw himself upon his knees by the bedside, and seized her hand.

It was cold, and in it was clenched a curl of black hair.

"My hair!" cried Zodomirsky, bursting into sobs. "Yes, yours," said the old nurse, "your hair that she cut off herself on quitting you at St Petersburg. I have often told her it would bring misfortune to one of you."

If anyone desires to learn what became of Zodomirsky, let him inquire for Brother Vassili, at the Monastery of Troitza.

The holy brothers will show the visitor his tomb. They know neither his real name, nor the causes which, at twenty-six, had made him take the robe of a monk. Only they say, vaguely, that it was after a great sorrow, caused by the death of a woman whom he loved.

HIGH AND MIGHTY

Tim Lebbon

Although some wars of the nineteenth century are firmly registered in our minds (the Napoleonic Wars, the Crimean War and the American Civil War perhaps being the most memorable) there are others which are virtually forgotten. Amongst these are the two wars Britain fought with China over the trade in opium – the so-called Opium Wars.

Britain tried to force China to open its ports to trade because opium was important to British commerce in the Far East. It was as a result of the First Opium War, which dragged on from 1839 to 1842, that Hong Kong was occupied and eventually ceded to Britain. The following story is set at the start of the First Opium War. Tim Lebbon is a relatively new author whose books Mesmer *(1997) and* Faith in the Flesh *(1998) attracted a lot of attention. His stories, several of unrelenting horror, have appeared in many small-press magazines. The following was written specially for this anthology.*

Everything here was different: the smells, the sounds, the sights. The air held echoes of a magical past, and even the water seemed to move unusually past the slicing bow of the boat. Soon, Captain Riley knew, the peace in this small part of China would be broken and people would begin to die. Soon it would be time for war, in a place where peace seemed to fit the landscape as snugly as a glove. For now, though, and until the fighting began, he had his own private battle. A fight for acceptance and understanding from his men. A struggle to convince himself he had made the right choice joining the marines, when his uncle had offered a perfectly respectable partnership in his cabinet-making business. The never-ending conflict with his nerves, traitors whenever faced with a threat. He fisted his hands and his nails dug into his palms. The pain convinced him that he was still alive . . . alive, and going to war.

It was 1839 and a new decade would soon begin, yet conflicts still erupted over the most trivial of matters. This time, drugs. The import of opium, to a China whose government objected. So foolish . . .

Riley sighed and closed his eyes, sensing his body following the rhythms of the swell. There was no reason for his men to mistrust him, he knew, other than . . . well, if they didn't need to know, he wouldn't have to tell them. Some things are best left unsaid, forever. It was their first mission together, true, but if it did get sticky they were all highly trained and perfectly capable of taking care of themselves. They were Royal Marines, after all. So he concentrated on nothing in particular, let his senses move with their surroundings, and soon he was relaxed and, almost, content. The motion of the boat, the quiet chatter of the soldiers, the singing of strange wildlife, the whisper of water smoothing the hull, their wake tumbling onto the riverbank behind them . . . lulling, soporific. Sensations that belonged nowhere near a battlefield.

The impact came like the thump of a cannon in his ears. Riley tried to jump to his feet but the deck of the boat thwarted him, spilling him sideways into the cabin, then back towards the gunwhale as the bow rose up three feet into the air. Arms spinning, he felt himself heading for a drenching. Shouting and cursing exploded around him. There was a splash as someone fell into the river, then another, followed closely by spluttered coughs.

A hand clasped Riley's upper arm and hauled him down to the deck. He fell heavily onto his left cheek and a rush of blood down his throat made his stomach turn.

"Alright, Sir?" a voice said.

Riley looked into the scared but calm eyes of one of his riflemen. He was ashamed that he could not remember the lad's name. "Yes. Thanks."

The men were already ushering order into the situation, some of them looking automatically to Riley, others checking their equipment or helping the two who had fallen overboard climb back into the boat. The boat, which was now bow-up and pivoting on the submerged rock that had pierced its hull.

"Get yourselves together, you lot," he said gruffly, more for his own benefit than for that of his men. If he acted quickly he would not have time to think about what had happened. "You, you, get below and check out what's happening. You . . . Sergeant Edwards . . . can you swim?" Edwards was a bull of a man, tall and stout, a mass of muscle and bad attitude, who Riley had already marked as someone to get under his control as soon as possible. No room for loose cannons or looser tongues out here.

" 'Course I can," Edwards said, with just too little disrespect to warrant comment. "You want me to tow the boat, Sir?"

Riley shook his head and realized he was spraying blood. He wiped his mouth, felt a brief but terrible moment of nausea and dizziness sweep through him . . . to collapse at the sight of his own blood, what the hell would they think, how in Heaven would he recover from that? . . . before he nodded at the shore. It was thirty feet away, the banks hidden by a beard of undergrowth nosing down to trail tendrils into the water.

"Want you to tie a line around yourself, swim to the bank and secure it to a tree. We'll tie the other end here. Make it high up so we can get the supplies across without getting them wet."

"Sir." Edwards held up his arms while another soldier tied a rope around his chest.

"Circling us already, look, like we're fresh meat," one of the young marines said, staring up into the burning blue sky.

Riley followed his gaze and saw several birds – too far away to identify – circling the stranded boat. At that moment the two men he had sent below came back up with the captain and the crew from the engine room.

"We're finished, Sir," one of them said. "A hole as big as a house in the front of the boat, we'll go down as soon as the tide lifts us from this rock."

Edwards splashed into the river and set out for the bank, pulling his way through the water with long, strong strokes. He cut through as if there was no such thing as tide, and within minutes he had climbed a tree and tied the rope six feet above river level.

With one more glance at the circling birds Riley nodded to his men, and they set about transferring all their equipment ashore. He wondered just what any Chinese army units would think of the birds if they happened to spot them from a distance. And all too soon he found out.

The first shot splashed into the water between two of the soldiers. The second and third missed as well, but the fourth spat a gob of blood from the neck of one of the boat crew and the lad slid quickly below the water and out of sight.

Riley gasped. He'd seen men die, but never this close, never this bloodily. And never under his command. "Shore!" he shouted. "Shore, covering fire!" He barely realized that none of them knew just where the shots were coming from.

The men on shore opened up, popping shot wildly into the foliage along the bank. The returning fire was calm and patient. By the time Riley had hauled his way through the rushes at the riverbank his heart was an almost indistinguishable blur, his breath misted blood into the air from his slashed tongue, and the boat captain and a marine were dead.

"Into the trees!" he said quickly, but the order was unnecessary.

They turned right almost immediately, in their previous direction of travel. The Manchu troops' matchlock rifles still coughed behind them, but the firing was aimless now that they were hidden from view.

"Come on," Riley said, "let's get some distance between us."

"Don't you want to leave a couple of men to lay down some covering fire?" Edwards asked.

For a moment Riley was confused. Of course, this man had seen battle several times before, he'd been in the thick of it and he held a shoulder-full of scars to prove it. He must know what he was on about. He must be right. But Riley shook his head, training overcoming nerves and fear and other human things, things the military tried to ignore.

"No, we all go. We're not here to engage the enemy, we're here to rescue some stupid bloody traders and a drunken old priest." He nodded to a private who stood with his back against a tree. "Wilkins, you lead the way. North, always north."

Riley stood back and let the men set off ahead of him, ducking occasionally as a Chinese soldier took an opportunistic shot into the treeline. As Edwards brushed by, Riley tapped him on the shoulder and held him with his stare. "Edwards, I respect the fact that you've seen more action than me. But you're my sergeant. You're here to back me up, not question my orders."

"I'm here to make sure I don't die, Sir. You think I want to get killed because some English toff gets in a bloody twist because he can't buy his Chinese goodies any more? Sometimes it's wrong to fight, as a soldier you should know that more than anyone."

"I don't care for your morals, Edwards, I care about my command. And if it's compromised by you again, you'll be arrested as soon as we get back to our own side. Got it?"

Edwards nodded.

"Got it?"

"Got it, Sir."

"Right. Let's go. And no hard feelings, Edwards?"

Edwards shook his head. "You're the boss. Sir."

★   ★   ★

When Riley was fifteen his father told him that he was a runt, a wastling, and that he would never amount to anything. His father was a cruel man, someone who rarely considered the results of his actions, nor wondered why people spent so much time crying around him. In a way Riley felt sorry for him now, because he truly believed that he had not been an intentionally nasty man. He had no feelings for anyone, but then he had no thoughts for himself either. His soul was a vacuum. When he died, few mourned, but his mother followed on soon after.

His father's brother – his uncle the cabinet maker – had tried to encourage Riley to seek education rather than wallow in the unfairness of life. Riley thought the offer of a partnership had been more out of pity than anything else, and that's why he had refused it. That was why he was now a soldier instead of a cabinet maker, dodging bullets in a wooded valley thousands of miles from home instead of honing, filing, fixing and jointing. And there lay the worst dilemma – Riley wanted that job with his uncle more than anything. He'd never thought of himself as proud. Perhaps with his refusal he had proven himself wrong.

There were sixteen of them rushing through the trees, flinching occasionally as a matchlock sounded from somewhere far behind. They were well out of range by now – the Chinese obviously had not been able to follow them – but the sounds harassed all the same. Strange birds took flight, startled by the running men and the intermittent shots. Riley had made his way to the front and replaced Wilkins; an unusual role for a captain, but he was keen to prove himself, both to himself and his men.

He should have been mapping, he knew, noting landmarks and plotting the course of the river for any future incursions. But he was too frightened. With every step, he expected a rifle to poke between the trees and blow his brains out. With every step he began saying his goodbyes, but each thought was halted and restarted again by the next footfall.

They had a good idea of where the traders and the priest were holed up. One of their number had escaped and floated down-river on a fallen tree, miraculously evading capture and eventually drifting far enough into the bay to be picked up by an East India Company steamer. He was delirious from thirst and half-baked by the sun, but he still gave directions to locate the rest of his party. Hearing them third hand and following them on the ground, however, were two different things.

Two hours after setting out from the river, they came to the edge of the woods.

"This the right village?" Edwards asked.

Riley nodded, shrugged. "I think so." He guessed they had come around four miles since the boat had been holed. It felt like forty. His clothes were still wet, his boots tightening as they dried, pinching his skin into blisters. He looked at the faces of his men, pale and expectant where they stood around and awaited his decision. Not for the first time he experienced a rush of panic at the responsibility he had; they respected Edwards more, he was sure, but he was the officer, he was in charge, his was the task to get them where they were going and home again. They looked up to him, even as they looked down upon him.

His father would have surely laughed.

Before them was a flooded rice field, the glittering spread of water interrupted here and there by the humps of rocks protruding from the ground. Its edges were raised to form walkways, and hedges stood at either side to separate it from the adjoining fields. Beyond the field lay the first of the buildings, with their gracefully curved roofs and patterned walls. Way beyond the village, a range of low mountains sat shrouded in mist.

"Right, Wilkins and you . . . er, Patterson. Try to get around the edge of this field, keep low, keep close to the trees in the hedge, use their shadows. Get as close as you can to the buildings on the outskirts and try to see up into the village. According to the chap who came out, Tenghi has a temple at its northern extreme. If you can see it, I reckon we might have the right place. But I want to be sure."

"Why not just storm in there," one of the marines said. He chewed on tobacco and scratched at mosquitoes nestling behind his ears. "We've got surprise on our side, and if you don't mind me saying, Chinese riflemen probably close up our arse."

There was a general mumble of agreement and Riley let it live on for a while. Once more his confidence hunkered down, settling back under the penumbra of doubt as he realized that these men had already fought together, long before he had been with them. They would know what they were talking about; they were wise in the practice of war, whereas he scored only in mere theory.

He shook his head. "No." And for an awful few seconds he thought they were going to scoff.

"Captain's right," Edwards said. "We don't know for sure this is Tenghi. We don't even know for sure that madman gave the right directions. So we post three men five hundred yards behind us and Wilkins and Patterson do as Captain Riley says. What if we storm the village and find a dozen barrack buildings full of heavily armed Chinese? There's no way I want to kiss all your horrible backsides goodbye!"

Expressions changed, heads nodded. Wilkins and Patterson moved off immediately into the field.

Riley nodded his thanks at Edwards, but he received nothing in return. His uncle had once explained the art of jointing. It was not just cutting and chiselling to fit, he had said, it was anticipating the join, estimating the shrinkage or expansion due to moisture, following the grain, allowing for stress and strain. A good joint between two pieces of wood would be as strong as the wood itself, so that a quality piece of furniture may as well have been carved out of one tree. Riley tried to compare how he and his men were fitting together, and it was not a pretty sight. Joints split and splayed. The wood splintered. Weak. Three dead already, drifting in a foreign river because they had not had a chance to retrieve their bodies.

Riley leaned back against a tree and closed his eyes. But he saw only black, so he opened them again to watch the two men approach the village.

Wilkins went first, stepping gingerly through the waters at the edge of the field. Patterson followed close behind. They had both left their weapons – if they were spotted the men in the trees would have to give them covering fire to aid their escape. They reached the raised perimeter and edged around the field using bushes and shadows as cover. Soon they were invisible, so Riley concentrated on where he thought they *might* be.

Minutes dragged by. The hustle of the village gave Riley a strange longing for home. The language was different, the sights and smells were different, but here was a community of people happy in their day, comfortable with each other. If only he could say the same.

The men reappeared suddenly, and a few of those staring across the field jumped and raised their guns. Wilkins and Patterson grinned and scurried beneath the trees, straightening and twisting the aches and groans from their backs.

"It's Tenghi," Wilkins said. "The temple's in the right place, anyway." He went to flick a leaf from his beard and a gout of blood exploded from his neck.

The gunshot sounded as Wilkins slumped to the ground. In the woods shapes were racing through the trees, dodging left and right with frightening dexterity. Whatever trail they had left, the Chinese had found it.

Behind them, an attacking force. In front of them, an enemy village, perhaps with army units stationed inside.

"Across the field, now!" Riley called.

"What!?"

He did not know who had shouted the incredulous question; he never did find out. The world exploded into a chaos of bullets and bangs, screams and shouts. And they were running for their lives.

As he splashed ankle-deep across the field, Riley had a strange sense of things coming apart. The tenuous joints and junctions in the unit were already at breaking point, and the panic caused by the sudden attack added the strain necessary to cause permanent fractures. The wind rushed through his hair from one direction and he felt the breeze of passing bullets from the other. Both ways spelled trouble, but one way spelled certain death. His order could not have been wrong, could it? Was there anything else they could have done?

Someone fell just in front of him, one of the men whose name he did not know, one of his men. An anonymous death in a foreign field . . . but he was not dead. As Riley ran with the rest of the men he heard the fallen soldier begin to scream, partly in agony, partly from fear of what the Chinese would do when they caught up to him. There were stories, terrible stories . . . Riley did not believe a word of them, of course . . . but still . . .

He turned and saw the pursuing Chinese swarm from under the cover of the trees. They rapidly approached the fallen, screaming soldier and passed him by. In the rage of the moment, Riley did not see what happened to him.

Death was here, now, pecking at his back, and it would only be a matter of luck if he survived the next few moments.

They were almost across the field and into the village. Edwards and Patterson reached the first of the buildings, slid to the ground and turned their rifles on the advancing enemy. Riley heard and felt bullets tearing the air both ways around him as a stand-off developed, the Chinese falling to their stomachs in the field and perhaps, for the first time, realizing their mistake.

Riley and the rest of his men reached the village, found cover and laid down a defensive fire over the heads of the Chinese. Water splashed as shot impacted, and occasionally other stuff would spurt into the air and a scream or a grunt would mark another direct hit. This was war, death, pain and useless suffering. Not for the first time in his short career, Riley wished he could simply stand, hold up his hand and instigate a ceasefire. Then he could go and talk with the enemy, try to get over to them how pointless this all was, how bloody foolishly pointless . . . and he knew that was his uncle talking in his head, planting surreptitious seeds of pacifism in the mind of a soldier.

"Where to?" he heard one of his men shout.

For a second Riley almost followed his idea through. He went to stand, raise his hand, but he knew that he would be dead in an instant. Peace was a fine idea, but it was about as likely as constant daylight. Instead he looked back into the village and saw that their battle had already cleared the streets. Dogs ran here and there, a few horses hoofed the ground in agitation, shifting their carts back and forth.

"Edwards!" he called. The sergeant was several feet away, hunkered down behind a low stone wall. "What do you think?"

Seemingly unsurprised at his commanding officer asking his advice, Edwards came out with his answer straight away. "If we go back into the village and lose ourselves in the buildings, we drop our advantage: numbers. I say we stay together and try to get to where the traders are holing up. Then wait for rescue when the fleet realizes we're trapped."

Riley nodded and hoped he kept the grimace from his face. *Rescue*, he thought. *Not likely*. But that was for later, not now. Now, they had to stick together.

"Fall back!" he shouted. "Through the village. Patterson, lead the way."

The men did not need to hear the order twice. Loosing another couple of rounds into the rice field they scurried back, low and fast, moving into the village so that there were more sheltering buildings between them and the angry enemy. Riley went with them, keeping his eyes glued on Patterson where he worked his way through the village towards the temple at the far end.

Faces peered from behind doors, frightened faces, hands clawed around the door jambs like claws, eyes wide open and white with fear. Children screamed and mothers shouted, dogs barked and doors slammed as the men dodged their way from house to house. Army boots thundered on a timber walkway, each footstep sounding like another gunshot in the cacophony of battle.

From the shouting behind them Riley knew that the enemy had entered the village.

"You and you," he said, pausing to talk to the two men behind him, "stay here and try to hold them off for a couple of minutes." He tried not to look into the eyes of the soldiers to whom he had just issued suicidal orders. He wondered what his uncle would think, but tried to push the thought aside instantly. Head down – still terrified, but that feeling now tempered by an acidic shame – Riley ran on. The stale taste of fear coated his tongue. He thought he could feel the very spot on his back where he was going to be shot.

He heard a frantic few seconds of gunfire and then the sounds of pursuit once more.

Patterson had reached the temple and was crouching down on its steps, seemingly confused about which direction to take. The enemy's gods watched Riley wave his men to the right, and soon they exited the village into a wild field of long grasses, dips in the landscape, rocky outcrops and lonely clumps of trees to hide behind. Once more the men laid down a covering fire, trapping the Chinese at the outskirts of the village, reversing the position of minutes before but still maintaining the advantage.

"Edwards!" Riley called, glad to see that the big man had kept close to him. "The traders are hiding a couple of miles east of here, if that chap's story was true. We need to get there."

Edwards nodded. "I agree. We can hold this lot off and wait for rescue."

Riley cringed inside. There would be no rescue. This was a mistake, it was all a dreadful mistake, but he could not bear to tell Edwards that, not yet, not now. Not while death still buzzed by their heads.

"We need to leave two men behind to hold them for a while," Riley said quietly.

Edwards nodded. "I'll stay and—"

"Not you. You come with me." Riley hoped Edwards could not hear the desperation, the fear in his voice. It was not something the big man would respect. Riley hurried off across open ground to talk to two men sheltering behind a rock.

"Give us a couple of minutes if you can, then follow," he said to wide, frightened eyes. He did not want to know what these men were thinking as he issued them their death sentence. "We're going due east, about two miles, hopefully we'll find the trading party there. If you can hold them off . . . give us enough time . . . they may not find us again. And you can lay low and join us when they've given up looking." A shot whined off the rock above his head and Riley flinched, his heart jumping, sudden images of splintered timber leaking fresh sap leaping to mind.

"Right, Sir," one of the men said. The other – barely more than a boy – could only nod. He reminded Riley of himself ten years younger.

He ran back to Edwards. "We'll pull back directly away from the enemy, keeping cover, try not to let him see we're moving."

"Why can't we just give them a stand-up fight?" Edwards asked, but quietly. However much he lacked respect for Riley, at least he still honoured his position.

"We've lost seven men already," Riley said. "I don't want to lose any more."

"But—"

"Do you know what it's like, Sergeant? Asking someone to stay behind and let the bulk of us pull back? Have you any idea?"

"They're trained. They're paid to fight."

Riley looked at the two soldiers readying themselves to die. "I only see two boys."

Don't fight with the wood, his uncle had said. Let it show you what's inside it; don't force it out. Nature has a way about it, all you have to do is to feel it and you'll be a success.

Riley had tried, he really had. But things never seemed to flow around him. He was like a dam, stemming the tide of natural progression, forcing all the junctions in his life into shapes and contortions that did not fit right at all. Now, in a foreign country with its soldiers doing nothing more than trying to protect their own, he sensed the tenuous joints of his company finally springing loose. They may be running together, hiding together – dying together – but in many ways, it was already every man for himself.

They found the trading party half an hour later. There was a dip in the hillside – perhaps an old mine working – which was now virtually covered in with trees and shrubs. As they passed there was a whistle from beneath the trees and a figure emerged from the shadows. The marines, shaken and exhausted by the running fight from the river, almost opened fire. But the man was obviously European: tall and pale; plainly dressed; smoking a pipe.

"Wondered when you people would get here," he said sardonically. "Come on in. We're having a party."

Riley stepped forward. "Who are you?" he asked breathlessly.

"Murphy." He puffed his pipe for a few more seconds as he gave Riley and his men a frank appraisal. "So Peter actually got through and made it downriver? Never thought the mad bastard would survive."

"Someone was picked up out in the bay. I assume he was your man."

Murphy laughed out loud, spitting a spray of saliva over Riley's still-wet uniform. "You bloody officers," he gasped, "always so proper! 'My man', as you called him, is a whinging bloody idiot most times." He shook his head and stared at his pipe, compressing the contents of the bowl with a rough, callused finger. "Though on this occasion, he may just have saved out lives."

"You have a priest with you?"

Murphy looked to the sky and then shrugged. "Our Christian mercenary. Chap think he's Lord God Almighty. A little too much of our product, truth be told."

"He's drugged?"

"Drugged himself. Found him indulging in my opium the first day we were trapped, he's not let up since." Murphy looked warily over Riley's shoulders, back across the rolling landscape towards the village hidden behind sleeping hills. "Still, he's entertaining. You a religious man, Captain . . .?"

"Riley."

"Captain Riley . . . you a religious man?"

Riley nodded because he knew that he should.

Murphy smiled and turned. "You'll not like our priest, then."

The traders had been in the cave for four nights. Its entrance was hidden beneath a lip of rock, which itself was sheltered by the wooded hollow from which Murphy had first emerged. There were three traders and the priest, Father O'Dwyer, who was much as Murphy had suggested – inebriated on opium and with an aggravated sense of self-importance. He sat regally in the corner, a bundle of robes and smoke, and occasional shouted curses towards anyone watching him.

On entering the cave the marines had immediately relaxed and let the cool atmosphere draw the tension from their bodies. Edwards posted two men in the hollow, overlooking the landscape they had just traversed and watching out for any pursuing Chinese. An hour after their arrival the two soldiers from the rear guard appeared across the fields, and the men in the hollow signalled them over. One had a bullet graze to his head, but other than that they were fine. They were sure they had not been followed, they said. Yes, they were positive. Absolutely.

Their reappearance – their survival – should have made Riley elated. But he was far too tired.

He sat back against a rock and closed his eyes, listening to the heavy breathing around him as the men caught their breath. Murphy was busy telling them all about how they had evaded capture, hidden themselves away, how he should have been a soldier . . .

"So when they killed that priest upriver and the Chinese army moved in, we knew we had to go. They'd confiscated opium from other traders and destroyed it – killed a couple of the traders, ate them too, evidently – so I thought, bugger that, I'm not getting eaten. Off we went, then we were spotted and . . ."

Soon, Riley knew, he was going to have to tell his men the truth, come clean, probably put himself in danger of a lynching. And there was no easy way of explaining what he had done other than sounding like a complete fool: *I wanted to prove myself.*

Who to? they would ask. *Me. And you. And the Admiralty.* Oh yes, that would go down very well. They'd likely shoot him.

"So are you the rescue party?" Father O'Dwyer asked sarcastically, pre-empting Riley and paving the way for his confession.

"Yes, but I suppose we need rescuing now." Edwards did not even glance up, but still Riley felt every soldier's cool attention suddenly focused on him.

Surely they could not lay blame? The rock in the river was not his fault; the ambush was bad luck; and at least they'd found the trading party and shelter. But there was a real feeling of antagonism in the cave, and seven dead men outside. Maybe nothing could make things any worse.

"There won't be a rescue," Riley said quickly.

"What?" Edwards snapped.

"I . . . volunteered us for this mission. In and out on our own. No other resources."

"You volunteered? And you didn't tell us? Why the hell would you want to do that?" Edwards was already on his feet, hands fisting by his sides.

Because I wanted to prove myself, Riley thought again. But he could never say such a thing. "All that matters is that we get back," he muttered instead.

"What about Wilkins and Jonesy, and those others lying dead across the bloody landscape?"

Riley looked down at his feet, unable to answer.

"What about them, you useless bastard!" Edwards shouted.

Riley sensed the big sergeant leaping at him, but there was no impact. When he looked up he saw a struggling shape on the floor, and it took him a few seconds to realize that it was Edwards and Murphy, rolling and punching and grunting. The soldier was big and strong but Murphy was wiry and supple, and Edwards was tired from the excesses of stress over the last hour. Soon the fight calmed down. Murphy sat on Edwards, who was face down on the floor of the cave.

Guns came to bear.

Soldiers aimed at traders, the very people they had come to rescue.

The moment thickened and stretched. It was very ugly. *Make or break*, Riley thought. It was a phrase his uncle used when he was trying to repair damaged goods.

From the corner of the cave a bitter laugh broke out, then a hacking cough, and then the priest stood slowly and walked in front of the guns. "Murder me, you bastards, and you'll see the fury of God!"

Riley stood and backed away, sure for a terrible moment that the guns would cough death and the purpose of their mission would be no more. But then someone laughed. It may have been Patterson, or perhaps it was one of Murphy's traders. Whoever, it caused an infectious amusement to shimmer through the cave, provoking more giggles when the inebriated priest opened his arms wide and stared at the rocky ceiling, inviting sacrifice.

"Bloody fool," Murphy said, standing and helping Edwards to his feet. The big sergeant brushed himself down and glared across at Riley, but the fight had gone from him.

"Be cruel in the eyes of God, you damn murderers, and you'll know his wrath!"

"We're not murderers," one of the soldiers said.

"All of you are, all of you."

"Shut up and smoke some more, Father."

"Killers, murderers, rapists—"

Murphy hit him. It was a slap more than a punch but it carried some force. The priest staggered sideways for a while, then leant against the wall, sliding down slowly and mumbling to himself all the way. When he was finally sitting he puffed some more at his pipe, pressed the contents down and glared around him.

"Now then," Murphy said, and the first shots rang out.

It all happened so quickly that Riley did not have a chance to think, let alone consider issuing orders.

The cave entrance darkened for a time as several dashing shapes came in. There were shots, screams, the clash of steel against steel as bayonets and swords sparked in the gloom. More shots, then Edwards shouting out a hoarse cry. Riley could make no sense there; it was a war cry, a scream composed of terror, rage and vigour. The big man charged at the several Chinese soldiers who had rushed the cave. He shouldered the first one aside, slashed out at the second as he reached him, shot the third. His men opened up as well, charging forward, knowing from experience what Riley was only just beginning to realize from his months of sterile training: that if they were trapped inside the cave, they would be finished. The Chinese would burn them out or starve them to death.

Riley unsheathed his sword and leapt forward. He saw Murphy hugging himself into the shadows, crouching down to offer as small a target as possible. Bullets kissed sparks from the rock and showered them down onto the trader's shoulders. He buried his face in his hands.

At the cave entrance there was a knot of men shouting in different languages, all words bearing the same meaning. This was life or death, a hand-to-hand fight to the end, with bayonets and fists and teeth if necessary; shot twisting its way indiscriminately into flesh and bone, blood smearing stone, screams echoing within and without. Riley held back, saw Edwards struggling under two Chinese soldiers, stepped forward and slashed out at one of them. The man's head whipped to the side, part of it flicking upwards on a red mist. Riley had never killed a man before.

Edwards was up on his knees, bashing his arms suddenly into his second aggressor's crotch, then stabbing him in the face when he was down. The sergeant merely glanced at Riley before standing and charging through the cave mouth, out into the open where the sunshine could expose the blood splashed across his uniform. Riley followed. There was little else he could do. On his way outside he stepped on dead and dying men.

Edwards and two others were already crouched down, shooting at the enemy. Chinese soldiers were perched on the lip of the hollow, peering beneath the overhanging trees to see where the shots were coming from. Just as Riley reached Edwards the big man stood once again, an image of hell in his blood-spattered uniform, his hip and trouser leg dark from blood that may have been his own. He shouted again, another guttural, animal cry, and ran up the small slope. His men followed. Riley followed them.

Even before he could see across the surrounding fields and hillside, Riley knew that the Chinese were retreating. He heard their panicked shouts moving away and the gunfire had changed, too. Where before it was incoming and outgoing, now it was only his own men firing.

"Now we're done for!" one of the men shouted, sweat and tears staining the neck of his uniform. "Done for now! No rescue, they know where we are, only a matter of time until—"

"Shut it!" Edwards roared. The battle had enlarged him, opening up his fearsome soul and affording him a terrible gravity. He was the man in charge, Riley realized. Edwards was the leader here, the one they all looked up to. He was the fighter, the warrior, the cold-blooded killer. He held the life of every remaining soldier in his hand, and in him they found some form of comfort.

Riley was just a sad man's son who should have been a woodworker.

And then Edwards turned to Riley, his face mucky and spotted with another man's blood. "What now, Sir?" he asked.

Riley tried not to look aghast. Over the last few hours he had come to know the inadequacy of his command, the fact that his musings on the morality of war lessened his ability to fight it. He had turned to Edwards at every step, and now here was his sergeant, awaiting his orders like any good soldier. It was for effect, of course. It was to make sure things held together in the eyes of the men. Edwards was the glue that would bind the wounded group, and if they were skilful enough the break may never be seen.

Riley stood and glanced over the rim of the hollow. A shot rang out and he ducked down, gasping for breath sucked out by fear. "Pinned down," he said. "We don't know how many of them there are."

"Could be lots more by morning," Edwards said carefully.

He's steering me, Riley thought. *Nudging me towards what he thinks is the right decision. Fight our way out. Shoot our way back to the river.*

"How is the powder and shot?" he asked.

"Low."

"We've got a mad old priest, a few traders who we were sent to save—"

"Sent?"

Riley glanced past Edwards' shoulder, unable to meet his gaze. "Who we came to save, then. Whatever. We run out into that, we all die."

"And the alternative is?" Edwards was doing it again, trying to edge him towards issuing the order to run and fight, fight and run . . .

Riley knelt and stared up into the tree canopy. He wondered what sights these trees had seen in their hundred year life, and what they would see in the future. Would they hold those visions in their gnarled arms until someone came along – a woodworker perhaps – to peel away the pretence and expose the ideas for what they were?

Crazy thoughts, but comforting. At least they took him away from where and when he was, if only for a moment.

One thing Riley did not want them to see was another dead man.

"We stay," he said. "If we run, we die. If we stay, there's a chance we can think of another way out."

"You've doomed us, you stupid bastard. Every last one of us!" Edwards spat into his face. Riley stood his ground, though his heart sought to topple him. And that was the only time Edwards ever openly offended him.

Five men remained at the edge of the hollow, exchanging the occasional shots with the Chinese when the enemy became daring and tried to crawl too near; then reloading, firing again. The Manchu forces' excited chatter could be heard over the birds and the breeze in the trees, and Riley knew it was only a matter of time before they rushed in and forced a showdown. But for now it was stalemate; a very uncertain one, perhaps, and probably uneven. But there still may be time to think of something else.

In the cave, the priest was on form. And there was a distinct change in atmosphere.

Murphy was sitting towards the dark rear of the cave, hidden in shadows and talking quietly, nostalgically of home. His men were brewing tea for the marines, explaining excitedly how they had bought it from a village up in the hills, it was fresh and pure. It was like nothing they'd ever tasted before. They drank, the marines drank, faces were pulled. Something was wrong with the water; perhaps because they'd collected it dripping from the cave walls.

"Pray to God, you murdering bastards!"

Murphy stood and strode casually to the priest, and Riley saw that he was smoking his goods as well. "Father, there's no time at the present for war or religion. But I'm sure we'll have need of them both again soon." He looked up at Riley and smiled.

Riley could not smile back. Somehow, the display was obscene. There were three dead men in the cave, Chinese, hauled across the floor and left against the cave wall. Their wounds had painted tracks on the rock, firelight flickered in glassy eyes giving a horrible semblance of life. No, this was no time for joking.

Riley sat down and watched his troops. The men he had condemned to probable death. By rights they should have shot him long before now, but training was always the last stumbling block against true anger. He realized, perhaps for the first time, what an alien he was to them. An officer, a toff – it may surprise them to know what a humble background he had come from – someone employed to lead them into battle and death. They could obey him, but they did not have to respect and trust him. Those things had to be earned.

He had to get them home.

He vowed there and then that when they made it back to the fleet, he would resign immediately. Take up cabinet-making when they arrived back in Britain.

He closed his eyes, wishing he had his pipe. And opened them again. And breathed in deeply. And suddenly the uselessness descending like a fine mist was dispersed by the heat of an idea.

"Sergeant!" he called.

Edwards sauntered over, still wiping at his bloodied face with a damp cloth, holding his side where a stray bullet had nicked the skin.

"Edwards, listen. I have an idea to get us out of here. And not one more man has to die, on either side."

Grudgingly, the big man sat down to listen.

There were three of them: Edwards, Patterson and Riley. It was not his job, Riley knew, going out into the field. He should have ordered one of the men to take his place. But guilt wore a heavier burden than duty this day.

His idea was a simple one, but it had almost been scuppered before it even began. The traders did not want to give up their stock. Riley had bargained with them at first, saying that for half of their stock they would be paid with their survival. Still Murphy and his men said no, no way, they were taking their goods with them when they escaped. Riley's frustration simmered. If this did not work, then they would have to launch themselves into a running battle. The results of that . . .

And then Edwards had changed things around. Blooded and bloodied, his eyes wide and still full of the fight, he only had to rest his hand on his pistol holster for Murphy to change his mind. A few words with his men, a couple of seconds arguing and the heavy bags were thrown at the soldiers' feet.

It was a crazy idea. Any number of things could, and probably would go wrong. But it was also audacious and unexpected, and the surprise element more than anything would work to their advantage.

There was the possibility that the Manchu soldiers had already had a taste of opium. Maybe they would welcome some more.

They left in different directions under the cover of darkness. The soldiers remaining behind popped off the occasional shot to keep the enemies' heads down, and Riley was pretty sure he had not been seen.

He crawled on his stomach through the long grass. The sun was bleeding redly across the horizon, putting an end to this day of carnage and, hopefully, welcoming in a peaceful night. In the twilight he could just make out the ground before him . . . and this was where most risk lay. If he misjudged the distance, he was liable to crawl straight into an enemy soldier. If he stopped short, the breeze may ruin the whole plan. There was so much that could go wrong, and such a small margin of success that, alone and exposed under the darkening sky, he began to realize what a foolish escapade this was.

Edwards had gone for the idea without question. Riley could not believe it was through respect for an officer, because he had done nothing to earn any respect. It must be because the big sergeant believed it could work.

Crazy.

When Riley thought he was nearer the enemy than his own men, he reached back and untied one of the prepared hessian bags from his belt. It was as big as his fist and wrapped a dozen times, hopefully providing something that would burn long and slow. He set it alight and buried it under several handfuls of grass. As it began to smoke he scurried away quickly, setting several more of the packages in this path. It took only five minutes to place them all. The night was silent around him save for the occasional furtive shuffling from the direction of the Chinese, and intermittent warning shots from his men back in the hollow.

His part of the plan complete, Riley threaded his way through the high grasses and back to his men. As he slipped in over the lip he saw Edwards come in from another direction, Patterson having already arrived back safe and sound.

Murphy sat at the cave mouth with a couple of his traders, making sure the priest did not run out ranting and raving, agitating the enemy even more.

"They'll be making their own plans, y'know," Murphy said.

Riley nodded. "Let's hope ours works first."

"Ours?" Edwards asked, an open display of mistrust aimed at his commanding officer.

Riley did not answer. There was nothing he could say. This was it, make or break, and he truly did not believe that they would have any more chances. If this did not work, they would have to rush the enemy: soldiers; traders; mad priest. What a sight they would make, sprinting down the hillside, falling left and right as the Chinese, safely concealed in the landscape they knew so well, picked them off one by one . . .

A silent half-hour later, they heard the first hint of laughter from the darkness.

"We should wait a bit longer," Murphy said. "Let them get the full effect." He was smiling in the dark, moonlight glinting off his uneven teeth. He looked calm and content.

Riley shrugged. "You're the boss." For some reason this seemed extremely funny, and the maniacal laughter coming from within the cave seemed to prove the point. But he was not in the cave, he was outside. In the night. Listening to laughter drifting in across the fields like an artillery barrage.

"Now's the time," Edwards said. "Listen to them. Listen." Even the big sergeant seemed subdued, and Riley was sure he'd seen at least one smile in the last ten minutes.

There was virtually no wind. The fumes and smoke wafted from the burning parcels in the field, spreading like ripples on a pond until the men of both sides breathed it in. It itched at Riley's throat, a strong and stinging presence which quickly became something warmer, and softer.

"I agree," said Riley. "I'll go." And with that he stepped quickly out of the hollow and was on his way across the fields.

He knew that the worst part of forming any wood carving was the final minute adjustments. His uncle sometimes carved features for furniture, simple pieces but perfect nonetheless. Riley had watched him once, edging his way around the piece after most of the work had been done, scraping here, sanding there, his touch as delicate as a butterfly kiss. And the time he had watched was the time his uncle had slipped, sending a chisel across the grain and biting a chunk out of the Madonna's face. Half a second ending several days' work. So much lost.

The art was in the detail.

Riley knew that any mistake in the next few minutes would cancel whatever advantage his small group had gained. And it was his face that would be broken by the results of that failure. He did not want to take a bullet, even if much of the mess they were in was down to him.

The laughter still reached him, and the nearer he edged to the Chinese lines, the more he thought some of it was coming from behind him. The night was cool and clear and calm; surely there could never have been any fighting going on here? Killing, slaughter, hatred of any kind?

He walked on.

Grass kissed his boots and whispered across the material of his trousers. The cool night air danced with the sounds of laughter. And always, the hint of smoke planting acid kisses on the back of his throat.

There were three Chinese soldiers in front of him. They squatted on a bare patch of ground behind a rock formation, all facing inwards, one of them telling a story to the other two. Their shoulders shook, they rumbled with barely restrained hysteria. They turned to look at Riley and their faces changed. The humour dropped from them as if emotion was suddenly subject to gravity.

Riley went to say something, to hold up his hands, to talk. But all he could manage was a pointless, aimless smile.

"We can leave," Riley said.

"What?" Edwards was stretched out against a fallen tree in the hollow, his boots off, his feet bare to the night.

"Quickly. Quietly. And quickly."

"Those guys want to buy any more, you think?" Murphy said, standing and nodding across the dark fields towards the laughter in the dark.

"Quickly and quietly," Riley said again. "That's how we can leave." He frowned and then smiled at the expressions on the other men's faces.

"You murdering bastards!" shouted a voice from the cave.

Riley felt tears melting his face because, in a way, the priest was so very right.

They left in single file. Riley went back to the three soldiers he had met and took Edwards with him. When they arrived they found the three had grown to a dozen, most of whom smiled and waved and muttered in Chinese, grabbing the men's arms and hauling them to the ground to share some unidentifiable meat they had spitted over a fire. Edwards was nervous but calm, Riley was trying to piece things together, sort out exactly what had happened so that he could explain it in his report when they returned. He realized soon enough that there was no real explanation, at least none that would be accepted.

So he ate some of the meat, encouraged Edwards to do the same, and accepted a drink proffered from a water sack.

They departed as soon as they could and caught up with the others. They were no longer a whole unit, but those left held together all the way back to the river and the bay. There was something cementing them now, a grudging respect for the officer none of them even knew.

As the effects of the opium wore off, Riley realized how unlikely all of this was. And he also began to think about what he would carve to grace his first finished piece of furniture. He thought, perhaps, it would be something Chinese.

PERDITA'S WAR

Daphne Wright

At the same time as the First Opium War was happening in China, the First Afghan War had erupted in Afghanistan, with the British seeking to curb Russian expansion. Daphne Wright's interest in the war had been aroused by reading, amongst other books, Emily Eden's Letters from India *(1869) and Lady Sale's remarkable* Journal of the Disasters in Afghanistan *(1843), based on her first hand experience. These books provided the many factual minutiae that flavour Wright's first novel* The Distant Kingdom *(1987), from which the following episode (set in January 1842) has been extracted and revised by the author. The success of that book allowed Daphne to break free from working in publishing to become a full-time writer. She has now established a solid reputation as a writer of crime novels under the name Natasha Cooper.*

It was dark before she woke fully and tried to get up. Her head felt odd, and there were all sorts of small pains pulling at her. A peculiar smell filled her nostrils, sickening in its mixture of rawness and corruption. She traced it to a filthy *poshteen*, which was all that lay between her and the hard-baked earth. Some memory returned and she knew who she was: Perdita, wife of Marcus Beaminster of the 121st Foot. The regiment had been posted to Afghanistan as part of the English garrison. Why was she lying alone on a disgusting sheepskin coat in the dark?

She wondered if she had had another fit and as soon as her brain produced the proposition knew that it must be true. Her tongue was bitten and her head ached as though someone had hit it with an iron bar. She was so tired her limbs felt as though they were made of lead. It must have been a fit. But she couldn't think what she had been doing to bring it on. More smells became recognisable. There were horses close by. It wasn't only their smell she recognized: she could hear bits jangling and hooves knocking against the stony ground, and there was the comforting familiarity of their snorts and whickerings. Had she been riding out? If so, her groom should have been with her.

"Aktur?" she said vaguely.

"Yes, lady-sahib, I am here." She looked towards the voice and saw that he was squatting at the foot of a mulberry tree, watching her, an expression on his dark face that she had not seen before. He looked awed. She dismissed the thought impatiently and held out one hand for him to help her up.

When he had adjusted her stirrup and she had arranged her long, dark-blue serge riding skirt discreetly over her boots, she took the reins. Thanking Aktur, she asked him to tell no one except the lord-sahib what he had seen. Slightly to her surprise, he agreed fervently. They rode back to the cantonment in silence, passing the sentries who saluted her. She hardly saw them as she wrestled with her loathing of the shameful fits that overcame her so rarely but so devastatingly. It was lucky that there had been only Aktur to witness this one.

When she reached the bungalow, she found Marcus waiting

for her in a fret of impatience. Usually the gentlest of men, he glared at her as she stumbled through the doorway.

"There's mud on your skirt. And blood on your lips. Where have you been?"

"I am sorry, Marcus." She put a gloved hand to her head, holding in the pain. "I rode with Aktur to Baba's tomb and then I had one of my turns."

She wondered what his brother-officers and their wives would say when they heard what had happened. They had always thought she was the most unsuitable wife for a man like him, with her lack of breeding, her clumsiness and shortage of conversation. Only Marcus himself seemed to believe she was worth anything very much, but there were still times, even now that they had been married for six years and had a son and daughter, when she felt like a stranger to him, too.

"I thought I was cured," she said apologetically. "I am truly sorry, but I cannot stop the convulsions."

"My dear, forgive me," he said at once, taking her hand and kissing it, "but I was concerned for you. Lieutenant Flecker was fired at this afternoon by a party of tribesmen and I was afraid something of the sort must have happened to you. Come, come and sit down."

He said no more then, but later he asked her not to ride outside the cantonment without his escort or that of another British officer. She agreed hesitantly, unable to ignore the good sense of his prohibition even though she knew she would miss her escape from the stultifying gossip that filled the houses of the English officers.

At first her new imprisonment made little difference, for in the aftermath of the convulsion, she felt too weak to ride and she could not throw off the nagging headache. The children sensed her weakness and behaved so wildly that she left them to their ayah whenever possible until she was strong enough to deal with Charlie's noisy rages and Annie's fears.

Perdita's health recovered soon enough, but as the summer drew into autumn, her longing to escape became more urgent. The cantonment was surrounded by Afghan tribes, usually fighting each other but now threatening to overwhelm the garrison itself. More and more of the wives whispered that it was time to abandon the attempt to keep peace between the tribes and the British. Soon their husbands began to voice the same thought. The whispers became louder. No one had any faith left in the Envoy or the Commanding Officer. All of them wanted to return to the safety of India.

There were only two routes back, both through narrow mountain passes that were guarded by tribesmen, who extorted money from anyone wanting a safe passage, but did not always grant it. Stories of unspeakable horror reached the cantonment, screwing up the tension day by day. General Sale and his brigade were sent to clear a way through the northern route by force.

But he was wounded and sixty of his men killed. The news came that they had been fired at from behind every rock in the precipitous, narrow pass by Ghilzai tribesmen: sixty of them according to the first report Perdita heard, two hundred according to Lady Sale, who dismissed the first paltry number as an insult. Perdita could not see that the higher numbers of enemy made the situation any better, except for saving English pride. General Sale and his men had fought on, but Perdita was sure that none of the occupiers were going to get out through the northern route.

In the intervals of trying to contain her fears and keep the children safely occupied inside the bungalow, she consoled herself with the thought of the southern passes home. But then came news of a Mrs Smith, the wife of a collector, who had been travelling through them with a small guard when her escort was attacked. The guards fled and Mrs Smith got out of her *palkee* and ran as fast and as far as she could before she was caught and hacked to death.

Perdita listened to the story in dismay. If neither route could be guaranteed, there seemed little hope. She thought of her father, waiting in Simla. She thought of the children, whose lives had hardly begun. And she thought of herself. Once, years earlier, the idea of dying had seemed almost comforting, but since then she had learned how to be happy. She couldn't bear the thought of staying in Kabul; but she was terrified of what they would face if they left.

Day after day Sale's guns could be heard from the cantonment, and departure was postponed again and again. More and more wounded were brought back with the news of attacks and treachery. Every caller who came to the house strengthened Perdita's anxiety, even Captain Lawrence, the Envoy's military secretary, who was always trying to reassure. Negotiations were being undertaken with the tribes to ensure the army's safe conduct back to India he told her.

One day Aktur begged permission to talk to the lady-sahib and she went out on to the verandah, wrapped in a huge black and red shawl, for it was growing very cold. He told her that he would not be able to work for her any longer.

"But why, Aktur?" she asked in the halting Pushtu she had been trying to learn with such difficulty. "Have we displeased you in some way?"

"No, lady. But it is hard for me to leave the city each day to come to you. And something terrible is going to happen. We do not know what, but you should be on your guard. Something will happen."

Creeping despair and a conviction that they would all die or at best be made slaves had seized almost everyone in the cantonment, when at last a loophole seemed to open. Akhbar Khan, the fighting second son of the Dost Mohammed Khan, arrived at Kabul and assumed leadership of the chiefs of all the tribes with whom the English had been attempting to negotiate. The terms he offered for their safe return to India were stiff – and humiliating – but they offered hope at last.

When news of the agreement leaked out, Perdita felt waves of astonished relief. To get out of the hated country, with an escort of tribesmen to see them through the passes! In the sudden exhilaration that attends any release from paralyzing fear, she and the rest of the wives set about their packing. The idea of a long journey in the cold and snow was unattractive, but few wanted to wait until spring. Perdita looked out all the warm furs and skins she could find for her family and servants, and gave orders for the best arrangements for the transport of all the furniture and silver she had brought with her from India.

Marcus warned her that with so many of the camels having died, it was unlikely that she would be able to take it all. Cheerfully she unpacked the less favoured pieces and had them chopped up for firewood for the last few days in Kabul. Once again the house became really warm, and the Beaminsters found themselves immensely popular.

Visitors called at all hours to sit over Perdita's fires talking, now hopefully, now in despair, about their prospects of survival. Lady Sale's servant, Mohammed Ali, had warned her to beware of treachery, and Aktur forced his way into the cantonment once more to deliver a similar warning to Perdita, begging her not to risk her life and the life of her children in the passes. She smiled as she found enough Pushtu to say:

"I will tell the sahibs, but I think they will march even so."

Aktur looked at her with a strange intensity in his dark eyes, saying urgently:

"If that is so, do not ride with the other memsahibs, but among the *sowars*. And wear these." He presented her with an unsavoury bundle of sheepskin coats and coarse turbans.

"That sounds wise counsel, Aktur. But what of my children? They cannot ride with the men."

"They must. They must wear the same and go nowhere near the camels and the English women. They must ride with you."

Perdita repeated the warning to Marcus later in the day. He nodded, his face bleak with endurance.

"I can well believe we are to be attacked. But there is nothing to be done. We cannot stay. Some will get through and that is better than all dying here. We must go as soon as we can." He paused and then, seeing in her eyes that she knew what they faced, added: "And may God have mercy on our souls."

Perdita had never been so cold or so afraid. She was half-lying, half sitting in a nest of sheepskin she had built over the snow, when the column halted to bivouac for the first night of the march. Marcus, on his way to see to his men, had urged her to take the children at least into a tent that had been pitched for the officers' families. But, remembering Aktur's advice, she had insisted on camping among the troops at the head of the column, in spite of the children's tearful protest and wailing demands for their ayahs and their beds. As Marcus had walked away, she had called after him:

"Come back when you can. We shall be warmer all together."

As darkness fell, the sky to the west of the bivouac was lit with an orange-red glow that was unpleasantly reflected in the moonlit snow. Perdita asked a passing officer of the 121st what it could be.

"It's the cantonment burning. They started the sack even before the last of our fellows got away." He strode off, leaving Perdita to try to ease her aching back and wait.

Once she was sure the children were asleep, she took her arms from around their shoulders, then she turned awkwardly to scoop up a mound of snow under the sheepskins to make a back rest. The relief she felt as she leaned against it was almost piercing, and she believed after all that she might survive until Marcus returned.

He came nearly an hour later, with Captain Thurleigh, his greatest friend, who had known him so much better and so much longer than Perdita. She buried her true feelings and welcomed him as though she, too, depended upon him. At her urging, Marcus added his sheepskin coat to her nest and lay down close to the children. Thurleigh hesitated, as he saw Marcus slide between the heaps of skins, but the cold was so intense that he saw the sense of it, and lowered himself down beside his friend. Marcus watched him, then turned to his wife.

"Perdita, my poor dear, are you very uncomfortable?"

She summoned up a smile. "Not so bad. If only there were some water! But any thirst is better than staying in Kabul, so I am not complaining. How far have we come?"

The two men looked aross the heap of coats that covered them all, and Thurleigh said roughly: "About five miles."

The horror of it silenced Perdita. They had ninety to go, and in a whole day's painful marching had only achieved one nineteenth of the total. There was no wood for camp fires, no fresh water, and the baggage train was in such disorder that no food had been distributed. She and the children had dined off biscuits soaked in sherry, the only liquid that was available. They could not survive many days like this one. She turned on her side and tried to sleep.

When the grey dawn came, releasing her and the men from the necessity of pretending to sleep, always trying to keep still in case they should inadvertently wake the others, all three were unsure whether or not they had actually slept at all. But at least they were warm, except for their faces, which were pinched and reddened from the cold. Perdita brought one of her hands out of the sheepskin covering to brush something from her eyelids and discovered that her eyelashes and brows were frozen hard. She was trying to thaw her face, wincing in the pain, as she saw the others struggle out of their coverings. Marcus said:

"I have to see to the men. But I'll try to find some breakfast for you and the children."

She thanked him, trying to keep down the panic that threatened to choke her. Thurleigh was tidying his clothes, so she turned away.

When Marcus came back to them fifteen minutes later, his face was unhappier than she had ever seen it. She started towards him.

"This is catastrophe," he said. "The worst mess anyone could have imagined. The rear guard did not reach the bivouac until two this morning; most of the baggage has been lost, and with it the entire commissariat. But worse, far worse . . ." He broke off and actually groaned. Before Perdita could urge him to tell her the worst, Thurleigh gripped Marcus's arm above the elbow and they walked a few steps away, talking in low voices.

"Then there is nothing to be done now, old fellow," Thurleigh said more loudly, "except see that the march is pushed forward with all speed, to get the living to some kind of shelter."

"Will one of you please tell me what has happened?" said Perdita with a force that was new to them all.

"Most of the Indian troops have suffered severely from frostbite, Lady Beaminster," Thurleigh said, turning back to face her with a grimness even he rarely showed. "Many of Marcus's men are dead . . ."

"From cold?"

"They were not allowed to wrap leggings around their boots as some of them wanted," Marcus said bitterly, "and they had no bedding. Some of them took off their clothes to burn as fuel in order to feel some warmth before they died. The camp followers are in worse condition, if possible. There are bodies all over the road; they just lay there and died."

"Ayah," came Charlie's voice sleepily from beneath the *poshteen*. Perdita gestured to her husband to be silent. "Ayah, bring my clothes." He spoke imperiously in Hindustani.

Perdita answered in English: "Ayah is not here, my son. And you are wearing your clothes. Look. We are on our way to Jellalabad, remember? Annie, here, let me help you to sit up."

"Breakfast, Mama. What is for breakfast?"

"I don't really know, old chap. Marcus, did you . . .?"

"Oh, yes," he said, feeling in his pockets. "Johnson has given me some Kabul cakes and tea for you all. But didn't you tell me you had some raisins and grain in your saddle bags?"

"Yes, but if we are marching at only five miles per day, and the army has rations for only five days even if they have not been lost, we shall need everything before we reach Jellalabad."

"I don't think it right to take Johnson's food while you have your own," said Marcus.

Perdita was so angry that she felt the blood warm and pounding in her cold cheeks.

"I cannot fight," she said. "But my duty is to ensure that the children reach Jellalabad alive. If that involves keeping the food I brought in spite of all the official reassurances that rations would be provided, I shall do it."

Marcus, who had never seen her so definite and was in any case too worried to argue, handed over the flask of tea and the collection of flat greyish-brown wheat cakes, and went back to his company without another word.

Perdita did not see him again all day. She coaxed the children on to their ponies and tried to keep them cheerful and confident throughout the long, cold, frustrating day as they rode the rocky path, crossing and re-crossing the river that wound between the high sides of the hills. Shots spattered down on them all day and the screams of the wounded terrified Annie. Perdita's voice was hoarse by evening, and she was exhausted with the effort of reassuring the children and keeping them riding onwards.

Reaching the night's bivouac, she refused all entreaties to take refuge in the only tent there was. Her race and her rank meant she would have been welcomed. But Aktur's warning beat in her brains. Once more she arranged a heap of skins in the open and made her family bed down in them. Snow fell on their faces. Charlie hid his discomfort in boyish truculence and Annie tried not to cry, but she was shivering and looked desperately fragile. Perdita ignored everything, all the other women, their infants, her own fears, and searched for something to make a shelter for her children's faces. Hunger made her stomach ache, but she would not touch the raisins that they would certainly need before they reached safety.

She heard a groan and the sound of hooves digging into the snow; and then Thurleigh's voice, calling her name. She turned to see Marcus swaying in his saddle, supported by Thurleigh and a *subadhar*. There was blood on his breeches.

"He's been wounded in the knee, and the ball is lodged in him," Thurleigh said, his harsh voice making her start. "Help me."

Together they got Marcus off his horse and laid him on the pile of sheepskin coats. He groaned once before biting deeply into his bottom lip to silence himself. Perdita pulled away the coverings.

"Charlie, please go to Mrs Sturt and ask if she has any of that sherry left for Papa. Annie, come here and hold Papa's head for me."

They did what they could to make Marcus less uncomfortable, which was not much, until Charlie came back with a bottle and the news that Captain Sturt was badly wounded.

"Worse than Papa. He can't speak and there's lots of blood. He's making a horrid noise."

Perdita put a hand to her eyes, unable to stop tears of horror. They seemed to be welling more and more quickly under her fingers and hard as she tried to stop them, she could not. She felt her arm gripped tightly and heard Thurleigh's voice, harsh and demanding: "Stop. There is a time and place for such nonsense. This is not it. Do something for your husband."

By nightfall, Doctor Brydon had found time to dress the wound, having roughly dug out the bullet. He took Perdita to one side.

"It will be painful, but he is not in danger, except of fever." Then he told her quickly of some of the others who had survived.

Captain Sturt was dying, he told her, and Maria Jamieson was already dead, although two of her children had got through alive; the sepoy leading their camel had marched doggedly through the pass in spite of his wounds. Mrs Trevor still lived with seven of her children, and young Mrs Mainwaring had heroically walked most of the way, carrying her child, and struggling over the bodies of men and cattle as she went. Little Mary Anderson, Annie's best friend, had been taken by some tribesmen, as had some other children Perdita did not know. It was thought that nearly three thousand had already died.

Perdita's mind could hardly take in the horror of it: so many men and women she had known, murdered, their bodies left to rot. And the children: they had had to watch such things, dying in pain and terror, or, worse perhaps, taken captive by their tormentors. In the face of such carnage to have survived unhurt seemed almost shameful; and yet the determination to live burned in Perdita still.

The sufferings of the living were not at an end. As night fell the firing continued and the survivors lay down in the snow, colder than ever, hungry, many of them hoping they would not wake again. As usual, Thurleigh joined the Beaminsters as soon as he could leave the general's side, and as usual they made their *poshteen* bed and tried to sleep. This time they were afraid to lie in a circle in case someone accidentally kicked Marcus's wounded leg, and so Perdita arranged them in a row, with Marcus at one edge, Thurleigh at the other.

Perdita had the satisfaction of seeing the children sleep almost at once, and soon afterwards she dropped into an uneasy doze, punctuated by nightmares and the sound of screams and groans that seemed part of the dreams. She was woken by a convulsive start in Marcus, lying beside her, and opened her eyes to see a young boy in Afghan dress kneeling over him. She was struggling out of the skins that covered her, hampered by her wet and clinging serge skirts, when Marcus screamed.

Seeing moonlight gleam off a knife in the boy's hand, Perdita lunged at him, grabbing his right wrist. He must have been only twelve or so and, although he was wirily strong, with her superior weight she managed to roll him on to his back on the ground. She dared not turn to see to her husband, for the boy squirmed and kicked under her hands.

All around her she could see Afghan men and children running through the camp, slashing, stabbing at the wounded and the dead. Some of the sepoys and their officers tried to fight the tribesmen off; others lay apathetically, allowing themselves to be killed or hacked about, as though too battered by the horrors they had suffered to care whether they lived or died.

Perdita heard Thurleigh's despairing voice: "His eyes, dear God, his eyes."

Suddenly she understood what the boy beneath her had done to Marcus. Quicker than thought, impelled by hate and terror, she knelt astride him to keep him still and taking her hand from his wrist wrenched the knife from his hand. He writhed between her thighs, shrieking curses. She drove the knife into his chest, pushing hard through the tough leather of his *neemchee*. The blade slid in quite easily, and the body stilled. She could not believe that killing was so easy, and wrenched the knife out again to drive it back into the boy, and again once more.

She felt a man's hand on her shoulder and heard a rough English voice, saying: "Enough, ma'am. Enough. The wretch is dead."

Dazed and sickened, she allowed the man to help her stand. He bent down to pick up a handful of snow and used it to clean the blood off her left hand. She raised the right, and in the thin light saw that it was dark with blood: sticky between her fingers and horrible under her nails. She looked at the hand as though she did not know what it was. Then her eyes dilated.

"Marcus?"

The man turned her round and she saw her husband lying with his head in Captain Thurleigh's lap, blood all over his face.

The children were huddled under the sheepskins, looking at their father, both in tears but neither making a sound. Perdita turned back to the man and at last recognized him.

"Sergeant Deane, thank you. Please find Doctor Brydon, or any of them, and tell him to come."

"Mama, Mama, why is Papa crying like Captain Sturt?"

Perdita stroked Charlie's forehead, wincing at the sight of the drying blood on her fingers.

"He has been hurt, Charles. We must all be as quiet as we can so that we do not disturb him. Lie down again. I'm coming in beside you, Annie. There is nothing to frighten you now. Lie down."

They obeyed, but she was afraid they would not sleep. She herself sat beside them to spend what was left of the night straining to see if anyone was approaching them through the murky moonlight, bitterly reproaching herself for sleeping earlier and asking herself how any twelve-year-old child learned the cruelty necessary to do what had been done to Marcus. She knew that blinding was a traditional punishment for any ruler overthrown in Afghanistan, or an enemy defeated, but the reality of it far outstripped even her most grotesque imaginings. She thought it would be less evil to kill than to maim in such a way.

Morning brought the usual shambles. Just after dawn there was a tremendous commotion as most of the fighting men and practically all the camp followers started to move off towards the next pass before the orders had been given. Individuals were grabbing ponies or camels where they could, and the air was thick with noise and panic. Perdita lost no time in getting the children up, rolling their sheepskins and strapping them to the ponies. Then she helped Thurleigh to lift Marcus into the saddle.

With his face set in vicarious pain, Thurleigh said: "I cannot stay. I must go to Elphinstone. Will you take his reins?"

"Of course. Marcus, can you stay in the saddle or shall I find a place in a camel pannier for you?"

He made a ghastly effort to smile in the direction of her voice and said: "I'll stay on."

"Very well, but you must tell me if I go too fast, or if you want to stop. Annie you must ride with Charlie today so that I can help Papa." She lifted the child up in front of Charlie, detaching her clinging hands as gently as possible.

They rode off, joining the milling force that straggled across the valley. As they passed the small tent in which the surviving English wives had spent the night, she saw piles of Indian corpses. It was not until much later that she learned how the poor wretches had tried to force their way in to share the only available warmth. Repulsed, they had simply lain down outside and died in the snow.

Perdita and her family had not ridden half a mile before an order rang out to halt.

"Oh, Christ, what now?" she said, unaware that she was blaspheming like a soldier.

As usual ignorant chaos reigned. Someone said that the whole force was to be turned round; others that still more dangers awaited them around the next bluff; yet others that Akbar Khan was genuinely going to provide them with an escort and food this time if they would only wait. Messengers, both English and Afghan, came and went and no one took any notice of a party of tribesmen riding down on the right of the column until they had seized Perdita's bridle, and Charlie's, and dragged their ponies away from the column. A few sepoys raised their muskets, and one or two even fired, but so wide that no one was hit.

Perdita was too frightened to speak and looked wildly back at

Marcus, only to realize that he could not help her; now she was responsible for him as well as the children.

"What is it, Perdita? Why are we riding away from the column? Who is firing?"

"Marcus," she began, "they are taking us . . ." She stopped, hearing wild shouts and the crunching of a pony's hooves in the snow behind them. She narrowed her eyes against the painful glare and then said in deep relief: "Marcus, Captain Thurleigh is coming."

"Thank God."

But the tribesmen had heard him, too, and two detached themselves from the raiding party, wheeled round and thundered down towards him. He took aim with his revolver; but before he could fire it, they were on him and had snapped his hands behind his back, roughly tying them with harsh-looking cord.

They were driven quickly away from the rest of the column. Horrific pictures flashed one after another through Perdita's mind: of poor Lieutenant Loveday's starved beheaded body found at Kehlat-y-Ghilzai; of Colonel Stoddart in the mad Nasrullah's unspeakable prison; of young Mrs Smith running for her life among the rocks north of Kandahar.

Although there had been moments last night when the thought of lying down to sleep and never waking again had held some comfort for Perdita, the idea of death now filled her with terror, and bitter bile rose in her throat at the thought of what the tribesmen might do to the living bodies of her children. She choked it down and at last found her voice.

"Where are you taking us?" she said in Pushtu to the man who was leading her pony and Marcus's. "What do you want of us?"

He turned and from under the coarse blue turban seemed to smile like a fiend.

She shuddered, and was grateful for the sound of Captain Thurleigh's English voice:

"Do not give them the satisfaction, Lady Beaminster. What is coming will come, and all we have now is our pride."

Marcus, lost in his fog of blindness and pain, and shivering under the weight of his damp and icy clothes, said again: "What is happening?"

"A group of tribesmen has overpowered us." Thurleigh's voice was calm, almost as though he was delivering an official report. "They seem to be taking us away from the valley into the hills. We do not know what they want with us, but they have shown us no violence."

"Perdita?"

"Yes, Marcus?"

"Have they hurt you?"

"No. Neither me nor the children." She turned back to look down the valley, but the struggling, intractable column was now hidden from her by a spur of the hills. She sat back in the saddle and tried to think of nothing but the sight of the man leading the children's pony.

He appeared to be entertaining them, making strange faces and whistling. She had once heard that all Afghans love children, but after what she had seen on the retreat, she could not have believed that such affection could encompass the offspring of their enemies.

They rode on. Perdita's eyes burned with tiredness, and all her joints ached with cold and exhaustion. Her icy clothes stuck to her body, and she felt degraded by the dirt and blood that soiled her.

Then, as the ponies climbed the last few yards towards a squalid-looking mud village, which she realized must be the end of their journey, she deliberately looked around her in search of some kind of peace before whatever was to come. To her surprise she found that she could see a certain beauty in the place. The little village might be poor and mean, but the mud of its walls had dried to a calm beige that echoed the snowless slopes of the bald mountain above it. The snow that lay on the plateau and dusted the higher slopes was dazzlingly white, and the bright sun picked out silver lights on the bare, fastigiate trees within the village walls. A frozen river was stilled by its icy imprisonment and a bird sang somewhere. There was peace there, and a strange loveliness.

Perdita turned to face the village, saying to James Thurleigh:
"Now we shall know."

They both looked towards the headman who was waiting for
them. As they came nearer, Perdita could make out his dress
and features. His greyish-white turban was wound above a
broad face, creased and burnt brown. His eyes, hazel as an
Englishman's were narrowed against the glare and seemed to
her to express the loathing of her race she had come to recognize
in Kabul, and his mouth looked as full and sensually cruel as the
Dost's. She kept her eyes on his as her captor helped her to
dismount, and she waited for the khan to speak.

Without moving, he said in slow, carefully enunciated Pushtu:

"Welcome. We have food for you. Come."

Wearily, she translated what he had said for the others and,
leaving Thurleigh to help Marcus, turned to the children. They
were happily standing by their escort, carefully repeating a
series of words he was teaching them. Mystified and extremely
frightened, Perdita followed the headman into one of the bigger
houses.

They walked into a grimy littered compound, in one corner of
which an old woman tended a large, steaming iron pot on a
primitive mud stove. The man gestured towards a low doorway
on the left and said, again very slowly:

"We have little room. Go in. Food will be brought to you."

They went in obediently and found a bare windowless room,
dimly lit by an oil lamp. There was a small ragged carpet on the
floor, but nothing else. Perdita turned back to the door to ask for
the sheepskins from their ponies. One of the brigands who had
brought them to the place nodded and ducked down through
the compound door.

While they waited, Perdita looked questioningly at Captain
Thurleigh. He shrugged.

"God knows. They don't appear to be hostile. But these
tribesmen are treacherous bastards." He paused. "I beg your
pardon, Lady Beaminster. What I meant was that it is impossible to trust any of them. We all know that Akbar Khan has

betrayed every promise he has ever made to us. Still, if these people feed us that will be something. They may have taken us for ransom; if so they must keep us alive at least."

Only moments later, a man arrived with the bundles of sheepskin coats, to be followed almost immediately by the old woman carrying her iron pot. She dumped it unceremoniously on the floor and departed without a word. A savoury scent issued from it in wreaths of steam. Perdita felt the saliva spurt into her dry mouth. Her clenched stomach ached for the hot food. The children darted towards the pot, but she stopped them.

"Captain Thurleigh, do you think it safe to eat?"

He looked at her and, having settled Marcus by the wall, walked to the tantalizing pot, bent down to smell its contents, then dipped in his hand. He ate a little.

"As far as I can tell it is only mutton and rice. Very greasy but wholesome enough."

She released the children, who dug their hands into the mess and crammed their mouths with the first warm food they had had since leaving Kabul. Perdita then filled her hands with the sticky rice and went over to squat on the mud floor beside Marcus. She tried to make him take the food. He was so weak and dispirited that he could not make the effort, and so she fed him, rolling the rice into small glutinous balls, and picking out bits of meat and pushing them into his mouth. Only when he said, "No more now," did she herself eat.

Never had she imagined that there could be such pleasure in swallowing something so unpalatable as the congealing rice and mutton fat from the bottom of the pot.

Later, when the children slept and Marcus had lapsed into a kind of half-consciousness in his corner, Perdita looked at James Thurleigh, worried by his physical proximity as she had never been while they camped out in the open, sharing the dangers of the last few days. Now that they were under a roof of sorts she found herself deeply embarrassed by him. She longed to ease her stays, which felt as though they were biting into her flesh, to strip off her sodden clothes and somehow try to dry and warm her skin, and she needed desperately to relieve herself.

He was in much the same case, but lacked most of her shame. Making an unspecific apology, he went to the furthest corner of the room and turned his back. She could be in no doubt about his purpose and closed her eyes and tried to stop her ears. Nevertheless, in spite of his example, she made herself wait until he was asleep to follow it.

They had all been awake, hungry and stiff from lying on the hard floor, for what felt like hours, before they heard someone at the simple lock on the outside of the door. The room was pitch black, for the lamp had long since run out of oil. Perdita held the children's hands firmly.

The door opened outwards, and they could see a square of brilliant light for a moment, before most of it was blocked by the stooping figure of a burly tribesman carrying another dim lantern. He said in the slow, clear Pushtu the headman had used:

"Come now. Outside." His voice seemed to hold no belligerence. Nevertheless, Perdita felt her pulse pounding, and the back of her knees were clammy with sweat. She tried to reassure the children, but her voice croaked and would not shape the right words. She managed only:

"He wants us outside."

It was Thurleigh who said: "Well, let us go. We have to know some time. Let it be now. Come, Marcus." He put his hands under his friend's arms and hauled him up. Putting Marcus's left arm across his own shoulders, Thurleigh helped him to limp out into the daylight. Perdita followed with the children, her mind now mercifully blank.

The light hurt her eyes, and she whispered to Charlie and Annie:

"It is too bright. Keep your eyes closed and it will not hurt so much."

They stood in a row, one truly blinded, the others unable to see for the moment. Perdita was trying to focus through the glare and fizzing in her eyes, when a voice said:

"Lady-sahib, do not fear. There are no Ghilzais here and my father will protect you."

All she could see against the sun was the outline of a man in shaggy trousers, loose tunic, *poshteen* and huge turban, but something in his voice broke through her bruised mind.

"Aktur?"

"Yes, Lady-sahib. Do not fear. You will be safe here."

They stayed in the village through the winter, helping where they could. Perdita joined the rest of the women on the twice-daily march to fetch water from the distant river, but that was her only distraction. Every night they were locked in their room, but no one offered them any violence.

As she came to know the harshness and poverty of their lives, she could also begin to understand the legendary and much-mocked Afghan liking for money, and indeed the rapacity of the tribes who controlled the passes. But understanding did not bring acceptance. It seemed to her that their lives need not be so difficult; that there would be easier ways to provide the necessities of life, and to leave time for the pursuit of civilization and gentleness.

But then she would ask herself how much civilization her own people showed, or why the Afghans should be gentle with a foreign army that had invaded their country, whatever the spuriously legal excuse they had given for it. Her mind seemed like a cage of wild animals, prowling angrily round and round. As soon as she persuaded one uncomfortable thought to lie down, another would rise and snarl in its place.

In spite of her gratitude for their safety, she came to hate the village, and she knew that Captain Thurleigh hated it too. She had no idea what were the thoughts that so clearly tormented him, but she saw their effect and tried to help.

Her efforts were clumsy, though, and her words so irrelevant to his concerns that he hardly heard them, saying only:

"What was that you said? Leave? I expect they'll let us go in the end. If they had other plans they'd have done something to us by now. No, I think you can take it that we're being allowed to live." The sneer in his voice was too obvious to miss.

The next morning she went as usual to fetch their meagre breakfast as soon as the door to their room was unlocked, leaving him to deal with the unspeakable latrine jar. When she came back carrying a pile of flat, greyish wheat cakes and a water jar, she saw him standing outside the door, staring out at the mountains, with a pistol in his right hand. She understood at once and ran to stand in front of him. With her hands full of food and her blue eyes blazing with anger, she said:

"How dare you?"

He looked down at her and said unemotionally:

"I have to." Then, seeing her look of uncomprehending anger, he added unemotionally: "I'm a deserter. It's a matter of honour."

The stupidity of it, the wickedness, held her mute for a full minute. Then she bent down to put her burden on the filthy ground and straightened up to say bitingly:

"If you think it more honourable to shoot yourself here, causing God knows what trouble, than to live to help me get a blind man and two children safely through eighty miles of enemy-held mountain passes to Jellalabad you must be demented. And better dead."

He leaned forward and scrambled on to his knees, pressing his face into her dirty and stinking skirts and gripped her body.

"Oh, God, what will become of me?"

She put both hands on his rough, caked hair, feeling yet another louse under her fingers. Pushing her disgust away, she said:

"Don't weep, James. With God's help, we shall all live. When we get to Jellalabad, all will be well. You shall rejoin the regiment. No one will think that you have deserted. There are truly times when life is worth more than honour."

As though the word had triggered something in him, he dropped his arms and withdrew from her. Turning his head away, he got up and said in a barely audible voice: "I beg your pardon, Lady Beaminster." And he walked away.

Perdita stood looking after him, wondering how they could all live cramped in their one room for much longer. She saw Aktur and waved to him.

"Aktur, what is the news?"

"Nothing new, lady-sahib. They say that at Jellalabad the general has refused to make a treaty with the Ghilzais. They tried to take the fort, but they cannot. Even when a great earthquake threw down the walls, the *feringhees* built them up again before the Ghilzais could overcome them."

Taking a deep breath to steady her voice, Perdita said: "Then, Aktur, do you think we could leave soon? If the division is safe in Jellalabad and the tribesmen are preoccupied with the earthquake, would it not be better if we went now?"

"The cold and snow will stop you."

"But if we wait for spring it will be worse. There will be rain, and all the rivers will flood. I think you should send us now."

He looked at her as though weighing up what she had said against unvoiced arguments of his own. The fear that lived just below the surface broke through again and Perdita remembered the endless broken promises.

"I go to speak to my father and my brothers. Wait."

Five days later they marched, with Aktur as their guide. In the end Perdita and James Thurleigh parted from the village with regret. Filthy, uncomfortable and verminous it might have been, but it had provided sanctuary. Now that they were setting off across wild mountains, expecting to face bands of vengeful Ghilzais, they knew how to value safety.

The view in front of them was breathtaking: rank after rank of mountain peaks glittering under a sun that blazed in a sky as pale and clear as enamelled glass. Across the plateau she could see the river where the women went for water, and above it the magnificent sight of a frozen waterfall. The air was so clear that even from that distance she could make out the great ice stalactites that hung from the black rocks, and the curtains of ice that spread downwards into the still liquid pools.

On the evening of the fourth day of their march, when they

had made their bivouac and shared the ration of dried fruit and bread, Aktur said slowly to Perdita:

"Jellalabad lies over those hills there." He pointed directly opposite the declining sun, which had dyed the sky and the mountains a deep orange-gold. "Tomorrow I must leave you. But if you follow this track it will take you across the hills and you will see the fort."

"Must you leave us?"

"Yes, lady-sahib. I must go to my people. I cannot ride into the *feringhee* camp."

Next morning she thanked him formally for what he had done for them all.

"Go with God," he said, unsmiling as usual, before he turned and rode away, leaving them alone in the wilderness of snow and rock . . .

"Come," Perdita said briskly, "we have only twenty miles now. Just over those hills and then we shall see the fort. Charlie, roll up that blanket. That's right. Will you do Annie's too?"

"Mama, why did Aktur go?"

"He had to get back to his village, Charlie. We shall be all right now."

"Yes, I know," he said, but he kept looking back. "Does Uncle James know the way?"

"Yes. And so do I. This track goes all the way to the fort. Aktur said we had only to follow it and we would get there."

It was not until about midday, judging by the height of the brazen sun in the sky, that anything untoward happened. There was a distant rumbling, a crashing of rocks a little closer, then a peculiar heavy stillness. Just there the track ran round a highish craggy mountain, and less than a hundred yards ahead turned out of their view.

"Another earthquake," said Captain Thurleigh into the silence. "Wait here and I'll find out what damage has been done to the road."

"Be careful," Perdita said involuntarily.

He had barely been out of sight for three minutes before the same, sickening noise came again. Into the silence that seemed even more eerie than before came the screams of an animal in pain. Perdita thrust the leading rein at her son.

"Charlie, take Papa's rein. I must see what has happened."

She rode nervously round the bluff, picking her way through the rocks and boulders strewn all over the track. Scars on the mountainside above showed where they had come from. The screams became more distinct with every pace her pony took, but she could see nothing. She dismounted and walked on, following the sound and peering over the edge of the track.

A vast boulder had pinned James's pony against a rocky wall above a tiny depression. Perdita knew what she had to do and took out the pistol Aktur had given her. She cocked it as she took aim at the poor broken creature's head. It was not until she stood over the pony that she saw James.

He too lay under the rock. One of his arms was free and he was jerkily feeling about him, touching and rejecting the stones in a desperate search for something. Perdita uncocked her weapon and knelt down.

"James, James, can you hear me?" She took his searching hand in her own.

"Perdita." He was gasping for breath. "I can't find my gun."

"Don't worry. I shall shoot the poor pony for you, and then we'll get you out of here."

His hand grasped hers. "You cannot. I can't feel anything below my waist. I know what that means. My back is broken. You will have to shoot me. But you must do it first, before the pony, so that Marcus and the children will hear its screams after the shot and think you missed."

Perdita recoiled in horror. To kill in cold blood someone who was not an enemy – who did not threaten the life of anyone she loved – was not possible.

"Sweet Christ, you must do it."

Looking down at his agonized face, she made herself imagine the alternative. She could see that he was right, that she could never shift the vast boulder to free him. If she left him to try to bring back help from Jellalabad, he would die before they returned. And it would not be a quick death or an easy one.

He would be suffering a pain that she could see from his face was already tormenting him. Even if he had been an enemy she could not have found it in herself to consign any human to that living hell.

"Perdita, please," he begged in anguish. The pony screamed as he could not.

"Hush," she said, as she used to say it to Charlie in baby-hood. "I shall do it for you." She felt his hand relax and looked at his face with terrible pity. Sweat stood out on the greyish skin in large drops and deep lines had been scored from his mouth by the pain. There could be no shrinking in the sight of his nightmare. She used both hands to recock the heavy pistol. Then she took his hand again.

His heavy eyelids lifted once more, and the dark eyes looked into hers. He must have felt the cold muzzle on his skin, but he gave no sign.

"Don't tell Marcus," he said calmly. "Don't ever tell."

She tried to smile. "I won't." Forcing herself to keep looking into James Thurleigh's eyes, she pulled the trigger.

Bitter vomit rose in her throat and her breath broke in a dry gasping sob. She looked away from his shattered head and the reddening snow. Lifting the weapon once more, she put the pony out of its agony.

Then she stood up, her knees shaking and the sickness making her stagger. She knew she had to make herself walk past James Thurleigh's body to take the life-saving blanket and food from his pony's saddle. Jellalabad might be only a few miles away, but they could have lost the right path and take days to reach it. She could not gamble with the children's lives to save herself this grim task.

When she struggled back to the road with the half-unrolled blanket, she saw the hem of her dress was dabbled in blood and so were her hands. She wiped them against her bodice.

As she rounded the bend that protected Marcus and the children from what she had done, she saw Charlie waiting for her. His face was greenish-white and his eyes stared.

"It is over, Charlie," she said with difficulty, swallowing

hard. "The poor pony's legs were broken. But I have shot it now and there will be no more pain." She put her free hand on his head to comfort him and saw that she was wiping blood into his blond hair.

Annie's eyes widened at the sight of them both. Perdita tried to reassure her, then turned to Marcus.

"He was dead," she said as gently as she could. Marcus flinched, but the expression on his face did not change. She struggled on. "The rocks had caught him and must have killed him immediately. He had hardly bled at all, so it must have been quick. Merciful."

"Are you sure he was dead? How could you tell?"

"I listened to his heart, Marcus, and held the gun to his lips. There was no breath to mist it. He was dead, my dear."

"I heard two shots."

My hand was shaking so much I did not kill the poor pony the first time."

"Yes, I heard it scream." His voice was quietly polite, but his hands were shaking. She wanted to touch him, but the knowledge of James's blood on her hands made that impossible. All she could do was watch as Marcus brought the trembling under control.

"My poor dear," he said at last, "you should not have had to do such things. Do you want to rest?"

"Rest? No. No," she said more violently than she meant. "We must reach Jellalabad before dark."

Once past the place where James had died, they rode on in silence. Annie was whimpering with tiredness and fear until Charlie told her roughly to be brave. Perdita could not intervene. She coaxed her pony and Marcus's forward, allowing them all to rest only when it seemed that they could not go on.

There were no more tremors, and eventually the track brought them to the edge of the hills above the fort, just as Aktur had promised. When they emerged on to the plain, dusk was already falling, but they could see the flag flying bravely from the ramparts, and sentries who were hanging lanterns on the walls.

THE CROSSROADS AT CHURUBUSCO

John T. Aquino

Texas had won its independence from Mexico in 1836 but disputes continued and, in 1845, Texas became the 28th state of the United States. This annoyed Mexico even more and within a year Mexico was at war with the United States. It was a disastrous war for Mexico because upon the victory of the United States in 1848 Mexico lost the territory that now comprises the states of California, Nevada, Utah, and most of Arizona, New Mexico, Colorado and Wyoming. The war introduced many colourful characters who would remain indelibly stamped upon history, not least Robert E. Lee. The following story is built around one of those remarkable incidents that make history so fascinating and which is revealed at the end of the story. John T. Aquino (b. 1949) is an American author with a special interest in Arthurian legend and the Elizabethan age. His stories have also appeared in The

Camelot Chronicles, Royal Whodunnits *and* Shakespearean Detectives.

Robert E. Lee barely knew his father, who had died when he was just 11. But he became certain that he was the son of "Light Horse" Harry Lee when he heard himself say to General Smith, "I will cross the Pedregal. I will find General Scott."

The sun was disappearing under the Mexican horizon, chased by the shirt-soaking, bone-drying heat. But the heat did not follow the sun and instead had stayed to split the darkening sky with lightning and shake it with thunder. Brigadier General Persifor Smith, who commanded a brigade under Twiggs' 2nd Division, was conferring in his tent with Captain Lee of the Army Engineers and Brigadier General George Cadwalader of the 3rd Division. They were situated at San Gerónimo off the San Angel Road, due west of the Pedregal, a mass of lava rock that was shaped like an egg and ran five miles east to west. Majestic Mexico City was nestled in a drying river bed. If the city was the head of a body, then the Pedregal was its stomach, with San Angel and San Gerónimo to the west and San Antonio to the east forming the arms. Roads ran through these towns like arteries toward Mexico City. Not surprisingly, both Mexican and American troops were positioned on both roads.

General Smith, with moisture blisters forming on the canvas over his head, had laid out his situation to the two officers – the words coming in his New Orleans drawl with the precision of the Princeton-schooled Orleans lawyer he had been before President Polk had declared his Mexican war in 1846.

"First," he had said, pacing, with his square-toed boot kicking up the sand, "General Valencia, in spite of his success this morning, has neither advanced nor withdrawn from his position south of us near Padierna and is, therefore, prime for an attack. It will be another vital step on our road to Mexico City. Second, to cover the assault, I need a demonstration in my's position. Third, given General Scott's ... of command, I feel obliged to inform him of my ... demonstration, but fourth, I will wait only so long ... not hear from our dear general by three o'clock, I will att... my own at dawn. Ergo, I need someone to carry a message to the general across the fastest and most direct way to his position near Mount Zacatepec – across the Pedregal.''

Lee, who had spent the last year in Mexico mostly standing in the back of meetings, stepping forward only when the commanding general Major General Winfield Scott asked him if he and the engineers could find a way around or through a certain area, stepped forward and volunteered at once. Smith, who seemed mildly surprised, looked the captain up and down and took in his perfectly combed black mustache and the officer's gloves showing no more than a quarter-inch of wrist. Deciding that the volunteer was dependable within his scope, Smith quickly accepted the offer, dismissed Lee, and turned back to Cadwalader. Within the quarter hour, Lee, two enlisted men, and a young Mexican named Juan or Raoul, Lee wasn't sure, were approaching the Pedregal on foot.

As they left the camp, the four men passed a musical mirror of themselves, a quartet of musicians, villagers really, squatting on the ground, idly strumming guitars in the halting running rhythm of this place, and singing requests to birds and angels to fly to their loves with messages of passion. When Lee and his men walked away, the music clung to their legs and pants and hung for a while until it dropped into the dust and disappeared.

The sun was all but gone behind them, which caused the ridges of lava rock to bury them in shadows. As they climbed upon the slippery shell, the three soldiers and civilian entered darkness as if through a door. Climbing by feel, Lee realized that for all the good his companions were to him he was walking alone. He was in the lead, with only his own sense of direction as his guide.

This was not an unusual feeling, he reminded himself. He had been second in his class at the Military Academy at West Point, and he had done this by studying virtually all the time, thereby missing much of the camaraderie and highjinks at Benny Haven's that filled the days and nights of his classmates. Many of the officers here had been in his class, and they knew him and showed him respect and courtesy but kept the distance that had been formed a dozen years before. Lee knew this much – this climbing effort was the most strenuous he had undertaken since training at the academy, and his forty-year-old bones knew it.

The night was silent except for the spotted thunder, the roar of rain as it pelted his back and then moved on, and the scraping of his boots against stone.

After ten minutes of feeling his way in the dark, Lee learned to court the lightning as he would a woman. He would wish for it, dream of it, feel it coming, and when it slashed the dark like an axe does a bush in one's path, he would embrace it as if a lover and remember all it did to everything around it. And then it would go, and he would wish for it again, dream of it, and feel it coming.

To his own surprise, he found he had been counting seconds – 1,800 seconds meant a half hour, and at this pace he reckoned they had gone a half a mile at best. But he had always had a mathematical mind. Not like his father. His father, "the swashbuckler," as Rector Meade had called him. "Light Horse" Lee, who had stormed Paulus Hook during the War of Revolution, seldom thought before he acted, which was the reason why, forty years after Paulus Hook, he had faced a mob alone and been near-blinded and disfigured by the hoodlums. Lee had come to know his father best when, in study hall at the Academy, he had read the autobiography that had been published posthumously from his father's notes. And sometimes, in Lee's reverie and half-sleep, his father would talk to him, in the words of the book.

"Why do men fight, father?" he had asked the shade across the library table one afternoon when the sun was also setting, a sun two thousand miles away and many years before. His father, an image of the etching in the book, the bold and brash, white-wigged member of General Washington's staff, was younger than Lee actually remembered him.

"My son," his father's voice was reedy – this Lee's imagination copied from life – "mankind admires most the hero; of all the most useless, except when the safety of a nation demands his saving arm."

And you were a hero, father, though not much of a father, Lee thought to the darkness. Useless. Why was Lee thinking of his father, the hero? Is that why he volunteered, Lee wondered, to please or to impress – as his boots slid on the slick stone and he toppled sideways, with shards of stone falling about him like sleet. He could not move his arms as rock buried his feet and surrounded his hips. He remembered family fears of being buried alive – his half-brother's wife, grief-stricken at her young daughter's death, addicted to the morphine given to quiet her, pronounced dead and prepared again and again for burial, only to revive and scream at the sight of the black box.

As he struggled, Juan or Raoul grabbed his hand under the wrist to keep him up and visible to the two soldiers who reached under his arms and pulled all six feet of him free. "*Engana,*" the young Mexican hissed, "*Usted no sabe lo que significia a esa 'pedregal'?*"

Lee had learned some Spanish in his year in Mexico and breathlessly answered, "I may indeed be a 'fool,' young man, so tell, what does 'pedregal' mean?"

The Mexican blushed at having his blunt assessment of the captain's intelligence understood. But as he answered, he stared at Lee's face, and almost stammered, "*Significa el rio de la roca que flue con las piedras.*"

"Ah," Lee understood. "The river of rock that flows with rock."

"*Si. Uste debe fluir con éi.*"

"Yes, my friend. I will flow with it." But Lee noticed that the young man continued to stare at his face. He wondered if the torment he was feeling was shining from his eyes.

They continued onward, and soon Lee's counting reached 12,439. They could see the shape of Mount Zacatapec but not of General Scott's camp. The tents were gone, the fires cooling. "*Virgen Marie de Guadalupe,*" the Mexican whispered.

"Well," Lee said to himself. "At least he is praying for me and not calling me '*Engana*.'" He turned to the two soldiers and announced, "We have missed the general. I must continue on to San Augustin, which is at least three more miles away. You may return to General Smith, with my thanks. As for you," he said to the young man, "*Gracias*," and tossed him an American dollar. "*Via con Dios*," he told him in his poor Spanish, praying that he would go his way with God's blessings, and turned and walked forward without looking back.

As he struggled to keep his feet pressed firmly down over the slick and malicious rock, with the rain pelting him at its whim, he thought of the young Mexican and his mention of the Virgin Mary of Guadalupe – a vision of Mary, the mother of Christ the Lord, that had appeared three hundred years before to a man in the city of Guadalupe, three miles north of Mexico City. Lee had seen the painted and carved image of the lady – a woman with her eyes cast down and hands folded in prayer – for nearly a year. Villagers knelt before it and prayed for the Lady's intercession to her son for their crops and their children, who were either in the womb or in the war.

So much of the land around him was steeped in what in Lee's Virginia – the state named after the "Virgin Queen" Elizabeth and not the Virgin Mary – was not unkindly called the papist or Catholic religion. The names of the towns – San Augustin, San Antonio, San Angel, San Gerónimo, San Mateo – not to mention the opposing general Santa Anna – were named for men and women whose piety and holiness had been honoured by Lee's ancestors until the break with the Pope of Rome by an English king; when the prayers for the intercession of saints in the daily lives of those of Lee's faith had all but vanished. This place of saints was now to be a field of battle, and their silent stone faces would bear witness.

The lightning crackled dully in the sky directly above. Lee smiled, uncertain if he should accept that as approval of his thoughts or reproof. Lee believed in God, more than he believed in life. He just preferred to practise his belief within himself rather than with an outward flourish. There was order in belief, more than in the world in which he walked. At prayer at Christ's Church, he understood so much. He was at home in prayer. At his confirmation, Rector Meade had had to shake him from his meditation in order to continue the ceremony. But when he left the church and set foot on the street, his certainty evaporated like dew from the grass at dawning.

And you, father, he said to the empty chair in study hall, did you believe? You, who when you were crippled by the angry mob abandoned your family and left for the Indies to live with pagans? Perhaps it was the lightning, but he thought he heard a thin voice quote the Bible, something about judging not, lest ye be judged. Lee again thought of the image of the Lady of this place. General Scott was no papist – although it was rumoured that his daughter Virginia had converted to Catholicism, become a nun, and recently died in a Georgetown convent in Washington, D.C. But he had ordered his officers to attend Catholic Mass as a sign of courtesy to the priests of the towns they were bloodying. Lee had heard and learned the prayers, if only by repetition, and so he said them now, to atone for his bitterness and in requiem for his late, lost father: "*Cure nestra penas, nuestra miserias y dolores, perfecta siempre Virgen Santa Maria* – cure our sins, our miseries, and our sorrows, faultless, always virgin, blessed Mary."

Lee reached a peak overlooking the town of San Augustin and saw the fires of General Scott's camp. Sensing someone behind him, he slowly covered the butt of his pistol with his palm, turned and saw the young Mexican, hanging back and looking out for him. The two soldiers had gone. Lee grinned and nodded in silent thanks, telling himself that the lightning had been both a sign of approval and reproof. There was certainty around him, he told himself, if only he could understand it.

Lee beckoned the young man to join him, but he shook his head and turned back. The storm was ending, and the air was crisp and still. Lee heard the Mexican mutter, crossing himself as he descended, "*Los que están a punto de morir ven siempre fantasmas.*"

Lee's face brightened the dark as it whitened with fear. The young man had seen his thoughts after all. Translating what the boy had said, probably a wise saying of his town, Lee whispered it back to the dark: "Those who are about to die always see ghosts."

The prospect of death is with a soldier more times than others. It is especially there when mentioned. Lee had written to his wife and children that evening and left the letter in his kit. If something happened, the quartermaster would find it and see that it was delivered. What his father did not write in his book, he thought, was that duty brings a soldier to war, and war leaves no choice. Lee started down the hill toward the lights of General Scott's camp.

When Captain Lee was ushered into the commanding general's tent, General Scott was silently writing orders – things that a subordinate could easily do but not, the general thought, as well. The full-faced Scott, whose sixty-first birthday his army had celebrated in June, looked up at Lee, his uniform, torn both at the shoulder and calf from his fall, his hair matted with rainwater and mud, in a glance took in what the officer had been through and nodded in appreciation. Lee gave his report and before he had finished, Brigadier General David E. Twiggs, with a brown beard that hung to centre chest, and the sculpted-faced Major General Gideon J. Pillow, who, though thirty years younger than Twiggs was his superior officer, arrived. Twiggs was limping on an injured foot. They too had gone to Zacatepec to find General Scott, only they had ridden around the Pedregal. "Gentlemen, there is much to do," General Scott announced, rising and reaching for his feathered hat.

Captain Lee heard himself ordered to return with General Twiggs and along the way to scrape up troops for General Smith's attack. While horses were being found for both of them, Lee sketched out the path he had taken for the Corp of Engineers, with instructions to clear the way immediately for troop movement.

General Antonio López de Santa Anna was sitting at dinner

at his temporary headquarters in San Angel, west of the Pedregal and just north of General Smith's position. The stump of
his left leg, with two bones protruding, the results of a botched
amputation nearly ten years before, was propped up on a red
velvet monogrammed pillow. The victory at Veracruz had led
to his second presidency. However, since his return to power
had lasted less than five years and had been followed by another
period in exile, the pillow had been his sole tangible gift from a
grateful nation. But now, thanks to the arrival of the Americans,
he was president for a third time. He sliced his roast with
finality, chewed it thoroughly, and sent after it a red wine that
had been vatted in his honour. The general was content in the
knowledge that General Valencia should have exterminated
Smith's brigade by now.

Soon, as he was draining his glass of Irish crystal of its last red
drops, he heard a commotion in the hall. He shouted from
where he sat, and quickly two of Valencia's aides were brought
in. Santa Anna could tell it all from their looks. Valencia had not
moved.

Since neither could Santa Anna, he flung his glass in fury at
the men and roared with his face to the ceiling, "*Tráigame sus
cerebros*," meaning, "Bring me his brains!" Just as quickly, the
general made preparations to move his troops to Mexico City,
just as a precaution.

Lee and Twiggs rode at a half-gallop in the light of the moon,
which was peeping its head through the clouds, checking to
make sure the storm was really over. It was just past midnight,
and they had three hours before Smith's troops moved out.
Twiggs was having difficulty staying in the saddle but did not
complain to his companion. They had been riding just a few
minutes when they approached a brigade. Twiggs started to
rein back, but Lee signalled him not to with a chop of his hand.
"If they are Mexican, we must get by them. If they are ours, we
will be there sooner."

They were Americans, a brigade under Pillow's 3rd Division and commanded by Brigadier General Franklin Pierce.

Pierce was there. He was even more handsome than Pillow – tousled black hair and dimpled chin – but he was crippled like Twiggs, having fallen from his horse the day before. Ninth Infantry Regular, Colonel T. B. Ransom, whom Lee did not know, was in temporary command. Lee and Twiggs explained the plan to both commanders. Ransom began to speak, but suddenly, the battle a reality, the chance for glory at his fingertips, Pierce cut him off. "I will resume command, Ransom." He timidly placed his foot in the stirrup, while his voice was anything but diffident. "Gentlemen, tell General Scott he may count on this brigade. Tell him –" As he mounted, Pierce's back arched, and he keeled back in a faint. Lee and Ransom both ran forward, Ransom to catch him, Lee to block the scene from the sight of Pierce's men. The medical officer was clandestinely sent for.

"The general can count on our brigade, Captain," Ransom said softly to the two officers. "General Twiggs, will you take command?"

"I am injured as well. You are in command, Colonel. I will stay with General Pierce."

"Captain Lee, can you direct us around the Pedregal?"

"I will be your guide, Colonel. But we must take a path through the Pedregal, not around it. I have just been through there by foot. My engineers are at hand and will clear our way. It is five miles, and it is hard, but we will not be seen."

Lee re-mounted and scanning the hills, he saw a solitary standing figure gazing down on the brigade. It was the young Mexican, still looking after him.

At first, General Gabriel Valencia's troops had been happy that the attack had not been ordered. "It is always better not to die," the old saying was repeated. The onset of rain and thunder had made this feeling even stronger. But came the dawn and the ground was wet and soggy and the cooks were nowhere to be found, not to mention the defending pickets, who had retreated to shelter in the storm. And as the soldiers emerged slowly, crankily, and angrily from their tents and blankets, they were able to see in the distance Santa Anna's troops retreating toward Mexico City.

It was then that Ransom and Lee led the frontal attack, on horse and foot. While the Mexicans had been angry, this did not stop them from being quick. They fired on the charging brigade from an elevated position. Men fell down and about Lee, strangers and brothers. He'd been in battle before, but usually setting up guns, never in charge, never shot at at point blank range.

There was then a roar of volleys from the crest of the hill behind the Mexican guns. Lee saw blue coats, pouring down, more brothers in arms, courtesy of General Smith. Valencia's troops broke and ran wildly in all directions, sometimes firing behind them but mostly not. Valencia himself barely escaped, avoiding the road to San Angel, having heard of Santa Anna's order to blow out his brains.

From San Angel, Santa Anna could see Valencia's troops, which only made him retreat to Mexico City all the faster. He had sent messengers ahead to the city, and from the walls its people could see the retreat from the roads on both sides of the Pedregal.

General Winfield Scott rode into the pursuing brigade, followed by Pillow, Twiggs, Major General William J. Worth of the 1st Division, and their junior officers. They rode in circles around Lee, shouting, cheering, hollering, clapping his back, mussing his hair. It was as if they were back in school at an Academy exercise. They were young again and friends. But Lee's mind went back centuries more and saw this band of brothers as Arthur's knights of the round table, fresh from Badon where King Arthur had carried the image of the Virgin Mary on his shoulder.

Scott, in his role as Arthur, was jubilant and loud, shouting for Lee, but never stopping, telling him as he passed, "If I were not on horseback, young man, I would kiss you! Gentlemen, if West Point had only produced the Corp of Engineers, that alone would make our country proud."

With Valencia's men retreating, Scott jumped off his horse, called for his officers, and knelt on the ground. Lee bent forward to see what General Scott was doing. Worth hesitated because it was unseemly, Pillow because it was dirty, and Twiggs because of his foot, but Scott did not wait for them, drawing in the mud with his finger. "As we know, the crossroads at Coyoacan controls the road to Mexico City. It is divided, with the Northern fork going to Churubusco where it is joined by the road from San Antonio. Pillow," the general had to kneel after all to see what Scott was asking him to do, "you will move up from San Angel to Churubusco. Worth, return to San Augustin, and when Pillow reaches the crossroads, cut the road from the rear and then pursue the enemy as they retreat, past the Convent of San Pablo and past this large ranch whose name I cannot pronounce. I will follow you. But Lee, you go before and reconnoiter the lower fork for Pillow."

Pillow, Lee, and Twiggs started to get up, but Worth, whose disdain of the commanding general was not unknown, said, "Wait a minute. General, with all due respect, this violates the most ancient and respected rule of warfare – do not divide your army in the presence of a superior foe."

Scott kept his eyes down in an attempt to control his temper. "It is a rule. Here's another one, General. And I learned it not from Plutarch or Herodotus but from General Andy Jackson during the War of 1812 – when you tree a cougar, you don't show him your rear. You get one of you to stare him in the eye, while another comes at him from behind. But you get him – before he gets you. Santa Anna's our cougar. Pillow and his brigades will come from one side, you from the other, and I'm going to stare him in the eye until he leaps. Any questions?"

The Arthurian camaraderie had lessened a bit but not much. Lee's horse was still fresh, so he mounted and rode in advance of Pillow's troops. His blood was up, his spirit soaring. He was alone again, leading, but he was getting used to it. The Mexican heat was back, his jacket was already soaked, but it did not matter. Perhaps he had misunderstood the young Mexican. Maybe he had really said, "Those who *face* death always see ghosts," rather than "those who are about to die." But no matter. The moment was now, the past was past.

The terrain was curved like a blown glass, and so a mile ahead

Lee could clearly see the retreat toward the crossroads at Coyoacan, the bridge at the Churubusco River. As he rode forward, Lee's eyes smarted and stung, and he realized it was from blowing smoke. As the soldiers retreated, they were setting fire to the corn, and the fields were all smouldering, since the crop was wet from the rain. The smoke would not cut off the movement of the troops as a fire would have, but it might slow them down.

Lee turned and saw Pillow's brigade behind him. If he could see them, he reasoned, they could see him. So he pointed and yelled and yanked his borrowed horse away from the smoke at an angle toward the bridge.

The brigade was following him, the villagers were fleeing ahead, and as Lee pulled his head back and forth one to the other, their images joined, with Lee riding faster and faster, his eyes filled with smoke. But one element was out of place – a single villager was running toward him. It was the young Mexican, waving his arms and shouting.

Lee reined up and dismounted as his walking companion ran to him, raising his little voice above the roar of fire and battle. "What is it, my friend?" Lee asked him.

"*El convento de San Mateo es un desvio. Han dado vuelta la casa del Dios en una fortaleza.*"

"You mean the Convent of San Pablo, not San Mateo, don't you?"

"*Engaña—*"

"All right, all right, I'm still a fool, but you say the Convent – of San Mateo – is a trap. How many soldiers?"

"*Muchos.*"

"*Gracias, amigo.* By the way, *como te llamas,*" Lee said, asking him his name.

"*Juan.*"

Lee mimicked his friend and waved his arms to attract General Scott, who reined his horse in with such force and so quickly that he almost threw him. When Lee told him what he had said, Scott looked down at the young Mexican, who reminded him of runaway Chippewas and Blackhawks from years back. "Can you trust him, Captain?"

"He has been my guide, sir. With my life I will trust him. And, incidentally, he says the name of the convent is 'San Mateo.'"

Scott reined his horse high. "I will keep that in mind," he shouted down, then barked at his lieutenant to pass the word. He then rode back to Lee. "What should we do, Captain? Your advice?"

"Continue your plan sir, only double it. Divide the force again as you approach the bridge, with brigades going around to the north of Churubusco, and seize the road from the back, blocking the enemy's retreat and putting him in a vice."

"Risky. The enemy's forces are hidden. But we have the momentum, Captain, like sweet whiskey from a jug. You will take two of General Shields' volunteer brigades around the Churubusco."

As Lee and the brigades approached the river, they saw masses of infantry on the wooden bridge. Lee drew his troops away from the river and toward Mexico City until he reached the ranch known as "De Los Portales" on the road to the city three quarters a mile in the rear of the bridge. Quickly, Lee threw the left of the brigade on the main building and the right on a building in the rear.

General Shields was forming a line obliquely to the Mexicans, who, responding, extended theirs. Pierce's brigade followed. Meanwhile, General Worth was proceeding up the road from San Antonio toward the bridge. A young stockily-built lieutenant named Grant with a scraggy beard in Colonel John Garland's brigade was straining his neck, leaning almost out of the saddle so he could see the movement of troops all the way to the bridge and to the city. There was gunfire raining down from the convent, and the lieutenant heard others say that these were the San Patricios, army deserters, who were said to fight like demons from hell, knowing what the United States did to deserters. But his reverie was ended by sniping from the enemy who were hiding in irrigation ditches, proving General Scott to be right.

Twiggs and his division were attacking the convent and gradually bringing the San Patricios down. General Shields, whose brigades were to hold the road, saw that the ground was boggy from the rain of the previous day. Deciding that the only offensive possible was a frontal attack upon the road, he ordered his divisions forward. The fire was thick, the bullets flying like lead-tipped bees. Lee was shouting to a hesitant lieutenant to move the howitzer battery forward. And then, the mass of the American army had suddenly and finally come together – Worth's troops crossed the bridge, meeting Shield's, who were being joined by Twiggs's, the convent having been taken.

The bridge and all behind it was theirs. Again, there were schoolboy cheers, but they were fleeting, vanishing north, as the army as a whole pursued the fleeing Mexicans toward Mexico City.

Lee hung behind, breathless, and seeing to the battery, the six and twelve pounders, while the heavy pieces were back at the convent. He saw the army go and would follow – but he stopped to think. He felt like a member of an audience when the play was ending and the illusion of reality was gone. If "Light Horse" Harry Lee's ghost had really been there, Lee hoped he had been proud and satisfied and would now rest. As for Lee himself, he felt he now knew what command was really like, as well as the camaraderie. He shook his head to think how in the past twenty-four hours he had helped clear roads through the Pedregal, walked six miles across it twice, joined in a vital demonstration before Padierna, and led a charge around the bridge of Churubusco. Not bad for a solitary man of forty.

Lee later learned that Mexican losses from the day were 6,000 nearly a third of the entire army, while the Americans had lost just over 1,000. After a brief truce, Mexico City was taken. Meanwhile, at Churubusco, as the men from General Worth's division had almost all crossed the bridge, Lee started to follow. Out of the corner of his eye he saw a rifle sticking from under the bridge and aimed directly at him. Lee was frozen in place, too exhausted to reach for his pistol or leap away. But before the man could fire, three bullets from a revolver drilled the wood, the rifle flew in the air and then plopped into the river beneath, a sound followed by that of a falling lifeless man.

Lee turned to see to whom he owed his life and caught a fleeting glance of a stocky lieutenant with a scrubby beard, pistol in hand, following his fellows, taking little notice of what he had done, acting as if shooting a sniper was just what a regular soldier does. Lee started to run after his saviour, but suddenly the day's labours weighed deep within him, and he was winded before he started, left to watch the lieutenant disappear into the rest of the army. Lee knew he would never forget the man's face and looked for him the next few days, but he could not find him.

Nearly forty years later, as he was dying, Ulysses S. Grant, former president of the United States and commanding general of the Union forces during the war between the states, wrote his memoirs in order to support his family after his death. He described his experiences as a young lieutenant during the Mexican-American War of 1846–7 and mentioned the late Robert E. Lee only in passing in that context. He instead dwelt in great detail on the day of 9 April 1865 at Appomattox Court House when Lee, as commanding general of the opposing Confederate forces, had surrendered to him. Grant wrote,

In my rough traveling suit, the uniform of a private with the straps of lieutenant general, I must have contrasted very strangely with a man so handsomely dressed, six feet high and of faultless form. We soon fell into conversations about old army times. He remarked that he remembered me very well in the old army, and I told him as a matter of course that I had remembered him perfectly, but from the differences in our rank and years (there being about sixteen years' difference in our ages), I had thought it very likely that I had not attracted his attention sufficiently to be remembered by him after such a long interval. And when I mentioned this to him, he smiled, a strange but gentle smile.

DAMNED RANKER

Paul Finch

We now turn our attention to the Crimean War, the subject of the next four stories. For once in military history Britain and France were allies and had joined forces with Turkey to arrest Russian interest in the Balkans. War was declared on 28 March 1854 and an expeditionary force, under the command of Lord Raglan and Marshal Jacques St Arnaud, landed in the Crimea in September with the intention of blockading the port of Sevastopol. The first major engagement was the Battle of the Alma on 20 September, which is where the following story begins. Paul Finch (b. 1964) is a journalist and former police officer, who has used his background in writing several scripts for the television series The Bill.

The first line to go up was the Rifle Brigade, its lads' emerald tunics shimmering in the mid-day haze. An obstacle they immediately came to was the river's north bank, where a maze-work of rock wall compounds enclosed the village vineyards. The Rifles threaded through it in their normal practised way, but then had the shallow waters of the Alma itself to cross, and now distant guns could be heard, round-shot coming whistling down the valley, though at present falling short. Some of the troops began to laugh . . . they could clearly see the missiles' heavy impacts on the barren soil to the south of the river.

Private Thaxted raised the brim of his shako and mopped dusty sweat from his brow, before gazing up at the heights. Here and there, blots of smoke earmarked the cannon currently at work, though more interesting were the dense masses of grey-clad Russian infantry making their perilous way down to defensive positions. Their own skirmishers, dismounted Cossacks for the most part, were concealed on lower ground, and were now beginning to exchange fire with the Rifles. Thaxted cupped his hand over his eyes to get a better view; the enemy's strength in numbers was formidable, but his positioning was also good. The southern slopes of the Alma were frightfully steep, while on this eastern flank, at least two hefty breastworks were visible, from which repeated plumes of smoke indicated that several well-stocked batteries were discharging. This would be a monumental task, the trooper realized, and on the back of six days' heavy marching from Kalamita Bay . . .

Thaxted would have chuckled in his usual ironic way, if he hadn't felt growing concern that such an impossible battle might cheat him of his goal. He glanced left along the line. Despite doggedly marching the arid coastline for the best part of a week, the majority of the 7th were in splendid array, heads tossed, bayonets at the ready, the white cross-belts startling on their vivid crimson tunics. At their western extremity, Major Lockhart sat astride his horse, proudly upright. To do the dashing warrior justice, he always made himself visible, though it might not be a wise ploy on this day. Thaxted shook his head, bewildered by the inconsistencies of officers.

"The Light Division will advance!" cried General Codrington, appearing at the front, almost hoarse in his efforts to be heard over the rising bombardment. "Trick yourself smart and watch your dressing! Remember who you are and where you are!"

"Trumpeter!" shouted Colonel Yea, taking up position at the battalion point, distinctive in his blue frock coat and cocked hat with ostrich plume. He was pulling on his gauntlets; the sabre shone at his hip. The requisite bugle call was made, and the men went stiffly to attention. "Fusiliers!" the Colonel called. "Fusiliers . . . forward, *march!*"

Similar cries went up along the line . . . "Duke of Wellington's . . . !"; "Royal Welsh . . .!"

And then, with a crash like a collision of railway locomotives, a nine-pound shell burst directly over their heads. Shattered corpses were flung in all directions, with in many cases only strips of charred uniform holding the chunks of butchered meat together. Other men went down to their knees screaming, clutching blinded eyes, broken eardrums. Thaxted's own head was ringing, but he pressed on determinedly through the smoke, as did the bulk of the line. The first shock of cannonade was always a terror, even to the stoutest hearts; men might go amok, seeking cover anywhere they could – boulders, broken-down walls – though it afforded them little protection. Many would die where they crouched, others be ripped to pieces as they marched. The veterans, however – troopers like Ben Thaxted – would bear through it unblinking, though possibly muttering prayers. They well knew this was no matter of expertise. When the true barrage began, only luck or the Lord could save you.

Not that he wasn't at least a mite concerned. He wanted to check, for instance, that Major Lockhart hadn't been killed . . . and a quick glance located the officer's shock of leonine-gold hair. Apparently, his shako had been blown off, but he was otherwise unhurt and cantering down the slope towards vineyards now cratered and burning. The private felt a surge of relief, though in conditions like these it was bound to be short-lived, and indeed it was . . . for a moment later the Russian artillery opened with grape and canister, sending screeching blizzards of steel fragments through the acrid pall. The rows of lush vine-plant were visibly shredded, the men already weaving through them struck down *en masse*. Directly ahead, the glittering waters of the river began kicking and spurting to the red-hot hail.

"Come on, you lazy fucking whoresons!" Sergeant Bowden bellowed, stalking among them, dragging them and pushing them onward. "That means you, Thaxted . . . show me your killing-face!"

"I'll show you the end of my bloody bayonet!" the trooper retorted under his breath.

As always, the NCO's hearing was pinprick accurate. "That's a charge!" he roared, as the thrusting tide of men forced them apart. "That's a charge, you damned ranker, damn your fucking eyes!"

"Ben . . . Ben, wait!" gasped young Noggs, staggering hurriedly up.

"Come on lad, we're at war now."

"Ben . . . you shouldn't talk to 'em like that," the boy stammered. He was seventeen if a day, and as always, a sweating, blinking bundle of nerves, though now greener at the gills than usual, for he'd spent this morning of his first ever action puking his insides out. "They'll flog the hide off you!"

Thaxted hawked and spat; the vile taste of burnt powder was filling his mouth. "They've already *tried* that. Now stay close, you hear. Down when I tell you."

The boy nodded and smiled in his nervy, rabbit-like way.

"Jesus, Mary and . . . *DOWN!*" Thaxted shouted.

They ducked, and the ground erupted before them, throwing both soldiers back onto their arses, deluging them with tattered vine and clods of soil. Others weren't so lucky – shards of shrapnel sliced them like blades, tore off their limbs, crushed their skulls. Their screams of pain were torture on the ears.

"J . . . Jesus!" Noggs stuttered. "It's a slaughterhouse . . ."

The older man hauled him to his feet. "Come on!"

For another ten minutes, they picked their way through

blasted allotments strewn with dead and dying men. Ahead, as
the banks of smoke drifted, the far shore of the Alma hove into
view and the green line of the Rifles was visible advancing
uphill, though this too had been severely enfilladed. Dozens of
green figures littered its wake like sticks of grass fallen to the
scythe. Thaxted would have crossed himself at the sight, had he
believed in anything other than his own personal mission.
When a drummer ten paces in front suddenly flew back, a hole
punched though his middle so big you could see daylight in it,
the seasoned trooper closed his eyes and simply stepped over
the corpse. Beside him, Noggs panted and strained under the
weight of his pack, but Thaxted could offer no condolence. The
heat was unbearable, but no words from *him* would alter the
fact.

"Let's hope Sevastopol's worth the game, eh?" cried a gruff
but rousing voice to the right of them.

They gazed round and saw Lockhart gallop past, his sabre
drawn. The officer was middle-aged, but still a fit man, and his
enthusiasm was admirable. Unlike so many senior ranks, he was
a renowned inspiration to his troops, but Thaxted could only
picture him a stinking fly-blown scarecrow, clad in rags and
huddled in the corner of some dank and filthy room . . . a
wasted thing, his skin filmy tissue stretched taut on the bones of
his starved and wretched face . . .

"Come on! Look lively!" Before them, Colour-Sergeant
Maybury was directing everyone through a narrow farm-gate
onto the northern bank of the river.

There seemed no other way forward, but beyond that gate a
phalanx of men from the Sherwood Forest regiment were
already assembled . . . most begrimed with smoke and dust,
many bearing bloody wounds. Clearly they were lost and out of
position. Even as the rain of grape swept over and around them,
Colonel Yea rode back and forth in their midst, arguing with
their subalterns. "The 95th is hindering my advance!" he
bellowed. "God damn it, you're a bloody shambles . . . where's
your deployment!"

Only muted responses came back, and Major Lockhart, in an

effort to prevent his support-companies bottling up the gateway and presenting easier targets to the gunners beyond the bridge, bade them all lie in the trampled foliage. "Cover!" he shouted. "Cover . . . on your bellies, now! Flat!"

They did as they were told, Thaxted and Noggs in the shadow of the river-facing wall, and for moments they were able to breathe again. As he waited, Thaxted drew the shotgun from his pack, broke it open and inserted two heavy ball-cartridges. It was an odd-looking thing, its fat barrels sawn down to virtually nothing, but its metal plating ornately carved with flowers and fish. Its stock had been whittled to a single-hand grip. According to Queen's Regulations, this was unofficial weaponry, but as was the way of many seasoned troopers, Thaxted had purloined it for himself and now kept it tight in his personal armoury.

The boy licked his thin lips. "You reckon we'll get near enough for that to be any use, hey, Ben?"

Thaxted tried to smile encouragement, but it was difficult. Above their heads, more shells exploded; the wall shook and spat out dust. "Reckon so, lad."

Noggs nodded and hefted his rifle.

"You've got that to start with," the man added. "The Minie . . . big advantage over the Russian smooth-bore. More accurate, twice the range."

Again the boy nodded. "You sound like a drill-pig . . ."

"The 7th will advance!" came the sudden voice of Colonel Yea. "Ignore these damn 95th riff-raff . . . walk right through them if they won't get out of the way!"

Thaxted grabbed his own rifle, slapped Noggs on the shoulder, and leaped to his feet. A moment later, they were over the wall and crossing the river. On a dry September day like this, it ran shallow, but the expanse was broad and bodies were floating past from further upstream. Thaxted glanced westward as they waded through, and saw the forward companies of the 2nd Division – the Borderers and the East Lancs – in similar disposition. The sight of them was a boost to morale, though they were taking a heavy pounding. The water boiled around them as fire rained down.

There was a momentary fright on the river's southern shore. Thaxted and Noggs came up unscathed, only to see Major Lockhart lying astride the gutted hulk of his horse. Whether he'd trodden on a mine or been hit from above was uncertain, but the animal was clearly dead, its innards littered around it in a glistening pulp. Its rider, his uniform blackened and smouldering, had been stunned to insensibility, but was at least alive. As Captain Monck and several infantrymen hurried towards him, he appeared to recover and started issuing orders again. "Up . . ." he coughed. "Up . . . all of you."

Again Thaxted was relieved; again he was impressed.

"They'll crack," the Major added, still egging on his men as he clambered to his feet. "Get up there lads . . . they'll crack and run!"

The men began their ascent . . . towards the larger of the Russian redoubts, which though six hundred yards away at least, still loomed over them like a fortress. The giant steel barrels of the enemy batteries were now visible, projecting down from the mighty earthworks, firing salvo after salvo in clouds of belching flame. These too had become targets, however. British artillery on the northern shore was hurling missiles at them. Smashing blows were struck against the ramparts; splinters flew like arrows; a cannon upended and blew itself apart – even above the deafening cacophony of battle, the screams of dying gunners were audible. The Rifles were also making an impact – they'd actually made it to the redoubt, though their numbers were horrendously thinned. Scarcely an officer higher than lieutenant remained, but most of the ranks had managed to take up sniper positions and were sharpshooting the defenders, picking them off with unerring accuracy.

Below meanwhile, the bugle-call to halt was sounded, and the men sank to their knees, gasping. Colonel Yea began the quick business of re-dressing. "We advance in line or not at all!" he shouted. "Break the line too often, and we're all easy meat!"

As he waited for his own squad to be called, Thaxted glanced leftward towards the lesser redoubt, where the 77th Middlesex were ascending only in fits and starts, the grey ranks of Russians coming boldly down to meet them, their muskets blooming smoke. On this part of the battlefield, however, the British were at last returning quality fire, blazing into the Czar's ranks with their murderous Minies, at that proximity raking massive gaps.

Thaxted stared at the Russians, fascinated. Everything said about them – namely, that they fought like disorganised rabble – appeared to be true. They came downhill in a mob, almost to a man clad in grey, ankle-length greatcoats, though the fur bonnets and gaudy vestments of Cossack horse-troops were also visible among them. As well as muskets, they had swords, hammers, reaping-hooks . . . many sported flintlock pistols, yet officers were almost indistinguishable from even the lowliest ranks. Inevitably, in such disorganization, they fell by the dozen . . . which again, was a heartening sight to Thaxted.

"Come on, Noggsy," he urged, as the order to advance was given. "We'll do for this lot in no time."

"Oh Jesus, Ben!" came the boy's querulous reply. "Oh Lord . . . look there!"

Thaxted gazed uphill and saw that Russian infantry were now starting to emerge on the flanks of the larger earthwork, and startlingly, these were not the unruly ruffians of before, but solid rank and file, in smart caps and jackets, their bandoleer-belts bulging with ammo. What was more, there were rivers of them; suddenly, they were spilling down from the heights like ants.

"Kazans!" someone shouted. "Special Guard!"

"We can match them!" cried Major Lockhart re-appearing on the point, sabre in hand. He mopped blood from his fore-head, and laughed scornfully. "At 'em, boys! Kill 'em all!"

Back in rigid formation, the thin line of the 7th went forward . . . a surely suicidal action which seemed to stump the Czar's troops, bringing them to an abrupt and staggering halt. Elite they may have been, but moments of bedlam followed as they were shunted forward by the swollen numbers behind, and thus unable to load or aim. And a split-second after that of course, the British were pouring volleys of shot into them from eyeball-to-eyeball range, taking a fearful toll immediately, dropping them in complete rows. Those Russians in support came gamely forward, loading and firing, but they too were peppered with leaden balls.

At several points the rival forces closed completely, and those were crazy, terrifying moments of flailing fists and slashing blades. The muggy air echoed to the din of ghastly shrieks and butchering blows, and was suddenly rank with the stench of sweat and blood and opened bowels. Thaxted and Noggs found themselves in the midst of it, lunging madly with their bayonets, though straight away the older man transfixed a hefty fellow, and his blade snapped at its base. Immediately, he pulled the shotgun from his pack, and with the first barrel-load, floored six Kazans, blowing multiple holes in each one of them.

"That's an illegal weapon, Private Thaxted!" roared Maybury.

The trooper only laughed. "'But for these vile guns, he would himself have been a soldier!'"

"Get on with it, you bugger! Don't quote your psalms at me!"

"*Psalms*, Colour-Sergeant?"

"Get forward, blast you!"

Thaxted laughed again, then emptied his second barrel, slamming another three from their feet, those around them now beginning to retreat. In fact, for all their Praetorian status, the Kazans were suddenly falling back in disorder, the sight of which served only to enthuse the Fusiliers, many of whom charged madly in pursuit, though Thaxted made sure he wasn't among them. He stopped Noggs too, pointing up to the redoubt . . . where a Union Jack was rising. It was fringed with burn and shot full of holes, but it was a Union Jack all the same. The standards of the 23rd Foot and 33rd fluttered beside it. A wild cheering could be heard.

"Oh my eye!" said the lad gleefully. "Does that mean it's over? Have we won?"

"There's better yet," said Thaxted. "See!"

Far to the right of them, in the lower portion of the valley, the smoke was still dense, but the various Scots regiments could now be seen advancing along the central Post Road to Sevastopol, in glittering echelon . . . the Black Watch, the Royal Highland, a triumphant wail of pipes rolling before them. For the weary troops who'd already fought their way onto the heights, it was a joy to behold. Even now, at this late stage, be-kilted, bear-skinned figures would suddenly flop down dead, but the dressing was immaculate, the progression fearless. And the moment the ghost-like shapes of Russians flowed up from their dugouts, a controlled firing commenced, withering fusillades knocking them down like skittles. Within minutes, the sons of Scotland were trampling a fresh carpet of fallen foes . . .

"*HERE THEY COME AGAIN!*" came a sudden croaking cry.

Noggs and Thaxted looked wildly back to their own front, and saw the Kazans in full-furied counter-attack, avalanching downhill. British shells now landed among them, each detonation throwing up fountains of dirt and stones, the rent and broken bodies of grey-coated men spinning through the air like rag-dolls, but they were coming nevertheless. The Fusiliers to the fore held their ground, though in many places they were overrun, and now Thaxted saw – to his consternation – that Major Lockhart was in dire peril, soaked all over in blood, his uniform riven to pieces, but slashing right and left with his sabre.

"Form square!" came the cry of Colonel Yea, but for the moment all was death and confusion, and no-one obeyed.

Bullets were zipping past, men began dropping again. Still, however, Thaxted could only gaze at the frenzied form of Lockhart as he battled the entire Kazan Regiment virtually on his own. "That damn fool's going to get himself killed!" he shouted, starting forward.

Noggs tried to hold him back. "Wait, Ben . . . what are you doing!"

"Lockhart's going to be killed!"

"So . . . let him, if he's that much a fool!"

"You don't understand, boy!" Thaxted yanked his arm free and rounded on the youngster. "If anyone kills him, it's me! Do you understand . . . *me!*"

Even under its greasy mask of powder-soot, Noggs's face paled. "What . . .?"

"Give me your Minie!" Thaxted said, snatching the boy's rifle. "This is *my* mission!"

"Ben, are you mad . . . you only laid eyes on him today!"

But the older man had fallen to one knee, rifle to his shoulder. "It *has* to be me."

"No . . ." the boy stammered. "I'll not let you hang yourself . . . *NO!*" And wildly, he grabbed at the rifle, the resulting shot going wide.

"God damn it!" Thaxted leaped to his feet and pushed Noggs away. Furiously, he began to reload. "You think I've come all this way for love of empire?"

"Ben . . . what are you saying?" Despite everything else, tears now glazed the boy's eyes. Frantically, he grabbed at his mentor's tunic. "Don't do this, please . . ."

But he never finished his sentence. A stray shell – British, no less – came shrieking down, though neither man saw nor heard it 'til it was virtually upon them. Thaxted had only one fleeting chance to cry "*NOGGS!*" before a calamitous explosion turned the world upside-down . . . seared that world black on white, white on black . . . fragmented all reality . . . reverberated for endless moments in a bottomless, icy darkness . . .

Days were long in the Marshalsea.

And not just for the debtors confined there. For the dependants who lived with them, for those friends and acquaintances who now and then felt they were obliged to visit. In all cases they found it a world apart. The unchanging shadows in its cramped rooms and dark, damp stairwells; the quiet of it – in the tight stone corridors; in the long narrow yard where the inmates walked. Scarcely a sound was ever heard in the Marshalsea. It was as if time was standing still between its high, spike-topped walls. The solitude of that place, especially considering that it stood in the heart of

London, was almost impossible to imagine for those who didn't know it.

The schoolmaster and his wife went there as unwillingly as all the rest. They'd never been in debt before, but they knew what it meant. They were taken by the tipstaff, who they assured all the way over Blackfriars Bridge that, having arranged a requisite loan, they'd be out again shortly, though he never once said a word to them, not even to announce their arrival on the narrow thoroughfare called Angel Court. The prison, which adjoined it, was a massive faceless building of no recognisable design. Its mighty walls were constructed from black brick – huge blocks set together with old mortar; the shadows it cast filled the tiny street. The schoolmaster and his wife could only gaze up in horror at the awesome structure.

An obese turnkey, in a crumpled green tailcoat and dusty tricorn, passed them through the first gate, and already sheer walls hemmed them in. To the left was the door to the warden's house, beyond that the entry passage with the arched roof. Down there, a second, equally shabby turnkey admitted them through a second gate, and at this point, they were ordered into the "lodge", so they could be "sized up for portrait". The schoolmaster's wife, a gentle mouse-like creature, but already four months pregnant, turned to her husband, frightened. He squeezed her hand bravely and told her: "There, there". They'd be paying their way out directly . . . at which the turnkey fell about laughing.

Thaxted opened his eyes in a world of torture.

Someone, it seemed, had hammered an iron spike into his skull. At least, it felt that way. His limbs . . . he wasn't sure if they were still attached to his body or not, for when he tried to move them, there was no response. At least his stomach was still his own, for it was freezing cold and he was sick to the pit of it. Likewise his eyes . . . he could see, though only dark, wavering forms, as if candle-fire flickered somewhere close by. In fact, the longer he gazed, the brighter that light became, until at last he saw a lantern and blurred figures crouching around him, mumbling together. He wanted to speak with them, but he couldn't . . . his mouth was crusty-dry, his throat constricted.

When he made an effort, he all but swooned, and fireworks of pain shot up from his deepest places.

Coarse hands, he realized, were now fumbling and snatching at him. In the dull glow, he could finally see faces . . . bearded, dirty, wolfish. And then, in an instant, Thaxted knew what this was . . . good God, the carrion crows! The scavengers and thieves who lurked around every battlefield! Many a good soldier, wounded but helpless, had died to the blows of their cudgels and thrusts of their knives . . .

Not this one . . . no, not this one.

Wildly, with every ounce of strength left, Thaxted began to struggle. At first taken by surprise, they grunted and hissed and wrestled him down all the harder, but when his bloody fingers clawed at their eyes and swiping fists connected with their chins, they swore loudly and openly, and knelt on him with all their colossal weight . . . and at last the breath wheezed out of him, and the soldier fell back into a black pit of delirium.

The wall was scabrous – once plaster, now soggy and crumbling, though the floor was worse – stone-slabbed, yet thick with slime; not just mud, but faeces, urine, vomit . . .

Thaxted found himself gazing at it for several minutes, before reality hit him, and it only did then because the stink suddenly became intolerable. He gagged, put a limp hand to his mouth, tried to roll away on his bed of mouldering straw, but found that he'd been thrown in a corner and there was nowhere to roll to.

"How you doing, mate?" came a thickly accented voice.

Very feebly, the trooper looked round. Beside him, a thin man in torn, grimy livery of the Rifle Brigade was sitting up on his own bed of straw. Thaxted saw that one of the fellow's legs was missing, his trouser tucked in around what had once been his left knee. If the bone-saw had left him in agony, though, he didn't seem distressed. In fact, under his ragged beard, and dirty straggles of grey hair, he was grinning.

"Where . . . is this?" Thaxted stammered.

"Hospital, mate."

"Ho . . . hospital?" Thaxted almost went dizzy. There were others in there, he could now tell; he could hear groans, coughing, the occasional deranged or drunken laugh.

"Aye," the Rifleman replied. "Scutari. Well . . . not *much* of a hospital, if I'm true. Derelict barracks more like. Turkish. Bit of a shit-hole."

The fellow's dialect was raw, guttural . . . he was clearly from the North Country somewhere, though the Fusilier was hardly interested in that. He glanced up. Close by there was a doorway. He didn't know where it led, but any doorway was preferable to none. Very slowly, gasping at the effort it took, he tried to climb to his feet. There was no strength there however, and he pitched heavily down again.

"Easy, mate," counselled the Rifleman. "You been hurt, remember."

Thaxted was nauseated by the fall; pins and needles ran riot over his body, and it was several seconds before he was even able to look down and assess his wounds. The first thing he saw was his uniform, or rather the fragments of it which remained – his tunic, for instance, was ripped almost to scraps and had been tossed over him as a sheet. What he could see of his flesh was cut and bruised beyond recognition. Here and there, bindings had been applied, all now loose and sticky with gore, and trailing off in caked, putrefying strips.

"The . . . fight," he said slowly, now recalling. "The fight . . . at the Alma."

The Rifleman sniffed. "Yeah . . . we won. Leastwise, that's what I 'eard."

With more exertion than he'd ever imagined, but now driven by desperation, Thaxted managed to climb to his feet again, though even then his head began to swim. Only by sliding along the wall was he able to reach the door, though beyond it lay a dark and foetid passage which bade no entry.

The Rifleman was still talking. "Got clobbered in Bourliouk, myself. Bastard Ruskie grenade . . ."

"Noggs . . ." Thaxted muttered, sweat dripping from his brow. "There was another man with me. Well . . . a boy.

Norman Coggin. Private Norman Coggin." The Fusilier looked round. "He here?"

"Don't know, mate . . . teeming, this fucking place."

And teeming it was. For the first time, the Fusilier was able to see the full extent of the room. It was a large chamber, at one time a barrack-stable but now a ward, though little had been done to cleanse it from its original purpose. To make matters worse, it was grossly overcrowded, the casualties – many still swimming in blood – lying shoulder-to-shoulder. Some were conscious . . . even playing cards together. Others, however, were dying . . . burned, disfigured, missing arms or legs or both. Several already *had* died, and were being used as pillows. Rats and beetles scurried among them, flies swarmed on lakes of noisome scum which clearly overflowed from the privies. There was a miasmic stench of gangrene . . .

"Am I dead?" said Thaxted, sinking to his knees. "Dead and in Hell?"

"Think it's bad in here, you should see the cellars?" the Rifleman replied. "If you've got any money, of course, you can buy yourself a little extra. The orderlies . . . they're not proud, if you get my drift."

But the Fusilier knew without needing to look, that nothing remained of his purse or personal belongings. The corner where they'd dumped him was empty. Not that he'd owned too much of value . . . with one exception. "I . . . I had a gun," he mumbled.

"Blimey, mate . . . didn't we all!"

Thaxted closed his eyes as he heard that gun . . . a loud and echoing report, muffled by the high, spike-topped wall, but regular as clockwork; every five minutes on the minute, crashing aloud in the hot, still, stifling air . . .

The main yard was perhaps ten feet in width and encircled the prison's residence – a clutch of old buildings, built back-to-back and so dilapidated that only the fact they were leaning against each other seemed to hold them up. There wasn't a window-frame, it seemed, with a shard of glass in it, not a crack in the stonework where weeds didn't grow.

On their arrival, the schoolmaster and his wife were led up a steep draughty stair to a garret room that was dank, bare, ingrained with filth, its ceiling clotted with cobwebs. Again the schoolmaster reassured his wife, telling her that at least he had space for his bagful of books, now the only thing of value they possessed.

The turnkey expressed doubt at that, however. It wouldn't be easy, he said. Three other families shared that room.

The orderlies at Scutari were all the things the one-legged Rifleman had hinted at, and worse. They wore official blue smocks, but were for the most part dirty, idle and disinterested. At a guess, their previous occupations included criminal, harlot, vagrant. Often, they went around drunk or intoxicated by drugs left for the patients. Their chief overseer was a man called Byers, a swarthy brute, from whose thick leather belt a truncheon swung. Why a hospital orderly should carry a truncheon was never explained.

Only after Thaxted had been at Scutari three days did he spot a proper medical officer . . . a tall, lean colonel, with lush white sidelocks. He was striding through the ward at speed, his cloak wrapped tightly around him. He was evidently on a spot-check, with apparently no intention of stopping to examine or treat anyone. By this time, the Fusilier knew why. Things were bad at camp, but in a warren of filth and hopelessness like this, dysentery and cholera would spread like wildfire. The trooper knew he had to get out.

"Sir," he said. "Excuse me, sir."

The surgeon looked round, startled that someone had spoken to him. When he realized it was a patient, he went even paler than he had been before. "What . . . what do you want?" His tone was clipped, nervous.

"Just wondering . . . what's wrong with me, sir? And when I'll be well?"

The surgeon made no effort to come closer, but he looked Thaxted over. "By the state of you . . . multiple wounds." He shrugged. "You can leave here when you feel fit enough to rejoin your battalion." And with that he turned to leave.

"Oh . . . sir!" The doctor glanced back, visibly agitated. "Just . . . wondered if you had any information on Major Lockhart?"

"Lockhart?"

"Royal Fusiliers, sir. Stood beside him on the Alma, I did. He was hurt too."

The doctor considered. "Er . . . yes, yes, I remember hearing about a certain Lockhart. Seems he was wounded but survived. Fought admirably, as I recall. He'll probably get a medal or something, in reward."

Thaxted couldn't resist a smile. " 'Let them, for their reward, be soon brought to shame . . .' "

The colonel gave him a curious, almost haunted look, then hurried from the room.

"What's that then?" asked the Rifleman, whose name was Charlie Lansing.

"Book of Common Prayer," Thaxted replied. "Never read it?"

Lansing snorted. "You're a funny one, Ben-mate. Seem plenty well-educated?"

Thaxted shrugged. "Much good it's done me."

The man taught the boy with all his teacher's skill, though it wasn't easy, as the boy had to work long hours in order that they might pay their "chummage", and buy their bits of coal and candles and what-not. Nothing was cheap in the Marshalsea, neither ale nor bread, not even water . . . mainly because the turnkeys had a smart mark-up on everything they permitted to be sold.

Certain winters, when the frost was particularly hard, and fuel scarce even for ready coin, the man had no option but to put some of his books on the paltry fire, and this hurt him grievously, though no more so than the repeated bouts of 'flu and jail-fever which reduced him very quickly to a withered husk too sick and weak even to write his regular letters of entreaty.

The boy, who attended all his lessons with vigour and determination, because the man told him his "poor, departed mother" would have wished it, was often curious about these letters, and would ask the man who he was writing to, and the man would simply say: "Someone who might help us, if he's a mind to . . . though I suppose ten pounds is a lot to be owed in times like these, even for an officer and a gentleman."

Thaxted came to enjoy the company of Rifleman Lansing. The doughty old Lancashire lad bore his injury bravely, and kept his grizzled chin up despite the fact his future looked grim. One-legged, he'd be little use in any kind of paying-work, and his pension would be negligible . . . in truth, it didn't bear thinking about. So Lansing did not think about it. And Thaxted never mentioned it.

"I seem to have spent my whole life in institutions," said the Fusilier, as they shared a bowl of oatmeal. All around them, the ordeal went on, the squalid stink of blood and faeces pervading the hovel like smog . . . yet even this they'd managed to grow accustomed to. A sharp and wintry chill was the problem now.

"Insti-what?" said the Rifleman.

"Shit-holes."

"Oh yeah . . . me too." Lansing sniffed. "Born in a lodging house, Foundry Road, Preston. Me old ma popped it a month later. Never knew me dad. Climbing for the parish sweep by the time I was four."

"I was coal-whipping, myself," Thaxted replied. "Wapping docks. Six to twenty-one, I did . . ."

Lansing nudged his arm. "Aye aye . . ."

The Fusilier glanced up to where new arrivals were suddenly spilling into the ward . . . all freshly tattered and bloodied. One young fellow, in the blue and gold of the Hussars, but now powder-burned and clutching a torn stump where his arm had been, stood rocking on his heels, ashen-faced.

"Where you from, mate?" Lansing asked him.

"Er . . ." The "cherry-picker" was clearly in shock. "Bal . . . Balaklava. There was . . . a battle."

"You don't say."

"We . . . they, er . . . they . . . decimated us."

"Decimated *who*?" said Thaxted.

"Er . . . 17th Lancers, 4th Hussars . . ." His words trailed off almost drunkenly.

The Fusilier relaxed again; he continued to eat. "Nothing like your pretty parades on Phoenix Park, then, hey? Well . . . if you're looking for a bed, there's none here. Spare a bit of floor, if you like."

The Hussar took the floor . . . and promptly died there. Afterwards, Thaxted stood by a window and gazed into the rainy courtyard, where the young man's body, stitched up in a sackcloth bag, was thrown onto a huge pile of other corpses all awaiting burial. As he gazed at the limp shapes, he thought of the pauper-pits at the back of the Marshalsea, and how he'd stood there in a similar storm one day in '39, and watched his father's sheet-wrapped remains slide down. The prison warden, a tall man, with skin the colour of iron and a mouth as hard as a trap, had been present in his topper and greatcoat, snivelling irritably as the parson went through the motions. After it was all over, the warden had spared a few brief words for the bereaved, and went through the normal routine of handing over a shilling from his own pocket. "Hope it's some recompense. Nasty thing for you, finding him up there like that."

"Nasty place for him to be," the youth had replied, refusing to take the money.

The warden had been outraged. "At least it gave you a roof over your head!" he'd barked. Then he'd grinned ghoulishly, a victor after all. "Not that it will, now." He'd nodded at the grave. "That's all your debts settled in full."

"Not nearly," the youth had mumbled, as they'd turned him out on the street. "Not even half . . ."

"Captain Lockhart?" said the sergeant, impressed. "Why yes indeed. He still serves in the Royal Fusiliers, and a fine gentleman he is too."

The tall young man with the thick black hair and sideburns, then ripped off his leather apron and stepped down from the coal-cart. "I'll take your poison chalice, Sergeant-Major."

"My what? You've a strange way of speech for a coster-lad and no mistake." Mumbles of agreement came from the ragged crowd gathered there in the gas-lit gloom of Bluegate Court. *"You sure you're not some recruiting officer yourself . . . a Guardsman maybe, incognito?"*

There was muted, vaguely bewildered laughter.

"Do you want me, or don't you?" said the young man. Not only was he impressively tall, but he had a dark and sullen look which the sergeant feared but also liked. Here was a soldier-in-waiting.

"Oh . . . we'll have you right enough." The sergeant slapped him on the shoulder, and bade him stand by the ensign. *"This is definitely the spirit, lads!"* he then shouted, turning back to the onlookers. *"Take a gander at this strapping chap . . . we'll have the ladies swooning after him right enough, when we get him out in his dress-coat and forager's cap."* His brusque tone rose up and up though the dank and overhung rookeries. *"I tell you, boys . . . you can waste your lives down here in the dregs if you want, spat on, stamped on, swilling everything away in a river of gin, but you join Her Majesty's finest, and things will be very different. We'll give you a reason to live . . ."*

Thaxted went to the overseer's office in the full darkness of midnight, working his way mole-like through the serpentine corridors, navigating by the groans and gasps. When he found the place – a niche of a room in the old barrack gatehouse – Byers was alone, sleeping as he always did . . . arse on his strong-box, head on the shelf beside a single candle. The flame flickered on his fat, bristling face. Thaxted was charmed by the fellow's vulnerability. Anyone who worked so hard, needed his sleep. And so thinking, he woke the man, shaking him by the shoulder. Byers sat up grunting.

"They sent me to India first," said Thaxted quietly. "But *he* didn't go . . . Lockhart. They said he had business affairs in England."

The orderly gazed at him, baffled. "Uh?"

"Can you imagine . . . fourteen years on the Punjab plains?" Thaxted shook his head wearily. "Battles, whippings, malaria

. . . and for what? It's taken 'til now, you see. But this time I'm going to do it. For real. First though, I want my cattle-gun."

"What you say?" Byers' dull, froggy eyes were crusted with sleep.

"My cattle-gun," Thaxted replied. "A handsome piece, as it turned out. Listened to it every day in the Marshalsea. Some slaughter-man was using it over the east wall, near the tannery-sheds. Every few minutes or so, every day . . . for nineteen years. That's an awful lot of cows, Mr Byers. I started feeling sorry for them, you see . . . I mean, we never got to eat meat anyway, so what the fuck? When they kicked me out, the very first thing I did was go round the corner and pinch the bloody thing. Might save some cows, I thought . . . *plus* . . . might find a use for it myself. Very appropriate for a job I had in mind."

The orderly had now regained sufficient sensibility to realize that it was still the dead of night, and that his gin-soaked head was thumping. He took a watch from his smock-pocket, glanced at it . . . then glared up. "Damn you for waking me . . ."

"*Damn me!*" Thaxted snarled, slapping the watch down and grabbing the man by his throat. "*They already have* . . . but I ain't going alone! You heard the phrase 'devil with devil damned', Byers?"

The orderly could only choke and struggle, and grab at his belt. To his horror, though, he found the cudgel missing . . . missing because this gaunt, black-bearded maniac was now wielding it himself.

"How about . . . 'Justice is truth in action!'" Thaxted hissed, and he crashed the weapon down on the orderly's balding skull. "Ought to know that one, Byers . . . Mr Disraeli only coined it three years ago!"

So ranting, he hit the man again and again, and finally dragged him bleeding and whimpering from off his strong-box.

"Open that chest," the soldier growled. "Do it now . . . and pray my cattle-gun's in there. *And* my money."

Trembling violently, the orderly dragged the keys from his pocket and within a moment had lifted the lid. A virtual treasure-trove was revealed . . . bottles of spirits, medicines, wads of paper-money, heaps of jewellery – mainly rings and neck-chains, plus several-dozen watches – and an earthenware chamber-pot packed to the brim with Turkish coins. There was even a diary or two, and a personal Bible imprinted with gold leaf. Without hesitation, Byers handed over a bundle of notes, then dug quickly down and in the bottom left-hand corner, located the curved hand-grip of the shotgun. Clearly relieved, he hauled it out, then rooted round until he found the leather pouch in which several dozen cartridges still remained.

The Fusilier cracked the weapon open, to check the mechanism. "Thought this fancy decor meant it was worth a bob or two, hey?" he said. "Didn't realise it was a slaughter-yard tool?"

Byers said nothing. He simply knelt there sweating, blood dribbling down his face.

The trooper leaned past him and dipped his hand into the Turkish money. "This presumably represents what you've so far managed to sell?"

Byers licked his lips, though the spittle began to dry on them when he saw his captor slot two cartridges into the breech of the gun and snap it closed.

"Well, allow me," Thaxted added, now casually trickling coins into the barrels, "to ensure you take some with you." He levelled the weapon. "Wherever you may go."

"Wait!" cried the orderly. "*Waiiiiiii . . .*" The shrill scream echoed through the filthy passages, only for two loud blasts to silence it forever.

"Private Thaxted reporting for duty, sir!"

The second-lieutenant had just taken the sheaf of documents handed to him by the new arrival, when the Russian artillery began to bombard and a salvo of case-shot hit him square-on, tearing his head, right arm and right shoulder clean off. The mutilated body stayed upright for a moment, the private's paperwork still clasped in its trembling left hand, then toppled heavily backwards, blood spraying from a plethora of severed arteries. Thaxted gazed down for a moment then stooped to retrieve his papers. As an afterthought, he also took the slain officer's revolver, and a handful of extra rounds, shoving them under his greatcoat as he picked his way down the trench.

In his absence, it was clear the once elite "Army of the East" had degenerated. Many of the men he now saw – a mixture of Fusiliers, Guards and North Lancs, mostly smoking their pipes or brewing tea as they waited to be called into the forward redoubts – were clad in uniforms sorely frayed and patched. Others wore pillaged Russian coats, or bits of fur and sheepskin. Toes were visible through the ends of boots, cheekbones were knife-blades in faces emaciated with hunger.

According to his written orders, he was now on "the Inkerman bastion", a fortified bivouac, lodged on high ground to the south of the Tchernaya River, where it could protect the right flank of the siege-lines at Sevastopol. None of this meant much to Thaxted . . . he couldn't picture the Crimean topography, and he hadn't seen anything even remotely approaching a town, let alone the great naval base they were allegedly assaulting. As far as he could make out, the usual bleak terrain lay to the front of the earthworks, not to mention behind them and on all sides. To make matters worse, it was now cloaked in drifting fog, though shell-holes were visible. A few of these still smouldered, and had shattered corpses strewn around them, most in the field-grey of Russian foot-sloggers. From what Thaxted had been told, several half-hearted attacks had already been repelled, though the big one was yet to come . . . and it wasn't as if the British hadn't already taken casualties. He glanced into the back of a cart and saw the body of General Sir George Cathcart, an illustrious figure at Horse Guards, one arm now shorn off, his belly burst open and entrails hanging out.

"Thaxted?" came a gruff voice. The Fusilier turned and saw Colour-Sergeant Maybury approaching along the trench. "Bollocks an' all!" said the NCO, a weak grin splitting his unshaved face. "Well, well my lad . . . you must have upset those doctors to end up back here."

"Requested it, Colour-Sergeant."

"Requested it?" The sergeant shook his head. "That bomb scrambled what little brains you've got."

They walked side-by-side into the section held by the remnants of the 7th. There were mumbled greetings, even a smile or two, but most men stared through their returning comrade as if they didn't see him. The searing cold was gnawing at them . . . apart from the gear they'd improvised themselves, few were in proper winter-wear.

"I see Lord Raglan's been tending to his supply lines," Thaxted grunted.

"It's a shambles," Maybury replied. "If His Grace, the Duke had been in charge, General Airey and the other quartermasters would be chained up and breaking fucking rocks. There's nothing surer. 'Cept they might have been hanged."

"Where's Major Lockhart, Colour-Sergeant?"

"On the Sandbag Battery, why?"

"Got a message for him."

Maybury held his hand out. "Give it here. I'll send the lancejack."

The private shook his head. "Personal, if you don't mind. A confidence."

The sergeant shrugged. "Well . . . report back here when you've done." He looked thoughtful for a moment. "You'd best be on your metal, son. Don't know if you've heard, but . . . well, they're going to try and sweep us off this plateau today. We've really got it coming."

The trooper nodded, then turned and set off towards the artillery posts. He knew time wasn't on his side. The Russian barrage was growing in intensity, and when he finally ascended the so-called Sandbag Battery – an abutment of higher ground, encircled with mealy-sacks, and sporting two nine-pounders and their crews – he fancied he could hear the jingling harness of cavalry, though drifting palls of mist still obscured much. Major Lockhart was in an even more forward position than the gunners, a slightly lower dugout all but invisible from the battery behind. At present he was alone there, except for a young corporal awaiting orders.

"Major Lockhart, sir?" said Thaxted, descending the ladder.

The officer lowered his field-glasses and turned. This was the first time Thaxted had been so close to him, and immediately it was apparent that much of the mythology about this man was true. He was fifty-five at least, but still had an aura of virility. Despite the privations of the last few months – and Lockhart was as dirty and smoke-stained as the rest – he bore himself with aristocratic dignity, but also a certain wildness which well suited his adventurous reputation. His shoulders were strong, his head broad and fierce like a lion's, the eyes chips of azure amid thick golden locks and mutton-chop whiskers. In most circumstances, Thaxted reflected, this would be a man worth serving. But appearances were deceptive.

"What are you?" Lockhart asked curtly. "A new recruit?"

The trooper smiled. "Return from sick, sir. Got myself some new kit. At least ten pounds' worth."

"What do you want, Private? I think you can see we're busy."

"Want to fight with you, sir."

"Uh?"

"Heard you always put yourself where the danger is."

Lockhart gave him a baffled stare, before looking back to the front. Hoarse voices were now calling to each other in the fog. Overhead, more shells were bursting, blasting the eardrums, throwing brilliant orange glares all along the line. The churned ground shook to each explosion. "Gaskins!" said the major.

The corporal stumbled forward. He was pasty-faced and trembling with fear. Even in the awful November chill, sweat stood on his brow.

"Pass the message. All squads to their positions."

Gaskins nodded and vanished from sight. Lockhart pursed his lips. Deep in the mist, bayonets glinted. Hooves were clearly drumming. He handed Thaxted his field-glasses. "You . . . whatever your name is, take a look. Tell me what you see."

The trooper took the glasses, but made no effort to look through them. "*Whatever my name is,*" he slowly repeated. "My name's Thaxted, sir. Not William, mind . . . but Ben. Ben Thaxted."

A moment passed before any recognition came into the major's eyes, though there was more bewilderment there than guilt. "Thaxted . . .?"

"You remember?" the private wondered.

"Sounds familiar, I . . ."

"So should ten pounds. But then you'd probably throw that away on the Soho gaming-tables in a single night, am I right?"

"William . . . William Thaxted?"

The trooper nodded, then suddenly reached over his shoulder and ripped the shotgun from his backpack, levelling it on the officer's chest. "This is for him, you see!"

Despite his famed courage, Lockhart backed up in fright. "What the devil . . ."

"Shut up!" A second passed as Thaxted pondered their position. The drumming hooves were closer. Orders were being shouted in the British redoubts. "I'd grin and enjoy this, Lockhart, but I'm not cruel. This is something *I have* to do, rather than want." Thaxted indicated the topmost firing-step. "Up there . . . now! When you die, I want them to think it was in battle. You'll benefit from that too, if you consider it."

The major made no move. He stared at the private, his eyes like beams of light.

"Get up, Major! Or I'll shoot you where you stand . . . it's immaterial to me."

"You think I fear you?" the officer asked. "When an enemy force eight times our size is here."

"You and your little war are of no concern to me," Thaxted replied.

"Before you pull that trigger, my lad, it might be as well to tell you that I don't know what the bloody hell this is even about!"

"Don't give me that," the trooper snarled. "Upwards of sixty letters, my father wrote you . . . begging for relief on that minuscule debt. Did you reply? Not even once. So he died in there. After nineteen years . . . *NINETEEN YEARS!*"

And only now did the chill of realization go through Major Lockhart, for in the strange brutal face of this intense and frightening man, he suddenly recognized the timid little school-master who'd once tutored his children, and who'd once bor-rowed a ten-pound note to settle some account so that his expectant wife could go into labour with peace of mind.

Almost casually, the trooper raised the gun to his shoulder and drew back its hammers. "You don't want to die a hero, Lockhart? Well . . . that's up to you."

"Thaxted . . . wait!"

"Farewell, Major."

"Wait . . ."

SCREEEEEEEEEEE . . .

The detonation was ear-shattering, for the blast went off very close to them. Mindless moments of fire and dizziness followed . . . then Thaxted was lying amid a debris of charred soil and splintered woodwork. Choking smoke enveloped him, sandbags had fallen down, and it was moments more before he realized that in the shock and concussion he'd dropped his weapon. Still blinded and coughing, he groped around for it, only to be drawn up sharp by the tip of Major Lockhart's sabre suddenly pressing at his throat.

The private slumped back into the wreckage. He could only glare up at the cold figure now regarding him. Among the many things he'd done in his life, Lockhart was alleged to have fought several duels, and to have triumphed in all of them. He never bore an insult lightly, so it was unlikely he'd let this pass. A moment later, however, the officer lowered his sword, though there was no mercy in his face. Instead, the flush of battle was appearing there, and behind him Thaxted now saw the Rus-sians, dense cohorts flooding up the moonscape slopes towards them. As so often, the Czar's men came without rigid forma-tion, infantrymen trundling alongside Cossack horse-troops, all shrieking in a blood-chilling dirge.

"Yes, Thaxted," said the officer tightly. "There's your real enemy! This is what you're here for!"

"I'm here for *you*, Lockhart."

"You hate me, yet you don't even know me?"

"I don't know *them!*" the private retorted.

Oddly, Lockhart grinned. He drew his pistol and lifted one leg over the sandbags. "Then come and meet them, man . . . if you've the courage. If you're genuinely a soldier. If you're not some cowardly malingerer who deserves to have spent his life in jail!" He chuckled. "I could kill you now, if I wanted to . . . but I know where my *real* duty lies."

"You'd be better killing me, Lockhart . . . I swear it!"

"Maybe later, Private Thaxted," the major replied. He stepped out onto open ground. "Maybe later."

"Damn you, Lockhart!" Thaxted scrabbled around for his shotgun.

When he found it and stood up however, the fight was already upon him. To either side of the battery, British troops were lurching up over the sandbag walls, raining shot down on the approaching foe. Straight away, the Russians began to fall, but as on the Alma, there were uncountable numbers of them in support, and now they too were returning fire, though as usual, Major Lockhart had taken a fearless forward position and was urging his men on.

"At 'em, boys!" he called, waving with his sabre. "Queen and country!"

With wild cries, his men followed him downhill, but the enemy musketry intensified, many in the Russian front rank dropping to one knee to take better aim . . . and soon British troops too were toppling over.

Thaxted watched, still vaguely dazed, only for a musket-ball to whine past his ear with inches to spare. He turned and saw a clutch of Russian infantry dashing over the mud towards him. From somewhere behind him, a nine-pounder on the battery boomed, hurling a ton of grape down onto them and slaughtering all but one, though *he* was left wounded and tottering. Thaxted fired at him with the shotgun, blowing him from his feet, then clambered from the dug-out and joined the advance. He still wanted Lockhart, but for the moment at least, the frenzy of battle made all else irrelevant. One cartridge remained in his shotgun, and he let it fly the moment he closed, hitting an infantryman squarely in the belly. The man went down and

Thaxted leaped over him. Volleys of lead still poured back and forth, but on all sides hand-weapons were appearing – blades, mattocks. Cossacks swarmed up, hurling their lances, slashing with their sabres. Thaxted drew the revolver and shot one though the neck. Another homed in from the side, his stallion grunting and puffing and blowing out clouds of steam. The Fusilier ducked the sweeping blade, then fired twice from point-blank range. The Cossack was hurled to the ground, black lung-blood erupting from his frothing mouth.

From all directions now there was a frantic crescendo of shouts, a mad crashing of gunfire. The stench of blood and powder filled the air. Bullets spun left to right, whistling and screaming. Then a musket-butt caught Thaxted between the shoulders. Agonized and winded, he toppled forward, but still managed to twist about as he fell and shoot the Russian sergeant behind, who crumpled down lifeless. The Fusilier staggered back to his feet, panting, cringing with pain from what he was sure were at least two fractured ribs. He glanced desperately around and spotted Colour-Sergeant Maybury. The brawny NCO had snatched a Cossack's sabre and was now hacking a thrown horseman to ribbons. Other members of the 7th were at it hand-to-hand, rolling and wrestling on the ground, many so plastered in mud that they were indistinct from their opponents. Sergeant Bowden was walking jerkily back to the trench, a rope of intestine dangling from a gaping wound in his lower left back. Fiery Welshman Private Jordan, bayonet levelled, was taking on all comers. In the blinking of an eye, he spitted two, but then a mortar-shell hit the earth at his feet and blew him to fragments.

Thaxted gazed dumbly, goggle-eyed. On all sides it was chaos, noise, blood, confusion. The company bugler stumbled towards him, blinded by a shot across his eyes. A second shot then hit the boy's head with sledge-hammer force, imploding his skull in a welter of brain-meal and bone-splinter. By now Colour-Sergeant Maybury was dead too. A sword-stroke to the neck had decapitated him. His killer was a dismounted Cossack of gigantic proportions. Colourful, flowing robes adorned his titan's frame. His head was the size of a boar's, and heavily bearded. On it, he wore steel helmet with bear-fur trimmings. His weapon was a massive hook-bladed scramasaxe. Thaxted raised his revolver and fired at the warrior. The chamber jammed harmlessly however . . . wet or blocked with dirt. The Cossack sighted him, and with a bellow, charged. He wore boots of wolf-skin, cross-strapped to mid-thigh. Beneath his robes, a cuirass glinted, and a shirt of chain-mail. What kind of war was this?, the Englishman wondered, astonished.

A moment later, the scramasaxe was hurtling down at his cranium. Only in the last fleeting second, did Thaxted throw himself to one side. The Russian raised his weapon for another mighty backstroke. Thaxted this time held his ground, stabbing his pistol into the barrel-chest, pumping the trigger. Still there was no response, and he was forced to duck a second blow, though on this occasion the sword-hilt caught his temple and hurled him stunned into the mud.

Grey phantoms of Russians hemmed him in. A few fell stiffly, shot off their feet. Most were advancing though. In some place high above, the triumphant Cossack gave a colossal belly-laugh, and drew back his blade for the *coup de grace* . . . only for a bayonet to pierce the back of his head and spring out through his mouth, severing his tongue at the root. With a gargling scream, the Russian tottered away, but Major Lockhart yanked his bayonet free, then lunged forward again, this time ramming it under the giant's arm and penetrating his heart.

"On your feet, trooper!" the officer roared down at Thaxted. "Feigning death is desertion!"

Thaxted snatched up the scramasaxe and scrambled to his feet. A Russian captain appeared from nowhere and took aim at them with his pistol, but the Fusilier was on him in an instant, splitting his skull like a melon. A Russian corporal came shrieking forward, but Lockhart stuck his rifle over Thaxted's shoulder and fired into the man's chest. When another Cossack wheeled round to face them, the major drew his revolver, and blasted a hole between the horseman's eyes.

"Lieutenant Grant!" Lockhart roared. "Lieutenant Grant!"

A grubby subaltern, streaming blood from a gash on his forehead, came stumbling forward.

"Find yourself a trumpeter and have the men retreat to the bags!" the major shouted. "I want organized firing-blocks, now!"

Nodding, the lieutenant hurried away and a moment later the call went out, and the troops began to pull back. It was no flight however, more a fighting-retreat. Volley after volley struck the pursuing Russians, clearing immense gaps in their ranks, but their battle-fury was carrying them forward all the same. The guns on the Sandbag Battery continued to spew payload after payload at them. Thaxted was emptying his shotgun and reloading it at such a rate that its barrels were soon too hot to touch. Each and every cartridge left four or more Russians mangled in the dirt, but still the combatants raged forward so that close-quarter fighting recommenced, men flying at each other with daggers and even rocks, slashing throats, smashing skulls. Thaxted swung the scramasaxe madly. When it broke, he used his shotgun as a club. He was vaguely aware that Lockhart was somewhere to the left, cutting frantically with his sabre.

"I see you're a soldier after all, Thaxted!" the officer shouted. "You'll see it close-up before the day's done!"

The major laughed aloud. "You may get your chance soon . . . look there!"

Thaxted risked glancing behind, and saw bodies of French Legionnaires appearing on the southern crest of the ridge, in pristine formation. From that high position, the covering fire of their rifles would be devastating . . . and indeed it was. A battery of field-howitzers was also hauled into view and let loose on the Russians. Under such intensive targeting, the Czar's men fell like stalks of wheat, and when the long-range eighteen-pounders in the British siege-train joined the barrage as well, hitting their centre repeatedly – ploughing infantry into the ground like chaff – their order began to disintegrate. Wave after wave of them still rolled forward, but the force of their attack was wilting badly.

Despite this, Thaxted was still in the midst of melee upon melee. He found he'd been driven leftwards, away from the battery itself, which the Russians had swarmed onto like apes, though the gun-crews were doing their best to battle them off with spades and ramrods. The Fusilier would have helped, but he was now almost too exhausted to stand. The reek of bones and gore filled his nostrils, of guts and mud and seething sweat. The shrieks of death and rage were pitched at a hysterical note, setting his head spinning. These were the last frenzied moments, he realized . . . it was make or break for the assaulting force. A dismounted cavalry officer came at him. The Fusilier grabbed up a discarded sabre, parried a thrust, then slashed into his neck. A Kazan infantryman blundered into view. Thaxted hit him with a blow so fierce the sword lodged in his bowels, blood spurting out in a boiling fountain.

And around him now, at last, the Russian assailants – many of their brigades cut down to mere handfuls – were finally falling back. The iron-hard French Legionnaires had advanced through the exhausted British ranks, a hedge of bayonets to the fore. Fusillade after fusillade they unleashed, scything the enemy down, pushing them backwards. The Czar's ravaged men hit them only with a single ragged line of fire before turning in chaotic flight, but even then their ordeal wasn't over. A unit of French horse-artillery also rode up and began firing grape into their flanks. Squalls of it scudded over them, knocking them down in swathes.

A furied cheering could now be heard from the Allied earthworks, though Thaxted, for one, wasn't convinced. He remembered a Russian retreat once before which had suddenly become a tumultuous counter-attack, and weary as he was, he quickly began scanning the vast flotsam of dead and dying men. A moment later he'd found himself a rifle, though it was empty. Hurriedly, he began searching pouches for rounds . . . only to be brought up short by the sight of something which instantly turned his blood to ice.

He slowly rose from his haunches. An eerie silence seemed to fall around him.

Several feet away, sprawled on a heap of Russian corpses . . . lay Major Lockhart. The officer was unmoving, and bleeding freely from a grisly chest-wound. Stunned, Thaxted approached. Almost warily, he knelt. In one limp hand, the major still clasped his sabre, notched and bloodied; in the other was the snapped-off grip of his revolver. His pallor had faded to a milky hue, but almost as if he sensed a new presence, his eyes flickered open. They were watery and bloodshot. He tried to move his lips, but at first no words came.

Thaxted cast the rifle away and slumped down onto his backside. Moments passed. The cracking of gunfire could still be heard in the near-distance, but a thundering silence now filled the shell-shocked air. For the first time, the gasps and cries of the wounded were audible. Eventually the trooper dug into his pocket, felt around for a moment, and sighed. When he drew his hand out, it was empty.

"I thought I'd saved one for you," he said. He pulled the shotgun from his pack, broke it open and showed the major its empty barrels. "These aren't cartridges you can pick up at Stores, you see. Had to buy them special." He shook his head. "Seems you've cheated me again."

"Tha . . . Thaxted," Lockhart managed to whisper. "You're a damned fool . . ."

"And you," said the private, "are a callous, heartless bastard." He glanced to his right, where a bayonet stood upright in the dirt. He extracted it, began to examine it. "And you'll still have your glory, won't you . . . Major? They'll never remember you for what you really were."

"Ben?" came a sudden wavering voice. "B . . . Ben Thaxted?"

Thaxted turned tiredly, and saw a private approaching over the wreckage of bodies. At first, he didn't recognize the man – he was thin, limping, spattered with mud. Like the rest of them, he sported a scruffy tangle of beard. There was something familiar about his haggard, youthful face, however. "Ben?"

Thaxted rose slowly to his feet. "Noggs?"

"By God!" The boy laughed aloud; he just checked himself

from dashing forward and embracing the burly trooper. "I thought . . . I thought you were dead?"

"Not likely, lad," said Thaxted. "But no thanks to our so-called doctors."

The boy laughed again . . . delightedly. Then he spotted Lockhart. "And the major, too!" He turned and shouted behind him. "Sergeant Linford . . . it's Major Lockhart! Ben Thaxted's found him." Noggs looked back. "Ben, I can't . . . I can't believe . . ."

He was still too overjoyed to speak coherently, and Thaxted himself had too many memories of the workhouse runaway he'd taken in at the barrack-door several years ago, to simply shrug off the reunion. He'd probably have grasped the lad and hugged him, had he not been clutching the bayonet . . . which Noggs suddenly noticed and then turned a shade paler at. The boy glanced again at the prone form of the major. Hurriedly, he hunkered down beside him.

"Gave you up, Noggsy," said Thaxted, fingering the blade. "On the Alma."

"Almost died, Ben." The boy's voice had become querulous again. He peeked up, watching the bayonet nervously. "Almost . . . but Major Lockhart here had a private tent set up. All the injured lads from his company were tended there. We had fresh air, clean lint . . . proper nursing and such."

Thaxted gazed at him, with mock-amusement . . . as if he believed it, but couldn't care less.

"Never . . . leave my men to die," Lockhart suddenly croaked. Gore was bubbling from his lips, but he seemed stronger now and was glaring up at Thaxted. "You'd have been taken from Scutari too," he stammered. "But you'll . . . you'll be the one who . . . fought with the men I sent. They said one fought . . . had . . . to leave him . . ."

"And did you send them for my father?" asked the trooper. "And did *he* fight them off?"

The major shook his head helplessly.

"Don't tell me . . . your accountants posted the bill for his debt? *You* knew nothing?"

Lockhart closed his eyes, grey-faced with pain.

"And the letters?" Thaxted spat.

"Ben . . ." Noggs pleaded.

"Well, Major? The letters? Presumably it was your secretary who tore those up? Before *you* saw them?"

"Don't remember . . ." the officer hissed.

Thaxted shook his head. "Either way, you're guilty as Hell. I'd . . ."

He was halted mid-sentence, for at that moment Sergeant Linford and a stretcher-party arrived. Thaxted turned and strode away a few yards, sliding the bayonet beneath his coat.

"General Pennefather's compliments, sah!" the NCO bellowed. "He says to tell you Prince Menschikov's attack is completely repulsed all along the line. Furthermore, that it was a glorious action, and you and your men were instrumental in it. You have the general's heartiest congratulations."

Lockhart nodded, still too pained to speak.

"Easy now, boys," the sergeant added as the men began to lift their CO onto his stretcher.

Throughout this, Noggs watched his old friend worriedly. The broad back was turned firmly on him, as if Ben was staring out over the hideous array of blood and butchery now stretching to the smoky horizon, though he plainly wasn't. There was a square, rigid look about him, as if at any moment he was about to turn and do something rash. Noggs knew nothing of Ben's civilian past, but he remembered the way the trooper had suddenly lost his senses on the Alma, and this new brooding was a chilling reminder.

"Alright now," Linford was saying, as they began to carry the officer away. "Easy does it. Woa . . . Coggin! We're not having you hanging round like a spare prick at the wedding. If you've nothing to do, I can find something."

"Yes, sergeant," the boy replied.

And then, just as he'd feared, Thaxted suddenly turned and walked swiftly after the stretcher-party. His grimy face was cut like steel. He reached determinedly under his coat. "Major Lockhart, sir . . ."

"No, Ben!" the boy shouted.

Sergeant Linford looked idly round.

"Something for you, sir," Thaxted added.

Lockhart glanced up, waxy-white but as fearless as ever.

"Memento of our time together," Thaxted said.

Frantic, Noggs unslung his rifle and raised it to his shoulder, but it was too late . . . the stretcher lads were blocking his shot. Ben was now leaning in over the major. He'd taken something out of his coat. He was staring intently down, his face pale as ice . . .

And then . . . then, he was stepping back all of a sudden. And the sergeant was whistling, and the major clutching something to his chest, gazing backwards at the big trooper as they carried him away . . . as if he too couldn't believe it.

Moments later, the stretcher-party had gone, vanished into the field-works. Thaxted turned and saw that Noggs was training a rifle on him, the youngster's face wet with sweat.

"A tenner," said the man casually. "I owed him a tenner."

"A . . . a tenner?"

"Been saving it quite a while, to be honest. Look . . . what you planning, Noggsy? Going to shoot me?"

A moment passed, then the private lowered the gun. He wore a twitching half-smile, though the humour didn't reach to his eyes. "I . . . I wouldn't shoot a man over a tenner, Ben."

Thaxted chuckled. "No?" He turned and strolled away. "Then you're a better man than me."

THE CALVARY CHARGE

Peter T. Garratt

If there is any single heroic moment that stands out in Britain's military exploits of the nineteenth century it is the Charge of the Light Brigade which took place at the Battle of Balaclava on 25 October 1854. Of the 673 soldiers involved, there were 272 killed or wounded. No matter how we might regard the foolhardiness of the action, and of the stupidity of the officers involved, we cannot deny the courage and bravery of the soldiers. Despite the results of the attack and the overwhelming odds, the soldiers were prepared to charge again. The event was immortalized in the poem by Lord Tennyson published within a few weeks of the disaster. It has been the subject of several stories and novels as well as at least two films – in 1936 (which established Errol Flynn as a star) and in 1968. The best known study of the action is The Reason Why *(1953) by Cecil Woodham Smith. The following story, specially written for this anthology, takes a new, almost transcendental look at the action. Peter Garratt (b.*

1949) is a clinical psychologist who has written scores of stories of fantasy and science fiction since his first sale, "If the Driver Vanishes . . ." (1985). His work also appears in The Mammoth Book of Men o' War.

We camped a few miles from the River Alma. I think we all knew the Russians would make a stand there. I slept badly for the first time since we had landed in the Crimea. I had a dream, of an age when I still had my innocence, but had already been touched by knowledge of war and death.

In that dream, I was again a child. I had been given childish books, tales of knights and daring deeds, but only for a short time. As soon as I could read passably well, I was given my own Bible. I was already aware of death, and that Our Lord had defeated Death, but was unsure how. I was told to read through the Gospel of St Luke from the beginning. When I reached the betrayal and trial of Our Lord, the dreadful scene where the mob is clamouring for His death, I peeked ahead and noticed that the next chapter seemed to be entitled: "Cavalry". I was called away before I could read on, but the story continued in my imagination: I wondered if Our Lord's escape from death had been aided by a charge of Christian cavalry, like that in which Sir Lancelot and his knights rescued Queen Guinevere. For years I had a dream of that impossible charge, yet when I bought my first, modest commission in the Lancers it became less frequent, and during my time in India it disappeared.

I rose early (I was on Lord Lucan's staff) and soon the dream was out of my mind. We inspected the men before dawn, Lancers, Hussars, and Light Dragoons, plus those of the Heavy Cavalry who had arrived. The men were smarter and cleaner than we had we had any right to expect, but we found there had been more cases of cholera in the night. I was getting a bad feeling about the Crimea: the men were unstoppable if only they were properly supplied and led, but unfortunately the same could be said for the officers. I myself, as a captain in the 17th

Lancers seconded to the staff, had seen more service in the field than anyone else in the Cavalry Division. This experience counted for little in official eyes as it had been gained in India. I had trained myself not to resent the promotions that men less experienced than myself were able to purchase: in England, it would have been pointless. In a vast and distant country, short of food and every kind of equipment, even of drinking water, facing an enemy whose numbers no one had counted, it was harder to not resent.

After the inspection, we had a meagre field breakfast of salt pork washed down with most of our remaining water. That day it would be down to cross the river or risk dying of thirst. The army set off soon after. As the marching bands of the infantry struck up, a lone rider approached the cavalry position, an *aide-de-camp* from General Lord Raglan. I was pleased to recognize Lewis Nolan, an old friend from my time in the Senior Department at Sandhurst. He was a fine-looking young man in Hussar's uniform, clean-shaven but for a small moustache, unlike the "Haw Haw" type so common in the cavalry with their elaborate whiskers. Nolan was rated the best horseman in Europe, a superb horse-trainer, and the leading expert on cavalry tactics to boot. He rode up to Lord Lucan, Major General of the Cavalry Division, saluted rather sloppily, and handed over a written order.

Lucan read it carefully. He was a man whose time had passed, in the view of most of his officers. Unlike many who purchased senior commissions, he had made a point of getting experience in the field, serving with the Russians in their last conflict with the Turks. But that had been decades ago, before, to the surprise and shock of many, we had sided with the Turks against the Russians. In any sanely run army, he would have been retired in favour of someone with recent experience in India. As it was, Lucan had more field experience than most of our other generals. He said: "Let's get this straight, Captain Nolan. The cavalry are to stay out of the action, conserve our resources. Which is good sense, given that we are little more than half strength. Disease, no food, no fodder . . . we scarcely need an enemy!"

Nolan bridled. He had made his reputation by demonstrating the possibilities of horsemanship and proclaiming the advantages of cavalry over the other arms. He had written things we all hoped were true; but in an age when guns were being improved faster than better horses could be bred, most of us in our hearts had doubts. Nolan himself had total faith in his ideas. I had seen him argue insolently with his seniors and only just get away with it. He particularly disliked Lucan, for no known reason. Dimmock, my batman, believed it was his Irish blood. Lucan held vast estates in areas blighted by the potato famine, and Dimmock believed that no Irishman, however distinguished, loved an English landlord. This time he merely said: "The orders are as written. Others will certainly follow . . . or if not, you must use your initiative!" Nolan was a great believer in leadership and initiative. He saluted smartly, as though dismissed, and rode off. In fact he rode up to me and patted my horse Subaltern on the head. "How's the old Satan doing, Morris old chap?"

"Very well, thanks to your advice!" Subaltern was a fine grey, whose ears were black and sharp, as if they were horns. When I had taken him on, he'd had a bad reputation, and some wag had carefully trimmed his tail into a devil's point. Now I was able to say: "Best horse I've ever ridden, thanks to your help!"

Some of the junior officers applauded. They adored Nolan. One said: "Vewy good howse-bweaking, Haw Haw!" Another quipped: "Exowcising the demon, Haw Haw!"

It was a fine day, and the army made a magnificent sight. Lord Cardigan was in the lead, with two regiments of light cavalry: then came two massive columns of infantry and artillery, the French and Turks nearest the sea, then the main British column, with the rest of the cavalry guarding the left flank. But we had not left disease behind: the men were too proud to go sick if they could just keep going, but from time to time I would notice one falling out of the column, just collapsing like recruits fainting on their first parade.

Cardigan had set out early, with two regiments of his Light

Cavalry brigade, as he usually did: but then they too were ordered to inactivity on the flank. They peeled slowly off to the left, then waited for us as the army overtook them.

James Brudenell, the Earl of Cardigan, was well over fifty, but had the figure of a much younger man. He wore the most magnificent uniform I had ever seen, Hussar's pelisse loose on his shoulders, so much braid on his chest that it could have been the gold breastplate of an Aztec emperor. He had on the tight red trousers, which had gained his 11th Hussars the nickname "cherry-bums". He had shaved the chin of his beard, but wore the rest like an elephant; his moustaches were long and pointed like its tusks, while his whiskers were as big as its ears. He saluted Lucan smartly, and Lucan returned his salute. Nevertheless, Cardigan started to complain at being withdrawn from the vanguard as if Lucan had done this himself, though the order had clearly come from his superior Lord Raglan. Since the landing, Raglan had constantly sent instructions for us to hold back and on no account to engage the Russians without orders. From time to time Cossacks had appeared, firing their pistols from beyond effective range and jeering when we did not respond. The jeers did more damage than the shots: it's hard to keep soldiers in a mood to fight and kill men they don't know, for a cause they scarcely understand, if they must also sit quietly dodging spent balls and listening to jeers. Though the orders originated with Raglan, officers and men alike assumed their inactivity could be blamed on Lord Lucan, whom they termed "Lord Look-on".

By this time the infantry were passing us, and we set off at a trot. I rode near Lucan and asked what he thought of the quality of Russian troops.

"They're brave enough, contrary to opinion in the newspapers and the Commons, but the infantry will be short of rifled guns and their tactics are out of date. In fact they prefer bayonet to musket and don't shoot well."

I was fascinated. No one else knew anything about Russian tactics. We spoke for a while about Russian cavalry, the famous Cossacks, and I wished my friend Nolan was there. Lucan went on: "Russians are an odd bunch. A few wish to keep up with the rest of Europe, most lag behind. And that's reflected in their army. Their artillery was always first-rate, but not the rest. They're gloomy devils. I think it's the climate. They grow up to think nothing is ever easy for long. But perhaps that's because of their greatest general."

"Who's that?" I hadn't heard of any great Russian general.

"General Winter. He's only on active service for half the year, but he's never late for duty, and he's never defeated."

We crested a ridge, the men eager for water as much as war, and gazed over the river to the Russians' serried ranks and fortified positions. Their numbers were as great as ours, and they were well dug in. The way back was long and thirsty: the only options open were attack or disaster. Raglan chose attack.

Others can write better than I of the great victory of the Alma. I saw little of it, and took less part. Foot officers will say that the great spirit of our soldiers carried the day, and that is true, but I suspect the Minie rifle with its greater range played a part also.

When we saw the enemy retreating, artillerymen making a particular effort to carry away their guns, Cardigan rode up to Lord Lucan and said: "Surely Sir, it is permissible to take some of those infernal guns away from the Russkies while they are in no position to fire them?"

Cardigan and Lucan had often been at odds, but the thrill of victory put both in a good mood. Lucan agreed and decided to ride with his staff with the 17th. Major Willet, the acting CO, greeted me warmly, though he had been ill and looked so thin and pale that I had earlier advised him to take sick leave. He called out to me cheerfully: "Look at this country, Morris! Ideal for cavalry work." He was right. The land was green and rolled gently, a cross between plain and downland. There was a scent of thyme.

I was glad to go into action with my own regiment. It was a hot day, and we were pleased to splash across the river. It was a joyful regiment of Lancers who rode on toward the broken Russians. Guns were being dragged away on limbers over unsuitable territory: in one fine swoop the cavalry would be able to redeem its earlier lack of action by capturing a great part of the enemy's strongest arm.

Near us, a gun was stuck with one wheel in a ditch. Despite the danger, the gunners worked desperately to free it as we galloped toward them. A big, bearded man, an officer by his uniform, got into the ditch and used strength I would not have credited to lift it out in one tremendous jerk: the wheel then came away entirely, and ignoring the sound of our hoofbeats he leaped back into the ditch to recover it.

The men were fired up for battle. I saw they were ready to ride down the gunners and give them no quarter: but these were Christian enemies, and I had to give them the chance I would have given Sikhs or Hindoos: I ordered the men to rein in and draw their pistols. We had them covered, two or three barrels to a man, and most put up their hands. The big officer still held the wheel, and hefted it as if wondering if he could use it as a shield or a weapon: I pointed my gun straight at him and shouted at him in French to surrender; at last he hurled the wheel away from him with an oath, saying something in Russian to his men as he raised his hands.

I ordered my prisoners away from the gun. I was detailing men to escort them to our camp, when an *aide-de-camp* rode up to us. "I say you chaps! Sowy you chaps, but you'we in the wwong place, Haw Haw! Awders of Lawd Waglan! All cavalwy units are to escawt owr gunners, not to chase the Wuskies! Now, where's Lawd Lucan?"

I looked at the damaged gun, wondering if it would be possible to get it back to camp, or if we would have to spike it. Before I could decide, a general movement back began. Lord Lucan rode up to me in a rage, my first real exposure to the famed Lucan temper. He shouted: "Are these prisoners?"

"Yes Sir. I was wondering if we can get this gun . . ."

"We're not allowed prisoners! We're not allowed near the enemy at all! What do you think you are, poachers! If Lord Raglan sees them, we'll all be court-martialled!"

"Sir, what are we to do with them?"

"Turn them loose, I suppose! What else!"

I was bewildered; but orders, however strange, have to be obeyed. I rode over to the Russian officer and said to him: "Monsieur, tu est . . . no . . . vous etes libre!"

He glared at me, then said crisply: "Nom, Ivan Stavinsky. Je . . ."

"Vous etes libre!" I snapped, then realized "libre" was a word the Russians probably couldn't translate into their language, I simply pointed to the retreating enemy and shouted "Allez! Allez!"

He stared at me as if I was mad, then saluted very smartly and marched away.

We made camp at the Alma to plan the next move and bury the previous day's dead. Nolan spent time in the cavalry camp, where there were no dead to bury, and, it was increasingly clear, no planning would be allowed. He had been with Raglan when the latter crossed the river with only his staff, not waiting for our men to secure the ground, and no one disagreed with his assessment that Raglan was the hero and Lord Look-on should not have interpreted the hero's orders in such a pedantic way. Nolan's theory of leadership required the leader to justify his initiative by results. If Lucan had thrown the full weight of the cavalry after the fleeing Russians, they would have been destroyed rather than just bloody-nosed, and the way to Sevastopol would have been open. As it was, we would now have to march right round the city, because the southern defences were thought to be weaker.

So it proved. It was a long dreary march, through rougher country than before. I had never seen vultures this far north, but from somewhere they appeared, circling the Alma, then following the army.

We were riding through an area of dense brushland, almost woodland, which Major Willet said reminded him of Ashdown Forest. The main column was somewhere to the right of the cavalry: we could not see it for low trees and high ferns, but the idea was to deter any ambush parties we might see. We were strung out in column down a long path, which according to the map supplied by the General's Staff led eventually to the undefended port of Balaclava, which was to be our main supply base for the siege of Sevastopol. Though the nights were turning cold, it was a warm day, an autumn smell of dead leaves in the air.

The map was wrong. The whole column halted as we came to a fork in the rough road. Lucan called for the map. "Where the devil can we be? No fork on this map!"

None of his own staff could interpret it. The ADC of Raglan's who had brought it was a typical lisping courtier, and he pronounced: "Well, the path to the wight leads diwectly to Balaclava, so that must be it!"

We started down the right-hand path. We continued for about a mile, then the path started to narrow and became increasingly overgrown. Finally, it just disappeared. We were lost, and like mariners far from shore, got out a compass and decided by dead reckoning to carry on the same way, trampling the ferns, now reinforced with briars and brambles, and where necessary dismounting and hacking our way through with our sabres.

It was hot, rough work, slow progress till we heard a commotion ahead, voices shouting in both Russian and English. No shots were fired, but the row continued intermittently. We hacked on as fast as we could, till a voice shouted from quite close on our left: "Over here, men! What the deuce is going on?"

It was Nolan. I could just see him above the wall of ferns and brambles. The whole column turned and hacked wildly towards him, followed more delicately by our horses, who were not of course hacks.

We found that Nolan was on the true course of the path. He waved his arm wildly, shouting: "Hurry up! Hurry up! General Lord Raglan is facing half an army with just his Staff!"

Back in the saddle, we made up for lost time, thundering down the path. How the General had overtaken us, I could not make out, unless he had ridden past when we were lost. We rounded a bend, and found a small group – I can hardly say a force – of our staff officers blocking it. They had with them a troop of horse artillery, which Nolan had not mentioned. Nevertheless, they were totally outnumbered: ahead the path ended abruptly in a road, along which a convoy of wagons was trundling, escorted by a huge force of Russian infantry. Nearest to them the aged but erect figure of Lord Raglan sat calmly on his horse; but his imperterbable demeanour snapped when Lucan rode up, and he yelled at the top of his voice: "You're late, Lord Lucan, you're late!"

The rest of us galloped on, eager for action at last. We swept past Raglan like a stampede of the legendary wild horses of the Americas, but the noise of our approach went before us, and before we reached the road at the end of the path, the Russians had taken to their heels, abandoning their baggage train, even though they probably still had the numbers of us. Of course we went after them, but before a weapon could be used, we heard the bugle calling us back.

Lucan's gloom deepened after this farce. He felt he had no choice but to keep to the letter of the orders which were branding him as "Lord Look-on", though obeying them earned him no better opinion than exceeding them would have.

At first Lord Cardigan was also targeted for blame, but he managed to avoid it by reminding Raglan that he was not in overall charge of the Cavalry Division, only the one brigade of Light Cavalry. He was an odd, controversial, character. Most of his officers thought even less of him than of Lucan, for he had a history of picking on them over petty matters, like the notorious episode of the Black Bottle, in which an officer's career had almost been ruined because he poured wine at a formal dinner from a black bottle, which resembled those from which we "Indian" officers took porter beer. Cardigan affected to despise things Indian even more than did others of his kind. But though he was a parade-ground bully to his juniors, I realized he was skilled enough as a courtier when dealing with those above him. Oddly, he was also quite popular with the other ranks, according to Dimmock, my batman.

*   *   *

South of Sevastopol the land was broken, great hills like steep-sided downs jutting from the rolling plains. We marched between two ranges, across a plain, and down a gorge to the port of Balaclava. It was one of the prettiest places I have seen; whitewashed houses with green-tiled roofs, fruits and grapes in the gardens. There was no resistance, and the Staff declared that this would be the main port of supply for the British expedition. The town being very crowded, the French de-camped to a supply-base of their own. After a brief respite, the artillery and the main body of infantry set out for the hills which overlooked Sevastopol from the south, leaving the cavalry, one regiment of Highlanders, and some Turks to guard the supply route.

Much needed supplies were carted with difficulty up the gorge, on a track I would not have dignified with the term road, to the plain, where the track joined the far superior Woronzoff Road. This crossed the plain on a causeway that then wound north to the best point for scaling the heights. There were other ways up and down, mountain tracks really, but they were difficult even without back-breaking loads.

The cavalry moved out of Balaclava and made camp on the plain, to the south of the causeway. The causeway itself was defended by a series of redoubts, garrisoned by Turks, lest the Russians try to cut the road. Behind them, to our right, the Highlanders guarded the track to Balaclava.

Ships were arriving, and the whole expedition looked more professional. Food was short, but we had tents, and no one needed to sleep in the open. This was a great relief, as it was now October, and the nights were much colder than at home.

Among the ships was Lord Cardigan's yacht. He was the oldest man on active duty with the cavalry, the rasp in his voice clearly indicating a bronchitic chest. He was still a stickler for absurd points of discipline, when not preoccupied with efforts to undermine Lord Lucan. Nearly all his officers hoped he would declare himself sick and sail home. Instead Lord Raglan gave him permission to spend his nights on the yacht, resuming his command during the day.

Major Willet looked in far worse shape than Cardigan. There was a hospital of sorts in Balaclava, and I urged him to repair there, or at least get lodgings in the town. I persuaded him to dine with Nolan and myself at a tavern near the port, hoping to get him to stay there for a while. We dined on beetroot soup . . . at least a change from salt pork . . . and in the absence of porter or decent wine, made our acquaintance with vodka.

We relaxed, and started to talk freely. The war would have seemed far away, had I not received a letter that morning which reminded me of my doubts about it. In an unguarded moment, I told them of a friendship I had formed with a young lady called Miss Irene Taylor. She was very well spoken, mannered, and educated, though her family were in trade. Her father had made most of his money by making and repairing steam engines.

Irene had sensible and well-informed views on a number of topics. Her religious faith was not loudly proclaimed and rigid, as was the fashion in her class, but quiet and serious like my own. However, she had a fixed opinion that it was wrong for a Christian nation to make war on another in defence of an unbelieving empire like that of Turkey. She had lived in India when her father built a railway there, and had been raised on tales of Muslim atrocities against missionaries. I had understood, and half-shared her concerns, but had failed to convince her, that as an officer and a gentleman, I belonged to the class which creates stability in society by forfeiting the right to question legitimate orders.

I took out the letter and read some of it: "Dear Captain Morris, I apologize if I gave any offence in our last meeting. I was just so concerned that our brave soldiers, who have so little choice about obeying orders, should be ordered into danger for unworthy reasons!"

Irene had sat for a portrait, not for a true artist, but for a photographer, and had sent me the result, or at least a print of it, for I understand several can be made. Nolan and Willet professed to admire my good fortune in having such a correspondent. I felt embarrassed. True, she was a fine looking girl, about twenty, not tall, but sturdily built without being overweight.

She was tastefully dressed in a gown of Indian silk, not low-cut or exactly tight, but clearly showing the femininity of her figure; and her curly brown hair was held by a magnificent peacock jewel. However, though she did not look vulgar, the silk of her dress would not have been worn by any Indian less in caste than a Maharani, and the jewellery she flaunted a duchess would have hesitated to wear. Unfortunately, I had let slip that to withdraw from the army and live on private means would not be a viable option for me; and she had suggested that I apply to her father for a position in his business! I had been astonished. She appeared well-educated, but was quite ignorant of the fact that an officer could no more resign his commission to engage in trade than a warhorse could become a pit pony. A fancy came to me that she intended me to drive one of his steam locomotives, or to collect the tickets. I burst out laughing, leaving her most offended.

Now, however, dining in a quite decent inn in a pleasant little town, I felt nostalgia for those distant and unfulfilled meetings. Irene would have made a better companion for an exploration of exotic but civilized places than any number of officers. But that was not the posting to which fate had assigned me.

Though I did not allow myself her doubts about the war, I did not think it required the devotion beyond the call of duty the ailing Willet was showing. I told him it would not have occurred to me to feign illness, but if I were as ill as he looked I would feel no obligation to soldier on.

He shook his head as vigorously as he could: "We've spent our lives doing a duty which promises action and excitement and delivers everything but. You seem to be a religious man, Morris, which I never was at your age. I took an oath before God to serve the Crown, and all I did for thirty years was polish buttons. Thirty silver buttons!" The pallor left his face and it started to glow: "Your lady friend was wrong. These Russkies can't commit themselves to be true Christians because they've no freedom and therefore no free will. They can only pray with the lips."

"We're not here to free them!" I said drily.

"No. But we can show that our way is better than theirs!"

Nolan interrupted. He was in compromising mood for once. Of course Willet should do his duty, but it wouldn't do him any harm to have a few days in a warm house in Balaclava till action resumed. "Once you hear gunfire, you can go to the quay and then ride up with the Noble Yachtsman." (He meant Lord Cardigan.)

Willet refused to say why he wasn't following the Noble Yachtsman's example. Instead he asked if it was true that a railway was soon to be built from Balaclava to the heights, and even an electric telegraph.

It was. A few days later, as one of Lucan's staff, I was detailed to show the area to some engineers, accompanied by a news reporter from the *Times*. It was early on a fine, crisp morning, the night's cold still dewing the grass. I had been up for some hours: Lucan insisted reveille and the day's first inspection should be before dawn. Nolan originated a rumour that starting everything early was the last desperate strategy of the incompetent mind. Dimmock said it was more to do with Lucan trying to get as much of the day over as possible before Cardigan arrived from his yacht.

I rode Subaltern to Balaclava when the chill was still in the morning, welcomed the engineers over hot coffee at the tavern, and led them up the gorge to the plain. There had been steady, continuous gunfire from the heights overlooking the city for three days now, and soon we could hear it more clearly. Two riders had been following us up the gorge: now they drew level. I started in amazement and almost forgot to salute. Lord Cardigan was wearing his Hussar's ceremonial outer jacket as a regular jacket, but I could hardly see it: over it he wore a loose knitted woollen jacket, in regimental colours but without any braid. Beside him rode Mrs Duberly, wife of an ADC, wearing a similar jacket in the colours of her husband's regiment.

Cardigan returned my salute crisply. "Ah, Captain Morris. This is the Pocket Hercules, Mrs Duberly, Haw Haw! Do you know what the firing is, Captain Morris?"

I said I did not, but that I thought our guns had been firing at

the defences for three days. I introduced the engineers, and
Cardigan said: "I dare say no one will know about the firing
unless they take a look, Haw Haw! I was just escorting Mrs D to
her husband. He's with Lord Rag's escort, y'know. Let's all
take a dekko!"

As we rode up the steep track to the heights, I reflected that it
wasn't surprising that Cardigan arrived late every day if he was
escorting Mrs Duberly to her husband at HQ. No doubt he
seized any chance to advance his complaints against Lucan.

The engineers meanwhile were preoccupied with the course
of the proposed railway. They didn't like the steepness of the
track we were on. By the time we reached the top we had a
marvellous view of the plain of Balaclava, spread below us
like a diorama – the tents of the cavalry, the men exercising
horses, the redoubts on the Woronzoff Road, the Turks
defending them and the naval guns which had been hauled
with great labour to the redoubts – all looked like toys, like
figures in a landscape unreal in its smallness. I pointed out
the difficulties: "The road is reached by a track. The road
itself is on a causeway which effectively divides the plain into
two valleys. The causeway doesn't look steep from here, but
it's a problem. Then the road winds on before it turns up to
the heights. What we need is something shorter and easier to
defend."

We rode on to a point where we could see the action.
Sevastopol was a different kind of diorama. Cardigan exclaimed: "Look! There are our fellows firing at the Russians,
and look, those other fellows are Russians firing back! But we
had those defences down two days ago. The bounders seem to
be rebuilding them in the night. Why don't we assault and drive
them off?"

No one seemed to know. The siege seemed to have reached a
stalemate, with no one daring to follow up the bombardment
with an assault. This alarmed me, for I had heard the engineers
say that there was no chance of having a railway running till
after the winter, and in that season any danger could oppress us.
Cardigan put up his field glasses and prepared to ride off,

saying: "I have never in my life seen a siege conducted on such principles, Sir!"

That evening the men were not stood down after supper. Lucan called his staff officers to his tent. "I have intelligence from the Turks that the enemy are planning a night attack in numbers on the redoubts."

I took the news to the 17th. Willet mustered the men and said: "This is it, men. Looks like they're stealing up on us like thieves in the night. For God's sake, don't think of any rumours of them having the numbers. Their numbers are serfs, driven into battle with whips and scorpions, and we're all volunteers, free men. So let's do our duty, and remember, though we ride through the valley in the shadow of Death, the Lord is our shepherd, He will be with us."

It was a long night, and the coldest yet. The men stood by their horses' bridles, waiting for the order to mount. An issue of hot rum was requested, but I pointed out that tea might be more appropriate. The night was not silent: soon after dark we heard the sound of a marching band. At first we hoped it was reinforcements coming down from the heights, but it was soon apparent that the music came from the opposite direction, from the interior of the Crimea, where great numbers of Russians had been reported manoeuvring. Before long the music got louder, not just nearer, and it was clear that the bands of many regiments were playing slightly different music. I rejoined Lucan, and he said: "What do you think, Morris?"

"It's not quiet enough out there, Sir. Surely they can't be planning a night attack making this racket?"

"Don't forget their tactics, Morris. They have the numbers, we have the range. They'll want to use the dark to get near enough to attack with the bayonet."

Around three the music started petering out. By that time our reinforcements were on their way, but I judged they were only halfway down the heights. It was a long two hours until the first hint of dawn reached the sky. There was little sound but for men coughing and when I walked up and down, frozen dew crunching on the grass.

Once there was light in the sky, we realized the reinforcements of infantry had just arrived, and were furious to have nothing to do but march back up the hill with no sign of an attack. Lucan decided to conduct his regular inspection. We were joined by George Padget, senior colonel in charge of the Light, no one having told the Noble Yachtsman of the alert. Padget was a Lord, and something of a dandy, but more intelligent and cynical than most of his kind.

The men stood rock-steady at their horse's heads, as if they were frozen men. Not a few had collapsed and been taken away. When we reached the 17th I noticed an odd thing. Willet was leaning against his horse's shoulder, one arm flung across, his head bowed. The horse seemed agitated, not moving its body, but constantly turning its head and trying to nuzzle him. Subaltern, by this time a perfectly behaved mount, let out a long distressed whinny. I rapidly dismounted and ran to Willet. I disengaged him from the horse and he collapsed onto the ground. Lucan barked: "What's the matter? Is the man ill?"

I tried to find a pulse. His wasted body felt to me as cold as the ice-dew on the grass: "I think he's dead, Sir!"

"Get him inside." Lucan turned to Padget. "Who's senior now, in the 17th?"

"Morris here, Sir. Maybe you should confirm him as acting CO, before the Noble Yachtsman shows up."

My first duty as acting CO was to organize Willet's burial. Three troopers had also died in the night. I was horrified that only half the regiment's total strength answered the roll-call, though a number of invalids made it to the funeral. Horses were, if anything, fewer than men. Many NCOs being ill, I promoted Dimmock.

Later that day, traders arrived from Balaclava. They were selling knitted woollen hats with chinstraps. These were grey, and looked like the helmets of chain mail worn by medieval knights. I bought enough for all the remaining 17th, thinking it a fitting tribute to Willet that the men he had so nearly led into action should look like crusaders.

Lucan did not suspend the pre-dawn inspections. On the third morning, we had finished and were about to order the men to breakfast when Lucan looked, as he always did at that time, toward the most important of the redoubts. The sun had not risen, but there was some light in the east: however, it had been a slightly milder night, and we were troubled by mist rather than frost. He called to Padget: "Can you see what I see? Two flags on the pole? That indicates a surprise attack!"

Before Padget could answer, a shot rang out, then another, then in seconds it sounded as if dozens of guns and hundreds of muskets were blazing away, as indeed they were! As we got the men to horse, the crash of shots became almost continuous, the few gaps being filled by the distant roar of charging men.

We advanced at a canter towards the action. There was no point in charging till we knew the exact disposition. About half-way, we met a Turkish officer called Abdul Abulbul who was riding like the wind with a message that the redoubts were being attacked by thirty thousand men. Despite these odds, it was clear that the first redoubt put up a terrific fight, but by the time we were in carbine range it was all over there: a few Turks were fleeing and a Russian flag was on the pole.

Worse was to follow. The firing was continuing from the next two or three redoubts, but the din was petering out. We saw the Turkish garrisons were accepting the logic of the numbers and fleeing for their lives, heading for Balaclava and the ships. Abdul managed to rally a few, but the rest fled.

Lucan had no choice. Two brigades of cavalry at half-strength through disease had no hope of recapturing the four redoubts. He made the best of a bad job and led us back to the gorge leading to the port. The sun was just rising, the heights behind us were glittering with dew, and a day of destruction had begun.

At the gorge we found the Argyll and Sutherland High-landers, some five hundred men, with a few recovering invalids and the Turks rallied by Abdul. They deployed on the reverse of a low ridge at the mouth of the gorge. We took a position on their left: if any Russians approached them, we could take the attackers in the flank. It was a good position, if poor odds. If any men were joining us from the heights, they had yet to set out: we received only the solitary reinforcement of Lord Cardigan.

Soon after, we received an even less welcome visitor: an ADC from Lord Raglan with a message that we should withdraw to a position much further from the Highlanders, just behind the two remaining redoubts. Lucan was furious, as indeed were the rest of us, but the message was clear, and we withdrew as slowly as we could, ashamed of our habitual obedience.

The new position was a poor one: between the foot of the heights and the highest part of the causeway. We could see the Highlanders we had abandoned, but not much else, indeed, we were surprised when Russian cavalry and horse artillery appeared from behind the causeway, crossed it, and started moving toward the gorge. Regiment after regiment poured over, three, four, perhaps five thousand men. It was a terrible moment. Our orders were to stay put unless attacked ourselves. We looked on as the Russians unlimbered their guns and started to bombard our comrades. Luckily, our men were in a good position behind the ridge, but the shells would be doing some damage. We saw men starting to run. I thought they were Abdul's Turks, but before I could be sure, a bugle sounded, the barrage ceased, and the Russian cavalry began its advance.

Cavalry charges do not start at a gallop. You begin at the trot, gradually building speed and momentum as you get nearer the enemy, and enter his effective range. The Russians were still trotting when a red line of Highlanders appeared on the ridge. It was steady, but only two deep. In seconds, we heard the crash of the first volley.

Such events are decided by men, not bullets. If the foot hold steady, they can do terrible execution on the horsemen. If they waver, they are lost. As for the advancing cavalry, with the odds the Russians had, if they had the will to go on and take losses, they could sweep the thin red line aside.

These Russians hesitated, I suppose surprised by the range at which they had been fired on: indeed the charge ground to a halt. Another volley sounded and did more execution: I saw men fall writhing on the ground, others pulling their horses round, then the retreat sounded, and the whole mass started to fall back.

There were cheers and sighs of relief from the Lancers behind me. For the moment, the worst danger had passed. I glanced at the heights. I could see Raglan and his Staff watching, looking no bigger than the carrion crows which were circling between us. Infantry were marching down the track to reinforce us but it was a long way down.

Bugles sounded from the Russian lines, the call carrying across the plain. Their cavalry were rallying, turning toward us . . . no, they were advancing toward the Heavy Brigade on our right. The lay of the ground put us uphill of the enemy; the Heavies, downhill. The Heavies were in a difficult position: they could take the charge standing, which no horseman likes to do, and nor does his horse; charge a stronger enemy uphill, or just run for it. While I was speculating, a marvellous thing happened: the Russian advance again ground to a halt, while the wings deployed.

As for the Heavies, no one thought of running. The charge sounded and the first line went forward, uphill and outnumbered, but against a stationary foe. I saw Lucan rushing around, deploying his small force, so the second line divided and took on the vast wings of the enemy.

As the first line of Heavies crashed into the stalled Russians, Cardigan turned his horse and started to ride up and down our line, muttering loudly to himself: "Damn those orders! The Heavies will have the laugh of us this day!"

I called out to him: "My Lord! The enemy aren't guarding their flank! This is a perfect opportunity . . ."

"No, Sir!" he replied loudly. "Dammit, our orders are to stay here unless we are attacked ourselves!"

"But they are downhill . . ."

"Dammit, they're not just Lucan's orders, they're orders from Lord Raglan himself!"

He wheeled, and returned to his position at the head of the Brigade. I was appalled. In India, we would certainly have been expelled from the continent if cavalry commanders had been denied the opportunity to attack the perfect target of a turned enemy flank. Meanwhile, the Heavies were doing well without our help. Again a thin red line made progress against the mass of the grey, but this time the fighting was hand to hand. We heard no shots, just roars, cheers, the clash of swords, the whinny of horses, and yes, the screams of dying men: that was, in the few moments when we ourselves were not cheering the Heavies. I heard a few men pray as well.

The charge petered out untidily. The Russians started pulling back, the gunners limbering their guns; but the momentum of the Heavies was spent, they were scattered and out of order, and I could see they were in no position to follow up. I rode up to Lord Cardigan and said: "Sir, the enemy are retreating in disorder, but not quite routed. It is our positive duty to attack them!"

He seemed to swell with enthusiasm for a moment, and I saw his hand inch toward his sabre: but then he shrank in his saddle and said: "No, no, Sir, our orders are to remain here!"

I looked at the enemy, dejected but not destroyed, and I remembered Nolan's maxim that a cavalry officer's judgement is vindicated by his results; I said: "Do allow me to take the 17th and ride them down! They are in disorder!"

He repeated the exact words he had used before: "No No Sir! Our orders are to remain here!"

I returned to my position, so full of anger that I was hitting my thigh with the flat of my sword, calling on officers and even men to witness that we were missing a great opportunity. I looked at the heights, wondering what Nolan would be thinking, ashamed so great an expert on cavalry should see us looking-on. I could not make him out, though I saw the column of reinforcements, snaking down the hill, and a mounted messenger hurrying past them.

The Heavies started to reform and return to their position. Meanwhile, the Russian cavalry reappeared on the far side of the causeway. They were over a mile from us, at the far end of a long valley. They too started to reform: wisely putting a battery of about a dozen guns from their horse artillery in front of their position.

The battle seemed to be reaching a stalemate, with plenty of looking-on but little to look at. Eventually, the messenger from Lord Raglan finished his agonizingly slow descent and approached Lucan. It seemed we were to attempt to regain the causeway, but not until the infantry joined us. The infantry, and some French cavalry, were still a long way off. Most of the officers allowed their men to dismount. Some lit pipes. I saw Lord George Padget puffing on a cigar.

A few guns were firing, but there was no movement except on the heights. Infantry were descending slowly. Another messenger had set out, and he was not going cautiously down the path, but plunging down the quickest route, which was steep and dangerous. He was making terrific time, and heads turned in admiration. Some of the wiser will have been wondering what message could be so urgent. We all knew the rider had to be Nolan, and I for one was looking forward to seeing him, to explain our inaction before the Lights were renamed the Look-on Brigade.

I assessed the situation. I could not see the redoubts we had to recapture, but the obvious plan was to move south. The Russians had concentrated their guns in the North Valley: horse artillery at the end, covering the north slope of the Causeway, and more guns covering them from the heights on the far side of the valley.

Nolan was dashing and leaping down the hill as if his mount was a giant mountain goat, or the winged horse Pegasus. He reached the bottom and galloped over the plain past the Lights toward Lucan's position between the two brigades. The men cheered as he sped by; someone shouted: "Odds on the favowite, Haw Haw!"

The 17th being at ease, I followed, as anxious to see my old friend as to hear the new orders. He continued at the same mad pace till he was alarmingly close to Lord Lucan, then got his horse to stop as suddenly as if he had been performing in a trick-riding show. He saluted, sloppily I thought, and handed over a written order. Lucan took his time over it, indeed, though it was a small scrap of paper, he was still reading it carefully when I rode up. Nolan scarcely noticed me. He was flushed and sweating, though the day was autumn bright and not quite warm, glaring at Lucan with increasing impatience. I was starting to share his feeling when Lucan said: "I don't understand. This doesn't make sense. What guns?"

Nolan's temper got the better of him, and he replied in an insolent tone: "Surely it's obvious! The order is to advance, and stop the enemy carrying away the guns!"

"I see no guns! What guns, Sir, what guns!"

Nolan waved his arm wildly and shouted: "There, Sir! There is the enemy! There are your guns!"

His insolence was so great I was afraid he would be put on a charge and arrested: meanwhile, a gasp of amazement and horror rose from the staff officers. I looked in the direction Nolan had indicated, and saw he had been pointing directly at the horse artillery battery at the far end of the North Valley, whose fire I had earlier assumed would stop us using that valley at all! Lucan was saying: "That is a useless order! Why, the enemy are not trying to carry . . ."

Nolan was shaking and twisting in his saddle, aware of his insubordination, but unable to control it, and he interrupted most disrespectfully: "Lord Raglan's orders are for the cavalry to stop looking on, and attack at once!"

He wheeled and rode off without being dismissed. Lucan hesitated no longer, but rode alone to Lord Cardigan's position. I did not hear the beginning of their conversation, but as I returned to my men, I heard Cardigan's loud voice. "Are you not aware, Sir . . ." (he too was almost impertinent to this point, but the tone evened out as he went on) ". . . that it goes against all the accepted principles of tactics for cavalry to charge a battery head on?"

Lucan shrugged. I heard him say: "I know. You *are* right. But these are Lord Raglan's direct orders. We have no choice."

Feeling gloomy and anxious, I got my men in order, telling them to put out their pipes and saddle up. I saw Padget doing the same to the second line, though he went easy on the pipes, perhaps because he was still smoking his cigar. He probably thought it his last.

We were ready to advance. I had lost track of where Nolan had gone, but now he rode up to me and asked permission to ride beside me at the head of the 17th. The men cheered to hear him: I seized the moment to tell them that it looked a hard task, but if we stuck together and didn't let the enemy break us up, we could still do it. Cardigan rode up and said: "You know the orders? It's a mad-brained scheme, but none of my doing."

I said: "We're game, Sir." I couldn't help adding: "Sir, if we get through this, I'll buy you a bottle of porter."

He looked shocked for a second, then remembered where he was, and he replied: "If we get through, Haw Haw! I'll drink it!" He rode to the front. I heard him say: "Here goes the last of the Brudenells!", but couldn't tell if I was meant to hear it.

I glanced back at the regiment, at the brigade. It was my last chance to do so, for a cavalry leader must trust his men to follow him during a charge. He cannot look round to see if they are there, for that would give the wrong impression to the waverers. Though at half strength through death, illness, and loss of horses, none of it caused by the enemy, less than seven hundred sabres by my reckoning, the brigade looked a magnificent sight, drawn up in three serried lines, every button on the uniforms as polished as for a parade. Nolan leaned over and held out his hand. "This is it, Morris! No more looking on! It's almost a religious moment, Morris, the redemption of cavalry against chemistry, of chivalry against arithmetic!"

I had once confided to him my old fancy of the Calvary charge. That would have been an uphill ride, had it ever happened, but it would not have been against guns. As for us, we pledged the ancient Faith of the crusaders against the deadliest war engines a new and godless age could devise.

The bugle sounded. Cardigan drew his sword; so did all the officers, and all the men, save in the 17th, where men, but not officers, carried lances. Cardigan said in his rasping voice: "Brigade will advance! Walk, March. Trot!"

The battle had almost petered out. No one was firing, shouting, or blowing trumpets as we trotted forward. We rode the first few yards to no sound at all but our hoofbeats and the jingle of equipment. The Russians on the heights and at the end of the valley looked on without reacting at first, as though our movement had nothing to do with them. They would have been justified in thinking it, in assuming we would soon wheel and head for a part of the field where we could be more rationally deployed. We passed the western end of the Causeway into the valley proper, and suddenly they jumped to it. The guns must already have been loaded, for the first salvo followed at once, a line of flashes, then thunder. That fire came too soon, the shot falling harmlessly to earth in front of us. Then more shots came from the covering batteries on our left, and those were nearer. We rode on steadily, not ready to increase speed, as the next salvo thundered from all round the valley.

There were more guns on our right, firing from the redoubts on the Causeway. I had not seen them from outside the valley. I looked over and saw that as well as those already firing, more were being manoeuvred painfully into position. It was a slow process, and I realized from their small wheels that these would be some of our own naval guns, captured earlier in the day, and now about to be turned on us.

We were still at the trot, advancing at quite a slow pace. I felt it was time to increase the pace, but Cardigan made no signal. Nolan seemed to feel the same way, for he spurred his horse into a canter without waiting for orders, indeed he covered the few lengths between our position and Cardigan's at a gallop, riding out in front of the brigadier. That was too quick, despite the terror of the bombardment, we had to be careful to not wind the horses before we reached the batteries. I called out: "No Nolan, that won't do at all! We have a long way to go and must keep steady!"

Nolan was level with Cardigan now, waving his sword and starting to shout something. I didn't hear a word, because a long ragged salvo drowned his voice: almost at once a shell exploded very near. Shrapnel hit Nolan. His body shuddered, like an immovable object struck by an unstoppable force: the sword fell from his hand, but his arm stayed in the air urging us forward. Nevertheless his horse panicked and turned, galloping back toward us and on through the ranks. I saw he was not quite dead but soon would be; for the whole side of his chest had been ripped away. For a second I fancied I could see his heart beating its last beats as it gushed blood onto the troopers in the front rank. One of his lungs was clearly ruined, but the other still functioned after a fashion; for as his mount carried him away he uttered the most terrible scream, the saddest cry I have ever heard. It made me think of the wail of the Banshee or even of the cry of Christ on the Cross.

I did not look back. I knew my friend was dead. Though we rode into the valley in the shadow of his death, we had to transcend it, to ride on: we were the Light Brigade and we would not turn back alive. We were riding, still trotting, into a great three-sided arena, like one of the evil theatres where the Romans put the innocent to death, and on all sides the Russian gunners were working madly to do the same to us. Shot was flying past me now, mostly hard shot, because I heard more cries behind me, oaths and the screams of horses, but few explosions. The rest of the Russian army may have fought poorly that day, but their accursed gunners were working like mad devils to make up for it. I could hear shouts of "Close up! Close up!" from the sergeants behind, and knew our men were closing neatly into the gaps left by the fallen. As we trotted with icy discipline in the best formation we could still manage, the artillerymen, with no thought of elegance, were working their guns like engineers on an express train which is trying for a speed record; swabbing, loading, ramming, running the guns forward. They didn't even let the recoil create more distance between us. They kept pushing them up, firing; smoke, flame, recoil and thunder; swab-load-ram, pushing them up and firing, smoke-flame-thunder.

Apart from Nolan, I had not seen anyone fall; I would not

look back, but I was not allowed to forget what was happening behind. The horses of the regiment had their own hierarchy, and saw Subaltern as a leader. Riderless steeds were starting to push forward from the decimated ranks and crowd beside us, as though he had some kingly power to protect them from round shot and worse. I would not look back, but I had to look from side to side. Maddened horses, some bleeding from their own wounds, whinnying with pain, others drenched with the blood of their riders on their accoutrements and neatly-trimmed manes, ran close to us.

We were half-way now, and the bombardment was so intense from all three sides that I knew I had to speed up, waving the men to follow. I drew almost level with Cardigan, but he increased speed only a little, holding his sword across our front and calling out: "Steady, steady, 17th Lancers!" So we rode on at our prescription pace, conserving the energy of those who might survive.

Ahead, the gunners showed no sign of breaking in fear of our advance. Instead they redoubled their effort, swab-load-ram-fire flame smoke thunder! I swear I never saw British guns fired faster, or to more dreadful effect, for the screams and cries behind me did not lessen. I knew those damned gunners thought they could destroy us all, kill us from afar as they had killed Nolan, that given a free hand and the dark Satanic mills to build bigger and worse guns, they could dominate the world, or destroy it. I shouted to the men, as if any could hear me above the roar, that it was our duty to kill the devils and drive them back to Hell, so that could never be and our friends could be avenged! I yelled that it was our duty if this was the last charge we ever made. I knew that for nearly all the men, it was also the first, but not one faltered: I heard them yelling in answer behind me.

By now the guns had produced so much smoke that I could hardly see the enemy, only the long line of flashes of the guns. There had been twelve when we set out and twelve were still firing. Smoke lay across the valley like an unnatural wall. If any ride ever more closely resembled charging into the mouth of

Hell itself, I never heard of it. By this time we were so close the enemy must surely be loading canisters of grape shot, the deadliest weapon at close range. There was nothing to be gained by saving the horses now, so I yelled: "Forward the 17th! Charge for the guns!" and galloped ahead flat out. Even Cardigan kicked his horse into a gallop. All were charging at full tilt onto the target, but I had been right about the grape shot: another salvo roared out, and the whole troop of four or five riderless horses on my right collapsed in a screaming, whinnying tangle. I myself was not hit, or by then I was past noticing it. The horses to my left were still going, and to judge from the yells behind me, I still had some men. We were almost on the guns now, I saw Cardigan gallop into a gap between two of them and disappear. It was like riding into a wall of night, but I could see the shadowy outlines of the guns and the mad demons who were working them. The hateful industrial fiends were straining to get off one last volley before we finished them. I saw it was close, very close. I was charging directly towards a gun that had just been pushed back into position, the crew were scuttling out of the way while the gun-captain ran back to fire it. I turned Subaltern round it, past the barrel – that was a chance of life, past the left-side wheel. The gun-captain was about to fire and I urged Subaltern into a mighty leap as though at a water-jump, leaning out from the saddle and swinging my sabre in an arc that caught the Russian on the jaw and lifted him off his feet in the same motion that struck most of his head off.

I had stopped him firing the gun but now I was riding pell-mell on a crazed Subaltern through the accursed, choking smoke. I never hated gunsmoke till that hour, but now I will hate it for the rest of my life. Then two things happened. I burst out of the smoke into the sunshine of a late October morning. At the same time the firing stopped. For a split second I felt as if I had leapt out of Hell and was poised in some netherworld, and that childhood dream of the Mount of Calvary returned to me.

And then reality returned. The great charge of the Light Brigade was over, but we were at the far end of the valley surrounded by enemies. To my right I could see a mass of grey-clad cavalry, motionless at the top of a low slope. In front, glaring at them as though they were his own men sloppily dressed on parade, was Lord Cardigan.

To my left, moving slowly towards me were more horsemen, Cossacks I think. I looked round for the first time and found a handful of my men who had ridden through, or round, the battery. Of a hundred and fifty Lancers who had set out, it seemed only about twenty were alive: then I realized that others were still in the cloud of smoke around the guns, yelling and cursing as they tried to drive off the artillerymen and spike their pieces.

The Cossacks came on hesitantly. Doubtless they thought we were madmen and would fight with the strength of ten. A single officer urged them on: if he succeeded we were done for, and the last of the Lancers would die there, at the far end of that bloody field. We had no choice but to charge on, as Nolan would have urged. I shouted: "Stick together men!" and rode straight at the officer. He didn't flinch and charged at me, swinging his sabre. I parried and as we passed I ran him through, but he too must have got a blow in, because suddenly the world was spinning, and water – no, this must be blood – was running down my face.

Few though we were, the Cossacks didn't fancy tangling with us, and they half-turned and began to shuffle away to the left. I was about to order a pursuit when I realized the din of fighting from the battery was not getting any less. Deep growling Russian voices seemed to be out-shouting our men. It was like the damned artillerymen to fight hand-to-hand better than ten times their number of Cossacks. I wheeled my few Lancers and rushed back to the battery, back into the accursed smoke. There, I found the second line of the Brigade had arrived, in slightly better shape than the first. Padget was there, spiking a gun, cigar stub still in his mouth. I noticed a couple of my loose horses, fighting with their hooves.

We found our way through the smoke to a gun where the Russians were still holding out. I yelled the charge and we rode full at them. One man with a ramrod fought on, dashing a lance from someone's hand, then getting another in the throat. The rest fell back. I dismounted, picked up a broken lance, and tried to use its point to spike the gun. I leaned over to look for the firing-hole, put my hand on the metal to steady myself, then screamed out loud for the first time in the battle. The damned piece was as hot from firing as the very throne of Hell! I rammed the lance-point into the hole with my good hand, trying to put my weight on it, not knowing if I was doing enough to disable it for long. Then everything went dark.

I came to on the ground, face down, my head splitting and dripping. The smoke had cleared a little, and I looked up and couldn't see any of our men. I was surrounded by Russians, though they did not come close. I realized that Subaltern was over me, rearing angrily and holding them off.

I tried to rise, uncertain if I had any chance to escape. I seemed to have no strength for it. Then there came a darker shadow than the smoke, and Subaltern stopped rearing. A vast figure stood over me, gripping his bridle, holding his head down by main strength. Of course, he would be biding his time, waiting a chance to pay back their devilish tricks with one of his own. I made a slightly more successful effort to get up, reaching my knees. The big Russian stood over me, grabbed my collar with his free hand, and pulled me to my feet. I recognized the bearded face of Ivan Stavinsky, the lieutenant I had captured at the Alma, and released on the petulant order of Lord Lucan. He glared at me for a long time, then suddenly relaxed and burst out laughing. He said "Libre!" in his rumbling voice, then hoisted me onto Subaltern's back, pointed him towards our lines, and shouted "Allez! Allez!"

Who can describe that awful ride back? Who would want to? There was some firing from the Causeway, but the battery on the heights had gone silent. I recognized the uniforms of French cavalry, Chasseurs d'Afrique, fighting up there. But it was not the firing that appalled me; I had lost all fear of that. Men and horses lay scattered and mutilated along the whole valley. We had lost at least as many as I feared. Many of the dying were trying to crawl back. Horses were thrashing with broken legs.

Ahead, men in better condition were making some progress. I saw many instances of the less injured on foot, leading the worse on their horses. Others were leading their own injured horses and sparing them their weight.

All through that awful retreat, the Russians kept up a half-hearted bombardment from the Causeway. They hardly hit anyone, and I wonder if they really wanted to. They were mainly firing the naval guns they had taken from us, as though to remind us they still had them. I saw horse teams and limbers on the Causeway, and remembered hearing that Lord Raglan had a great horror of losing guns, fearing the enemy would parade them as great trophies. So our former guns were firing a salute to their own capture. By then I was light-headed from loss of blood, and a thought came to me without any passion that these were the guns we had been meant to stop the enemy "carrying away". How Nolan had failed to realize this, I could not imagine. I felt so weak that the death of my friend and the devastation of his dream seemed unimportant, a dream themselves.

In this mood, nearly fainting, I came on Dimmock. He was unhorsed, and had injured a leg. He was making slow progress, leaning on his lance. I could see many men helping the wounded, and wanted to do the same myself. I said: "Dimmock! A chance to do something you've always wanted! A chance to ride Subaltern!"

He said: "I don't think so, Sir!" and then everything went black.

Someone got me onto a hospital ship bound for home. I was still very weak when I arrived, and was an invalid for over a month. This did not worry me, as to my amazement I found I had been given a colonel's commission without having to afford it.

That was important, for every day of my convalescence I received a visit from Miss Irene Taylor. She read the *Times* to me, the disputes between the generals, the terrible conditions our men endured under siege from General Winter. I knew my luck was in, and now I was no longer tempted to marry her for her money, I determined that I would marry Irene.

Cardigan came to the wedding. No one knew how he had escaped from the guns and the Cossacks, but he was there, looking a little embarrassed by his standards. He drank his bottle of porter like a man.

I was rated a hero, the new expert on cavalry. I knew myself to be a lucky man. But my luck was daytime luck. By night, as I sleep, I hear that voice, rasping above the guns, "Steady, steady, 17th Lancers!" I live again the Calvary Charge, that last, Pyrrhic charge of men on guns, of Faith against firepower. And on bad nights, very bad nights, I still hear Nolan's last scream.

VENGEANCE

Pamela Brooks

From the midst of some of the most atrocious conflicts emerge captivating and remarkable characters, as related in the following story. Pamela Brooks (b. 1966) is a prolific writer of historical, romantic and erotic novels under a variety of pen names including Lucinda Chester, Evelyn D'Arcy and Pamela Rochford. She has even written How to Write Erotic Fiction *(1998) and* Irish Babies' Names *(2000).*

Blood. Wherever you walked, you could smell it. Even if you washed your face in the river, pushed your head right under the freezing water so it would wash the stench from your nostrils, you would smell it as soon as you came back up for air. The whole place stank of blood: a thin, coppery reek. I could even taste the stuff, metallic and sharp, when I breathed in; there was a sickly-sweet undertone of gangrene and pus, mingled with the rich stench of the earth, thawed out by the body heat of the dying.

All around me, I could hear stifled groans from the men, whose socks never dried and who were lucky if their feet froze before the flesh rotted. Half of them couldn't even get their boots on, their feet were so swollen; so they went barefoot or cut the heels out and forced the leather round their flesh.

This was Hell. Worse even than the cramped, dark hospital John had worked in, in London. Those anguished cries, worse still for being muffled – because it would not do for an infantry-man to admit he suffered. And the little I could do to help was so very, very little, it was heartbreaking. I could barely stand it.

But I had to. For John's sake.

John was the reason I was here. John, my twin brother; he'd been the elder, by ten minutes. The brave one. Handsome, a little reckless. John, with that ready smile, the need to *do* something to right the wrongs of the world burning in his eyes. Eyes that had been dulled by the Crimea, by what he saw.

By the enemy within.

Even now, amid the noise of rifles being cleaned, men stamping their feet against the cold, dogs barking and horses whinnying, the groans of the sick, the screaming nightmares of those who managed to sleep – even now, I could still hear John's voice above them all. The rasp of his voice, disfigured by pain, as he told me what had happened. Over and over in my mind, I heard it, every word engraved into my heart. The more so because now I knew what he meant, at first hand. I was reliving my brother's nightmare, in every sense of the word.

You were right. I should have waited – I should have stayed here, in London. Not joined the 106th. But Jojo, if you'd seen them in the barracks at Windsor: they looked so proud, the buttons of their uniform gleaming and the coats of their horses burnished in the sunlight. How was I to know?

How, indeed.

I thought they'd fight for what was right, like our own Ninth Foot. That we'd stop the Russians wreaking havoc in the Mediterranean. That I could do even more good there, help the

*casualties, ease the suffering of the wounded and dying. And I could
have done it, but for one thing. I was a grocer's son, a tradesman's
son: I wasn't a gentleman.*

A gentleman. John was the gentlest man I knew. Far gentler
than I – because with every word he spoke, anger thickened and
froze my blood until I was ready to use a sword myself, to slice it
across the throats of his tormentors and hack their carcasses
until they were unrecognizable.

*I should never have asked Uncle Stephen to lend me the seven
hundred pounds to buy the lieutenant's commission. Maybe if I'd
been a private, they would have left me alone. But then I couldn't
have been a surgeon, too. I needed that commission.*

*They said . . . they said that I was short of class. I didn't talk
like them. I wasn't a heavy swell like them, a man who'd shoot and
hunt and fish and gamble, putting higher and higher stakes on the
dice. I couldn't knock back tot after tot of whisky and then walk in
a straight line.*

*But I'd been gazetted. They couldn't argue with the authorities.
So the only way they could get rid of me was to take matters into
their own hands. And then it started, the campaign against John
Barton. They put more energy into fighting me than into fighting
the Russians. If I went to sleep, someone would trip and spill a bowl
of water – or worse – over me and soak my bed. And if I protested,
they'd say it was an accident.*

The bastards. The bloody, bloody, bloody bastards. Not even
having the decency to let my brother sleep in a dry bed: it made
me grind my teeth, made me want to soak their own beds. To
make them sleep in a pool of piss, like they had done to him.

*And on the days when I escaped them, lost myself in my work,
tending the wounded in the battlefield, I'd come back to the tent and
my bedding would be wet, muddy, impossible to sleep in. My letters
. . . They were ripped before I could read them, and smeared with
mud or water so that even if I pieced them back together, I wouldn't
be able to make much sense of them.*

So the notes I'd carefully made for him about new inventions,
new theories in the world of medicine, had been useless to him.
And worse, the stupid, petty, spiteful behaviour meant that others

– men who were horribly maimed, even dying: men who could
have profited by my brother's knowledge – had suffered. The
knowledge made me angrier still. Such a waste. Such a stupid,
stupid, stupid waste. I wanted to go out there, go to the East and tie
them to a stake and make them listen. Force their ignorance back
in their faces. Make them realize what they'd really done.

*They ripped my photographs, Jojo: every last one was torn to
shreds. Everything I owned was smashed and ruined, even the
watch our parents gave me on our twenty-first. I saw Bruce do it. I
saw him stamp on the things most precious to me. He knew I saw
him, and he laughed. He laughed in my face. I wanted to kill him –
kill all of them. But they were my comrades in arms. They were
British. How could I fight them? Instead, I pretended that the
Russians had their faces. I killed, Jojo. I actually killed a man. No,
more than that: I killed me. I thrust my sword into their guts and
twisted it. And I enjoyed it.*

My brother – my brother, who wouldn't harm so much as a
spider – enjoyed killing. That's what they'd reduced him to.
The way they treated him, keeping him cold and tired and
hungry, the only thing left he could enjoy was killing. The very
thought turned my blood to burnished steel: steel that I wanted
to push through their hearts. Very, very, very slowly: so that
they knew who'd done it, and why: John Barton's twin.

And Grierson sent me into the breach.

Of course, the Lieutenant General didn't tell him what was
behind it. The fat, lying bastard probably didn't even know;
and, if he did, I doubt if he cared. He hadn't cared enough to see
what was going on in his own regiment. He'd probably even
joined Bruce and the others in baiting my brother.

And I was wounded.

That was litotes, if ever I heard it. My brother was virtually
ripped to shreds, and the salt air on the long sea voyage home
inflamed his wounds even further.

Avenge me, Jojo. Avenge me.

They were his last words to me. What else could I do?

It meant going East and facing his tormentors. I was prepared
for that. After John's death, I was prepared for anything.

Though I knew that there was no point in asking my parents. They'd have said it was impossible. Apart from anything else, they'd just lost one child and they didn't want to lose a second. The cost of a commission would have been too high for them, too: the grocer's business was doing well, but not *that* well. And the most they would have agreed for me to do was work in the hospital in Scutari; in their view, it would have been more fitting than going out to the front.

It would also have meant that I could do nothing to avenge my brother.

So the only person I could turn to was our godfather and tell him what John had told me. And after that, what could he do but agree with my strategy and get me the commission?

Three weeks later, I walked into their camp. J. Barton, esq. was back, in the form of John Barton's twin, also a doctor and a scholar. They didn't bother to check the records and see if I had obtained my degree in the same place as John, or if I had a degree at all: the way I talked was enough to convince them that I was another sawbones. And another target.

Though they had some additional things to taunt me about. The fact that I was careful about washing, that I insisted on privacy for it. That I wouldn't void my body in front of others. That the dog I'd rescued from their ill-treatment slept on my bed and kept me warm at night; and that I wouldn't rise to their jokes about nurses being prostitutes and drunkards, and doctors being not much better. That I was a "beardless boy", not growing the thick beard like theirs at the sides of their faces and under their chins, the neatly trimmed moustache of the "heavy swells".

John had warned me about their loutishness, the foul language and the constant gambling; when I, like he, declined to join in, they taunted me for it.

"You're more of a woman than Mrs Duberly," Sir Henry Bruce said, mimicking a mincing movement as he stalked past my bedding.

Mrs Duberly, whose husband was in the Hussars, and who rode the battlefields, peering at the wounded: they called her the Vulture, the French wrote a polka in honour of *l'Amazone*, and it was said that she was no lady of the drawing room.

More of a woman that Mrs Duberly. Indeed.

"Look at you. Thin, small – what kind of a man are you?" he sneered.

I smiled. "I dare do all that become a man; who dares do more is none."

He didn't understand my reference, of course. How could he? The nearest he could have come to a theatre would have been an actress's dressing room. Shakespeare, unless it were the name of a dog or a racehorse, meant nothing to him. I never saw Bruce or any of his cronies with a book or a letter, in the rare time we had to relax. The only things they seemed to read were playing cards and dice. Their counting seemed to be limited to money, too, accompanied by sneers and jeers at whoever lost at cards. Cards that were probably marked, in the first place.

And then there was the fact that I ate with my men, not with them. "But you don't want me eating with you, anyway," was my retort, when Bruce took me to task about it. I preferred to pool my officer's rations with the twenty-five men I commanded, as their lieutenant, rather than sit drinking all night in the mess tent with louts I couldn't bear. My men respected me for it, too. They teased me for being soft-spoken, for being different, but they respected me – because I treated them with respect, too, not like common scum to be ground down beneath the heel of my highly polished boot. They talked to me. I listened. And they could tell the difference between an officer who at least tried to find out what those bloody purveyors were doing and get proper rations and warm clothes issued, and an officer who simply smiled, waggled their hands a bit and said that there was a war on, you know, so you had to expect to rough it, then went back to swig best claret from a polished silver goblet.

John was always more of a hothead than I am; though maybe that was because I had always had to remain calm. I could do nothing else, in my position, but rage inside my head at the injustices. And maybe he let his tormentors see how much their behaviour hurt him: whereas my smile was as that of the

Egyptian sphinx, of *La Joconde*. What they said, what they did, was nothing. The more they tormented me, the more I ignored them. I would simply await my chance to avenge my brother. If they grew bored with tormenting me in the meantime, so much the better: but I could wait for the right moment.

And my chance came. We were camped about a quarter of a mile in the rear of the 2nd Division, on the slope of the ridge between the Tchernaya River and the Careenage Ravine. The men had been muttering, restless: the mist was thick and seemed to sink into our bones, making old wounds ache and feet swell. Sir Andrew Grierson, our esteemed Lieutenant General, was one of the old school; he'd fought under Wellington, and expected all his soldiers to be as hard as he was. So he ignored the complaints about the cold and insisted that the men wear dress uniform. Extra rags draped about the men to keep them warm were ripped off the first time Grierson saw them, and thrown into the fire, the second time. But although the men were cold, hungry and miserable, they feared Grierson more. Because the one rule he would break was the one about the forty-five lashes maximum on a flogging. And non-regulation uniform, in his eyes, was a flogging offence at the third time.

That morning – a November the 5th I will remember for the rest of my life – the Russians opened fire. Their infantry stopped and artillery shells swept the rest of our hill.

And then, after what seemed like hours – though it could only have been minutes – the order came. We were to go down the forward slope.

We could barely see in the mist. No wonder the Russians had managed to creep up on us. Rumours were everywhere: that the Russians had ten battalions, that there were fifty thousand men – a hundred thousand – waiting for us in the mist. But our orders were to go forward. Loud guns sounded either side, screams as shells hit their targets, the soft thuds as bodies hit the ground and were trampled by those behind. The sharp stinging smell of gunsmoke in our noses, mingling with the mist to make it even harder to pick our way through the undergrowth. Rough ground underfoot, small boulders and stones and unexpected holes ready to trip the unwary.

Now. Now was my moment.

But no. We had another battle to win, first. Once we'd won it: then I'd take my moment.

On we went, some firing the new muzzle-loading Enfield rifles, others using bayonets. I had my sword; it was a while since I'd practised fencing, but I'd been good with a sword in my youth. And now I was going to use it. Still with a graceful movement, but this time I'd push the point forward, not stop it politely against my opponent's clothes.

A light sword. "A lady's sword," my tormentors sneered. Indeed. It was perfectly suited to my grip, light but sure and very, very sharp. I'd sharpened it myself, and I kept it with me at all times, so it couldn't be "accidentally" blunted the way that John's had, in his last battle.

"Forward," I screamed, leading my men on. And they were behind me all the way, with bayonets and swords, jabbing and leaping and screaming for victory.

Russian after Russian fell before us, crying out in their strange tongue to their God. The clash of sword on sword. The crunch of bone as a bayonet forced its way through a ribcage. The smell of blood again, fresh and choking: the mist itself seemed to turn blood-red before my eyes. I even heard General Pennefather myself, riding through the fog and calling out to the men, urging us on with oaths and curses as much as smiles. But he was there with us, not skulking back like some I could mention: and it was enough to drive us on. We might be outnumbered, but we were the better fighters. We knew that.

And then, so quickly, it was over. Word came that General Siomonov had been killed, that the Russians were retreating. We'd repulsed the advance from Sebastopol.

I took out the watch from the inside pocket of my frock-coat. Forty minutes. That was all it had taken. And I felt as if I'd been fighting for a whole lifetime. Every muscle ached, my eyes hurt, and my throat was sore from the smoke and the screaming.

I dropped to my haunches, and regretted it when I realized

that I was sitting on a dead Russian, that the wetness under me was blood rather than mud. But I was too tired to get up again.

"Well done," I croaked to the men. "Well done."

"Yes . . . Lieutenant."

The tone of Sergeant Mundford's voice made me snap my head back and stare at him. He was staring at me.

And then I realized.

In the battle, I'd been too busy using my sword to realize that my frock-coat had been ripped by one of my opponents. Ripped enough to make life very difficult for me.

There was a long silence; then Mundford stripped off his coat. "I think you needs this more than me, ma'am," he said, his Hampshire accent broadening in embarrassment.

"Thank you," I said, using his coat to cover my modesty.

"We never . . . Well, we thought you was John Barton's younger brother, see."

"I never actually said that. I said I was his twin. Which I am." I grinned at him. "At ease, Sergeant."

"But ma'am—"

"But nothing. My brother was killed, and I know how it happened. I'm here to make things right."

His eyes widened. "But you're—"

"Just as qualified as John. I studied with him for the exams, though I couldn't take them." And that in itself had been a bitter blow, at the time. How I had railed at the sheer bigotry of Cambridge, refusing to let me sit an exam because I was of the so-called fairer sex. "His sword-master taught me, at the same time." That had been another issue, but at least I had won that one.

"But your ma and pa—"

"Oh, they despair of me," I said with a grin. Maybe it was our victory against the Russians; maybe it was just that all the secrets were over. For now. But I felt suddenly light-headed, happier than I'd felt for weeks.

"You said to call you Jojo, ma'am."

"That's what they call me at home. It's short for Joanna," I said. "But, Sam, I don't want this broadcast. Promise me."

"All right." He frowned. "But why?"

"Like I said, John was killed. I'm here to make things right."

"Revenge, you mean?"

"In a way."

He looked thoughtful. "You going to kill them?"

So the men knew about it, too. Why hadn't they done anything? But of course, they couldn't. In the army, you obeyed orders, whether you agreed with them or not. If any of the men had stood up for John, there would have been a flogging. Not for standing up for another human being – some excuse would have been found. A rifle not clean enough, an alleged disobedience. "Right now, I don't know. I'd like to." I stared at my sword. The bright metal looked rusty with dried blood. "And I'm capable of doing it."

"You're that, all right," he said.

I grinned back at him. That was the nearest thing I'd had to approval from anyone except my brother. "The Spanish women carried guns in the Peninsula war, you know."

"Because their men were too bloody cowardly to do it themselves. Beg pardon, ma'am." He'd obviously been taught not to swear in front of a woman. His eyes flickered. "It's different, here."

"I'm staying, Sam," I said quietly. "And I'd appreciate it if you kept this quiet. Tell the others, too."

He stared at me for a long moment. I thought he was going to refuse. Finally, he sighed. "All right. I'll tell them to keep it quiet."

"Thank you, Sam." I coughed. "Now, if you don't mind . . ."

He grinned. "We'll keep our eyes closed, ma'am."

"Sir," I reminded him, grinning back.

By the time I'd exchanged my jacket for his – a poor fit, as Sam was so much broader in the shoulders than I was, but at least it was modest – more orders had come. There was another Russian attack, at the Quarry Ravine. Our battalion was to protect the Sandbag Battery, a two-gun establishment with a good position, looking downhill for three hundred yards or so. The Russians didn't have a hope of taking it from us. I wasn't sure why we really needed to go, but orders were orders.

The mist still hadn't lifted. We trudged our way towards the battery, the noise of gunfire becoming louder and we grew nearer. I tried not to look at the dead and the dying; though one particular groan was so piercing that the doctor – albeit un-qualified – in me had to stop.

It was a Russian. His dark eyes were bloodshot, and he was lying as if he were trying to raise himself on one elbow. I could see his skull quite clearly, and there was a gaping hole in the middle of his chest. His clothes were soaked in blood.

"Leave him," a voice said beside me. "Unless you want to end up like that."

I knew that voice. Bruce. The worst of John's – and my – tormentors. I couldn't bear to look at him. "Have you no compassion?" Stupid question. I already knew the answer to that, firsthand.

"You can't do anything for him, Sawbones. Leave it."

But there was something I could do for the man. We didn't speak each other's language, but the Russian was telling me what he wanted, as clearly as anything. His dignity. Peace. I nodded, lifted my sword, and pushed it against his jugular. The skin pressed inward, inward; and then, finally, my sword pieced it and the vein. Blood gushed out, the soldier said something that could have been a thank you or could have been a prayer, and he was dead.

"Sentimental," Bruce scoffed.

I shrugged.

"And stupid. He was the enemy."

"And one of God's creatures," I reminded Bruce. The cruel smile on his thick lips made me want to vomit. "Why let him suffer more than he has to?"

"Stupid," Bruce repeated.

I reminded myself not to let him upset me. If he saw the effect he had on me, he'd win. And that wasn't going to happen. "Maybe one day," I said softly, "you'll be glad for someone to do the same thing for you." I nearly did it myself, there and then; although there were people round me, I knew that they would all claim to be elsewhere. I could simply wipe that smile off his face with my sword. Stab him through the guts, twist the blade . . .

But I restrained myself. Just. I marched off, surrounded by my men.

The captain of another company was giving orders to his men. I listened in; I had a feeling that his word would be better than that of Bruce's. Bruce was as useless as Grierson when it came to tactics. And I'd noticed that he was hardly sweating, let alone covered in mud and blood and filth as the rest of us were. He hadn't been doing too much fighting.

It seemed that we were to protect a line of rocks and the Sandbag. Three hundred yards downhill of the battery, there was dead ground. The Russians could disappear into this and regroup. We were to repulse them whenever they attacked.

Almost as soon as he'd finished speaking, the Russians launched their first attack. Screaming and yelling, they came for us, swords raised. The riflemen answered with a barrage of shots; the first wave of the enemy was down, but another was behind. And another. And another.

"Forward!" I yelled, springing up to the top of the parapet. "We must charge!" Sam was beside me.

"How many will follow?" I asked, but I didn't wait for an answer. I leapt down to meet our assailants, using my sword to clear the space around me. From the corner of my eye, I could see Sam bayoneting one of the enemy, and thrusting the corpse back to knock down the fellows behind him. Again and again we clashed with our opponents, sword against sword, bayonet smashing into bone. I could hear screams beside me, behind me, but I dared not turn and see who was down or what I could do to help. I had to fight on, on and on and on.

A Russian officer barred my way. He was a good foot taller than I was, and twice as broad. I didn't stand a chance . . . But I had to. I had to stay alive, so I could avenge John. I parried the other soldier's thrust, feinted, then lunged as hard as I could. Thank God, my sword hadn't been that blunted by the early morning struggle; it slid into his guts.

"Thank you, God." I mouthed the prayer as I pulled my

sword out and struck again and again, fighting for my country, my life and my chance to avenge my brother; and not in that particular order.

Every time I struck, I thought of Bruce's loathsome face. I thought of the way he sneered, the way he'd taunted John, the way he'd taunted me. And every blow was for him; just as John had done, I imagined that the Russians all had Bruce's face. It gave my arm an almost supernatural strength; all around me, men were fighting in small groups, hand to hand. Rifles were used as clubs as well as for shooting, the heavy butts cracking open skulls and smashing arms; bayonets were used as daggers, ripping through flesh and stabbing into eyes; and everywhere, there were screams and yells and the constant boom, boom, boom of the heavy guns.

Every time the Russians retreated into the dead space, we thought it was over; but before we could relax or celebrate, they were back again, stronger and stronger. Our line splintered into groups, smaller and smaller, one to one. On and on and on.

But at last, they were pushed back into the Quarry Ravine; the French artillery had arrived and started galloping down the forward slopes. And the two eighteen-pounder guns behind us blasted the note of victory.

A cheer broke out among the men, and another, and another; we surged forward, waving swords and guns and bayonets, and the enemy was fleeing back to their lines. And then finally, the guns on Shell Hill – named for the tiny white shells that covered it, rather than for the guns themselves – fell silent. The Russians had retreated. The battle was over.

I trudged back towards where I thought my men were. I hadn't thought about them in the battle – I hadn't had time – but I prayed that they were safe. My good, solid Hampshire-men, my allies and my friends.

"Barton?"

The voice was almost a croak, but I recognized it. A voice I hated from a man I despised. I stopped and looked down at the pitiful figure on the ground.

"I'm dying, Barton. Help me."

"Help you?" I wiped my sword on my overalls. Help him. Just like I'd helped the Russian soldier into a merciful death. It would only take a moment: the point of my sword against his neck, then leaning on it, the pressure of my body weight driving the steel through his body. Just as I'd dreamed of doing, killing him and the others who'd been so cruel to John, so harsh to the men they commanded. I'd be doing the world a good turn.

And I'd be doing him a good turn, giving him a quick death, rather than a slow one.

"Why should I help you, Bruce?"

"Dammit, it's an order! I'm your superior officer."

"But you're dying. And I might be deaf from the guns." The silence seemed so loud. It was hard to get used to, after the hubbub of the fight.

"Barton. I'm dying. My back's broke."

"Is it, now? Such a shame the poles never arrived for the stretchers –" Bruce had never once tried to chase up our missing supplies "– or I'd send for a couple of bearers."

He screamed; a spasm of pain had clearly hit him. "You – you're not going to leave me here, like this?" he asked, almost whining.

"Let me see. You bullied my brother: you pissed on his bed – and on mine. I saw you. You said I wasn't worthy of being an officer. And you want me to help you?"

"I . . . I . . ."

"The word is 'sorry', Bruce. But it's a bit too late. John's dead."

"I'll be dead, soon." His face, beneath the splashes of mud, was ashen with pain.

"You called me more of a woman than Mrs Duberly," I reminded him.

He drew a shuddering breath. "I saw you fight. You're not."

"A beardless boy. Small and thin." I quoted the words back at him. "Think about it, Sir Henry." I couldn't resist sneering his title at him. "Didn't it ever occur to you that John had a sister?"

"You said you were his twin!"

"I am." I smiled. "I'm his twin sister."

"But . . . But . . ."

I shrugged, enjoying the fear and horror on his face. "Doesn't matter, now. But you'll die knowing that the woman you despised was a better swordswoman than you. And you'll die knowing that your cowardice, the way you treated John, will be exposed. I'll fight side by side with your cronies until every single one of them's dead. And then I'll fight back home, until the army's reformed and creatures like you never get the chance to buy your way into power again."

"No. No." He shook his head wildly. "It's not true. I didn't. I—"

"You're a liar, a bully, a coward and a braggart," I told him. "And, with a broken back, you'll never survive." Actually, with proper care, he could: but I wasn't going to give him any hope. "You're going to die, Bruce. Slowly and painfully. But I'm not going to let you die in the comfort of your bed. You'll die here, in the mud, where you belong. And I'm not going to give you the dignity, the peace I gave that Russian. You sneered at me, then; so you won't want it for yourself, will you?"

"Barton, for the love of Christ . . ."

"Rot in hell, where you belong," I said.

And I walked away, back to my company, leaving my enemy screaming to his death.

Historical note

The 106th and Lieutenant General Sir Andrew Grierson are fictional, but based loosely on Sir Robert Garrett and his 46th South Devon Regiment, who fought at Inkerman, and whose bullying of Lieutenant Parry (the son of a tradesman) scandalized Victorian England in 1854.

The heroic exploits of the fictional Joanna Barton at Inkerman are based on those of Captain Burnaby of the Grenadier Guards.

Mrs Duberly followed her husband in the Crimea and published a book of her experiences in 1855. Colonel Shewell signed her application for a Crimea medal, including clasps for Balaclava and Inkerman.

THE SHARPSHOOTER

Garry Douglas

*Garry Douglas is the pseudonym of author Garry Kil-
worth (b. 1941), who has been writing science fiction and
fantasy since 1976, and is also the author of many popular
books for children. Under the Douglas name he has written
a series of novels set in the Crimea and featuring Sergeant
Jack Crossman of the 88th Regiment. The series includes*
The Devil's Own *(1997),* The Valley of Death *(1998),*
Soldiers in the Mist *(1999) and* The Winter Soldiers
*(2000). The following episode was specially written for
this anthology.*

The colonel heard the single shot from the Russian lines. A
soldier fell dead in the British trenches. The dead man had only
been half-alive anyway. It was January in the Crimean winter of
1855 and many British soldiers were dying of exposure, freezing
to death on piquet duty, or on the line. The uniforms they had

been wearing for almost two years now were in tatters and no winter clothing had arrived. There was nothing the colonel could do about this. The Commissariat, in charge of supplies, was a department which had become hopelessly entangled in bureaucracy and had all but ground to a halt.

Wrapped in a single blanket crackling with ice and frost, each soldier was like a grey shambling beast moving across a tundra.

The colonel's men were going through the motions of being alive, but the winter had driven the spirits from their bodies and left in its place a hard inscape of emptiness. Bleak faces with lacklustre eyes peered out of the hoods formed by the thin blankets. In most cases the skin was pitted where frostbite had ravaged the exposed cheeks and jaws. Raw noses with split skin poked from beneath the peaks of shakos. Chapped lips had been cracked open by the sharp winds which swept down from the steppes. The Russian winter had numbed these men almost beyond caring whether the next bullet was intended for them.

"Bastard!"

The hollow shout in an Irish accent had come from one of these living ghosts, directed at the Russian sharpshooter in the sangar, a fortified ruined windmill. They called him "The Hawk" because he never missed his prey. Once in his sights you were a dead man. The colonel had heard his Rangers arguing as to whether the Hawk had supernatural powers.

"It's not enough we should be freezin' to death out here," a soldier now grumbled, "but we have to put up with the likes of *him*."

The corpse was dragged away, along one of the communication trenches. He had been a member of the Light Company of the colonel's Connaught Rangers, who now occupied this position on the line. Some of the victim's fellow Rangers thought him lucky to be dead rather than severely wounded. All knew that if he had been merely injured he might have had to make the journey in one of the notorious death ships, across the Black Sea to Scutari Hospital at Constantinople, where sick and dying men languished in their own maggots and filth.

At least, some said, the cholera, or dysentery, or one of half-a-dozen other killer diseases had not sucked the life out of him. The .702 calibre conical ball had struck him on the temple, taking away most of the right side of his head. It had been quick and clean.

Still, the colonel and his Rangers hated the Hawk. They all knew the Russian regiment which lay behind the Hawk's position were crowing about their Goliath, who had the Rangers pinned to the walls of their trenches, unable to wave a finger above the parapet without it getting shot off. They knew this and they prayed for a David to come along, to rid them of this constant threat.

When the sharpshooter had first made his presence known, the colonel had asked one of his subalterns, "How is this man able to shoot so accurately? Surely not with a Russian smooth-bore musket?"

"We believe he has a Minié, sir," came the reply.

"Damn the man!"

A Minié rifle! Standard issue in the British army, but not so common in the Russian. In any case the Russians sand-rubbed their weapons, for drill purposes, until every piece of ironwork was loose and rattled in the stock. It made for a grand sound on the parade ground, but it rendered the weapons virtually useless for battle.

The colonel had seethed on receiving this information. They were being slaughtered by one of their own rifles: a four-and-a-half foot long Minié, accurate up to nearly a thousand yards. A single shot from this weapon had been known to pass through four men standing one behind the other. The Minié was not a breech-loader, but a good soldier could ram down and fire three rounds a minute. The Hawk used this weapon from behind the safety of an unassailable sangar halfway between the British and Russian lines. The sangar was part of what had once been a windmill, built on the crest of a wind-swept hill, behind which was a Tartar graveyard that swept down to a huge church.

It did not help the colonel's temper any to realize that if the miller who had built the windmill had done so a few hundred yards or so further on, the Hawk would have been killing

French soldiers instead of British, for that was where the allied line changed. Though the colonel did not detest Frenchmen as much as his commander-in-chief, he would prefer that the Hawk was shooting bluecoats, rather than redcoats.

As things stood, the Hawk was killing British soldiers – men from the colonel's mostly Irish 88th Connaught Rangers – and he was doing a job which satisfied his officers and comrades nestled in and around the great church behind him.

Not long after the dead man had been removed, the colonel learned that a second 88th soldier was shot that day. The soldier had moved to ease his cramp and his right shoulder had showed briefly above the parapet. A Minié bullet tore through it instantly, smashing and splintering the scapula, and causing the man to scream in agony. The Rangers had had enough. They had lost twelve men in a week to the Hawk and something had to be done about him. They complained bitterly to the colour-sergeant, who took their grievances to a lieutenant, and so on, until the complaint reached the ears of the colonel.

At the time the complaint was laid before the colonel he had been conversing with a Major Lovelace, spy and saboteur, who commanded a small *peleton* of misfits.

The beleaguered colonel expressed his frustration to the major.

Lovelace suggested, "Why not blast the sangar out of the way with artillery?"

The colonel shook his head, sagely. "We've been refused permission. Staff believes we may need all the cover we can get once we mount our own attack on Sebastopol. Ridiculous. It provides cover for a single man and then only when used from the west side. We are being led by a pack of nimcompoops, major."

Lovelace knew that. The British generals were either very elderly or too inexperienced to run a war. Their heads were full of old-fashioned ideas of warfare. Lord Raglan, the commander-in-chief, was himself more of a deferential administrator than a warrior. Raglan hated spies and saboteurs, calling them "skulkers" and had forbidden his generals to use them, which was why Major Lovelace performed his undercover duties unknown to anyone but Brigadier-General Buller, one of the few progressive and enlightened senior officers in the field.

"What about a quick frontal attack? Kill the sharpshooter, use the sangar for our own purposes?" said Lovelace.

"We've tried that. The sangar is only a few hundred yards from a Russian church bristling with troops. We have the same distance to cover, but ours is rough ground covered in rocks and with a steeper uphill slope. They have gravestones for cover on the plateau of that hill. If we try to mount an attack the sharpshooter signals to his comrades, they reach the position before we do and cut us down as we climb the slope to his position. It's hopeless."

"I'll tell you what, I'll put my best man onto it. He's good at solving puzzles. Sergeant Crossman."

The colonel's eyes narrowed. He knew of this sergeant. The one the troops called "Fancy Jack" because of his accent and manners. A man from his own regiment, along with two or three others, seconded to General Buller for duties dark and mysterious.

"I'm aware of this Sergeant Crossman," murmured the colonel. "They say he is an aristocrat going under an assumed name in the ranks. One wonders what he's doing there. The officers don't trust him because of his obvious breeding and education, and the men themselves are suspicious of him, believing he is there to spy on them."

"Oh, I'm sure he has his reasons, but they need not be underhand ones, colonel. Perhaps he could not afford the purchase price of a commission?"

"Then why join the army at all? The ranks of the British Army consist of the scum of the earth. A man from a good family amongst 'em? Why, there has to be a deeper motive than just wanting to be a soldier. My soldiers are brave lads, but they've cannon fodder just the same."

The colonel's views on Jack Crossman and the rank and file were directly in line with those of his fellow officers. One purchased a commission in the army. One didn't join as a common soldier. There could be no possible reason to do so, unless one was mad. The pay was negligible: a private was lucky to have tuppence a day left out of his wages after all his "extras" had been paid for. Conditions, especially in places like the Crimea, were appalling. When they had first arrived the troops had no tents and slept out in the open in all weather. When the tents did come they were so rotten they fell to pieces when they were handled. Much of the British soldier's war was being spent in a trench half-filled with freezing water, being shelled night and day from the defences of Sebastopol. Who would go for a soldier but a criminal, a man desperate for any kind of employment, or a madman?

Nevertheless, Crossman was sent for. He arrived at the colonel's tent from his billet in a hovel in Kadikoi, near the entrance to Balaclava harbour with two of his men: Lance-Corporals Peterson and Wynter. They were all veterans. Since arriving in the Crimea they had fought the battles of the Alma, Balaclava, and two battles on the Inkerman Heights, the second of these fought in mists and lasting several hours. Apart from these "normal" duties the three soldiers had undertaken many missions, or "fox hunts" for General Buller, involving espionage and sabotage.

The colonel disliked dealing directly with a sergeant. Especially one as unconventional as Crossman, who had entered his tent wearing a forage cap, a foul-smelling sheepskin, blue Turkish pantaloons and Russian boots. Nevertheless the colonel felt the situation was serious enough for him to put aside his prejudices for a short while. He explained the problem to Crossman. The sergeant, a tall, lean aristocrat of Scottish birth nodded.

"What happens at night? Does the Hawk sneak back to his own lines?"

"There's a slope down from the sangar. The Hawk can quite easily get back to the church for food and warmth without being seen. We believe the sangar is occupied by troops during some of the night hours to allow the Hawk some respite. When the problem first arose I sent a picquet out to the sanger at night, hoping it was vacant and we could occupy it before dawn. Both men were shot dead before they were halfway there. We don't really know whether the Hawk got them, or whether they were shot by ordinary Russian soldiers. We think it was him."

Crossman's eyebrows went up. "They were seen in the dark?"

"It must be assumed that he aimed at the sounds he heard."

"So, not only does our sharpshooter have the eyes of a hawk, he has the ears of an owl too! I am beginning to think this man is the stuff of myth. I wish I had my Bashi-Bazouk with me, but he's been loaned to the French Zouaves for a mission they have conceived."

"Your Bashi-Bazouk?" said the colonel, faintly.

"A Turk by the name of Yusuf Ali. He looks rather like someone's amiable uncle Albert, but he's as deadly as he is rotund. I would have no doubt he would sneak up and cut the throat of the Hawk with less sound than a beetle amongst the rocks, but as I say, he's unavailable. The Zouaves have got him for two weeks. He's out somewhere in the hills north of the Woronzoff Road and when Yusuf Ali is lost in the mountains there's no finding him until he comes out again."

"So, sergeant," said the colonel, "what do you intend doing about this rat we have in our wainscot?"

"Let's try Peterson first. He's one of my lance-corporals."

Crossman did not add that Peterson was a woman who had disguised herself as a man in order to join the army. She just happened to be the best shot Crossman had ever encountered. Her secret was well-kept by her sergeant and comrades.

"Your lance-corporal? You seem to own a lot of soldiers. One would think you had a private army, sergeant," the colonel could not help remarking with more than a little acidity in his tone. "I believe these men are in *my* regiment, are they not?"

"That is so, sir. They are mine only in the sense that they take their orders directly from me. It's my opinion that the army will devolve initiative down to ranks even lower than myself one day."

"That sounds like heresy to me. It is commonly held that only generals are permitted initiative, sergeant."

However, if the Crimean War had proved anything, it was that when the generals had failed to provide orders in the heat of the battle, colonels, majors, captains and lieutenants – yes, and even sergeants – had used their own intelligence and had acted on their own enterprise. The colonel knew this, though he would never have discussed it with a common soldier. He was uncomfortable with the idea that men could think for themselves. A disciplined army had its strength in its ability to move like an automaton, under the orders of generals and marshals.

However, he also knew that it had to be recognized, if only privately, that Inkerman would have been lost if everyone had stood around and waited for orders from generals. At Inkerman three or four thousand scattered, isolated and disparate groups of British soldiers had held out against 60,000 Russian troops and artillery. Orders from above had been few and had failed to reach most groups, who battled tenaciously in the fog to retain control of the Inkerman Heights. The common soldier had proved his ability to think for himself that day. Perhaps it was no longer appropriate to use Wellington's term "scum" for the Irishmen, Scotsmen, Englishmen and Welshmen who were the British soldiery?

"What will this Peterson do? Is he an assassin like your Bashi-Bazouk?" asked the colonel.

"No, he's a sharpshooter like the Hawk. One of the best. When he's not with me he's with Captain Goodlake's sharpshooters."

Peterson was ordered down to the trenches, along with Wynter, who whined about this their latest mission and his part in it.

"Kill a bloody sharpshooter? Why's that our work? The bastard might get me while I'm down there. Why do I have to come with you? Peterson's the one to do it, not me . . ."

Crossman said, "Stop complaining Wynter. If I'm going to be there, and Peterson, you're going to be there too. We might have to use you as a shield."

"What?" cried the long-suffering Englishman.

Crossman smiled. "A joke, Wynter, to lighten your day."

"That's not funny, sergeant. Not funny at all."

Peterson found a suitable spot from which to fire at the sangar, but failed to even glimpse the Hawk. The convex ruin of the windmill's wall was the perfect shield for the man behind it. She tried firing at the small hole through which the Hawk poked his rifle, but it had been shaped like an arrowloop, with just a slit on the side facing the British trenches. Only a very lucky shot would find its way through. Moreover, she began to draw fire from the Hawk in return, and found her position precarious. Once, a round creased her jacket on the shoulder. She moved position several times, but could find no real safe spot where she was able to expose herself with any safety when firing at the sangar.

"It's no good, sergeant," she said. "We'll be here a month of Sundays before I manage to hit him."

At the end of that day the Hawk had killed another man, a subaltern whose fresh young features were marred by the bullet wound where his nose had been. The boy had not died outright from the wound but had choked on his own blood. They carried him back in the darkness, to be buried the following morning. The colonel, who knew the boy's family, had the unenviable task of writing to them of their son's death. He said nothing of the real manner of the death, but described a minor skirmish in which their son had a hero's role. It was not too far from the truth to be called an outright lie, since there had been some activity in and around the trenches that evening.

That night Sergeant Jack Crossman went to the colonel's tent again with a dangerous plan.

"Well, Sergeant, been thinking for yourself again?"

The lamp cast shadows against the canvas wall of the tent as the two men stood facing one another. The colonel was grieved to notice that the sergeant's silhouette was taller and straighter than his own. He consciously made an effort to improve his own posture.

"Yes, sir, I'm afraid I have."

"Well, sir, you had better let me in on it."

Crossman said, "It's impossible to get the Hawk from this side. His position is unassailable. If we try to attack him in force, his own troops rally from the church beyond and he slips away between them. If we send out individual men, he picks them off. He is invisible to us, thanks to the shape and position of the sangar. The only way to kill him is from behind."

"And how is that to be accomplished?" asked the colonel, with a sarcastic edge to his voice. "Do we send a message to his own regiment to deal with the matter?"

Sergeant Crossman's voice was soft and low.

"No, sir. I find it is my mission to disguise myself as a Russian, infiltrate their lines, and shoot the Hawk in the back of the head."

The colonel was shocked and he showed it in his features.

"Do you know what you're saying, sergeant? You are proposing to become an *assassin*, under the cloak of the uniform of the enemy. Good God man, this is supposed to be a war. Where's the honour in such deeds? Where would they lead? Only to chaos, to bloody murder. It's unthinkable. Such a mission exudes evil from every pore. Despite these special duties you have, you wear the uniform of my regiment. I will not have the Connaught Rangers brought to dishonour."

Crossman had been prepared for such a reaction from the field officer. War was still played like cricket, or a single-combat duel, for the most part with fairness and honour. There were rules, there was even etiquette. There were things you did and did not do. Lord Raglan himself hated any departure from the unwritten code. He abhorred the idea of spying, even as a general rule to find out the numbers of enemy he was up against. Such a mission as this would have the commander-in-chief in a fit. He would hang such an assassin himself, from a high gallows, albeit that man was working for the British cause against the Russians. Lord Raglan, like most officers in the British Army of the East, would have called it murder.

Crossman had heard that only the other day, an Irish corporal, captured by two Russian soldiers, had snatched the musket of one of his captors and had killed both of them before escaping back to his own lines. The unholy suggestion of a medal for the sagacious Irishman had Lord Raglan frothing at the mouth. The corporal had been captured. He should have gone away quietly with his captors, who had graciously allowed him to live, and submitted to his changed status as a prisoner-of-war.

"Sir," said Sergeant Crossman to his offended colonel, "I am of a new breed of men, who believe in expediency."

"Machiavelli!" countered the colonel. "It is monstrous."

"Perhaps, but this war has to be won so that we can all go home and live peaceful lives. Do you honestly believe that the sharpshooter is any better? He sits there safe and sound, killing men one by one, without a qualm. Or if he has them, he ignores them. Is that not murder?"

"It is one of the *acceptable* faces of warfare."

"My methods, the methods of General Buller and Major Lovelace, will also become acceptable very soon now. The shape of war is changing, colonel. Weapons are becoming more deadly, more accurate. You do not suppose that the Hawk could do what he does with a smoothbore musket, which is inaccurate beyond two hundred yards? The Minié is the first of a type of rifled weapon with a ball which expands to grip the barrel. It is accurate up to 800 yards and can kill at twice that distance. Times are changing, colonel. Such wanton killing as this sharpshooter has shown must be nullified with methods we would have considered underhand in the Duke of Wellington's time."

"Do not even say his name, sergeant. The Duke would turn in his grave."

"I'm afraid our old heroes are also old fashioned. You have a choice, colonel. Do you want more of your men to die, or do you want me to assassinate this one man who will be the cause of their deaths? It's as simple as that. I can find a Russian uniform from amongst those of the enemy prisoners we hold. I speak enough Russian now to get by. All being well I can find the opportunity to sneak up behind this sharpshooter and blow out his brains. There would be an end to it all. Some of our men, who would otherwise not see the coming of next Spring, will live to dandle their grandchildren on their knees."

The colonel sighed and made a gesture of resignation with the palms of his hands.

"Thank you, sir," said Crossman. "I shall go tonight. If you have to, look on it simply as an attack from the rear. Tactics."

Something occurred to the colonel. "What weapon will you use? If you're disguised as a Russian, you will be carrying Russian arms."

Crossman reached inside his sheepskin coat and produced a pistol.

"This holds five shots. It's one of the very latest percussion revolvers being manufactured by Tranter."

"That is not standard issue, sergeant."

"No sir, it's a private pistol. I purchased it myself, before leaving London. Many of your officers have such weapons."

"You are only an NCO."

Despite himself, the colonel was fascinated by the new weapon.

"I see it has two triggers."

Crossman explained, "The one under the guard is to cock the pistol, the other is to fire it."

"Is it efficient?"

"Very."

The colonel recovered his former mood of disapproval. "And you will use this in your ambush? I find I still cannot support these methods, sergeant. You are nothing less than an assassin. It is the kind of warfare employed by brigands and bandits. By men with no principles or integrity. My father would be ashamed, if he were still alive . . ."

"Sir, with all due respect, your father never experienced the hell of trench warfare."

Crossman found a way into the Russian lines further to the north, where troops were thinner on the ground. He was dressed as a sergeant in the Ukrainski Jagers in one of the thankfully warm greatcoats and little round hats worn by that regiment. Major Lovelace, who relied on the intelligence reports he received from a small network of Bulgarian and Greek informers within Sebastopol, had told Crossman that this was the regiment encamped around the church behind the Hawk. If he was stopped on the way Crossman could produce a message, forged by one of the Russian prisoners held by the British, from his greatcoat pocket. It was addressed to a colonel in the Ukrainski Jagers.

Jack Crossman hoped he would not have to pass inspection in such a manner. The idea was to slip past the church and make his way to the sangar from the rear. If he were seen at that point, and challenged, the idea was to grunt a reply that he was taking soup to the sharpshooter.

Crossman carried a Russian smoothbore musket, with its thin brittle stock, but he did not intend to use this on the Hawk. In his greatcoat pocket was the Tranter. This additional piece of ordnance had saved his life a number of times, especially when faced by Cossacks out in the hills. The Cossacks had now placed a price on his head. They were desperate to find and execute the rogue sergeant who had ambushed and killed so many of their kind.

He also carried a German hunting knife, strapped to the calf of his right leg, for emergencies.

Crossman had been in and out of Sebastopol several times since the war had started. Once, he had been caught and tortured, only to be rescued by Wynter and Yusuf Ali as he was about to be hanged. On another occasion he had rescued his older brother, James, a lieutenant in the 93rd Sutherland Highlanders, who was serving with their father, a major in the same regiment. James was not aware that he had been saved by his younger brother, who had enlisted under an assumed name.

On these previous excursions Crossman had studied the landscape and now used known gullies and rises to travel south to the church. The Russians had known what they were doing, choosing a church for their barracks. Allied gunners were reluctant to shell such buildings, being Christians themselves.

Crossman was challenged and cursorily inspected twice by picquets as he passed through enemy border territory. He replied in his best Russian, learned from Yusuf Ali over the months, that he was a messenger. His awkwardness with the language did not go undetected, but did not arouse suspicion. There were many Poles, Hungarians, Czechs and other nationalities in the Russian Army. The man who had engineered the Sebastopol siege defences, Colonel Todleben, was a German by birth.

On reaching the church Crossman found it was lit within. He could hear the voices of the soldiers. Most of the men were inside, it being a freezing night, though there were one or two sentries in the graveyard, looking bored, wandering listlessly amongst the tombstones. Crossman silently skirted the cemetery. Out there in the darkness before him was the sangar. He could not see it from the church but he knew it to be about four or five hundred yards to his front. He hoped the Hawk would be there. If he was not Crossman intended to find some cover and wait for him.

He checked his Tranter. The hand-gun had been carefully loaded before setting out on the mission. Crossman felt its comfortable weight in his hand. He then stood for a moment and examined his own motives for this fox hunt. Surely they were entirely valid? In the sangar was a man who was to all intents and purposes an assassin himself. The Hawk could kill men at a distance with great skill and ease from an unassailable position. Crossman's skill, he told himself, was in his ability to penetrate enemy lines and go in close for the kill. Why should his talent be regarded as any less worthy than that of a sharpshooter's?

There were not many who could kill, hands on the victim, in cold blood. It was easier at a great distance. You did not have to witness the result of your work. You were not able to touch and feel the warmth, the life-blood, draining from your victim. You did not have to witness the hurt look in his eyes as he stared at you from just this side of death, blaming you for the fatherless family, the husbandless wife he had to leave behind him. You did not have to carry with you, for the rest of your life, the picture of a youth whose bloom you had savagely wrenched from him, lying sightless and soundless in the mud, a cry for his mother caught on his dead lips. It was surely harder, and therefore more honourable, to be an assassin who grappled with his victims close to, than a sharpshooter?

Crossman began the journey over that stretch of ground in a shallow arc, hoping to approach the Hawk from the north-west.

When he was halfway there he suddenly found himself in a group of about fifty or sixty men. They were lying in scattered groups in a shallow depression and he almost blundered over a prone body. Crossman dropped to the ground immediately, just as one or two of the soldiers nearest to him turned to peer at him with puzzled expressions. A Russian voice in the centre of the group whispered, "Who's making that noise? What are you, an elephant?" Crossman did not answer. His heart was beating fast. He realized almost at once that he was in the middle of a raiding party: one of those that went out at night and attacked allied soldiers in their trenches, just as Goodlake's sharpshooters sallied forth from the British side to strike fear and dread into the hearts of the Russians.

The Russians remained in the depression for an age. Crossman knew what they were waiting for: the first rays of dawn. Dawn is a time when men can see to kill, but it is also a time when things take on an unreal quality, when shadows drift into being amongst the boulders and rocks, and those watching and waiting begin to see things that are not there. Daybreak is a much trickier time than night, when nothing can be seen but blackness. Daybreak is a grey half-world, covered with the fleeting shreds of ghosts, that dart here and there, confusing the brains of watchers. At dawn the advantage is with the attacker, for the defender has spent time peering into the greyness, starting at every imagined movement, and he is jumpy, nervous and unsure of himself and his position.

Suddenly an order hissed from the lips of the officer.

"Forward!"

The shapes rose around Crossman and he found he had to get

to his feet and move along with the group. To have tried to break and run would have been madness. He was caught in the meshes of the raiding party and for the moment had to go along with them. Crossman kept an eye open for side gullies. He hoped he could slip away before the party reached their target trench. With this in mind he edged his way towards the periphery of the group. At the very worst he could feign injury – a sprained ankle in the darkness – and would hopefully be left behind. At this moment, however, he was in a mild panic, his best laid schemes having gone wildly astray.

There was a shout of "Who's there?" in English, followed very shortly afterwards by a shot which came perilously close to Crossman's ear. He was in danger of being killed by his own picquets! The Russians around him opened fire now, blasting away at a picquet post to the east. Burnt powder odours filled the night air. There were flashes from barrels, illuminating scared faces in the half-light for brief instants.

"Forward!" cried the officer. "Use the bayonet!"

The two British picquets were overwhelmed as they reloaded. Crossman had to watch, horrified as they were bayoneted to death by eager and frightened Russian infantry. The party went on, Crossman swept along with it, towards a trench which was now spitting fire and lead. There were angry shouts flying in the void between the combatants. The dawn air was full of invisible insects, humming around Crossman's head. To Crossman's left there was a noise like "*thwuck*" and a Russian soldier went down on his knees, instantly, as if he were about to pray. Crossman saw that the man had been hit full in the face and half the back of his skull was missing. A Minié bullet the size of a man's thumb makes a horrible mess of a human head.

The mortally wounded man fell forward with a gargled sigh.

For one brief confused moment Crossman was angry with the enemy. This man beside him was a comrade. He had been killed by those bastards in the trenches. Crossman almost fired his musket at the British. Then he remembered who he was, why he was there, and what he was there to do. While the small battle raged on around him, Crossman crept away, first to the edge, then to the rear of the yelling, firing Russian soldiers, who were only intent on reloading and discharging their weapons at those in the trench. He stumbled over the rough ground, back towards Sebastopol, until he was once more in line with the church to the south. When he reached it a grey light was stretching beyond its red roof and around the elaborate wrought iron cross which adorned is ridge. There were similar crosses to the one on the roof scattered about the graveyard behind him. Crossman wondered if he would remain in the Crimea with the owners of those crosses. It seemed likely in the circumstances.

Throwing away his Russian musket he painstakingly retraced his arc. The dawn rays glittered on the frozen ground and began chasing off the swirling mists. The harsh winds had blown away much of the snow from the heights, but there were scatterings of white in the folds of the hills and in the gulleys. Ice flashed from creases in the rocks. It was going to be a bright day and he was going to have to face his antagonist in its early light.

From a distance he could see the concave wall of the sangar, with a man crouched behind it. When Crossman's boots crunched on a thin sheet of ice the figure turned and stared. Crossman saw a white round face with very pale blue intense eyes set in its features. There was a wispy moustache below a thin aquiline nose. The Hawk! He studied Crossman for a few seconds, then turned his back again. What the Hawk had seen was a Russian sergeant approaching his position from Russian lines.

The sharpshooter's mittens were off, dangling from strings on his wrists. Crossman realized the Hawk had been about to shoot someone when he heard the sounds behind him. He was now back at his task, sighting along the barrel of the Minié. A man in the trenches was about to be flung into the void beyond life and the living.

Crossman took out his Tranter and cocked it. Approaching his victim he aimed at the middle of the man's back, to break his spine if possible, or if not hopefully to hit some vital organ. The idea was to pump four shots into his victim, saving one for any emergencies.

Just as Crossman's finger was squeezing the firing trigger, the Hawk relaxed his aim, put down his rifle and slipped his hands into his fur mittens. The Hawk's target had obviously gone. He would await another opportunity, once his hands had warmed again.

Crossman stared at the curved, broad back before him. His hand and the revolver in it started shaking. He tried to squeeze the trigger but found he could not bring himself to do it. After all his talk about the necessity of expediency in modern warfare, he found himself unable to shoot a man in the back. The society, the culture, which had made the regimental colonel had also made Crossman. It was all right to spout the theories which had been instilled in him by Major Lovelace: putting them into practice was another thing altogether. The vestiges of the chivalric code, still dear to many of the hearts of civilized gentlemen of most nations, rose to choke the Machiavellian ideals of the end justifying the means. A man of honour does not shoot another man in the back, without giving him at least a chance. To do so would be the dastardly act of a coward, and a gentleman would be ostracized by all who knew him.

Private Wynter could have done it, but not Sergeant Crossman.

At that moment the Hawk turned and saw the pistol pointed at him. He stared into Crossman's eyes in disbelief. Then, seeing something alien there, he leaped forward, flinging himself at the Scot. During his leap the Hawk divested his hands of his mittens. Crossman was knocked off his feet, his revolver went spinning from his grasp. The two men then began a desperate struggle in the ice and snow. The Hawk attempted to get his thumbs into Crossman's eyes to gouge them out. Crossman had one hand on his assailant's throat and the other reached down to his calf for his German hunting knife.

Crossman's head went back and forth, wildly, to avoid the thumbs. Thwarted in this idea the Hawk then began to pummel Crossman's face with his fists, at the same time he tried yelling for assistance from those in the church. Crossman's grip on his throat strangled the cry. The Ranger sergeant's right hand at last found the knife and he drew it. He began stabbing the Russian in the breast, but the man's clothing – his thick greatcoat and uniform underneath – resisted the heavy blade. The point penetrated but not to any great depth. After about half-a-dozen rents and tears had been executed on the Hawk's chest, with no visible success, Crossman seized a chance to attack the man's head. The knife stabbed at the sharpshooter's cheeks, finding more depth here.

On being wounded the Hawk struggled free and jumped up. He ran back to retrieve his rifle. By the time Crossman had got up from the ground, the Hawk was pointing the weapon at his body. There was a look of triumph in the Russian's eyes. A small curious smile played about his mouth. Crossman felt he was savouring his victory over his unknown adversary.

"Now you will die," came the Russian words. "Whoever you are, sergeant."

A single shot cracked across the dawn.

Crossman was astonished to see the Hawk's face explode. The man's arm's went limp and his weapon sagged. He staggered forward two or three paces then fell flat on his front. There was a hole in his head, just behind his left ear. He was as dead as a stone.

Retrieving his pistol, Crossman ducked down behind the sangar.

No Russian troops had left the church area. All they had heard until now was a single shot. They were used to such a sound coming from the direction of the sangar. No doubt they were chuckling amongst themselves, telling each other, "Another notch on the Hawk's rifle stock! When will those redcoats learn to keep their heads down?"

Extremely relieved and grateful to be alive Crossman shouted to the troops in the trenches below.

"British soldier! Don't shoot! Coming down!"

Tearing off his Russian greatcoat to reveal his 88th Connaught Ranger's uniform beneath, he stepped out and began a slow walk down the slope towards the trenches. A shot sang out, the ball passing by him at waist level. He stopped and shouted angrily, "Sergeant Crossman. British soldier! Are you blind, man?" The regiment had been warned to expect him. They should know he was coming. After a short wait he continued down the slope again. There were no more nervous fingers.

When he reached the trenches the colonel was there, waiting for him.

"Did you get him, sergeant?"

Crossman found his hands were shaking. He put them in his pockets to hide the fact. For a moment he just stood there, unable to speak. He was in mild shock, at having escaped death, of having had to assist in the delivery of death at close quarters. Those looking at him could see by his pale expression that he was not completely himself, not fully sensible. Then, with great effort, he managed to pull himself together. His voice sounded a little croaky, but the words came out clearly and firmly.

"The Hawk is no more," he told the colonel. "In trying to avoid being killed by my hand, he was shot dead by another."

A ragged but hearty cheer went up along the British line and the word began to go out immediately. The Hawk was dead. That was all they wanted to know. Revenge *was* sweet indeed. What did it matter how the fiend had come by his death, or whether Crossman's action was honourable or not? Men would be able to move around without fear of becoming just another victim of a crack shot. Jack Crossman's plan had worked, where all others had failed. Perhaps later, in hindsight, there would be accusers, critics, historians and researchers who condemned the act, but in the immediate now there was nothing but celebration.

Crossman looked along the trench and saw a grim-faced lance-corporal, a crackshot from his own small *peleton* of spies and saboteurs, leaning on her beloved Minié rifle.

"All I wanted was one small chance at him," said the soldier, "and you gave it to me, sergeant."

"Thank you, Peterson," said Crossman. "I am in your debt."

THE FALLEN PLUME

Tom Holt

*The following story is our first, but not our last, encounter
with the Zulus. It is set during the Zulu civil war of 1856
and is related by the historical figure of John Dunn, who is
one of those unbelievable and slightly eccentric Victorian
colonials that only the British could breed. He was a minor
bureaucrat working for the Natal agency who managed to
end up as a Zulu chieftain! He was also part of the
inspiration for Rider Haggard's famous character Allan
Quatermain in* King Solomon's Mines *(1885), and its
many sequels. Tom Holt (b. 1961) is probably best known
for his humorous fantasy novels such as* Who's Afraid of
Beowulf? *(1988),* Paint Your Dragon *(1996) and* Snow
White and the Seven Samurai *(1999), but he has also
published several serious historical novels including* Goat-
song *(1989),* The Walled Orchard *(1990),* Alexander at
the World's End *(1999) and* Olympiad *(2000).*

Sixty years ago, in the November of 1856, I crossed the Tugela
River in Zululand. In theory, I had been sent by the Natal
border agent to negotiate on his behalf with Prince Cetewayo,
whom my principal's office recognized as the rightful heir to the
Zulu kingdom, with a view to averting the civil war between the
sons of King Panda that seemed to grow more inevitable with
each new development. In practice, I went to offer my services
as adviser, tactician and warrior to Cetewayo's deadly rival,
Prince Umbiyazi. I was young, and English, and a born fool.
Two of these defects of character I have since remedied; the
third, I fear, I shall never be rid of.

As was only fitting for a knight errant, I took with me my
squires and men-at-arms; more precisely, four dozen Dwandwe
hunters who were (for reasons I could never understand) as
fiercely loyal to myself as they were inimical to the Zulu royal
house. The Dwandwe – ah, but if I begin to explain why
Dwandwe exiles hated the Zulu royal house, I should be
tempted to trace the quarrel back to Chaka and Zwide and
Dingiswayo, and my story would be crushed to death under a
great press of names and tribes and histories, all of them far
more significant and fascinating than the adventures of one fool
Englishman, and I would put aside my pen and sit looking
through my window at the stars. It is enough to say that my
loyal companions were accustomed to the handling of firearms,
and that I had provided each of them with an elderly but
serviceable Tower musket (my princely liberality being somewhat constrained by my resources, and these same muskets
being suddenly available at an affordable price owing to a
canceled order at Delagoa Bay), reserving for myself my double-barrelled *roer* and a pair of Adams' revolvers. Thus accompanied and outfitted, I rode my horse into the briskly-flowing
river, in spate at the change of the seasons, confident that it was
in my hands to manage the course of history, and that I was
competent to do so.

Prince Umbiyazi, with whom I was already slightly acquainted, received me and my band of brigands with polite
amusement. At the time, I recall, his attitude annoyed me

rather, since it was clear that he could do with all the help he could get. To be ruthlessly fair, his cause was neither popular nor just, being founded on the favour of King Panda, which hardly counted for anything at that time, and the fact that his mother had been one of the concubines of Panda's brother and most glorious predecessor Chaka, the founder of the Zulu kingdom, the Great Elephant, the "axe that cuts and keeps cutting", and so on and so forth. The connection, tenuous and dubious enough to a European observer, had been enough to ensure Umbiyazi a slow but steady movement of support from those of his father's subjects who resented Panda's long keeping of the peace and hungered after a return to the old ways of expansion and conquest; whence they had derived the name of their party, the Quosa, or "trickle". Cetewayo was, by contrast, the son of Panda's principal wife, an important distinction considering that Panda had twenty-nine sons and twenty-three daughters, and had already served his nation with distinction both on the battlefield and in more mundane capacities as effectual regent for his capable but discredited father. There was, in short, no real reason why anyone should support Umbiyazi except sentiment; certainly, that was what had prompted me to lend him my unsolicited and unsuspected aid.

Accustomed as I was to the modest but entirely practical accommodations of a Zulu kraal, which resembles nothing so much as a parcel of hayricks surrounded by a thatch curtain (a homely enough sight, and misleadingly familiar to an Englishman's eye) I found the camp an unsettling place. There was none of the meticulous order that marks the permanent settlements of the Zulu. I suppose this was only to be expected in a camp of war; and yet I could not help but wonder at it. To me it seemed as if the prince and his followers had no faith in their own cause, and therefore had not taken the trouble to do anything properly – a disturbing reflection for one who had just turned his back on his career, indeed on all his own kind, on a whim to join that same cause. I had expected to see the regiments drawn up in sharply-dressed ranks practising spear-and-shield drill, or diligently mending their gear, proudly oiling the gummed ring worn in the hair as a mark of a married man or grooming their head-dresses of ostrich feather and otter-skin in quiet readiness for the struggle that lay before them. Instead, the camp seemed all but deserted, with only a few men hurrying by on unknown errands as if they had too much to do and too little time to do it in. It was hardly an encouraging sight.

As a singular mark of honour, a stool was brought for me and the prince indicated with a grave nod of his head that I should sit before him. The prince himself sat on a three-legged stool that had belonged to his uncle, King Dingane, and before him to Chaka himself. I heard later that he had had it stolen from his father's house shortly before Panda sent him across the Tugela in the vain hope that separating the princes might keep them from each other's throats.

"We have seen you," he said (such is the fine if rather confusing style of courtly greeting among the Zulus, the equivalent of our *good morning* or *good day*). "You are John Dunn, the adjutant of the English governor in the north. May I ask what business you have here?"

I confess that at that moment I felt distinctly foolish. It was plain enough that Umbiyazi was extremely busy with pressing matters of strategy and administration; as well as the leadership of some six or seven thousand fighting men. His camp sheltered perhaps as many as twelve thousand Quosa civilians, together with their cattle and possessions, all of them in a highly nervous and excitable state. It was, I feel, typical of both the best and the worst facets of the Prince's character that he consented to see me at all under such circumstances.

Nevertheless, I had made my decision and could not unmake it without severe damage to my self-esteem. Accordingly I put on my most soldierly expression and told the prince that I had come to plant my spear beside his for the coming battle.

Umbiyazi smiled indulgently as he tipped snuff onto his thumb. "That you pledge me your spear is most gratifying," he said. "However, I have enough spears already. Now, if you were to bring me two thousand of your excellent guns, the kind that strike from a long way off by spinning the bullet round and round like a child's top, I would be even more delighted to welcome you. As it is, I must warn you that if it does come to blows between my brother and myself – which Heaven forbid – I fear that I shall be hard put to it to guarantee the safety of yourself and your men; and I should not want your master in Natal to notice his servant's absence and find him among the dead. His wrath would be a great matter for our people, regardless of whether my brother or I prevail."

This was not the reception I had anticipated; and, had I been wise, I would have taken it as a mortal insult and gone home again (as, I feel sure, Umbiyazi in his humanity intended me to do). It has been my experience, however, that the more a young fool is guided away from his folly, the harder he will struggle to pursue it. I told myself that the prince was misguided, not deliberately trying to offend me, and set about the task of convincing him of my worth.

"You may recall," I said, "that when you sent to my master in Natal for help, asking for men and guns or, alternatively, a safe place to go to, in the event that your brother drove you out of Zululand, he replied that it was not the practice of Her Majesty's colonial officers to involve themselves in the internal affairs of their neighbours. It was I myself, in fact, who gave that reply to your envoys, much though it pained me to do so." I paused for a moment, to let him savour the mild insults implicit in what I had said. It did not occur to me, needless to say, that it was hardly my place to insult the man I had come to serve. Fortunately, Umbiyazi had a good sense of humour, and seemed to enjoy the absurdity. "For my part," I continued, "I feel that my master is being short-sighted, and that a man who turns away his brother when he is hungry should not expect any better treatment when his own bowl is empty."

"I hear you," the prince said slowly. "Obviously your people understand service to their masters otherwise than we do, since we hold that the first duty of a servant is to obey orders, not to decide for themselves whether or not their master's decision was wise or foolish." He sighed then, and for a moment I could see in his face a shadow of the pain he was feeling. "However," he went on, "as you say, my bowl is empty, and since you have been gracious enough to put something in it, I thank you and accept what you have to offer. I have heard," he went on, looking over my shoulder, "that your people have studied the art of war for generations, taking great care to consider the mistakes of those who failed, thus making sure that they are never repeated. I am told that there are places where the best of your young men go to be taught nothing but how to plan battles and deploy regiments, and how to devise snares and tricks whereby the smaller army may overcome the greater and the weak and cowardly may defeat the strong and brave. If you have any of this learning, I would be glad if you would share it with me. We are very young in the art of war, and we go about the business in a very straightforward way. My brother has three times as many men at his disposal as I do, and I fear that if there is to be a battle, it will be over very quickly."

I should point out that my knowledge of the theory of warfare was extremely limited. I had parsed my way, painfully and without any great accuracy, through Caesar's Gallic Wars when I was a boy, and had read a book or two about the great and glorious wars of long ago. I had a vague recollection of the battle-lines of the Punic Wars, though I tended to muddle them so thoroughly in my head that I could never be sure if I was blending together the first part of Lake Trasimene with the latter part of Lake Trebbia, or that the side whose tactics I could best remember had won or lost. However, having been asked for my superior wisdom, I could hardly confess my ignorance. "I shall be delighted," I assured the prince, "to advise you on any matters about which you see fit to consult me."

He nodded, hardly overwhelmed by the splendour of my offer, but taking it seriously nevertheless. For my part, I was already regretting the haste with which I had allowed my apparent faith in my own abilities to outstrip my better judgment.

Ah, judgment! How elusive it is, and how easily we deceive ourselves into seeing it where it is palpably absent. The more we hunt it, the faster it runs away, and when it stands still and quiet we fail to notice it and pass it by. To make matters worse, judgment and opinion have ever been enemies, and the civil war they wage inside us lays waste all our noblest endeavours. It has been my misfortune throughout my life ever to side with opinion against judgment, either through whim or misguided reason. Many times I have committed all my resources to opinion, crossing disputed borders between wisdom and folly, between one loyalty and another; for some reason always; seeming to be drawn to the weaker side, as if there were some intrinsic merit in the lesser prevailing against the greater. Opinion, in fact, has ridden me in everything I have ever laid my hand to, misinforming my choices at every stage of my life and making me an instrument of havoc among my dearest friends. Most surprisingly, however, I have prospered and flourished, living out my wildest dreams, becoming at every turn the thing I imagined myself to be. I have been an *induna*, a king's counsellor – the only white man ever accorded that dignity by a Zulu king – and a great chief in my own right. I have been a mighty warrior, fighting single combats like Homer's heroes in front of the battle. I have disobeyed my masters and been rewarded for each betrayal with further and greater prosperity. And that is something I have never been able to understand.

Prince Umbiyazi moved his people into the valley between the Tambo and Nyoni Rivers, as Cetewayo and his faction, the Usutu, moved down the Mandeni valley from the north. Realizing that he would be unwise to retreat any further, Umbiyazi prepared to meet his brother on a ridge near the kraal Ndondakusuka, which had formerly belonged to a great *induna* of King Dingane. His position was perilous in the extreme. Should he fail to hold the ridge, there would be nothing to prevent Cetewayo from sweeping down into the valley and falling upon the defenceless Quosa civilians, as he was honour-bound to do. In short, the prince had so arranged matters that his defeat would ensure the annihilation of all those who had put their trust in him. To say that he chose to act in this manner would be to overstate the case. In the event, he had no more choice in the matter than driftwood on the sea. Nevertheless, the stoicism with which he and his followers accepted the position came close to infuriating me.

It was the prince's intention to sit still and wait for Cetewayo to come to him. I made it my business to advise him otherwise. Demanding an audience (which was granted in the same spirit of tolerant good humour as my first interview with him) I berated the prince at great length for his apparent lack of concern. Either he should take the initiative and attack while his brother's army was still making its preparations for battle, thereby at least adding an element of surprise; or he should try to find some way of ensuring the safety of his unarmed dependants in the event of defeat. As I spoke, the prince looked at me as if such possibilities for seizing control of his own destiny had not previously occurred to him; he admitted that both ideas had great merit, and then proceeded to waste what little time remained in debating with myself and his *indunas* as to which course of action he should pursue. By the time these deliberations had been resolved in favour of a surprise attack, the time for such an escapade had long since passed; it was almost nightfall, and there was nothing to be done except wait for the sun to rise.

The morning of 1 December 1856 was cold and uncomfortable, with mist, and light nagging rain lingering over the green hills. Our enemies made the first move, leaving their camp and advancing towards us in the now traditional formation of the bull's head, a manoeuvre that had been the standard practice of the Zulu nation since it was first introduced and developed by Chaka himself. In doing so, they had taken control of the battle before the first blow was struck, since all Umbiyazi could think of doing was to arrange his own forces in as close an imitation of his brother's as the terrain would permit.

The bull's head was a simple yet unquestionably effective way of deploying a Zulu army. Essentially, the available forces were divided into four parts. On each side, the regiments of younger men were placed to form the bull's horns, while the veteran regiments held the centre. The reserve, or bull's neck, stayed some way back from the centre, so that a sudden panic in those regiments would not communicate itself to those behind; the space between, in effect, forming a firebrake. The idea was for the horns to advance and envelop the enemy in the flanks, whereupon the centre would charge home to settle the matter. Should the battle on the edges go awry, the proven men in the centre were those best equipped to stand and resist with the greatest judgement and fortitude, just as the youth and impetuous valour of the junior regiments made them ideal for the more fluid stages of the conflict.

At my own request, my small force took its position on the left horn. As we were the only contingent of any size on either side who were equipped with firearms, I had hopes that the shocking effect we might have on Cetewayo's most volatile and inexperienced troops might in the event prove significant; if we could halt the onrush of his horn and throw it into disarray, Umbiyazi might possibly be able to execute the necessary encirclement himself and so win the day. In all honesty, as I told the prince, I could see no other way in which we might hope to prevail, given the enemy's greatly superior numbers. The prince replied that my suggestion seemed eminently sensible to him, and that since he had no firm plans of his own, he was content to try mine.

From our position we had a clear view of Cetewayo and his leading men as they stood up to perform the various rituals that inevitably precede any battle in Zululand. I confess that I have always found these affairs unconscionably dull, almost as tiresome as a pompous evensong in an English cathedral town, and I was moved by my impatience to suggest to the prince that if we were to attack suddenly while the attention of the Usutu was thus engaged, we might stand a chance of cutting off Cetewayo in front of his army and thereby securing a swift victory. (I had already made up my mind that Cetewayo's death was the only eventuality that could save us, since driving his army from the

field was clearly beyond our capabilities). Umbiyazi replied that
my plan was both daring and entirely feasible, and that "had
circumstances been otherwise" (I still have no idea what he
meant by that) he would have adopted it without hesitation.
Then he went back to leaning his chin on the edge of his shield
and watching his brother.

Prince Cetewayo had chosen to array himself in the uniform
of his favourite regiment, the Tulwana. He had bound up his
brows with a strap of otter-skin, crested with a single crane
feather, and he carried a dark shield with a single white spot on
the lower half. He had obtained, by theft, treachery or seren-
dipity, a Quosa shield, which he proceeded to throw down in
full view of both armies and, with the utmost solemnity, kneel
on – for all the world like a pious English gentleman kneeling in
church – thereby signifying to all the world that the Quosa were
thrown down and dispatched before the battle had even begun.
I was moved to laughter by the sight of this foolishness, but the
mirth died in my throat as I noticed that every man I could see
in the Quosa ranks was watching, silent and expressionless. At
that moment, a gust of wind dragged the tall-brave ostrich
plume from Umbiyazi's head-dress and dropped it at his feet –
the worst possible omen, as I was later informed, that anybody
could imagine. The prince's demeanour did not change at all.
He merely stooped gracefully, picked the plume up and tucked
it back in place.

Given Umbiyazi's curiously fatalistic attitude, it was inevitable,
I suppose, that Cetewayo should have opened the battle, sending forward his right horn to encompass our left. Unusually,
however, there was a degree of guile to their proceedings, for
they followed the line of the Mandeni River into the shelter of
the Nkwaku valley, where we could no longer see them. Umbiyazi promptly dismissed them from his thoughts; I, however,
realized what was happening and (in default of any orders from
the prince) made haste to marshal my small army and lead them
as quickly as I could to the banks of the tenuous Nkwaku stream
to contest the crossing.

It was, of course, the very first time I had ever taken part in anything even remotely resembling military action; my nearest comparable experience, I suppose, was flushing game from reed-beds, marshalling my line of beaters and taking my stand to shoot the quarry as it emerged from its cover. Certainly the fierce apprehension I had to endure as I waited was common to both occasions, and I believe the same analogy had occurred to one or two of my Dwandwe cohorts, for I overheard one ferocious old man, whose name now eludes me, muttering to his neighbour that on this occasion at least they didn't have to go and fetch out the lions, since they were headed towards us of their own accord.

I occupied my time with practical matters, checking that both my powder flasks were full and handy, and that both ball and caps were easily accessible for speed of loading. I have since followed the same ritual in every subsequent encounter, and have always found it soothing to my nerves. For their part, my Dwandwes followed their somewhat alarming custom of singing their own funeral dirge, on the grounds that in the event of our being defeated, there would be nobody else to perform this necessary function for them. The logic of this was faultless, but I found the mournful nature of their singing to be depressing in the extreme.

When the Usutu came into view, I was momentarily shocked into inactivity by the size of the forces opposing me and the corresponding magnitude of my own plight. Any Zulu army in deployment is a majestic, terrifying sight; imagine you are standing on a beach watching a great dark wave swelling in towards you, the white flecks of foam at the crest being the plumes, necklaces and wrist ornaments of the soldiers and the flashing white blades of their spears. Now imagine that, at the moment when the mass resolves into individual shapes, and for the first time you are able to identify single bodies and faces in the press, a great drawling cry goes up from the front rank – *Usutu! Us-u-tu!* – and all other sounds are drowned out by the unique and terrifying noise of spear-handles drumming against the stretched hides of the shields. I have been in our English factories and heard a somewhat similar noise – or rather felt it, for it is the rhythm rather than the sound that makes the most impression. On the occasion of my first such visit, I confess that I behaved in a most deplorable fashion, imagining that the Usutu were upon me once again and scampering from the building in great distress, (much to the disgust of my hosts, who were anxious to persuade me to invest money in the business).

When the enemy were two hundred yards distant from us, I ordered my men to cap and cock their muskets – a futile exercise on my part, since they had all done so long before – and to hold their fire, for God's sake, until such time as the foe were close enough to take the greatest possible harm from our first volley while still affording us enough time to reload. Silently, my men began to cram musket-balls into their mouths – a most convenient way of having them in readiness, I might add, with the additional advantage that the moisture of the mouth lubricates the ball for ease of ramming home. Deciding to copy this excellent invention of theirs, I took a handful of pistol balls from the magazine at my belt and pressed them greedily between my lips in the manner of a small boy gobbling sweets. Once they were tucked securely between gum and cheek I forgot all about them until after the battle was over, at which point I spat them out in disgust. How I managed to avoid swallowing at least one of them, I cannot for the life of me imagine.

At a hundred yards' range, I gave the order to fire. There is something merciful about the first volley of a battle. The cloud of smoke erupting from the muzzles completely obscures the enemy from one's view, so that for one blessed instant it is possible to believe that they have literally vanished in a puff of smoke and the danger has passed. While the haze was still thick, we laboured mightily at our loading, holding the piece steady with the left hand while throwing the powder charge with the right, fumbling a ball into the muzzle and ramming it home (a task that becomes steadily harder as the barrel fouls with the residues of combustion) and finally pinching a single cap from one's pocket to prime the nipple and complete the operation. As I mentioned earlier I was armed with my favourite double-barrelled elephant gun, and it was only as I rammed home the ball to replenish the fired barrel that I noticed the muzzle of the unfired tube (capped and cocked, needless to say) pointing squarely at my own forehead.

As the smoke dissipated enough to afford us a view of the enemy, I expected to see the Usutu already clambering up onto our bank of the river, their spears poised to strike. Instead, the front rank were standing in the water, confused and aimless, as their comrades in arms poured in beside them, choking the stream with human bodies. Some years later the leader of this detachment, Prince Dabulamanzi (who was to become the closest friend I ever had, even though I tried my very best to kill him at the battle of Kambula) told me that it was not so much the effect of our weapons that astonished them – we had managed to kill no more than a dozen of them – but the fact that we had suddenly vanished from sight behind a dense, foul-smelling white cloud. Some of the more excitable Usutu called out that we were *tagati* (bewitched) whereupon the advance immediately came to a dead stop. This is a curious facet of the Zulu character: utterly unconcerned by the prospect of death at the hands of a physical enemy, the mere thought of a super-natural foe unmans them completely. (I have seen mighty warriors scarred from head to foot with battle-wounds literally die of fright because of some calf's blood smeared by a witch on the gateposts of his house).

At the time, all I knew was that Providence had seen fit to bless me with a wholly unexpected opportunity. I ordered my men to fire by their ranks (so that half our number would be loaded at any one time, and also to reduce the density of the smokecloud, lest the enemy come upon us unseen) and proceeded to discharge my *roer* and one of my pistols in the general direction of the enemy. I took no aim to speak of; the Usutu were packed so closely together by now that it would have taken the ingenuity of an Archimedes to pass a ball through the press without striking something.

My wise choice of fire by ranks was very nearly my undoing, though at the time I was blessedly unaware of the reason. Because the smoke-cloud was thinner we were no longer vanishing completely after each volley and were remaining hidden from sight for a shorter time, which suggested to the enemy that our powers were waning and that we might after all prove vulnerable to mortal steel. Accordingly the front ranks rose up from the water with a terrible cry and rushed towards us. My front rank was loaded, and let fly at no more than ten yards' range, while I had discharged all five chambers of my one functioning revolver (to my unutterable disgust, the other had chosen the first shot of the battle to fail in the mainspring) before my men had finished their volley. Standing defenceless behind the obscuring curtain of smoke, firmly believing that the enemy were close enough that if I were to reach into the smoke with my hand, I should surely encounter one of them, I could think of nothing else to do but try to remove the loaded cylinder from the useless revolver and place it in the one that still worked; a singularly foolish notion, since it involved the slacking off of two screws and the withdrawal of two pins. By the time I had broken both thumbnails in a ridiculous attempt to turn the screws I was too dejected to care much what became of me. I put away both pistols in their holsters, tucked my gun under my arm and waited to see what would become of me.

The smoke melted away to reveal a quite extraordinary sight; the river clogged with bodies and the Usutu in headlong retreat. Later, Dabulamanzi told me that nothing, no promise of reward or threat of reprisal, would induce his men to stand against what they regarded as the most horrendous show of witchcraft. He explained that they were all too young to have taken part in Dingane's campaigns against the Boers and therefore had never experienced firearms discharged *en masse* before. I have always found it curiously fitting that it was smoke and superstition, not the horrifying casualties we inflicted, that put the gallant Usutu to flight.

This development in the fortunes of the battle, following precisely the pattern I had imagined as the best possible outcome we could hope for, was not lost on Prince Cetewayo. He knew that the sight of his right horn falling back in wretched disarray without having come within arm's length of the sorcerous enemy, could easily infect his entire army with panic and provide an opportunity that even his languorous brother would be hard put to ignore. Accordingly he ordered his left horn to attack with more than the usual degree of speed and vigour.

Once, when I asked a Zulu acquaintance why his people fitted such short handles to their spears, he smiled at me and replied that it was because his people preferred to fight close to the enemy. It was King Chaka who taught the Zulu how to close with the spear, dashing the face of one's shield against that of one's opponent and sliding it across and down until the back edge slipped behind his, before wrenching it hard to the rear, thereby exposing his left armpit to the broad blade of one's spear. The sound made as the spear goes home is quite distinctive, a sort of slick crunch, followed by a sucking hiss as the blade is pulled free. Then the victorious soldier yells *Ngadla!* ("I have eaten") as he strides forward to confront his next opponent in the same way. It is an honest way to fight, if there can be such a thing; the outcome is decided purely by speed, strength, confidence and skill, which are the virtues that most clearly epitomize the Zulu as a nation. Zulus do not fence or parry, duck or sidestep; the matter is over in a short, decisive moment, and the weaker man or the man who gives way to indecisiveness duly perishes. Lately I have read with interest a book by the notorious Mr Darwin, in which he asserts that the triumph of the stronger over the weaker and the better over the worse is the very essence of things, and has shaped the development of every living creature. The Zulus would agree with him – I, of course, do not, since at every stage my life has refuted his conclusions utterly – and they would add that not only is it inevitable that the strongest and fittest should prevail, but also that it is unquestionably right.

As the left horn of the Usutu rolled up Umbiyazi's right, so Cetewayo sent forward the solid chest of his army up the Mandeni ridge. Umbiyazi did not care to abide their coming.

At first he was able to withdraw his men in good order, but as they followed the course of the Tambo down into the valley they stumbled across a large contingent of their own civilians, so cunningly hidden that they failed to notice them until they were almost standing on top of them. So unnerved were they by this that they lost all order, becoming hopelessly tangled among their own women, children and cattle; whereupon the Usutu, clearing the crest of the ridge and charging down upon them, caught them squarely in flank and rear and swept them into the little river, where they cut them to pieces. Those that survived were herded into the reed beds on the banks of the Tugela, whence they were flushed out like game by the Usutu and slaughtered, those not perishing by the spear either drowning in the swollen fury of the river or feeding the crocodiles that have always plagued that spot. I have heard that of the twenty thousand Quosa, soldiers and civilians together, twelve thousand died there in a short time, so that for years afterwards the Tambo ran slowly, being clogged with the remains of the dead – a most curious coincidence, since the word *tambo* means "bones".

Where and how Umbiyazi died I have never been able to discover. It is even possible that he escaped, since his body was never certainly identified. At the time, I was not unduly concerned with the prince's fate, having my own to consider. When the Quosa broke, we were left standing bemused beside a mat of the enemy dead on the bank of the Nkwaku stream, with nobody seeming to be unduly concerned about us. It was a curious sensation indeed; one moment, to be the victorious spearhead of Destiny, the next to be an irrelevancy, left on the side of the plate as the hungry banqueter turns his attention to more nourishing fare. Thankfully, one of my senior hunters was rather more pragmatic than I; tugging first at my sleeve and then my ear, he told me in no uncertain terms that the battle was over and we should clear out with all possible haste, before Prince Cetewayo decided to take offence at our loitering there. As he spoke I caught sight of a large body of Usutu heading across the face of the ridge towards us; and if they were not unduly boisterous in their enthusiasm to close with us, neither did they show any real tendency to apprehension. I turned about, gathered up my ramrod, which I had dropped in the panic of the battle and not bothered to retrieve, and led my men away in the direction furthest from Cetewayo and his victorious army.

Some time after the battle, when I was safely back in Natal, though still understandably somewhat out of favour with my principals in the agency, a party of English traders presented themselves with a most strident complaint against the Zulus, and Prince Cetewayo in particular. It seems that they had been driving their cattle across the Tugela on the eve of the battle but had underestimated the ferocity of the spate. Accordingly they could get no further than a sandbank in the middle of the river and were stranded there when the battle began the next day. After the triumph of the Usutu, some of Cetewayo's men engaged in pursuit of the enemy swam across to the sandbank and, meeting no opposition from the terrified traders, relieved them of their cattle and went away.

My principal was not inclined to pursue the matter, taking the view that any stranger foolish enough to tarry in the vicinity of a civil war should count himself fortunate to escape with his life, let alone his chattels. I was, however, anxious to curry favour and re-establish myself within the administration, and volunteered to visit Cetewayo and seek redress for the traders' loss. My principal agreed, doubtless on the grounds that Cetewayo would instantly have me put to death and so rid him of a nuisance, and I set out for the prince's residence at Odini before he could change his mind. On reflection, I suppose I acted on a whim; it was certainly an ill-judged escapade by any reasonable standards.

Cetewayo knew perfectly well who I was, but my effrontery amused him enormously; he received me in great style, returned the traders' cattle without demur and, once they had been safely despatched under escort for Natal, invited me to stay with him at Odini for a while. To cut short a long and involved tale, I stayed with the prince at his kraal for a long time, talking often with him both in his moments of leisure and also as his adviser on more formal occasions, and was rewarded with the singular honour of being made an *induna*. With the title came a substantial grant of land (albeit in the south, where the recent wars had caused much damage and hardship), and there I stayed, the only white man ever to become a Zulu nobleman, until the outbreak of Lord Chelmsford's war in 1879. At that point I abandoned Cetewayo, who by then had succeeded his father King Panda on the throne, and my many friends among the Zulu and, spurred on by some romantic notion or other of duty to my native land, joined Lord Chelmsford's army as a scout and adviser.

I am not minded to discuss that war or my part in it. I am ashamed of both, which proves, I suppose, that I am no Zulu; for all that the stronger and fitter party prevailed, I deeply regret having betrayed my king and friend – and yet I made the decision to do so in an instant, hardly feeling that I had any choice in the matter. Had I held true to my allegiance, I have little doubt that I could have persuaded Cetewayo to modify his tactics in the war against the British, and that the outcome of the war would have been somewhat different. It would have been an unrivalled opportunity for me to manage the course of history, as I had so yearned to do on the day I first crossed the Tugela; by that stage in my career, however, I no longer felt sure that I was competent to do so, and accordingly sided with the strong against the weak. When Cetewayo's army annihilated a British column at Isandlhwana, I was tempted almost to smile, as if the outcome had been arranged solely for my benefit as evidence that destiny could not be deflected so easily.

After the war, and Cetewayo's defeat and humiliation, I returned to my lands and titles as a puppet of the British, and played with enthusiasm my part in the hateful civil wars stirred up by my people among the Zulus to keep them quiet and weak. When Cetewayo was restored briefly to his throne, I helped to drive him out and bring about the ruin of those loyal to him. I prospered mightily, helping to organize the recruitment of countless thousands of Zulus to work as hired hands on the estates of English settlers in the newly annexed territories. Now, as an old man returned to his native shore, left over from the previous century just as once before I was left over from the battle, I have the privilege of sitting in my splendour and reading in the newspapers about the terrible losses being inflicted on our armies in the trenches and mines of France by our German enemies. Given the number of times I have changed my loyalties and the colour of my coat, perhaps it is not surprising that when I fall asleep over my copy of *The Times* and dream of the horrors of this present war, I should see in my mind's eye among the banked-up mud great piles of slain Zulus, cut down in swathes by the German guns as they storm against the invulnerable lines in a futile repetition of all the battles that were ever fought. It seems to me then that I walk alone and unscathed through the deadly hail of bullets, unable to find an enemy to kill me among so many betrayed friends.

THE MAN WHO SAW

Talbot Mundy

*The Indian Mutiny broke out at Meerut and Delhi in May
1857 and soon spread throughout northern India. There had
been an undercurrent of dissatisfaction for several years over
the imposition of western and Christian values upon the
Indian cultures, but the immediate flashpoint was much more
mundane. The new Enfield rifle had been introduced and the
cartridge came in greaseproof paper which had to be bitten
for use. Animal fat had been used and worse – that it was
either the fat of cows (sacred to the Hindus) or of pigs
(unclean to the Moslems). The Hindu soldiers (or sepoys)
rebelled and insurrection flared. I have selected two stories
set during the Mutiny, and they could not be more contrast-
ing. The first is by Talbot Mundy (1879–1940) who, in his
day, was considered something of a successor to Rudyard
Kipling because of his rousing stories of soldiery and Empire.
He is probably best remembered for* King – of the Khyber
Rifles *(1916), made into a stirring film starring Tyrone
Power in 1954. But he wrote many exciting novels of*

fantastic adventure not unlike the exploits of Indiana Jones, especially his series about US secret agent James Grim, known to all as Jimgrim. The following is one of Mundy's earliest stories, first published in the popular American pulp magazine Adventure *in October 1912.*

I

He was a fine-looking man, was Michael Blackmore. There were six feet and two inches of him, broad in the back, deep-chested, and straight; he had a fine big, black moustache, and a strong, dark, good-looking face that made passers-by look twice at him; and his brown eyes were as level and unflinching and inscrutable as Fate itself. Moreover, he had a way with women.

He was sergeant-major of his regiment; and that was a fine thing to be even in those days, when the pay was less and the privileges were fewer than at present; and he was a prince among sergeant-majors in an army that has always had the finest sergeant-majors in the world.

The men realized his efficiency to their abiding disgust, and obeyed him with grudging admiration; and the officers drew comfort from it. The regiment was what it was because of him. And yet no one, either officer or enlisted man, looked on him as a friend, and no one either knew or cared what his private opinions were; he was known and admired from end to end of India as Black Mike of Jungalore; but no man loved him.

Black Mike retaliated in kind. He went his own way, kept his own counsel, and did his duty in a most efficient manner of his own; and when his day's work was done, and well done, he prosecuted his various and quite amazing love affairs without apparently knowing or caring who witnessed them.

He had a bad name in the bazaar, for the natives of India are not in the least partial to the attentions of white soldiers to their women-folk; but he could talk the language that is spoken round

Jungalore perfectly, and he had a vein of cunning in his composition that could pilot him through even the drawn curtains of the East. The natives hated him, and feared him; and Black Mike made love and went his way.

The regiment was the J.L.I.'s, and it had been a famous regiment. It paraded well, and drilled well, even in '57, thanks to Black Mike. But it had been stationed too long in Jungalore, which lies away and away to the northward of Cawnpore, in the middle of a densely-populated "babu" country.

The natives of that district never have been fighting men; they have been traders, and farmers, and manufacturers, and money-lenders for centuries – cunning, underhanded schemers, possessed of an amazing disregard for death, and an equally amazing dislike for getting hurt. They hated the English, and especially the English soldiers; but they have hated in turn, and just as cordially, every one of the conquering peoples that have overridden them and taxed them, and bullied them, through wave after wave of succeeding conquest since the birth of India.

They had over-developed brains with which to scheme against their conquerors, but they lacked always the courage and cohesion to overthrow them. It needed the Sepoy Rebellion to make them fight instead of talking fight.

So the J.L.I.'s grew fat and weary in cantonments. They guarded the big stone gaol in Jungalore, and that is no proper task for fighting men. They heartily despised the only enemy they might possibly be called upon to fight, and the reason for regimental discipline ceased to be so obvious; gradually their officers grew slack in the enforcement of it, and what should have been the very lifeblood of the regiment became a thing to cavil at and avoid by subterfuge.

After the fashion of those days they were harshly treated, and harassed by various annoying regulations, and they had plenty of time in which to resent their lot through the long, hot, lazy afternoons. By degrees they came to regard their officers as unreasonable martinets; that was the beginning of the trouble. Then they began to realize that officers are only human, and that each one had his private and peculiar weakness; they began to despise them; and from that point, stage by stage, they descended to the verge of mutiny.

Their full name and entitlement was the Honourable East India Company's Eighty-Second (Jungalore) Regiment of Light Infantry; but that name was much too long for general use. Like every other official thing in India, they were known by their initials, or part of them, and as the J.L.I.'s the regiment had left its mark, cut deep, on most of the battlefields of India.

It would have been all right now if the men had had a chance to fight and feel their feet; but stationed in that fat, green country, they had nothing much else to do but fight each other, and drink themselves into cells, half-sections at a time. And their officers were in no greatly better predicament.

There was no sport of any kind at Jungalore, and the British officer needs sport, and plenty of it, to keep him in condition. These particular officers were good enough men; they were quite devoid of cowardice, and they were bred and brought up in the same way as other officers whose names are famous; but it is not in human nature to continue for year after year guarding a big stone gaol instead of your country's honour, and retain your enthusiasm for a service that is supposed to be based on glory.

There was no glory at Jungalore, and uncommonly little fun; but the mess Madeira was magnificent. So, slowly, and by gradual degrees, the regiment became a mere trained mob, instead of the single-minded, many-handed unit it should have been.

Black Mike was the only man who suffered no deterioration. He saw the change that was taking place, for a good sergeant-major is in touch with officers and men, swinging like a pendulum between them; he should be the first person to know what is wrong with a regiment's morale, and to divine the reason for it.

Black Mike saw clearly enough, but he went through the routine of his business, and said nothing; the regiment still paraded clean and glittering as it ought to do, and the usual number of drills were gone through the usual number of times a day; the men feared him and obeyed him; there was no mur-muring while on duty, and there was even less than the usual

amount of crime. But a rot had set in the regiment, and Black
Mike knew it.

He went his way daily down to the bazaar on errands of his
own, and as time went on there were signs there that he could
not fail to recognize. There were always men of the regiment
down there, slouching about in twos and threes in and out of
native grogshops, spending money freely, but very seldom
getting really drunk. He came across them every now and then
talking in low tones to natives – a thing that the British soldier is
seldom prone to, and there was one native, Chundha Ram by
name, who seemed to be for ever fraternizing with the soldiers.

Black Mike knew Chundha Ram; he was a high-caste native,
whose religion forbade him as a general rule to associate with
foreigners, and Black Mike knew the caste rules as well as
anyone. But he kept on his course, and still said nothing; his
business lay always farther down in the bazaar, where a Hindu
girl thrummed on a stringed instrument, and waited for him.

His interludes with her were not in the least what the J.L.I.'s
would have suspected, had they wasted any time on speculation.
Once his love-affairs did come up for discussion in the canteen,
and a recently-joined youngster openly expressed his envy.

"Him?" said Bill Connors, who was reckoned shrewd by the
men and a "lawyer" by his officers. "Him? Why, he's the livin'
breathin' image o' Hanuman, the God o' Love, that's what he is,
with a different woman for every day o' the week, an' Hell
waitin' for him! Envy him, do you? I don't envy him! Mark
what he'll get by-and-by, an' then see if you envy him!"

That was the first openly-expressed hint that the sergeant-
major was included among the victims of their intended vengeance, and the low laugh that followed told more than words
could have done that he was less popular even than the officers.

Black Mike must have heard the whisperings; every now and
then he came on little groups of men, behind walls and around
unexpected corners, talking together earnestly in low tones and
arguing; he must have noticed, too, the scowls that followed him
everywhere, and he could hardly have helped hearing the
mocking laughter that was directed at him whenever his back

was turned. But he still said nothing, and he went on his daily walk to the bazaar with his back as straight and his walk as carefree and swaggering and independent as it had always been.

Whatever Connors might have to say about it, the whole regiment would have envied Black Mike if that Hindu girl of his had been less invisible. But though she had succumbed to his allurements, she was still a purdah-woman, hidden behind the inviolable curtains of the East. No white man save Black Mike saw her. She lay and longed for him, and thrummed on her guitar, and sang a native song, the ending of whose every verse was "They will make thee King, my master!" And when he entered, she flung the instrument aside and rose to greet him with a "Hail, Heaven-born!" He changed then, or seemed to change. The mask of iron indifference left him, and the man stepped out from beneath the mould of the sergeant-major.

Love-making in Hindustanee is a little different from the ordinary methods of the soldier-man; it is just as near to nature, but it is more like the flowers of nature, and less like the untilled weeds. Black Mike was past master of it, and he lay on the mat beside her and wooed his Indian sweetheart with honeyed words until her dark eyes glistened, and her teeth, like two rows of chosen pearls, peeped at him through the sweetest smiling lips in Asia. Then she would shake her head at him, and sing the last words of her song again, "They will make thee King, my master!"

"Little fool! Am I not thy King already?"

"Indeed art thou! But others need thee! There is no peace in Ind – nothing but intrigue and corruption and the matching of scheme with scheme. Men need a strong man to rule them, and thou art chosen. Aye, my beloved, thou art chosen!"

"By Chundha Ram?" Black Mike rolled over, face downwards, and bit his sleeve.

"Nay. But by those who sent him. Thou shalt rule the whole of Ind, Heaven-born!"

When he left her and faced the blazing sunlight beyond the curtains, the human element shrank once more inside him, and the sergeant-major strutted out again to stare at the world with level eyes; and as his straight, white-clad figure swaggered down the dusty road – almost before he was out of sight even – the fat, good-natured-looking babu, Chundha Ram, would enter the room that he had left. The girl did not rise to receive him, nor call him Heaven-born; but she expected him, and did not seem to resent his coming.

"Does he take it well?" asked the babu. She nodded.

"Even to-day, but a short hour ago, he chuckled with delight at the thought of so great an honour. He turned away from me and bit his sleeve that I might not hear him. Listen, Chundha Ram! Thou wilt spare his life?"

"I have promised," said the babu.

"Thy promises! What worth have they to me? How shall I know thou wilt not cause him to be slain with all the others?"

"I have promised!" said the babu once again. "But his life only! It is thy reward. The others die, all of them, before nightfall on the appointed day!"

"Thou wilt slay him too!"

"Nay! I have promised."

II

One afternoon Black Mike came on Private Connors loafing in the bazaar, and this time he stopped and spoke to him.

"Come over here!" he ordered.

Connors obeyed him sulkily.

"What's this talk about a mutiny, and what's Chundha Ram got to do with it?"

Connors' little slits of eyes opened wide, and he drew back like a scared snake.

"What d'you mean?" he asked.

"Out with it!" said the sergeant-major. "I know you're at the head of it, and I know Chundha Ram's version. I want yours."

There was no avoiding Black Mike's level eyes, that seemed able to read right down into the soul of a man; and Bill Connors, like many other talkers and ringleaders, lacked courage when single-handed.

"It's more than my life's worth to tell you, sergeant-major," he answered after a moment.

"Take your chance of that. If you don't tell me, you'll hang in hollow square in less than a week! I'll see to that. If there's to be a mutiny, I'm in it. If I'm not in it, there'll be no mutiny, or I'm not sergeant-major."

"We thought you'd side with the officers."

"You thought wrong. Now, out with it! Get it off your chest!"

So Connors told him. The scheme was to turn *fantee* – to go over to the natives. The officers were to be coaxed into the gaol under some pretext or other, and shut in there for the natives to deal with as they saw fit; then the whole regiment would lay down its arms and walk outside the fort.

Chundha Ram had promised them a life of luxury and idleness, and almost limitless sums of money, and had assured them that the same thing was about to happen to nearly every other British regiment in India. They had received liberal supplies of money in advance already, and had made up their minds to mutiny and get the rest; they were only waiting now for Chundha Ram to give the word.

"And where do I come in?" asked Black Mike.

Connors eyed him inquiringly, but the sergeant-major's face betrayed nothing.

"We reckoned you'd side with the officers," he repeated.

"Going to shut me inside the gaol with them?"

"No. That wasn't the idea."

"What then? Shoot?"

Connors nodded, and Black Mike smiled grimly.

"Nice lot of mutineers you'd be without me to lead you! D'you think Chundha Ram would keep his word with you, once you'd laid down your arms? He'd butcher the whole lot of you in cold blood within half an hour. Are the non-coms all with you?"

"Sure, all of 'em!"

"Well, I'm a non-com. I'm going to lead this business. I'll conduct the negotiations with Chundha Ram, and I'll fix it so that we keep our weapons. You tell the men from me that if they don't agree to that the mutiny's off. If I don't lead it, I'll put a stop to it."

"All right, sergeant-major, I'll tell 'em."

"And see here! You tell 'em to carry on as though I knew nothing about it. I'll talk to a few of them now and then, but no demonstrations, mind. Nothing that would excite suspicion. Remember, I'm sergeant-major until the thing comes off, and I'll be treated so."

"All right, sergeant-major."

Then Black Mike, committed to lead a mutiny, swaggered down to the bazaar again to have a talk with Chundha Ram; he talked for two hours, and then returned to barracks.

The men watched Black Mike after that as birds watch a prowling cat. They were afraid of him, and not quite sure of him, and they did not dare to kill him for fear that the fat would be in the fire too soon. They gave him no opportunity whatever to talk to the officers in private, although Black Mike showed not the slightest desire to do it; there was always somebody within earshot of him, and even in the bazaar he was kept in sight until he disappeared behind the purdah of the house where his girl waited for him. None of the men ever knew what he talked to her about, and nobody else cared.

Black Mike was one of the few men, though, who knew in advance of the impending Sepoy Rebellion, and he must have drawn his information from some such source. He had warned his colonel of it more than a year ago, but almost the most amazing thing about that rebellion was the way that the British officers ignored the warnings of it. They absolutely refused to believe that there was a chance of an Indian rising, and when Black Mike spoke of it his colonel laughed at him.

There was no language star against the sergeant-major's name on the muster-roll, and the colonel had taken the senior-grade examination in Hindustanee; it passed his comprehension that a non-commissioned man should know more of the language and the country than he himself did.

And yet Blackmore could make love in the native dialect to

three different girls at once, and keep them all guessing. There was more knowledge of India and the Indians in his little finger than in the heads of all his officers put together, and Black Mike knew it. His position, though, forbade any display of resentment or superior knowledge, just as his character precluded the possibility of risking a second snub – one such was enough for him. Besides, had he told his colonel that a mutiny of the regiment was impending, as well as an uprising of the whole of India, he would probably have been locked up in the guardroom as a lunatic, and the least thing that would have happened to him would have been reduction to the ranks.

He preferred to take his own line and quell the regimental mutiny himself; the colonel, he knew, would only set a match to the stored-up powder if alarmed, and the regiment would be doomed and damned for ever. He had the honour of the regiment at heart, and it seemed to him that he saw his way clear to preserve it.

Every now and then a delegation of the men, headed by Private William Connors, would waylay him for an interview; their conversation began invariably with threats of what they would do to him at the slightest sign of what they were pleased to call treachery on his part, and it ended with excited queries as to when and exactly how the blow they planned was to be struck.

"Ever see a file o' men lined up with their backs to the twelve-pounders?" he asked them. "Feel like trying it? You move before Chundha Ram gives the word, and the guns'll be over from Jullundra in half a jiffy. There's four batteries there, and it's only fourteen miles away."

The guns! They had not thought about the guns. With the short-sighted cunning of uneducated men they had laid a scheme cleverly enough to trap their officers; but they had looked no farther than their noses, and the mention of the guns brought terror to them.

The Bengal Horse Artillery was the finest branch of the East India Company's service; the men were magnificent, and loyal to the last drop of blood that ran in them. There were four-and-twenty sleek twelve-pounder guns at Jullundra, fourteen miles

away, and they were horsed and manned by the very best that
England could produce.

"What about the guns, sergeant-major? Chundha Ram said
all the other regiments were going to do the same – like us –
mutiny. How about 'em?"

"You leave the guns to me. Leave everything to me. Your
plan's all right enough about the officers. Stick to that, and
leave me to settle the rest. What you've got to bear in mind is
that these natives are as treacherous as they make 'em; I've fixed
it now so's we keep our arms and some ammunition, and we'll
be able to look after ourselves after it's all over; but unless we
stick together they'll turn on us like a shot as soon as they're in
possession of the gaol.

"We can loot all we want to so long as we're still a regiment
and don't seem afraid of them, but if we start looting afterwards,
one by one, there'll be mighty few of us left to loot within
twenty-four hours – you take my word for it!"

"What about Chundha Ram?" they asked him. "Is he square?"

"Square as the average run of natives. Don't let him think
that you're afraid of him – that's all. If he thinks that you're
afraid, he'll break his word and butcher the lot of you, or try to.
Keep the upper hand with him. Better still, leave him to me; I
know how to deal with him."

They began to have more confidence in Black Mike after that;
he seemed to be sincerely one of them; and along with their
growing confidence in him they began to be surer of themselves;
they had a strong man to lead them, and the regiment began to
cohere again. It was mutinous, but it began again to be a unit,
capable of acting uniformly, precisely, and on the instant.
There was less grumbling, and the men looked less sulky; they
began even to behave better, and one morning after six o'clock
parade the colonel addressed them and actually complimented
them on their good behaviour.

If he could have heard the ribald laughter in the barrack-
rooms afterwards he might have been enlightened, but it was
not considered good policy in those days to know the men too

intimately; instead of getting into better touch with them, he wrote a long report to the authorities in which he boasted, among other things, of his men's good conduct.

It was not only the J.L.I.'s who were anxious about those guns at Jullundra; the natives were worried about them, too, and Chundha Ram spoke to Black Mike about them.

"About the artillery, sahib? Would your men fight if the gunners got news of their mutiny and tried to interfere?"

"That all depends," said Blackmore. "If they got here before it happened, the men would be partly afraid and partly ashamed, and they'd call the thing off. If they came too late, the men would either fight or else scatter; they'd probably scatter – one regiment couldn't make much of a show against four batteries."

The babu nodded. He would like the regiment to scatter. It would be easier to deal with afterwards.

"The guns must not arrive – too soon!" he said deliberately.

"You can't prevent them coming unless you contrive to keep the news from them."

"They will get news, sahib – when all is over. That will be arranged. Then they will come galloping – there will be an ambuscade – and –" The babu shrugged his fat shoulders.

"Who'll arrange the ambuscade?"

"I will, sahib."

"Better let me hunt out the right place for you. I know more about that kind of thing than you do."

"Pardon me, sahib. Were you to wander out alone in the direction of Jullundra, knowing what you know, you would not return alive. That, too, would be attended to."

Black Mike grinned pleasantly.

"Come with me," he answered.

Chundha Ram eyed him in silence for half a minute; then he nodded. It suited his sense of humour perfectly that a British soldier's knowledge of warfare should be used for the undoing of his own countrymen.

"If you have time, sahib, we will go now," he answered.

*   *   *

The two men got into a native bullock-cart and drove out leisurely in the direction of Jullundra, while Chundha Ram chewed betel-nut reflectively, and Black Mike searched the surrounding country with eyes that took in every crease and fold in it, and burned them in his memory. Two-thirds of the distance to Jullundra he pointed out to Chundha Ram a place that was admirably suited as a trap for galloping artillery; they could be almost surrounded and shot down at close range from under cover.

"How many men can you spare for the ambuscade?" asked Blackmore.

"More thousands than you or I can count, sahib. All India is behind this uprising."

"You don't want too many. The chief element of an ambuscade is surprise. Your men must not be seen. If the ground scouts catch sight of them they'll lead the batteries round by another route, and your trouble'll all go for nothing; besides that, you'll have the guns to deal with at the other end. Send just as many as can be concealed in the cover here – say, a thousand, certainly not more – and clear everybody else away from the countryside.

"Concentrate your forces on the gaol. If the gunners see any bodies of armed men anywhere about, they'll be on their guard, and you'll never trap them. Clear the whole countryside, set your ambuscade right here, and make all the others close in on Jungalore – understand? Then, if any of the guns do get through, you'll have plenty of men near the gaol to deal with them."

"I understand, sahib; it shall be done as you say. And we will not be ungrateful to you; you will be better situated than a King when the English are no longer over-lords of India."

And Black Mike rolled over on his side in the bullock-cart, and once more bit his sleeve as he had done when the girl had prophesied.

"Now look here, Chundha Ram," he said, as the bullock-cart bumped and squeaked along the road to Jungalore again; "you've got to do this thing properly, and make no mistakes about it; otherwise there'll be a holy mess. Are you going to take my advice or aren't you?"

"You see that I take it, sahib. Otherwise, why should I ride with you in a bullock-cart?"

"True for you. Now listen. The men of the J.L.I.'s won't surrender without a parley. They've got to save their faces, you understand. You, being a black man, don't know about it, but there's such a thing as the honour of a regiment; take my word for it — it's so."

"Is it different from other sorts of honour?" asked the babu blandly.

"In some ways, no; in others, yes. Now, for instance, supposing you were to be surrounded by a gang of thugs while you were in this bullock-cart, and they ordered you to surrender — you'd surrender, wouldn't you?"

"Surely, sahib. I would be but one against many, and I would be afraid."

"That's the idea exactly. It's the same with a regiment; they're not going to surrender without some apparent reason why they should. I mean they won't just walk out and ask to be taken prisoners. You'll have to show up with a sufficient force, and then you'll have to talk to them and call on them to surrender. They can save their faces that way; it wouldn't be dishonouring the regiment — at least not to the same extent — to surrender to a vastly superior force. Understand?"

"I understand, sahib; and words are cheap. What shall I tell them?"

"Be more polite about it than the thugs I spoke of would be to you, but use the same sort of argument. Make it clear that they are surrendering because there is no alternative."

"I understand, sahib."

"And talk in Hindustanee, Chundha Ram. Sometimes when you're talking English you make mistakes, and there won't be room for anything of that sort. I'll be standing at the head of the regiment, and I'll translate what you have to say. I know just how to handle 'em, and you don't; you haven't lived among them for years and years as I have, Chundha Ram."

"I thank God I have not, sahib!" said the babu, smiling; "but everything shall be done as you say, and the white regiment shall save its honour. It is a small matter, and words are cheap."

The sergeant-major ground his teeth. The honour of the J.L.I.'s was not at all a small matter to him; he meant to save it, even if it cost his own life, and that of every single officer and man in the regiment, to do it.

"Is everything arranged finally for Sunday?" he asked.

"Sunday morning," said the babu, nodding, "at the usual time for church parade."

III

The regiment behaved itself, and waited in grimly concealed impatience until Sunday came. Not a man was in cells on any charge, but the big stone gaol was full of civil prisoners, and the colonel made his usual round of inspection just before church time, followed by all his officers. The rear of the procession was brought up by a sergeant, and the sergeant-major stayed with the regiment, mustering them company by company for parade.

The sergeant chanced to be one of the men's keenest ringleaders, and he had learned his part perfectly; as the junior subaltern followed the rest through the huge arched gateway into the gloom beyond, the sergeant stepped back quickly and slammed the immense teak doors behind him. As the clang of its shutting and the rattle of the big iron bolt told that the officers were prisoners within the gaol, a bugle-call rang out across the barrack square, and the regiment fell in in a hurry, breaking all precedent on church parade by bringing their rifles and ammunition-pouches with them.

Eyes glanced uneasily from left to right up and down the lines, looking for signs of flinching, but no one spoke. Men say little under the stress of that sort of excitement. They felt uneasy, for the lines seemed lonely and unusual without their officers.

"'Tshun!" barked the sergeant-major, and they came to attention, eyes straight in front of them, from force of habit. He gave them no time to think, for he read their condition exactly, and he saw fit to lead them to the climax as they were.

"Form fours!" he ordered.

Then he marched them round to the *maidan*, to the spot just outside the city wall where it had been agreed the surrender should take place. They were lined up outside the city almost before the imprisoned officers had had time to wonder what was happening, and why no one came to let them out.

The sergeant-major stood and faced them – the one lone man among nine hundred who was unafraid. The men were afraid of what they were doing, for it is not exactly every Sunday that a British regiment mutinies.

"Listen!" he ordered. "The success of this depends on your not letting these natives think that you're afraid of them. Remember that!"

A murmur answered him – a low growl, half wonder, half disgust. They were not afraid of natives.

"Leave the talking to me. I'll listen to what the Indian says, and then translate."

Then he turned his broad, well-hollowed back to them and waited for the babu, standing right out alone in front of the regiment like a white statue of drilled inscrutability; and behind him the regiment rustled and shifted feet with a noise such as trees make when a light breeze blows through them. Blackmore heard it and understood; the game was half won already – but only half won.

The ranks stiffened, and the sergeant-major stared steadily in front of him as Chundha Ram advanced across the *maidan*. He was followed by a big, silent mob of men – silent in expectation of coming loot and slaughter; they were clothed in every colour of the rainbow, and armed with every imaginable weapon, from matchlocks to service rifles, and from axes to spears made out of household implements.

It was a big, unwieldy mob, formidable only for its numbers. Chundha Ram halted it within two hundred paces of the regiment; then he stepped up to address the sergeant-major.

"Are you ready to surrender?" he asked, with just the least suspicion of insolence in his voice, but speaking in Hindustanee, as agreed.

Blackmore played his part promptly.

"And why should we surrender?" he asked. "And to whom?"

"You will see," said the babu oilily, and waving his hand in a magnificent gesture towards the mob behind him – "you will see that we have you at a great disadvantage – an overwhelming disadvantage. You are few, and we are many. Surely you would be afraid to fight. Your officers, too, seem frightened; they are hiding in the gaol."

Black Mike turned to the men behind him.

"This man says," he roared, pitching his rasping voice till it echoed against the city wall, and every single man heard every word he said, "that you've got to surrender to him or else he'll hand you over to his mob. He says that your officers are hiding in the gaol, and that you're too big cowards to fight that mob without them. He thinks that you're afraid of him."

The growl that followed that announcement disturbed Chundha Ram considerably. Black Mike eyed him with something not unlike amusement, and the babu flushed darkly underneath his olive skin.

"Well?" asked Chundha Ram.

"They don't seem quite to understand you. Try some more talk."

The babu tried it. He spoke now in English, ignoring the sergeant-major, and addressing the men directly; and with each sentence that he uttered he damned his cause more completely. Soon the men were too amazed even to listen.

"As promised, we will show you mercy!" said the babu, trying vainly to compromise between politeness to the soldiers and bombast for the sake of the mob behind him. The regiment rustled – too amazed to speak. He drew nearer, mistaking the shifting feet for a sign of indecision.

"You were only hirelings in the first instance. The Company has paid you little and has given you ill-treatment; now why should you befriend the Company when I offer you more money and kind treatment? Why should you be killed? Why should I order my men here to make an end of you? You should surrender to our much more powerful force, and accept our

clemency." He paused to regain his breath, and to let the effect
of his grandiloquent speech sink in.

"To hell with him!" shouted someone, and the murmuring
ranks began to roar wholesomely.

"What's your answer?" demanded the sergeant-major's rasping voice.

"Tell him to go to—!"

This from a hundred men; and there came the click and snap
of loading rifles. Black Mike leaped suddenly aside and slipped
to his proper place behind the regiment.

"At two hundred yards!" came his accustomed voice, the
voice they had heard and obeyed so often. "Ready! – present! –
fire!"

Chundha Ram never realized what hit him. He curled up and
died where he had stood, and seven or eight hundred bullets
sped past him to find their billets in the howling mob he had led.
The regiment was saved now and the game was won, if Black
Mike knew anything at all of men.

"Form fours!" he bellowed, and they hinged into the fresh
formation like a clockwork mechanism.

They were in fours, and ready to move in any direction before
the mob of Hindus had recovered from the shock of their terrific
volley, or even knew there would be no surrender.

"Right!" roared Black Mike at the top of his lungs. "By the
left – double! Left wheel!"

He led them at the run back along the city wall and through
the gate they had emerged from, and before even the men
themselves had had time to realize that they had sloughed their
rôle of mutineers, they were formed up, panting, before the gaol
gate, and facing the direction from which the enemy would
come. Then Black Mike swung the gaol door open, and let light
in on the astonished officers. The colonel emerged into the
sunlight first.

"What's the meaning of this?" he demanded.

"All present and correct, sir," answered Black Mike, licking
up his right hand to the salute. "Take charge, sir, quick! They'll
be here in a second!"

The colonel looked around him and took charge. A glutton he might be, and a bad officer in peace time, but he was a man of action and prompt decision when it came to fighting. There was surely no time to waste on argument, and his commands began to ring out loud and clear almost before the words were out of the sergeant-major's mouth. And the men obeyed them on the instant; they had had enough of mutiny.

Picked men, stationed by Chundha Ram on every roof-top, began an intermittent fire on the front of the gaol; these were the men who were to have shot down the soldiers one by one after their surrender, and the J.L.I.'s had a chance to see what fate had really awaited them. Nine or ten men were down already. The colonel marched them inside the gaol, and stationed them as best he could to defend the place – some on the roof, some at the embrasures, and the remainder down below as a reserve to act when needed.

IV

Then the amazing happened. It was one of those terrific things that happen once in a thousand years when the right man springs on the right horse, and rams his heels in at the right ten-thousandth of a second. The right horse was the colonel's charger – a chestnut Kathiawari gelding that had stood tied up outside the gaol gate, and the man was Black Mike, the sergeant-major.

He leaped on the horse, rammed in his heels, and rode – straight for the rebel ranks. The defenders of the gaol gasped as they watched him, for there were twenty thousand armed natives swarming towards the big square through every street and alley. They were scattered yet, but they saw him, and rushed in with a yell to meet him. Swords clove the air an inch behind him, bullets screamed past him, eddying whirls of black humanity scrambled to block his way. They grabbed at his rein, and he beat them off with a stirrup, brandishing the leather in his hand. They shot his helmet off, and riddled the flapping cloth of his open tunic with bullet holes, and men threw themselves prone, trying to hamstring the horse under him; but Black Mike rode straight as a die, at, through or over everything.

The maddened charger reared and plunged and leaped, and Black Mike flogged it with the leather strap; the natives howled and blocked the road in front of him, but as a shuttle shoots through a loom, he burst through a gathering mob of twenty thousand men – a flogging, flashing, unexpected bolt of grim determination – and getting clean through untouched, to the plain beyond, headed for Jullundra.

"The man's mad," said the colonel; "stark, staring, raving mad!"

"He's gone for the guns," said someone, and the colonel nodded.

"Now, men," he shouted, "the guns should be here within two hours; we've got to hold this place till they get here."

The guns! The men roared now at the thought of them. A week ago they were worried about the guns, but things had somehow altered.

You must go to India where the thing happened, and hear it from the lips of Indians whose fathers saw Black Mike ride, to get a real idea of how he saved the gaol and the lives of the men who held it. They will tell you that he rode straight through the ambuscade that Chundha Ram had set two-thirds of the way to Jullundra; he knew where it should be, for he had placed it, and he rode through it to be sure that it was there, and that his trip with Chundha Ram had not been a trick to throw him off his guard.

A hell of bullets greeted him, and a hundred men sprang out to seize his horse, but he rode straight through them – silent and untouched. They say there that a legion of devils rode with him, and that the Kathiawari gelding that he rode breathed fire from his nostrils and sent green fire flashing from his heels. That, of course, is nonsense, and the truth is that Black Mike was a man, and the gods of war favour such as he.

He burst like a bomb into Jullundra, and shouted the alarm; and he very nearly got locked up in the guard-room as a lunatic, for nobody believed him. But he convinced them somehow that at least there was need for action – the bullet-holes through his riddled tunic were proof enough of that.

So the four batteries thundered out on to the *maidan*, with their ground scouts spread out like a fan in front of them, and the gun teams plunging in answer to the lash. And in front of the ground scouts, on a fresh horse, rode Black Mike, the sergeant-major of the J.L.I.'s. He showed them where the ambuscade was hidden, and led them round it.

Grapeshot was too much for the mutineers. They melted before the guns like snow under a hot sun, and the gaol was saved.

Next day came news of the general outbreak that had burst out like a flame through disaffected India, and the guns and the J.L.I.'s set out to reach Delhi by forced marches, for every man was needed to strike a blow at the heart of the rebellion. As they filed behind the guns through the bazaar, two paces behind the regiment, in among the dust and flies and heat-haze, marched a straight-backed man who, loaded up with sixty pounds of haversack, preached the art of marching in raucous undertones:

"Keep your places in the fours here! Less talking, and keep some o' the dust out o' your throats! Save your breath for marching! Now then – Left! – Left! – Left!"

As he passed a corner house in the bazaar there came the tinkling of a stringed instrument, and a girl's voice sang in Hindustanee: "They will make thee King, my master!" He laughed aloud this time; there was no need to bite his sleeve. He needed no job as King; he was Black Mike, the sergeant-major of the J.L.I.'s, who had saved the honour of the regiment, and then the regiment itself, to fight for England. Three weeks hence he would salute his colonel and report, "All present and correct," in front of Delhi, having nursed the men all the way by forty-mile-a-day stages. Why make him King? The British army has built its reputation on the bones and brains of such as he.

FLASHMAN BESIEGED

George MacDonald Fraser

*Harry Flashman is one of the great creations of modern
literature. First encountered as the school bully in* Tom
Brown's Schooldays *(1857) by Thomas Hughes, he was
thankfully rediscovered by George MacDonald Fraser (b.
1925) who purportedly edited the Flashman papers starting with* Flashman *(1969). The series, now running to
eleven volumes, takes us through the Afghan Wars, the
Crimea, the United States, China and the Indian Mutiny.
The following episode, set at the bloodthirsty siege of
Cawnpore in May 1857, comes from* Flashman in the
Great Game *(1975). Despite the horror of the situation,
Fraser manages to retain the usual sparkle and total lack
of honour one has come to expect from Flashman.*

I'll tell you a strange thing about pain – and Cawnpore. That
ankle of mine, which I'd thought was broken, but which in fact

was badly sprained, would have kept me flat on my back for days anywhere else, bleating for sympathy; in Cawnpore I was walking on it within a few hours, suffering damnably, but with no choice but to endure it. That was the sort of place it was; if you'd had both legs blown off you were rated fit for only light duties.

Imagine a great trench, with an earth and rubble parapet five feet high, enclosing two big single-storey barracks, one of them a burned-out shell and the other with half its roof gone. All round was flat plain, stretching hundreds of yards to the encircling pandy lines which lay among half-ruined buildings and trees; a mile or less to the north-west was the great straggling mass of Cawnpore city itself, beside the river – but when anyone of my generation speaks of Cawnpore he means those two shattered barracks with the earth wall round them.

That was where Wheeler, with his ramshackle garrison, had been holding out against an army for two and a half weeks. There were nine hundred people inside it when the siege began, nearly half of them women and children; of the rest four hundred were British soldiers and civilians, and a hundred loyal natives. They had one well, and three cannon; they were living on two handfuls of mealies a day, fighting off a besieging force of more than three thousand mutineers who smashed at them constantly with fifteen cannon, subjected them to incessant musket-fire, and tried to storm the entrenchment. The defenders lost over two hundred dead in the first fortnight, men, women, and children, from gunfire, heat and disease; the hospital barrack had been burned to ashes with the casualties inside, and of the three hundred left fit to fight, more than half were wounded or ill. They worked the guns and manned the wall with muskets and bayonets and whatever they could lay hands on.

This, I discovered to my horror, was the place I'd fled to for safety, the stronghold which Rowbotham had boasted was being held with such splendid ease. It was being held – by starved ghosts half of whom had never fired a musket before, with their women and children dying by inches in the shot-torn, stifling barrack behind them, in the certainty that unless help came quickly that entrenchment would be their common grave. Rowbotham never lived to discover how mistaken he'd been: he and half his troop were lying stark out on the plain – his final miscalculation having been to time our rush to coincide with a pandy assault.

I was the senior officer of those who'd got safely (?) inside, and when they'd discovered who I was and bound up my ankle I was helped into the little curtained corner of the remaining barrack where Wheeler had his office. We stared at each other in disbelief, he because I was still looking like Abdul the Bulbul, and I because in place of the stalwart, brisk commander I'd known ten years ago there was now a haggard, sunken ancient; with his grimy, grizzled face, his uniform coat torn and filthy, and his breeches held up with string, he looked like a dead gardener.

"Good God, you're never young Harry Flashman!" was his greeting to me. "Yes, you are though! Where the dooce did you spring from?" I told him – and in the short time I took to tell him about Meerut and Jhansi, no fewer than three round-shot hit the building, shaking the plaster; Wheeler just brushed the debris absently off his table, and then says:

"Well, thank God for twenty more men – though what we'll feed you on I cannot think. Still, what matter a few more mouths? – you see the plight we're in. You've heard nothing of . . . our people advancing from Allahabad, or Lucknow?" I said I hadn't and he looked round at his chief officers, Vibart and Moore, and gave a little gesture of despair.

"I suppose it was not be expected," says he. "So . . . we can only do our duty – how much longer? If only it was not for the children, I think we could face it well enough. Still – no croaking, eh?" He gave me a tired grin. "Don't take it amiss if I say I'm glad to see you, Flashman, and will welcome your presence in our council. In the meantime, the best service you can do is to take a place at the parapet. Moore here will show you – God bless you," says he, shaking hands, and it was from

Moore, a tall, fair-haired captain with his arm in a blood-smeared sling, that I learned of what had been happening in the past two weeks, and how truly desperate our plight was.

It may read stark enough, but the sight of it was terrible. Moore took me round the entrenchment, stooping as he walked and I hobbled, for the small-arms fire from the distant sepoy lines kept whistling overhead, smacking into the barrack-wall, and every so often a large shot would plump into the enclosure or smash another lump out of the building. It was terrifying – and yet no one seemed to pay it much attention; the men at the parapet just popped up for an occasional look, and those moving in the enclosure, with their heads hunched down, never even broke step if a bullet whined above them. I kept bobbing nervously, and Moore grinned and said:

"You'll soon get used to it – pandy marksmen don't hit a dam' thing they aim at. It's the random shots that do the damage – damnation!" This as a cloud of dust, thrown up by a round-shot hitting the parapet, enveloped us. "Stretcher, there! Lively now!" There was a body twitching close by where the shot had struck; at Moore's shout two fellows doubled out from the barrack to attend to it. After a brief look one of them shook his head, and then they picked up the body between them and carried it off towards what looked like a well; they just pitched it in, and Moore says:

"That's our cemetery. I've worked it out that we put someone in there every two hours. Over there – that's the wet well, where we get our water. We won't go too close – the pandy sharp-shooters get a clear crack at it from that grove yonder, so we draw our water at night. Jock McKillop worked it for a week, until they got him. Heaven only knows how many we've lost on water-drawing since."

What seemed so unreal about it, and still does, was the quiet conversational way he talked. There was this garrison, being steadily shot to bits, and starving in the process, and he went on pointing things out, cool as dammit, with the crackle of desultory firing going on around us. I stomached it so long, and then burst out:

"But in God's name – it's hopeless! Hasn't Wheeler tried to make terms?"

He laughed straight out at that. "Terms? Who with? Nana Sahib? Look here, you were at Meerut, weren't you? Did *they* make terms? They want us dead, laddie. They slaughtered everything white up in the city yonder, and God knows how many of their own folk as well. They tortured the native goldsmiths to death to get at their loot; Nana's been blowing loyal Indians from guns as fast as they can trice 'em over the muzzles! No," he shook his head, "there'll be no terms."

"But what the devil – I mean, what . . .?"

"What's going to come of it? Well, I don't need to tell you, of all people – either a relief column wins through from Allahabad in three days at most, or we'll be so starved and short of cartridge that the pandies will storm over that wall. Then . . ." He shrugged. "But of course, we don't admit that – not in front of the ladies, anyway, however much some of 'em may guess. Just grin and assure 'em that Lawrence will be up with the rations any day, what?"

I won't trouble to describe my emotions as this sank in, along with the knowledge that for once there was nowhere to bolt to – and I couldn't have run anyway, with my game ankle. It was utterly hopeless – and what made it worse, if anything, was that as a senior man I had to pretend, like Wheeler and Moore and Vibart and the rest, that I was ready to do or die with the best. Even I couldn't show otherwise – not with everyone else steady and cheery enough to sicken you. I'll carry to my grave the picture of that blood-sodden ground, with the flies droning everywhere, and the gaunt figures at the parapet; the barrack wall honeycombed with the shots that slapped into it every few seconds; the occasional cry of a man struck; the stretcher-parties running – and through it all Moore walking about with his bloody arm, grinning and calling out jokes to everyone; Wheeler, with his hat on his head and the pistol through the cord at his waist, staring grim-faced at the pandy lines and scratching his white moustache while he muttered to the aide scribbling notes at his elbow; a Cockney sergeant arguing with a private about the height of the pillars at Euston Square station, while they cut pieces from a dead horse for the big copper boiler against the barrack wall.

"Stew today," says Moore to me. "That's thanks to you fellows coming in. Usually, if we want meat, we have to let a pandy cavalryman charge up close, and then shoot the horse, not the rider."

"More meat on the 'orse than there is on the pandy, eh, Jasper?" says the sergeant, winking, and the private said it was just as well, since some non-coms of his acquaintance, namin' no names, would as soon be cannibals as not.

These are the trivial things that stick in memory, but none clearer than the inside of that great barrack-room, with the wounded lying in a long, sighing, groaning line down one wall, and a few yards away, behind roughly improvised screens of chick and canvas, four hundred women and children, who had lived in that confined, sweating furnace for two weeks. The first thing that struck you was the stench, of blood and stale sweat and sickness, and then the sound – the children's voices, a baby crying, the older ones calling out, and some even laughing, while the firing cracked away outside; the quiet murmur of the women; the occasional gasp of pain from the wounded; the brisk voices from the curtained corner where Wheeler had his office. Then the gaunt patient faces – the weary-looking women, some in ragged aprons, others in soiled evening dresses, nursing or minding the children or tending the wounded; the loyal sepoys, slumped against the wall, with their muskets between their knees; an English civilian sitting writing, and staring up in thought, and then writing again; beside him an old babu in a *dhoti*, mouthing the words as he read a scrap of newspaper through steel-rimmed spectacles; a haggard-looking young girl stitching a garment for a small boy who was waiting and hitting out angrily at the flies buzzing round his head; two officers in foul suits that had once been white, talking about pig-sticking – I remember one jerking his arm to shoot his linen, and him with nothing over his torso but his jacket; an *ayah** smiling as she

---

* Native nursemaid.

piled toy bricks for a little girl; a stocky, tow-headed corporal scraping his pipe; a woman whispering from the Bible to a pallid Goanese-looking fellow lying on a blanket with a bloody bandage round his head; an old, stern, silver-haired mem-sahib rocking a cradle.

They were all waiting to die, and some of them knew it, but there was no complaint, no cross words that I ever heard. It wasn't real, somehow – the patient, ordinary way they carried on. "It beats me," I remember Moore saying, "when I think how our dear ladies used to slang and back-bite on the verandahs, to see 'em now, as gentle as nuns. Take my word for it, they'll never look at their fellow-women the same way again, if we get out of this."

"Don't you believe it," says another, called Delafosse. "It's just lack of grub that's keeping 'em quiet. A week after it's all over, they'll be cutting Lady Wheeler dead in the street, as usual."

It's all vague memory, though, with no sense of time to it; I couldn't tell you when it was that I came face to face with Harry East, and we spoke, but I know that it was near Wheeler's curtain, where I'd been talking with two officers called Whiting and Thomson, and a rather pretty girl called Bella Blair was sitting not far away reading a poem to some of the children. I must have got over my funks to some extent, for I know I was sufficiently myself to be properly malicious to him.

"Hallo, Flashman," says he.

"Hallo, young Scud East," says I, quite cool. "You got to Raglan, I hear."

"Yes," says he, blushing. "Yes, I did."

"Good for you," says I. "Wish I could have come along – but I was delayed, you recollect."

This was all Greek to the others, of course, so the young ass had to blurt it out for their benefit – how we'd escaped together in Russia, and he'd left me behind wounded (which, between ourselves, had been the proper thing to do, since there was vital news to carry to Raglan at Sevastopol), and the Cossacks had got me. Of course, he hadn't got the style to make the tale sound creditable to himself, and I saw Whiting cock an eyebrow and sniff. East stuttered over it, and blushed even redder, and finally says:

"I'm so glad you got out, in the end, though, Flashman. I . . . I hated leaving you, old fellow."

"Yes," says I. "The Cossacks were all for it, though."

"I . . . I hope they didn't – I mean, they didn't use you too badly . . . that they didn't . . ." He was making a truly dreadful hash of it, much to my enjoyment. "It's been on my conscience, you know . . . having to go off like that."

Whiting was looking at the ceiling by this. Thomson was frowning, and the delectable Bella had stopped reading to listen.

"Well," says I, after a moment, "it's all one now, you know." I gave a little sigh. "Don't fret about it, young Scud. If the worst comes to the worst here – I won't leave *you* behind."

It hit him like a blow; he went chalk-white, and gasped, and then he turned on his heel and hurried off. Whiting said, "Good God!" and Thomson asked incredulously: "Did I understand that right? He absolutely cut out and left you – saved his own skin?"

"Um? What's that?" says I, and frowned. "Oh, now, that's a bit hard. No use both of us being caught and strung up in a dungeon and . . ." I stopped there and bit my lip. "That would just have meant the Cossacks would have had two of us to . . . play with, wouldn't it? Doubled the chance of one of us cracking and telling 'em what they wanted to know. That's why I wasn't sorry he cleared out . . . I knew I could trust myself, you see . . . But, Lord, what am I rambling about? It's all past." I smiled bravely at them. "He's a good chap, young East; we were at school together, you know."

I limped off then, leaving them to discuss it if they wanted to, and what they said I don't know, but later that evening Thomson sought me out at my place on the parapet, and shook my hand without a word, and then Bella Blair came, biting her lip, and kissed me quickly on the cheek and hurried off. It's truly remarkable, if you choose a few words carefully, how you can enhance your reputation and damage someone else's – and it was the least I could do to pay back that pious bastard East. Between me and his own precious Arnold-nurtured conscience he must have had a happy night of it.

I didn't sleep too well myself. A cupful of horse stew and a handful of flour don't settle you, especially if you're shaking with the horrors of your predicament. I even toyed with the idea of resuming my Pathan dress – which I had exchanged for army shirt and breeches – slipping over the parapet, lame as I was, and trying to escape, but the thought of being caught in the pandy lines was more than I could bear. I just lay there quaking, listening to the distant crack of the rebel snipers, and the occasional crump of a shot landing in the enclosure, tortured by thirst and hunger cramps, and I must have dozed off, for suddenly I was being shaken, and all round me people were hurrying, and a brazen voice was bawling "Stand to! Stand to! Loading parties, there!" A bugle was blaring, and orders were being shouted along the parapet – the fellow next me was ramming in a charge hurriedly, and when I demanded what was the row he just pointed out over the barricade, and invited me to look for myself.

It was dawn, and across the flat maidan, in front of the pandy gun positions, men were moving – hundreds of them. I could see long lines of horsemen in white tunics, dim through the light morning mist, and in among the squadrons were the scarlet coats and white breeches of native infantry. Even as I looked there was the red winking of fire from the gun positions, and then the crash of the explosions, followed by the whine of shot and a series of crashes from the barracks behind. Clouds of dust billowed down from the wall, to the accompaniment of yells and oaths, and a chorus of wails from the children. A kettle-drum was clashing, and here were the loading parties, civilians and followers and even some of the women, and a couple of *bhistis*,★ and then Wheeler himself, with Moore at his heels, bawling orders, and behind him on the barrack-roof the torn Union Jack was being hauled up to flap limply in the warm dawn air.

★ Native water-carriers.

"They're coming, rot 'em!" says the man next to me. "Look at 'em, yonder – 56th N.I., Madras Fusiliers. An' Bengal Cavalry, too – don't I know it! Those are my own fellows, blast the scoundrels – or were. All right, my bucks, your old riding-master's waiting for you!" He slapped the stock of his rifle. "I'll give you more pepper than I ever did at stables!"

The pandy guns were crashing away full tilt now, and the whistle of small arms shot was sounding overhead. I was fumbling with my revolver, pressing in the loads; all down the parapet there was the scraping of ram-rods, and Wheeler was shouting:

"Every piece loaded, mind! Loading parties be ready with fresh charges! Three rifles to each man! All right, Delafosse! Moore, call every second man from the south side – smartly, now! Have the fire-parties stand by! Sergeant Grady, I want an orderly with bandages every ten yards on this parapet!"

He could hardly be heard above the din of the enemy firing and the crash of the shots as they plumped home; the space between the parapet and the barracks was swirling with dust thrown up by the shot, and we lay with our heads pressed into the earth below the top of the barrier. Someone came forward at a crouching run and laid two charged muskets on the ground beside me; to my astonishment I saw it was Bella Blair – the fat babu I'd seen reading the previous night was similarly arming the riding-master, and the chap on t'other side of me had as his loader a very frail-looking old civilian in a dust-coat and cricket cap. They lay down behind us; Bella was pale as death, but she smiled at me and pushed the hair out of her eyes; she was wearing a yellow calico dress, I recall, with a band tied round her brows.

"All standing to!" roars Wheeler. He alone was on his feet, gaunt and bare-headed, with his white hair hanging in wisps down his cheeks; he had his revolver in one hand, and his sabre stuck point-first in the ground before him. "Masters – I want a ration of flour and half a cup of water to each—"

A terrific concerted salvo drowned out the words; the whole entrenchment seemed to shake as the shots ploughed into it and smashed clouds of brick dust from the barracks. Farther down the line someone was screaming, high-pitched, there was a cry for the stretchers, the dust eddied round us and subsided, and then the noise gradually ebbed away, even the screams trailed off into a whimper, and a strange, eery stillness fell.

"Steady, all!" It was Wheeler, quieter now. "Riflemen – up to the parapet! Now hold your fire, until I give you the word! Steady, now!"

I peered over the parapet. Across the maidan there was silence, too, suddenly broken by the shrill note of a trumpet. There they were, looking like a rather untidy review – the ranks of red-coated infantry, in open order, just forward of the ruined buildings, and before them, within shot, the horse squadrons, half a dozen of them well spaced out. A musket cracked somewhere down the parapet, and Wheeler shouted:

"Confound it, hold that fire! D'you hear?"

We waited and watched as the squadrons formed, and the riding-master cursed under his breath.

"Sickenin'," says he, "when you think I taught 'em that. As usual – C Troop can't dress! That's *Havildar* Ram Hyder for you! Look at 'em, like a bloody Paul Jones! Take a line from the right-hand troop, can't you? Rest of 'em look well enough, though, don't they? There now, steady up. That's better, eh?"

The man beyond him said something, and the riding-master laughed. "If they must charge us I'd like to see 'em do it proper, for my own credit's sake, that's all."

I tore my eyes away from that distant mass of men, and glanced round. The babu, flat on the ground, was turning his head to polish his spectacles; Bella Blair had her face hidden, but I noticed her fists were clenched. Wheeler had clapped his hat on, and was saying something to Moore; one of the *bhistis* was crawling on hands and knees along the line, holding a chaggle for the fellows to drink from. Suddenly the distant trumpet sounded again, there was a chorus of cries from across the maidan, a volley of orders, and now the cavalry were moving, at a walk, and then at a trot, and there was a bright flicker along their lines as the sabres came out.

Oh, Christ, I thought, this is the finish. There seemed to be hordes of them, advancing steadily through the wisps of mist, the dust coming up in little clouds behind them, and the crackle of the sharpshooters started up again, the bullets whining overhead.

"Steady, all!" roars Wheeler again. "Wait for the word, remember!"

I had laid by my revolver and had my musket up on the parapet. My mouth was so dry I couldn't swallow – I was remembering those masses of horsemen that had poured down from the Causeway Heights at Balaclava, and how disciplined fire had stopped them in their tracks – but those had been Campbell's Highlanders shooting then, and we had nothing but a straggling line of sick crocks and civilians. They must break over us like a wave, brushing past our feeble volleys—

"Take aim!" yells Wheeler, "make every shot tell, and wait for my command!"

They were coming at the gallop now, perhaps three hundred yards off, and the sabres steady against the shoulders; they were keeping line damned well, and I heard my riding-master muttering:

"Look at 'em come, though! Ain't that a sight? – and ain't they shaping well! Hold 'em in there, *rissaldar*, mind the dressing—"

The thunder of the beating hooves was like surf; there was a sudden yell, and all the points came down, with the black blobs of faces behind them as the riders crouched forward and the whole line burst into the charge. They came sweeping in towards the entrenchment, I gripped my piece convulsively, and Wheeler yelled "Fire!"

The volley crashed out in a billow of smoke – but it didn't stop them. Horses and men went down, and then we were seizing our second muskets and blazing away, and then our third – and still they came, into that hell of smoke and flame, yelling like madmen; Bella Blair was beside me, thrusting a musket into my hand, and hurrying feverishly to reload the others. I fired again, and as the smoke cleared we looked out onto a tangle of fallen beasts and riders, but half of them were still up and tearing in, howling and waving their sabres. I seized my revolver and blasted away; there were three of them surging in towards my position, and I toppled one from the saddle, another went rolling down with his mount shot under him, and the third came hurtling over the entrenchment, with the man on my right slashing at him as he passed.

Behind him pressed the others – white coats, black faces, rearing beasts, putting their horses to the parapet; I was yelling incoherent obscenities, scrabbling up the muskets as fast as they were reloaded, firing into the mass; men were struggling all along the entrenchment, bayonets and swords against sabres, and still the firing crashed out. I heard Bella scream, and then there was a dismounted rider scrambling up the barrier directly before me; I had a vision of glaring eyes in a black face and a sabre upraised to strike, and then he fell back shrieking into the smoke. Behind me Wheeler was roaring, and I was grabbing for another musket, and then they were falling back, thank God, wheeling and riding back into the smoke, and the *bhisti* was at my elbow, thrusting his chaggle at my lips.

"Stand to!" shouts Wheeler, "they're coming again!"

They were re-forming, a bare hundred yards off; the ground between was littered with dead and dying beasts and men. I had barely time to gulp a mouthful of warm, muddy water and seize my musket before they were howling in at us once more, and this time there were pandy infantrymen racing behind them.

"One more volley!" bawls Wheeler. "Hold your fire, there! Aim for the horses! No surrender! Ready, present – fire!"

The whole wall blasted fire, and the charge shook and wavered before it came rushing on again; half a dozen of them were rearing and plunging up to the entrenchment, the sabres were swinging about our heads, and I was rolling away to avoid the smashing hooves of a rider coming in almost on top of me. I scrambled to my feet, and there was a red-coated black devil leaping at me from the parapet; I smashed at him with my musket butt and sent him flying, and then another one was at me with his sabre, lunging. I shrieked as it flew past my head,

and then we had closed, and I was clawing at his face, bearing
him down by sheer weight. His sabre fell, and I plunged for it;
another pandy was rushing past me, musket and bayonet extended, but I got my hand on the fallen hilt, slashing blindly; I
felt a sickening shock on my head, and fell, a dead weight landed
on top of me, and the next thing I knew I was on my hands and
knees, with the earth swimming round me, and Wheeler was
bawling,

"Cease fire! Cease fire! Stretchers, there!" and the noise of
yelling and banging had died away, while the last of the smoke
cleared above the ghastly shambles of the parapet.

There seemed to be dead and dying everywhere. There must
have been at least a dozen pandies sprawled within ten yards of
where I knelt; the ground was sticky with blood. Wheeler
himself was down on one knee, supporting the fat babu, who
was wailing with a shattered leg; the frail civilian was lying
asprawl, his cricket cap gone and his head just a squashed red
mess. One of the pandies stirred, and pulled himself up on one
knee; Wheeler, his arm still round the babu, whipped up his
revolver and fired, and the pandy flopped back in the dust. The
stretcher parties were hurrying up; I looked out over the
parapet, across a maidan littered with figures of men that
crawled or lay still; there were screaming horses trying to rise,
and others that lay dead among the fallen riders. Two hundred
yards off there were men running – the other way, thank God;
farther down the parapet someone sent up a cheer, and it
gradually spread along the entrenchment in a ghastly, croaking
yell. My mouth was too dry, and I was too dazed to cheer – but I
was alive.

Bella Blair was dead. She was lying on her side, her hands
clutched on the stock of a musket whose bayonet was buried in
her body. I heard a moan behind me, and there was the riding-
master, flopped against the parapet, his shirt soaked in blood,
trying to reach for the fallen water-chaggle. I stumbled over to
him, and held it up to his lips; he sucked it, groaning, and then
let his head fall back.

"Beat 'em, did we?" says he, painfully. I could only nod; I

took a gulp at the chaggle myself, and offered him another swig, but he turned his head feebly aside. There was nothing to be done for him; his life was running out of him where he lay.

"Beat 'em," says he again. "Dam' good. Thought . . . they was going to ride . . . clean over us there . . . for a moment." He coughed blood, and his voice trailed away into a whisper. "They shaped well, though . . . didn't they . . . shape well? My Bengalis . . ." He closed his eyes. "I thought they shaped . . . uncommon well . . ."

I looked down the entrenchment. About half the defenders were on their feet at the parapet, I reckoned. In between, the sprawled, silent figures, the groaning, writhing wounded waiting for the stretchers, the tangle of gear and fallen weapons, the bloody rags – and now the pandy guns again, pounding anew at the near-dead wreck of the Cawnpore garrison, with its tattered flag still flapping from the mast. Well, thinks I, they can walk in now, any time they like. There's nothing left to stop 'em.

But they didn't. That last great assault of June twenty-third, which had come within an ace of breaking us, had sickened the pandies. The maidan was strewn with their dead, and although they pounded us with gunfire for another two terrible days, they didn't have the stomach for another frontal attack. If only they'd known it, half the men left on our parapet were too done up with fatigue and starvation to lift a musket, the barrack was choked with more than three hundred wounded and dying, the well was down to stinking ooze, and our remaining flour was so much dust. We couldn't have lasted two minutes against a determined assault – yet why should they bother, when hunger and heat and the steady rate of casualties from bombardment were sure to finish us soon anyway?

Three folk went mad, as I remember, in those forty-eight hours; I only wonder now that we all didn't. In the furnace of the barrack the women and children were too reduced by famine even to cry; even the younger officers seemed to be overcome by the lethargy of approaching certain death. For that, Wheeler now admitted, was all that remained.

"I have sent a last message out to Lawrence," he told us

senior men on the second night. "I have told him that we have nothing left but British spirit, and that cannot last forever. We are like rats in a cage. Our best hope is that the rebels will come in again, and give us a quick end; better that than watch our women and little ones die by inches."

I can still see the gaunt faces in the flickering candlelight round his table; someone gave a little sob, and another swore softly, and after a moment Vibart asked if there was no hope that Lawrence might yet come to our relief.

Wheeler shook his head. "He would come if he could, but even if he marched now he could not reach us in under two days. By then . . . well, you know me, gentlemen. I haven't croaked in fifty years' soldiering, and I'm not croaking now, when I say that short of a miracle it is *all up*. We're in God's hands, so let each one of us make his preparations accordingly."

I was with him there, only my preparations weren't going to be spiritual. I still had my Pathan rig-out stowed away, and I could see that the time was fast approaching when, game ankle or no, Flashy was going to have to take his chance over the wall. It was that or die in this stinking hole, so I left them praying and went to my place on the parapet to think it out; I was in a blue funk at the thought of trying to decamp, but the longer I waited, the harder it might become. I was still wrestling with my fears when someone hove up out of the gloom beside me, and who should it be but East.

"Flashman," says he, "may I have a word with you?"

"If you must," says I. "I'll be obliged if you'll make it a brief one."

"Of course, of course," says he. "I understand. As Sir Hugh said, it is time for each of us to make his own soul; I won't intrude on your meditations a moment longer than I must, I promise. The trouble is . . . my own conscience. I . . . I need your help, old fellow."

"Eh?" I stared at him, trying to make out his face in the dark. "What the deuce—?"

"Please . . . bear with me. I know you're bitter, because you think I abandoned you in Russia . . . left you to die, while I

escaped. Oh, I know it was my duty, and all that, to get to
Raglan . . . but the truth is –'' he broke off and had a gulp to
himself ''– the truth is, I was *glad* to leave you. There – it's out
at last . . . oh, if you knew how it had been tormenting me these
two years past! That weight on my soul – that I abandoned you
in a spirit of hatred and sinful vengeance. No . . . let me finish! I
hated you then . . . because of the way you had treated Valla . . .
when you flung her from that sledge, into the snow! I could
have killed you for it!''

He was in a rare taking, no error; a Rugby conscience pouring
out is a hell of a performance. He wasn't telling me a thing I
hadn't guessed at the time – I know these pious bastards better
than they know themselves, you see.

"I loved her, you see," he went on, talking like an old man with
a hernia. "She meant everything to me . . . and you had cast her
away so . . . brutally. Please, please, hear me out! I'm confessing,
don't you see? And . . . and asking for your forgiveness. It's late in
the day, I know – but, well, it looks as though we haven't much
longer, don't it? So . . . I wanted to tell you . . . and shake your
hand, old school-fellow, and hear from you that my . . . my sin is
forgiven me. If you can find it in your heart, that is." He choked
resoundingly. "I . . . I trust you can."

I've heard some amazing declarations in my time, but this
babbling was extraordinary. It comes of Christian upbringing,
of course, and taking cold baths, all of which implants in the
impressionable mind the notion that repentance can somehow
square the account. At any other time, it would have given me
some malicious amusement to listen to him; even in my dis-
tracted condition, it was interesting enough for me to ask him:

"D'ye mean that if I *hadn't* given you cause to detest me,
you'd have stayed with me, and let Raglan's message go hang?"

"What's that?" says he. "I . . . I don't know what you mean. I
. . . I . . . please, Flashman, you must see my agony of spirit . . .
I'm trying to . . . make you understand. Please – tell me, even
now, what I can do."

"Well," says I, thoughtfully, "you could go and fart in a
bottle and paint it."

"What?" says he, bewildered. "What did you say?"

"I'm trying to indicate that you can take yourself off," says I. "You're a selfish little swine, East. You admit you've behaved like a scoundrel to me, and if that wasn't enough, you have the cheek to waste my time – when I need it for prayer. So go to hell, will you?"

"My God, Flashman . . . you can't mean it! You can't be so hard. It only needs a word! I own I've wronged you, terribly . . . maybe in more ways than I know. Sometimes . . . I've wondered if perhaps you too loved Valla . . . if you did, and placed duty first . . ." He gulped again, and peered at me. "Did you . . . love her, Flashman?"

"About four or five times a week," says I, "but you needn't be jealous; she wasn't nearly as good a ride as her Aunt Sara. You should have tried a steam-bath with that one."

He gave a shocked gasp, and I absolutely heard his teeth chatter. Then: "God, Flashman! Oh . . . oh, you are unspeakable! You are vile! God help you!"

"Unspeakable and vile I may be," says I, "but at least I'm no hypocrite, like you: the last thing you want is for God to help me. You don't want my forgiveness, either; you just want to be able to forgive yourself. Well, you run along and do it, Scud, and thank me for making it easy for you. After what you've heard tonight, your conscience needn't trouble you any longer about having left old Flashy to his fate, what?"

He stumbled off at that, and I was able to resume my own debate about whether it was best to slide out or stay. In the end, my nerve failed me, and I curled up in the lee of the parapet for the night. Thank God I did, for on the next morning Wheeler got his miracle.

THE PRIVATE HISTORY OF
A CAMPAIGN THAT FAILED

Mark Twain

*The American Civil War began in April 1861 after eleven
southern states had seceded from the Union and established
their own Confederate States of America. The causes of
the war were complex, and were as much tied up with the
opposing economic attitudes that the North and South took
to the expansion westward as it was with the issue of the
emancipation of slaves. The war would stretch over four
bloody years and cost the lives of some 618,000 soldiers. I
have selected five stories about the war, three of them by
people who lived through it. Mark Twain, the pseudonym
of Samuel Langhorne Clemens (1835–1910) is best remembered for* The Adventures of Tom Sawyer *(1876)
and* The Adventures of Huckleberry Finn *(1884).
Clemens had served briefly in the Confederate Army
during June 1861 but his division rapidly deserted when
they realized how frightening and dangerous war was.*

*Clemens spent the rest of the war in the west where he
became a journalist. The following story is a lightly
fictionalised account of Clemens' own experiences at the
start of the war.*

You have heard from a great many people who did something in
the war; is it not fair and right that you listen a little moment to
one who started out to do something in it, but didn't? Thousands entered the war, got just a taste of it, and then stepped out
again permanently. These, by their very numbers, are respectable, and are therefore entitled to a sort of voice – not a loud one,
but a modest one; not a boastful one, but an apologetic one.
They ought not to be allowed much space among better people
– people who did something. I grant that; but they ought at least
to be allowed to state why they didn't do anything, and also to
explain the process by which they didn't do anything. Surely
this kind of light must have a sort of value.

Out West there was a good deal of confusion in men's minds
during the first months of the great trouble – a good deal of
unsettledness, of leaning first this way, then that, then the other
way. It was hard for us to get our bearings. I call to mind an
instance of this. I was piloting on the Mississippi when the news
came that South Carolina had gone out of the Union on the 20th
of December, 1860. My pilot mate was a New-Yorker. He was
strong for the Union; so was I. But he would not listen to me
with any patience; my loyalty was smirched, to his eye, because
my father had owned slaves. I said, in palliation of this dark fact,
that I had heard my father say, some years before he died, that
slavery was a great wrong, and that he would free the solitary
negro he then owned if he could think it right to give away the
property of the family when he was so straitened in means. My
mate retorted that a mere impulse was nothing – anybody could
pretend impulse; and went on decrying my Unionism and
libeling my ancestry. A month later the secession atmosphere
had considerably thickened on the Lower Mississippi, and I

became a rebel; so did he. We were together in New Orleans the 26th of January, when Louisiana went out of the Union. He did his full share of the rebel shouting, but was bitterly opposed to letting me do mine. He said that I came of bad stock – of a father who had been willing to set slaves free. In the following summer he was piloting a Federal gunboat and shouting for the Union again, and I was in the Confederate army. I held his note for some borrowed money. He was one of the most upright men I ever knew, but he repudiated that note without hesitation because I was a rebel and the son of a man who owned slaves.

In that summer – of 1861 – the first wash of the wave of war broke upon the shores of Missouri. Our state was invaded by the Union forces. They took possession of St Louis, Jefferson Barracks, and some other points. The Governor, Claib Jackson, issued his proclamation calling out fifty thousand militia to repel the invader.

I was visiting in the small town where my boyhood had been spent – Hannibal, Marion County. Several of us got together in a secret place by night and formed ourselves into a military company. One Tom Lyman, a young fellow of a good deal of spirit but of no military experience, was made captain; I was made second lieutenant. We had no first lieutenant; I do not know why; it was long ago. There were fifteen of us. By the advice of an innocent connected with the organization we called ourselves the Marion Rangers. I do not remember that any one found fault with the name. I did not; I thought it sounded quite well. The young fellow who proposed this title was perhaps a fair sample of the kind of stuff we were made of. He was young, ignorant, good-natured, well-meaning, trivial, full of romance, and given to reading chivalric novels and singing forlorn love-ditties. He had some pathetic little nickel-plated aristocratic instincts, and detested his name, which was Dunlap; detested it, partly because it was nearly as common in that region as Smith, but mainly because it had a plebeian sound to his ear. So he tried to ennoble it by writing it in this way: *d'Unlap*. That contented his eye, but left his ear unsatisfied, for people gave the new name the same old pronunciation – emphasis on the front end of it. He then did the bravest thing that can be imagined – a thing to make one shiver when one remembers how the world is given to resenting shams and affectations; he began to write his name so: *d'Un Lap*. And he waited patiently through the long storm of mud that was flung at this work of art, and he had his reward at last; for he lived to see that name accepted, and the emphasis put where he wanted it by people who had known him all his life, and to whom the tribe of Dunlaps had been as familiar as the rain and the sunshine for forty years. So sure of victory at last is the courage that can wait. He said he had found, by consulting some ancient French chronicles, that the name was rightly and originally written d'Un Lap; and said that if it were translated into English it would mean Peterson: *Lap*, Latin or Greek, he said, for stone or rock, same as the French *pierre*, that is to say, Peter: *d'*, of or from; *un*, a or one; hence, d'Un Lap, of or from a stone or a Peter; that is to say, one who is the son of a stone, the son of a Peter – Peterson. Our militia company were not learned, and the explanation confused them; so they called him Peterson Dunlap. He proved useful to us in his way; he named our camps for us, and he generally struck a name that was "no slouch," as the boys said.

That is one sample of us. Another was Ed Stevens, son of the town jeweler – trim-built, handsome, graceful, neat as a cat; bright, educated, but given over entirely to fun. There was nothing serious in life to him. As far as he was concerned, this military expedition of ours was simply a holiday. I should say that about half of us looked upon it in the same way; not consciously, perhaps, but unconsciously. We did not think; we were not capable of it. As for myself, I was full of unreasoning joy to be done with turning out of bed at midnight and four in the morning for a while; grateful to have a change, new scenes, new occupations, a new interest. In my thoughts that was as far as I went; I did not go into the details; as a rule, one doesn't at twenty-four.

Another sample was Smith, the blacksmith's apprentice. This vast donkey had some pluck, of a slow and sluggish nature, but a soft heart; at one time he would knock a horse down for some impropriety, and at another he would get homesick and cry. However, he had one ultimate credit to his account which some of us hadn't; he stuck to the war, and was killed in battle at last.

Jo Bowers, another sample, was a huge, good-natured, flax-headed lubber; lazy, sentimental, full of harmless brag, a grumbler by nature; an experienced, industrious, ambitious, and often quite picturesque liar, and yet not a successful one, for he had had no intelligent training, but was allowed to come up just any way. This life was serious enough to him, and seldom satisfactory. But he was a good fellow, anyway, and the boys all liked him. He was made orderly sergeant; Stevens was made corporal.

These samples will answer – and they are quite fair ones. Well, this herd of cattle started for the war. What could you expect of them? They did as well as they knew how; but, really, what was justly to be expected of them? Nothing, I should say. That is what they did.

We waited for a dark night, for caution and secrecy were necessary; then, toward midnight, we stole in couples and from various directions to the Griffith place, beyond the town; from that point we set out together on foot. Hannibal lies at the extreme southeastern corner of Marion County, on the Mississippi River; our objective point was the hamlet of New London, ten miles away, in Ralls County.

The first hour was all fun, all idle nonsense and laughter. But that could not be kept up. The steady trudging came to be like work; the play had somehow oozed out of it; the stillness of the woods and the somberness of the night began to throw a depressing influence over the spirits of the boys, and presently the talking died out and each person shut himself up in his own thoughts. During the last half of the second hour nobody said a word.

Now we approached a log farm-house where, according to report, there was a guard of five Union soldiers. Lyman called a halt; and there, in the deep gloom of the overhanging branches, he began to whisper a plan of assault upon that house, which made the gloom more depressing than it was before. It was a crucial moment; we realized, with a cold suddenness, that here was no jest – we were standing face to face with actual war. We were equal to the occasion. In our response there was no hesitation, no indecision: we said that if Lyman wanted to meddle with those soldiers, he could go ahead and do it; but if he waited for us to follow him, he would wait a long time.

Lyman urged, pleaded, tried to shame us, but it had no effect. Our course was plain, our minds were made up: we would flank the farm-house – go out around. And that was what we did.

We struck into the woods and entered upon a rough time, stumbling over roots, getting tangled in vines, and torn by briers. At last we reached an open place in a safe region, and sat down, blown and hot, to cool off and nurse our scratches and bruises. Lyman was annoyed, but the rest of us were cheerful; we had flanked the farm-house, we had made our first military movement, and it was a success; we had nothing to fret about, we were feeling just the other way. Horse-play and laughing began again: the expedition was become a holiday frolic once more.

Then we had two more hours of dull trudging and ultimate silence and depression; then, about dawn, we straggled into New London, soiled, heel-blistered, fagged with our little march, and all of us except Stevens in a sour and raspy humor and privately down on the war. We stacked our shabby old shotguns in Colonel Ralls's barn, and then went in a body and breakfasted with that veteran of the Mexican War. Afterward he took us to a distant meadow, and there in the shade of a tree we listened to an old-fashioned speech from him, full of gunpowder and glory, full of that adjective-piling, mixed metaphor and windy declamation which were regarded as eloquence in that ancient time and that remote region; and then he swore us on the Bible to be faithful to the State of Missouri and drive all invaders from her soil, no matter whence they might come or under what flag they might march. This mixed us considerably, and we could not make out just what service we were embarked in; but Colonel Ralls, the practised politician and phrase-juggler, was not similarly in doubt; he knew quite clearly that he had invested us in the cause of the Southern Confederacy. He closed the solemnities by belting around me the sword which his neighbor, Colonel Brown, had worn at Buena Vista and Molino del Rey; and he accompanied this act with another impressive blast.

Then we formed in line of battle and marched four miles to a shady and pleasant piece of woods on the border of the far-reaching expanses of a flowery prairie. It was an enchanting region for war – our kind of war.

We pierced the forest about half a mile, and took up a strong position, with some low, rocky, and wooded hills behind us, and a purling, limpid creek in front. Straightaway half the command were in swimming and the other half fishing. The ass with the French name gave this position a romantic title, but it was too long, so the boys shortened and simplified it to Camp Ralls.

We occupied an old maple-sugar camp, whose half-rotted troughs were still propped against the trees. A long corn-crib served for sleeping-quarters for the battalion. On our left, half a mile away, were Mason's farm and house; and he was a friend to the cause. Shortly after noon the farmers began to arrive from several directions, with mules and horses for our use, and these they lent us for as long as the war might last, which they judged would be about three months. The animals were of all sizes, all colors, and all breeds. They were mainly young and frisky, and nobody in the command could stay on them long at a time; for we were town boys, and ignorant of horsemanship. The creature that fell to my share was a very small mule, and yet so quick and active that it could throw me without difficulty; and it did this whenever I got on it. Then it would bray – stretching its neck out, laying its ears back, and spreading its jaws till you could see down to its works. It was a disagreeable animal in every way. If I took it by the bridle and tried to lead it off the grounds, it would sit down and brace back, and no one could budge it. However, I was not entirely destitute of military resources, and I did presently manage to spoil this game; for

I had seen many a steamboat aground in my time, and knew a trick or two which even a grounded mule would be obliged to respect. There was a well by the corn-crib; so I substituted thirty fathom of rope for the bridle, and fetched him home with the windlass.

I will anticipate here sufficiently to say that we did learn to ride, after some days' practice, but never well. We could not learn to like our animals; they were not choice ones, and most of them had annoying peculiarities of one kind or another. Stevens's horse would carry him, when he was not noticing, under the huge excrescences which form on the trunks of oak-trees, and wipe him out of the saddle; in this way Stevens got several bad hurts. Sergeant Bowers's horse was very large and tall, with slim, long legs, and looked like a railroad bridge. His size enabled him to reach all about, and as far as he wanted to, with his head; so he was always biting Bowers's legs. On the march, in the sun, Bowers slept a good deal; and as soon as the horse recognized that he was asleep he would reach around and bite him on the leg. His legs were black and blue with bites. This was the only thing that could ever make him swear, but this always did; whenever his horse bit him he always swore, and of course Stevens, who laughed at everything, laughed at this, and would even get into such convulsions over it as to lose his balance and fall off his horse; and then Bowers, already irritated by the pain of the horse-bite, would resent the laughter with hard language, and there would be a quarrel; so that horse made no end of trouble and bad blood in the command.

However, I will get back to where I was – our first afternoon in the sugar-camp. The sugar-troughs came very handy as horse-troughs, and we had plenty of corn to fill them with. I ordered Sergeant Bowers to feed my mule; but he said that if I reckoned he went to war to be a dry-nurse to a mule it wouldn't take me very long to find out my mistake. I believed that this was insubordination, but I was full of uncertainties about everything military, and so I let the thing pass, and went and ordered Smith, the blacksmith's apprentice, to feed the mule; but he merely gave me a large, cold, sarcastic grin, such as an ostensibly seven-year-old horse gives you when you lift his lip and find he is fourteen, and turned his back on me. I then went to the captain, and asked if it were not right and proper and military for me to have an orderly. He said it was, but as there was only one orderly in the corps, it was but right that he himself should have Bowers on his staff. Bowers said he wouldn't serve on anybody's staff; and if anybody thought he could make him, let him try it. So, of course, the thing had to be dropped; there was no other way.

Next, nobody would cook; it was considered a degradation; so we had no dinner. We lazied the rest of the pleasant afternoon away, some dozing under the trees, some smoking cob-pipes and talking sweethearts and war, some playing games. By late suppertime all hands were famished; and to meet the difficulty all hands turned to, on an equal footing, and gathered wood, built fires, and cooked the meal. Afterward everything was smooth for a while; then trouble broke out between the corporal and the sergeant, each claiming to rank the other. Nobody knew which was the higher office; so Lyman had to settle the matter by making the rank of both officers equal. The commander of an ignorant crew like that has many troubles and vexations which probably do not occur in the regular army at all. However, with the song-singing and yarn-spinning around the camp-fire, everything presently became serene again; and by and by we raked the corn down level in one end of the crib, and all went to bed on it, tying a horse to the door, so that he would neigh if any one tried to get in.*

* It was always my impression that that was what the horse was there for, and I knew that it was also the impression of at least one other of the command, for we talked about it at the time, and admired the military ingenuity of the device; but when I was out West, three years ago, I was told by Mr A. G. Fuqua, a member of our company, that the horse was his; that the leaving him tied at the door was a matter of mere forgetfulness, and that to attribute it to intelligent invention was to give him quite too much credit. In support of his position he called my attention to the suggestive fact that the artifice was not employed again. I had not thought of that before.

We had some horsemanship drill every forenoon; then, after-noons, we rode off here and there in squads a few miles, and visited the farmers' girls, and had a youthful good time, and got an honest good dinner or supper, and then home again to camp, happy and content.

For a time life was idly delicious, it was perfect; there was nothing to mar it. Then came some farmers with an alarm one day. They said it was rumored that the enemy were advancing in our direction from over Hyde's prairie. The result was a sharp stir among us, and general consternation. It was a rude awakening from our pleasant trance. The rumor was but a rumor – nothing definite about it; so, in the confusion, we did not know which way to retreat. Lyman was for not retreat-ing at all in these uncertain circumstances; but he found that if he tried to maintain that attitude he would fare badly, for the command were in no humor to put up with insubordination. So he yielded the point and called a council of war – to consist of himself and the three other officers; but the privates made such a fuss about being left out that we had to allow them to remain, for they were already present, and doing the most of the talking too. The question was, which way to retreat; but all were so flurried that nobody seemed to have even a guess to offer. Except Lyman. He explained in a few calm words that, in-asmuch as the enemy were approaching from over Hyde's prairie, our course was simple: all we had to do was not to retreat *toward* him; any other direction would answer our needs perfectly. Everybody saw in a moment how true this was, and how wise: so Lyman got a great many compliments. It was now decided that we should fall back on Mason's farm.

It was after dark by this time, and as we could not know how soon the enemy might arrive, it did not seem best to try to take the horses and things with us; so we only took the guns and ammunition, and started at once. The route was very rough and hilly and rocky, and presently the night grew very black and rain began to fall; so we had a troublesome time of it, struggling and stumbling along in the dark; and soon some person slipped and fell, and then the next person behind stumbled over him and fell, and so did the rest, one after the other; and then Bowers came, with the keg of powder in his arms, while the command were all mixed together, arms and legs, on the muddy slope: and so he fell, of course, with the keg, and this started the whole detachment down the hill in a body, and they landed in the brook at the bottom in a pile, and each that was undermost pulling the hair and scratching and biting those that were on top of him; and those that were being scratched and bitten scratching and biting the rest in their turn, and all saying they would die before they would ever go to war again if they ever got out of this brook this time, and the invader might rot for all they cared, and the country along with him – and all such talk as that, which was dismal to hear and take part in, in such smothered, low voices, and such a grisly dark place and so wet, and the enemy, maybe, coming any moment.

The keg of powder was lost, and the guns, too; so the growling and complaining continued straight along while the brigade pawed around the pasty hillside and slopped around in the brook hunting for these things; consequently we lost considerable time at this; and then we heard a sound, and held our breath and listened, and it seemed to be the enemy coming, though it could have been a cow, for it had a cough like a cow; but we did not wait, but left a couple of guns behind and struck out for Mason's again as briskly as we could scramble along in the dark. But we got lost presently among the rugged little ravines, and wasted a deal of time finding the way again, so it was after nine when we reached Mason's stile at last; then before we could open our mouths to give the countersign several dogs came bounding over the fence, with great riot and noise, and each of them took a soldier by the slack of his trousers and began to back away with him. We could not shoot the dogs without endangering the persons they were attached to; so we had to look on helpless at what was perhaps the most mortifying spectacle of the Civil War. There was light enough, and to spare, for the Masons had now run out on the porch with candles in their hands. The old man and his son came and undid the dogs without difficulty, all but Bowers's; but they couldn't undo his dog, they didn't know his combination; he was of the bull kind, and seemed to be set with a Yale time-lock; but they got him loose at last with some scalding water, of which Bowers got his share and returned thanks. Peterson Dunlap afterward made up a fine name for this engagement, and also for the night march which preceded it, but both have long ago faded out of my memory.

We now went into the house, and they began to ask us a world of questions, whereby it presently came out that we did not know anything concerning who or what we were running from; so the old gentleman made himself very frank, and said we were a curious breed of soldiers, and guessed we could be depended on to end up the war in time, because no government could stand the expense of the shoe-leather we should cost it trying to follow us around. "Marion *Rangers!* good name, b'gosh!" said he. And wanted to know why we hadn't had a picket-guard at the place where the road entered the prairie, and why we hadn't sent out a scouting party to spy out the enemy and bring us an account of his strength, and so on, before jumping up and stampeding out of a strong position upon a mere vague rumor – and so on, and so forth, till he made us all feel shabbier than the dogs had done, not half so enthusiastically welcome. So we went to bed shamed and low-spirited; except Stevens. Soon Stevens began to devise a garment for Bowers which could be made to automatically display his battle-scars to the grateful, or conceal them from the envious, according to his occasions: but Bowers was in no humor for this, so there was a fight, and when it was over Stevens had some battle-scars of his own to think about.

Then we got a little sleep. But after all we had gone through, our activities were not over for the night; for about two o'clock in the morning we heard a shout of warning from down the lane, accompanied by a chorus from all the dogs, and in a moment everybody was up and flying around to find out what the alarm was about. The alarmist was a horseman who gave notice that a detachment of Union soldiers was on its way from Hannibal with orders to capture and hang any bands like ours which it could find, and said we had no time to lose. Farmer Mason was in a flurry this time himself. He hurried us out of the house with all haste, and sent one of his negroes with us to show us where to hide ourselves and our telltale guns among the ravines half a mile away. It was raining heavily.

We struck down the lane, then across some rocky pasture-land which offered good advantages for stumbling; consequently we were down in the mud most of the time, and every time a man went down he blackguarded the war, and the people that started it, and everybody connected with it, and gave himself the master dose of all for being so foolish as to go into it. At last we reached the wooded mouth of a ravine, and there we huddled ourselves under the streaming trees, and sent the negro back home. It was a dismal and heart-breaking time. We were like to be drowned with the rain, deafened with the howling wind and the booming thunder, and blinded by the lightning. It was, indeed, a wild night. The drenching we were getting was misery enough, but a deeper misery still was the reflection that the halter might end us before we were a day older. A death of this shameful sort had not occurred to us as being among the possibilities of war. It took the romance all out of the campaign, and turned our dreams of glory into a repulsive nightmare. As for doubting that so barbarous an order had been given, not one of us did that.

The long night wore itself out at last, and then the negro came to us with the news that the alarm had manifestly been a false one, and that breakfast would soon be ready. Straightway we were light-hearted again, and the world was bright, and life as full of hope and promise as ever – for we were young then. How long ago that was! Twenty-four years.

The mongrel child of philology named the night's refuge Camp Devastation, and no soul objected. The Masons gave us a Missouri country breakfast, in Missourian abundance, and we needed it: hot biscuits; hot "wheat bread," prettily criss-crossed in a lattice pattern on top; hot corn-pone; fried chicken; bacon, coffee, eggs, milk, buttermilk, etc.; and the world may be confidently challenged to furnish the equal of such a breakfast, as it is cooked in the South.

We stayed several days at Mason's; and after all these years
the memory of the dullness, and stillness, and lifelessness of that
slumberous farm-house still oppresses my spirit as with a sense
of the presence of death and mourning. There was nothing to
do, nothing to think about; there was no interest in life. The
male part of the household were away in the fields all day, the
women were busy and out of our sight; there was no sound but
the plaintive wailing of a spinning-wheel, forever moaning out
from some distant room – the most lonesome sound in nature, a
sound steeped and sodden with homesickness and the emptiness
of life. The family went to bed about dark every night, and as we
were not invited to intrude any new customs we naturally
followed theirs. Those nights were a hundred years long to
youths accustomed to being up till twelve. We lay awake and
miserable till that hour every time, and grew old and decrepit
waiting through the still eternities for the clock-strikes. This
was no place for town boys. So at last it was with something very
like joy that we received news that the enemy were on our track
again. With a new birth of the old warrior spirit we sprang to
our places in line of battle and fell back on Camp Ralls.

Captain Lyman had taken a hint from Mason's talk, and he
now gave orders that our camp should be guarded against
surprise by the posting of pickets. I was ordered to place a
picket at the forks of the road in Hyde's prairie. Night shut
down black and threatening. I told Sergeant Bowers to go out to
that place and stay till midnight; and, just as I was expecting, he
said he wouldn't do it. I tried to get others to go, but all refused.
Some excused themselves on account of the weather; but the
rest were frank enough to say they wouldn't go in any kind of
weather. This kind of thing sounds odd now, and impossible,
but there was no surprise in it at the time. On the contrary, it
seemed a perfectly natural thing to do. There were scores of
little camps scattered over Missouri where the same thing was
happening. These camps were composed of young men who
had been born and reared to a sturdy independence, and who
did not know what it meant to be ordered around by Tom,
Dick, and Harry, whom they had known familiarly all their

lives, in the village or on the farm. It is quite within the probabilities that this same thing was happening all over the South. James Redpath recognized the justice of this assumption, and furnished the following instance in support of it. During a short stay in East Tennessee he was in a citizen colonel's tent one day talking, when a big private appeared at the door, and, without salute or other circumlocution, said to the colonel:

"Say, Jim, I'm a-goin' home for a few days."

"What for?"

"Well I hain't b'en there for a right smart while, and I'd like to see how things is comin' on."

"How long are you going to be gone?"

"'Bout two weeks."

"Well, don't be gone longer than that; and get back sooner if you can."

That was all, and the citizen officer resumed his conversation where the private had broken it off. This was in the first months of the war, of course. The camps in our part of Missouri were under Brigadier-General Thomas H. Harris. He was a townsman of ours, a first-rate fellow, and well liked; but we had all familiarly known him as the sole and modest-salaried operator in our telegraph-office, where he had to send about one despatch a week in ordinary times, and two when there was a rush of business; consequently, when he appeared in our midst one day, on the wing, and delivered a military command of some sort, in a large military fashion, nobody was surprised at the response which he got from the assembled soldiery:

"Oh, now, what'll you take to *don't*, Tom Harris?"

It was quite the natural thing. One might justly imagine that we were hopeless material for war. And so we seemed, in our ignorant state; but there were those among us who afterward learned the grim trade; learned to obey like machines; became valuable soldiers; fought all through the war, and came out at the end with excellent records. One of the very boys who refused to go out on duty that night, and called me an ass for thinking he would expose himself to danger in such a foolhardy way, had become distinguished for intrepidity before he was a year older.

I did secure my picket that night – not by authority, but by diplomacy. I got Bowers to go by agreeing to exchange ranks with him for the time being, and go along and stand the watch with him as his subordinate. We stayed out there a couple of dreary hours in the pitchy darkness and the rain, with nothing to modify the dreariness but Bowers's monotonous growlings at the war and the weather; then we began to nod, and presently found it next to impossible to stay in the saddle; so we gave up the tedious job, and went back to the camp without waiting for the relief guard. We rode into camp without interruption or objection from anybody, and the enemy could have done the same, for there were no sentries. Everybody was asleep; at midnight there was nobody to send out another picket, so none was sent. We never tried to establish a watch at night again, as far as I remember, but we generally kept a picket out in the daytime.

In that camp the whole command slept on the corn in the big corn-crib: and there was usually a general row before morning, for the place was full of rats, and they would scramble over the boys' bodies and faces, annoying and irritating everybody; and now and then they would bite some one's toe, and the person who owned the toe would start up and magnify his English and begin to throw corn in the dark. The ears were half as heavy as bricks, and when they struck they hurt. The persons struck would respond, and inside of five minutes every man would be locked in a death-grip with his neighbor. There was a grievous deal of blood shed in the corn-crib, but this was all that was spilt while I was in the war. No, that is not quite true. But for one circumstance it would have been all. I will come to that now.

Our scares were frequent. Every few days rumors would come that the enemy were approaching. In these cases we always fell back on some other camp of ours; we never stayed where we were. But the rumors always turned out to be false; so at last even we began to grow indifferent to them. One night a negro was sent to our corn-crib with the same old warning: the enemy was hovering in our neighborhood. We all said let him hover. We resolved to stay still and be comfortable. It was a fine warlike resolution, and no doubt we all felt the stir of it in our veins – for a moment. We had been having a very jolly time, that was full of horse-play and school-boy hilarity; but that cooled down now, and presently the fast-waning fire of forced jokes and forced laughs died out altogether, and the company became silent. Silent and nervous. And soon uneasy – worried – apprehensive. We had said we would stay, and we were committed. We could have been persuaded to go, but there was nobody brave enough to suggest it. An almost noiseless movement presently began in the dark by a general but unvoiced impulse. When the movement was completed each man knew that he was not the only person who had crept to the front wall and had his eye at a crack between the logs. No, we were all there; all there with our hearts in our throats, and staring out toward the sugar-troughs where the forest footpath came through. It was late, and there was a deep woodsy stillness everywhere. There was a veiled moonlight, which was only just strong enough to enable us to mark the general shape of objects. Presently a muffled sound caught our ears, and we recognized it as the hoof-beats of a horse or horses. And right away a figure appeared in the forest path; it could have been made of smoke, its mass had so little sharpness of outline. It was a man on horseback, and it seemed to me that there were others behind him. I got hold of a gun in the dark, and pushed it through a crack between the logs, hardly knowing what I was doing, I was so dazed with fright. Somebody said "Fire!" I pulled the trigger. I seemed to see a hundred flashes and hear a hundred reports; then I saw the man fall down out of the saddle. My first feeling was of surprised gratification; my first impulse was an apprentice-sportsman's impulse to run and pick up his game. Somebody said, hardly audibly, "Good – we've got him! – wait for the rest." But the rest did not come. We waited – listened – still no more came. There was not a sound, not the whisper of a leaf: just perfect stillness; an uncanny kind of stillness, which was all the more uncanny on account of the damp, earthy, late-night smells now rising and pervading it. Then, wondering, we crept stealthily out, and approached the man. When we got to him the moon revealed him distinctly. He was lying on his back, with his arms abroad; his mouth was open and his chest heaving with long gasps, and his white shirt-front was all splashed with blood. The thought shot through me that I was a murderer; that I had killed a man – a man who had never done me any harm. That was the coldest sensation that ever went through my marrow. I was down by him in a moment, helplessly stroking his forehead; and I would have given anything then – my own life freely – to make him again what he had been five minutes before. And all the boys seemed to be feeling in the same way; they hung over him, full of pitying interest, and tried all they could to help him, and said all sorts of regretful things. They had forgotten all about the enemy; they thought only of this one forlorn unit of the foe. Once my imagination persuaded me that the dying man gave me a reproachful look out of his shadowy eyes, and it seemed to me that I could rather he had stabbed me than done that. He muttered and mumbled like a dreamer in his sleep about his wife and his child; and I thought with a new despair, "This thing that I have done does not end with him; it falls upon *them* too, and they never did me any harm, any more than he."

In a little while the man was dead. He was killed in war; killed in fair and legitimate war; killed in battle, as you may say; and yet he was as sincerely mourned by the opposing force as if he had been their brother. The boys stood there a half-hour sorrowing over him, and recalling the details of the tragedy, and wondering who he might be, and if he were a spy, and saying that if it were to do over again they would not hurt him unless he attacked them first. It soon came out that mine was not the only shot fired; there were five others – a division of the guilt which was a great relief to me, since it in some degree lightened and diminished the burden I was carrying. There were six shots fired at once; but I was not in my right mind at the time, and my heated imagination had magnified my one shot into a volley.

The man was not in uniform, and was not armed. He was a stranger in the country; that was all we ever found out about him. The thought of him got to preying upon me every night; I could not get rid of it. I could not drive it away, the taking of that unoffending life seemed such a wanton thing. And it seemed an epitome of war; that all war must be just that – the killing of strangers against whom you feel no personal animosity; strangers whom, in other circumstances, you would help if you found them in trouble, and who would help you if you needed it. My campaign was spoiled. It seemed to me that I was not rightly equipped for this awful business; that war was intended for men, and I for a child's nurse. I resolved to retire from this avocation of sham soldiership while I could save some remnant of my self-respect. These morbid thoughts clung to me against reason; for at bottom I did not believe I had touched that man. The law of probabilities decreed me guiltless of his blood; for in all my small experience with guns I had never hit anything I had tried to hit, and I knew I had done my best to hit him. Yet there was no solace in the thought. Against a diseased imagination demonstration goes for nothing.

The rest of my war experience was of a piece with what I have already told of it. We kept monotonously falling back upon one camp or another, and eating up the farmers and their families. They ought to have shot us; on the contrary, they were as hospitably kind and courteous to us as if we had deserved it. In one of these camps we found Ab Grimes, an Upper Mississippi pilot, who afterward became famous as a dare-devil rebel spy, whose career bristled with desperate adventures. The look and style of his comrades suggested that they had not come into the war to play, and their deeds made good the conjecture later. They were fine horsemen and good revolver shots; but their favorite arm was the lasso. Each had one at his pommel, and could snatch a man out of the saddle with it every time, on a full gallop, at any reasonable distance.

In another camp the chief was a fierce and profane old blacksmith of sixty, and he had furnished his twenty recruits with gigantic home-made bowie-knives, to be swung with two hands, like the *machetes* of the Isthmus. It was a grisly spectacle to see that earnest band practising their murderous cuts and slashes under the eye of that remorseless old fanatic.

The last camp which we fell back upon was in a hollow near the village of Florida, where I was born – in Monroe County. Here we were warned one day that a Union colonel was sweeping down on us with a whole regiment at his heel. This looked decidedly serious. Our boys went apart and consulted; then we went back and told the other companies present that the war was a disappointment to us, and we were going to disband. They were getting ready themselves to fall back on some place or other, and we were only waiting for General Tom Harris, who expected to arrive at any moment; so they tried to persuade us to wait a little while, but the majority of us said no, we were accustomed to falling back, and didn't need any of Tom Harris's help; we could get along perfectly well without him – and save time, too. So about half of our fifteen, including myself, mounted and left on the instant; the others yielded to persuasion and stayed – stayed through the war.

An hour later we met General Harris on the road, with two or three people in his company – his staff, probably, but we could not tell; none of them were in uniform; uniforms had not come into vogue among us yet. Harris ordered us back; but we told him there was a Union colonel coming with a whole regiment in his wake, and it looked as if there was going to be a disturbance; so we had concluded to go home. He raged a little, but it was of no use; our minds were made up. We had done our share; had killed one man, exterminated one army, such as it was; let him go and kill the rest, and that would end the war. I did not see that brisk young general again until last year; then he was wearing white hair and whiskers.

In time I came to know that Union colonel whose coming frightened me out of the war and crippled the Southern cause to that extent – General Grant. I came within a few hours of seeing him when he was as unknown as I was myself; at a time when anybody could have said, "Grant? – Ulysses S. Grant? I do not remember hearing the name before." It seems difficult to realize that there was once a time when such a remark could be rationally made; but there *was*, and I was within a few miles of the place and the occasion, too, though proceeding in the other direction.

The thoughtful will not throw this war paper of mine lightly aside as being valueless. It has this value: it is a not unfair picture of what went on in many and many a militia camp in the first months of the rebellion, when the green recruits were without discipline, without the steadying and heartening influence of trained leaders: when all their circumstances were new and strange, and charged with exaggerated terrors, and before the invaluable experience of actual collision in the field had turned them from rabbits into soldiers. If this side of the picture of that early day has not before been put into history, then history has been to that degree incomplete, for it had and has its rightful place there. There was more Bull Run material scattered through the early camps of this country than exhibited itself at Bull Run. And yet it learned its trade presently, and helped to fight the great battles later. I could have become a soldier myself if I had waited. I had got part of it learned; I knew more about retreating than the man that invented retreating.

THE LITTLE REGIMENT

Stephen Crane

Stephen Crane (1871–1900), who died tragically young of tuberculosis, established a formidable reputation with his second novel, The Red Badge of Courage *(1895). The novel explores the dilemmas faced by a young soldier in the Civil War who contrasts the heroic ideals of war with the frightening and violent reality. Even though Crane had been born six years after the war ended he succeeded in capturing the atmosphere and above all the psychological drama of the conflict. He wrote several short stories also set during the war of which "The Little Regiment" (McClure's, June 1896) is one of the best.*

I

The fog made the clothes of the men of the column in the roadway seem of a luminous quality. It imparted to the heavy infantry overcoats a new colour, a kind of blue which was so pale that a regiment might have been merely a long, low shadow in the mist. However, a muttering, one part grumble, three parts joke, hovered in the air above the thick ranks, and blended in an undertoned roar, which was the voice of the column.

The town on the southern shore of the little river loomed spectrally, a faint etching upon the gray cloud-masses which were shifting with oily languor. A long row of guns upon the northern bank had been pitiless in their hatred, but a little battered belfry could be dimly seen still pointing with invincible resolution toward the heavens.

The enclouded air vibrated with noises made by hidden colossal things. The infantry tramplings, the heavy rumbling of the artillery, made the earth speak of gigantic preparation. Guns on distant heights thundered from time to time with sudden, nervous roar, as if unable to endure in silence a knowledge of hostile troops massing, other guns going to position. These sounds, near and remote, defined an immense battle-ground, described the tremendous width of the stage of the prospective drama. The voices of the guns, slightly casual, unexcited in their challenges and warnings, could not destroy the unutterable eloquence of the word in the air, a meaning of impending struggle which made the breath halt at the lips.

The column in the roadway was ankle-deep in mud. The men swore piously at the rain which drizzled upon them, compelling them to stand always very erect in fear of the drops that would sweep in under their coat-collars. The fog was as cold as wet cloths. The men stuffed their hands deep in their pockets, and huddled their muskets in their arms. The machinery of orders had rooted these soldiers deeply into the mud precisely as almighty nature roots mullein stalks.

They listened and speculated when a tumult of fighting came from the dim town across the river. When the noise lulled for a time they resumed their descriptions of the mud and graphically exaggerated the number of hours they had been kept waiting. The general commanding their division rode along the ranks, and they cheered admiringly, affectionately, crying out to him gleeful prophecies of the coming battle. Each man scanned him with a peculiarly keen personal interest, and afterward spoke of him with unquestioning devotion and confidence, narrating anecdotes which were mainly untrue.

When the jokers lifted the shrill voices which invariably belonged to them, flinging witticisms at their comrades, a loud laugh would sweep from rank to rank, and soldiers who had not heard would lean forward and demand repetition. When were borne past them some wounded men with gray and blood-smeared faces, and eyes that rolled in that helpless beseeching for assistance from the sky which comes with supreme pain, the soldiers in the mud watched intently, and from time to time asked of the bearers an account of the affair. Frequently they bragged of their corps, their division, their brigade, their regiment. Anon they referred to the mud and the cold drizzle. Upon this threshold of a wild scene of death they, in short, defied the proportion of events with that splendour of heedlessness which belongs only to veterans.

"Like a lot of wooden soldiers," swore Billie Dempster, moving his feet in the thick mass, and casting a vindictive glance indefinitely; "standing in the mud for a hundred years."

"Oh, shut up!" murmured his brother Dan. The manner of his words implied that this fraternal voice near him was an indescribable bore.

"Why should I shut up?" demanded Billie.

"Because you're a fool," cried Dan, taking no time to debate it; "the biggest fool in the regiment."

There was but one man between them, and he was habituated. These insults from brother to brother had swept across his chest, flown past his face, many times during two long campaigns. Upon this occasion he simply grinned first at one, then at the other.

The way of these brothers was not an unknown topic in regimental gossip. They had enlisted simultaneously, with each sneering loudly at the other for doing it. They left their little town, and went forward with the flag, exchanging protestations of undying suspicion. In the camp life they so openly despised each other that, when entertaining quarrels were lacking, their companions often contrived situations calculated to bring forth display of this fraternal dislike.

Both were large-limbed, strong young men, and often fought with friends in camp unless one was near to interfere with the other. This latter happened rather frequently, because Dan, preposterously willing for any manner of combat, had a very great horror of seeing Billie in a fight; and Billie, almost odiously ready himself, simply refused to see Dan stripped to his shirt and with his fists aloft. This sat queerly upon them, and made them the objects of plots.

When Dan jumped through a ring of eager soldiers and dragged forth his raving brother by the arm, a thing often predicted would almost come to pass. When Billie performed the same office for Dan, the prediction would again miss fulfilment by an inch. But indeed they never fought together, although they were perpetually upon the verge.

They expressed longing for such conflict. As a matter of truth, they had at one time made full arrangement for it, but even with the encouragement and interest of half of the regiment they somehow failed to achieve collision.

If Dan became a victim of police duty, no jeering was so destructive to the feelings as Billie's comment. If Billie got a call to appear at the headquarters, none would so genially prophesy his complete undoing as Dan. Small misfortunes to one were, in truth, invariably greeted with hilarity by the other, who seemed to see in them great re-enforcement of his opinion.

As soldiers, they expressed each for each a scorn intense and blasting. After a certain battle, Billie was promoted to corporal. When Dan was told of it, he seemed smitten dumb with astonishment and patriotic indignation. He stared in silence, while the dark blood rushed to Billie's forehead, and he shifted his weight from foot to foot. Dan at last found his tongue, and said: "Well, I'm durned!" If he had heard that an army mule had been appointed to the post of corps commander, his tone could not have had more derision in it. Afterward, he adopted a fervid insubordination, an almost religious reluctance to obey the new corporal's orders, which came near to developing the desired strife.

It is here finally to be recorded also that Dan, most ferociously profane in speech, very rarely swore in the presence of his brother; and that Billie, whose oaths came from his lips with the grace of falling pebbles, was seldom known to express himself in this manner when near his brother Dan.

At last the afternoon contained a suggestion of evening. Metallic cries rang suddenly from end to end of the column. They inspired at once a quick, business-like adjustment. The long thing stirred in the mud. The men had hushed, and were looking across the river. A moment later the shadowy mass of pale blue figures was moving steadily toward the stream. There could be heard from the town a clash of swift fighting and cheering. The noise of the shooting coming through the heavy air had its sharpness taken from it, and sounded in thuds.

There was a halt upon the bank above the pontoons. When the column went winding down the incline, and streamed out upon the bridge, the fog had faded to a great degree, and in the clearer dusk the guns on a distant ridge were enabled to perceive the crossing. The long whirling outcries of the shells came into the air above the men. An occasional solid shot struck the surface of the river, and dashed into view a sudden vertical jet. The distance was subtly illuminated by the lightning from the deep-booming guns. One by one the batteries on the northern shore aroused, the innumerable guns bellowing in angry oration at the distant ridge. The rolling thunder crashed and reverberated as a wild surf sounds on a still night, and to this music the column marched across the pontoons.

The waters of the grim river curled away in a smile from the ends of the great boats, and slid swiftly beneath the planking. The dark, riddled walls of the town upreared before the troops, and from a region hidden by these hammered and tumbled houses came incessantly the yells and firings of a prolonged and close skirmish.

When Dan had called his brother a fool, his voice had been so decisive, so brightly assured, that many men had laughed, considering it to be great humour under the circumstances. The incident happened to rankle deep in Billie. It was not any strange thing that his brother had called him a fool. In fact, he often called him a fool with exactly the same amount of cheerful and prompt conviction, and before large audiences, too. Billie wondered in his own mind why he took such profound offence in this case; but, at any rate, as he slid down the bank and on to the bridge with his regiment, he was searching his knowledge for something that would pierce Dan's blithesome spirit. But he could contrive nothing at this time, and his impotency made the glance which he was once able to give his brother still more malignant.

The guns far and near were roaring a fearful and grand introduction for this column which was marching upon the stage of death. Billie felt it, but only in a numb way. His heart was cased in that curious dissonant metal which covers a man's emotions at such times. The terrible voices from the hills told him that in this wide conflict his life was an insignificant fact, and that his death would be an insignificant fact. They portended the whirlwind to which he would be as necessary as a butterfly's waved wing. The solemnity, the sadness of it came near enough to make him wonder why he was neither solemn nor sad. When his mind vaguely adjusted events according to their importance to him, it appeared that the uppermost thing was the fact that upon the eve of battle, and before many comrades, his brother had called him a fool.

Dan was in a particularly happy mood. "Hurray! Look at 'em shoot," he said, when the long witches' croon of the shells came into the air. It enraged Billie when he felt the little thorn in him, and saw at the same time that his brother had completely forgotten it.

The column went from the bridge into more mud. At this southern end there was a chaos of hoarse directions and commands. Darkness was coming upon the earth, and regiments were being hurried up the slippery bank. As Billie floundered in the black mud, amid the swearing, sliding crowd, he suddenly resolved that, in the absence of other means of hurting Dan, he would avoid looking at him, refrain from speaking to him, pay absolutely no heed to his existence; and this done skilfully would, he imagined, soon reduce his brother to a poignant sensitiveness.

At the top of the bank the column again halted and rearranged itself, as a man after a climb rearranges his clothing. Presently the great steel-backed brigade, an infinitely graceful thing in the rhythm and ease of its veteran movement, swung up a little narrow, slanting street.

Evening had come so swiftly that the fighting on the remote borders of the town was indicated by thin flashes of flame. Some building was on fire, and its reflection upon the clouds was an oval of delicate pink.

II

All demeanour of rural serenity had been wrenched violently from the little town by the guns and by the waves of men which had surged through it. The hand of war laid upon this village had in an instant changed it to a thing of remnants. It resembled the place of a monstrous shaking of the earth itself. The windows, now mere unsightly holes, made the tumbled and blackened dwellings seem skeletons. Doors lay splintered to fragments. Chimneys had flung their bricks everywhere. The artillery fire had not neglected the rows of gentle shade-trees which had lined the streets. Branches and heavy trunks cluttered the mud in driftwood tangles, while a few shattered forms had contrived to remain dejectedly, mournfully upright. They expressed an innocence, a helplessness, which perforce created a pity for their happening into this cauldron of battle. Furthermore, there was under foot a vast collection of odd things reminiscent of the charge, the fight, the retreat. There were boxes and barrels filled with earth, behind which riflemen had lain snugly, and in these little trenches were the dead in blue with the dead in gray, the poses eloquent of the struggles for possession of the town until the history of the whole conflict was written plainly in the streets.

And yet the spirit of this little city, its quaint individuality, poised in the air above the ruins, defying the guns, the sweeping volleys; holding in contempt those avaricious blazes which had attacked many dwellings. The hard earthen sidewalks proclaimed the games that had been played there during long lazy days, in the careful shadows of the trees. "General Merchandise," in faint letters upon a long board, had to be read with a slanted glance, for the sign dangled by one end; but the porch of the old store was a palpable legend of wide-hatted men, smoking.

This subtle essence, this soul of the life that had been, brushed like invisible wings the thoughts of the men in the swift columns that came up from the river.

In the darkness a loud and endless humming arose from the great blue crowds bivouacked in the streets. From time to time a sharp spatter of firing from far picket lines entered this bass chorus. The smell from the smouldering ruins floated on the cold night breeze.

Dan, seated ruefully upon the doorstep of a shot-pierced house, was proclaiming the campaign badly managed. Orders had been issued forbidding camp-fires.

Suddenly he ceased his oration, and scanning the group of his comrades, said: "Where's Billie? Do you know?"

"Gone on picket."

"Get out! Has he?" said Dan. "No business to go on picket. Why don't some of them other corporals take their turn?"

A bearded private was smoking his pipe of confiscated tobacco, seated comfortably upon a horse-hair trunk which he had dragged from the house. He observed: "*Was* his turn."

"No such thing," cried Dan. He and the man on the horse-hair trunk held discussion in which Dan stoutly maintained that if his brother had been sent on picket it was an injustice. He ceased his argument when another soldier, upon whose arms could faintly be seen the two stripes of a corporal, entered the circle. "Humph," said Dan, "where you been?"

The corporal made no answer. Presently Dan said: "Billie, where you been?"

His brother did not seem to hear these inquiries. He glanced at the house which towered above them, and remarked casually to the man on the horse-hair trunk: "Funny, ain't it? After the pelting this town got, you'd think there wouldn't be one brick left on another."

"Oh," said Dan, glowering at his brother's back. "Getting mighty smart, ain't you?"

The absence of camp-fires allowed the evening to make apparent its quality of faint silver light in which the blue clothes of the throng became black, and the faces became white expanses, void of expression. There was considerable excitement a short distance from the group around the doorstep. A soldier had chanced upon a hoop-skirt, and arrayed in it he was performing a dance amid the applause of his companions. Billie and a greater part of the men immediately poured over there to witness the exhibition.

"What's the matter with Billie?" demanded Dan of the man upon the horse-hair trunk.

"How do I know?" rejoined the other in mild resentment. He arose and walked away. When he returned he said briefly, in a weather-wise tone, that it would rain during the night.

Dan took a seat upon one end of the horse-hair trunk. He was facing the crowd around the dancer, which in its hilarity swung this way and that way. At times he imagined that he could recognise his brother's face.

He and the man on the other end of the trunk thoughtfully talked of the army's position. To their minds, infantry and artillery were in a most precarious jumble in the streets of the town; but they did not grow nervous over it, for they were used to having the army appear in a precarious jumble to their minds. They had learned to accept such puzzling situations as a consequence of their position in the ranks, and were now usually in possession of a simple but perfectly immovable faith that somebody understood the jumble. Even if they had been convinced that the army was a headless monster, they would merely have nodded with the veteran's singular cynicism. It was none of their business as soldiers. Their duty was to grab sleep and food when occasion permitted, and cheerfully fight wherever their feet were planted until more orders came. This was a task sufficiently absorbing.

They spoke of other corps, and this talk being confidential, their voices dropped to tones of awe. "The Ninth" – "The First" – "The Fifth" – "The Sixth" – "The Third" – the simple numerals rang with eloquence, each having a meaning which was to float through many years as no intangible arithmetical mist, but as pregnant with individuality as the names of cities.

Of their own corps they spoke with a deep veneration, an idolatry, a supreme confidence which apparently would not blanch to see it match against everything.

It was as if their respect for other corps was due partly to a wonder that organizations not blessed with their own famous numeral could take such an interest in war. They could prove that their division was the best in the corps, and that their brigade was the best in the division. And their regiment – it was plain that no fortune of life was equal to the chance which caused a man to be born, so to speak, into this command, the keystone of the defending arch.

At times Dan covered with insults the character of a vague, unnamed general to whose petulance and busy-body spirit he ascribed the order which made hot coffee impossible.

Dan said that victory was certain in the coming battle. The other man seemed rather dubious. He remarked upon the fortified line of hills, which had impressed him even from the other side of the river. "Shucks," said Dan. "Why, we—" He pictured a splendid overflowing of these hills by the sea of men in blue. During the period of this conversation Dan's glance searched the merry throng about the dancer. Above the babble of voices in the street a far-away thunder could sometimes be heard – evidently from the very edge of the horizon – the boom-boom of restless guns.

III

Ultimately the night deepened to the tone of black velvet. The outlines of the fireless camp were like the faint drawings upon ancient tapestry. The glint of a rifle, the shine of a button, might have been of threads of silver and gold sewn upon the fabric of the night. There was little presented to the vision, but to a sense more subtle there was discernible in the atmosphere something like a pulse; a mystic beating which would have told a stranger of the presence of a giant thing – the slumbering mass of regiments and batteries.

With fires forbidden, the floor of a dry old kitchen was thought to be a good exchange for the cold earth of December, even if a shell had exploded in it and knocked it so out of shape that when a man lay curled in his blanket his last waking thought was likely to be of the wall that bellied out above him as if strongly anxious to topple upon the score of soldiers.

Billie looked at the bricks ever about to descend in a shower upon his face, listened to the industrious pickets plying their rifles on the border of the town, imagined some measure of the din of the coming battle, thought of Dan and Dan's chagrin, and rolling over in his blanket went to sleep with satisfaction.

At an unknown hour he was aroused by the creaking of boards. Lifting himself upon his elbow, he saw a sergeant prowling among the sleeping forms. The sergeant carried a candle in an old brass candle-stick. He would have resembled some old farmer on an unusual midnight tour if it were not for the significance of his gleaming buttons and striped sleeves.

Billie blinked stupidly at the light until his mind returned from the journeys of slumber. The sergeant stooped among the unconscious soldiers, holding the candle close, and peering into each face.

"Hello, Haines," said Billie. "Relief?"

"Hello, Billie," said the sergeant. "Special duty."

"Dan got to go?"

"Jameson, Hunter, McCormack, D. Dempster. Yes. Where is he?"

"Over there by the winder," said Billie, gesturing. "What is it for, Haines?"

"You don't think I know, do you?" demanded the sergeant. He began to pipe sharply but cheerily at men upon the floor. "Come, Mac, get up here. Here's a special for you. Wake up, Jameson. Come along, Dannie, me boy."

Each man at once took his call to duty as a personal affront. They pulled themselves out of their blankets, rubbed their eyes, and swore at whoever was responsible. "Them's orders," cried the sergeant. "Come! Get out of here." An undetailed head with dishevelled hair thrust out from a blanket, and a sleepy voice said: "Shut up, Haines, and go home."

When the detail clanked out of the kitchen, all but one of the remaining men seemed to be again asleep. Billie, leaning on his elbow, was gazing into darkness. When the footsteps died to silence, he curled himself into his blanket.

At the first cool lavender lights of daybreak he aroused again, and scanned his recumbent companions. Seeing a wakeful one he asked: "Is Dan back yet?"

The man said: "Hain't seen 'im."

Billie put both hands behind his head, and scowled into the air. "Can't see the use of these cussed details in the nighttime," he muttered in his most unreasonable tones. "Darn nuisances. Why can't they—" He grumbled at length and graphically.

When Dan entered with the squad, however, Billie was convincingly asleep.

IV

The regiment trotted in double time along the street, and the colonel seemed to quarrel over the right of way with many artillery officers. Batteries were waiting in the mud, and the men of them, exasperated by the bustle of this ambitious infantry, shook their fists from saddle and caisson, exchanging all manner of taunts and jests. The slanted guns continued to look reflectively at the ground.

On the outskirts of the crumbled town a fringe of blue figures were firing into the fog. The regiment swung out into skirmish lines, and the fringe of blue figures departed, turning their backs and going joyfully around the flank.

The bullets began a low moan off toward a ridge which loomed faintly in the heavy mist. When the swift crescendo had reached its climax, the missiles zipped just overhead, as if piercing an invisible curtain. A battery on the hill was crashing with such tumult that it was as if the guns had quarrelled and had fallen pell-mell and snarling upon each other. The shells howled on their journey toward the town. From short range distance there came a spatter of musketry, sweeping along an invisible line and making faint sheets of orange light.

Some in the new skirmish lines were beginning to fire at various shadows discerned in the vapour, forms of men suddenly revealed by some humour of the laggard masses of clouds. The crackle of musketry began to dominate the purring of the hostile bullets. Dan, in the front rank, held his rifle poised, and looked into the fog keenly, coldly, with the air of a sportsman. His nerves were so steady that it was as if they had been drawn from his body, leaving him merely a muscular machine; but his numb heart was somehow beating to the pealing march of the fight.

The waving skirmish line went backward and forward, ran this way and that way. Men got lost in the fog, and men were found again. Once they got too close to the formidable ridge, and the thing burst out as if repulsing a general attack. Once another blue regiment was apprehended on the very edge of firing into them. Once a friendly battery began an elaborate and scientific process of extermination. Always as busy as brokers, the men slid here and there over the plain, fighting their foes, escaping from their friends, leaving a history of many movements in the wet yellow turf, cursing the atmosphere, blazing away every time they could identify the enemy.

In one mystic changing of the fog, as if the fingers of spirits were drawing aside these draperies, a small group of the gray skirmishers, silent, statuesque, were suddenly disclosed to Dan and those about him. So vivid and near were they that there was something uncanny in the revelation.

There might have been a second of mutual staring. Then each rifle in each group was at the shoulder. As Dan's glance flashed along the barrel of his weapon, the figure of a man suddenly loomed as if the musket had been a telescope. The short black beard, the slouch hat, the pose of the man as he sighted to shoot, made a quick picture in Dan's mind. The same moment, it would seem, he pulled his own trigger, and the man, smitten, lurched forward, while his exploding rifle made a slanting crimson streak in the air, and the slouch hat fell before the body. The billows of the fog, governed by singular impulses, rolled between.

"You got that feller sure enough," said a comrade to Dan. Dan looked at him absent-mindedly.

V

When the next morning calmly displayed another fog, the men of the regiment exchanged eloquent comments; but they did not abuse it at length, because the streets of the town now contained enough galloping aides to make three troops of cavalry, and they knew that they had come to the verge of the great fight.

Dan conversed with the man who had once possessed a horsehair trunk; but they did not mention the line of hills which had furnished them in more careless moments with an agreeable topic. They avoided it now as condemned men do the subject of death, and yet the thought of it stayed in their eyes as they looked at each other and talked gravely of other things.

The expectant regiment heaved a long sigh of relief when the sharp call: "Fall in," repeated indefinitely, arose in the streets. It was inevitable that a bloody battle was to be fought, and they wanted to get it off their minds. They were, however, doomed again to spend a long period planted firmly in the mud. They craned their necks, and wondered where some of the other regiments were going.

At last the mists rolled carelessly away. Nature made at this time all provisions to enable foes to see each other, and immediately the roar of guns resounded from every hill. The endless cracking of the skirmishers swelled to rolling crashes of musketry. Shells screamed with panther-like noises at the houses. Dan looked at the man of the horse-hair trunk, and the man said: "Well, here she comes!"

The tenor voices of younger officers and the deep and hoarse voices of the older ones rang in the streets. These cries pricked like spurs. The masses of men vibrated from the suddenness with which they were plunged into the situation of troops about to fight. That the orders were long-expected did not concern the emotion.

Simultaneous movement was imparted to all these thick bodies of men and horses that lay in the town. Regiment after regiment swung rapidly into the streets that faced the sinister ridge.

This exodus was theatrical. The little sober-hued village had been like the cloak which disguises the king of drama. It was now put aside, and an army, splendid thing of steel and blue, stood forth in the sunlight.

Even the soldiers in the heavy columns drew deep breaths at the sight, more majestic than they had dreamed. The heights of the enemy's position were crowded with men who resembled people come to witness some mighty pageant. But as the column moved steadily to their positions, the guns, matter-of-fact warriors, doubled their number, and shells burst with red thrilling tumult on the crowded plain. One came into the ranks of the regiment, and after the smoke and the wrath of it had faded, leaving motionless figures, everyone stormed according to the limits of his vocabulary, for veterans detest being killed when they are not busy.

The regiment sometimes looked sideways at its brigade companions composed of men who had never been in battle; but no frozen blood could withstand the heat of the splendour of this army before the eyes on the plain, these lines so long that the flanks were little streaks, this mass of men of one intention. The recruits carried themselves heedlessly. At the rear was an idle battery, and three artillery men in a foolish row on a caisson nudged each other and grinned at the recruits. "You'll catch it pretty soon," they called out. They were impersonally gleeful, as if they themselves were not also likely to catch it pretty soon. But with this picture of an army in their hearts, the new men perhaps felt the devotion which the drops may feel for the wave; they were of its power and glory; they smiled jauntily at the foolish row of gunners, and told them to go to blazes.

The column trotted across some little bridges, and spread quickly into lines of battle. Before them was a bit of plain, and back of the plain was the ridge. There was no time left for considerations. The men were staring at the plain, mightily wondering how it would feel to be out there, when a brigade in advance yelled and charged. The hill was all gray smoke and fire-points.

That fierce elation in the terrors of war, catching a man's heart and making it burn with such ardour that he becomes capable of dying, flashed in the faces of the men like coloured lights, and made them resemble leashed animals, eager, ferocious, daunting at nothing. The line was really in its first leap before the wild, hoarse crying of the orders.

The greed for close quarters which is the emotion of a bayonet charge, came then into the minds of the men and developed until it was a madness. The field, with its faded grass of a Southern winter, seemed to this fury miles in width.

High, slow-moving masses of smoke, with an odour of burning cotton, engulfed the line until the men might have been swimmers. Before them the ridge, the shore of this gray sea, was outlined, crossed, and recrossed by sheets of flame. The howl of the battle arose to the noise of innumerable wind demons.

The line, galloping, scrambling, plunging like a herd of wounded horses, went over a field that was sown with corpses, the records of other charges.

Directly in front of the black-faced, whooping Dan, carousing in this onward sweep like a new kind of fiend, a wounded man appeared, raising his shattered body, and staring at this rush of men down upon him. It seemed to occur to him that he was to be trampled; he made a desperate, piteous effort to escape; then finally huddled in a waiting heap. Dan and the soldier near him widened the interval between them without looking down, without appearing to heed the wounded man. this little clump of blue seemed to reel past them as boulders reel past a train.

Bursting through a smoke-wave, the scampering, unformed bunches came upon the wreck of the brigade that had preceded them, a floundering mass stopped afar from the hill by the swirling volleys.

It was as if a necromancer had suddenly shown them a picture of the fate which awaited them; but the line with muscular spasm hurled itself over this wreckage and onward, until men were stumbling amid the relics of other assaults, the point where the fire from the ridge consumed.

The men, panting, perspiring, with crazed faces, tried to push against it; but it was as if they had come to a wall. The wave halted, shuddered in an agony from the quick struggle of its two desires, then toppled, and broke into a fragmentary thing which has no name.

Veterans could now at last be distinguished from recruits. The new regiments were instantly gone, lost, scattered, as if they never had been. But the sweeping failure of the charge, the battle, could not make the veterans forget their business. With a last throe, the band of maniacs drew itself up and blazed a volley at the hill, insignificant to those iron intrenchments, but nevertheless expressing that singular final despair which enables men coolly to defy the walls of a city of death.

After this episode the men renamed their command. They called it the Little Regiment.

VI

"I seen Dan shoot a feller yesterday. Yes sir. I'm sure it was him that done it. And maybe he thinks about that feller now, and wonders if *he* tumbled down just about the same way. Them things come up in a man's mind."

Bivouac fires upon the sidewalks, in the streets, in the yards, threw high their wavering reflections, which examined, like slim, red fingers, the dingy, scarred walls and the piles of tumbled brick. The droning of voices again arose from great blue crowds.

The odour of frying bacon, the fragrance from countless little coffee-pails floated among the ruins. The rifles, stacked in the shadows, emitted flashes of steely light. Wherever a flag lay horizontally from one stack to another was the bed of an eagle which had led men into the mystic smoke.

The men about a particular fire were engaged in holding in check their jovial spirits. They moved whispering around the blaze, although they looked at it with a certain fine contentment, like labourers after a day's hard work.

There was one who sat apart. They did not address him save in tones suddenly changed. They did not regard him directly, but always in little sidelong glances.

At last a soldier from a distant fire came into this circle of light. He studied for a time the man who sat apart. Then he hesitatingly stepped closer, and said: "Got any news, Dan?"

"No," said Dan.

The new-comer shifted his feet. He looked at the fire, at the sky, at the other men, at Dan. His face expressed a curious despair; his tongue was plainly in rebellion. Finally, however, he contrived to say: "Well, there's some chance yet, Dan. Lots of the wounded are still lying out there, you know. There's some chance yet."

"Yes," said Dan.

The soldier shifted his feet again, and looked miserably into the air. After another struggle he said: "Well, there's some chance yet, Dan." He moved hastily away.

One of the men of the squad, perhaps encouraged by this example, now approached the still figure. "No news yet, hey?" he said, after coughing behind his hand.

"No," said Dan.

"Well," said the man, "I've been thinking of how he was fretting about you the night you went on special duty. You recollect? Well, sir, I was surprised. He couldn't say enough

about it. I swan, I don't believe he slep' a wink after you left, but
just lay awake cussing special duty and worrying. I was surprised. But there he lay cussing. He—''

Dan made a curious sound, as if a stone had wedged in his
throat. He said: "Shut up, will you?"

Afterward the men would not allow this moody contemplation of the fire to be interrupted.

"Oh, let him alone, can't you?"

"Come away from there, Casey!"

"Say, can't you leave him be?"

They moved with reverence about the immovable figure,
with its countenance of mask-like invulnerability.

VII

After the red round eye of the sun had stared long at the little
plain and its burden, darkness, a sable mercy, came heavily
upon it, and the wan hands of the dead were no longer seen in
strange frozen gestures.

The heights in front of the plain shone with tiny camp-fires,
and from the town in the rear, small shimmerings ascended from
the blazes of the bivouac. The plain was a black expanse upon
which, from time to time, dots of light, lanterns, floated slowly
here and there. These fields were long steeped in grim mystery.

Suddenly, upon one dark spot, there was a resurrection. A
strange thing had been groaning there, prostrate. Then it
suddenly dragged itself to a sitting posture, and became a man.

The man stared stupidly for a moment at the lights on the
hill, then turned and contemplated the faint colouring over the
town. For some moments he remained thus, staring with dull
eyes, his face unemotional, wooden.

Finally he looked around him at the corpses dimly to be seen.
No change flashed into his face upon viewing these men. They
seemed to suggest merely that his information concerning
himself was not too complete. He ran his fingers over his arms
and chest, bearing always the air of an idiot upon a bench at an
almshouse door.

Finding no wound in his arms nor in his chest, he raised his hand to his head, and the fingers came away with some dark liquid upon them. Holding these fingers close to his eyes, he scanned them in the same stupid fashion, while his body gently swayed.

The soldier rolled his eyes again toward the town. When he arose, his clothing peeled from the frozen ground like wet paper. Hearing the sound of it, he seemed to see reason for deliberation. He paused and looked at the ground, then at his trousers, then at the ground.

Finally he went slowly off toward the faint reflection, holding his hands palm outward before him, and walking in the manner of a blind man.

VIII

The immovable Dan again sat unaddressed in the midst of comrades, who did not joke aloud. The dampness of the usual morning fog seemed to make the little camp-fires furious.

Suddenly a cry arose in the streets, a shout of amazement and delight. The men making breakfast at the fire looked up quickly. They broke forth in clamorous exclamation: "Well! Of all things! Dan! Dan! Look who's coming! Oh, Dan!"

Dan the silent raised his eyes and saw a man, with a bandage of the size of a helmet about his head, receiving a furious demonstration from the company. He was shaking hands, and explaining, and haranguing to a high degree.

Dan started. His face of bronze flushed to his temples. He seemed about to leap from the ground, but then suddenly he sank back, and resumed his impassive gazing.

The men were in a flurry. They looked from one to the other. "Dan! Look! See who's coming!" some cried again. "Dan! Look!"

He scowled at last, and moved his shoulders sullenly. "Well, don't I know it?"

But they could not be convinced that his eyes were in service. "Dan! Why can't you look? See who's coming!"

He made a gesture then of irritation and rage. "Curse it! Don't I know it?"

The man with a bandage of the size of a helmet moved forward, always shaking hands and explaining. At times his glance wandered to Dan, who saw with his eyes riveted.

After a series of shiftings, it occurred naturally that the man with the bandage was very near to the man who saw the flames. He paused, and there was a little silence. Finally he said: "Hello, Dan."

"Hello, Billie."

MERCY AT GETTYSBURG

John Jakes

John W. Jakes (b. 1932) is the best-selling author of the eight-volume historical saga the Kent Family Chronicles which began with The Bastard *in 1974 and of the Civil War novel* North and South *(1982). The success of* North and South *resulted in two sequels,* Love and War *(1985) and* Heaven and Hell *(1988). He has also written* California Gold *(1989) and, most recently,* On Secret Service *(2000), about the start of organized government espionage during the American Civil War. Jakes began as a writer of science fiction, fantasy and detective fiction, producing many stories for the pulp and digest magazines during the fifties and early sixties. He created the Conan-like hero Brak the Barbarian who through several stories and novels continues to fight his way to Khurdisan. Jakes began writing historical novels under the alias Jay Scotland, including* Sir Scoundrel *(1962),* Veils of Salome *(1962) and* Arena *(1963). The following story is one he often reads at public lectures, seldom leaving a dry eye in the house.*

War came to our home in July of 18 and 63.

Our house and the remains of the smithy stood on the Hagerstown Road, southwest of the sleepy little town of Gettysburg, in the hills of Pennsylvania. General Bob Lee had invaded the North. It was a desperate throw of the dice for the Rebs, who were fighting for black bondage and something called secession, which at age eleven I didn't understand.

Rumors of great armies just over the horizon reached us almost daily during the last week of June. I am sure there was fear in every heart in Adams County. Except my father's.

On Tuesday, June 30, a terrified family passed by from the west, saying the Rebs were advancing behind them. My father, a huge, strong man hurt by his blindness, threw his cane aside and fumbled his rifle down from over the hearth.

"If they do come, Daniel, I'll kill a Reb for your brother," he said to me. "You will help."

He raised the rifle over his head and exulted. "God be praised."

My father and mother, Jenny, were Bible people. My mother lived by moral principles without any thought of the cost. Once, right after pa's accident, when we had almost no money, a grocery clerk making change returned an extra dime. That dime would have bought a lot. My mother courteously pointed out the error and handed him the dime. My mother read the New Testament gospels mostly. For pa, she read aloud those books that he preferred – the Old Testament, all full of holy anger and vengeance. I suppose he cherished them because of what happened to my older brother Toby, who marched away with General McClellan on the Peninsula and never came back . . .

Sure enough, before noon on July 1, Reb horsemen came storming down upon us. Wil Sharp who had the next farm west galloped through, yelling that the Reb dust cloud was visible from his place.

"Help me, Daniel," my father exclaimed. "Carry my rifle, and set me up on the rail fence where I can shoot at them. You'll tell me when to fire."

"And they'll shoot back, and you'll both be dead," my

mother said. My little sister Lisbeth covered her eyes and bawled. Mother told her to hush.

Pa wouldn't be put off. Leaning on my shoulder, he walked out of the house and I set him up with his elbows resting on the top rail and his rifle pointing down the pike. The July day was hot and humming with insects.

We waited perhaps ten minutes, pa with his rifle, me with my heart thumping in my breast, certain I was enjoying my last summer on earth. Then a dust cloud rose above the next hill. My mouth was so dry I could barely croak.

"There they are."

"How close?"

"Other side of the ridge."

"God strengthen my arm and steady my hand." He could have put on a robe and grown his beard long and passed for one of those Old Testament prophets full of rage for justice. My brother had taken a Confederate ball in his vitals at some little Virginia creek, and then – I learned this later, when my mother thought I could bear hearing it – Reb scouts had outraged his body with bayonets. Or so his commanding officer wrote.

"I've got to kill at least one for Toby," Pa said as the tan cloud rolled down the hill like a cyclone. I remember his voice gentling then. "Scared?"

"Oh Lord yes, pa." He must have believed me, since he didn't reprove me for speaking the Lord's name in an irreverent way. He found my head and ruffled my hair, then appeared to gaze down the road, squinting his pale blind eyes. Lightning had set fire to the smithy one spring night in '59. Pa rushed inside to save his tools and two horses he was shoeing, and a blazing beam fell on top of him, right across his eyes – one bright glory and then perpetual dark. Except for ma tutoring the children of some families in town, we'd have starved.

I saw the horsemen then; I have always supposed they were mounted scouts on the right wing of Heth's division. Swords flashed like lightning inside the cloud. "I hear them," pa cried, for their hoofbeats sounded like drums. He laughed loudly.

A moment later, the Reb riders veered north and swept away, behind our property, out of sight.

"They're gone," I said, thinking we were saved. I guided pa back to the house, joyful that I might live another summer.

Ma tried to take the rifle from him. He was mad with disappointment and wouldn't let go. Lisbeth tugged at my sleeve.

"There's a sojer out back. I think he fell off his horse, he's all bloody."

Little fool, she didn't whisper softly enough. Pa heard. "What's that? A soldier?"

My mother seldom showed anger, but she gave Lisbeth an eyeful of it then. "Jenny," my father said, "take me to the soldier. This instant."

She was a dutiful wife, my mother. She led pa out past the jumbled black timbers of the smithy. He walked with his shoulders back, steel and death in his blind eyes again. Mother walked with her head bowed. I was a ways behind, with Lisbeth hanging onto my waist and mewing in an annoying way.

Then we heard him. Not a loud cry, but heart-wrenching all the same. Like an animal holed up with a broken paw.

I saw him sprawled in the tall weeds at the ruined corner of the smithy, a soldier in Confederate butternut, all covered with dirt and blood. The bloodiest was his left leg, where someone had shot him. He must have lost his horse, right enough, and maybe in all the dust and noise no comrade had seen him fall. You could hear him breathing.

"Aim the muzzle for me, Jenny," pa said, hoisting his rifle. "Aim at his head."

The Reb was dazed but awake; he saw what my father intended. He tried to thrash backward into the tall weeds but he was too weak. His eyes fixed on my father. They were big brown eyes, almost girlish. I don't suppose he was eighteen yet.

"Damnation, woman, hurry up. I'm going to kill the bastard." Behind me, Lisbeth was gasping; she was little but she knew that when pa stooped to bad language, the sky was falling.

"Jerusha Lamb, you can't," mother said with a keen look at me, then one at Lisbeth, which was wasted. "I must take care of this boy, he's a Union boy. You can't see him but I can, he's wearing Union blue. He must have been chasing those others."

Bees were buzzing. Up toward the Chambersburg Pike, cannon began to bang away; a big battle. I thought I'd wash away, so much fearful sweat was rolling down inside my shirt.

"Woman – woman, if – if you –" Pa was shaking. He loved my mother too much to accuse her of lying. But he knew how to discover the truth:

"Lisbeth? Daughter?"

Lisbeth's eyes got huge with tears; she couldn't lie to pa. Knowing I might go to hell for it, I put my hand over her mouth and clamped her to my side and said, "She went back to the house, pa, she's a scairdy cat."

My father held still a minute, then put his head back and gazed at the unseen sun and cried out, "Toby. Toby."

He walked away into the weeds with his rifle, weeping; ashamed of being unmanned.

I never saw the Reb again. My mother insisted on tending him by herself, keeping him warm and well fed in a little lean-to she made from a blanket and sticks. In the morning he was gone.

"Oddest thing," my mother said to me then. "His last name was Tobin. Toby – Tobin – isn't that odd?"

The battle of Gettysburg ravaged the town and the land round-about for three days. We mostly hid in the root cellar. After General Pickett's doomed charge, thousands of men and boys mowed down as they marched through an open field, right into the Union guns, General Bob Lee retreated south and never came back. Many said he lost the war that July in Pennsylvania.

My father died two years later, never having received the payment he thought he was owed.

In 18 and 66, my mother got a letter from a Leverett Tobin of Wytheville, Virginia. He had survived the war, married his sweetheart after the surrender, and recently opened a hardware store. He praised my mother's compassion that July day.

My mother gazed at the letter laid in her lap. Her face showed no joy; there isn't any in war, or memories of war.

"Daniel," she said, "I pray that when I come to judgement, God can forgive my untruths."

"Mine too, mama. But I think He will." I put my hand over hers in a clumsy way. "Yes, I'm sure He will."

FROM A SOLDIER'S WIFE

Bella Spencer

I'm afraid I know next to nothing about Mrs Bella Zilfa Spencer. It looks like she died young. The Library of Congress records her dates as 1840 to 1867. She produced two novels: Ora, the Lost Wife *(1863) and* Tried and True; or, Love and Loyalty *(1866), plus a collection of stories:* Right and Wrong *(1870). I have no doubt that she wrote from direct and bitter experience of the Civil War. I am grateful to Paul Di Filippo who discovered the following story in the October 1864 issue of* Harper's Magazine. *The battle of Shiloh took place on 6 April 1862.*

At Paducah, Kentucky, I first realized what it required to be a soldier's wife. I had seen much before, and borne a great deal, yet it seemed but little comparatively when I came to take leave of my husband, and turned back to my lonely room to await his return.

True, I had expected this—was prepared for it in a measure; yet a strange and overpowering sense of my position came over me that I had not felt before, when I stood by the window to catch a last glimpse of a beloved form. He was standing upon the deck of a large boat, with hundreds of others around him; yet I seemed to see him only, his sad face turned to me in a mute farewell as the bell clanged and the ponderous vessel swept slowly out into the stream, and turned her prow toward the mouth of the Tennessee. It was but a moment, during which I leaned against the casement, breathless, agonized. There the waters lay cold and glittering under the spring sunbeams, and the sadness of utter desolation seemed to have fallen upon my spirits.

I am ashamed to say that I shut every ray of the bright, beautiful sun from my room, feeling as if it was a mockery too bitter to endure in that hour; that I threw myself upon my couch and wept as if my heart would break, for the time forgetful that there were any in the world more sorrowful, and with deeper cause for sorrow than I. But it is true, and here I confess my selfish weakness repentantly, glad to be able to say that I have since that time learned to think less of myself and more of others on whom the hand of affliction has fallen heavily, while I am still unscathed.

After the first burst of grief I roused myself with the question, "What shall I do?" and the answer came so quickly that my cheek was dyed with shame. What should I do, with three hospitals in sight of my window? No need to ponder the question long. The call of duty was loud and strong, and I obeyed it without delay.

It was about two o'clock in the afternoon when I first entered the Presbyterian church, which had been converted into a hospital, and walked up its aisle under the gaze of a hundred eyes. The very remembrance of that time thrills me again with the same sensation of pity and pain that rose in my heart as I looked upon the pale, emaciated faces around me. Near the pulpit two men were standing, whom I rightly supposed to be the doctor and steward. Toward them I went directly, and addressed the tallest of the two.

"Is this the attending physician of the hospital?"

"It is, madam. Dr L——, at your service. What can I do for you?"

"Tell me, Sir, how I can make myself useful to others. My husband has gone to Pittsburg Landing, to be away for several weeks, perhaps, during which time I shall have nothing to do, unless you make me useful here. Can I be of service?"

"Look about you and see. There has not been a lady within these walls since I came, nearly five weeks ago. Your voice is soft, your hand light and skillful – all women's are – and I have no doubt but your eyes will be quick to see what should be done. I shall be glad to have you come."

"Thank you. I may come to you for advice when I want it?" I asked.

"Certainly. I shall be happy to assist you at all times."

I bowed and turned away, feeling as if about to realize, indeed, some of the terrible consequences of war.

In a few moments I had laid aside my hat and cloak, rolled my sleeves away from my wrists, and constructed an impromptu apron of an old sheet which I found among the bandages in the linen room. Thus prepared for the work which I saw before me, I went out to the kitchen and obtained warm water, a tin wash-basin, and some towels. For combs and brushes I was compelled to send out before I could do any thing.

Then the work began in earnest. Commencing with the lower berth, I went up the entire length of the aisle, taking each patient in his turn until I got through. Grimed faces and hands were to be bathed, hair and beard trimmed and brushed – a long and distressing task. But I had undertaken it with a will, and though my arms and neck ached, I would not yield until the last sufferer had been relieved.

It was half past eight o'clock in the evening before I had done, and when I reached the hotel I could scarcely stand for very weariness. Such duties were new to me then, and the excitement helped to wear away my strength. But the memory of grateful thanks, tearful eyes, and broken, trembling exclamations of relief more than repaid me. Even as I sat beside them, passing the cool sponge over their faces or brushing the tangled hair, many of the sufferers had fallen asleep.

I slept little that night. It was vain to attempt sleep after such an experience. Moreover, an idea came to me that filled me with unrest. I had observed when tea was brought in how coarse and unpalatable the food was, and that many turned from it with loathing. There was hard, brown bread crisped to a blackened toast; some fat bacon, and black tea without milk served to the men on that evening. The tea was sweetened with very coarse brown sugar, stirred into it with large iron spoons. They drank from tin cups and ate from tin plates. This would have made little difference had the food been nice and palatable, which it certainly was not. Some of the men told me, in answer to my questions, that they could not have swallowed a mouthful to save their lives.

I rose very early the following morning, filled with the idea that many of those brave sufferers were actually starving, and determined to look into the matter more closely. But few of the nurses were astir in the hospital, and I went to the kitchen, where the cook had just commenced the preparation of the morning meal, and was greeted with a surly "Good-morgen" in mixed German-English. In a moment I saw that I should not have a very pleasant time in my examinations. After a few careless remarks, to set the man in a good-humor, I asked him to show me the hospital stores for the day's consumption, which he did ungraciously enough. A moment's observation filled me with horror and indignation.

"Do you tell me that you are going to cook all this stuff for those men in the other room?" I said, indignantly. "Look at this tea, black and mouldy as it can be, and this bacon is one living mass! Here are salt fish laid upon boards over the sugar-barrel, brine dripping through into the sugar! I hope you have not been using this for their tea."

"It is not my fault. I am not ze prowider fur ze hospital," growled the cook in response. "I does my duty so fur as I can. I cooks ze rations zat is bring to me, and zat is all so fur as I go."

"Well, that is farther than you will go in less than a week from now!" I answered, quickly. "If you had the soul of a man in you you would refuse to have any thing to do with such horrible things as those! Poor boys! No wonder they turned away from such food in disgust. Some of those men are starving to death. Do you know it?"

He stared at me aghast and made no reply.

"It is really true, and I know it. How can they eat such bread and meat – drink such tea as this? They are weakened by illness, and require delicacies. It would be utterly impossible for many of those men to swallow coarse food, even if clear and palatable. How then can they eat this?" I repeated, looking at him steadily till his head drooped, and I began to suspect that he was even more guilty than at first appeared. Afterward I found that he had carefully put aside all the delicacies that found their way to the hospital and feasted upon them, while those for whom they were intended faded and pined day by day under his eyes.

When Dr L—— came I went to him at once and told him how I had been engaged, and what I had found in my researches. He looked so much surprised that indignation was redoubled, and I could not forbear expressing it in plain words.

"Can it be possible that you, the physician in charge of a hospital, do not know, after five weeks' service, what your patients have to eat?"

"I am not here when the meals are served. I give orders for such diet as my patients must have, and my steward's business is to carry out my instructions."

"Do you never inquire into the condition of the stores? Have you never examined to see if they were as they should be? It seems to me you ought to know all about what is going on here. If three hundred lives were in my hands as they are in yours I should not dare to trifle with them thus!"

"You are severe, madam!"

"Ask yourself if I am unjustly so, Sir. I do not desire to appear rude or assuming; but indeed I won't look upon this unmoved. What I saw last night and this morning has opened my eyes to a condition that is a shame to any hospital. See the confusion all around us! Remember how long helpless men have lain without even a face bath or a wound dressed for three days, to say nothing of the more dreadful slow starvation to which they are subjected! If all hospitals are kept like this God pity the poor soldiers!"

"Since you see the evils so plainly, perhaps you can suggest a remedy," remarked Dr L——, sarcastically.

"I will try, if you will act upon the suggestion," I answered, quickly.

"Well?"

"In the first place, then, what do you do when a man fails to draw his regular rations?

"He is entitled to its value in money if he wishes it."

"Then why not refuse to draw such rations as those, and with the money buy food that can be eaten?"

"It might be done if there was any thing to buy. I am afraid it will be hard work if you attempt it."

"No matter; it must be done. If you will furnish me with a boy to do errands, I will see if I can not get fresh butter, eggs, and chickens, at least – perhaps milk also. These would prove invaluable just now. To-day I intend to send to a Society for some sheets and mattresses; and, if you have no decided objection, will try to bring order out of chaos, if possible."

"I see you are one of the working kind," said the Doctor. "Do all you wish, and call upon me when I can render any assistance."

"That will be very frequently, I assure you." And with that I turned away, still too much incensed to treat him civilly. He was willing enough to let other people take his work off his hands, since he would come in for a full share of the credit in the end. At least that was my uncharitable thought at the moment; and I am not sure now that I was far wrong, as I know his character better.

The same day I went to him again about the boy, but he had forgotten all about the matter, so I went to the Quarter-master instead. He furnished a horse, and I sent my own waiting-man out to the country for supplies, making him take a receipt for every penny he paid in his purchases. This was for the purpose of ascertaining precisely how much was spent, as I desired to render a faithful account of my stewardship. I was fully aware that the ground I was taking might easily prove a dangerous one should I fail to keep precise accounts of my expenditures, and resolved to give no chances for misrepresentation. Every receipt and bill of sale, after being duly copied in my own account-book, was carefully filed in the Quarter-master's office, subject to the inspection of any who chose to examine them.

Mr P——, the Quarter-master, was a kind, gentlemanly man, in whom I found an ever-ready assistant. He had received a donation in money, for the benefit of the wounded, from some one in Illinois, which he begged me to use as designed, and I did so gladly. Even with that I had not enough, and was often compelled to draw from my own purse the means wherewith to supply the many wants of the patients.

It took me a week to get fairly started in my vocation as hospital nurse. There was such an entire absence of system in the establishment, that it seemed almost impossible to bring it into any thing like order. The nurses were detailed each day from the convalescent corps – weak, spiritless men, who thought more of themselves than of the charges placed in their hands. I had seen them lounging about and sleeping while the sicker men, failing to make them hear, would try to struggle into a sitting posture to get at the medicines to be taken from time to time.

All this had to be changed, and strong, able men detailed for duty. The ward-master drank fearfully, and I was compelled to report him and get another man put into his place. With the assistance of these, however, after the changes were made I got along very well. Every morning we had the floor nicely washed, and when the sun shone the windows were opened to let in the fresh, balmy air, the effect of which was almost magical; eyes would brighten, and lips wreathe in pleasant, hopeful smiles, beautiful to behold.

It was with more joy than words can express that I observed the rapid improvement of the men under careful attention. When the new sheets and comforters, with pillows and mattresses came, we were able to keep the place perfectly fresh and comfortable. But it required the most constant attention. I went to my hotel only for my meals, devoting the day, from half past five in the morning to nine in the evening, to the care of the sick. I must be there at every meal, or many would go without any thing at all. Some of the feeblest had to be fed like children, and what they ate could be prepared by myself only. I must toast the bread and make the tea; then I must sit down and support their heads with my left hand, while with the right I conveyed the food to their lips. Such constant care was very wearing, and I was often tempted to steal away for an hour's rest, trusting to some one to take my place for a time; but when I gave it a second thought the temptation faded. Suppose the man should die, could I feel that I had done all in my power to save him? Not if I should yield to the inclination I felt to abandon my post; so I remained, and tried to be patient.

Two hours each day were devoted to letter-writing for those who were unable to correspond with their friends. And sometimes, after tea, I would send for my guitar and sing for them, at the request of the music-loving ones under my charge. So the days sped, and all things began to run smoothly – for a time, at least. Death was not banished from our midst, however. Sometimes it was my fate to walk up the aisle in the morning and find some berth empty in which a favorite patient had lain. I might here go into particulars, and detail some of the most touching scenes in life; but I will here speak of only one case:

One evening I was sitting by a dying man, reading a favorite chapter in the Bible, to which he listened eagerly, even while his eyes drooped under the shades of death. One clammy hand groped for mine, and clasped it with a feeble, tremulous touch, and as I finished his lips moved painfully: "Write to my wife and children. Tell them I can not come to them, but they may soon follow me to that place of which the Saviour said, 'In my Father's house are many mansions: I go to prepare a place for you.' Oh, how sweet and comforting! 'Let not your hearts be troubled: ye believe in God; believe also in me.' Jesus, Saviour,

I do believe in thee. Receive thou my spirit!" And the voice sank softly. A few moments later the last fluttering breath went out, and the mysteries of the unknown world were mysteries to him no longer.

Tears fell fast as I pressed the white lids over the blue eyes, thinking of those who were far away, and denied the sad privilege of paying the last tender rites to the dead. Poor children! Poor mother! How my heart ached to think that mine must be the task to tell them the story of death, of which, perhaps, they were not dreaming now!

Before I had finished a boy came in hurriedly and said something to the steward, of which I caught only the words, "been fighting all day . . . rebels attacked them this morning . . . had a very hard time of it."

I grew for a moment sick with a terrible fear. A battle had taken place, and who should say how many lives in a few short hours had been crowned with the thorny wreath of affliction? It might be that I, too, was destined to feel the force of an awful blow. If so, God help me!

I could gain no particulars at the hospital, and was forced to wait until I reached home. There I learned that an attack had been made upon our forces Sunday morning, and the Confederates had occupied our camps for some time. Afterward they were driven out again, but we had lost many lives. They were still fighting an hour before nightfall. Further than this nothing was known.

All night I walked the floor in an agony of suspense and dread. Would the morning's dawn come to me with a message of gladness; or should I rank among the doomed, who henceforth must walk the earth in the darkness and gloom of utter desolation?

Ah, how I prayed that night! How I wrestled with my own fearful heart, and chided myself for the lack of faith which should have borne me up in that hour!

Monday came, freighted with death to thousands! All day the battle raged, and at night it was said that the Federals had achieved a great victory. A victory it was; but oh! at what a fearful cost! How many hundreds of young heads were that day laid low in the dust, never to rise again! How many hopeful hearts throbbed their last impulses of human aspirations and ambition!

Tuesday and Wednesday brought hundreds from the field of action. Some of the wounded were transported to Paducah, and I was called upon to dress their wounds and to assist in amputations, which required all the strength I possessed. The duty was a terrible one; but I nerved myself resolutely to perform it, hoping that, if need be, some one would as willingly attend to one of whose fate I had as yet learned nothing.

On Thursday morning the St Francis Hotel was alive with officers from Shiloh, but still I was left in ignorance of my husband's fate, and the suspense was becoming insupportable. Every excuse that could be made for a delay of tidings had been utterly exhausted, and I felt now that he was either killed or wounded.

In the hope of hearing something definite I went out to the table for the first time since the battle, and took my usual seat, near which sat two wounded officers. One had his head bandaged; the other's arm was in a sling; and both were pale and weary-looking. But they were talking of the late contest, and after listening for a few moments I yielded to an uncontrollable impulse and asked the one nearest me if he knew any thing of the fate of the — Regiment.

He turned politely, with a look of interest I could but remark, and answered:

"I am sorry to say, madam, that it fared very badly. Some other regiments of the same division showed the white feather, and, perfectly panic-stricken, broke ranks and fled. That gallant regiment alone stood its ground, and was literally cut to pieces. Those who were not killed were taken prisoners, only a few escaping."

"And the officers – were they all –?" I could not finish the sentence for the deathly sickness that was choking my utterance, and he answered it gently:

"I believe every one was killed. Did you have any friends among them, may I ask?"

"My husband," I gasped. "Captain S——."

I saw them exchange glances; and then, as if in a dream, a voice seemed to murmur afar off amidst the rushing of waters.

"Poor thing! He fell in the first onset. But see! She is falling!"

A strong hand grasped my arm, and a glass of water was pressed to my lips; but the shock of that deadly blow was too heavy, and I sank slowly into utter oblivion, conscious of a wish, as sight and sound faded, that I might never waken again!

It was an hour before they brought me back to a sense of my bereavement, and then I turned from the kind faces clustered about the couch to which I had been borne, and gave vent to a bitter cry.

"Ah! why did you not let me die? The world is so cold and desolate!"

Two firm, soft hands clasped mine, and drew them away from my face, and I saw the mild, reproachful eyes of a stranger gazing into mine. He was an old man, with hair as white as the snows of winter, and a voice soft and gentle as a tender mother's.

"My child, you are rebellious! Rouse yourself, and learn to say, Not my will, but thine, O Lord, be done!"

"I can not! – I can not bring myself to feel that there is any mercy or love in the power that could deal such a blow. God knew that he was all I had on earth, and he has taken him from me. It was cruel!"

"Hush! Resignation will come when you have time to think. Perhaps, after all, it is a mistake. There has been no official report of your husband's death, and he may only be wounded or a prisoner."

I started up, wild with the hope his words awakened.

"Nay, be not too hasty! I only say it may be possible."

I was silenced, but the hope was not crushed. It stung me to life again, and made every idle moment seem like an eternity of agony.

In a few moments they began to leave the room, and only one

or two ladies remained in conversation with the old gentleman, who was a physician, and had been summoned hastily when I fainted. Seeing them thus engaged, I formed a sudden resolution, and raised myself from the pillows.

"What are you going to do?" asked the doctor, turning his face toward me.

"Find my husband – dead or alive," I answered, getting off the bed.

"My dear child, you are mad!" he expostulated. "You can not do any thing. Look at your face – it is as pallid as marble, and your eyes would frighten any one."

"That is because I have not slept or eaten scarcely since last Saturday night," I said, in reply. "Besides, I have been half mad with suspense. Only for the sick at the hospital, who claimed my care, I don't think I could have borne it at all."

"Go back and lie down on the bed," pleaded one of the ladies. "It makes my heart ache to look at you."

"How dreadfully you must have suffered!"

"God and my own heart only know how much," I answered, gulping down a sob. Her tone of womanly sympathy shook my strong self-control till I trembled. Then I broke down entirely, and with a bitter cry fell upon my knees by a chair.

"O Charley, Charley! my heart is breaking!"

Instantly her kind arms were twined round me – her soft lips pressed to my forehead. She held me to her heart, and suffered me to weep until the fountain of my tears was exhausted.

"There! you feel better now, don't you?" said the doctor, kindly. "You must lie down and keep quiet a while, or you will be ill. Your hands are like two burning coals now, while only a moment since they were like ice. You must not fall ill."

"Oh no! I can not afford to be ill. I must search for my husband," I answered, rising. "There – it is over now! I am done with tears for the present, and am ready to work. If I do not, I shall soon lose my reason. Don't talk to me, any of you!" I cried, as I saw them about to remonstrate. "I am determined to go up the river, and if I should never return, try to remember me kindly."

"The authorities will not permit you to go," said the doctor. "An order has been issued to allow no lady to pass up the river, and Colonel N—— has locked himself up to escape the importunities of the people."

"I shall go, nevertheless," was my reply.

"How will you manage it?" asked the old man, curiously.

"I don't know yet. But I shall go. Before night I will be on my way to Pittsburg Landing."

They looked at me pityingly; but I paid no attention further, and when they left the room I began to pack some articles in a small trunk which I could easily take with me.

About noon a boat, chartered at Cincinnati and sent after the wounded, touched at Paducah, and I obtained passage. Fortune seemed to favor me here, for I not only found myself able to carry out my design, but came into the midst of sympathizing friends, who received me cordially, and did all in their power to make me comfortable.

There were a number of surgeons and their assistants on board. Three Sisters of Charity and two ladies from Cincinnati completed the list, and in about an hour we entered the mouth of the river and proceeded on our sorrowful errand.

I will not dwell upon the tediousness of the trip. To me it seemed like an eternity of misery. On Thursday, about one o'clock, we left Paducah, and did not arrive at Pittsburg Landing until Saturday night, near eight o'clock.

I shall never forget that night or a single incident connected with it. As we made fast to the shore I was standing upon the hurricane deck, looking abroad, with my heart full of a wild and bitter fear. Here was Shiloh! There were the black, forbidding bluffs directly over my head, the banks of the river lined with boats from which profane and noisy men were unloading Government stores. Across the river two or three gun-boats stretched their black, snake-like lengths along the waters, and from them only a fiery gleam was now and then discernible. Above, the sky was clear and blue, and studded with myriads of stars that looked, oh so calmly! down upon that terrible spot. There, where rivers of blood had flowed, lay the silvery white

moonbeams, and on the death-laden air floated the rich per-
fume of spring flowers.

Even while I stood looking around me the *Continental* swung
loose from her fastenings, and rounded out into the stream
followed by half a dozen others. Now the lights blazed from
every vessel, and a band struck up "Dixie" in the most spirited
manner.

General Halleck was going up the river to destroy a bridge,
and, convoyed by two of the gunboats, they started two and two
abreast, keeping in this order until a sudden turn hid them from
sight.

Turning my face once more toward the shore, some dark
objects became visible lying some distance up the side of the
hill; but I could not discern precisely what they were, and the
next moment my attention was absorbed in a painful scene
taking place on the deck of a boat just along side of the *Lan-
caster*.

There were a number of men lying upon berths in the open
air, and around one of them was a surgeon and his group of
assistants. The wounded man had his arm bared to the
shoulder, and had I not seen the glittering of instruments in
the light of the numerous lamps held around him I should still
have divined his fate. Poor fellow! I heard him sob and plead
piteously, "Oh, doctor, don't take my arm off! If I lose it my
little sister will have no one to work for her. I'd rather die!"

"Die you will if it does not come off, and that very soon," was
the response. "No help for it, boy, so be a man and bear it
bravely."

The next moment a handkerchief was held to his face, and
after a brief struggle he yielded to the powerful influence of
chloroform. I hear the deep, quick gasping so painful to the
listener and the tears ran down my cheeks unrestrainedly.

Captain V—— came up to me.

"Mrs. S——, I have been making inquiries for you, and can
gain no intelligence whatever concerning your husband. I see
no way but to wait until daylight, and then I will find a
conveyance and send some one with you."

"Can not I go to-night? It seems as if it is impossible to wait."

"No, it is out of the question. The mud is two feet deep on shore, and it is quite dark in the woods. I am sorry for you, but it will be only a little while longer. Try to be as patient as you can."

"Thank you, I will. But it is very, very hard."

"I am sure of it. But let me say a word to you here, Mrs. S——. I fear you are hoping too much. Remember he fell early on Sunday, and the chances are that he was hastily buried with many others in the trenches."

"For Heaven's sake go no further!" I implored. "My husband buried in a trench! Oh, God forbid!"

He took my hand, and drawing it within his arm led me to the ladies' cabin, which now presented a singular appearance, converted as it was into a hospital, and peopled by the wounded which the men were carrying on board.

There were three rows of mattresses spread upon the floor, the one in the middle capable of accommodating two patients, and one on each side a single man.

All these were filled already, and the clamor was terrible. Some called for food, others for water, and a few lay moaning piteously, their hunger and thirst forgotten in the sharp pain of undressed wounds.

One boy near the stern of the boat seemed to be in such distress that I hastened to his side and bent over him.

"Where are you wounded?" I asked.

"In the shoulder. I got it Monday, and it's never been dressed. I can not get at it myself."

Hastily getting a basin of water, sponge, and bandages, I exposed the inflamed and swollen shoulder and began to bathe it carefully. He regarded me for a moment with wide, fearful eyes, then as he felt the gentle touch and cooling sponge, his eyes closed and he heaved a great sigh of relief.

"Ah, that is so nice!" he murmured, presently. "I tell you it's hard enough to be shot down like a dog; but when it comes to lying out for a whole week in the open air, with only a blanket, a cracker, and a slice of dried beef, with an occasional drink of water, it's harder still. I thought I should starve to death before they could get a boat to take us off, and if I could only have had my shoulder dressed! Oh, how good that feels!"

I had just laid a folded napkin wet with ice-water over the wound, and it was this which called forth such an exclamation of delight.

"I am glad you feel better. Now I am going to bring you a cup of tea, with some bread and butter. If you are so nearly starved, it is time you should have something to eat."

"Oh, thank you!"

I hastened away, and in a few moments came back with the tea and bread, which he ate like a man who was indeed starving. The glare of his large dark eyes was perfectly terrible.

"More, more!" he gasped pantingly, swallowing the last drop of tea at a draught.

"Not now. In half an hour you shall have more. To give it you now will do you more harm than good. We must try to keep down fever. Now, shall I bathe your face and hands for you?"

"If you please," with an eager, wistful look at the empty cup and plate that made my eyes grow humid.

While I was engaged in the operation Doctor P——, from Cincinnati, passed me.

"Who taught you to nurse?" he asked. "I wish all women would take right hold of the boys as you do. There would be less suffering."

"They have surely earned this much at our hands, at least," I said, in reply.

"Ay, to be sure. But I know plenty who would never get down on their knees on the floor as you are doing, and take hold of an object like that."

"I hope not. I believe there are few who would not do it if in such circumstances. There is not one who has a father, brother, or husband in the service who would refuse to do it, I am sure."

He passed on with some careless reply, and I continued attending the soldiers until it grew late. After three o'clock I threw myself upon a sofa in the chamber-maid's room, and slept until half past five. Then I rose and went again among the wounded until such an hour as I could set out upon my journey over the field.

I will here mention a case that may seem incredible to many; but if so, it will not surprise me, for I could scarcely believe the evidence of my own senses, when one of the surgeons came to me directly after I entered the cabin the night before, and asked me to come and "see a sight." I told him I would as soon as I finished "feeding my patient;" and did so, he meeting me half-way when he saw me coming.

About midway of the cabin lay a rebel prisoner, badly wounded in the head. A ball had passed behind his eyes, forcing both upon the cheeks, where they lay in a most horrible and swollen condition. From the wounds in each temple a portion of the brains was slowly oozing, and the doctor pointed to it, saying,

"In all my life I have seen nothing like that. He has been lying here for the last ten minutes in that condition, quarreling with this Federal soldier just opposite."

"Surely he can not know what he is saying!" I ejaculated.

"Yes, he does, perfectly. You should hear him."

I had an opportunity soon, for in a moment he called out:

"Say! look here, Yank! I want a drink of water!"

"All right! You shall have it in a moment," answered one of the men in waiting.

"I'm tending to a feller, and shall be done in a minute."

"Oh yes, I'll be bound you'll tend to your Yanks before you do to me! But when a man's on his last legs you might stop a moment to give him a drop of water. I sha'n't ask it of you more than an hour or so longer. Then I'm going straight to—!"

I shuddered and retreated from the spot. Such profanity and recklessness upon the very brink of eternity! It was awful!

"Poor wretch! God pity and have mercy upon you!" said the doctor. "You have none for yourself."

"I don't want any of your cant, Sir," said the man, in reply. "My soul is not yours, and you need not trouble yourself about it in the least."

When I came again into the cabin the following morning he

was just breathing his last – going home to his Creator hardened, reckless – utterly careless of the fate that awaited him.

An hour later Captain V—— sent for a conveyance, but could get none, to carry me over the field in search of the camp from which I hoped to gain some intelligence that should end suspense. While striving to devise some means the medical director of the Division came on board, and offered me one of his horses, proposing himself to guide me to the place where the Regiment was camped. There were but few left, he said, but what there were had pitched their tents about five miles distant, and he thought he could take me to the place without difficulty.

Thanking him warmly I accepted the offer, and erelong found myself mounted and laboring through the mud up the side of the bluff.

The path led round it, ascending gradually to the top, and once upon the shore, I discovered the dark objects that had puzzled me the night previous were human bodies lying under the broiling sun waiting for burial.

Through the mud, over fallen trees, broken artillery, and pieces of shells, the carcasses of horses and mules, and by strips of woodland cut down like grass by the rains of iron and lead! How strange and solemn and fearful it seemed! Giant trees pierced by balls and shorn of their bark till the trunks showed a hundred grinning scars; boughs severed and hanging by a single fibre, or lying prone upon the ground, trampled and blood-stained!

Our progress was slow. It was long past noon ere we reached the little hollow in which the tents I sought had been pitched; and then, as we came in sight of the little blue wreaths of smoke, and saw a few solitary men moving about, I began to tremble. I knew that I was about to meet my fate, and the thought of what it might be almost deprived me of the necessary strength to go on to the end.

Presently, after passing through several encampments, we descended into the hollow and alighted before the officers' quarters, which seemed almost deserted. There the doctor bade me go in and wait while he made inquiries of those around outside.

On first entering I saw nothing but a berth, on which lay a man with his face turned from me; but the next moment I discovered that another was seated beyond, his head resting against the side of the berth, fast asleep. A pillow supported the right arm of the invalid, and by the bandages I knew he had been wounded. My heart swelled with pity, and stealing softly toward the bed, I leaned over to catch a glimpse of his face.

Pale – oh, so pale and wan! with the rich brown hair pushed back from the broad brow, pure and white as marble. The blue eyes were half closed, and the lips parted with such an expression of suffering that a loving woman's heart might almost break in looking upon it. Yet I did not moan, nor faint, nor cry out. I only fell upon my knees, and taking the white, clammy fingers of the left hand in my own, covered it with warm tears and gentle kisses – for it was my own dear husband, whom God had spared to me, and I had found him at last!

"I thank Thee, O my Father!" was the cry of my soul in that hour, and my lips breathed it audibly. With the sound Charley opened his eyes and looked into my face with a bewildered stare. Then a light broke all over his pale face, and his glad smile sent happy tears raining over my cheeks.

"Is it you, darling? I thought you would never come!" he breathed faintly. "But you are here now, and you will not leave me again, will you?"

"No, indeed. I will take care of you, and get you well again. Ah, how you must have missed me!"

"Missed you! It has been an eternity of misery since I fell, and I have called your name vainly a thousand times."

"They told me you were killed!" I said, chokingly. "I waited for tidings from you till I thought I should go mad, and then they said you were dead, and when I declared my intention of finding you, tried to keep me from coming. But I would not be stayed, and, thank God! I have found you alive."

"Ay! Thank God from your soul, for it is one of His greatest blessings that he is here now!" said the doctor, who had entered and laid his hand upon my head.

"Tell her all about it," whispered my husband's faint voice, and as his fingers clasped mine closer the old man sat down upon a camp-stool and began:

"I have just heard the story from one of the boys, and it is a wonder to me how he lived through that long time without the least care. He must have crept into the thicket where they found him very soon after falling, and there remained for four days. There was a dead soldier near him, and from his canteen and haversack he managed to obtain water and food; but his wound bled terribly. They say, to judge by the stains around and where they came across him, he had just a spark of life left. He will need you now to nurse him back to life again, and it will take nice nursing too."

"Will he lose his arm, doctor?" I asked, in a suppressed voice, lest Charley should hear.

"I will tell you after a while," was the answer; and accordingly "after a while" he examined it closely. As he left the tent I followed him out.

"Well, doctor?"

"All right, my little anxious woman! The Captain can carry that arm through several campaigns yet, I hope," he said, heartily; and I went back to my boy, my eyes wet with glad tears.

Three weeks later we were within our own quiet home, where I was nursing him back to strength to be ready for the Fall campaign.

ONE OF THE MISSING

Ambrose Bierce

Ambrose Bierce (1842–1914?) fought on the Union side in the Civil War and was involved in some of the fiercest battles. Although not a pacifist he later became disillusioned about the cause for which he fought and refused back pay from the army because he came to regard himself as a "hired assassin". He settled in San Francisco and turned to journalism in 1868 establishing a profound reputation over the next twenty years for his acid wit and misanthropic outlook on life, as a consequence of which he became dubbed Bitter Bierce. He later turned to writing short stories, most of them soaked in his sardonic humour and frequently all the more horrific for that. The following story, first published in 1886 was later collected in the rare volume Tales of Soldiers and Civilians *(1891). The battle of Kennesaw Mountain, which took place on 27 June 1864, was a particularly bloody confrontation with an estimated 4,000 casualties suffered in a little over an hour-and-a-half.*

Jerome Searing, a private soldier of General Sherman's army, then confronting the enemy at and about Kennesaw Mountain, Georgia, turned his back upon a small group of officers with whom he had been talking in low tones, stepped across a light line of earthworks, and disappeared in a forest. None of the men in line behind the works had said a word to him, nor had he so much as nodded to them in passing, but all who saw understood that this brave man had been intrusted with some perilous duty. Jerome Searing, though a private, did not serve in the ranks; he was detailed for service at division headquarters, being borne upon the rolls as an orderly. "Orderly" is a word covering a multitude of duties. An orderly may be a messenger, a clerk, an officer's servant – anything. He may perform services for which no provision is made in orders and army regulations. Their nature may depend upon his aptitude, upon favor, upon accident. Private Searing, an incomparable marksman, young, hardy, intelligent and insensible to fear, was a scout. The general commanding his division was not content to obey orders blindly without knowing what was in his front, even when his command was not on detached service, but formed a fraction of the line of the army; nor was he satisfied to receive his knowledge of his *vis-à-vis* through the customary channels; he wanted to know more than he was apprised of by the corps commander and the collisions of pickets and skirmishers. Hence Jerome Searing, with his extraordinary daring, his woodcraft, his sharp eyes, and truthful tongue. On this occasion his instructions were simple: to get as near the enemy's lines as possible and learn all that he could.

In a few moments he had arrived at the picket-line, the men on duty there lying in groups of two and four behind little banks of earth scooped out of the slight depression in which they lay, their rifles protruding from the green boughs with which they had masked their small defenses. The forest extended without a break toward the front, so solemn and silent that only by an effort of the imagination could it be conceived as populous with armed men, alert and vigilant – a forest formidable with possibilities of battle. Pausing a moment in one of these rifle-pits to apprise the men of his intention Searing crept stealthily forward on his hands and knees and was soon lost to view in a dense thicket of underbrush.

"That is the last of him," said one of the men; "I wish I had his rifle; those fellows will hurt some of us with it."

Searing crept on, taking advantage of every accident of ground and growth to give himself better cover. His eyes penetrated everywhere, his ears took note of every sound. He stilled his breathing, and at the cracking of a twig beneath his knee stopped his progress and hugged the earth. It was slow work, but not tedious; the danger made it exciting, but by no physical signs was the excitement manifest. His pulse was as regular, his nerves were as steady as if he were trying to trap a sparrow.

"It seems a long time," he thought, "but I cannot have come very far; I am still alive."

He smiled at his own method of estimating distance, and crept forward. A moment later he suddenly flattened himself upon the earth and lay motionless, minute after minute. Through a narrow opening in the bushes he had caught sight of a small mound of yellow clay – one of the enemy's rifle-pits. After some little time he cautiously raised his head, inch by inch, then his body upon his hands, spread out on each side of him, all the while intently regarding the hillock of clay. In another moment he was upon his feet, rifle in hand, striding rapidly forward with little attempt at concealment. He had rightly interpreted the signs, whatever they were; the enemy was gone.

To assure himself beyond a doubt before going back to report upon so important a matter, Searing pushed forward across the line of abandoned pits, running from cover to cover in the more open forest, his eyes vigilant to discover possible stragglers. He came to the edge of a plantation – one of those forlorn, deserted homesteads of the last years of the war, upgrown with brambles, ugly with broken fences and desolate with vacant buildings having blank apertures in place of doors and windows. After a keen reconnoissance from the safe seclusion of a clump of young pines Searing ran lightly across a field and through an orchard to a small structure which stood apart from the other farm buildings, on a slight elevation. This he thought would enable him to overlook a large scope of country in the direction that he supposed the enemy to have taken in withdrawing. This building, which had originally consisted of a single room elevated upon four posts about ten feet high, was now little more than a roof; the floor had fallen away, the joists and planks loosely piled on the ground below or resting on end at various angles, not wholly torn from their fastenings above. The supporting posts were themselves no longer vertical. It looked as if the whole edifice would go down at the touch of a finger.

Concealing himself in the débris of joists and flooring Searing looked across the open ground between his point of view and a spur of Kennesaw Mountain, a half-mile away. A road leading up and across this spur was crowded with troops – the rear-guard of the retiring enemy, their gun-barrels gleaming in the morning sunlight.

Searing had now learned all that he could hope to know. It was his duty to return to his own command with all possible speed and report his discovery. But the gray column of Confederates toiling up the mountain road was singularly tempting. His rifle – an ordinary "Springfield," but fitted with a globe sight and hair-trigger – would easily send its ounce and a quarter of lead hissing into their midst. That would probably not affect the duration and result of the war, but it is the business of a soldier to kill. It is also his habit if he is a good soldier. Searing cocked his rifle and "set" the trigger.

But it was decreed from the beginning of time that Private Searing was not to murder anybody that bright summer morning, nor was the Confederate retreat to be announced by him. For countless ages events had been so matching themselves together in that wondrous mosaic to some parts of which, dimly discernible, we give the name of history, that the acts which he had in will would have marred the harmony of the pattern. Some twenty-five years previously the Power charged with the execution of the work according to the design had provided against that mischance by causing the birth of a certain male child in a little village at the foot of the Carpathian Mountains, had carefully reared it, supervised its education, directed its desires into a military channel, and in due time made it an officer of artillery. By the concurrence of an infinite number of favoring influences and their preponderance over an infinite number of opposing ones, this officer of artillery had been made to commit a breach of discipline and flee from his native country to avoid punishment. He had been directed to New Orleans (instead of New York), where a recruiting officer awaited him on the wharf. He was enlisted and promoted, and things were so ordered that he now commanded a Confederate battery some two miles along the line from where Jerome Searing, the Federal scout, stood cocking his rifle. Nothing had been neglected – at every step in the progress of both these men's lives, and in the lives of their contemporaries and ancestors, and in the lives of the contemporaries of their ancestors, the right thing had been done to bring about the desired result. Had anything in all this vast concatenation been overlooked, Private Searing might have fired on the retreating Confederates that morning, and would perhaps have missed. As it fell out, a Confederate captain of artillery, having nothing better to do while awaiting his turn to pull out and be off, amused himself by sighting a field-piece obliquely to his right at what he mistook for some Federal officers on the crest of a hill, and discharged it. The shot flew high of its mark.

As Jerome Searing drew back the hammer of his rifle and with his eyes upon the distant Confederates considered where he could plant his shot with the best hope of making a widow or an orphan or a childless mother, – perhaps all three, for Private Searing, although he had repeatedly refused promotion, was not without a certain kind of ambition, – he heard a rushing sound in the air, like that made by the wings of a great bird swooping down upon its prey. More quickly than he could apprehend the gradation, it increased to a hoarse and horrible roar, as the missile that made it sprang at him out of the sky, striking with a deafening impact one of the posts supporting the confusion of timbers above him, smashing it into matchwood, and bringing down the crazy edifice with a loud clatter, in clouds of blinding dust!

When Jerome Searing recovered consciousness he did not at once understand what had occurred. It was, indeed, some time before he opened his eyes. For a while he believed that he had died and been buried, and he tried to recall some portions of the burial service. He thought that his wife was kneeling upon his grave, adding her weight to that of the earth upon his breast. The two of them, widow and earth, had crushed his coffin. Unless the children should persuade her to go home he would not much longer be able to breathe. He felt a sense of wrong. "I cannot speak to her," he thought; "the dead have no voice; and if I open my eyes I shall get them full of earth."

He opened his eyes. A great expanse of blue sky, rising from a fringe of the tops of trees. In the foreground, shutting out some of the trees, a high, dun mound, angular in outline and crossed by an intricate, patternless system of straight lines; the whole an immeasurable distance away – a distance so inconceivably great that it fatigued him, and he closed his eyes. The moment that he did so he was conscious of an insufferable light. A sound was in his ears like the low, rhythmic thunder of a distant sea breaking in successive waves upon the beach, and out of this noise, seeming a part of it, or possibly coming from beyond it, and intermingled with its ceaseless undertone, came the articulate words: "Jerome Searing, you are caught like a rat in a trap – in a trap, trap, trap."

Suddenly there fell a great silence, a black darkness, an infinite tranquillity, and Jerome Searing, perfectly conscious of his rathood, and well assured of the trap that he was in, remembering all and nowise alarmed, again opened his eyes to reconnoitre, to note the strength of his enemy, to plan his defense.

He was caught in a reclining posture, his back firmly supported by a solid beam. Another lay across his breast, but he had been able to shrink a little away from it so that it no longer oppressed him, though it was immovable. A brace joining it at an angle had wedged him against a pile of boards on his left, fastening the arm on that side. His legs, slightly parted and straight along the ground, were covered upward to the knees with a mass of débris which towered above his narrow horizon. His head was as rigidly fixed as in a vise; he could move his eyes, his chin – no more. Only his right arm was partly free. "You must help us out of this," he said to it. But he could not get it from under the heavy timber athwart his chest, nor move it outward more than six inches at the elbow.

Searing was not seriously injured, nor did he suffer pain. A smart rap on the head from a flying fragment of the splintered post, incurred simultaneously with the frightfully sudden shock to the nervous system, had momentarily dazed him. His term of unconsciousness, including the period of recovery, during which he had had the strange fancies, had probably not exceeded a few seconds, for the dust of the wreck had not wholly cleared away as he began an intelligent survey of the situation.

With his partly free right hand he now tried to get hold of the beam that lay across, but not quite against, his breast. In no way could he do so. He was unable to depress the shoulder so as to push the elbow beyond that edge of the timber which was nearest his knees; failing in that, he could not raise the forearm and hand to grasp the beam. The brace that made an angle with it downward and backward prevented him from doing anything in that direction, and between it and his body the space was not half so wide as the length of his forearm. Obviously he could not get his hand under the beam nor over it; the hand could not, in fact, touch it at all. Having demonstrated his inability, he desisted, and began to think whether he could reach any of the débris piled upon his legs.

In surveying the mass with a view to determining that point, his attention was arrested by what seemed to be a ring of shining metal immediately in front of his eyes. It appeared to him at first to surround some perfectly black substance, and it was somewhat more than a half-inch in diameter. It suddenly occurred to his mind that the blackness was simply shadow and that the ring was in fact the muzzle of his rifle protruding from the pile of débris. He was not long in satisfying himself that this was so – if it was a satisfaction. By closing either eye he could look a little way along the barrel – to the point where it was hidden by the rubbish that held it. He could see the one side, with the corresponding eye, at apparently the same angle as the other side with the other eye. Looking with the right eye, the weapon seemed to be directed at a point to the left of his head, and *vice versa*. He was unable to see the upper surface of the barrel, but could see the under surface of the stock at a slight angle. The piece was, in fact, aimed at the exact centre of his forehead.

In the perception of this circumstance, in the recollection that just previously to the mischance of which this uncomfortable situation was the result, he had cocked the rifle and set the trigger so that a touch would discharge it, Private Searing was affected with a feeling of uneasiness. But that was as far as possible from fear; he was a brave man, somewhat familiar with the aspect of rifles from that point of view, and of cannon too. And now he recalled, with something like amusement, an incident of his experience at the storming of Missionary Ridge, where, walking up to one of the enemy's embrasures from which he had seen a heavy gun throw charge after charge of grape among the assailants, he had thought for a moment that the piece had been withdrawn; he could see nothing in the opening but a brazen circle. What that was he had understood just in time to step aside as it pitched another peck of iron down that swarming slope. To face firearms is one of the commonest incidents in a soldier's life – firearms, too, with malevolent eyes blazing behind them. That is what a soldier is for. Still, Private Searing did not altogether relish the situation, and turned away his eyes.

After groping, aimless, with his right hand for a time he made an ineffectual attempt to release his left. Then he tried to disengage his head, the fixity of which was the more annoying from his ignorance of what held it. Next he tried to free his feet, but while exerting the powerful muscles of his legs for that purpose it occurred to him that a disturbance of the rubbish which held them might discharge the rifle; how it could have endured what had already befallen it he could not understand, although memory assisted him with several instances in point. One in particular he recalled, in which in a moment of mental abstraction he had clubbed his rifle and beaten out another gentleman's brains, observing afterward that the weapon which he had been diligently swinging by the muzzle was loaded, capped, and at full cock – knowledge of which circumstance would doubtless have cheered his antagonist to longer endurance. He had always smiled in recalling that blunder of his "green and salad days" as a soldier, but now he did not smile. He turned his eyes again to the muzzle of the rifle and for a moment fancied that it had moved; it seemed somewhat nearer.

Again he looked away. The tops of the distant trees beyond the bounds of the plantation interested him: he had not before observed how light and feathery they were, nor how darkly blue the sky was, even among their branches, where they somewhat paled it with their green; above him it appeared almost black. "It will be uncomfortably hot here," he thought, "as the day advances. I wonder which way I am looking."

Judging by such shadows as he could see, he decided that his face was due north; he would at least not have the sun in his eyes, and north – well, that was toward his wife and children.

"Bah!" he exclaimed aloud, "what have they to do with it?"

He closed his eyes. "As I can't get out I may as well go to sleep. The rebels are gone and some of our fellows are sure to stray out here foraging. They'll find me."

But he did not sleep. Gradually he became sensible of a pain in his forehead – a dull ache, hardly perceptible at first, but growing more and more uncomfortable. He opened his eyes and it was gone – closed them and it returned. "The devil!" he said, irrelevantly, and stared again at the sky. He heard the singing of birds, the strange metallic note of the meadow lark, suggesting the clash of vibrant blades. He fell into pleasant memories of his childhood, played again with his brother and sister, raced across the fields, shouting to alarm the sedentary larks, entered the sombre forest beyond and with timid steps followed the faint

path to Ghost Rock, standing at last with audible heart-throbs
before the Dead Man's Cave and seeking to penetrate its awful
mystery. For the first time he observed that the opening of the
haunted cavern was encircled by a ring of metal. Then all else
vanished and left him gazing into the barrel of his rifle as before.
But whereas before it had seemed nearer, it now seemed an
inconceivable distance away, and all the more sinister for that.
He cried out and, startled by something in his own voice – the
note of fear – lied to himself in denial: "If I don't sing out I may
stay here till I die."

He now made no further attempt to evade the menacing stare
of the gun barrel. If he turned away his eyes an instant it was to
look for assistance (although he could not see the ground on
either side the ruin), and he permitted them to return, obedient
to the imperative fascination. If he closed them it was from
weariness, and instantly the poignant pain in his forehead – the
prophecy and menace of the bullet – forced him to reopen them.

The tension of nerve and brain was too severe; nature came to
his relief with intervals of unconsciousness. Reviving from one
of these he became sensible of a sharp, smarting pain in his right
hand, and when he worked his fingers together, or rubbed his
palm with them, he could feel that they were wet and slippery.
He could not see the hand, but he knew the sensation; it was
running blood. In his delirium he had beaten it against the
jagged fragments of the wreck, had clutched it full of splinters.
He resolved that he would meet his fate more manly. He was a
plain, common soldier, had no religion and not much philosophy; he could not die like a hero, with great and wise last words,
even if there had been some one to hear them, but he could die
"game," and he would. But if he could only know when to
expect the shot!

Some rats which had probably inhabited the shed came
sneaking and scampering about. One of them mounted the pile
of débris that held the rifle; another followed and another.
Searing regarded them at first with indifference, then with
friendly interest; then, as the thought flashed into his bewildered mind that they might touch the trigger of his rifle, he

cursed them and ordered them to go away. "It is no business of yours," he cried.

The creatures went away; they would return later, attack his face, gnaw away his nose, cut his throat – he knew that, but he hoped by that time to be dead.

Nothing could now unfix his gaze from the little ring of metal with its black interior. The pain in his forehead was fierce and incessant. He felt it gradually penetrating the brain more and more deeply, until at last its progress was arrested by the wood at the back of his head. It grew momentarily more insufferable: he began wantonly beating his lacerated hand against the splinters again to counteract that horrible ache. It seemed to throb with a slow, regular recurrence, each pulsation sharper than the preceding, and sometimes he cried out, thinking he felt the fatal bullet. No thoughts of home, of wife and children, of country, of glory. The whole record of memory was effaced. The world had passed away – not a vestige remained. Here in this confusion of timbers and boards is the sole universe. Here is immortality in time – each pain an everlasting life. The throbs tick off eternities.

Jerome Searing, the man of courage, the formidable enemy, the strong, resolute warrior, was as pale as a ghost. His jaw was fallen; his eyes protruded; he trembled in every fibre; a cold sweat bathed his entire body; he screamed with fear. He was not insane – he was terrified.

In groping about with his torn and bleeding hand he seized at last a strip of board, and, pulling, felt it give way. It lay parallel with his body, and by bending his elbow as much as the contracted space would permit, he could draw it a few inches at a time. Finally it was altogether loosened from the wreckage covering his legs; he could lift it clear of the ground its whole length. A great hope came into his mind: perhaps he could work it upward, that is to say backward, far enough to lift the end and push aside the rifle; or, if that were too tightly wedged, so place the strip of board as to deflect the bullet. With this object he passed it backward inch by inch, hardly daring to breathe lest that act somehow defeat his intent, and more than ever unable to remove his eyes from the rifle, which might perhaps now hasten to improve its waning opportunity. Something at least had been gained: in the occupation of his mind in this attempt at self-defense he was less sensible of the pain in his head and had ceased to wince. But he was still dreadfully frightened and his teeth rattled like castanets.

The strip of board ceased to move to the suasion of his hand. He tugged at it with all his strength, changed the direction of its length all he could, but it had met some extended obstruction behind him and the end in front was still too far away to clear the pile of débris and reach the muzzle of the gun. It extended, indeed, nearly as far as the trigger guard, which, uncovered by the rubbish, he could imperfectly see with his right eye. He tried to break the strip with his hand, but had no leverage. In his defeat, all his terror returned, augmented tenfold. The black aperture of the rifle appeared to threaten a sharper and more imminent death in punishment of his rebellion. The track of the bullet through his head ached with an intenser anguish. He began to tremble again.

Suddenly he became composed. His tremor subsided. He clenched his teeth and drew down his eyebrows. He had not exhausted his means of defense; a new design had shaped itself in his mind – another plan of battle. Raising the front end of the strip of board, he carefully pushed it forward through the wreckage at the side of the rifle until it pressed against the trigger guard. Then he moved the end slowly outward until he could feel that it had cleared it, then, closing his eyes, thrust it against the trigger with all his strength! There was no explosion; the rifle had been discharged as it dropped from his hand when the building fell. But it did its work.

Lieutenant Adrian Searing, in command of the picket-guard on that part of the line through which his brother Jerome had passed on his mission, sat with attentive ears in his breastwork behind the line. Not the faintest sound escaped him; the cry of a bird, the barking of a squirrel, the noise of the wind among the pines – all were anxiously noted by his overstrained sense.

Suddenly, directly in front of his line, he heard a faint, confused rumble, like the clatter of a falling building translated by distance. The lieutenant mechanically looked at his watch. Six o'clock and eighteen minutes. At the same moment an officer approached him on foot from the rear and saluted.

"Lieutenant," said the officer, "the colonel directs you to move forward your line and feel the enemy if you find him. If not, continue the advance until directed to halt. There is reason to think that the enemy has retreated."

The lieutenant nodded and said nothing; the other officer retired. In a moment the men, apprised of their duty by the non-commissioned officers in low tones, had deployed from their rifle-pits and were moving forward in skirmishing order, with set teeth and beating hearts.

This line of skirmishers sweeps across the plantation toward the mountain. They pass on both sides of the wrecked building, observing nothing. At a short distance in their rear their commander comes. He casts his eyes curiously upon the ruin and sees a dead body half buried in boards and timbers. It is so covered with dust that its clothing is Confederate gray. Its face is yellowish white; the cheeks are fallen in, the temples sunken, too, with sharp ridges about them, making the forehead forbiddingly narrow; the upper lip, slightly lifted, shows the white teeth, rigidly clenched. The hair is heavy with moisture, the face as wet as the dewy grass all about. From his point of view the officer does not observe the rifle; the man was apparently killed by the fall of the building.

"Dead a week," said the officer curtly, moving on and absently pulling out his watch as if to verify his estimate of time. Six o'clock and forty minutes.

THE STORMING OF THE FORT

Walter Wood

The Second Afghan War broke out in 1878 when the British once again feared that the Russians would extend their influence over Afghanistan through their treaty with the Amir, Sher Ali. The hero of the war was Major-General Sir Frederick Roberts who, through his remarkable command, achieved notable victories at Peiwar Kotal, Kabul and, most notably, relief of the siege at Kandahar. The following story takes place during the Second Afghan War, although the story is almost prophetic. A year after this story was published (in August 1896), the Gordon Highlanders achieved a major victory on the Indian Frontier when they won the Heights of Dargai in October 1897. Wood could almost have been writing about that assault. But then Walter Wood (1866–1961) was no stranger to imagining the future. He wrote a number of stories whipping up a jingoistic zeal at the threat of an invasion of Britain, as in The Enemy in Our Midst *(1906) and most notably in the short story "The Tunnel Terror" (1907), where the Channel Tunnel has to be protected against the might of Germany.*

Gordon's Own were under canvas, and from the lines all men could see the gloomy fort which was to be stormed and captured. The fort lay in a little hollow at the foot of the lowering hills, looking like a prison to which men might be sent who were cut off from the world for evermore. It was 90 yards square, with walls 8 feet thick, and 20 feet high, and at each of the four corners was a tower which rose 20 feet above the wall. Three sides were flanked by hills, and one only was open to the plain, and in that the single gate of the fort was placed. The flat roofs of the huts shone dully in the burning sunshine, and the towers rose heavenward, like silent sentinels. Within the massive walls there was no mark of life; the place was as dormant as a city of the dead. But swarthy men stood, grim and patient, in the watch-towers, waiting for their prey to deliver itself up to them. Their eyes glowed as they swept the plain where Gordon's Own were quartered, and a grating sound arose as they slowly changed their arms from one hand to the other. The banner of the Prophet drooped from a flagstaff on the tallest tower, and the hillmen looked from that to the camp and from the camp to the flag again. They could see the sentries of Gordon's Own, and looked at them with lazy curiosity.

A private of gigantic stature was on sentry nearest the fort, and he stopped on his pendulum-like march to gaze for a moment at it. His form was boldly outlined, and a knot of tribesmen in an outer tower watched him with savage admiration. But the thirst for blood was strong within them, and one man raised his awkward weapon and thrust the barrel gently through a loophole. The sentry stood there like a statue. He was looking dreamily at the fort, and wondering about his own home in the hills across the sea, in more generous climes than these.

He saw a puff of smoke and a tiny fork of flame from one of the towers, and before he guessed its meaning he felt a sharp pang in his shoulder, and staggered back a pace or two. The wound was slight, and the sentry had no wish to call attention to it. He was within range of the fort, and might go down at any moment; but that was a concern of his commanding officer. If he saw fit to alter things, it was well; if he did not, it was still well. The officer commanding could do no wrong.

The sergeant of the guard had seen the puff of smoke, and he hastened up to the sentry. The man was plugging the wound with a finger and was telling, in audible tones, what he thought of the hillmen and where he wished they were. "And I'd have it specially hot for 'em, too," he added, as he saw the sergeant.

The sergeant laughed. "Well, you'll be able to fire up a bit when we storm the place to-night," he said; "that is, if you're not too much hurt."

"Hurt," said the sentry, scornfully, "hurt by an old slug-slinger like yond? I'd scorn to think it. I'm as fit as may be, and don't even want relieving."

"Two inches lower down," said the sergeant, eyeing the wound critically, "and it would have plumped through your heart."

"But for an accident of birth I might have been King of England," answered the sentry.

"That's so," said the sergeant; "all the same, you'll get relieved, and take a walk round and see the doctor. If you hadn't such a thundering big carcass you wouldn't be such a good target. That sort of thing reconciles one to being rather small of stature."

The sentry was relieved, there were no more shots, and night came down from the hills. No man went to rest in camp, but the soldiers in the fort, secure in the strength of their retreat, lay down to sleep with their arms beside them. Their minds were at rest, for a certain priest had given them his blessing and said, "The sons of pigs who are in the plains are few in number, and their fate is sealed. To-night they will try to rush the fort, but fear not, for the walls are thick and the gates are strong, and their bones will bleach in the wind and rain." He had given them his blessing and had gone farther up the hills, mistrusting greatly his own prophecy.

The colonel and his second in command walked forth from the lines as the day gave place to night, and the two looked long and earnestly at the fort.

"You'll find," said the senior major, "that the place is too strong for us, and that it can't be done."

"Can't be done!" exclaimed the colonel.

"Can't be done! Why, if the odds were ten times as big as they are, I'd undertake the risk – and win, too. Can't be done! There's no such word as 'can't' for Gordon's Own!"

"I'm not saying it won't be attempted," said the senior major, sadly. "God knows I'd be the last to do so. The order's come, and we've got to go. You know what I mean, Stevens – we'll talk as friends now, and not as chief and second. When I say 'can't,' I only mean that what happened to Charley will happen again, and perhaps cause to others just the bitterness it caused to me. Someone bungled then, and someone has bungled now: but that doesn't mend matters."

"Someone blundered at Balaclava," said the colonel, "but think of the glory of it."

The major smiled wearily.

"The glory part of the profession never appealed much to me," he said, "and now that I'm getting somewhat into the sere and yellow leaf it doesn't offer any new charms. Charley used to talk of glory – and what was the end of it?"

"I admit that that little affair in the hills was a bad business," said the colonel, uneasily; "but you know, Raylton, it wasn't done on purpose."

"The result was just the same," said Raylton, grimly. "If a father's curses could have withered the life of the man who was responsible for that day's sorry work, he would have gone the way of all flesh long ago."

"You know what the chaplain said on Sunday about forgive and forget," said the colonel, but rather lamely, for he had no great faith in sermons.

"The first I did long ago," replied the major; "but the second – not if I lived till the crack of doom. And if you had had a son of yours sent on to death as Charley was sent, you'd think as I think now."

"The lad was mentioned in despatches," said the colonel, "and his bravery was officially recorded in the *Gazette*."

The major smiled again, but grimly this time. "And when his mother saw it – what then?" he asked.

"It was the suddenness of the shock," replied the colonel, "and the state of her heart. You know, a shock like that often kills."

"I lost Charley out here, and my wife at home, in one week, all through the bungling and incompetence of a general officer commanding," said Raylton, "and yet you talk to me of glory. I remember how every one of the small force was butchered, and you remember just as well. Never a soul survived, and yet when you are ordered to do the same sort of thing you scoff at the notion of its impossibility, and refuse to hear of such a word as 'can't.'"

"I do, and I say again what I said then," exclaimed the colonel. "By the men of Gordon's Own the word 'can't' has never been recognised; you know that it's one of the traditions of the regiment that the word is barred. As for Charley and that miserable business in the hills, you cannot know how sorry and sore I've been about it. Why, Raylton, only one man on earth suffered more than I did, and that was yourself. Come, come; the worst was bad enough, without adding to it. Remember that, and give me your support now, when I need it more than ever before. If *you* fail me, Raylton, where am I to look for guidance and assistance? Forget the past, and help me to make the present such that people will hold it in eternal remembrance. Think of the records of Ours, and what it would mean to have this achievement added to them! Why, there would be nothing to surpass it in our annals!"

The colonel was a man of enthusiastic temperament, and had a way of communicating his enthusiasm to others. The major was a cold man at best, the soldier of a system, with but meagre receptivity for what he called the bunkum of glory; but the fire of his chief and comrade was thawing him. The sternness of his face relaxed, and he felt a tingling sensation as the blood coursed faster through him.

"Kismet!" he said, at last. "What will be will be. I crave the post of greatest danger. If the worst comes to the worst, why, what's the end of it? – the sooner to be with her and Charley."

The colonel watched him as he strode away. "That's the spirit for a forlorn hope. If I were certain that it would fill every officer and man of the battalion," he mused, "I'd storm the gates of the Inferno itself. But I'm not, in spite of what I said to Raylton, for half the men are fresh from home and the other half are untried. In twelve hours we shall know the worst, and know what stuff the men are really made of."

When the colonel got back to the lines he found that all was ready for the assault. A captain and half his company had fallen in, and the pioneers with the powder-bags and their picks and spades were in front. The captain's instructions were clear and simple, for the colonel was a man of few words. He was to advance noiselessly to the gates, and, having laid his powder-bags, was to blow them up. The explosion was to be the signal for the general assault.

The party marched off, and the colors moved the battalion nearer to the fort, so that his men should be ready to rush the entrance as soon as the gates were blown down.

The explosion came at last. There was a blinding flash and a dull roar, followed by shouts of startled men within the fort. The battalion dashed up to the gates, with bayonets fixed, but only to meet the captain and his party falling back.

The powder had been exploded, but the bags had been poorly laid in the darkness and the gates were still standing.

"Never mind," shouted the colonel, "we'll make the assault, all the same. The gates are bound to be weakened, and we can knock them in with spades and axes. Come on, Gordon's Own, remember Ghuznee!"

The men who heard him rallied, but those who did not, and they were most in number, remained where they were, sullen and immovable in the darkness. The front of the battalion got to the gates again, and there was a hammering sound of axe and spade. But the gates were stout and strongly barred, and the soldiers within the walls were firing smartly, with heavy loss to the assailants, and never a casualty to themselves.

Who really gave the cue for it no one could tell, but someone shouted that it was no good standing there to be shot down like sheep, and as everyone seemed to be of his way of thinking, there was a general and disorderly retreat.

Men ran helter-skelter back to the lines, where shame overcame them, and they formed up – not quite as steadily as on parade, but as well as could be expected, seeing that the legs of half of them felt as if they had plenty of running power still left, and would like to find an outlet for it.

Day had broken when the battalion had formed up, and in the weird and uncertain light the men began to look uneasily and distrustfully at each other. Each would have liked to ask the other what had possessed him to fly, but as each was quite well able to answer the question, it was not put. The light grew stronger, and when the day had completely broken, the battalion, thinking for the moment as an entire being, began to wish that things had been otherwise – that it had not, for instance, fallen back in such unseemly haste; and particularly to wish that the colonel did not look so unholy as he strode to the front and made as if he would address them.

The spirit of "I told you so!" possessed the major for the moment, and he could not keep from reminding the colonel of the talk they had had. "It's scarcely worth mentioning," he said, as he stood beside his chief, for no officer was mounted, "but I ventured to remark that it couldn't be done."

"And I ventured to reply," returned the colonel, hotly, "that it not only could be done, but should be done. We've fallen back for the time being, but we shall storm the fort again, and I'll either take it or lose every officer and man in the battalion."

"In the teeth of language like that," said the major, warmly, "I should be more than coward to say another word to turn you from your purpose. I'm with you to the death, and by way of showing it, I propose to volunteer to place some more bags of powder against the gates and blow an opening through them. If I can't get any men to do it, I'll run the risk alone."

"I'll ask for twenty volunteers for you," said the colonel; "but first of all I've something to say to the battalion."

The colonel was not a pleasant sight to see. He had been shot in the shoulder, and the blood had thickened on his Khaki jacket. One of his own men, in the confusion of the retreat, had stuck his bayonet into his helmet, and had cut through it and on to the colonel's brow, where the marks showed red and fresh. His face was blackened with the battle-smoke, and his eyes glowed in their sockets.

There was dead silence as the chief faced his battalion, and it was broken only by his angry voice.

"Gordon's Own," he began, "what can I say to you? I don't know; words won't come, the words I ought to utter I daren't."

The men shuffled uneasily, and the officers kept their eyes on the ground.

"And yet," exclaimed the colonel, fiercely, "why should I spare you? My feelings are nothing to you; why should your's concern me? What you are you know as well as I do – you are cowards, poltroons; dogs who turn tail and fly from the enemy, and whose blood turns to water at the sight of the sword and the smell of powder!"

There was more shuffling in the ranks, and the colonel heard low growls of disapproval. The officers lifted their eyes from the ground, and looked defiantly at their leader. His language could be justified to some extent, but there was a limit to what even he might say. Not a sign escaped the colonel's eyes, not a sound was made that did not reach his ears. He began to feel his battalion, and to know that at last all was well. He tried another sentence, and was then sure of his ground. "I wish," he said, "that God had spared me the shame of seeing this night's work. Is there one of you man enough to say 'Amen' to that?"

The soldiers found their tongues at last, and there was one loud answer, "Yes."

"Is there one man among you who wants to fall out – who

feels as if he couldn't storm the place again?" asked the colonel. "If so, there's plenty of room at the rear." He uttered the last sentence in tones of withering contempt, and it galled his hearers to the quick. There was a savage shout of "No."

"I give you two minutes to think it over," said the colonel, "and if any man's heart is faint, let him fall out. This isn't the place for his sort."

The colonel took out his watch and held it in his hand. "One minute's gone," he said, after a pause.

No man stirred. "A minute and three quarters," said the colonel. Still no man moved. "Only five seconds left," he said, but the ranks remained unbroken.

"Time's up," said the colonel, replacing his watch. "And you've proved yourselves men." He had meditated saying that the chance for withdrawing had passed, and that the sergeants were to shoot any man who tried to run away, and that the officers were to shoot any sergeants who did the same; as for the officers, he would keep an eye on them. But he knew that further threats or condemnations were not needful, and he went on: "There never was a simpler and easier bit of work than this. Major Raylton wants twenty volunteers."

The battalion stepped forward like one man, took two paces to the front, and halted. The whole movement was done without a word of command, and the colonel's heart was glad. "Thank God," he said, "for that spontaneous advance. Major Raylton will choose his men. The work is as easy and simple as marching past. All we have to do is to wait for the explosion, then rush the gates once more, and the fort is ours. You hear what the niggers are playing on the tom-toms and howling? It's their song of victory, and they're thumping and shrieking it because they think they're licked us. We've got to change their music for them, and we'll do it. When we're within a hundred yards of the gates, the bugles and the drums will strike up something like that infernal air; and, lads, we'll beat 'em to their own confounded tune!"

After that not even the colonel could have kept them back. The major and his little band stole off, and marched under a heavy fire to the gates. There was dead silence in the ranks, as officers and men waited for the flash of the powder and the boom of the explosion.

It came at last. There was another great blaze, and another deep, loud roar as the powder was exploded. The flames died away, but the sound of the explosion went rumbling over the plains and up the hills. It smote upon the ears of the prophetic priest, and he was glad that the spirit had moved him to go up higher.

A shower of small stones and pieces of wood rained upon the ranks of Gordon's Own, but they hurt no man seriously. The voice of the colonel was heard once more, and the battalion dashed forward to the assault. The men went bodily and solidly towards the fire which the explosion had made. When a hundred yards from the fort, the buglers and the drummers obeyed the command which had been given to them, and with one great shout Gordon's Own swept towards the gates. There was not much music in the tune; but that was all the better for the bandsmen, for their state of mind and body was such as to make fine music impossible. They could thump the drums, however, and make the bugles blare, and this was the only sort of tune that could be made audible above the shouts of the fighters, the rattle of the hillmen's jezails, and the clank of steel. When the gates were reached, drums and bugles were thrown aside, and with cold steel only Gordon's Own swept through the opening into the fort.

Many a man went down before the fort was won, but Gordon's Own got in at last, and the banner of the Prophet was hauled down to make way for the hoisting of the Queen's Colour. The old torn sheet of silk went slowly up, and the chief of Gordon's Own was satisfied.

The colonel was a man of method, and when he had got his prize he wished to know the cost.

"What's the roll-call like?" he asked.

"It's dwindled sadly," answered the adjutant. "There's many a man lying under the walls of the fort who'll hear the 'Last Post' no more."

"They'll do something more than that," said the colonel, with a glow of enthusiasm; "they'll hear the 'Réveillé.'"

"That's true, sir," said the adjutant, gravely. "I'd overlooked that for the moment. As for the roll-call: Major Raylton, Captain Hawkes, and Lieutenant Waite are among the killed."

The colonel sighed. "God rest their souls – they were all good soldiers," he said.

"Six N.C.O.'s and seventy rank and file went down, too," proceeded the adjutant; "and, not counting ourselves, there are half-a-dozen officers and a hundred men pretty badly wounded."

The colonel drew himself proudly up. "That's a heavy and a sorry list in one way," he said, "but what will the general say, and what will they say at home when they read of it?"

"They'll be talking of it to-morrow," said the adjutant. "The newspapers will be full of it."

"God grant that those who've gone will know about it, too," said the colonel. "Fall in the burial parties, and let both officers and men be laid to rest on the little hillock there. People shall know it henceforth as the Hill of Gordon's Own."

LOVED I NOT HONOUR MORE

Amy Myers

*Border problems between an expanding South Africa and
a strong Zulu nation led to an outbreak of hostilities in
January 1879. Soon afterwards, an army of Zulus massacred a British camp at Isandhlwana. So began the short
but memorable Zulu War. This is the background to the
following story by Amy Myers, who has written a number
of historical novels under the pseudonym Harriet Hudson.
Under her own name she is probably best known for her
series featuring the Victorian/Edwardian chef-cum-sleuth
Auguste Didier.*

*Remember me, remember me! A posy of blue forget-me-nots for
Mary Halliday . . .*
   Bodies everywhere, assegaied, shot, mutilated, black and

white in heaps tumbled together – white as the boulders and
stones of this accursed slope and black as the guilt of those who
saw no need to fortify this camp; those whose reconnaissance
could find no sign of the vast Zulu impi, and who ordered half
the remaining forces here to ride out to seek the foe, leaving
20,000 Zulu warriors to fall upon the 1,800 at Isandhlwana Hill
under the merciless heavens. Scorching heat and death, that was
Isandhlwana camp, every body ripped open by assegais; men
disembowelled, beheaded, hung up like butcher's carcasses.
After all was lost there was no escape for the pitifully few
survivors, even in flight. The ground was red with the blood of
Her Majesty's Imperial Army, the blood spilt for England.

"Faster, Coomassie, for our lives!"

Captain Jack Cavendish of the 2nd/24th urged his horse on.
To call his mount Coomassie might bring him good fortune in
his quest for honour. He wore the Ashantee War Medal for
Wolseley's '74 expedition to capture Coomassie and had won
promotion there for bravery, but the achievement did not sit
lightly on him. He must live up to it, not only for his own but for
Mary's sake. He had hoped this war against the Zulus would
provide the opportunity, but, dear God, not like this. What
chance for glory in the midst of this nightmare massacre?

God Himself had hidden His eyes this day. In the midst of
the fighting, the sun had blacked out, as though He could not
bear to watch. Evening had fallen upon them, so it seemed to
Jack, dazed by catastrophe in which time had no meaning. Then
once more the pitiless heat burned down from above, as well as
all around. The smell – the acrid stench of heat, blood and guts
– stifled his nostrils, enfolded him like a blanket, and he longed
only for the waters of the Buffalo River. If he could reach that
blessed Jordan, everlasting life might yet be his. But first the
hell, the fires and torments of damnation, for the Buffalo lay a
few miles from the camp over stony hilly ground with no tracks.

The forces left to defend Isandhlwana camp today had been
meagre, but even so they would have held it until relieving
forces could arrive, had they been packed densely together
inside a laager formed by wagons. Their training, fire power

and unlimited ammunition would have carried the day, but no such command had been given. Lord Chelmsford had ordered the 2nd Battalion 24th Regiment of Foot to march at daybreak in the belief he could trap the enemy to the east in the Nkandhlas hills, and Colonel Pulleine, left in command of the camp, had his authority superseded by Colonel Durnford, who had later arrived at Isandhlwana with his Natal Native troops. Small groups of Zulus had been sighted, and so Durnford too had marched forth in mid-morning to seek the enemy. Worse, the camp was further weakened by companies despatched as outposts a thousand yards and more from the tents and wagons.

Madness! Why had no one even suspected the small groups of Zulus might turn out to be the main Zulu impi?

Too late, Durnford must have realized his mistake and turned back to aid the camp. Jack's company had been on the right of the line of defence with the mounted men, and, falling back under the Zulu onslaught when the line broke, had mustered in a desperate last attempt to save the camp at the saddle between Isandhlwana Hill and the rocky koppie. There they had found themselves side by side with Durnford's men, but against such numbers they were slaughtered where they stood.

Jack Cavendish cursed his lot. He should have been riding safely with Colonel Glyn, not fleeing for his scant chance of life. Ill fortune had put his company on picquet duty last night, only to be relieved at 4 am, too late to join the marching forces with the rest of his battalion.

There was no dishonour, he knew, in this desperate flight. He had done his duty by his men, and now there was none to save, except himself. He had seen men he had laughed and joked with only yesterday cut down and torn open, heard their cries as they fell, knowing what kind of death was about to descend on them. He had seen as they made their stand at the saddle the horrors of the camp that lay straddled across the path; officers, men and boys butchered together, Zulus everywhere, looting and mutilating. Death for Queen and Country had sounded fine and glorious as they embarked in England, but where lay glory here?

The only chance of escape had lain across the saddle, for beyond it lay the track to the camp at Rorke's Drift. Yet that path too had been swarming with the enemy. The Zulus' tactics of horns and chest had ensured that one horn could sweep round the camp to the rear of the hill. There was no choice but to ride south, down this trackless slope strewn with boulders and stones, in the hope of reaching the Buffalo. Yet here too the few survivors with their red tunics were easy targets, and the black shapes of Zulus loomed up over every crest and from behind every rock, bounding with ease over this hostile terrain. The white men, hampered by heavy boots, their ammunition gone, were being slaughtered on all sides, and their black troops with them. The Natal Native forces were tearing off the head-bands that proclaimed their allegiance to the Great White Queen – in vain, for they too were cut down.

"Good old Coomassie." Was that choking voice, the tears mingling with the sweat, all that was left of Jack Cavendish and his dreams of glory?

Only those who were mounted, as Jack was, stood any chance of escape from this hell, and even that was small, for on this ground the Zulus could run as fast as any horse.

"*uSuthu!*"

A Zulu shot up from behind a large boulder before him, assegai in hand, chanting the now familiar war cry. Coomassie reared up, throwing the Zulu from his aim and Jack despatched him with one of the precious remaining bullets in his revolver. Coomassie was plunging out of control now, he would kill them both, and Jack struggled to calm him, as they reached the thorny shrubbery bordering a treacherous-looking dry gully, littered now with the bodies of those who had chosen the nearest crossing place, without thought for the rocks and danger beneath.

Following the path of others in an attempt to find a safer way, Jack dismounted to lead Coomassie through the all but impenetrable thorns. One foot landed on the mutilated body of some poor devil, his innards torn from him, but he hardly registered the fact. Sweat streamed from his face, clung under his helmet, and made his uniform dark with wet and smelly stickiness.

On this bank there were fewer Zulus, but behind him, ahead of him, the noise of war cries and screams deadened his mind to all but the instinct of survival in this race with death. There were fewer gunshots now; the Zulus behind him had looted rifles from the dead at Isandhlwana to add to their own, but in front of him must be gathering the same horn that cut the Rorke's Drift track, whose chief weapons would be assegais.

He remounted, following the example of the half-dozen or so fleeing men ahead of him. Across the gully at last and he could see another slope, crawling with Zulus pursuing the trickle of survivors. A huge Zulu leapt towards him, and another, both poised to kill, but Coomassie swerved and it was the fellow in front whose horse caught the brunt of the assegai, bringing its blue-tunicked rider crashing down. The Zulus moved in for the kill.

As the man cried out, it crossed Jack's mind that he could kill both the Zulus, even pick up the white man. He tried hard to dismiss the thought; it was suicide to stop on this frantic ride, but he had promised Mary he would return to her with honour, when a year ago he had ridden off to war. He could achieve it now, but he had two bullets only – he might need them for himself to save his life, or, he gulped, to end it. And yet . . .

Suddenly Jack realized he was icy calm. Here at last was the opportunity he had longed for to display the reputation he had so dearly won at Coomassie. He thought of the locket he had given Mary, with Lovelace's words written in delicate script inside:

> Tell me not, sweet, I am unkind,
> That from the nunnery
> Of thy chaste breast and quiet mind
> To war and arms I fly.
> I could not love thee, dear, so much
> Loved I not honour more.

He was even humming the regimental march, "The Warwick-shire Lads", as he reined in Coomassie, took aim and shot both Zulus. "For the Twenty-fourth" he shouted. Those who lay dead and mutilated in the camp that should have offered them defence. Those whose bones would lie bleached on this hillside. His ammunition was gone, his revolver useless now; he had only his sword and already more black warriors were gathering, bounding towards them, shields up and assegais glinting in the sun. For precious seconds, he was paralyzed, unable to move to grasp his slim chance of outriding them in this crazy race to the river.

The man had scrambled clear and was staggering towards him. It was madness, Jack told himself, for Coomassie could not bear them both to safety, and yet he found he was hauling up the soldier on to Coomassie's back behind him. Perhaps the blue patrol tunic of the man he'd rescued would bring them both luck, for the Zulus' first instinct seemed to be to attack the red tunics that outnumbered the blue. Ahead of them Jack saw the last hill before the river, and it seemed to him the Zulus were thinning out. Could there be a chance, even for both of them?

He turned to glance at the man he had rescued. *And in the midst of this hell the devil was laughing at him.*

"My thanks, Jack."

"Harry," he croaked. Dear God, he had saved the life of Harry Lyle, had chosen to ride through this pit of death with Harry Lyle, if he fell to a Zulu assegai or bullet how could fate have been so vicious as to make Harry his companion in death?

Sergeant Harry Lyle of the 1st/24th grinned, as Coomassie plodded on agonisingly slowly now. The blue eyes, which Jack thought until a few hours ago had been banished from his life for ever, still mocked him.

"I'll race you to Mary's arms yet," he laughed.

"Have you no sense of honour?" Jack yelled.

"No. I find it a great disadvantage in life, don't you agree?"

Jack's heart sank as he realized the steepness of the hill before them. "Coomassie will never carry the two of us," he cried. "One of us has to lead him."

"I vote for you, Jack," Harry laughed. "Coomassie, eh? What a joke."

A joke? Did the man have no shame? Very well, Jack would prove to him that there was some honour in the world, that he trusted Harry not to seize the reins from his hands and ride off. He dismounted, leading Coomassie and stumbling at his side as Harry dug his heels in. Coomassie managed to struggle onto the ridge, but he could not last much longer. Beyond them lay the blessed sight of the Buffalo River – but something else as well.

"God's teeth!" Harry whistled. "Cetewayo's welcoming party."

"Half the Zulu impi," Jack groaned, scrambling up in front of Harry again. "The river's our only hope now."

Dear Lord, what was he to do? Ahead lay certain death for one, and probably both. Anyone but Harry would dismount and take his chance alone, but if by a miracle Harry lived, how would that tarnish Jack's love for Mary? Would he ever be free of those mocking eyes? The thought of Mary as he had seen her last, bright eyed, laughing at him, so lovely in her blue gown, her lips so soft, sent a stab of pain shuddering through him. Why this hell, this torment? Men were tearing others to pieces, all in the name of honour: the honour of the Queen, of the army, of the regiment – and one's own.

Coomassie twisted sharply as they stumbled across the flat to the Buffalo River, and the Zulus had seen them now. Jack's weight was thrown back against Harry, who was slipping from the horse, and he reached out for him. With all his efforts Harry could not hold on, and he fell from Coomassie, his tunic tearing open as he did so.

And then Jack saw it. Surely he was mistaken? It was the hallucination of a doomed man. No, the image was starkly clear, as was his mind; it was the last twist of fate's assegai. Round Harry's neck, earlier held from Jack's sight by the tunic, was a torn piece of cloth, now fluttering free over Harry's chest as he lay sprawled on the ground. There was no doubt it was part of the regimental colour of the 2nd/24th, his own battalion's, not Harry's. Jack knew the regimental colour of the 1st Battalion had been left in camp at Helpmakaar, and he'd seen the red silk, with its XXIV, quite clearly on Harry. All calm vanished. The regiment had lost a colour at Chillianwallah in 1849. Was he, Jack Cavendish, to be singled out by fate for failing to seize the opportunity to rescue one, even though only a mere scrap of it remained?

How the hell had Harry come to have it, when it must have been in the command tent in the centre of the camp? He and Harry had been close together in the line of defence, and by the time what survivors there were escaped the attentions of the Zulus, the camp was a stench of death; there had been no hope of an individual fighting his way in through the Zulu mob. But what to do now? Surely God could not demand of Jack to rescue Harry Lyle just for the sake of that scrap of cloth? Merely to turn Coomassie back once more would spell certain death with only the sword as a weapon. And yet Jack turned his head, to see Harry lying still on the ground, either wounded or winded, and four Zulus racing towards him. "Tell Mary I died a hero," Harry yelled painfully. "On your honour, Jack."

Jack was weeping in his agony. He had already done enough to win a Victoria Cross in rescuing Harry. Was that not honour enough? Should he gallop on? No one would know about the colour but him. Or should he turn back to be a dead hero? Surely that could be asked of no one, even to rescue the colour? To gallop on, to turn back, which?

Why, oh why, had Harry Lyle burst back into his life in the early morning of this nightmare . . .

This camp was the best yet, Jack decided, even though with Isandhlwana Hill behind them, a gradual slope and plain before them, a full camp and plenty of supplies, little attention had been paid to the regulations for camp defence. It was unnecessary, for here nature had provided its own. Jack had been out here in South Africa for ten months now. Before that, 2nd Battalion had been stationed at Chatham, close to Mary Halliday's home at Boxley, and his long and patient courtship had been sweet.

The battalion had come out here in '78 to reinforce the eastern frontier of Cape Colony and had beaten back countless rebel native attacks at Haynes Mill, Zanyorkwe valley and Mount Kempt; by July Jack had been well seasoned as to the way of things out here, though so far the fighting had mostly been in brief skirmishes. When they'd moved on to Natal to wait for the inevitable war with King Cetewayo of the Zulus, he was impatient to get his first real crack at the enemy. Now six months later it had come. At last they'd moved to Helpmakaar and then Rorke's Drift, and eleven days ago on 11th January, when the ultimatum to Cetewayo had expired, they had crossed the river Buffalo into Zululand. The invasion had begun and soon the Zulu capital Ulundi would be theirs. Yesterday Jack's battalion, artillery, and other troops had marched with Colonel Glyn's column the nine miles to Isandhlwana and there they had camped to prepare to face Cetewayo's impi. Jack was eager for action, confident that good warriors though some of the Zulus undoubtedly were, they would be no match for the firepower of Chelmsford's forces. Soon he would be able to write to Mary of victory, of the capture of Ulundi and of Cetewayo himself.

The 2nd/24th was camped near to one side of the track to Ulundi, next to the Mounted Infantry. The 1st Battalion were on the far side of the track, and the whole camp was protected by the oddly shaped Isandhlwana Hill, or the Little Sphynx as it was already jokingly called from its likeness to the regimental badge. The two battalions of the 24th, the Warwickshires, were all but strangers, for the 1st had been out here in South Africa for some years. It was from their ranks that the Mounted Infantry had been chiefly drawn – a grand name for a hotchpotch of a few regular soldiers and anyone able to ride a horse who was willing to volunteer.

Jack was still smarting with annoyance that while he was on guard duty most of 2nd Battalion had vanished along with other troops with orders to join Lord Chelmsford to fight the foe ten miles away. The first chance of a real engagement with the enemy, and here he was stuck in camp. Few honours were won that way.

"Jack Cavendish, as I'm alive and well."

To his horror, outside the HQ tent, walking by as bold as brass he saw Harry Lyle with all his old damned impudence. Jack had not seen him for nearly five years, and had hoped never to do so again. Harry gravely saluted his superior.

"What the devil are you doing here?" Jack asked, sick at heart. Was there no escape?

Hary shrugged. "One second lieutenant 2nd/24th dismissed the service for cowardice in the face of the enemy, one lowly private name of Harry Smith joins 1st/24th Regiment of Foot conveniently leaving shortly for South Africa. I'm highly thought of here, Jack. I'm a sergeant, promoted to Mounted Infantry. Not bad, eh?"

"I thought the Colonel took the Mounted Infantry with him earlier this morning."

"So he did. There was I all dressed up in my blue, resigned to following the drum, but then I managed to duck out. Too many Zulus and too few rations out there for my liking. They wanted thirty volunteers to stay behind in camp for the good of the regiment, so I sacrificed my eagerness to die."

"You haven't changed, have you?"

"I'm too fond of my own skin, old fellow. You don't mind me calling you old fellow, do you? Against the rules and all that, but we've known each other a long time. Are you going to spill the beans and have me drummed out of the regiment?"

"No," Jack replied savagely. "There's Mary to consider. It would upset her. We'd hoped never to hear of you again."

"Ah yes, my lovely Mary. Are you married yet?"

"We are to marry on my next leave."

"Does she still wear forget-me-nots on her gown?"

"She does, but she wears them for me, Harry, as she always did. She has forgotten you now."

There had been a brief time, a terrible time, when Jack feared he might be losing her to Harry, but then the stars had fallen from her eyes.

"Ah yes," Harry's eyes glittered dangerously, "but suppose Harry were to come marching home again, and charm her into a fairy-tale that it was you deserved that court martial, not I?"

Jack laughed. "She wouldn't be taken in again by you, Harry. Not now. You may have beguiled her in our youth, but she is a woman now and loves me."

Late in the autumn of '73, Second Lieutenants Cavendish and Lyle of the 2nd/24th, inspired by an admiration for its leader, Sir Garnet Wolseley, had volunteered their services under Captain Charles Bromhead for his expedition to subdue the Ashantee. It had been five years ago almost to the day that the advance to Coomassie had begun, and by mid-February the town was in ruins and the peace treaty signed. They were home again in March, Jack to commendation and promotion, Harry to a court martial for cowardice in the face of the enemy.

It was an unpleasant story, and Jack had done his best to wipe it from his mind. They had been detailed to escort back to camp two Swiss missionaries and their baby daughter who had been imprisoned in Coomassie and released by the Ashantee after the treaty. On their way, they had been attacked by a group of hostile warriors who seized the child, to whom they had apparently taken a fancy during its parents' imprisonment, and disappeared into the jungle. The soldiers had no option but to follow. The Ashantee were good warriors, but it was not that that they feared, only their rumoured blood sacrifices – and worse. Although they were outnumbered, Jack had managed to return the baby to its parents in camp. There had been no sign of Harry, however, until that evening when he sheepishly turned up. "Congratulations on saving the baby," was all he said. Jack had had to testify that Harry had turned and run, leaving him to fight off the Ashantee alone. Harry had been seen by the CO, and a fellow officer, emerging white-faced and swordless from the forest, physically sick with terror. The result was a foregone conclusion.

Harry had been vastly amused at the verdict. "So I landed up in the stewpot after all," was his only comment.

And no doubt he had been equally amused to rejoin the regiment by trickery.

"You don't believe I could charm her back? A wager on it, Jack, or don't officers bet with NCOs?"

"Not over the honour of a woman, Harry."

"You fear to lose? I have a persuasive tongue – and lips. She may recall them – and more."

Jack lost his temper. "Keep away, God damn you. By God, if you come near Mary again—"

"You'll do what, Jack? Run me through with your sword? Hardly honourable, since I'm merely a sergeant now. Besides, remember our Chillianwallah pact. How old were we? Nine? Ten? The 24th was about to storm the Sikh outpost on the mound, and General Campbell spurred us on by recalling the glorious deeds of the 24th in the Peninsula. When ordered to storm a battery at the point of the bayonet alone, we were in the only unit that had obeyed the order, taking the position without firing a shot. God, they were splendid days, we said. I gravely intoned the General's words at Chillianwallah: 'Now let it be said that the 24th carried the guns, with the bayonet'.

"We shook hands, you and I, Jack, before we attacked that Sikh battery, agreeing that we should come to the rescue of the other come hell or high water. You broke the enemy line, single-handed, I recall. I captured the guns and rallied the men into regrouping after retreat into the jungle became inevitable. We returned to the fray after heartening our men, and between us we carried the day. The regimental loss was heavy, however. I died nobly, in defence of the Queen's colour, which was lost forever. You died in the midst of rescuing the regimental colour which in your dying throes you handed to Private Richard Perry for him to bear triumphantly back to the regiment. What rot, it all seems, Jack. What point the colours, I said even then, if the regiment is lost. The colours are the regiment, you replied. Do you still believe that rubbish, my dear old fellow?"

"Yes," Jack replied stiffly. The regiment's honour was his honour. "Now get out, Harry. I have work to do here."

"Perhaps not for long, Jack. Methinks, if I were a Zulu, I would see a splendid target in this camp."

"It's excellently sited."

"For the Zulus, yes. I tell you, Jack, if I thought I stood a chance, I'd cut and run."

"Leave your post? Hardly a soldier's duty, but then, as you said, you do not believe in it."

"Honour is a curious thing," Harry said reflectively. "I wonder what the Zulus think of our famed English sense of honour now we have invaded their homeland on a mere pretext."

"They have threatened Her Majesty's territory. We have no option."

"But endeavour to deprive them of their king and country? What will they think of the Great White Queen who kills their people and seeks to take their land?"

"Harry, I might feel as you do, but our duty is to obey, and I for one shall do so."

"Not to question why?"

"*Afterwards*. Not now," Jack said quietly. "Who are *you* or I to put our opinions above those of our generals? Sometimes I wonder why you ever joined the army."

Harry, for once, said nothing.

By now Jack could see that the Buffalo River ahead was no sweet Jordan; it was a torrent of swirling water in flood, sweeping men and horses along with its force. Zulus were leaping from the bank among the helpless who had been parted from their horses, adding their blood to the water, and for those few who were struggling out the other side, there were more Zulus to meet them. Nevertheless, the river provided a faint chance of escape for himself and Coomassie if they slipped into the water unnoticed and kept to the bank . . .

If – but behind Jack was Harry Lyle. Suppose he went back, just suppose he *could* rescue him, would Mary's heart be moved once again by Harry? No, this was black fantasy. Mary would never be swayed again; no words or blandishments from Harry could seduce her now. She loved him – Jack – but he tried in vain to suppress the stab of doubt. If Harry survived, moreover, he would have saved the colour; he would undoubtedly get a

Victoria Cross, be rehabilitated, old scores forgotten, his slate wiped clean and piled high with honours. Harry, with his charm, his unscrupulous devilish ways . . . Jack hated Harry Lyle.

And yet years ago they had sworn a pact to come to each other's aid. Childhood games, maybe, and he had long since forgotten it. Harry hadn't though, and he had reminded Jack of it. An oath was an oath, whether sworn at nine or ninety.

Jack had an unspoken, unwritten pact with the regiment too, as did every man in it, to save the colours at all costs. Whether or not anyone from the 24th returned to tell this story, no one would blame him for not returning to pick Harry up a second time, past or no past, but failing to save the colour would be viewed differently. He had no choice. Or did he?

No, not if he were ever to gain the honour he so craved. He wheeled Coomassie round to return to the man he loathed.

Harry was crawling painfully over the stones towards the trees bordering the river, and Jack realized he must have been hurt in the fall or shot by the Zulus. The four racing warriors were almost on him, eager to make the kill, and Jack had only his sword. One sword, if Harry could get to his feet, against four assegais and probably rifles too.

Jack reached Harry, with the Zulus only yards away. No time to drag him up onto the horse. "The colour, Harry," he shouted, reaching for the cloth. "It must be saved. I'll take it, and you run on Coomassie's far side as best you can. It's our only chance."

"Not me, old chap. I'm holding onto the regimental stuff and nonsense. You can take it from my dead body. What ho, Jack, I've decided to be a hero at last. That's worth a death."

The fool. Didn't he see the colour had to be saved? Jack's way, both might survive. Harry's way meant death for both of them. He wouldn't even shelter behind the horse. Instead, Harry was supporting himself against Coomassie, bayonet in hand.

The Zulus were on them. Two were attacking Harry, two concentrating on Jack. Height gave Jack the advantage; he hardly heeded the slicing cut at his leg, as his sword found a target. Coomassie was kicking and plunging now, and if he was thrown it meant certain death.

Harry must have seen, for he yelled, "Take it, Jack. Get out the best you can."

The devil was still smiling, as with one hand he drew the colour from around his neck, and threw it up at Jack.

There were still two Zulus left alive, and there was no way of escape even if by a miracle he stayed on Coomassie. One was attacking Harry; the remaining Zulu was so close Jack could stare into his eyes. The smell of the sweat and heat of the Zulu coupled with his own stench stifled him; the assegai was poised. His only chance was to slip from Coomassie's back to stand side by side with Harry, and he took it. Harry was slithering down under the weight of the Zulu. The last thing he saw was the swinging assegai.

"Tell Mary –" but he could manage no more.

He saluted the colours in the memorial window, placed by the regiment in St John's Priory church and read once more the inscription beneath it to the officers and men of the 24th who had fallen at Isandhlwana. In the camp as the Zulus attacked had been 850 Native troops and 950 Europeans. Of the latter nearly 900 had died, two-thirds of them from the 24th Regiment of Foot. They gave their lives for Queen and Country. Jesu mercy.

His beloved wife Mary was at his side. He remembered her weeping when he had ridden away to war all those years ago; her love for him had never faltered even when she feared he was dead, and they had been married four weeks after his return. They had been coming here together every 22nd January for thirty years.

There was no mention of the colours on the memorial, nor was any scrap of the regimental colour of the 2nd/24th to be seen in the regimental museum. It lay on the battlefield of Isandhlwana or in some Zulu homestead. Did he come to this church to honour the regiment, or the memory of a man who had once been his friend? He had only escaped by the merest chance, as he slid from under the wounded Zulu, under Coomassie, and managed to mount. The scrap of the colour lay unheeded on the ground where it had fallen, and this time it would not be rescued.

Where, after all, did honour lie? A coward too scared to save his friend at Coomassie had won a posthumous Victoria Cross for trying to save the colour, since Jack had honourably told the full story on his return. The same words had been flung at him at Coomassie: "Get out the best you can," and he had been left to fight off six Ashantee alone. He remembered it without bitterness, just as he remembered the deliberate push from Coomassie's back that had so nearly meant his death. The cock would never crow thrice, however.

Mary sighed, as she looked at his photograph, that lay proudly by the VC so honourably won. "How brave he was. Dear Jack."

Harry kept his own counsel.

FOR VALOUR

L.T. Meade and Clifford Halifax

*Throughout the nineteenth century there was conflict
between the British in India and the Burmese. The British
had annexed Lower Burma, including Rangoon, in 1852,
and a tension continued between the Burmese ruling dy-
nasty and the British. In 1885 the third Burmese War
broke out, leading to the annexation of Upper Burma by
the British in 1886. That is the background for the
following story by L.T. Meade (1854–1914). Elizabeth
Thomasina Meade was a prolific writer of mystery stories,
girls' stories and adventure stories of every kind, appearing
in most of the popular magazines at the turn of the last
century. She frequently appeared with a collaborator who
provided some of the technical detail, whereas she did all of
the writing. Clifford Halifax was a doctor. This story
comes from a series headed "Stories of the Red Cross –
being the strange experiences of Surgeon Major Dale." It
was published in* **Pearson's** **Magazine** *in 1897.*

That most democratic and distinguished of all decorations, the Victoria Cross, given "For Valour" shown on the field of battle, does not in every case fall to the lot of the man who has earned it. On this roll of fame some grand names are omitted. The deed of heroism is done, but it leads to neither glory nor public recognition. I recall an instance of this sort which happened to a great friend of my own.

The story which I am about to tell happened a few years ago in a remote part of Upper Burmah. We were stationed at a place called Alipore, and our force was under the command of a very distinguished general officer, Sir Henry Redfern. In the regiment to which I was then attached Phil Luttrell happened to be the youngest captain. He was a regular boy in manners and appearance, and amused us, one and all, by his ways and doings. He was the most modest fellow I ever met, with a lot of cool pluck, and that sort of intellectual force and insight into character which invariably tells.

He had no fear, and when he set his heart on a thing he, as a rule, obtained it; but he was fond of keeping in the background, and, in consequence, did not always get the credit he deserved. He was a man with remarkable qualities, and was bound sooner or later to come to the front. But he was so jolly and bright that he was a universal favourite. He took chaff well, and had a merry smile and a gay word for all.

The time was a time of danger, and brave men for the honour of their country held their lives but lightly. The natives were in a state of high disaffection, and we did not know from day to day what might take place.

Luttrell had been born in Burmah, and knew the country well. He was highly popular with the men of his company, and began in this difficult time to render good service by the indefatigable manner in which he kept them together. Our Governor-General expected any day to go to the front. In the meantime we waited, enduring the suspense as best we could. If our women and children were safe in England, we felt we should mind nothing else, but with the memory of the Mutiny in our hearts, we could not but tremble for the fate which might lie before them.

In the meantime the usual entertainments went on, for Alipore was a gay place. Wherever fun was, Luttrell was in the thick of it – waiting on the ladies, returning the idle chaff of his fellow officers, his laugh ringing out free and merry, and his eyes dancing with fun and fire. He was a good-looking chap, slightly above the average height, clean cut, lean, and active as a cat. His eyes were of a good bright hazel, and well open. They had a look in them which I have sometimes seen in those of a trusty dog, but seldom in a human being. They were capable of great expression, and when he wanted to plead his cause most ably, he allowed his eyes to speak while his tongue remained silent.

Towards the end of the winter, and just when military affairs were most critical, General Redfern's only daughter appeared on the scene. Why she came to India at such a time I cannot say, but that is neither here nor there. The General had been excited about her before she came, talking of her to his most intimate friends, and expressing the highest satisfaction at her advent. It needed but a glance to show that she was as the apple of his eye, and when she arrived we little wondered that this should be the case.

She was a young and very fresh-looking girl, with a face full of tenderness, radiance, and beauty. I cannot recall now, often as I looked at her in those anxious days, whether she was dark or fair, or what colour her eyes were, but the moment you saw her, somehow or other you gave her your heart, and you could never think of another girl while she was by. Even the women were not jealous of sweet Dolly Redfern. They could not be, for she was so gently sympathetic and kind. In some ways she was like a creature apart – not a bit worldly in the ordinary sense I mean, and yet she was the most human girl I ever met.

She did us all good. We liked to see her and to listen to her. We felt bravest of the brave when she was by, and less afraid of any direful consequences which might be near. To think that danger could possibly touch her was enough to nerve every man in the place to fight for her with all his strength and courage. Yes, her advent did us good, although we often expressed our surprise at the General willingly bringing his only child into a scene of possible danger.

He was a queer man, and the most obstinate I have ever seen. In thinking over everything now, I am inclined to believe that he had a mad vein in him somewhere, and that Dolly brought it to the fore. It was plain to be seen that he was terribly ambitious for her. Before she came he was a bit of a martinet, and also a strict disciplinarian, but he was as just a man as you could find in the army. Now he became fretful and anxious, and even began to show most unsoldier-like jealousies. He talked about Dolly to some of his friends, and quite openly explained his views.

Dolly's mother had been the daughter of an earl, and Dolly herself, when peace was once more re-established, was to return to England and marry well. Her father would go with her and see to the whole thing. Dolly's husband must be a man of rank. Wealth did not so greatly matter, but rank she must have at any cost. On one occasion the General said all these things to me, and as he did so I noticed to a marked degree the restless sparkle in his eyes and the unnecessary vehemence in his manner. He tugged at his moustache, and began to walk up and down.

"If any of you young fellows were to aspire to my daughter's hand, I could be cruel, Dale, I could be cruel," he reiterated.

"I don't believe it," I answered; but, as I spoke, my heart sank, for I glanced into his face, and was forced to see that his words bore the impress of truth.

"Dolly shall be a duchess before I die," he continued. "She has beauty and sweetness enough to win anybody. You'll see, Dale, if you live long enough, you'll see."

Now if these were Redfern's ideas for his daughter, Dolly's own views for herself were widely apart. A humble home lit up with love would abundantly content her – she wanted love and nothing else.

Meanwhile we one and all soothed the General and petted Dolly, and I for one trusted that no tragedy would occur.

This hope was soon destined to be shattered, for, of course, the likely thing happened, and Phil Luttrell – who had no rank of any sort, and was a mere nobody – fell over head and ears in love with the General's daughter. He took the complaint badly, and we scarcely knew him for a bit. Soon everyone in the place knew the state of affairs. Luttrell was in love with Dolly, and Dolly fully returned his affection. Now, indeed, General Redfern showed the rough side of his character. He was furious, stamped about like a veritable madman, and would not hear of an engagement. Luttrell asked him point-blank for Dolly, and got a point-blank refusal. The young man did not say a word, but in his own way he was as quietly determined as Sir Henry himself. Dolly also was heard to declare her intention of never giving in.

In the midst of this state of things – Dolly defiant, Phil furious and determined, the General scarcely on speaking terms with him – orders arrived from headquarters for the troops to march at once to Cholier, which was declared to be in a dangerous state of disaffection. Luttrell rushed into my quarters with the information.

"We are off to-night," he exclaimed; "isn't it glorious fun?"

I answered in the affirmative, for I was as glad of a chance of seeing a bit of real fighting as any other young fellow.

"I believe that my luck is in the ascendant," continued Luttrell, rubbing his hands; "the General will surely be satisfied if Dolly marries a man of mark. I intend to distinguish myself during this campaign."

I looked at him and smiled.

"I see what you are thinking about," he continued; "you believe that I am a conceited ass and all the rest, but I have simply made up my mind. Now that we are really off to Cholier, I have got just the chance I want. Cholier happens to be my native place; I understand not only the language, but the natives. One of their women was my ayah when I was a kid, and for the first five years of my life I grew up in their midst. I have never shaken off the old affections or the old ties, and I believe that I can use my knowledge and information now to the benefit of our force; you wait and see."

I looked into Phil's clever, serious face, and half believed him.

His pluck was well known, and he was desperate. He wanted to win the girl he loved, and would go through fire and water on her behalf; but even without her, Phil was the sort of man to lay down at any moment his life for his Queen and Country. With a double motive, therefore, what might he not achieve?

We were to leave Alipore in the evening, and on the afternoon of that day I received a message from Sir Henry. He had been kind enough to take me up lately, and often sent for me to have a chat. I did not suppose that he wanted me for anything particular, but strolled across the compound to his house. I found him looking perturbed and anxious.

"Here you are, Dale!" he cried; "come in, won't you? The fact is this, I am awfully sorry that you are coming with us."

"Why so?" I asked. "I should be deeply disappointed if I did not join the expedition."

"Well, you are a clever doctor, and, of course, will be useful, and there is a great deal of cholera about; still, if you remained at Alipore you could have looked after Dolly. I am not quite happy about her; she has no friends here, at least there are no women with whom I especially care to leave her; the cholera is near, and" – he paused, waiting for me to say something.

I made a commonplace rejoinder, something about the water Dolly was to drink and the usual precautions. He shook his head.

"Something ails her," he cried; "there is something worrying the child, and I don't like it, not a bit."

Now, of course, I knew very well what was worrying Dolly Redfern, but, glancing at the General, I saw that this was no time to remind him of the fact. He might have guessed my thoughts, for he looked restless and more anxious than ever.

"I did wrong to bring her out," he continued. "I ought to have left her in England for at least another year; but I was lonely without the child, and she wanted me; I saw it in her letters. The temptation was too much for me, but a motherless girl in Burmah just now is a facer. God knows what may happen here at any moment. Dolly's position is a horrible one, and it weighs on me. I have a presentiment that something bad will happen."

"Why don't you send her to England by the next boat?" I asked. "Surely you could get an escort to take her to the coast."

"No, no; and if I did she would not go. She is as staunch as God makes women, and that says a great deal. She has no fear in her – bless her. No, it is the thought of leaving her, and the trouble in her eyes; and, then, suppose she gets cholera, and there is no one here to look after her? I could almost find it in my heart to take her with me, but, of course, that is impossible. Dale, you have often wondered at me; I see it in your face."

"Well, you are a complex character," I answered.

"I am – I am; and where Dolly is concerned, as I have said already, I could be cruel. Of course, you have heard that Luttrell had the cheek to propose for her?"

"I do not see any cheek in it," I answered stoutly. "Luttrell is as good a fellow as you could find in the service. He'll come to the front some day. He has a brave heart, and he loves Miss Redfern well."

The General stared at me, his face, which had been flushed, became almost purple, the pupils of his eyes were distended, his lower lip dropped. Before he could utter a word, however, the room door was softly opened, and Dolly came in. There was a change in the girl. Her face, which had been so fresh, looked already slightly worn; big black shadows accentuated the pathetic expression of her eyes. She looked very young, and sad.

The General gave her a glance, which showed me how he worshipped her; then he opened his arms, and folded her up in them.

"I wish you were back in England, little girl," he cried.

"Then I'm right glad I'm not, father," was the spirited reply. "It is dreadful to feel that you are going off and into danger, and – and all the others. If it were not for that" – she stopped abruptly, and to my astonishment, and to the General's discomfiture, burst into tears.

"Why, what is it, Dolly, my dear, what is it? Tell me what is troubling you?"

"It is this," answered Dolly stoutly. "I don't mind Dr Dale knowing a bit. I cannot bear to part from Phil, father; I cannot bear it."

The General frowned. His tone, which had been full of compassion and tenderness, changed. He pushed Dolly from him.

"Don't let me hear you talk such folly," he cried.

She flushed up, and the tears dried on her cheeks.

"It is not folly, and you have no right to say it," she answered. "I love Phil better than anyone else in the wide world."

"I will not listen to any more of that sort of nonsense," cried the General. "You are little more than a child. You know nothing about such matters."

"But I do, father. See here, I have come to talk to you. You have a minute or two to spare, and Dr Dale is present. I like Dr Dale – I am very fond of him. He is Phil's friend, and I don't mind his knowing everything. Now you must listen to me. No, I am not going to be afraid. I know you can be terribly, terribly angry. I know there are two sides to your nature. The noble, splendid side, and the side which – Oh, father, father, there is a part of you which could kill me! which could drag me into my grave! but I am sure the better side will conquer. Father, you must listen!"

I stared at Miss Redfern while she was speaking. I scarcely knew her. Hitherto I had thought her a very sweet, womanly girl, no stronger in any way than the majority of her sex, but now in her quiet, grave tones, in the confidence of her words, I read strength.

"I love Phil better than anyone else in the world," she repeated. "I shall never marry anybody else. I do not wish to disobey you, and I will not marry him without your leave, but I shall never marry another. He is going away to-night, he is going with you, and into danger. He may never come back again. I may never see him any more. I want to be engaged to him with your sanction and blessing, before he goes. Will you allow it?"

"Never!" cried General Redfern. "Dolly, you madden me.

Am I the sort of man to give in to a girl's caprice, and so ruin her for life? No more on the subject, my dear. The fellow has the cheek of a – what is he? – a nobody."

"He will be somebody yet," answered Dolly, "and in any case he is the man I love; therefore he is somebody to me."

She took the General's hand; he tried to withdraw it.

"I thought perhaps you would refuse," she continued, still speaking in that very quiet, constrained voice, which somehow or other, made each word tell; "I had hoped you would say yes, but I thought it might be the other way, knowing you as I do, – yes, knowing you as I do. You want me to marry some day, don't you?"

"Certainly, my love, but I have no time to talk on the matter now."

"But this is so important, father, and there is the chance that I may never see you again."

The General winced, and his face turned pale.

"You want me to marry," continued Dolly, "and you would like me to marry a brave man and a distinguished man."

"Yes; that goes without saying."

"Then if Phil becomes distinguished – we all know that he is brave – if he wins the Victoria Cross, for instance, may I have him? I will not marry him without your leave unless he gets the Victoria Cross. That is a great distinction – a high honour. You will say yes to that. Father, you will, you must."

"You press me too hard, Dolly." The General fidgeted, and looked out of the window.

"I do not press you hard enough. I mean to go on begging and imploring until you yield. If Phil wins the Victoria Cross in this campaign, may I have him? If he gets it for valour on the field, or for any other noble and brave action, may I be his wife? Is it yes or no? If you say yes, I shall be well and happy, if no, then—" Her face turned white, the energy suddenly left her little figure, her head drooped as though she were a withered flower.

"You had better yield, sir," I cried suddenly. "Miss Redfern's proposition is a most reasonable one. If Luttrell should win the Victoria Cross, he is certain to come to the front; his family is good, he is not without private means, you could have no possible objection to the match, and they love each other. There is a great deal of cholera about," I continued, as if it were an afterthought, "and a depressed state of the nervous system—"

"What do you mean, Dale?"

"A depressed state of the nervous system lays a person dangerously open to contracting the disease."

"Is your mind unalterably set on this, Dolly?" inquired her father.

"It is, father. The thought of the coming separation nearly kills me; but if I have your word, I shall rest."

"Then, listen. I yield on a condition. It is this – that you do not see Luttrell before he goes."

Dolly started. The General went on inflexibly:

"You do not see Luttrell again; and if he does *not* win the Victoria Cross in this campaign, you give him up."

"Oh, you are cruel!"

"I yield on no other terms."

"Then I submit – I must."

"That is good. He won't get the Victoria Cross – not a chance of it, but if he does, I also keep my part of the bargain. Now, leave me, for I am busy."

That evening the ladies of the different regiments saw us off. Dolly was amongst the number. She held her head like a queen, and when we moved off to danger, glory, or death, she, with the others, accompanied us to the end of the valley. I looked back twice, and each time saw her smiling face. It was white as death, but she was waving her hand, and kept on smiling. I thought I had never seen a fairer nor a more stimulating sight.

Luttrell was far away from her in command of his own men, but the young pair managed to throw glances of fire from one to the other which no one could intercept, and Phil's feet stepped lightly over the ground as we marched off, and were lost to view.

Some days later we reached Cholier. Cholera had already broken out in our midst and our anxieties were great. Cholier was in a high state of disaffection, but the arrival of our force had an immediate and salutary effect, and the General had not much trouble in taking possession of the outskirts of the town. The great palace in the centre, however, had yet to be won before the place could really be considered ours.

During these anxious days I saw very little of Luttrell, but his brother officers were loud in their praise of him, and often brought me stories of his unselfishness, zeal, and pluck. I longed to whisper a certain word in his ears, but it seemed to me that honour forbade, and after all he was plucky enough to do what Dolly expected of him without knowing how grave was the issue which hung upon his valour. The time was near when he was to be put to the test.

After a most gallant fight we forced our way into the centre of Cholier, and the enemy were obliged to retire into the adjacent hills. By 3 pm on this eventful day the whole of this block of hills was cleared of the enemy, and was also in our possession. Guns were captured, but the enemy still kept up a heavy fire on us from two guns on the parade, from the fort, and from the palace which occupied the heart of the town.

I shall never forget the keen excitement. The heat was the most intense I had ever experienced, and with the heavy firing our men were falling on all sides. By four o'clock that day we had practically taken the town, and had come up in front of the palace. Its courtyard and buildings were occupied by a large number of armed men, whose intentions were evidently war to the death. Having taken the outposts, the moment had arrived when we must storm the citadel.

This was no easy task; our loss would doubtless be considerable, and it would be extremely difficult to dislodge the enemy. The terraced roofs of the palace were screened by a parapet; thus our foes were sheltered, and could fire on us without mercy. The place was held, too, by desperadoes, who would fight to the last breath. The palace of Cholier was not only strongly fortified, but was full of treasure, the destruction of which could never be replaced.

If we were lucky enough to save this magnificent building, we should obtain the goodwill of the Tsawbwa, who was now absent, and in all probability the disaffection, which might spread at any moment through the length and breadth of Burmah, would be summarily put an end to. If, on the other hand, the palace was battered by our guns, it would be war to the knife.

By orders of Sir Henry Redfern, our force was formed for an advance, and, although we had ceased firing at that moment, at any instant the bombardment of the palace might begin. While we all waited in suspense, I saw Luttrell put spurs to his horse and ride forward. He came up to the place where the General had paused to give final directions. I happened to be within ear-shot, and heard what he said.

"If you will allow me, Sir Henry," he cried, "I will volunteer to ride forward alone and endeavour to obtain the surrender of the palace to the British force without bloodshed."

I saw the General's eyes flash with sudden fire. Just for a moment a look of strong admiration filled them; then they darkened, and I saw him give the young fellow a contemptuous glance from head to foot.

"What do you mean?" he said briefly.

"What I say," replied Luttrell. "It is most important that the palace should be saved for the Tsawbwa, and that heavy loss of life should be averted. It is possible to save the place by diplomacy without a shot being fired. If you will give me permission I am willing to make the attempt. At the worst I can but fail; but I was born in Cholier and know the place. I also understand Burmese. May I take the risk?"

Some men who were standing near raised a shout of approval, for the offer was in truth a most gallant one, and Luttrell's face spoke volumes. My heart almost stopped beating as I listened for the General's reply. Just for a moment his brow fell, and his eyes sought the ground; then he nodded his head in token of assent. The order was immediately given to the column to halt, and Captain Luttrell rode up to the gateway which formed the entrance to the courtyard of the palace.

The moment he did so muskets were levelled at him from every quarter, but, wonder of wonders, no one fired. It was easy to see from the post where we remained that the men inside the palace were in the wildest confusion. I felt certain that they were determined at all risks to fight our troops.

There was no gate, but the ingress through the gateway was barred to a horseman by a beam of wood which was fixed to a socket in the wall at either side, and for some minutes Luttrell's life was in the gravest peril. The confusion inside made it impossible for his voice to be heard, but he could be plainly seen, and muskets from every quarter were levelled against him. Suddenly a lithe Mussulman started up; he was standing near the gateway. He glanced at Luttrell, and then uttered a shout. We heard his words from where we stood.

"It is Luttrell sahib," he cried. "Luttrell sahib speaks the truth; let him in."

Immediately three or four men rushed forward, the barrier to the gateway was removed, and Luttrell dashed into the court-yard and was lost to view. Then there followed a heavy silence. Would the brave fellow ever come out again alive? For an act of cool daring I had seldom seen anything to equal what he had just done. Many a man in the heat of excitement will go up to the cannon's mouth, but there was nothing here to excite or stimulate him but his own sense of the importance of the duty he had volunteered to perform.

Half-an-hour passed, the armed men in the palace were silent, the troops outside remained motionless. Suddenly, to our intense delight, Luttrell reappeared. He dashed up immediately to Sir Henry's side, and spoke eagerly.

"It is all right," he cried. "I told the Chief that I would guarantee that all lives in the palace would be saved if they would obey orders, but there must be no delay, as the British force was prepared and eager to attack them."

"Well?" said the General briefly.

"At first he refused to give in, and told me that they would hold the place for the Tsawbwa, and would only give it up to him on his coming; but that nothing would induce them to surrender it to the English. In that case I assured them that the place would be stormed, and that not a man would escape. They saw that I was determined, held another consultation, and finally said: 'We will do what you order.'"

"Good," said the General; his mouth twitched. I gave him a keen glance. I wondered if at that supreme moment he remembered Dolly, and the promise she had wrung from him. Luttrell continued to speak with a ring in his voice.

"There was still great danger, for if one of our troops, by the merest chance, fired, it would be all up, as the fire would be immediately returned, and the word of the chief would go for nothing.

"In order, therefore, to avoid such a risk, I directed every man to get at once inside the building, and to remain there perfectly quiet until they had directions to leave, or orders were issued by you, sir, for their disposal. The Chief grumbled at this, but in the end he yielded, and now the removal of the armed men from the outside of the palace has been effected. The Chief and his fellow leaders are responsible for the conduct of their men, and for the preservation of the interior of the palace building, and I have come to ask you, General Redfern, to send a party of our men immediately, to post for the security of the palace."

"I will do so," answered the General. "Luttrell, I thank you; you have behaved with splendid bravery, courage, and tact."

General Redfern's words were heard by all the men who stood round. Luttrell's face, which had been flushed and animated, grew pale from intense emotion; he bowed his head and turned aside. The next moment the General had given the necessary orders, a couple of companies immediately went forward to the palace, Luttrell going with them.

In this way the Tswabwa's palace was taken by the British force without a single shot being fired, or a drop of blood shed. Luttrell had won the victory.

I can scarcely speak of the excitement and rejoicing which ensued. I felt in my heart of hearts that all was now well. Luttrell would be recommended for the Victoria Cross which he had so nobly earned, and the General would keep his word to Dolly.

"You had cool daring," said a Major in our own regiment, who came up to the young fellow to congratulate him. "If Sir Henry does you the justice you deserve, you will not only win the Cross, but get the rank of Major."

"Luttrell, your action was simply a brilliant one," said his Colonel later that day.

To these remarks Luttrell answered very little. He was never a fellow to brag; as I said before, he was as modest as he was plucky. We all wondered what mention would be made of him in the dispatch which Sir Henry would send home within the next few days. The Victoria Cross was, at least, a foregone conclusion.

Weeks and even months passed by. Cholier was ours, the moment of peril had been safely tided over – the insurgents had seen the folly of their ways, and all was once more peace. Some of Sir Henry Redfern's force had already been distributed to other parts of the country, but the regiment to which I was attached was still at Cholier.

One day news like an electric shock ran through the place. The English mail had arrived. Sir Henry Redfern's dispatch home had been copied from the London Gazette into the daily papers. These papers had reached us. The dispatch gave a gallant and spirited account of our short campaign, but there was no mention whatever of Luttrell's name.

It was Luttrell himself who came to tell me.

"I knew the General would do for me," he cried. "I always felt he would, but I did not think he was quite base enough for this."

My indignation was so great that I had scarcely words to reply.

He flung some English papers on my table.

"Never mind that now," he continued. "After all it is not on this subject, important as it is, that I have come to speak to you. I have heard from Alipore, and have had very anxious news about Dolly. She has been failing for some time. I feel queerly nervous about her. If anything happens, I believe I shall shoot myself."

"No, you are far too manly for that," I answered. "Now look here, Phil, things are past bearing, and I shall interfere. I am going off this very minute to interview the General. If he knew of Miss Redfern's illness, I am certain he would do something. The fact is she is fretting for you, Luttrell. Hers is a warm heart, and love and separation are too mighty for it."

"I shall do my best to get leave of absence and go back to her," said Luttrell. "But there," he added passionately, "I am hemmed in on all sides; the General has it in his power to prevent me, and he hates me."

I did not dare to tell him what I knew. It was all too plain that General Redfern had been base enough to omit Luttrell's name from the dispatch because of his promise to Dolly.

I was just about to speak when an orderly came hastily to my quarters. He brought a note with him – it was from General Redfern, asking me to go to him at once. I hurried off in some wonder. When I arrived at the General's house I found everyone in the greatest consternation. Small wonder! It needed but a glance to show me that Sir Henry had been seized by cholera in its most acute form, and that his life was in danger. A cruel and more terrible foe than shot and shell had him in its grip.

I watched by him all night doing what I could to relieve his agonies, but the poison was so virulent that his strength was immediately undermined, and he lay prostrate, scarcely fighting for the life which was so rapidly ebbing away. Towards morning his sufferings became less, and he called me to his side.

"Mine is a bad case, is it not?" he asked.

"It is," I replied; but then I added: "We must hope for the best – keep up your courage."

He did not speak but closed his eyes, a frown knitting his brows. Grave collapse had begun to set in. The temperature of the body fell, the surface became cold and clammy. As I looked at it I could scarcely recognise Sir Henry's face. The features were drawn, the eyes sunken; the expression denoted terrible anxiety. It needed no second glance to assure me that he was dying. His muscular power was already diminished, but as yet his intelligence was unclouded.

"I want to say something to you, Dale," he whispered hoarsely.

"Anything," I replied.

"You are sure that it is all up with me?"

I made no answer.

"Come, doctor, don't hesitate. I am not afraid. Death comes once to all men. You believe that I am about to die?"

I nodded my head.

"It is harder to go coldly and silently like this than in the heat of battle," he continued, "but all men go once, and this is my hour. Now I want to say something. It is this – I die as I lived."

"Most men do, sir," I replied. "I do not believe in deathbed repentances or anything of that sort. Besides, you have not" – I paused; the memory of what Luttrell had just told me swept over my brain.

"Oh, yes, I have something to repent of," he interrupted me quickly. "It would now be in the correct order of things for me to make restitution, and to—"

"What do you mean?" I asked.

"What I say. Twenty-four hours ago I was in the full possession of my faculties. I had then absolutely made up my mind that Luttrell should never marry Dolly. I am still of the same way of thinking. He shall not have her."

"But your promise," I cried. "General Redfern, he has done the deed of valour, and by all that is just in heaven above or in earth beneath, the Victoria Cross is his."

"Stoop down, Dale," said the dying man. His voice grew more hoarse. I could barely distinguish the words. "Luttrell will never get his V.C."

"What do you mean?"

"What I say. I willed it so. My dispatch has already been received and published. *I have, on purpose, omitted all mention of his name!*"

"Good God!" I cried. "You cannot mean what you are saying, Sir Henry?"

"I have done it, Dale – I have done it."

"On account of Dolly?" I asked.

"No matter why – it is done."

"Then, do you know what you really are?"

"Quite well," he said steadily. "A black-guard, and worse; but as compared to Dolly's future, my own character goes for nothing. She was to marry him, with my consent, if he got the Victoria Cross. He does not get it, and whether I am alive or dead, she cannot in honour become his wife."

"But this is fearful." I said. "Even now, you can repair the mischief you have done. For Heaven's sake, General Redfern, don't go to your Maker with this sin on your soul."

"He shall not marry Dolly, nor get the insignia due to valour. I die as I lived. I always said that on this point I could be cruel."

"My God, you are!" I answered. I could scarcely speak. The attitude of the man whose moments were numbered utterly appalled me. It was with difficulty I could attend to my medical duties. But still graver symptoms of the fell disease aroused me. The pulse flagged, and the intelligence, hitherto so bright, became clouded. Sensibility and even capacity of movement were almost gone. I felt that all was hopeless, and was debating in my own mind what possible steps I could take when like a flash an idea occurred to me.

"General Redfern," I said, bending over him, and speaking in a loud, clear voice, "can you attend to me for a moment?"

The sunken eyes were opened and fixed on my face.

"What is it?" he asked.

"Have you heard lately from your daughter?"

Even at the brink of the grave these words troubled him. He started up and said excitedly:

"I have not heard for some weeks. I cannot account for the silence."

"But I can," I answered. "Miss Redfern does not write because she is ill."

"What, ill? Dolly?" he said. Strength came back to his eyes and voice, his pulse beat rapidly. Just at that supreme moment I heard someone speak in the outer room. A voice clear as a bell sounded in my ears.

"By Heaven, Dolly herself!" I cried under my breath. "Dolly

in Cholier – how in the name of fortune did she get here, and now?"

I rushed from the room to confront her on the threshold. Her sweet face was full of anxiety and fear. She stretched out her hand to motion me to let her pass.

"My father, is he as bad as they tell me?" she asked.

I did not reply. She hurried forward and fell on her knees by the sick man's side. "I was ill and miserable, and could stand it no longer," she began. "Mahomet Khan came with me, and I am here. I heard the news, of course, and what Phil had done. He has won the Victoria Cross. Dear father, you will now fulfil your promise."

No other voice would have roused the dying man, but Dolly's did. He looked at her attentively.

"Phil has won the Victoria Cross," she repeated. "You have recommended him, of course; you have spoken of him in your dispatch. He will get it."

"Did you hear anything more?" he asked in a strange, low whisper.

"Nothing; nothing except what he has done and the bravery of the action. All Burmah rings with it. You will now fulfil your promise."

The General looked at her with knitted brows. There was a very perceptible change in her face; she looked worn and ill, the eyes were far too bright and anxious for health.

"You have been suffering?" he said briefly.

"Yes; but that is nothing. Phil has won the Victoria Cross, and you will fulfil your promise."

The General continued to gaze into her changed face. "Leave me for a moment," he said abruptly.

I motioned to her to go from the room. The moment she did so Sir Henry Redfern turned to me.

"Is my daughter in danger?" he asked.

"Yes, but happiness will save her," I replied.

"Then I yield; she shall be saved. Is it possible to hide the truth from her about the dispatch?"

"Luttrell will never tell her."

"Send him to me immediately."

I rushed from the room. No need to ask me to put wings to my feet. I hurried across the compound, and was lucky enough to find Luttrell in his own quarters.

"Come back at once," I said, "Dolly is here – how she managed to get to Cholier Heaven only knows. The General is dying; he has but a few moments to live; you are wanted. Be brave, Luttrell, and, as you are a man, forgive as you hope to be forgiven."

"Oh, I'll do that; I only want Dolly," was the answer.

"But a grave and terrible wrong has been done you, my boy."

"No matter. I only want Dolly," was the reply.

We both entered the sick room. The General was alive, but little more. Dolly knelt by the bed, holding his hand. Luttrell crossed the room and bent over the old man.

"I am sorry to see you so bad, sir," was his remark.

"Ah, yes; I am going, Luttrell. I did you an injustice and I – *don't* repent. Were I to live I should stick to it. As it is, I beseech of you to respect my memory to my child, and be her protector, if you will."

"With all my heart."

"Then go both of you. Dale, ask them to leave me."

They went out of the room.

"I had a hard fight to give in even now," whispered the old General; "but see, Dale, see that she never knows the truth about that dispatch." The grip of death was at his throat as he spoke.

Dolly lives, and is happy; but Luttrell's name has never been added to the roll of the Victoria Cross heroes. His wife thinks that bitter injustice has been done him by those in the highest authority. She will never guess the real reason.

SPHINX

Clotilde Graves

*We end in the Sudan. One of the great heroic stories of the
nineteenth century is the defence of Khartoum by General
Gordon against the mighty forces of the Mahdi. Gordon
succeeded in holding Khartoum, against overwhelming
odds, for ten months. However just two days before a
belated relief force arrived, the city walls were breached
and Gordon and his entire garrison were massacred. It was
to be thirteen years before the British at last defeated the
Mahdi's successor Abd Allah, the Khalifa, at the battle of
Omdurman on 2 September 1898. My thanks to John
Eggeling for drawing the following story to my attention.
It is an early work by Clotilde Graves (1863–1932), who
had already established a reputation in the 1890s for her
books with strong feminist themes. However her best remembered books are those with military themes, a fascination no doubt inherited from her father, who was an Irish
army officer. She became well known for* **The Dop Doctor**
(1910), written under the alias Richard Dehan, which is

set during the Boer War, where a doctor, struck off the list
for conducting an abortion and now turned to drink,
becomes a hero during the Siege of Mafeking. Two
Thieves *(1912)* is a broad sweeping novel, set mostly
during the Crimean War, and based on the real life
character of Jean-Henri Dunant, the founder of the
Red Cross.

Of course, it was at Lady Paddington's ball, that closed the
London summer season of 1898, that I dared to tell Sphinx
Rowcliffe how I loved her. Had I known it, I could not have
chosen a more unlucky moment; for the 1st Battalion Grenadier
Guards sailed from England the next day, and the girl's heart
was going with the regiment, comfortably buttoned inside
Carisbroke's khaki tunic.

Should I have held back if I had known? Perhaps not. I was
wild over her; drunk with her beauty; maddened by the great
dark-lidded, unfathomable eyes, that only looked on me with
friendly indifference. There was some excuse. Where other
men and women of Society – decked in their ancestors'
braveries, made up in exact imitation of family portraits, or
representing characters figuring between the boards of the
Pictorial History of Europe from the fifteenth century down to
the reign of Anne the tea-drinker – where they seemed like
dolls, limp, inanimate, and stiff, *she* lived and moved and had
her being as an Egyptian Princess. She *was* an Egyptian
Princess, with the lithe and lovely line of her form scarcely
hidden by the sheath-like dress of green and gold and black
tissue, with her enamelled head-dress, modelled in represen-
tation of a guinea-fowl, whose crested head and diamond eyes
crowned those wonderful level brows of hers with wonderful
effect; with her mother's Cairene chain of *scarabei* about her
exquisite brown throat, and emerald-headed asps of gold for
bracelets.

I asked her to marry me. I also called her Violet for the first time. The inappropriateness of the name struck me, but the occasion possessed some solemnity.

She was ambiguous. She said she cared for me too much to think of anything of – of that kind.

My reply was that I cared for her so much that I could think of nothing else. Then she tried to turn the conversation.

"Even if I did . . . think of you in that way," she said, expressing the most important parts of her sentence in blanks, as women will, "it would not be right. My father goes out to the Soudan with the Second Brigade in August; he is to be Assistant Adjutant-General at headquarters—"

"I know," I said.

"And until then he should have all my care and all my affection," said the darling humbug, with the corners of her delicate lips quivering. "No one else should share what he may never claim from me again."

She broke off as the opening chords of Strauss's last valse crashed out from the ball-room, and a handsome, brown-haired, blue-eyed man – I never failed to do the good looks and good manners of Captain Angus Carisbroke justice, be that said for me! – appeared to claim Miss Rowcliffe for the dance. The scarlet and gold of his full-dress uniform, the Eastern magnificence of her robes, united with the remarkable beauty of the woman and the frank wholesome comeliness of the man, made them a couple worth looking at. As I reluctantly admitted this, a hearty blow fell on my shoulder, and the jovial voice of Major Rowcliffe said, close to my ear—

"Practising killing attitudes, Wyvern, for the benefit of the ladies? Don't try, my dear chap, don't try! Leave elegance to other men. A reputation for daredevilry and cheek like yours stands a man in better stead than pink and white prettiness and a waxed moustache. Hang it all! Do you think people don't remember the day when you dropped from the skies into the garrison at Chitral, in '95, disguised as a Sunyasi, and told Sir Robert Lowry you'd come up for a little hill-air and local colour? Do you think they've forgotten the Tochi Valley, and your fight with the three Waziris who'd been sent to cut the telegraph-wires between Siltha and Bhamra? You bobbed up in Egypt in '97, got wounded at Dongola—"

"And was stoker on the first engine that ran between Cairo and Berber," I put in, rather weary of the ancient warrior's reminiscences. "Come, Major, don't you want to lay the dust after all this? I guarantee the champagne-cup. Lady Pad's head butler is a man who can take a hint as well as a tip."

And I dragged the Major, without much exercise of force, to the refreshment-buffet. Thence he despatched me to find Miss Rowcliffe.

The dance was just over as I entered the ball-room. People were promenading, sitting in alcoves, or enjoying the air upon the broad balconies, sheltered by the awnings and embowered in hothouse roses and palms. With the clairvoyance of love, I found Sphinx Rowcliffe before I had been a minute in the room.

She was on one of the balconies with Carisbroke. I did not mean to spy, but as I set foot on the threshold of the glass door, that stood open to the cool, starry night, I saw that they stood with clasped hands, and that their faces were very close together. In that moment, too, I saw that I had no chance. A woman only looks at *one* man of all the world of men – as Sphinx Rowcliffe looked at Angus Carisbroke.

"I love you!" she said. "I loved you in the beginning, when our eyes first met. I shall love you until the end. In truth or in falsehood I will be yours: in happiness or misery, yours: in life as in death, yours! Is that enough? Now go. We shall not meet again before you sail for Egypt. But remember, when you go you leave your wife behind you!"

He stooped and kissed her hands, and left her, passing by me with eyes that were blind with tears. I nerved myself for the thing, and stepped forwards, offering her my arm.

"The Major sent me for you," I said in as natural and cheerful a tone as I could manage. She caught my arm and clung to it, panting and trembling.

"You were there . . . you overheard! You know that I love Angus Carisbroke! And I tell you!" All her composure was gone, sobs that rent my own heart seemed to tear her bosom, and she clutched my arm with a nervous strength her small, slight fingers might not have been credited with possessing. "I tell you, if they kill him I shall die!"

"Do you think he would let them kill him?" I broke out. "Do you think he would be such a idiot as to die – with you waiting for him at home?"

That made her smile, and when her eyes were quite presentable I took her to the Major, said good-night, and went home – to pack my own kit for Egypt.

II

Never did I learn whether Sphinx and her lover saw each other again before he sailed for Egypt. It may have been! I myself went out with the Second Brigade some weeks later as Special Warco for the *Daily Volt*. The big bustle did not stimulate me, as of yore, to pleasing excitement; my spirits ran thick and muddy as the cocoa-coloured Nile itself.

"You're as sick as a camel who has eaten her sun-bonnet," said Grainger, stout and jolly Jimmy, of the *Recorder*, as we sat together eating our first breakfast taken under canvas in camp at Atbara. "I wonder," he went on, "whether the cast-iron toughness of the turkeys and chickens is a special dispensation of the Father of the Faithful. Ordinary human jaws furnished with the usual number of grinders and incisors are useless when you come to deal with tendons like these." He held up a muscular leg as he spoke. "What really is required is a buzz-saw or a chaff-cutter!"

"Egyptian Tommy comes off better than English Tommy in the grub line," said I. "Dates and dhurra porridge washed down with sour milk or sherbet are all the human engine really wants to keep it going in a climate like this. But if English Tommy were asked to exchange tough goat-mutton and cartilaginous cow-beef for such 'fodder,' as he would call it, there would be shines in the tents of Shem, or I am not acquainted with the gentleman. Come for a stroll round camp, and let us see a little more of him." I got up and shook some cockroaches out of my well pipe-clayed helmet, and put it on. "His dogged determination to stick to what he is used to accounts for the rapidity with which civilisation follows in his footsteps, and springs up on his left hand and his right."

"It's true," Grainger said, looking over the busy scene that not many days previously had been a sand-driven waste. A thriving bazaar had sprung up on the banks of the Nile. Within the confines of the huge camp, sherbet-bars, canteens, and Greek cafés catered for the wants of Egyptian sepoys, English soldiers, Arabs, and rail-head fitters. Bands played, elevated on mud platforms and sheltered by canvas awnings, the familiar melodies dear to the ear of the Cockney-bred warrior. The strains of the "Cavalleria Rusticana" were inwoven with the familiar tunes of " 'E Don't Know Where 'E Are" and "Yankee Doodle," rendered extremely popular at the moment by America's recent conquest of Havana. "They've made a city – a big, bustling, profane, prosperous city – out of nothing, in next to no time. And over on the opposite side where the Lancers are" – he pointed to the camp of our late charges – "there will be another in a day or two."

"And a telegraph-cable laid across the Atbara," said I, "with a land-line to Shabluka, and an overhead communication across the water-gates, so that Warcos may delude a confiding home public with rapidity and ease. I loathe lying by camel-post."

"We spoke of civilisation just now," remarked Jimmy, "in reference to band-stands, cafés, and open-air theatres, which have sprung up round us like mushrooms. But one other social institution, lacking until a few moments ago, we may now pride ourselves on possessing – I allude to Woman! Not as she is, but as man imagines her to be! Woman, lovely woman! at this moment landing from a stern-wheel paddle-steamer, amidst the respectful admiration of British rank-and-file and the sugared politeness of British officers. To-day she descends upon us. To-morrow will see her manœuvring in the Desert in every variety of formation for attack. Why, you lucky devil! one of them knows you. She beckons with a lily-white sunshade! Go and render homage without delay!"

Next moment, as I hurried down the wharf, I held the hand of Sphinx Rowcliffe in mine.

"How brown you are, Walter!" she cried gleefully. "How your campaigning kit becomes you! Are you glad to see me? Do you think my father will be? This is my dear friend Mr Wyvern, Mrs Bennett," she went on, putting her slight hand affectionately through the arm of the elder woman, a pretty, vivacious, *passée* American. "Now you know each other, you must be friends."

"You will guess the trouble we had to get up here," said Mrs Bennett. "The miles of red tape that your officials wound around us! My! We felt like two bugs in a spider's web. And then, Herbert – I guess you'll like my husband when you know him, Mr Wyvern – Herbert did a smart thing. That is, smart for Herbert. He let it leak out accidentally that we were near relatives of the Sirdar, and that it would ease his mind to have a short conversation with us over family affairs before going into battle! But, all the same, we had to give an undertaking that we'd turn round when we got here and go right back. And I think it's a shame! You're all real cosy here, and want nothing but a little ladies' society to cheer you up, I should think."

So the charming lady prattled on, besieging me with questions which she did not give me time to answer, and recounting thrilling experiences of the voyage up river which she omitted to finish.

III

Major Rowcliffe was indignant with his daughter for what he termed her wilful disobedience, but after a while the veteran's wrath calmed down. The Guards gave the heroic ladies an ovation, and the Sirdar himself presided at a dinner given in their honour under the hospitable roof-tree of the regimental mess-tent.

Afterwards there was an open-air performance in the regimental theatre. How well I remember the scene! The farce "Freezing a Mother-in-Law" was played, beardless privates sustaining the feminine characters, and the roars of laughter that went up from the brawny throats of their comrades seemed to shake the great white Desert stars that the little oil-lamps blinked at. Afterwards there was a variety entertainment, with burnt-cork witticisms, which seemed to tickle the natives, though probably the listening Hamids and El Shendis understood not a word of what was spoken.

And a few yards from where we lingered Sphinx Rowcliffe and Angus Carisbroke, a manly, handsome figure in his khaki uniform, leggings, and pipe-clayed helmet, stood together, oblivious, it was plain, of everything in the world but each other, basking in the love-light of each other's eyes.

The ladies slept in camp that night, in a tent adjoining that of Major Rowcliffe, placed at their disposal by one of the Guardsmen – Captain Carisbroke, I believe. And as in the night a duststorm broke over us and nearly buried the Anglo-Egyptian Army beneath stifling drifts of hot sand, they naturally enjoyed the experience. They were to leave at daybreak of the third day following their arrival, and, under the protection of the intelligent Herbert, return to Assouan.

"But before we go," said Mrs. Bennett, "we're going to attend a grand parade of all the troops, and see some practice zareba-ing – don't you admire how technical I am? And we're going to make an excursion to Omar's deserted camp at Wady Hammam, under a guard furnished by the Sirdar – just as though we were Royalty! – and visit Omar himself."

I knew she spoke of the Khalifa's captured General, Omar Zain Mohammed, the Emir of Abu Gubat. I could not prevent the excursion, which I looked upon as in the highest degree risky, but I could, by accompanying it, add the strength of one more strong man, well armed, to Miss Rowcliffe's defence, if defence should be needed, against any stray party of wandering tribesmen who might chance to attack us. Danger in the prison, which I knew to be well guarded by Egyptian soldiery, I did not anticipate. How blind we are, the most keen-sighted of us! how dull of apprehension! The danger lay *in* the prison, after all!

How well I remember that ride to Wady Hammam! We

reached the fortified gate of the prison at about half-past five in the afternoon. Some Soudanese in chains – murderers for the most part – crouched by the walls. We crossed the large courtyard, guarded by soldiers with loaded rifles, and entered a smaller one, where one armed sentry paced to and fro. A single cell opened out from it. At a call from the prison official who accompanied us, Omar stepped across the threshold and confronted us, with folded arms.

He wore a white Arab *jibbeh*, or shirt, and an Emir's turban. Red slippers were on his bare feet. He was black as coal, and the Arab type in his features was mingled with that of the negro. In height he towered to an altitude of nearly seven feet. He was unchained, and his fierce eyes rolled upon us as though he would have liked to tear us to pieces with his small, muscular, sharp-taloned hands.

Some among our party spoke Arabic fairly, myself, Major Rowcliffe, and Sphinx, who prided herself upon her knowledge of her mother-tongue.

There was nothing cringing in the imprisoned Emir's manner. He bore himself like a chief, and regarded us evidently with contempt, though he replied to our inquiries—

"Am I comfortable here?" He echoed a question of the Major's. "By Allah! I am as comfortable as a lion in a net or a fish out of water. Where a Dervish feels at ease is when his charger's hoofs spurn the sand of the desert, and his spear or his gun is levelled at the accursed faces of his enemies. Or" – the whites of his eyes rolled upwards sanctimoniously, and he stretched his arm out towards the south – "when he bows at the tomb of the Prophet in the great mosque at Omdurman, where the true believers assemble to call down destruction upon the head of the infidel."

"Are there many Dervishes in Omdurman, O Chief?" I asked.

"Praised be Allah! yes," said Omar. "When the faithful gather to prayers in the Mosque, there are forty-seven rows of fighting-men, and in each row there is fifteen hundred. Wait until you get to Omdurman, you and your Sirdar! You will not

only see the Dervishes, but feel them!" He grinned sneeringly.
"They will drive you as the north wind drives the dust – you
will fly before them to the ends of the earth. I have said it!"

"The driving will be the other way, I take it," said Carisbroke, laughing. "Your people are very foolish. Why not submit
instead of waiting to be killed?"

I saw by Omar's ferocious scowl and the frown that gathered
between his coarse black brows that, whether he understood
English or not, the manner of the speaker was offensive to him.
But before Major Rowcliffe could translate, Sphinx turned
upon her lover quite fiercely.

"They may be foolish," she cried hotly, "but they are brave!
Were I a man of their race and tribe, I would fight to the last, as
they have done and will do again, and fire my last shot at the
enemies of my faith, with the death-rattle in my throat, as they
do!"

The Dervish's full black eyes rolled towards her.

"What does the Egyptian woman say?" he asked, addressing
Miss Rowcliffe in the third person, commonly employed by the
Arab in conversation with the sex he deems so much inferior to
his own.

Before her father could stop her, Sphinx had translated her
words. Omar smiled.

"It is well, O my sister!" he said. "Thine eye and thy features
proclaimed thee of Arab race ere thy tongue testified to it. What
dost thou among the infidels, O Rose of the Oasis, who shouldst
blossom only in the bosom of a son of the Prophet?"

His smile was horrible as he looked at the shrinking girl. My
blood boiled at it.

"You insult the lady, Emir!" I burst out fiercely. "She is of
English blood; she will be the bride – please Allah! – of an
Englishman, and she spits upon the unwashed fanatics who lick
the Mahdi's tombstone five times a day in your stinking dog-
kennel of a mosque at Omdurman!"

Omar started, and turned upon me the glare of a ferocious
beast, ere the click of the sentry's accoutrements as he shifted
his rifle reminded him that a bullet would probably be the

reward of any violent demonstration of anger. He folded his muscular arms upon his breast, inclined his head – a salutation intended only for Miss Rowcliffe – and turned upon his heel.

"I have spoken. Remember! We have learnt much since Atbara. We shall make a good fight of it when the next time comes. Life is nothing to us – death is much. Peace be with you, O lady!" He drew from the folds of his *jibbeh* a red cord, upon which some kind of a talisman or charm was suspended, threw it towards Sphinx, so that it touched her in falling, and vanished into his cell. "Keep the token!" said the deep voice from within. "Keep the token until we meet again!"

"Why, I do believe he's fallen in love with you, Violet!" exclaimed Mrs Bennett delightfully, as she stooped and lifted the talisman from the earthen floor. "Don't say you're going to be so mean as to refuse his keepsake!" She offered the thing to Sphinx as she spoke.

"Throw the vile trash away!" said Angus Carisbroke imperiously. His tone nettled me, and Sphinx's rich brown cheek glowed scarlet as she heard. For answer, she took the talisman from the hand of her friend and, casting a defiant glance at Angus, put it in her pocket.

IV

A startling surprise was ready for us next morning. When the camp was fairly astir, the hive of men was roused to wild excitement by the sudden intelligence that Miss Rowcliffe was missing from the tent she shared with her friend.

Mrs Bennett, hysterical and indignant by turns, could not account in any way for the girl's disappearance. Waking with the dawn, she had missed her – that was all. A subaltern of the Guards, returning at midnight to quarters from patrol duty, had seen two Arabs, as he thought, in flowing *jibbehs* pass down one of the alleys of wood and canvas dwellings, and vanish in the broad shadow cast by the mess-tent of the Guards. And in the sandy desert fifty yards beyond the zareba, at a point upon the north side, one of the sentries on outpost duty lay dead, his throat cut from ear to ear by the slash of a broad-bladed Dervish knife. And the sand bore the broad V-shaped impression of a camel's feet, as well as human footprints, some of them made by the soldier's clumsy boots, others the impressions of a muscular naked foot, others the double dents made by the toe and heel of a small Parisian shoe in the yielding, dun-coloured dust. Thenceforward the camel tracks led northwards, curving south by degrees, as the armed scouting parties despatched by the Sirdar followed them up, until upon the river bank, some twenty miles south of the camp, after sharp brush with a party of Fuzzies, we came upon a dead camel, a high-bred Bisharin, surrounded by vultures and crows, eagerly feasting upon the scarcely cold carcase. Then the trail came to an end, with the discovery of an unmistakable clue to the identity of *one* of the riders of the dead beast.

"It's a woman's veil! English-make, and tied to the saddle!" I said, showing my prize to Carisbroke.

He took the veil, though it rent my heart to let him have it – it was his by right – and kissed it and thrust it in his breast. Then, remounting, we rode back with the scouting party to Atbara.

There startling developments awaited us. Omar had escaped early in the previous night from the prison at Wady Hammam. Whether by connivance or by accident, a swift riding camel happened to be tethered beyond the walls, and of this the flying Chief had availed himself. It was a coincidence which brought to me – perhaps alone of all those who assembled in council before the Sirdar's quarters that night – the conviction that by some unexampled act of daring and treachery Major Rowcliffe's daughter had fallen into the hands of the Khalifa's fierce General – had been borne by him a captive, who knows where, probably to Omdurman.

"Hush!" I said, gripping Jimmy's arm as the staff emerged from the canvas pavilion, where, by the light of candles flaring in hooded tin sconces, the Sirdar had held a war council with his chiefs. The light of the torches outside fell upon the soldierly figures, the grave, keen-eyed faces – one of them seamed and haggard with the grief which had changed Major Rowcliffe in the space of two days from a middle-aged man into an old one. In the crowd of officers I caught a glimpse of the white face and brooding eyes of Carisbroke, and then I lost sight of him, my attention being fixed on the Sirdar. He touched his helmet in response to the cheer that rang out from the seething crowd of soldiers about him, then lifted his hand, and silence fell.

"Gentlemen," he said, "our advance will continue from to-morrow, under—" He named the Generals who were to lead the various divisions, and cheer after cheer greeted the names of popular men. "The work of concentration has been completed. To-morrow this camp will be deserted, and our entire force will be upon its way to Kerreri and Omdurman."

"*Hurrah!*" What a mighty cheer went up to the Desert stars from thousands of British throats! The triumphant yelling and drumming of the friendly Arab tribesmen were swallowed up in that immense volume of sound. The Sirdar spoke again—

"Men and officers, comrades all, England counts upon your loyalty and devotion to wipe the stain of General Gordon's unavenged blood from the flag of our country, to free this harassed land from the dominion of a cruel tyrant, at the cost of our lives if necessary – that is the task that lies before us. You will not fail when the time of trial comes. One other duty devolves upon us. There are English prisoners in Omdurman. One of them, by information received to-day from an Arab refugee who has fled from the Khalifa's threatened stronghold to the shelter of the English zareba, we believe to be the daughter of my friend, Major Rowcliffe, the unhappy young lady who was treacherously abducted from our camp a few days ago, we believe by a band of Arab spies of the Khalifa's, who thought she would prove a valuable hostage. By the strength of British arms and the help of God" – the General lifted his helmet reverently – "we will not only conquer Omdurman and take Khartoum, but save that lady! Good-night!"

The soldiers dispersed, the camp sank into silence. Only the challenge of the sentries and the grunts of the camels, mingled with the solid and continuous snoring that rose from the sleeping brigades, sounding like the beating of waves upon

the shore, were audible. The Sirdar's quarters were illuminated
– the staff were likely to remain in palaver until daybreak. No
time was to be lost if I was to carry out an idea that had occurred
to me. I sent an orderly with my card, bearing a pencilled
entreaty for a moment's interview. He returned after a short
delay, and ushered me into the presence of the Sirdar. In as few
words as possible I detailed my plan.

"It's madness!" said Sir Herbert, as Major Rowcliffe grasped
my hand in silence. "But I will give you the order and the
countersign. Do you really speak Arabic well enough to be
mistaken for a Jaalin?"

I nodded, and Sir Herbert wrote a few lines on a scrap of blue
paper and handed it to me.

"The gun-boat *Fateh* goes up-river to-night, to reconnoitre
with the electric searchlight and pick up refugees. Give this to
the officer in command! He will take you as close to Omdurman
as he can. As for getting ashore . . ." The Sirdar shrugged his
shoulders.

"I shall swim," I said shortly. "My stain won't wash off."

"Whether it does or does not, Mr Wyvern," said the Chief
gravely, "you run a fearful risk. Why not wait until the odds are
less desperate?"

"I've a bet on, for one thing, with Grainger of the *Recorder*,"
said, "that I shall be the first Warco to get into Omdurman.
And I mean to win. And while I am about it, I can look up Miss
Rowcliffe; that's all in the day's work, you see. So *au revoir*, Sir,
and good luck to all of us!"

V

Now when I decide upon a line of action, I am generally prompt
to act; and the plan I hit on will at once be perceived was one not
without danger.

"It's a gorgeous make-up," said the Lieutenant in command
of the *Fateh*, surveying me critically from top to toe as I stood
up in the gun-boat's little cabin under the swinging electric
light.

"You're a Dervish, every inch of you, and a d—d ugly one, too."

We went on deck. The night was still and quiet, save for the cracking of Dervish Martinis from the earthworks along the shore, and the occasional sharp crack of a bullet on an armour-plating, as we steamed along at some eight knots, sweeping the river with the broad V-shaped flare of the searchlight.

"Shut off, Martin, and run her in as close under the port bank as you can!" said my friend the Lieutenant.

Out went the light. A dropping volley of rifle-shots from the shore greeted the *Fateh*, and in the same instant I dived from the starboard side and struck out for the right bank of the river. The downward sweep of the current was strong, but I was a good swimmer, and had, moreover, provided myself with a small log, upon which I rested my breast and shoulders when, having battled my way against the flood some hundred yards, I turned and let myself drift slantwise towards the shore. Presently I was swept against the bank, not quite hard enough to stun me but hard enough to knock all the remaining breath out of my body. Holding on to a water-sodden log that projected from the mud, I looked up. Mud ramparts loomed above me to the height of twelve feet, perhaps. Digging my fingers and toes cautiously into the crevices, I had swarmed up a little way when I heard the crack of a Martini, and from a loophole near my head a tongue of flame sprang and licked my hair as the bullet whizzed harmlessly past my head.

"Why didst thou shoot, Muhamed?" said a guttural Arab voice upon the other side of the wall. "The devil-boat has turned and gone back; and, could thy bullet strike her, it would but flatten on her iron skin. They build everything of iron; Allah curse the outcasts!"

"I deemed I heard the breathing of a swimmer, O brother!" said Muhamed, "and something dark swung down upon the stream." He must have had good eyes, that chap, to pick out my abandoned log among the shadows. "Thou knowest that hourly cravens desert us, and, clinging to logs or camel-bladders, drift down to the camp of the White Khalifa" – he spat piously – "whom may Allah confound to burnings with all his followers!"

The Arabs passed on. I climbed the mud rampart and dropped to the filthy ground below. I had won my bet with Grainger. I had reached the capital of Khalifa Abdullah before him. I was in Omdurman. But – how to accomplish the task that lay before me? How to save Sphinx Rowcliffe from the fearful fate that threatened her – that would most surely befall her on the morrow!

I had brought a turban with me, Arab slippers, and a *jibbeh*, wrapped in a piece of native wax-cloth and tied about my body. I unrolled and put them on. As I stood up fully dressed, a score of white-clad figures similar to my own passed me in the bluish twilight of a stifling Egyptian night. The cries from the mosque towers continued. The Faithful were assembling to prayers. I mingled unperceived with a band of true believers, followed them to the doors of the Great Mosque, a gigantic quadrangular building of glimmering whitewashed brick with a central dome and a turret at each corner. I left my slippers at the door with other true believers, and entered barefoot the Kaabeh el Mahdi.

The interior of the building was packed to suffocation with white-clad, groaning Dervishes. The prayer was being led by a gigantic priest, who stood with outstretched arms beneath the central dome, before the black-draped wooden sarcophagus that contained the Mahdi's remains. The din, the heat, the stench were suffocating. I edged along by the wall, chanting as loudly as any fanatic present some scraps from the Koran. A doorway was within a few yards of me, screened by a striped curtain. I seized my opportunity, and as a tall, lean Dervish, wearing the headdress of a Syud, passed behind the curtain, I slipped through after him. We were in a dimly lighted passage, at the end of which was another doorway, guarded by two Dervishes with their terrible, broad-bladed spears. As they saluted the Dervish who preceded me, they made him some sign of warning. He turned round instantly, and I fell at his feet.

"Who art thou?" he demanded sternly.

"I am of the Jaalins, Lord," I answered, with my face pressed to the earth. "I am the camel-man who sent the pigeon! And the infidels suspected me, and I fled yesterday from the camp. And, I pray you, let me be heard by the Khalifa and the Emirs. For I bring important news. I have spoken."

The green-turbaned Syud, I felt, scrutinised me closely as he bade me rise and follow him. We passed into the chamber beyond. It was long, large, and lofty, and illuminated by rag torches dipped in naphtha, and emitting no very pleasant smell. The upper part of it, situated beneath one of the smaller domes of the Mosque, was divided from the rest of the chambers by a screen of carved and inlaid wood. Groups of Dervishes – Emirs by their turbans – stood about conversing in bated whispers; from beyond the screen came the sound of harsh, imperious voices, raised in argument or discussion. The Syud advanced. I followed closely on his heels. In another moment we were in the presence of the Khalifa Abdullah.

What passed at that interview?

I hardly recollect. I know that I prostrated myself as a good Dervish before the Commander of the Faithful. When a rasping voice addressed me, bidding me look up and speak the truth, I looked up, and told all the lies I had about me. They seemed to satisfy the Khalifa – a forbidding-looking, elderly man of negroid type, but less black than his brother, Yakoub Emir, the commander of the Dervish forces, a splendid figure in his shirt of mail and towering turban – and the Generals of the staff, among whom I recognised the villainous-looking Omar. It was he who spoke.

"Thou hast done well to come hither if thou hast good news, O man of the Jaalins. If thou bringest bad, it is not so well for thee.

"Regarding the woman of Egyptian blood whom the Emir Omar snatched from the harem of the White Chief, dost thou know whether the Commander of the infidel army set high value upon her or small?"

"O Light of the Earth!" I answered with a beating heart, "there are more Englishwomen than one in the infidels' camp.

Unless I saw the woman face to face, I could not say for
certain."

There was a pause. Then—

"Let the camel-man look upon the woman," said the Khalifa.
"Bring her here!"

There was a slight bustle, and an order was given. Perhaps
ten minutes passed, and then—

Then she came, guarded by Dervishes, the woman I loved,
the woman whose life I meant to save, or, if I could not, die with
her. She was draped in the voluminous garments worn by Arab
women. The yashmak did not screen her face, and I saw that it
was pale and wan with weeping. But her great lustrous eyes had
fire in them, and pride, and scorn, as she looked upon her
captors, and when it rested upon Omar, her glance was one of
defiance and most utter hate.

"Thou seest the woman," the Khalifa said to me. "Now say,
O Camel-man, if thou canst, what rank her beauty holds in the
heart of the White Chief?"

I rose to my knees and squatted on my heels, and stared at
Sphinx Rowcliffe coarsely, shading my eyes, for a reason, with
my stained hand.

"As the One God sees me, O Khalifa!" I cried, "this woman
is nothing to the Sirdar. She is but the bride of a Captain of his
Guard. Ask her if this be not truth that I have spoken."

"She hath declared the same thing ere now," said the Emir
Yakoub, with an angry glance in Omar's direction. "Wherefore I
hold that her life or death will be of small account in the eyes of the
English Chief and his generals, and that thy menace, O my
brother!" – he turned to the Khalifa – "will no more stay the
advance of the British brigades to-morrow than a grain of sand.
At the prompting of the Emir Omar, therefore, hast thou done a
vain thing, and our beards are laughed at and we are put to shame.
But" – he touched the iron handle of his long crooked sword –
"there be some of them who will laugh no more after to-morrow,
and whether the day be ours, O Lord of the Earth! or whether I
die beside thy black standard ere noon of to-morrow, with the
hosts of the Faithful, it is one! Death is sweeter than Life to him

that dies for the Faith!" He shouted, and the domed roof gave back the war-cry, "*Allah! Allah! Rasul Allah el Mahdi!*"

"Allah!" a hundred Dervish throats echoed. Then Yakoub saluted the Khalifa and strode from the chamber, leaving doubt and perplexity behind him.

"Thou art a fool, O Emir!" said the Khalifa sullenly, after a whispered conference with some of his ministers, addressing Omar, who seemed decidedly out of favour. "But none the less that she is of small account in the eyes of the White Chief shall this woman die. See that my sentence concerning her be carried out as I have commanded, to-morrow, when the first English shell falls into our holy city. Until then," he stood up and beckoned his generals and ministers to follow him, "she is thine. Pluck the rose, O Omar! for the bush that bears it will be cut down before noon. By the beard of the Prophet! our torches are beginning to fade in the daylight already. Morning has stolen on us unperceived."

Boom! boom! crash!

O God! the thunder of the howitzers, the splitting roar of bursting shells! As the dome above us shivered to fragments, mud and bricks falling in showers about our ears, the Khalifa, Omar, and the other generals dashed from the room. I was left with the woman whom I had come to save!

"Touch me not!" she said sternly in Arabic, as I darted toward her with a cry of joy. She drew back into an angle of the wall, her eyes sternly fixed on me. She put one hand to her bosom. I guessed she had a weapon hidden there.

"Sphinx – Miss Rowcliffe, it is I – Walter Wyvern!" I cried. And then, with a shriek of joy, she threw herself into my arms.

"Is it you – is it really you?" she sobbed, over and over again. When she was a little calmer, she told me the story of her abduction by Omar from the zareba, on the night following her visit to the prison at Wady Hammam.

"An Arab whose face I knew brought me a message," she said. "'An English officer begged to speak to me for one moment . . . He was waiting close by,' the man said. And I thought that it was Angus. We had had our first quarrel," her voice broke: "I wanted to see him and make it up. So I followed the Arab. Then as we passed into the shadow of the Guards' mess-tent, a wrapper was thrown over my head – I was overpowered, stifled. I must have fainted, for when I recovered it was to find myself bound on a camel, before Omar's saddle. and flying through the desert like the wind. Then we met a party of tribesmen. They killed the camel for some reason, and we made the rest of the journey on horses. They took me to the Khalifa's harem when we reached Omdurman – some of his wives were kind to me. But for the past two days I have been imprisoned here. And I have feared—" she shuddered and broke off.

Did she know, I wondered, what really was to be feared? And as the thought crossed my mind, the thunder of the guns broke out again. A volley followed and a reply-volley. The battle had begun in good earnest. I snatched up a spear leaning in an angle of the wall.

"Where does that staircase lead to?" I asked, pointing to a winding flight of steps in the opposite corner of the room. Without waiting for an answer, I darted up. The morning air, hot yet moist with the dampness of the river mists, met my smarting face. I looked northwards, and saw a glorious sight. Fronting me lay spread upon the plain the Anglo-Egyptian army. Its flanks rested upon the river, its line extended from the Nile westwards, its formation resembling three sides of an irregular square. Suddenly I perceived that Sphinx had not followed me, and I sprang down the staircase.

I regained the chamber below not a minute too soon. Omar was there with two other Dervishes, fierce-eyed, bloodstained zealots, eager to fulfil the Khalifa's command. He held Sphinx in a fierce grasp as he argued with the two Dervishes who sought to drag the girl from him.

"Let her be!" he cried. "Ye shall not slay her till I am weary of her. If we evacuate the city she shall go with me. Did I not take her from the English? Is she not mine?"

"She is the Khalifa's, as thou art and all of us," screamed one of the Dervishes. "And the word of Abdullah has gone forth: she is to die."

"Then she shall die by this hand, not by thine!" said Omar. He drew a keen curved dagger-blade from the shawl-girdle that bound his coat of steel links about his lean, sinewy figure, and crushed the half-fainting girl more closely in the sinewy embrace of his left arm. Despair lent me the strength of three men. Unseen till that moment, I rushed in, and slew one of the Dervishes. As I drove the point of the broad leaf-shaped spearblade home against Omar's mail-clad breast he staggered, and the dagger fell from his hand, so unexpected was my onslaught. And next moment, as the remaining Dervish recognised in me no ally, but an enemy, we were engaged in a hand-to-hand fight – his iron grip upon my right arm, his keen blade seeking to drink my blood. As the sword passed through my body, he loosed his hold, and I had the satisfaction of shooting the brute before consciousness left me, and I fell headlong into what seemed like a bottomless pit of nothingness.

But I came up out of the depths and opened my eyes to see – what? The light of day through the shattered walls of the Mahdi's Tomb, English faces round me, and my head supported in the lap of the woman I would have given a thousand lives to save. You know the thrilling story of the victory; there is no need to tell again the tale the newspapers told so well many weeks ago, ere we came back to England, and Sphinx Rowcliffe gave her hand to the gallant Guardsman who already owned her heart. But a corner of that heart belongs to a certain battered War-Correspondent of whom you have heard before and will hear again, perhaps, unless we turn our Maxims into garden watering-engines, and, our Lyddite-shell mortars into ornamental flower-pots, to please His Imperial Majesty the Czar!

APPENDIX

Stories of the Victoria Cross

The Victoria Cross, the highest award for bravery and valour, was instituted by Queen Victoria in 1856 after the Crimean War. The Crosses are cast from the metal of the guns captured at the siege of Sebastopol. Between then and today, 1,350 men have been awarded the VC, three of whom have won it twice. The following are a few personal accounts of how the VC was won, compiled and introduced by H. Greenhough Smith (1851–1935), the editor of The Strand Magazine.

No tales of heroism are more thrilling and exciting than the narratives of the exploits which have gained the coveted reward of the Victoria Cross; and a story never has so much reality and vividness as when it comes first-hand from the performer of the deed. Accordingly, we have asked a number of the heroes of the Victoria Cross – a truly noble army – to relate in their own language how they came to win the most glorious decoration open to a soldier, the plain bronze cross "For Valour." The narratives which follow require no further introduction, and will, we think, be found to possess an interest which is all their own – the interest and impression of reality.

1 SERGEANT ABLETT

One of the most gallant acts which can be conceived is seizing a live shell and casting it away, so as to prevent mischief from its explosion. A second's delay may be fatal, and the man who picks up the shell cannot tell whether the second in question will be allowed him. If it bursts in his hands it means certain death. Not only the greatest, but also the promptest, courage is needed for such an act of courage. Among the few who have performed such a feat is Sergeant Ablett, late Grenadier Guards, whose own modest account is as follows:

On the 2nd September, 1854, when in the trenches before Sebastopol, the sentries shouted "Look out there!" a shell coming right in the trenches at the same moment and dropping amongst some barrels of ammunition. I at once pulled it from them. It ran between my legs, and I then picked it up and threw it out of the trench; it burst as it touched the ground. From the force of it I fell, and was covered by its explosion with gravel and dirt.

Sergeant Baker and others picked me up, and asked if I was hurt. I said, "No; but I have had a good shaking." There was a great number in the trenches at the time, but I am glad to say no one was hurt. The Sergeant reported the circumstances to the officer in charge.

On coming off duty I was taken before the commanding officer, and promoted to the rank of Corporal, and then Sergeant. He also presented me with a silk necktie made by her most gracious Majesty. I was at the battles of Alma, Balaclava, Inkerman, and the capture of Sebastopol after eleven months' siege. This is all I think I need say as to myself and the Victoria

Cross. My likeness is to be found in Victoria Cross Picture Gallery, Crystal Palace, and Alexandra Palace.

2 MAJOR JOHN BERRYMAN

Among those who won the Victoria Cross at Balaclava none gained it more worthily than Major John Berryman, who served in the Crimea as Troop-Sergeant Major in the 17th Lancers. This is how Major Berryman describes the charge of the Light Brigade:

"Gallop!" was the order as the firing became general. And here a discharge from the battery in our front, whose guns were doubly shotted, first with shot or shell, and then with case, swept away Captain Winter and the whole division on my right. The gap was noticed by Captain Morris, who gave the order, "Right incline," but a warning voice came from my coverer in the rear rank (Corporal John Penn), "Keep straight on, Jack; keep straight on." He saw what I did not, that we were opposite the intervals of the guns, and thus we escaped, for the next round must have swept us into eternity. My attention here was attracted to James Melrose, a Shakespearian reciter, calling out, "What man here would ask another man from England?" Poor fellow, they were the last words he spoke, for the next round from the guns killed him and many others. We were then so close to the guns that the report rang through my head, and I felt that I was quite deaf for a time. It was this round that broke my mare's off hind leg, and caused her to stop instantly. I felt that I was hit, but not till I dismounted. Seeing that the mare's leg was broken, I debated in my own mind whether to shoot her or not, when Captain Webb came up to me, and asked me, was I wounded? I replied, "Only slightly, I thought, in the leg, but that my horse was shot." I then asked, "Are you hurt, sir?" He said that he was, and in the leg, too; what had he better do? "Keep to your horse, sir, and get back as far as you can." He turned, and rode back. I now caught a loose horse, and got on to his back, but he fell directly, the brass of the breast-plate having been driven into his chest. Seeing that there was no hope of my joining the regiment in the *mêlée*, and the 11th Hussars being close upon me, I moved a little to the right, so as to pass through the interval between the squadrons. Both squadrons closed in a little, and let me pass through. I well remember that Sergeant Gutteridge was the right guide of the 2nd squadron. Finding that Captain Webb had halted, I ran to him, and on inquiries found that his wound was so painful that he could not ride any further. Lieutenant George Smith, of my own regiment, coming by, I got him to stand at the horse's head whilst I lifted the captain off. Having accomplished this, I assisted Smith to mount Webb's horse, and ride for a stretcher, taking notice where we were. By this time the Russians had got back to their guns, and re-opened fire. I saw six men of my own regiment get together to recount to each other their escapes. Seeing their danger, I called to them to separate, but too late, for a shell dropped amongst them, and I don't think one escaped alive. Hearing me call to these men, Captain Webb asked what I thought the Russians would do?

"They are sure to pursue, sir, unless the Heavy Brigade comes down."

"Then you had better consult your own safety, and leave me."

"Oh no, sir, I shall not leave you now."

"Perhaps they will only take me prisoner."

"If they do, sir, we will go together."

"Don't mind me, look to yourself."

"All right, sir; only we will go together, whatever happens."

Just at this time I saw Sergeant Farrell coming by. I called to him. He asked, "Who is it?" When told, he came over. I said, "We must get Captain Webb out of this, for we shall be pursued."

He agreeing, we made a chair of our hands, lifted the Captain up, and found that we could carry him with comparative ease. We had got about 200 yards in this manner, when the Captain complained that his leg was very painful. A private of the 13th being near, Malone, I asked him would he be good enough to support Captain Webb's legs, until we could procure a stretcher? He did so, and several of the officers passed us. Sir G. Wombwell said, "What is the matter, Peck?" (Captain Webb's nickname.)

"Hit in the leg, old fellow. How did you escape?"

"Well, I was unhorsed and taken prisoner, but when the second line came down, in the confusion I got away, and, seizing the first horse I could, I got away, and I find that it is Morris's."

Sir W. Gordon made the same inquiry, and got the same answer. He had a very nasty cut on the head, and blood was then running down his face. He was carrying his dress cap in his hand. We had now reached the rear of the Greys, and I procured a stretcher from two Infantry band boys, and a young officer of the "Greys" gave me a "tourniquet," saying that he did not know how to apply it, but perhaps I might. I put it on the right thigh, and screwed it up. Doctor Kendal came here, and I pointed out what I had done, and asked was it right?

"I could not have done it better myself; bring him along."

I and Farrell now raised the stretcher and carried it for about fifty yards, and again set it down. I was made aware of an officer of the Chasseurs d'Afrique being on my left by his placing his hand upon my shoulder. I turned and saluted. Pointing to Captain Webb, but looking at me, he said:

"Your officer?"

"Yes."

"Ah! and you sergeant?" looking at the stripes on my arm.

"Yes."

"Ah! If you were in French service, I would make you an officer on the spot." Then, standing in his stirrups and extending his right hand, said:

"Oh! it was grand, it was *magnifique*, but it is not war, it is not war."

This officer was General Morris. We resumed our patient, and got to the doctors (Massy and Kendal). I saw the boot cut off and the nature of the wound, the right shin bone being shattered. Farrell made an exclamation, and I was motioned to take him away. I told him that I should go and see the end of it. He said that he was too exhausted to do any more. Finding a horse in the lines, I mounted him, although the animal belonged to the 4th Light Dragoons, and thus dropped in behind the Duke of Cambridge, and heard what passed. The Duke, speaking to Lord Cardigan, said:

"Cardigan, where's the Brigade, then?"

"There," said Cardigan.

"Is that all of them? You have lost the finest Brigade that ever left the shores of England."

A little further on he spoke to Captain Godfrey Morgan (Lord Tredegar):

"Morgan, where's the regiment, then?"

"Your Royal Highness, that is all of them!"

"My poor regiment, my poor regiment!"

I now took my place in the ranks, and, in numbering off, being on the extreme left, I counted 22. We fell back during the night, and, being dismounted; I, with my servant, was left behind. I suffered intensely with my head, and got a napkin and tied it as tightly as possible round my brows. I also had time to examine my wound, which was inside the calf of my leg. A small piece about the size of a shilling had been cut clean out of my leg; but except that the blood had run into my boots, I felt but very little inconvenience from it. Cold water bandage was all I used; but, unfortunately, scurvy got to it, and it was a long time healing.

3 PRIVATE WILLIAM NORMAN

Private William Norman, of the 7th Regiment, in a true modest and soldier-like style thus describes the exploit which won for him the Victoria Cross:

On the night of December 19, 1854, I was placed on single sentry at some distance in front of the advanced sentries of an out-lying picquet in the White Horse Ravine – a post of much danger, and requiring great vigilance. The Russian picquet was posted 300 yards in our front. Three Russian soldiers advanced under cover of the brushwood for the purpose of reconnoitring. I immediately fired my rifle, which was the signal of alarm, and then jumped into the trench almost on the top of the three Russians, two of whom I succeeded single-handed in taking prisoners, and marched them into our lines, the other one having fled back to the Russian lines.

My feelings I can hardly describe, as what I did was on the spur of the moment. But it was no doubt the means of saving our position.

4 DEPUTY INSPECTOR-GENERAL J. JEE, CB, VC

Though military surgeons are technically non-combatants, yet practically they are as much exposed to peril as other officers, and frequently have to perform work demanding the greatest care and calmness under the most disturbing dangers. In gallantry and devotion to duty no other class of soldiers has surpassed them. The following is the story of the exploit of one of these brave men, Surgeon Jee, as told in his own words:

On the advance of the force to relieve the garrison of Lucknow, under Generals Havelock and Outram, my regiment, the 78th Highlanders, led the way. General Outram's order on leaving Lucknow ran as follows: "I have selected the 78th Highlanders for covering the retreat of the force; they had the post of honour on the advance, and none are more worthy of the post of honour on leaving it."

There was very hard fighting from the Alum Bagh till we arrived close to Lucknow, when I was told an officer was severely wounded. I dismounted from my horse to attend him, and found he was dead. At that moment a very rapid ordnance and musketry fire commenced close to us, and I was pulled into the bastioned gateway of the Char-Bagh Palace by some soldiers, to whom probably I owed my life, as the round shot passed by us in quick succession. Captain Havelock (now Sir Henry Havelock) then rode up to me, with a bullet hole through his topee, and said, "We have taken that position, at all events, at the point of the bayonet." That proved to be the bridge over the canal at the entrance of Lucknow, defended by heavy guns, which had evidently been well served, judging by the numbers of dead lying around them.

When the main body of the force arrived and crossed to the other side of the bridge, the Generals heard that the streets in the city, leading direct to the Residency, were entrenched and barricaded. It was, therefore, decided to take the outside route by the very narrow road to the right by the canal, leaving the 78th to hold the position until ordered to advance after the column. Captains Drummond-Hay and Lockhart were then ordered to proceed with their companies to a pagoda some little distance up the street leading from the bridge. All was pretty quiet for some time, and the force had got some distance away, when a message was sent down to the Colonel by Captain Drummond-Hay that the enemy were coming down upon them in great force with two guns. The Colonel sent up an order for them to charge them, which they did, and spiked the guns and brought them down and threw them into the canal, all the while hotly pursued by the enemy. I then got between twenty and thirty wounded men in a few minutes.

I was then informed that the regiment had disappeared round the corner of the canal after the force, and that we should all be killed if I remained to dress the wounded upon whom I was engaged, as the enemy was firing at us from the corner of the street. So I sent to the Colonel for men to carry the wounded on their backs till we came up with the dhoolies. I was thus enabled to save them for a short time. It appeared that Captain Have-lock, the Assistant Adjutant-General, had been sent back by his father to order the 78th to follow the force, when he was badly wounded in his arm. Luckily I came across two dhoolies, in which I placed him and a lieutenant of the 78th, who was mortally wounded. The rest I put into sick-carts drawn by six bullocks; but shortly after all of them were massacred within sight of us, as unfortunately a native hackery containing round shot fell over, and completely blocked the road. One poor fellow, Private Farmer, held his watch out from one of the carts, asking his comrades to come and take it rather than the enemy should get it, but no one responded, as the danger was too great.

One man had his lower jaw blown off by a round shot, whom I am seen dressing in my V.C. picture at the Crystal Palace.

When we reached the force Captain Halliburton, 78th Highlanders (afterwards killed in Lucknow), took charge of the wounded with his company. We lost our way in the city, and were led by a guide, who showed us the way to the Residency into the enemy's battery, where we suffered considerable loss. After this we wandered about the suburbs of the city, under an awful cannonading and shelling from the opposite side of the River Goomtee, being fired at from loopholes in the houses of the streets when we entered them, from which parties of natives, clothed in white, often issued. We took refuge in the Mote-Mahul, as it was too late at night to advance further. The Mote-Mahul is a square courtyard with sheds round it, and two large gateway entrances. This was crowded with soldiers, camp followers, and camels, so that you could scarcely move. I had Captain Havelock and Lieutenant Woodhouse (right arm afterwards amputated), 84th Regiment, with me under the shed. The firing during the night was deafening, and gongs were sounding the hour, and we knew not how far the Residency was. Some who had been with the main body said the 78th were all killed, and they could not tell what had become of the rest of the force. At daylight the next day Brigadier Cooper gave us some tea, as we had taken nothing since leaving Alum Bagh early the morning before. Our men then commenced making loopholes in the wall of the shed to shoot the enemy on the other side, and I heard them told not to make too many or they would be shooting some of us, and soon afterwards Brigadier Cooper was shot through one of them, and fell over me. I often had to cross a gateway that was being raked up by bullets, to dress the wounded of both the artillery and my own men, against the remonstrances of my apothecary, Mr de Soura, and others.

I then volunteered to attempt to get the wounded into the

Residency, and was told by Captain Halliburton, if I succeeded, to tell General Outram to send him reinforcements or they would all be killed and the guns lost. I soon came across Colonel Campbell, wounded in the leg (afterwards amputated in Lucknow, and he died), and I got one of his men to carry him on his back (who would have been recommended for the V.C. if he could have been found, but he was supposed to have been killed). I then wandered on, and had to cross a shallow stream under fire of the guns of the extensive Palace of the Kaiser Bagh, where the enemy were said to have 20,000 men. I was then hailed by an European sentry at the gate of a very high wall, which I had the unpleasant feeling was the Kaiser Bagh, and that I was on the wrong road, but to my great relief he told me it led to the Residency, and that I must keep well under the wall on the way to it, to avoid the firing that was going on. On arriving at the Residency I delivered my message to General Havelock, who congratulated me on my escape, as I was reported killed.

Of course I lost a great many of my wounded, and one could see their skeletons lying outside the Palace, which we afterwards took, during the two months we were besieged in Lucknow. I did not see my horse (that is painted in my V.C. picture from a photograph) till after I arrived in Lucknow, where he was captured. He was badly wounded by a large slug or bolt about two inches long (which I have now) entering deeply on the side of the chest, and which was afterwards found most difficult to extract with bullet forceps. Yet the horse lived to aid Outram's relief outside Lucknow, and afterwards was sold as a very valuable charger for £160.

5 LANCE-CORPORAL WILLIAM GOATE

The following account, written by himself, of the military career of William Goate, and of the heroic act of devotion for which he was rewarded with the V.C., speaks for itself and needs no introduction:

*　　*　　*

My father died when I was only five years old, and left mother with a family of eleven of us, so as I grew up I had to work in the fields till I was big enough to mind horses. Then after a bit I got tired of the country, although it was a pretty village in Norfolk, called Tritton, close to Norwich; so I thought I would go to Norwich and get a job as a groom, which I did, and stopped till I was 18. Then I thought I would like another change, so up to London I went, and I had a wish to be a soldier. I was a smart lad and fresh-looking, so I went to Westminster in November, 1853, and enlisted in the 9th Lancers, and being a groom I was quite at home in a cavalry regiment; and I confess to being proud of our gay uniform and fluttering pennons. Well, after serving four years I was destined to ride in many a wild charge and see men and horses go down like ninepins, but I never thought of danger. When we got the order to charge, away we went determined to win, and I can tell you it must always be a terrible sight for any troops, let alone Sepoys, to see a regiment of cavalry sweeping down upon them.

Our fighting began at Delhi. We were at Umballa when the Mutiny broke out, and we were ordered to join in the operations against Delhi. I was present at the siege and capture of that city. I will tell you of a little adventure of my own at this time. Before the city was taken I was on despatch duty at an advanced post with orders to fetch reinforcements when the enemy came out. One day I saw six men trying to steal round by the river into our camp. Believing them to be spies, I asked the officer in charge of the picket to allow me and two men to go and ascertain what their intentions were. He gave us leave. We had a very difficult job to get down to the riverside on account of the rocks, and when we got up to the men they showed fight. We shot three of them with our pistols – one each. Being on horseback we then attacked them with the lance. One daring fellow struck at me, and I couldn't get at him. He slightly wounded my horse and then made a run for the river. I jumped from my horse, and, going into the water after him, ran him through with my lance. Meanwhile, the other two of my companions had settled the two remaining men. All this while a heavy fire had played on us from the enemy's battery. We had now to ride for our lives. On getting back to the camp, the officer in command sent me to the camp with a note to the Colonel of the regiment, who made me a lance-corporal then and there.

I might say I was two years in the saddle, almost continuously fighting. I was with Sir Colin when he retook Cawnpore from the Gwalior rebels. We went to the aid of General Wyndham, who had been repulsed. We crossed the bridge of boats under a heavy fire, but forced our way in. As soon as our brave leader got his men in position, he carried everything before him. We could still see traces of Nana Sahib's atrocity in June, and every soldier vowed vengeance. The affair that I was in when I gained my Victoria Cross was before Lucknow, the second time. Early in 1858 the rebels had strongly fortified the place, and it became necessary for Sir Colin to take it. Our regiment had some hot work. It was on March 6 that I won the Cross, in action at Lucknow, having dismounted in the presence of the enemy and taken up the body of Major Percy Smith, 2nd Dragoon Guards, which I attempted to bring off the field, and after being obliged to relinquish it, being surrounded by the enemy's cavalry, going a second time, under heavy fire, to recover the body, for which I received the Victoria Cross.

I will try and describe the fight, and what I saw of it. The enemy appeared in great force on the race-course outside Lucknow, and the 9th Lancers, the 2nd Dragoon Guards, and two native cavalry regiments were ordered to charge. The brigade swept on in grand style, and clashed into the enemy. We had a fierce hand-to-hand fight; but our troops behaved splendidly, and at last we broke them up. Then we were obliged to retire under a heavy fire. As we did so Major Smith, of the Dragoons, was shot through the body, and fell from his horse. Failing to catch him, I sprang to the ground, and, throwing the bridle-rein over my arm, raised the Major on to my shoulder; in this manner I ran along-side of my horse for some hundreds of yards, until I saw the enemy's cavalry close upon me. Clearly I couldn't get away with my burden, so I determined to do what I could for myself.

Springing into my saddle, I shot the first Sepoy who charged, and with my empty pistol felled another. This gave me time to draw my sword, my lance having been left on the field. The Sepoys were now round me cutting and hacking, but I managed to parry every slash and deliver many a fatal thrust. It was parry and thrust, thrust and parry all through, and I cannot tell you how many saddles I must have emptied. The enemy didn't seem to know how to parry.

Taking advantage of this, I settled accounts with a jolly lot. I was determined not to be taken alive. At last some of the Lancers saw me and came to my rescue. Thinking the major might still be alive, I went again to rescue him, but it was not until the enemy's forces were driven back that we got his body.

After the action, General Sir Colin Campbell, General Sir Hope Grant, and some of the cavalry officers shook hands with me and complimented me.

In regard to the sword and lance, I certainly prefer the lance; the lance is so keen, it goes through a man before he knows it. I was always very careful never to let a swordsman get under my lance, and in fighting with cavalry I made full use of the pennon to baffle an enemy's horse.

The weapons of troops on active service are made as keen as razors, and it was a common thing during the Mutiny to see a party of soldiers under the shade of a great tree waiting their turn to get their blades sharpened and the dints removed, ready for the next fight with the rebels. Our gallant little army was like a ship cleaving its way through the sea, for wherever we went, the enemy, like the waters, closed in behind.

6 PRIVATE JAMES DAVIS

The attack on Fort Ruhiya on April 15, 1858, gave an opportunity for much display of courage and devotion. Among those who conspicuously distinguished themselves was Private James Davis, of the 42nd Highlanders. This gallant soldier, who had previously served throughout the Crimean War, also saw much fighting during the Indian Mutiny, and for his conduct at Fort Ruhiya was awarded the Victoria Cross.

The following is his account of the feat which won for him the much-prized honour:

I belonged to the Light Company, under the command of Captain (now Sir John) Macleod. We got orders to lie down under some trees for a short time. Two Engineer officers came up and asked for some men to come with them to see where they could make a breach with the artillery. I was one who went. There was a small garden ditch under the walls of the fort, not high enough to cover our heads. After a short time the officers left. I was on the right of the ditch with Lieut. Alfred Jennings Bramley, of Tunbridge Wells, as brave a young officer as ever drew sword, and saw a large force coming out to cut us off. He said, "Try and shoot the leader. I will run down and tell Macleod." The leader was shot, by whom I don't know. I never took credit for shooting anyone. Before poor Bramley got down he was shot in the temple, but not dead. He died during the night.

The captain said, "We can't leave him. Who will take him out?" I said, "I will." The fort was firing hard all the time. I said, "Eadie, give me a hand. Put him on my back." As he was doing so he was shot in the back of the head, knocking me down, his blood running down my back. A man crawled over and pulled Eadie off. At this time I thought I was shot, the warm blood running down my back. The captain said, "We can't lose any more lives. Are you wounded?" I said, "I don't think I am." He said, "Will you still take him out?" I said, "Yes." He was such a brave young fellow that the company all loved him. I got him on my back again, and told him to take me tight round the neck. I ran across the open space. During the time his watch fell out; I did not like to leave it, so I sat down and picked it up, all the time under a heavy fire. There was a man of the name of Dods, who came and took him off my back. I went back again through the same fire, and helped to take up the man Eadie. Then I returned for my rifle, and firing a volley we all left. It was a badly managed affair altogether.

7 PRIVATE W. JONES

No action in recent warfare is better known than that of the heroic defence of Rorke's Drift. We are here able to give the narratives of three soldiers who gained their Cross for bravery in that day's gallant struggle. Here, first, is Private Jones's account of the affair:

About half-past three o'clock on the afternoon of the 22nd of January, 1879, a mounted man came galloping into our little encampment and told us that the Zulus had taken the camp at Isandlwana, and were making their way towards us at Rorke's Drift. We at once set to work, and with such material as we had at hand formed a slight barricade around us; this was formed of sacks of mealies (Indian corn), boxes of sea biscuits, &c., of which we had a good supply. We also loopholed the walls of the two buildings. We had scarcely completed our work when the Zulus were down upon us.

The hospital being the first building in their line of attack, they surrounded it. Having twenty-three sick men in the rooms, our officer, Lieutenant Bromhead, ordered six men into the hospital, myself being one of the number, to defend and rescue the sick from it. We had scarcely taken our post in the hospital when two out of our number were killed in the front or verandah, leaving four of us to hold the place and get out the sick. This was done by two (viz., Privates Hook and Williams) carrying the sick and passing them into the barricade through a small window, while myself (William Jones) and my comrade (Robert Jones) contended each door at the point of the bayonet, our ammunition being expended. The Zulus, finding they could not force us from the doors, now set fire to the thatched roof. This was the most horrifying time. What with the blood-thirsty yells of the Zulus, the cries of the sick that remained, and the burning thatch falling about our heads, it was sickening. Still we kept them at bay until twenty out of the twenty-three sick men were passed into the barricade under the fire of our own men; the other three sick I have every reason to believe must have wandered back into one of the rooms we had cleared, as they were men suffering from fever at the time. By this time the whole of the hospital was in flames, and as we could not stay in it any longer, we had to make our own escape into the barricade, by the window through which the sick had been passed. This we did, thank God, with our lives.

8 PRIVATE HENRY HOOK

On January 22nd, 1879, Private Henry Hook, with his company, under Lieutenant Bromhead, was stationed at Rorke's Drift, to guard the ford and hospital and stores. He thus tells his gallant story:

Between three and four in the afternoon, when I was engaged preparing the tea for the sick at the out-of-door cooking place, just at the back of the hospital – for I was hospital cook – two mounted men, looking much exhausted, and their horses worn out, rode up to me. One was in his shirt sleeves, and without a hat, with a revolver strapped round his breast; the other had his coat and hat on. They stopped for a moment and told me that the whole force on the other side of the river had been cut up, and that the Zulus were coming on in great force. They then rode off. I immediately ran to the camp close by and related what I had heard. We were at once fallen in and set to work to strengthen the post by loopholing the windows of the buildings, and to make breastworks of biscuit boxes and mealie bags. About half an hour later the Zulus were seen coming round a hill, and about 1,200 yards off. We were then told off to our posts. I was placed in one of the corner rooms of the hospital.

About this time Captain Stevens and all his men, except one native and two Europeans, non-commissioned officers, deserted us, and went off to Helpmakair. We were so enraged that we fired several shots at them, one of which dropped a European non-commissioned officer. From my loophole I saw the Zulus approaching in their thousands. They begun to fire, yelling as they did so, when they were 500 or 600 yards off.

They came on boldly, taking advantage of anthills and other cover, and we were soon surrounded. More than half of them had muskets or rifles. I began to fire when they were 600 yards distant. I managed to clip several of them, for I had an excellent rifle, and was a "marksman." I recollect particularly one Zulu. He was about 400 yards off, and was running from one anthill to another. As he was running from cover to cover, I fired at him; my bullet caught him in the body, and he made a complete somersault. Another man was lying below an anthill, about 300 yards off, popping his head out now and again to fire. I took careful aim, but my bullet went just over his head. I then lowered my sight, and fired again the next time he showed himself. I saw the bullet strike the ground in a direct line, but about ten yards short. I then took a little fuller sight, aimed at the spot where I knew his head would come out, and, when he showed himself, I fired. I did not then see whether he was struck, but he never showed again. The next morning, when the fighting was over, I felt curious to know whether I had hit this man, so I went to the spot where I had last seen him. I found him lying dead, with his skull pierced by my bullet.

The Zulus kept drawing closer and closer, and I went on firing, killing several of them. At last they got close up, and set fire to the hospital. There was only one patient in my room with a broken leg, and he was burnt, and I was driven out by the flames, and was unable to save him. At first I had a comrade, but he left after a time, and was killed on his way to the inner entrenchment. When driven out of this room, I retired by a partition door into the next room, where there were several patients. For a few minutes I was the only fighting man there. A wounded man of the 24th came to me from another room with a bullet wound in the arm. I tied it up. Then John Williams came in from another room, and made a hole in the partition, through which he helped the sick and wounded men. Whilst he was doing this, the Zulus beat in the door, and tried to enter. I stood at the side, and shot and bayoneted several – I could not tell how many, but there were four or five lying dead at my feet. They threw assegais continually, but only one touched me, and that inflicted a scalp wound which I did not think worth reporting; in fact, I did not feel the wound at the time. One Zulu seized my rifle, and tried to drag it away. Whilst we were tussling I slipped in a cartridge and pulled the trigger – the muzzle was against his breast, and he fell dead. Every now and again a Zulu would make a rush to enter – the door would only let in one man at a time – but I bayoneted or shot every one. When all the patients were out except one, who owing to a broken leg could not move, I also went through the hole, dragging the man after me, in doing which I broke his leg again. I then stopped at the hole to guard it, whilst Williams was making a hole through the partition into the next room.

When the patients had been got into the next room I followed, dragging the man with the broken leg after me. I stopped at the hole to guard it whilst Williams was helping the patients through a window into the other defences. I stuck to my particular charge, and dragged him out and helped him into the inner line of defences. I then took my post behind the parapet where three men had been hit just before. One of these was shot in the thick part of the neck, and was calling on me all night to shift from one side to the other. On this side the blaze of the hospital lighted up the ground in front, enabling us to take aim. The Zulus would every quarter of an hour or so get together and make a rush accompanied by yells. We let them get close, and then fired a volley – sometimes two. This would check them and send them back. Then after a time they would rally and come on again. About 3 am day began to break, and the Zulus retreated. A party, of which I was one, then volunteered to go across to the hospital, where there was a water cart, and bring it in to the inner enclosure, where there was no water, and the wounded were crying for it. When the sun rose we found the Zulus had disappeared. We then went out to search for our missing comrades. I saw one man kneeling behind the outer defences with his rifle to his shoulder, and resting on the parapet as if he were taking aim; I touched him on the shoulder, asking him why he didn't come inside, but he fell over, and I saw he was dead. I saw several others of our dead ripped open and otherwise mutilated. Going beyond the outer defences I went, as I have said before, whither I had killed the man at whom I had fired three shots from the hospital. Going on a little further I came across a very tall Zulu, bleeding from a wound in the leg; I was passing him by when he made a yell and clutched the butt of my rifle, dragging himself on to his knees. We had a severe struggle which lasted for several seconds, when finding he could not get the rifle from me, he let go with one hand and caught me round the leg, trying to throw me. Whilst he was doing this I got the rifle from him, and drawing back a yard or two, loaded and blew his brains out. I then was fetched back to the fort, and no one was allowed to go out save with other men. Then several of us went out together, and we brought in several wounded Zulus. By this time it was about eight or nine o'clock, and we saw a body coming towards us; at the same time Lord Chelmsford's column came in sight, and the enemy retired.

Lord Chelmsford, soon after he arrived, called me up to enquire about the defence of the hospital. I was busy preparing tea for the sick and wounded, and was in my shirt-sleeves, with my braces down. I wanted to put on my coat before appearing in front of the General, but I was told to come along at once, and I felt rather nervous at leaving in such a state, and thought I had committed some offence. When Lord Chelmsford heard my story he praised me and shook me by the hand. The Cross was presented to me on August 3, at Rorke's Drift, by Sir Garnet Wolseley.

9 PRIVATE ROBERT JONES

At the gallant defence of the fort at Rorke's Drift, every man fought like a hero, but some were fortunate enough to attract the particular attention of their superiors. Among these was a private of the 24th Regiment, named Robert Jones, who obtained the Victoria Cross for his conduct on the occasion. His story is as follows:

On the 22nd January, 1879, the Zulus attacked us, we being only a small band of English soldiers and they in very strong and overwhelming numbers. On commencing fighting, I was one of the soldiers who were in the hospital to protect it. I and another soldier of the name of William Jones were on duty at the back of the hospital, trying to defeat and drive back the rebels, and doing our endeavours to convey the wounded and sick soldiers out through a hole in the wall, so that they might reach in safety the small band of men in the square. On retiring from one room into another, after taking a wounded man by the name of Mayer, belonging to the volunteers, to join William Jones, I found a crowd in front of the hospital and coming into the doorway. I said to my companion, "They are on top of us," and sprang to one side of the doorway. There we crossed our bayonets, and as fast as they came up to the doorway we bayoneted them, until the doorway was nearly filled with dead and wounded Zulus. In the meanwhile, I had three assegai wounds, two in the right side and one in the left of my body. We did not know of anyone being in the hospital, only the Zulus, and then after a long time of fighting at the door, we made the enemy retire, and then we made our escape out of the building. Just as I got outside, the roof fell in – a complete mass of flames and fire. I had to cross a space of about twenty or thirty yards from the ruins of the hospital to the leagued company where they were keeping the enemy at bay. While I was crossing the front of the square, the bullets were whishing past me from every direction. When I got in, the enemy came on closer and closer, until they were close to the outer side of our laager, which was made up of boxes of biscuits on sacks of Indian corn. The fighting lasted about thirteen hours, or better. As to my feelings at the time, they were that I was certain that if we did not kill them they would kill us, and after a few minutes' fighting I did not mind it more than at the present time; my thought was only to fight as an English soldier ought to for his most gracious Sovereign, Queen Victoria, and for the benefit of old England.

10 GUNNER JAMES COLLIS

Gunner James Collis tells his story in these words:

On the twenty-seventh of July, 1880, we were encamped at Khushk-i-Nakhud, in Afghanistan. At 4 a.m. that day we – Battery E, Battery B Brigade – marched with the rest of the force on Maiwand to meet Ayub Khan. About 9 a.m. we came in sight of him in position under the hills. We were on the open plain. Major Henry Blackwood, commanding my battery, gave the order "Action front." I was a limber gunner that day. We began firing with common shell from the right of the battery. After we had fired a few rounds, their artillery replied. The first shot struck the near wheel of my gun, killing a gunner, wounding another, and Lieutenant Fowler.

The limber box upon my gun was smashed by a shell which also killed the wheel horses, but did not touch the driver. Several riding horses of my battery were killed, and a good deal of damage done to guns and carriage. Four gunners and Sergeant Wood, the No. I of my gun, were killed, and two men wounded, leaving only three men to work the gun. I took Sergeant Wood's place.

At about 1.30 p.m., some of Jacob's Rifles, who were lying down about ten yards in rear of the trail, began to be panic-stricken, and crowded round our guns and carriages, some getting under the carriages. Three got under my gun. We tried to drive them away, but it was no use. About that time we ceased firing a little, the enemy having set the example. During that pause the enemy on the left got pretty close. To check them, General Nuttall formed up the 3rd Bombay Cavalry and the 3rd Scinde Horse to charge. Gunner Smith of my gun, seeing what was going to be done, mounted his horse and joined the cavalry. General Nuttall led the charge, Gunner Smith being at his side. After going about 300 yards, the enemy being about 200 yards off, the whole line, with the exception of the General, the European officers, and Gunner Smith, turned tail, forming up when in line with the guns. General Nuttall with the officers, finding themselves deserted, returned, General Nuttall actually crying from mortification. Gunner Smith dashed on alone, and was cut down.

About 4 p.m. a large body of the enemy's infantry charged the left of the battery, the men of the left division 5 and 6 being compelled to use their handspikes and charge staves to keep them off. Major Blackwood on this ordered the battery to limber up and retire. When Lieutenant Maclaine heard this order he said, as I was afterwards informed, "Limber up be damned! Give them another round." We limbered up and retired at a gallop about 2,000 yards. In the meantime Major Blackwood remained behind with Lieutenant Maclaine's guns and was killed, Lieutenant Osborne by his side, Lieutenant Maclaine fighting to the last. At length, seeing no use in stopping, he galloped after us – we had got separated from the right division – and called out to us, only two guns, "Action, rear." We fired two rounds with shrapnel. Captain Slade, who had been in temporary command of the smoothbores, finding Major Blackwood dead, came up with his smoothbores and took command of all the guns. Colonel Malcolmson a moment later ordered Captain Slade to retire, saying, "Captain Slade, if you and the Lieutenant keep those two guns, he will lose them the same as he has lost his own." We then limbered up and went off. Just then a shell burst open our treasure chest. Many of the troops and camp followers stopped to pick up the money and were overtaken and killed. Just after that some of the enemy's cavalry caught up the guns. One of them wounded me on the left eyebrow as he passed. He wheeled round and came at me again; I took my carbine, waited till he was within four or five yards, and let drive, hitting him on the chest and knocking him off his horse. As he fell his money fell out of his turban, and Trumpeter Jones jumped off his horse and picked it up. He escaped, and is now corporal R.H.A., and wears the Distinguished Service medal for his conduct at Maiwand.

It was now beginning to get dusk, and I got off to walk by the side of my gun. Seeing a village close by, and some men at a well, I followed them and got some water. Just as we got to the well the enemy charged and drove us off, killing a good many.

On my return I missed my gun, and picked up with No. 2, which I stuck to till I reached Candahar. It was now dark, and we were with a stream of men of all regiments, camp followers, camels, and waggons. Going along I saw a lot of sick and wounded lying by the side of the road, and I picked them up and put them on the gun and limber. I had about ten altogether; they were all 66th men, and a colonel whose name I do not know and never heard of.

We had been fighting all day, marching all night and next day without a bit of food or a drink of water. I did not feel it so much, as I was so occupied, but I saw several dying by the roadside from thirst and fatigue. About four in the afternoon of the 28th, we came to a place called Kokeran, 7½ miles from Candahar; I saw a village where I could get water for the men who were with me. I went off and brought the water back and the men with me. On going to the village I saw Lieutenant Maclaine mounted; when I came back I saw two horses without a rider. I then went again for more water. I was about 150 yards from the gun when I saw ten or twelve of the enemy's cavalry coming on at a slow pace towards the gun. The gun went off and I lay down and allowed the gun to pass me, and began firing with a rifle which I had got from a wounded 66th man, in order to draw their fire upon myself, and stop them from going forward with the gun. I was concealed in a little nullah, and I fancy they thought there was more than one man, for they stopped and fired at me from the saddle. I shot one horse and two men. After firing about thirty-five rounds General Nuttall came up with some native cavalry, and drove them off. When I first saw the enemy they were about 300 yards off, when they left they had got 150 yards. General Nuttall asked me my name, saying, "You're a gallant young man, what is your name?" I said, "Gunner Collis, of E. of B, R.H.A." He entered it into a pocket-book and rode off. I then followed up my gun, which I found some 500 yards distant by the side of a river. The enemy's fire, which had been going on all the way from Maiwand, now became hotter, the surrounding hills being full of them. Some of the garrison of Candahar met us about four miles from the Fort and escorted us in. I arrived about seven p.m.

On the occasion of the sortie from Candahar in the middle of August, 1880, the fighting was going on in the village situated about 200 yards from the edge of the ditch of the fort. I was standing by my gun on the rampart, when General Primrose, General Nuttall, and Colonel Burnet came up. I heard them talking about sending a message to General Dewberry, who had succeeded General Brooke, who had been killed. I spoke to Colonel Burnet and said that I would take the message over the wall. After a little hesitation General Primrose gave me a note. I was let down a distance of about thirty or forty feet to the bottom of the ditch by a rope. When half down I was fired at but not hit by matchlock men about 250 yards distant, and I scrambled up the open side of the ditch and ran across to the village. I found the officer commanding in the middle of it, and fighting going on all round. I delivered the note and returned. When half way up the rope I was fired at again, one bullet cutting off the heel of my left boot. General Primrose congratulated me and Colonel Burnet gave me a drop out of his flask, for what with not having recovered from the fatigues of Maiwand and the exertion and excitement of this trip, I was a bit faint.

I was recommended for the Victoria Cross without my knowledge about September 10, by Sir F. Roberts, on the report of General Nuttall and Colonel Burnet. It was given to me July 28, 1881.

COPYRIGHT AND
ACKNOWLEDGMENTS

My thanks to Bernard Cornwell for his foreword and for his interest in the project. My thanks also to Christine Clarke of the Sharpe Appreciation Society for her initial help; to Dorothy Lumley and Sara Fisher for their guidance and encouragement; and to Paul Di Filippo and John Eggeling for their discoveries.

All of the stories are copyright in the name of the individual authors or their estates, as listed below. Every effort has been made to trace the holders of copyright. In the event of any inadvertent transgression of copyright, the editor would like to hear from the author or their representatives, via the publisher.

"The Crossroads at Churubusco" © 2000 by John T. Aquino. Original to this anthology. Printed by permission of the author.